For Dharma

PREFACE

"Do you understand why you're here, Mary?"

Darkness. Her head was spinning, and her body felt numb. She could feel her eyes trying to focus as they slowly tried to flutter open.

"Mary? Now there's a girl. Keep coming toward my voice, Mary."

As she began to regain consciousness, Mary could hear a hushed trickling of water, droplets echoing like whispers in a cave. It smelled like human waste and grime, accompanied by a harsh dampness in the air that was beginning to make her skin crawl. At once, Mary recognized where she was, and knew that the people they brought down to the sewers never returned home.

She felt a hand come below her chin to gently lift her head off her chest, and suddenly without warning ice cold water was thrown into her face. The shock snapped Mary back to reality like waking from a nightmare; though unfortunately for her, this was no nightmare. Choking to catch her breath, Mary's eyes at last took in her surroundings, and a shadow of dread slowly crept over her body.

Sitting down in a rickety wood chair, her feet were restrained to the legs and her arms bound behind her. The ropes were so tight she could no longer feel her feet or her hands, and her limbs burned like they were on fire. She ached in a way she had never experienced, and abruptly without cause, Mary suffered such an intense pain in the side of her head she thought she might pass right back out again. It wasn't until one of the men spoke that she even really noticed their presence in front of her.

"Welcome back, Mary. We have been waiting."

As her eyes found his face, Mary identified this man – Mr. Murphy – the man who was her boss' boss, and she had only met him on one other occasion before she had been officially hired to do their books. Mary was one of the few Irish women in New York who could read, write, and do math, and that had made her very valuable to her people in their rise to political power. It had been her idea… she was eager to make a living on her own. She recollected the Madame warning her repeatedly that if she did this job she needed to be quiet and compliant, and she had. At least until she found that things were not quite adding up: in the beginning, payments were being made to her boss' "corporation" that she was told not to register. Money was going out to undisclosed personnel in large quantities, and to make sure no one knew, Mary was abrasively coerced into falsifying names and numbers as camouflage. Then, as more time passed, even great evils reared their ugly heads…

It didn't take long for her to discover that the so-called "cleansed" Tammany Hall was more corrupted than it ever had been in the Tweed regime; they had just found a puppet to distract the people while they continued their underground operations, and no one was aware of who was pulling the strings. "Honest John" as they called him, was in fact honest because he was absolutely oblivious to it all, and the proof was in the books she had been scribing. The devious bastards had played the people like a fiddle, and their tune was winning them the Irish and the rest of New York back to their cause. Only Mary knew it was one giant lie.

"How long have you been running the books for Mr. O'Neill, Mary?" he asked her. Seamus Murphy was a tall, strong man with broad shoulders and piercing green eyes that were prominent amidst his robust facial hair. His usual top hat and coat were missing and the sleeves of his white shirt were rolled up to his elbows. With his arms crossed over his chest he glared down at her, unflinching and relentless. Mary was terrified, yet realized if she even tried to feign ignorance, they would see right through it. Those consequences wouldn't be in her favor.

She cast her gaze down to her feet in an attempt to avoid his stare. "After Tweed had been ousted, sir. Kelly wanted someone doing the books…that…that was one of us, and that was…untainted by the Tweed scandal. The Madame always had a good relationship with Tammany and she…she suggested me. She taught me the math when I was just a girl." Mary gulped back tears of pain, praying for some kind of mercy.

There was a long pause. "When did you decide to start all the fucking blabbing, Mary?" said the other man at Mr. Murphy's side, standing a few feet behind him. Mary glanced his direction, and as he took a few steps toward her, she was surprised to discover she had never seen him before. Though not as tall as Mr. Murphy, this man was somewhat stout and looked as strong as a bull. His sand colored hair, long nose, and blue eyes would have made him handsome, however his general demeanor was so severe she couldn't imagine anyone looking at him and feeling anything but intimidation. Her head began to spin again.

The unknown interrogator leisurely made his way closer to Mary, greatly contrasting Mr. Murphy in his appearance by dressing in what she assumed was his Sunday best, and he squatted down with his eyes peering directly into hers, their faces only inches apart. Mary could smell the egg and beans he had for breakfast.

"You love your son, don't you, Mary?" he went on. At the sheer mention of Thomas, Mary felt her skin get hot and her body tense violently. The man smiled, seeing he had struck a nerve.

"Good. Well if you want Thomas to live through the remainder of the day, you will answer whatever questions I ask you. Prompt-ly. Is that understood?" She remained silent but nodded her head heavily in reply. Her insides were turning over as the gravity of her situation sank in slowly… she would probably never get out of the sewers alive…

He stood up and made a motion to Mr. Murphy, who then hast-ily took three paces her way and slapped Mary fiercely across the face. For a moment, the blinding agony made her see nothing but stars. She blinked hard, her body lurching forward as her long red hair covered her eyes, and shuddered. The thought of Thomas kept her conscious as rage flowed through her veins. She needed to hold on and be strong, or any hope for her or her son seeing the sunrise tomorrow would disappear. If she couldn't save herself or any of the others, she had to save him.

Mr. Murphy retreated, and the other man's back was to her now as he spoke unsympathetically. "I am sorry – I realize this is not how ladies are supposed to be treated. But you've done this to yourself. These times are trying for us, and I need to know what you know, Mary. If you tell me what you know, I can help you through this bullshit. But you must cooperate."

Mary could feel bile rising in her throat. "I will tell you any-thing. Just don't hurt Thomas. What do you want to know? What do you want from me?!"

He abruptly turned to face her, eyes blazing. "Who did you tell? That is all I want to know. We need to clean this up now, and I know that you know exactly what I am talking about, Mary. Who did you tell?!"

Mary was quiet again. She had, in truth, told four – the first be-ing the Madame, who had been her benefactor all her life and who she had believed was her guardian. While she hadn't told her more than a few small details, a part of her wondered if that conversa-tion was the reason she currently sat tied in this chair. The second was Harry, a man who had loved her for many years yet had only remained a dear friend. She ensured he was long gone after her talk with the Madame, and Mary hoped he was halfway to California by now. The last two men were Pinkertons who aided in the original sacking of Boss Tweed, and Harry arranged a meeting between the four of them. Al and John were determined to bring down Tammany Hall for good, and they promised Mary complete confidentiality and a new life for her, Thomas, and little Esther. They had only desired the evidence to support their case…the evidence only she knew how to find. Mary was on her way to discreetly retrieve the pages from their hiding place when Mr. Murphy snatched her off the street, and she thanked God that she was not on her returning trip when he found her, or she'd probably already be dead.

There was no way she could give this man what he wanted – Mary was clueless as to the whereabouts of Al or John, and Harry had already left town. It didn't matter whom she'd told at this point…she would take the hit for all of them. And that being the case, there was no way in hell she'd rat out the others to try and stay alive for a few measly hours in the sewers.

Mary took a deep breath and hardened her face, willing him to believe her. "One evening I had gone to see a friend of mine after a frustrating day. I had too much whiskey and told him something was not right with the money, and that it made me suspicious of the man that hired me. When I realized what I had done…how stupid I had been…I went to tell the Madame, and she reprimanded me and had me pay off the man to leave town. Which I did, with her help, and I believe he is on his way back to Ireland to be with his family. That is all I did. I swear on my son's life. Please believe me…it was all just a stupid mistake…"

The man kept his eyes on Mary, studying her. "I believe you, Mary. And I hope you know that you should never lie to me, and I will never lie to you. If you do lie to me, I will always find out, and in this particular case, your deception will get both you and your son killed. Now, as for me being honest, this is a special case…" He let his voice trail off as he nodded to Mr. Murphy again, who hesitatingly strode over to Mary's chair with a blade out and began cutting the binds on her ankles and wrists. "I need time to make sure you are not hiding something me, and because you betrayed your employer with no grounds, I do not trust you to be loose on the streets running your mouth. The Madame seems to have lost her grip on those closest to her, which I will discuss this with her later. In most circumstances Mary, I kill the bastards who betray us. Myself. However, I am by no means the type to want the blood of a woman on my hands. So we will keep you put away for now, or until I feel it is safe for you to be free again."

Mary was confused, nearly loose from bindings. "Put me away? Where? Jail?"

With her arms and legs unexpectedly free of the rope, she could feel the blood rushing back, giving them sensation. She had half a mind to turn and run, though she would never make it far; trying to stand would only result in her collapsing after so much time without blood in her limbs. As if reading her thoughts, Mr. Murphy shot her a warning glance, staying closely by her side.

"You will be taken to a special place that you probably call the island, were we put women who have...well...lost touch. You will remain there until I decide it is safe for you to have your freedom again."

Mary froze, stricken with horror. "Oh no. Please...don't send me there. You can't. I am not crazy...you can't put me in that place... please don't...."

"If you behave," he continued. "It won't be long before you are out and with your son once more. Don't push your luck, Mary. You are lucky to have the prospect of a life after what you have done. If you go quietly you won't have to put up with another beating from Mr. Murphy. Don't make me change my mind."

Mary struggled to keep herself from fighting and shrieking out for help – it was no use. The whole reason behind taking their victims down to the sewers was because there was no one to hear their screams.

"Please…please tell my son I am alive. That I will come home… please…"

"Your son will be told by the Madame that you have left to start a new life with your friend…Harry I think was his name? I will ensure Thomas will be looked after by the Madame and her giant French goon. And Mary? You will never mention this incident from the minute you arrive at Blackwell." With that final verdict, the man spun on his heels and began pacing away, disappearing into the blackness.

As Mr. Murphy shuffled her along, a pistol thrust into her side, Mary started to cry and choked aloud, "I don't even know your name…."

Her answer came from somewhere through the rumbling, damp tunnel: "Croker."

PART 1:
NEW YORK CITY, 1874

I.

It was early morning when the rain began to fall, and Thomas thought the dreary climate paralleled the dark and wistful clouds hanging over his own heart. He sat on the windowsill lost in memories as he watched the city go mindlessly through the habitual motions to start the day, unable to stop speculating where his mother could possibly be, or worse, to what end she might have met. It was nearing six and a half days since Mary vanished. Thomas hadn't slept more than a few hours, and that was solely the result of sheer exhaustion. In addition, he found he was constantly lying to Esther to keep her at ease. Thomas had formed a routine, every night sneaking out quietly after putting her in bed, on to desperately hunt the streets of New York in the hopes of finding a trace or hint of Mary's whereabouts. Though it wasn't easy, Thomas sought out most of Mary's friends, acquaintances…anyone he believed his mother conversed with at one time or another all to no avail. Even the Madame appeared to be in a state of despondency over Mary's inexplicable absence, which was more emotion than he'd witnessed from her in years. It was as if his mother evaporated into thin air – and there was no proof to persuade him otherwise.

On that first evening, Thomas and Esther arrived home at their apartment above the barbershop only to discover it empty. Devoid of any worry, Thomas' immediate assumption had been Mary was caught working late again, or that she needed a whiskey after the daunting hours she typically endured at her job. Mary ran the books and numbers for a general store in Hell's Kitchen, and while Thomas never liked her employer much, he genuinely did not suspect he could have anything to do with Mary's disappearance. Billy O'Neill was a slimy son of a bitch, but Mary was smart, and Thomas was certain if his mother couldn't talk her way out of a situation with him, she would physically have the advantage given the man was nearly a head shorter than her and constantly had a half bottle of whiskey under the table. It had been hard for her to convince O'Neill to hire her – good, honest work for a woman was hard to come by. Mary won out in the end by proving her education far exceeded every employee he had put together and, as a result, their little family had been earning almost triple what they were before. As that first night neared dawn, Thomas grew increasingly worried, and mistakenly suppressed his conscience. While the sun ominously rose, he anticipated any second for her to walk through the front door, yet her footsteps never came up the back stairs, and when the time came to wake Esther, Thomas sensed that something was very, very wrong.

Nearly a week had come and gone since then, and still Thomas found no answers. He now sat watching the rain pour from the grey sky, an endless array of horrific possibilities swirling through his head, and it didn't take long for him to conclude the odds of seeing Mary again were not in his favor. They had taken care of each other from the beginning, just the two of them, and for years Thomas thought he was on his way to being a self-sustaining man; however the sudden reality of his circumstances made him see how emotionally unprepared he was to be alone. New York City was one of the most treacherous places in the entire world, where people were murdered in the streets and disappeared every day, and here he sat, almost ashamed this incident had taken him by surprise. His ignorance and his lack of a grasp of the world around him were both hard truths he found difficult to swallow. The agitation and overwhelming sadness he'd been purposefully pushing down these long few days at last escaped and surfaced from his heart, and then slowly those feelings became rage...rage at being utterly unable to control anything around him. It wasn't until there was a tap on his shoulder Thomas noticed he'd been crying, and he turned to find the stare of a tiny, apprehensive Esther at his side.

"Tommy? What's wrong? Why are you crying?" Her eyes were still half asleep as she ambled closer, wrapping her small arms around his chest and squeezing tight. Thomas immediately wiped the tears from his cheeks with the back of his hand and smiled down at her, trying the best he could to mask his pain and frustration.

"Es, what are you doing awake? The sun has only just come up." Standing, Thomas scooped her into his arms and walked back toward her room. "Back to bed. You've still got at least another hour until you need to be up."

Esther comfortably nuzzled into his arms and yawned, pushing her long dark hair from her face. "But you were...you were crying again. What's wrong?"

With one hand, he opened her bedroom door, sighing. "I think it might just be you and me for a little while, Es. Is that all right with you?"

"You mean Mary's not coming back?"

Thomas placed her down into her bed and under the covers, not sure how to respond. "I am going to go make us some breakfast. Back to sleep."

Without any protest, Esther was already dreaming by the time Thomas closed the door softly behind him. Nearly two years prior, Mary brought Esther home with her and explained to Thomas they had acquired a new member of the family rather than orphaning her to the streets, and Thomas hadn't done anything to challenge his mother's decision. Esther easily assimilated to their lifestyle, and

Thomas was relieved to have her now as a companion, at least until he could decide what in the hell to do next.

He drew in a long, deep breath to get himself composed. Thomas aspired to maintain an air of normalcy around Esther to prevent her from being panicked or frightened. She had only just turned ten years old and, considering her own personal history, Thomas didn't want her to feel abandoned, even if he did. Wandering over to the windowsill once more, he resumed his post, trying to work through the devastating idea that the life he'd known no longer existed. When lower-class people went missing in New York City, they were almost never found or heard from again — it was a hazard of where they lived, one he came to terms with at a very young age after seeing more violence than most directly outside his window. Regardless of this, Thomas could not move on without at least the smallest sense of resolution…an inkling, even, would be sufficient to put his heart and mind at rest. Mary had never been the type of woman to do anything sporadically or on a whim, and she worked hard to earn as much as she could for the small life they lived. It was impossible to imagine she would desert everything she'd built to simply pick up and leave a son she loved and a little girl she took in to nurture. No, there had to be foul play in one way or another, and someone had to know something. Perhaps he had just been looking in all the wrong places…

The church bells chimed loudly outside, and the devout made their way down the road to mass that Sunday morning to say prayers for those they loved. At last, the misty rain was fading and the sun began to peek through the clouds. If Mary were here she would be walking out their door at that exact moment to join them. But she wasn't…and Thomas' anger at God for doing this to him kept him right where he was, carrying on in his presumptions, trying in spite of himself not to miss her.

When the crowd had filtered through and left the streets slightly less crammed, Thomas took a few coins from his and Mary's stash and went out on an extended search for fresh eggs and bread, wanting to make him and Esther a big, special breakfast to start a new day…a new chapter in their lives. After bartering with the baker for his largest loaf, using Mary's disappearance to extend his money as far as it would take him, he found eggs at the corner market and made his way back to the apartment. The cool, post-storm breeze and social encounters did him justice, providing some clarity from the fog of his grief. It was then a thought struck him: he hadn't heard from the Madame since the day he informed her of Mary's disappearance, and while he gave her space to let her do some digging on her own, such an extended silence was not in her character. Perhaps he should drop in on her…Thomas couldn't recall the last time he'd gone more than four days without at the very least having her drop by the apartment…

Thomas returned to wake Esther for their meal and to dress for the day ahead, formulating a plan as to what he might do once she was at the Hiltmores'. Not long after Esther's arrival into their home, the Madame found Esther work as a domestic servant for a very prominent society family in Midtown. The Hiltmores hired her, undoubtedly due to a favor they owed the Madame, and Esther became a maid for their young daughter, Celeste, who was only two years older and ecstatic to have another girl in her midst. Mary saw this as the perfect opportunity for Esther to learn proper conduct as well as to be educated, and without any protestation, Mr. and Mrs. Hiltmore conveyed they had no objections to Esther sitting in on their daughter's tutoring once or twice a day if she completed her tasks at the residence. Within weeks, Esther quickly picked up the basics of French, was learning arithmetic, and her reading and writing were progressing far beyond anyone's expectations. It wouldn't be long before she surpassed Thomas' own capabilities, and he could only hope the Hiltmores' generosity would take her in the right direction as she grew older.

The storm had completely dissipated by the time they were fed and ready for the day, though unfortunately the crowd reconvened. The damp and muddy cobblestone streets were packed endlessly with people, livestock, and wagons shoving their way to and fro. After locking up the apartment, Thomas took Esther's hand tightly in order to not lose her in the masses. She jogged along behind him as he swerved in and out of the pack, hoping that in six or seven blocks they would be free from the claustrophobia of their neighborhood.

Finally making it to fresh air, Thomas let go of her and the two strolled on for another few minutes until Esther broke their silence, slowing her pace.

"Tommy…I need to tell you something…"

"What is it, Es?"

She kept her eyes downcast, her expression guilty. "I know you told me not to tell Celeste about Mary…but…I…I did. It was an accident, though, I promise! She asked why I had been sad, and I can't lie to her. Or to anyone! You know I'm a terrible liar! I just…I couldn't do it…I'm sorry."

Thomas let out a slight chuckle and shook his head, not at all surprised. "Es, it's nothing to be ashamed of. I knew you'd tell her sooner or later. Little girls aren't supposed to keep secrets. That's for when you're older." She paused at his words, her sparkling green eyes more than a little confused, and he resolved not to explain his joke. "I'm not mad in the slightest. Everyone will find out eventually, and I know Celeste is your best friend."

"You promise you aren't mad?"

"I promise."

She seemed to be satisfied with his reply, and tugged his hand to resume their commute. "I have a French lesson this afternoon! Well, Celeste has a French lesson…I just get to listen. I've gotten so much better, Tommy…"

Esther chatted merrily on for the remainder of their journey and Thomas indulged her by appearing wholly engrossed in her lessons and the gossip of the Hiltmores' household staff. Internally, however, he went back and forth considering the inclination he'd had earlier that morning to pay the Madame a visit once Esther was settled, praying she might have some explanation for him. If anyone managed to uncover Mary's fate, it would be her, and the fact that it had been nearly a week without any contact from the Madame made Thomas increasingly suspicious.

Thomas saw Esther to the servant's quarters at the rear of the house and changed his direction west toward the edge of Central Park. As he walked, he replayed the previous days in his head – out of every person Thomas questioned in his pursuit of Mary, the conversation he'd had with the Madame suddenly became the most disconcerting. There was no denying she was the most well-connected person he'd ever met and the closest thing to family he had left. Nevertheless, since Thomas initially told her the news, her voice and opinions were noticeably missing whereas typically, they were the most prominent, and not by his choice. There were only two plausible explanations: that the Madame was as unsuccessful as Thomas had been, which he strongly disbelieved, or that she uncovered something and didn't want to tell him. Either way, this was the only option Thomas had left. He just hoped it hadn't been a late night – the one thing she hated more than being woken up was unexpected visitors, and Thomas would in all likelihood be both of those upon reaching at The Palace.

It took him thirty minutes to navigate from East Midtown to where The Palace was located, and unlike the nighttime hours, the early morning was tame and subdued. He marched to the front gate and unlatched the lock; like clockwork, a grinning Louis stepped outside the front door and nodded hello to Thomas.

"Good morning, Tommy. Always a pleasure to see you," he greeted, his French accent scarcely obvious.

"Hi, Louis. Is the Madame awake? I need to speak with her."

He shrugged. "You know she almost never sleeps. Everything all right?"

Thomas almost smirked, meeting him at the top of the stoop. "Louis, you know not everything is all right. Can I see her?"

"Aren't you supposed to be at mass, Thomas?" came the Madame's familiar tone bellowing down the staircase, and he saw her hastily descending over Louis' shoulder. "What on earth are you doing here on a Sunday?" Her voice was filled with condescension and annoyance.

"We need to talk," he replied, pushing past Louis' large frame to meet her at the bottom of the staircase. She was still fully dressed in her provocative yet fashionable ensemble from the previous night, and Thomas wondered if she'd spent the whole evening awake for the same reasons he had.

Defensively, the Madame glared at him and crossed her arms, not bothering acknowledge his demands; instead, she merely rotated around and made her way back up to her office, and Thomas took this as an invitation to follow.

From the outside, any average pedestrian saw the The Palace as another luxurious mansion at the western foot of Central Park; what was hidden beneath its exterior housed the most lavish whorehouse in New York City, catering only to the rich and powerful, as most could not afford to set foot inside. Every item of décor was imported specifically from a supplier in Paris and each piece was one of a kind, making Thomas hypothesize exactly how far the Madame's power truly reached into the realm of the world. The main chandelier looked as if it were made entirely of diamonds, glistening like water on the dark marble floors below their feet and along the perfectly painted beige walls. The artwork impeccably decorating the rooms was said to have been a gift from an old foreign client, and the deeply romantic and racy tones set the mood perfectly for any arriving customer. Base boards and crown molding were all delicately adorned in gold trim, the furniture and tables detailed in the same hue to match. The ambiance was meant to make each client feel like royalty, which some of them were, and anything they could possibly need or want was provided effortlessly. The Madame offered absolute discretion to her customers, and in turn, earned certain favors and enough leeway to make her one of the most influential women in the city. Whatever her girls learned through the very meticulous and careful methods they shared with her, and this information was catalogued and used to the Madame's advantage to increase both her wealth and power. The Vault, as they called it. She had run her business for close to twenty years. Miraculously, she managed to look as if she had not aged a day in all the time Thomas had known her, as if both The Palace and the Madame would remain timeless, no matter what storms they weathered. And as Thomas recalled there had been many storms.

As soon as they reached the second floor, the Madame headed straight through the giant oak doors of her office to give them privacy, and Thomas closed both doors shut behind him. He took a seat on the armchair in front of her enormous desk, or the 'throne' as he mockingly referred to it, where she was perched eyeing him closely. They sat in silence for a few seconds, Thomas thoughtfully debating over how to begin, when she rapidly got to her feet and went over to the drink cart, pouring herself a large glass of whiskey. Lifting it, the Madame held it level to her eyes, as if suspect of the quality, and then threw the glass back to finish it in one gulp.

"Would you like one, Thomas?" she asked, letting out a staunch exhale. "I think I will have another."

Without waiting for his response, she refilled her own glass along with one for him. Thomas was accustomed to having a glass of whiskey with her every once in a while, typically on special occasions or when times were hard on them. In this case, he could feel something was different. She knew why he was here and what he wanted, she simply didn't want to tell him the truth, and he could see it in her face. The Madame picked up their glasses and floated over toward him, leaning back against the front of her desk. She handed him his whiskey and took another sip of her own. Thomas struggled to remember the last time he had been this close to her, and realized it had been months, if not years. She was exquisite to see up close, beyond beautiful in every aspect of her features. Though she would never admit her age, the only evidence the Madame exceeded thirty were the deepening crow's feet around her honey and grey colored eyes. Her dark hair was amazingly littered with red, not grey, and her petite frame and porcelain skin gave her a deceivingly angelic exterior, though anyone who spent more than a few minutes on her bad side would know better. Thomas had witnessed the Madame once or twice in her most menacing form, and he preferred to keep that part of her personality dormant while he was in her presence.

Thomas had a drink from his glass. "Rough night?" he started, trying to edge into the discussion.

She sneered. "You could say that – nothing like catering to a bunch of bastards from Georgia who still think the Confederacy will rise again," she laughed to herself. "Fucking imbeciles."

He couldn't resist a grin, relaxing slightly. "Never one to sugar coat it."

"We both know that's not how I work. What is it you need, Thomas?"

"And I thought we were being straightforward? You know why I'm here."

"Oh do I?"

"You promised me you'd try and find her," he retorted, annoyed and mildly insulted. "And you know it's bullshit that I am here after almost a week begging you to tell me what you know."

Her eyebrows rose. "Ah, so this is just about your mother, then."

Thomas couldn't believe what he was hearing. "How can you even say that? You're acting like she doesn't even matter to you when we both know that's not true!"

"Watch your fucking mouth, Thomas, and if you don't I'll have Louis knock a little sense into your thick skull," she shot back, taking another gulp of whiskey as her face hardened.

Thomas' temper took over. "I'm not one of your damn marks, for Christ's sake, and you swore you'd find out something…anything for that matter! You have been avoiding me purposefully because you don't want to tell me what it is you found. I know you better than you think, Madame."

"I've had my fucking eyes and ears everywhere, Thomas, and no, there's been nothing. For days nothing. I've been reaching out with no response, and that fucking ape who runs the store doesn't know a God damned thing either. So no, Thomas, I have nothing new to report. And you're right. I have been avoiding you because of that."

From the way she spoke there was no room for her usual stretch of the truth, and Thomas' head and spirit sank.

"No one has talked? How is it that not a single person she knows can tell us anything? It just doesn't make any fucking sense! You know her…she wouldn't just…just leave…she wouldn't…"

The Madame shook her head. "Thomas, listen to me, and these words will not be easy to hear. We have to assume the worst – that she's dead and we'll never know when or why. I want nothing more than to find Mary, believe me, but we have no clues to lead us in any direction. The trail went cold. We just have to continue moving forward."

He sat still for a moment, frozen. A spark lit in Thomas' head as he went over the Madame's words again. There was no way to know for certain, but something in the way the Madame addressed him caught Thomas' attention, and he could sense it must have been rehearsed. In times of stress she was always candid with her words, which were typically littered with profanities and vulgarity…unless, of course, she was putting on an act, and after years of beholding it firsthand, Thomas saw through the cover. Discreetly, he observed his surroundings, considering the entire scene with scrutiny. Her countenance was placid, her eyes sorrowful, and her body language lacked usual poise. She had even added the personal touch of being nearer to Thomas, along with the gesture of pouring a whiskey for him…it all came together to make a perfect and easy play for her. Obviously, the Madame was attempting to emotionally compromise him… to convince him there was nothing more to the story. The Madame loved his mother; the three of them had been family since Thomas could remember. Giving up and letting go was not one of her strong suits, yet protecting others by hiding her secrets was how she'd become the woman who currently stood in front of him. There was no way through the armor, and Thomas didn't know what else to do. Accusing her wouldn't get him anywhere other than in a screaming match, and he didn't want Louis giving him a black eye because of it.

A loud knock on the door interrupted them, and without a second thought the Madame set down her glass, her demeanor wholly transforming.

"What is it, Louis?" she demanded in irritation, proceeding around the desk to sit down on her throne.

"Madame, you have a few guests downstairs wanting to see you on urgent business," Louis called. "I put them down in the parlor room and poured them each a whiskey."

"The ones I've been waiting on?" she pressed, her interest clearly heightened.

"Yes, Madame."

She smiled. "Tell them I will be right down, Louis." Straight away she was on her feet, strolling out of her office. "Finish your whiskey and stay here if you wish to resume our talk. Otherwise, I will plan on seeing you later tonight at the apartment." She paused at the door to adjust her dress and make sure her appearance was adequate, and right before she left him, the Madame turned back. "I'm sorry, Thomas. You're…you're like a…well, you know what you and your mother mean to me. I don't want you to think there's any hope when there isn't. The world is a fucked up place, and I'm just trying to keep you safe…in my own way. I hope you can understand that."

He nodded, acknowledging her sentimentality, and she whipped around and out the doors, closing them and leaving Thomas alone in the office. Mulling over what to do next, the phrase 'no hope' rang loud in his ears. On the contrary, Thomas refused to believe the Madame spent the previous week accepting the shrugs and confusion of others as gospel – when the Madame wanted something,

22

she got it no matter the cost. Her excuse was not plausible, and with no other leads to follow, there was only one thing left he could do. His gaze fell on the desk in front of him. Silently, Thomas got to his feet and tip toed over to the office doors, listening to be sure no one was lingering outside before bolting them shut. There would only be a small window of opportunity for him to take. She'd had enough confidence to leave him without supervision in her office…alone with her desk…and Thomas realized it was one place the Madame never dreamed he would dare to look through.

The surface proved to be more decorative than informative, and after piecing through its external contents, Thomas ransacked every drawer, reading and examining each piece of paper or object he found. As he searched it eagerly from top to bottom, Thomas felt his frantic pursuit was in vain, and an overpowering frustration set in. He cursed under his breath, slamming the last drawer closed, glaring down at the insignificant things he'd come across. The desk, like so many aspects of The Palace, was only a decoy, and he reprimanded himself for thinking he could possibly outsmart the Madame. Did he really think anything of value would be left out in the open for someone to find? Sitting into the Madame's chair, Thomas slammed his fist down on the desk, and instantly stopped dead. Once more he slammed his hand down, and a grin crept to his lips.

It was brilliant.

Lightly tapping, Thomas was aware that there was something hollowed out underneath the top...something metal. The Madame kept everything under lock and key in The Palace, why would her own desk be any different?

Thomas dove underneath the desk and uncovered a small, locked iron safe. His thoughts raced with the possibilities of what to do next: a key was needed to open it, and he lost himself for a minute or two, seriously contemplating breaking the desk apart, and then he remembered the whiskey decanter. There was a key that hung around the outside of its neck. Up to that very second, he'd only thought of it as a decoration or keepsake with no idea what it was really for…no idea until now. He got to his feet and hustled toward it, becoming convinced with every passing second there was something she was hiding deliberately from him in the safe, though he wasn't sure why. Carefully, Thomas grabbed the key and returned, lowering himself under the desk and hurriedly twisting open the lock.

What he found was not at all what he expected. His eyes first focused on an old, fully loaded revolver covered with a thin film of dust. Gently, he picked it up in his shaking hands, blowing away the grime and examining it closely. It was a Griswold, a gun he'd heard his Master Lawrence ramble on about but had never had the privilege of observing firsthand. The metalwork was unlike anything Thomas had ever seen, detailed to a degree that didn't quite add up for a mass-produced weapon of the war. A little in awe, he set it down on the ground to his right and kept digging. Next, Thomas found a small stack of paper money, and his eyes grew wide when he counted almost five hundred dollars altogether, which was more money than he'd ever heard of anyone possessing at once. Uneasy with having that much in his hands, he set the bills down beside the Griswold. Moving on and underneath his first two discoveries sat a handful of letters and documents, which after a quick skim, proved be legal documents claiming the Madame owned not only The Palace, but also multiple other properties scattered throughout the city, including the apartment he, his mother, and Esther called home. Once he'd flipped through those with amazement, the safe was empty, and Thomas' defeat made him ashamed for sneaking when he knew he shouldn't have. Perhaps she hadn't lied…perhaps for once, she'd told him everything…

Just as he was about to replace what he'd found, Thomas caught a glimpse of a very tiny piece of satin sticking up in the back part of the floor inside the safe. Without hesitation, he instinctively lunged forward and pulled the tiny piece of fabric, and to his delight, the bottom of the safe came up, revealing an immense stack of papers he could easily make out to be personal letters of correspondence. Thomas' heart pounded as he removed the letters, and after a quick peek, saw they were the only contents in the hidden compartment. Straightening up to filter through what he'd unearthed, Thomas thought he must be hallucinating. Every one of the letters was addressed to the same person, and that person was not the Madame. It was his mother.

A far off rustling of footsteps up the staircase caught his attention. Thomas stopped dead and listened intently, thankful to recognize the heavy tread of Louis' leather boots and not the light clacking of the Madame's heels ascending steadily toward him. There wasn't much time. Thomas thrust the floor of the safe back into place, put one hundred dollars of the money back into the safe along with the property deeds and closed the hatch, locking it tightly. His hands steadied with adrenaline as he placed the Griswold, letters, and cash into his jacket and folded it up. The best choice he had was to take the key with him along with everything else in the hopes that the Madame's spare was not close at hand, thus giving him a greater head start. With everything tucked away neatly, Thomas heard Louis down the hallway and raced to the door, unbolting the locks, and then hurried to his chair, throwing back the last of the Madame's Casper's whiskey and trying to appear composed and casual as Louis knocked and entered the office.

"Ah good, you're still here. Madame wanted me to tell you her meeting will take some time but you're more than welcome to stay."

If he had any clear chance at an undetected escape with the Madame's stolen goods, it would have to be while the Madame was preoccupied elsewhere.

"Tell her it's all right, and I will just plan to see her later," he told Louis, rising from the chair. Thomas realized as he got up he had been moving so frantically his whole body was soaked with sweat, and sincerely prayed Louis wouldn't take any notice.

Louis loitered at the door, his face pained. "Tommy…if there is something I can do to help…anything at all…all you need to do is ask. I am sorry about your mother. I truly am. We loved her dearly."

Thomas kept his distance and tried to innocently remain a few feet away. "Thank you, Louis, that really means a lot to me." Louis was the Madame's right-hand man and her muscle, never leaving her side unless ordered directly by her to do so. Throughout Thomas' life, Louis paid special attention to him and to Mary; the threatening scowl he reserved for most visitors was always brushed aside in their presence, and in its place was a constant, encouraging smile. Oftentimes he was the only one Thomas could turn to when his mother or the Madame were both driving him out of his mind. For anyone else, however, Louis was a force to be reckoned with: at six feet tall, his long and burly limbs could crush stone if requested to do so, and his shaved head and blonde goatee made him all the more intimidating. Nonetheless, Louis was a friend, one of the few Thomas had, and he hoped this breach of the Madame's trust wouldn't affect their longstanding relationship.

"How is Esther?" he asked. "How is she dealing with this?"

"Fine," Thomas said plainly, shifting nervously on his feet. "She's taking it in stride. Es is tough, tougher than me I think."

"Yes, I can see that," Louis agreed, teasing. "You're back working with Lawrence tomorrow morning?"

"Horseshoes until lunchtime."

"Good. That metal work will help you work through it. Having an outlet for your emotions during days like these is necessary since obviously you've been doing nothing but hiding from them."

Thomas was startled. "I have not—"

Louis held up a hand to stop him. "Just hit the fucking the hammer hard tomorrow. For me. Now take one of these and get out of here." He took a step forward and tucked one of his hand rolled cigarettes into Thomas' shirt pocket, the scent of fresh tobacco hitting Thomas' nostrils, and winked. "Got a fresh batch in yesterday. Your favorite. Damn fine if I do say so myself."

"Thank you, Louis," he replied, gripping the bound up jacket on his arm even tighter, "I'll see you later this week." With a small nod,

Thomas set off out of the Madame's office and down the stairs, reciting a Hail Mary over and over again in his head until he reached the street outside, trekking south. He contemplated how much time he had until they figured out what he'd done.

When Thomas finally reached the apartment, he was out of breath from the elevated pace of a near full-on sprint for the majority of his trip home. He wasn't sure why, but a strong pang of paranoia was consuming him, and rather than take any chances Thomas locked the door to the apartment, trying to slow his heartbeat. Once his lungs recovered, he rushed straight to the loose floorboard in his room, where he and his mother designated their secure spot to hide their earnings from work or otherwise, and only the two of them were aware it existed. Together, they had been planning to go west for almost three years, wanting to start a new life away from the madness and growing dangers of New York. Last week they had been just ten dollars short and on the verge of arranging their travels to the frontier. With the hundreds of dollars he now possessed in his jacket, he and Esther would have more than enough money to comfortably travel on their own and fulfill that dream, taking them to a place of opportunity much different than the city. From what Thomas regularly observed, it was evident that New York was worsening with each passing day, and if Thomas could survive it for seventeen years, he was convinced he could survive anywhere in the world. Secretly, Thomas believed he understood the real reason Mary wanted out of New York: she wanted to escape from the hold of the Madame, and while she never personally confided this in him, it was obvious to Thomas his mother desired something more out of her life. The Madame was an overbearing force and involved in every major decision they made. His mother sought a place that was their own, and Thomas rejected the idea of giving that up entirely. In his heart, he didn't want to stay any longer in that suffocating, filthy place…particularly with Mary gone. If his mother was dead and watching over him, Thomas was determined this is what she would have wanted him to do; Mary was never one to dwell on anything she couldn't control. "It's all in God's way," she used to tell him, and a part of him debated over if she actually believed it, or if it was the only way she could accept the world around her.

As he got to his room, Thomas shut himself inside. He proceeded to place the Griswold and cash onto the floor and commence the task he couldn't complete at The Palace. Dumping the letters on his bed, he scattered them around while he considered where to begin. The Madame locked these away for a reason – not a single one belonged to her, and he doubted whether or not his mother even knew they existed. The paper must have been years old and, judging from their external condition, the letters were heavily worn from a long journey. Thomas couldn't wait any longer. He snatched one up into his hands and initiated reading the words on the page.

August 1860

Mary,

I have been thinking of you incessantly, and I am excited to report I think this conflict may at last be coming to a close. We are planning a march into enemy territory in just a few weeks' time, and I am quite certain these Eastern armies have no knowledge of the firepower of the Imperial Navy. If all goes accordingly, I will be sailing home to England and then back to you in the spring. So much has happened while I have been away, and I have much to tell you about. But most importantly, I want you to come back to England with me. My fortunes have changed to a degree that has completely altered my life and our future. There we can begin our life together and live at ease and in comfort.

I miss you more than I could ever say in this letter, and I hope you know my love has only grown stronger in our time apart. I promise I will be with you soon.

Yours & etc.,

Edward

Thomas stared at the letter unblinking, feeling as if a wave of cold water hit his entire body. Struggling to assemble the pieces of the puzzle, Thomas could only conclude with an explanation that seemed impossible. From an early age, he had been told his father perished during his childhood in the early battles of the Civil War. Since then, Mary made it clear she never wanted another man in her life and rarely spoke of him, and Thomas didn't push the subject, maintaining it to be too heartrending for her. But there was something indisputable in this letter that made Thomas' hair stand on end. Right on the page was all the evidence needed to corroborate the old story was a farce: it was the name of the letter's author, because Edward, he'd been informed, was the name of his father. And there was no chance it was purely coincidence.

Heart pounding hard in his chest once again, Thomas grabbed another letter and read it from top to bottom, this one nearly identical to its predecessor. Then another. And another. It took well over an hour for him to read them all, and once he finished, Thomas completely fell apart where he stood, dropping down to his bedroom floor with the final letter in his hands. It had been a giant lie…a lie perpetrated to provide him with closure in reference to his absent father. Letting the paper slip from his fingertips, Thomas pulled at the hair on the back of his head, shutting his eyes tight in aggravation. Oddly, the most despairing notion was that the one person he wanted to confront was no longer there to answer his questions, forcing Thomas to sort out Edward's story on his own using the seventy-one letters he had at his disposal.

From what he could gather, Edward Turner was the second son of a very wealthy English tradesman. The way he discussed his family made Thomas assume his elder brother took the helm of the business when the time came, and therefore Edward chose to enlist in the Royal Navy due to his love of being on the sea. He excelled and before long captained his own ship with a rowdy but loyal crew. In the summer of 1856, Edward came to New York City to see his cousin's nuptials to an American bride. Since birth, Edward and his cousin apparently were extremely close, and Edward considered him to be another brother as well as his best friend. It was this summer that Edward met Mary, and the pair fell in love right as he departed to a war in the South Pacific. After four years of being away, Edward planned to sail to England and then onto New York City in order to claim Mary and bring her home across the Atlantic with him. Then, out of the blue, Edward found he was not only a Lord but also the sole heir to their family fortune. What's worse, on his return trip, Edward became dangerously ill with malaria and many thought he would not survive. It took months for him to recover, and due to the gravity of his family's situation, he was honorably discharged from the navy. He faithfully wrote to Mary and told her everything that happened, though it became apparent in Edward's pleas to hear from her she must have stopped responding to his correspondence not long after the war. Thomas was amazed at Edward's diligence; he never faltered in his devotion to Mary, and he couldn't help feeling perplexed at his mother's lack of constancy as he read on. It wasn't until he found the final letter that the reason behind this was revealed.

Madame,

I greatly appreciate your letter. I had not heard from Mary in quite some time, and was also beginning to wonder if my nightmares had become a reality. My deepest condolences to you as well, and I hope you know Mary will forever remain the love of my life.

If there is anything I can assist you with, please do not hesitate to write with your request. I would also like you to consider burying her here on my estate where she ought to have lived the rest of her days, as she is the only woman I would ever want to be buried by my side.

Please let me know if this wish could be granted. I am devastated to know she has been taken from me before our life together could even begin.

Sincerely Yours & etc.,

Lord Edward Turner

The letter was clutched so forcefully between his hands it was a miracle it didn't rip. Thomas' eyes scanned over the words again, the frustration building faster. A fury rose in Thomas – one he had never experienced at such a high intensity, and he was barely able to contain himself. It all made sense. Mary hadn't wanted to discuss Edward because she had honestly never known what became of him. The Madame must have started intercepting their letters and told his father Mary died. Edward must have had no idea that Thomas even existed, and Thomas was in such shock the only thing he could do was gape at the pile of letters on his bed. There was so much anger…so much resentment…it took every ounce of his willpower to not explode into a rampage.

Fighting hard to concentrate and keep a clear head, Thomas succeeded in convincing himself no good would come from lashing out. If anything, it would end with a beating, and he would be on the worse end of it for daring to betray the Madame despite his overpowering desire to strangle her with his bare hands. The truths and answers he sought he would never find in her. In her, there would only be excuses and more fabrications. The bigger mystery was why his mother had never told Edward about having a son, and the possibility that he could be the child of anyone else now seemed groundless – he'd done the math in his head, and being born in the spring of 1857 meant these letters were no longer circumstantial. Thomas took a few deep breaths and let them go loudly, cursing his mother for leaving him in such a mess. His gaze wandered over the paper still in his hands, his forced composure steadying his anger. It was at that second Thomas' eyes grew wide as they locked on Edward's return address.

There was his answer – his one and only opportunity. If he wanted a father, and if he wanted to seek the facts, he had nothing else to lose. A man he never presumed he would meet was just a letter away, and it gave him hope that maybe he wasn't as alone as he supposed…that maybe this man, if he loved Mary that dearly, would want nothing more than to hear from Thomas and find him.

Standing abruptly, Thomas took the last letter with him into the kitchen, where he poured himself a large glass of whiskey and sat down at the table. For a moment he wavered, glancing at the letter: he was at a crossroads, and the decision he made in the next few seconds would greatly affect the rest of his life. During the week of Mary's absence, Thomas felt as if he'd aged ten years. It had been the hardest thing he'd ever had to cope with, and he was forced to comprehend the weight his mother suffered dealing with so much on her own. He needed to do this for her, and she'd be damned to let someone else dictate the way his life would be lived. Thomas threw back his glass of whiskey and rose to his feet, going to grab ink and paper from his desk. When he got back to the kitchen table, he sat down and wrote a letter to someone he firmly believed could change everything, and he no longer cared if it was for better or for worse.

Lord Turner,

This is a very difficult letter for me to write. I was unaware that you existed until a few moments ago, and I am reaching out to you now hoping you can give me answers to the numerous questions I have. I discovered letters you wrote to Mary Daugherty many years ago, and I am unhappy to report they were cut off without my mother's knowledge. For many years she lived on while you believed she was dead, and I am sorry to say it was a lie.

I am writing you today because I believe I am your son. My mother disappeared no more than a week ago with no hint of her whereabouts. I think if you knew my mother as well as I do, the thought of her ever abandoning people she loved seems ridiculous, and I can only imagine the worst. I came across your letters in my search for her, and I pray that wherever she is, she is at peace.

I don't know if you have any interest in ever meeting me or in writing to me. I am in New York City, as I have been my entire life, and I ask that if you want to reach me you do so immediately. Otherwise, I will be leaving the city and starting anew elsewhere in two months time.

Thank you, and I apologize for any inconvenience this may cause you.

Thomas Dougherty

As he finished, Thomas folded the letter and sealed it, setting it aside on the table. He poured himself another whiskey and leaned back in his chair, letting the day sink in. What was becoming the most difficult to swallow was the impending notion he would never see his mother alive ever again.

Throughout the passing days, Thomas held onto a small sliver of hope he was wrong, that somehow this was all some sort of nightmare, but it wasn't. It was a disillusioned fantasy. He may never know how or why, and apart from that, he couldn't go on lying to himself that everything would be all right. A lump rose in his throat as he recalled the last time he'd seen her, and how doting her smile was that morning before he left for work. Trying to stifle the tears in his eyes, Thomas rose from his chair and walked toward her room. He pushed the door open delicately and welcomed the familiar scent of rosewater, peering around at what she'd left behind. The bedroom was dark save for a small beam of light sneaking through her handmade curtains, and he noted the dust accumulating on the surface of her tiny desk by the window. Mary's vanity in the right corner looked as though she just left it, stool scooted out and hairpins scattered on the shrouded linen cloth that covered its surface. His mother had made her bed perfectly that morning prior to going to work herself, and Thomas cringed thinking she had no clue it would be her last. In those few minutes, he allowed himself to miss her until it was much more than he could bear. Thomas took a final peek, absorbing the contents of the room, and closed the door, his heart consequently shattering into a thousand pieces.

His decision was made. Thomas paced over to the kitchen table and retrieved his letter to Lord Turner, setting off to the post office in urgency. A few blocks down the road, he tactfully bribed the postmaster with an extra quarter to see that his letter left the next morning, and the man estimated it would take two weeks to reach its recipient, making a response probable within a month. Feeling content, Thomas thanked him and left. One month and he would have a reply, and if two passed without one, there was no cause for him to wait. Starting over was his only objective, and he didn't care where it was or with who, as long as he was out of New York. Thomas dove back out into the busy street, and instead of heading home the way he'd come, he took to wandering the city, reminiscing as he aimlessly rambled on. He wasn't sure how long he strolled, though eventually, he recognized where he was…a place he hadn't been in many years that still gave him chills. It was where he had been with his mother when the draft riots started, one of the first memories he had as a boy, and there hadn't been a time since when he was more terrified. Mary fought tooth and nail to get them home, undergoing a nasty knife wound from a man trying to rob her even though they had no money on them. Thomas tried and repeatedly failed to forget his mother desperately clawing the man off her and taking off running through the crowd with Thomas in her arms, bouncing against her hip as he clung to her. The screams echoed in his ears, and they nearly starved from not leaving the apartment for days until the army put an end to the riots.

He thought back to right after the war ended, and New York was the one place in America doing the worst despite the best efforts of those with money or power. He and his mother worked hard and were lucky to make enough to eat, and just when all seemed calm violence sprang up like a dormant weed never fully plucked by its roots. The class divides grew larger, and racism and hatred ran thick through the veins of the natives, especially with the increasing number of immigrants. Mary had shown him the areas of town to avoid, highest on the list being the Five Points and Bowery, home to the inexorable hub of gangs, murderers, thieves, swindlers, cons, and pickpockets.

Mary provided for the two of them along with a little help from the Madame until Thomas was of working age. He hadn't been sure how the Madame secured their small apartment above the barbershop without much fuss and without any other residents; however, after he found the property records earlier that afternoon, it now made perfect sense. The sheer thought of her made Thomas' palms sweat with spite, and he hoped he would be able to control his anger the next time they were face to face. It wouldn't be long before she found the key missing and figured out what he'd stolen, and Thomas felt a malicious grin forming: it was far too late, and there was nothing the Madame could do to undo it. For the first time in his seventeen years, Thomas had the upper hand on her, and he had to admit...it was an intoxicating feeling – one he really wouldn't mind getting used to.

He realized then he had forgotten for most of the day about the one person he did still have to care for, and deliberated what he probably should and definitely shouldn't tell Esther. Her company brought a little more light into their lives during the past few years, and he'd not once doubted his mother's decision to keep her and raise her. Esther was timid at first, but quickly became accustomed to Mary, Thomas, and her new way of life. In those early days, Thomas taught Esther the basics of how to read and write, and their mutual attachment blossomed, as neither had ever had a sibling or many friends. Mary loved her as if Esther was her own daughter, and together, the three of them formed a family, one Thomas presumed was unbreakable.

A stupid, young man's fallacy.

All he could do was await a letter from his father, and if that never came, Esther would never have to know. For the time being, Thomas had to be patient. Everything hung by a very thin string, and he had no interest in testing those limitations just yet.

With a loud crack of thunder, a strong, steady rain fell as it had that morning, and the clouds darkened overhead. People rushed from the streets to take cover wherever they could; Thomas, on the other hand, dawdled to watch them scatter while his clothes soaked through, halting mid stride in what he found to be a somewhat refreshing summer shower. He tilted his head back toward the sky, arms stretching out as if to embrace the water, thunder rumbling only a few miles off. All the memories of who he had been with his mother, the boy he'd been and the world he thought he knew began to fade away as the water washed him clean. All the regret, the sadness, the hopelessness and anger subsided, leaving his conscience with a blank slate. He lowered his arms, smiling, perceiving with a full heart this was the sign of something greater. In those few seconds, Thomas felt as if the rain rinsed away the binding sense of guilt...relieving him of his crippling disgust and cleansing who he always he pictured he was.

Ahead lay a path he never dreamed he might take, and Thomas did not know where it would lead him. The rain was an omen to him, an omen of new things to come. And in the rain, Thomas felt reborn; he was ready for a new journey to begin.

II.

It took all the strength in Esther's tiny arms to pull the tall
upstairs windows closed after dusting and scrubbing them spotless. As she leaned outward on her tip toes, her balance teetered
for a half second and, in a slight panic, she abruptly thrust herself
backward and caused the structure to swing hard with her, loudly banging closed and causing her to topple to the ground. Across
the room, Celeste burst into a fit of giggles, and Esther attempted
to ignore the scowls Madame Moreau was sending her direction
for distracting her pupil. Esther got to her feet and brushed herself off, pleased to see her hard work was progressing: the windows
sparkled, looking better than they had in months. She had nearly
finished cleaning the drawing room where Celeste's French lesson
was taking place, but in spite of her diligent efforts, there was no
way she would be done in time to actually participate, much to the
delight of Madame Moreau. That arrogant woman despised Esther
more than foul milk, and it was no secret she considered having to
deal with Esther's presence outrageously beneath her. The two of
them would face off almost every lesson, each challenging the other just enough to stir their respective tempers without getting into
too much trouble. Thankfully, there was nothing more enjoyable

to Celeste than watching her French tutor lose her cool, and she jumped on every opportunity to witness Madame Moreau's face turn purple at Esther's clever retorts.

While their lesson went on, Esther picked up her pace – she still had three widows and the drapes to clean with teatime fast approaching. In spite of her disappointment Esther loved every minute of her time in the drawing room; it was her favorite room in the household, and she especially loved the dazzling silver curtains around each window, which perfectly matched a shimmering sea basked in sunlight. The walls were decorated with landscape portraits, detailing the beaches and oceans of the northeastern coastline and together with the deep blue, silver, and white shades of furniture and fixtures, Esther would get completely lost in the feeling that she was indeed at the waterfront. The room also held an exquisite pianoforte, which Celeste could play brilliantly, along with a colossal fireplace that kept them all warm during New York's brutal winter months. A great deal of the Hiltmores' residence reminded Esther of where she and her mother lived not too long ago, and she couldn't deny it saddened her to recall how quickly her mother's adoration transformed to burdened resentment. With a sigh, Esther drove the memory from her mind. Those days were far behind her, and she had bigger worries to concern herself with.

She woke earlier than usual that morning, though Esther wasn't exactly sure why until she found Thomas at the windowsill in the foyer, crying and staring outside into nothingness. On his face was the same look that hadn't left since Mary vanished: he was beaten down, tired, and resigned that Mary wasn't coming back. Esther knew he tried to hide it from her, and while she searched to find the right words, she couldn't find a way to explain that she understood exactly how he felt…that very same feeling of abandonment, of not knowing what to do and everything spinning out of control. None of that was new to her. She felt it every day for months when she first was given to the Dougherty's. Her mother deserted her at The

Palace without a second thought, and that recollection was one that still brought her to tears. No matter what Esther might say or do to try to ease the pain, Thomas would only find relief in time, like she had. Or at least she had done the best job she could convincing herself that was the case.

In the two years Esther lived with the Dougherty's, Mary was always gracious, gentle, and kind to her, but Esther's loss of her own mother in such a heartless manner stripped away the ability to trust in anyone, the only exception being Thomas. From her first night to that very day, he made sure to build their relationship gradually and on absolute honesty. He never lied, he never made a promise if he couldn't keep it, and he had never let her down…not that Mary had. Maybe it was the role Mary had to fill in Esther's heart that made it so hard to let her in. Thomas was easy to love and open up to, and it wasn't as if Esther didn't love Mary or appreciate what she'd done for her. On the contrary, Mary was given a task she wouldn't ever be able to fulfill, yet Esther made sure to keep those sentiments to herself and treat her new family as if they were her own.

Now, Mary was gone, and Esther had spent the last few days punishing herself, hoping she was never ungrateful; a time would never come to thank Mary, and without her, Esther would not have survived. Unlike Thomas, Esther knew from the second day of her absence Mary wouldn't return. She wished she could have told her how much their life meant to her, and she made a vow to say it in her prayers every night, even if it was for nothing.

Much to Esther's dismay, rumors were swirling around the Hiltmore house, all centered around what was to be done with Esther following such a drastic turn of events. She overheard many conversations, usually hiding away in the maid's stairs, squatted down with her ear pressed against the door, grateful that eavesdropping was a skill she perfected as a child. Most thought Mary had been killed in some sort of tragic incident and would never be discovered; others thought she left Thomas and Esther to run away with a man, though who they couldn't say. Esther didn't know what to believe, and with the theories growing wilder, she became more and more certain Mary was dead. Against her wishes, Celeste told her parents, and both Mr. and Mrs. Hiltmore met with Esther and asked how she and Thomas were coping, their expressions doubting Esther's assurances they were doing fine. It had nearly been a week, and every gaze she met in the hallway was filled with pity and condolence. It made Esther's fists ball up in anger – she didn't want or need anyone's sympathy. Not from them at least.

"If there is anything we can do, Esther, anything at all, we are at your disposal," Douglas Hiltmore reminded her each morning, his worry clearly building. Esther thanked him but denied it was necessary. She greatly respected and admired the Hiltmores, however there was no real way they could do anything even if she asked. All she could do was go on with daily life as if nothing happened.

"Esther!" Celeste's voice rang out as she finished dusting the last curtain, snapping her to the present. "We are almost done here! Did you need Madame Moreau to go over anything you might have missed while cleaning?"

"Non!" she called, smiling at her friend.

"Oui!" Celeste acknowledged and turned to face the unfaltering disdain of Madame Moreau, who was turning a deep scarlet.

"Time for the little maid to fetch your tea, I think?" Madame Moreau spat, on the brink of being unable to control her outrage.

Taking the hint, Esther completed the last curtain and made her way to the servant's passage across the room, hastily descending down to the kitchen. Celeste and her mother took tea together nearly every day following her lessons in the drawing room, and Esther was always the one to serve them at their request. After a few twists and turns through the narrow staircase, she emerged into the kitchen to find a riled up Mrs. Shannon barking out orders to the staff as the dinner rush commenced. As everyone darted about tending to their respective tasks, Mrs. Shannon's hawk-like eyes found Esther.

"You've only got a few minutes, Es, so hurry your ass up!" she yelled, hustling her along as fast as she could. Mrs. Shannon more or less ran the entire Hiltmore household, and had for over a decade, keeping her main station in the kitchens where she could reprimand any of her workforce openly without disturbing the family. The woman was unapologetic and meticulous in her ways, wearing a conservative black dress daily and her hair tightly knotted in a bun on her head, accentuating her thin lips and light brown eyes. When she requested something of anyone, it was done without a fuss, because it was well known the outcome of not fulfilling that duty was far, far worse than any household chore.

Esther rushed around, scrambling to get together everything she needed. Once the tray was set with teacups, silverware, and plates, she threw on a kettle of water to heat up the brew, which never took more than a few minutes and gave Esther extra time. Half of her morning was spent dedicated to making lemon tarts for Celeste, which were her friend's favorite pastry, and Esther dashed down into the cold cellar to retrieve them along with a few cucumber sandwiches. Neatly, she placed the pastries on a stand and the sandwiches on a plate, slicing up a fresh lemon on the side for their tea.

As she rounded up her preparations, Esther poured the contents of the kettle into the teapot and picked up the heavy tray, happy to see Mrs. Shannon holding the door to the stairs open.

They had grown fond of one another in her time with the Hiltmores, and while Esther was close with all the staff, the majority of them frowned upon her relationship with Celeste. Esther promptly found out how straddling the line of maid and companion could have unfair consequences. Celeste wasn't privy to the hardships that came with their unconventional friendship – they fell solely on Esther, and on specific days, the staff's teasing would turn bitter, particularly amongst the younger maids. It was like she was trapped between two worlds, and often would have days she went home both grateful for her friend and frustrated with her at the same time. Mrs. Shannon, on the other hand, never treated her any differently and didn't mind telling off those who did during their daily meetings.

A few days earlier, when the time came that she couldn't hide it any longer, Esther informed Mrs. Shannon about Mary's disappearance, and she could see the ache in the older woman's face. After a small, troubled apology, Mrs. Shannon sent Esther onto her chores; yet, in the following days when Esther struggled to wrap up a few extra tasks, she found them already completed without anyone to take the credit. She assumed Mrs. Shannon had been the one to help, and it made Esther rest a little easier knowing she had Mrs. Shannon on her side.

"Stop!" Mrs. Shannon halted her as Esther was about to amble past with her tray. She looked her up and down, then grabbed the edge of her own apron and wiped away what Esther assumed was smut from her cheek. "There you go. Keep your balance up those stairs and don't drop the tray."

"I've never dropped a tray!" Esther cried.

"Doesn't mean you won't someday," she replied coolly. "Now scoot!"

With a roll of her eyes, Esther started to climb the stairs.

Nearing the top, she could hear Celeste and Mrs. Hiltmore talking merrily with one another, and as she pushed the door open they were laughing in loud, high spirits. Esther walked over leisurely, not wanting to disturb them; nevertheless, it only took a few seconds for Celeste and Catherine to notice her approach.

"There she is!" Mrs. Hiltmore exclaimed, clapping her hands together. "Celeste and I were just discussing her lessons. She says your French is almost better than hers is!"

Esther set the tray down cautiously at their table and curtsied before pouring them each a cup of tea with fresh lemon.

"Thank you, Mrs. Hiltmore, for the compliment, but my French is nowhere near as good as Celeste's."

"Oh please," Celeste interrupted, reaching for a lemon tart. "Esther has such a good memory. Much better than mine is. I don't think she's ever forgotten a word!"

"Is that right?" Mrs. Hiltmore asked curiously. Esther flushed and kept her eyes down, wanting to remain as inconspicuous as possible. Being the praised subject of any dialogue no matter how trivial was not something she was used to, especially because of her social station.

Mrs. Hiltmore was a society darling. Her outgoing and bubbly persona made her a delight to have as an acquaintance, primarily because she was the constant center of attention at any group event, and that was just the way she liked it. Esther did not ever let it show, but she found it difficult to enjoy her time with Celeste's mother. Constantly there seemed to be a hidden agenda underneath her jovial exterior, and she took pride in being extremely intimidating to those around her. Along with that, she was so beautiful Esther had a feeling she had never been contradicted, making her all the more self-assured in her observations. Both mother and daughter were nearly identical: tall and graceful, with light blue eyes, button noses, and shimmering blonde hair that cascaded for miles. Together, they were quite a sight. To Esther's relief, however, and in spite of their matching physical attributes, Celeste took after her father in personality. Rather than putting Esther on edge, being with Celeste was relaxing for her and extremely easy to handle. Celeste was calm, collected, and sincere where Mrs. Hiltmore was boisterous, extroverted, and at times, her wit was insensitive and brash. As Esther finished serving their tea, she realized she could not have been a greater contrast in comparison with the pair, and it reminded her of her real place. Esther was only a maid, and she was not and would not ever be one of them, regardless of Celeste trying to convince her otherwise.

And then out of the blue, Catherine Hiltmore changed all that.

She took a sip of tea and her eyes locked on Esther. "Esther, dearest, would you want to join us for tea today? Be one of us girls?

I have some things I would like to talk to you about, and I would feel a lot better knowing you felt more…included."

Esther froze, stunned by such a formal request, unsure of how to react to the invitation. On several occasions she had been treated to tea, and yet that had only been with Celeste and on their own, typically when the Hiltmores were entertaining guests downstairs. From the look on Celeste's face, she was just as blindsided as Esther was, gaping at her mother with astonishment. Mrs. Hiltmore pretended not to notice the rising nervous tension as she snacked on one of the cucumber sandwiches.

"Celeste, why don't you take Esther back to your dressing room and put her in something…a little more elegant? Something suitable for tea?"

Esther thought her legs might give out, and while she tried to find the words to protest, Celeste got there first.

"Uh…why yes, of course! Give us just a few minutes, mother."

Celeste leapt up, taking Esther by the hand and leading her off down the hallway. In whispers, Celeste was striving to be cordial and reassuring; nevertheless, Esther didn't hear. Her head had gone foggy, the world around her silent. There was something about this that made her feel uneasy, toyed with even, but it was too late to decline the offer. Celeste escorted her with a grin, squeezing her friend's hand in hers, and when they reached Celeste's rooms she threw the doors open, nearly scaring Laura to death, who at the time was putting fresh sheets on the bed.

"Laura, I need you to go to my closet," Celeste ordered without hesitation, and Esther promptly closed the doors behind them. A bewildered Laura dropped the bed linens where she stood and darted over to Celeste's wardrobe, doing what was instructed despite her alarmed confusion.

Celeste continued: "Esther, you go behind my changing board. Undress quickly. Laura? Grab my dark red satin gown, the one that I outgrew last season and was being sent to the tailor. It should fit her perfectly." Esther took her place behind the dividers and stripped to her undergarments, the whole thing like some sort of strange dream. Within a few seconds, Celeste marched over and handed the dress around the side to her, and Esther warily pulled it on, terrified she might tear or ruin it. Just as she'd gotten her arms through the sleeves, Celeste commanded she come out for them to see and assist.

Esther came forward, and the look on both their faces made her heart skip a beat. Sarah immediately went to her side and adjusted the gown, buttoning the back up for her. The dress was a simple princess cut in a dark red hue, making Esther's green eyes pop, and as she caught a glimpse of herself in Celeste's vanity mirror, she couldn't believe how different she appeared. The butterflies in her stomach fluttered violently whilst Celeste smoothed the lining of the skirt and expertly pinned her hair up on top of her head the way she'd done with her own a thousand times.

Esther swallowed. "I don't…I don't know Celeste…"

"What do you mean you don't know?" she posed, her words slurred from the pins in her teeth as she kept working. "Hold still. This piece doesn't want to stay…"

"This isn't…I mean I've never worn anything so…so fine…I just don't understand what's going on…"

"It's my mother. God knows what is going on in that brain of hers."

Laura let out a slight giggle, which lessened Esther's anxiety. "What would she want to talk to me about though?"

"I don't know, Es. We both are going to find out together. Don't worry. It's going to be fine I promise." Celeste put two more pins in and took a step back, examining her work. "You're perfect. You are just stunning. Right Laura?"

"Stunning," Laura agreed, nodding compliantly.

"Good. Now come on, we can't keep her waiting much longer."

In under ten minutes, Esther felt transformed, like a caterpillar to a butterfly, and the two girls rapidly shuffled through the hallway toward the drawing room hand in hand, excited for whatever occasion this surprise might warrant.

Entering the room together, Mrs. Hiltmore rotated to greet them. "My, my!" she cried when they strode through the doors. Her gaze scrutinized Esther closely, and after a moment, she gave an approving smile. "Look how beautiful you are, Esther! A wonderful choice of dress too, Celeste. Now, the two of you sit. We have some important things to discuss at our tea time." Celeste and Esther took their respective places eagerly on either side of Catherine, glancing at each other with anticipation. Esther noticed in her absence a place had been set for her with a cup of tea as well as a plate with a lemon tart seated neatly in the middle. She stretched out to grab for her tea and then thrust her hands into her lap, seeing how shaky they were and not wanting to embarrass herself in Mrs. Hiltmore's presence.

"What is going on, mother?" Celeste pressed, picking up her previously half-eaten pastry.

Mrs. Hiltmore set down her teacup. "Well, as you already know Celeste, Esther is in an unfortunate dilemma. Her guardian has, to our dismay, disappeared without a trace. It has been a week since, and we are…sadly, Douglas and I are not sure she will return to resume caring for Esther." Esther's heart fearfully skipped a beat, wondering if this was some sort of masquerade to make her feel special before firing her. "Douglas and I have discussed it, and while we love Thomas and how courteous he is when he has been in our home, we do not believe he is a suitable caretaker for a young lady with Esther's potential."

Esther didn't quite understand what Mrs. Hiltmore was implying, and she grew defensive of Thomas. "Tommy takes good care of me. He is always kind and wanting to do what's best for us."

"Of course, dear, that is exactly what I mean," Catherine persisted supportively. "I think you have a promising future, yet I do not believe staying in the…the living situation you are in now will benefit you in any way. In fact, I think it will do you much more harm than good."

Celeste saw Esther's ears redden and spoke up first. "What do you mean?"

"Celeste, every one of your tutors, and that includes that insufferable Madame Moreau, have all told me Esther's aptitude for knowledge is astounding. She excels with less teaching than some of the smartest students they have ever had. Douglas and I believe she would be an asset to you, and to society, with the right...the right coaching."

A smile crept onto Celeste's face, and again her hand found Esther's under the table. "Are you saying...?"

Mrs. Hiltmore took another sip of tea. "I am saying that we have decided to take on Esther as a ward of our household, if she would agree to move in, and continue her time here as your companion, not as your maid. What do you say, Esther? Could you agree to such an offer?"

Esther nearly fainted out of her chair. "A-a ward?" she stuttered. "You mean...I would no longer be a servant?"

Mrs. Hiltmore shook her head. "You will be at Celeste's side where you belong, not behind her. You are a beautiful girl, Esther, and it is not often a mother has the chance to help someone of your class and know it will better each one of our lives, not just yours. I want to give you an opportunity you've only dreamed of. What would you say to that?"

Esther smirked, doing her best to ignore the insult. "Can I just ask one question?"

"Of course you can! What is it, dearest?"

"Why?"

Catherine let out a small cackle. "Esther, this is why I adore you. You're always the first to want to peek at what's underneath the surface, and that is something I hope you pass along to my daughter. It is, after all, an offer that requires more explanation than your success in Celeste's lessons. Douglas and I love our daughter, Esther. We want what is best for her, and to have a loyal, well-rounded friend at her side will aid her in transitioning into society with a spotless reputation. You are her confidant, the closest thing to a sister she'll ever find. Your importance to her makes you important to us. There are lots of bad apples in our midst, Esther, and the last thing any young girl needs is to fall victim to those people and temptations. And that goes for both of you. We want to take you in as one of our own and make you a part of our family. What do you say?"

The initial shock of the Hiltmores' offer finally gave way to happiness, and Esther beamed from ear to ear. "I…well yes! I absolutely will. Thank you so much for your generosity, Mrs. Hiltmore. I just…" The moment the words left her lips, however, her enthusiasm diminished as her thoughts went to the one person who mattered most.

Celeste could perceive something was wrong. "What is it?"

"I don't know how I am going to tell Thomas," she admitted, guilt-ridden.

"Esther, listen to me," Mrs. Hiltmore said softly, leaning forward and resting her hand on Esther's shoulder delicately. "It is deplorable what has happened to his mother, a complete tragedy. I cannot imagine how hard things have been for him or for you. But you need to consider what lies ahead for you in the future. It was his mother who has vanished, and his life is going to change drastically. A young woman living with a young man she is not related to is generally frowned upon in this day and age, regardless of how tolerable the world is starting to become. Do you understand what I'm telling you?"

Esther knew she was right and nodded reluctantly. "I do understand. I am not sure he will, though."

"He will get over it, Es!" Celeste added encouragingly. "He can visit whenever he wants, right mother?"

Catherine let her hand fall from Esther's shoulder and grinned at Celeste. "Indeed. We want to make this a smooth transition for both of you."

Esther stared at Catherine Hiltmore, wise enough to grasp that deep down she was lying through her teeth. The promises were decorated and put together to try to hide the fact that Esther was nothing but a charity case for Mrs. Hiltmore – something to brag and boast over, carrying on to all her friends about her good deeds while downing champagne at the opera. The minute she left Thomas behind that woman would make sure he was gone for good, not wanting anything in her daughter's wake that might soil the perfect world she'd built for Celeste. Then again, there was no denying this was the greatest opportunity Esther would ever receive, freeing her from her fate as a domestic servant to become a real lady...something she never thought could be possible. Esther had to accept – Mrs. Hiltmore's intentions were selfish, yes, though she had been spot on. If Esther continued to live with Thomas, any hopes of fine things and high society would vanish...just as Mary had. She would never again be handed a fresh start along with a step up into a world of luxury, and therefore would have to say yes, no matter if that meant hurting and leaving behind the only person she had always counted on.

Her hands finally steady, Esther reached out for her cup and took a drink of her tea. "I will tell him. Can I have a few days to think of what I want to say and talk it over with him?"

"Absolutely," Mrs. Hiltmore confirmed. "Whatever is necessary."

There was a brief pause before Celeste squealed aloud in delight, and the three ladies carried on to discuss the upcoming details of Esther's move into their residence and tutoring alongside Celeste. One of the guest bedrooms would be Esther's permanently, and she was to have an appointment made with a tailor to fashion a few dresses for her the following week. The whole afternoon was such a whirlwind Esther could barely keep up with their banter, and eventually took to simply smiling and nodding along with Catherine and Celeste's plans.

When their tea concluded, Celeste took Esther back to her rooms to change into her work clothes, talking animatedly about the days ahead. Esther played along while her heart was taken in by a flurry of emotions. For as long as she could remember, her life had been chaotic and filled with ups and downs, and Esther learned to deal with the sudden changes as they came. Thomas' life had always been steady and consistent, like his personality, and this would hurt him more than he would ever let on. It was an agonizing situation with no easy way out, and she could only hope this way would be the best for them both. Esther did not want to be a burden on him, and more importantly, didn't want to make him feel obligated to care for her.

The remainder of the day passed in a daze for Esther, and she went through the motions engrossed in how she would bring up Mrs. Hiltmore's offer with Thomas. She lent a hand to Mrs. Shannon and Anthony in preparing dinner to try and subdue her thoughts, and afterward traveled upstairs to dress Celeste for the evening. Sensing her own discontented state, Esther took her time trudging up the steps, struggling to force herself into a lighter mood. When she reached Celeste's rooms she was surprised to find her friend sitting on the bed, waiting for her.

"Come in and sit here," she said, patting the spot next to her on the mattress.

Esther did as she was asked and folded her hands in her lap, her eyes on the ground. "If you changed your mind, I don't blame you."

"Don't be ridiculous!" Celeste exclaimed. "Listen, Es, I know this week has been hard on you and Thomas, and I know you don't want to leave him. But I swear I will take care of you. You are the sister I have always wanted! Thomas may be upset but he will also know this is the right thing, and he can visit us whenever you'd like. I'll do everything I can to make it up to you. You won't regret it, I promise. Okay?"

Esther felt a hot tear stream down her cheek. "Okay," she sniffed. "I hope you know how happy I am. It's just…this week… losing Mary…"

"I know," she told her. "But you are so smart, Es. You should be able to be given the prospects you deserve! By the time we are eighteen we will have all the eligible men eating out of our palms, and we can have children who grow up best friends just as we are. Don't you want that?"

"I…I do…of course I do…"

Celeste pulled her in and hugged her tight. "I need you, Es. My mother and my father see that. I need a sister to rely on and to have confidence with, just like you do. Being alone won't do either of us any good. We need each other!"

Esther wiped her eyes. "I know you're right. You always are."

"Hardly!" Celeste declared, releasing her. "But we were meant to have this together. My parents love you. We can be a family… the four of us!"

"I really am so thankful for this. I wish you could see that."

"I can," she comforted her and smiled. "And Es? There is no reason to be so upset. It will all be fine. All right?"

"All right."

"Good!" Celeste giggled and got to her feet. "Now, let's get me dressed for dinner. I'll never hear the end of it from mother if I'm late."

A short time later Thomas arrived to retrieve Esther from work. She was dining with the rest of the staff, who were abuzz from her afternoon tea with Celeste and Mrs. Hiltmore. Esther smartly decided it was best not to tell them it was anything other than a treat, and after she deliberately avoided answering their questions, they dropped their inquisition, filling Esther with relief. When Thomas entered the kitchen, everyone paid their respects as usual and miraculously didn't mention anything regarding her afternoon to him. Esther was seated at the servant's dinner table, and she drained the remainder of her stew from the bowl and said goodnight, not wanting to press her luck and linger too long. Grabbing Thomas' arm, she led him out the back door, wanting to leave the Hiltmores' before someone spoke up.

"How was your day?" he asked when they reached the street.

"It…it was fine. Just…busy."

"Busy? Oh no! Did you get to sit in on French today?"

"No, I couldn't. The curtains took longer than I thought they would. They get so dusty during the summer months with all this wind, I can never finish them in time!"

Thomas chuckled. "What a shame. Well I hope tomorrow you can listen in. Should I take you in a little earlier so you can get your chores done earlier?"

"Okay." Esther struggled for a few seconds and failed to muster the courage to tell Thomas about tea. It made her stomach turn.

"Are you all right, Es? You look pale." He stopped and bent down to feel the temperature of her cheek.

"I feel fine. I think I'm just tired," she lied.

Thomas rose, though from his face he didn't believe her, and the pair renewed their walk home. "I don't envy you, Es. It must be hard to work for the Hiltmores with Celeste as your friend. I know it isn't easy to see everything they have compared to us. Just remember, sometimes things that look wonderful and pleasant from the outside aren't that way on the inside. Do you understand what I mean?"

"I think so."

"Really?"

"I mean, I don't like Mrs. Hiltmore either."

Thomas laughed heartily. "So you do know what I meant."

"Yes," she confided. "She's worse than my mother used to be. But they do treat me well, Tommy."

He sighed as they turned a corner. "I know, Es. I just want to make sure you see people's true colors. That's all."

They took their time wandering home, and for the remainder of their trip Esther tried again to practice in her head what exactly she wanted to say to Thomas on the subject of the Hiltmores' offer. When they got home, Esther went straight to the kitchen table and sat down, her mouth ready to speak the words until Thomas disrupted her thoughts. He tossed a book down on the table in front of her, and Esther picked it up, examining it closely.

"What is this?" she asked, taking it into her hands.

"I found it in a shop today. I thought you might enjoy a little reading, though it is a little outdated…"

"*Betsy Thoughtless*?"

Thomas pulled a chair up next to her. "It has to do with young girls coming of age. The guy at the store recommended it. Apparently, it's supposed to teach you lessons of what not to do, especially as you get older."

Esther was touched. "You got this for me?"

"Just for you! I mean, you don't think I want to read it, do you?"

She giggled. "No, I guess not." Esther opened the book and couldn't resist a grin. "Thank you, Tommy. Can we read some tonight?"

"Sure. Why don't you get ready for bed and we can read a bit of it before you go to sleep?"

Esther ecstatically jumped to her feet, running to change into her bedclothes. Her determination to tell Thomas was readily pushed aside for tomorrow. After all, why did she need to tell him right away? There was no reason to ruin the night after he brought her such a nice gift. Their upcoming talk would not be easy to have, and her eyes were already growing heavy from a long day of dusting and scrubbing floors.

They were ten pages into Eliza Haywood's novel when there was a loud knock on the door. Thomas and Esther were both cuddled up in her bed while she read aloud to him, and the sound of a visitor at such a late hour made them jump.

Thomas did not loiter – he was instantaneously on his feet heading toward the doorway of her room. He halted as he reached it and turned to face her.

"Listen to me, Es," he whispered urgently, his eyes humorless. "You lock your bedroom door as soon as I close it. All right? You lock it and don't come out until you hear my voice saying it's okay to come out."

Esther was petrified yet did as she was told; the second the door closed behind Thomas she rushed over and locked the deadbolt tight. Being safely secured inside, Esther slid down to the floor, hugging her knees to her chest and pressing her ear against the door, unsure of what to expect and praying it was someone…anyone they might know, or some kind of misunderstanding.

Through the barrier between her and the foyer, she could hear Thomas shuffling through the apartment frantically. The knock came again, this time louder and harder.

"One moment!" he shouted, and Esther could sense a slight panic in his tone. Instead of going directly for the front door, Thomas went to his room first, where he rummaged for a moment and then made his way to open the door. As the sound of the lock releasing echoed to her, Esther closed her eyes and held her breath, trying not to make a sound.

"Oh, for fuck's sake!" she heard a familiar voice cry. "What in the hell do you think you're doing with that, Thomas? You going to kill me with my own fucking gun?" Esther heard what she assumed was a slap, followed by Thomas mumbling something inaudibly. It was the Madame.

"You think I wouldn't piece together that you took the fucking key, Thomas? Do you really think I'm that God damned stupid to not notice the key was gone the minute I arrived back in my office? And now here you are with the gun from my own safe in your fucking hand. I could have you arrested for burglary, you stupid bastard!"

Esther couldn't be sure, but she thought she heard another much softer tick, which she could only presume was Thomas uncocking the gun.

"Sit down," was all he said, followed by a tense silence and the noise of chairs moving against the hardwood. Esther's pounding heart began to decelerate, happy their late night call was someone they both knew so well; still, she could sense something was amiss, and she wished she could see what was happening rather than stuck struggling to hear through the door.

"Louis will beat you for this, Thomas…"

"He won't. Not after he finds out the truth. Sit down, please."

A hushed curse was followed by the squeak of a chair, implying the Madame conceded to Thomas' demands. There was a clinking of glasses and the sound of liquid being poured, and then at last Thomas continued.

"You stole my mother's letters. I want to know why in the hell you took the letters. And why you've been lying to her and to me for so long. Do you realize what you've done? You ruined my mother's…you ruined our lives!"

"Put the gun away, Thomas."

"I will put the gun away when I damn well please!" he bellowed furiously. "Tell me the real reason why you took them!"

Esther bit her lip – she couldn't remember a time she'd ever heard Thomas so mad.

"I don't have to tell you anything!" the Madame snapped. "You can threaten me all you want, Thomas, I know sure as shit you won't shoot me. And if you do, the truth about Mary will die with me. Do you want to spend your whole life with that on your fucking conscience? Do you?!" The Madame paused, giving him ample time to retort. When he didn't respond, goose bumps rose on Esther's arms and down her spine.

The Madame went on. "A few men came to see me today. I've got a lead at last. I am on my way there after I see you tonight, and I am damn sure I will find out the real story. So can you please put the fucking gun down?"

Something heavy dropped to the table, hinting the Madame was no longer at Thomas' hostage. "A lead?"

"The only one I have gotten, and most likely, the only one we'll ever fucking get."

"And how can I trust you? You've destroyed the small amount of trust I had in you in the first place!"

"What do you want me to say, Thomas? Do you want me to tell you why I took the fucking letters? Fine. I took those God damned letters from your mother because I was afraid, Thomas. More afraid than I'd ever been."

Thomas snorted. "Afraid of what?"

The Madame let out a loud, frustrated exhale. "Clearly you don't understand how this works. Mary has been the only family I've ever had. You may fail to grasp this, darling, but the thought of losing her, and then you, was enough to make me lose my mind. I made an irrational decision, and even though a part of me didn't want to do it, there was no changing my mind. I had to make your father disappear. You were born out of wedlock…a bastard to a family that would have only viewed you as a burdensome, illegitimate child. Your mother may have thought he loved her, and maybe he did, but a family like his wouldn't have given a rat's ass about love – they're all about their fucking reputation being upheld. Mary fought me at first, but after his letters…stopped unexpectedly…I think she saw the real picture."

"You mean the picture you painted for her to see?"

"No, Thomas. You can live in denial if you wish, but I am justified in what I did. I saved you and your mother from a lifetime of pain and disappointed hopes. It was a shitty thing to do, yes. But I did what was fucking necessary to protect my damned family, and I refuse to be ashamed of that."

"The choice wasn't yours to make! You should have let her make the choice!"

"I wouldn't give you up, all right, Thomas? To a man your mother barely fucking knew for a summer? I wasn't going to let him take your mother away from me. I refused to let that happen. So I did what I had to do."

Esther's head started to hurt from pressing her ear so hard

56

against the door, barely to keep up with all they said, and she shook it off and noiselessly changed positions, rotating around to use her other ear.

"When did you start taking the letters?"

"Just after he left China…he wrote to your mother about being ill and she fucking panicked. Wanted to spend all her money and take you to England to meet him…fucking insanity. It would have been a disaster. I told her to wait until she heard from him when he was safely home in England, and from that point forward she never did. She was still living with me then, and hiding the letters was much easier than I thought it would be. After a few months, I convinced her he had either died of his sickness or decided to give her up. It wasn't until almost a year later, after intercepting every letter after that his health returned, I learned the depth of his inheritance. Because of this, the odds of him marrying someone of Mary's class became even more minimal. In order to make sure he never came looking for her, I wrote to him and told him she had died. And that is all the God damned truth I have for you. It was my own fucking scheme to keep my family in one piece. I have no regrets. I couldn't let Mary take that risk, so I stopped it from happening altogether."

Esther was stunned. All of this was so unexpected, and nothing could have ever prepared her for it. Thomas hadn't mentioned finding any letters on their walk home or anything about his father. The strange thing was, Esther actually found herself sympathizing with the Madame and what lengths she went to to keep Mary and Thomas out of harm's way. It had been wrong of her to lie, yet Esther could understand those actions, wishing jealously her own mother had fought as hard for her as the Madame did for Mary and Thomas. And they weren't even related.

Seconds later, the familiar noise of liquid pouring into their glasses reached Esther's ears, and the whiskey was an indicator Thomas' temper was subsiding.

"Where are you going tonight?" he inquired.

"To the Points," the Madame declared. "I am going to meet someone who claims to know some sort of information about Mary and her last seen whereabouts."

"Do you really think you'll find out anything?"

"Let's just say a prayer there will at least be some fucking closure. We have no other option, Thomas. And if I am being frank, I don't think anything I discover tonight will be a comfort. The men that came to see me are by no means the type to dick around if she were really in the trouble they claim she was in."

"Men? As in multiple?"

"As in multiple. Irish fucking goons. I can only guess I'm meeting whoever their ring leader is tonight."

"You can't go by yourself. I won't let you."

"Louis is with me."

"It sounds dangerous, even for Louis. The Points along with Irish pricks threatening you added together? You can't go down there and expect nothing is going to happen. And it's not like Louis will get a warm welcome, either. I at least know enough to understand Louis isn't…allowed there on his own terms."

Everything went quiet until the Madame muttered under her breath: "How could you know that?"

"Mary had a loose tongue when she had too much whiskey," Thomas divulged.

"Ah. And now you're so worried about what fucking happens to me, then? With or without Louis, I can take care of myself, Thomas."

"It's not the same anymore. It's gotten worse since the riots. You know that."

"Hah! We'll see about that. In the meantime, you also need to keep your head down, because there's a God damn target on it. You've been doing a lot of digging around, and if there is something someone is trying to hide, you'll be the first person they fucking come after." The room once again went silent for a few seconds, yet the Madame didn't let up. "Oh yes, Thomas. Whoever your mother pissed off has put us in some seriously hot water."

"I don't…I don't understand. Who are these people?"

"A group of people I don't want to fuck with, Thomas. People who could hurt us badly. She left nothing but a shit storm for me to figure out, and her son being tailed like fresh meat."

"You don't even care, do you?"

"Care? About what, Thomas?"

"Look at you!" he suddenly lashed out. "You aren't even…even upset! You walk into our home and just pragmatically tell me you took my dad from us with no regret whatsoever, and then you claim my mother is supposedly dead with a straight face and expect me to just sit here and take it? You want to know what I think? Do you? I think she's the only thing that made you feel human, and now that she's gone you've lost whatever was left of your own fucking heart and are left to be the cruel, cold bitch you really are!"

"Well! Look who finally has the balls to stand up to his dear old Aunt!" she thundered in return. "Yes, I am a cold bitch because it's the only fucking way to survive in this town, and you'd better get a thicker skin, Thomas, or the wolves will tear you to shreds. I have done nothing to you but make your life the best it could be. You have no idea the shit I have been through to keep you and your mother safe all these years, and clearly I've been sheltering you from too fucking much. The world is brutal, Thomas, and you'd better accept it. Your mother is gone and we can't get her back. Grow up, for your own sake, or there's nothing I can do to help you anymore."

Esther heard a chair fly back and clamor against the ground. It had to be Thomas', and she could feel him pacing to and fro, with heavy, frustrated breathing. No one said a word for what felt like hours, and Esther was tempted to go out to investigate when at last the Madame broke the staleness.

"What did you do with the letters?"

"They're in my room."

"Keep them. And will you do me one favor, Thomas?"

"I don't owe you a fucking thing."

"Thomas, please. I will take all the fucking blame for Edward, but don't blame what happened to your mother on me. I am doing everything I can, and I know you believe that. Please, Thomas." Her last few words were slightly choked, though she attempted to hide it.

"What is the favor?"

"Let go of your father. Please. Don't pursue finding him. Imagine he has moved on, to a new life with a new family, with no knowledge of any of this. The last thing this man needs after a life of unhappy fucking memories is to have his illegitimate son draw him back into his past. Don't do that to him, Thomas. You don't want to be responsible for ruining someone else's happiness...believe me. It's not something that goes down easy, no matter how much whiskey you drink."

"I'm keeping the letters."

"Good."

"And the Griswold."

"Fine," she answered with a hint of annoyance. "Do with them whatever you desire. Just don't be seen in public with it or people with have questions. And...try to trust I'm doing what's best for you. In the meantime, I must be on my way."

There was a scoot of the chair and footsteps toward the door. "Wait."

"Yes, Thomas?"

"What...what was he like?"

"Your father?"

"Yeah."

"Well..." Another sigh. "Christ, I only knew him a short time, and most of what I do know stems from what Mary confided in me."

"Please," Thomas pleaded. "Anything you can share."

The Madame let out an amused scoff. "Well, to be honest, you look almost identical to Edward...his splitting image, I'd say. It's uncanny...fucking uncanny. Anyway, I will be late. Goodnight, Thomas."

Esther stayed where she was for as long as she could bear after hearing the front door close, and when she couldn't stand it any longer, she unbolted her bedroom door and ran out to Thomas. He sat at their kitchen table with his shoulders hunched over, his head in his hands. As he heard her coming, Thomas turned: his eyes were red and puffy, his face worn down and defeated, and he opened his arms to her, allowing Esther to jump to his embrace. Esther squeezed tight, knowing that despite how hard she thought her day had been, it in no way compared to his. Everything that was said between him and the Madame was heavy and, in her opinion, extremely worrisome, and she hoped whatever danger Thomas had been in would be over soon.

They stayed that way for quite some time before Thomas finally let go of Esther and spoke, his voice cracking. "If I know you, Es, you heard every word of my argument with the Madame."

"I know I shouldn't have…"

"It's all right," he assured her, setting Esther down in the chair next to him. "Listen to me, Es. I don't know what is going to happen these next few weeks. It's going to be different, new, and scary for us. But we will make it through…it's just the two of us from now on, and looking out for each other is all that matters."

A rush of shame blasted her. "Tommy, I…" she tried to articulate the words but couldn't. Not at this moment, when Thomas needed her support more than ever.

"What is it, Es?"

"I…I want to know about the letters. About…Edward…?" She made it up on the spot, though it wasn't an all-out fib.

He smiled, and his dejection seemed to lift off his shoulders. "Ask me anything, and I'll do my best to tell you what I've found out."

After a few minutes of talking, Thomas went to his room and retrieved the letters, and he let her read a few back to him as they tried to piece together the puzzle of who Thomas' father was. She loved to see him laugh and let go of his hurt – he had always been the positive force in their home, and not having that in her everyday life made her weary of how she would get on without him. Esther didn't want to desert him. It would kill her to say goodbye to their partnership, to the one person she'd grown to really adore and appreciate, and she could only pray their last few days together would be just like that night turned out to be – full of hope, good memories, and joyfulness.

As Esther fell asleep tucked away into bed an hour later, she dreamt of strolling through the streets of New York City with Celeste, years older and donning the same beautiful red dress from that afternoon while they laughed merrily under a sunny sky. She woke the next morning with the notion that her dream had been a premonition of her future, and the bliss she felt by far outweighed her ache of responsibility toward Thomas. There was also a very real fear that if she didn't take this opportunity, she would not be asked a second time, and that notion she couldn't live with.

While getting dressed for the day, Esther kept flashing back to what the Madame had said to her the day her mother abandoned her at The Palace. It was only the two of them in her office, and Esther sat across from that giant, menacing desk, not afraid…but more in awe. There was no solace or pity in what the Madame told her. In fact, if Esther recalled correctly, she could appreciate that her advice was a warning from a woman who had made a similar mistake before.

"If you try to hold a drowning man above water, you'll flounder with him. Better to take your chances on your own than die together."

She and Thomas needed to swim on their own, or she would sink down with him. And for Esther, sinking would never be an option, no matter how much she loved Thomas.

Like the Madame, it must not be in her nature.

III.

The Madame stepped outside of Mary and Thomas' apartment and stopped, taking a deep breath in of the cool night air as she replayed the evening again in her head. Her visit with Thomas was positive in the end, and while the Madame hated having to deceive him with false grief, his youth and immaturity would never allow him to understand she had cried the totality of her tears long before she reached adolescence. Growing up an orphaned girl along with so many others in the Points was an unremitting vicious battle amongst the sort of people Thomas knew in the worst of his worst dreams. Only the strongest survived, and survived she had. At the time when Mary happened to fall into her realm of responsibility, the Madame made a vow to God that she would not let Mary suffer the way she had suffered all those years. It was by no means an easy feat to take on at her age, yet it was the most rewarding thing the Madame had ever done. This past week had been unbearable for her with no end or vindication in sight. She loved Mary, more than she would admit to herself. But falling to that weakness was no way to go about business, especially when it became clear the men Mary double-crossed weren't just the everyday idiotic bastards she was used to. Nonetheless, the Madame refused to give into the victim mentality. Tonight she would regain control and get the answers she needed. It was time to be the predator and not the prey…and she sincerely hoped it wouldn't be a fucking bloodbath.

Louis was waiting for her at the bottom of the wooden staircase, his back to her, eyes scanning the area around them, and she smirked: her ever-watchful guard dog. When she was collected and ready, the Madame descended down to him and halted at Louis' side, staring out into the empty street.

"Went well?" he muttered quietly.

"Yes. Time to go."

"Carriage is around the second block. No tails, no spies. For now."

"Good."

Their driver patiently sat at the helm of the coach, nodding in acknowledgement as they drew closer. The moment Louis and the Madame slipped into the passenger car, the driver flicked the reins to get moving. They'd both been careful, constantly checking their tracks to be sure they weren't being followed. Until they could identify their enemy and the source of their troubles, no chances could be taken. There were no reservations in the Madame's mind that Thomas was being kept under surveillance, and she hoped that by the end of the night, his newly acquired shadow would be called off.

Her eyes fell on Louis, who appeared nervous. "What the fuck's gotten into you?" she posed.

"Fucking Whyos. You know I am not supposed to set foot in the Points. Under any circumstance."

"And technically neither am I. Pull yourself together, for Christ's sake. We're not dealing with any of the shithouse Bowery gangs. This is someone much higher up the fucking totem pole."

"Who could it be?" Louis pressed. "It's not like Mary was working for big money uptown. O'Neill is just a worthless Irish prick."

The Madame shook her head. "It's not money, Louis. It's worse."

"What's worse than money?"

"Politics. Politics and power, darling. Because in the eyes of those bastards, they can never have enough."

"Can we handle this?" he asked. "Are we prepared?"

She glanced out the window to try to disguise her insecurity. "I don't know yet, Louis. I just don't fucking know."

About ten minutes later, the carriage came to a standstill, indicating they had indeed arrived in the Points. With only a quick peek at each other, the Madame and Louis communicated what was at stake, and that time was of the essence. She flung the door open and set off down the street, staying three paces ahead while allowing Louis to continue surveying the darker alleys and doorways as they passed. The Madame and Louis had been an enigmatic team since the very beginning, and hiring him as her protection had paid off tenfold in their years together. During the early days of her business venture when they were still located downtown, it was often suggested she ought to hire protection for her and her girls, yet the Madame despised the idea of not being able to defend herself in her own establishment. However, just after reluctantly giving in and signing on Louis at Mary's suggestion, a woman nearly gutted the Madame outside the old Palace over her loose husband's antics. This incident swiftly made the Madame warm up to the idea of a bodyguard due to the fact that Louis got there in the exact right moment to save her skin. When the excitement was over, the Madame beat the woman senseless with her bare hands to send a loud and clear message, though by no means was she fool enough to think she would be alive without Louis. In conclusion, that episode sold her on Louis for good, and much to her satisfaction, no one had come that close to her since.

And she wanted to keep it that way.

Off in the distance, the Madame heard church bells chime and moved faster. Eleven. She had some ground to cover but would be right on time. Her morning appointment following Thomas' unforeseen social call was an intriguing turn of events. A man by the name of Seamus Murphy that the Madame had never met before and two of his goons came to meet with her on account of Mary's disappearance. These so-called gentlemen started their negotiations firmly, insisting Mary betrayed the trust of their mutual employer as well as his clients, and therefore she had been "disposed of." Seamus and the other imbeciles explained they were there to make sure any search or investigation by the Madame or Thomas would be suspended indefinitely, and threatened to kill Thomas and burn down The Palace if she didn't cooperate. It was hard for the Madame not to laugh in their faces, though somehow, she managed.

Seamus and his friends made the presumption they could squeeze her, and who could blame them? Those poor bastards didn't know who she was or what she was capable of. Of course, in practiced fashion, she and Louis struck like lightening. Armed with pistols as they always were with new faces, the Madame and Louis drew their guns upon being threatened, unwavering in their ferocity. The color drained from their visitors' cheeks, realizing they had made a monumental mistake, and the three men left with their tails between their legs. They returned an hour later with a counter offer from their "employer:" he would meet with the Madame tonight at St. Michael's in the Five Points at a quarter past eleven. This, for her and Louis, was unchartered territory, and still the Madame agreed. There was nothing else she could do. She needed to find resolution, for her and for Thomas' sake.

What bothered her most was she should have seen it coming all along. The Madame warned Mary just prior to taking her new job with O'Neill that it wasn't precisely upstanding work, let alone legal. Mary ignored the Madame's arguments, and she couldn't blame her. The pay nearly quadrupled what Mary had been making at her former workplace, and for a time she seemed to uphold the discretion she was required to. Eventually, it did begin to wear down her moral compass, and a few months into running O'Neill's books Mary made one detrimental mistake: she told an innocent bystander, her old friend Harry, that she was cooking the books. From there everything escalated out of control.

The job was by no means only about running O'Neill's numbers at the store. The Madame was convinced Mary came across more than a few nasty secrets during her short time in that position. Within weeks, Mary looked as if she'd aged five years, and was timid and uncomfortable whenever the subject of her employment was brought up, thus making the Madame heavily contemplate if she needed to intervene. During their final conversation, Mary admitted to her the books she thought were for O'Neill's general store were for a whole other sort of operation; however, despite her persistent queries, Mary did not disclose any details of the content to the Madame, though it was apparent Mary had gotten herself involved in some sort of illicit activity.

The Madame cursed aloud to the empty street – she should have kept pushing and broken down those barriers rather than allow Mary to flounder right in front of her. A small piece of the Madame's conscience took the blame for Mary's fate...for not taking care of a problem she could have solved with the snap of her God damned fingers.

She was too late. Now Mary was, in all likelihood, long dead.

Late one night, Mary went to meet Harry for a drink after a long day, and five whiskeys later her discontent surfaced, leading her to confess to Harry what had been shredding her morale bit by bit. Harry had been Mary's shoulder to cry on for many years for things she wouldn't bother the Madame with, and Harry, like any other man, had ulterior motives despite Mary making it clear on several occasions the two would only remain platonic friends.

The morning following the occurrence, Mary fled to the Madame in a panic, conceding to her mistake in getting Harry involved. Harry was paid by the Madame and Mary to leave town a week later, and he complied without much dispute. Mary believed it might save him from meeting a terrible end, and also possibly save her own skin. On the sly, however, the Madame left out a tiny detail of her plan. In a last ditch effort to clean up the mess Mary created, Harry was unluckily the collateral damage. The day Mary disappeared, Harry's body was found thirty miles outside of the city by the police. She had given the order for the hit, and Louis carried it out by her instruction. Unfortunately, her interference was in vain.

St. Michael's was daunting in the distance: the dark stone walls of the church and foggy mist in the air gave it the appearance of an old medieval cathedral, and the haunting gargoyles on the rooftop seemed to watch her every move as she drew closer. The Madame strode toward the bottom of the stone staircase which lead toward the large iron-trimmed doors. She halted for a moment. Glancing back to Louis, she saw he lingered just off to her right, and with a quick nod, the Madame rotated and began to climb the stairs unhurriedly. Louis would await her return outside unless the Madame gave the signal – she really didn't want it to come to that.

The doors were much lighter than she remembered, and the Madame inconspicuously stepped inside the church. Once inside the doorway, she gently closed both doors shut behind her and habitually recited a hushed Hail Mary, lightly dipping her hand in the holy water and making the sign of the cross. The entire inside was dark, yet beautifully lit by candlelight – it was tranquil, silent, and empty of worshipers, giving her a sense of solace contrary to the real reason she was there. Moving onward, the Madame sat in the seventh pew from the rear as previously directed. Her unknown company would arrive soon, and she attempted to keep her heart steady through long, deep breaths. Whoever might show had the clear cut advantage; the Madame was on their turf, and until she met the man behind this catastrophe, the only things that mattered were Mary's whereabouts and what was at stake for her and for Thomas.

Suddenly, the Madame was very aware she was no longer by herself in the church. A figure came to the pew and into her peripheral vision, though she didn't bother to turn her head. Instead, she kept her eyes forward, and the man wordlessly slid into her row and sat down right beside her, leaning back to rest on the bench.

"I know why you are here, and I want to help you," he started, his words clear and articulate. "But I hope you also understand that this is business. You of all people should know it's just how things are done if you want to move up in this city."

It took another deep exhale for her to refrain from attacking him outright, and on the contrary, the Madame settled with a shrewd smile.

"I do understand," she replied. "I came here for an explanation only, with no hidden agenda, and to make sure I leave with a clean slate." Her hands gripped into fists beneath her crossed arms, and she could feel her nails digging into her palms through the leather gloves. Composure wasn't her fucking specialty. Pivoting to face him, the Madame was astonished when she recognized who he was, and her muscles became tense.

"I can see that you know who I am," he observed, amused.

She swallowed her anxiety. "I do. I guess what I can't understand is why a member of the Hall is involved in something so… well…like this, Mr. Croker. It doesn't exactly live up to the new standards Tammany has spent every dollar they have left promoting."

Croker scrutinized at her for a few seconds, and the Madame thought she may have already crossed the line. "Standards are a pretense for the beginning of any regime. In truth, it's impossible to have standards in a place like New York City…it's a corrupt piece of shit that lives in hypocritical denial and is run solely by the mob. Investors purposefully shield their eyes from the hell this place really is. It's an eat or be eaten world, Madame, and that's not news to you considering your…elaborate history. Particularly in these parts." His eyes were ice cold as he spoke, lacking any sentiment. "In the case of Mary, I was invested. I needed to see it through that any risks were handled promptly, and correctly as any good businessman might do. As you yourself would do."

"Handled?" The Madame found it hard to keep her voice relaxed, irate with the arrogant tone he took with her.

"She should have listened to your advice from the beginning and not taken the job," he declared, "but money has a sway over people they sometimes cannot overrule. O'Neill explained her role and that the details of what she did were not to be discussed with anyone. Are you aware of what exactly she was doing there?"

"Enlighten me, Mr. Croker."

He seemed almost pleased by her ignorance. "My colleague, Seamus Murphy, does a lot of business with Mary's former employer, a man by the name of Carol. I assume you are acquainted with him?"

"Yes I am."

"Months ago, Carol bragged to Seamus one day about the overly intelligent woman he had more or less running the store for him. Through a little maneuvering and under some watchful eyes, Mary was found to be just what we required for our operations: an Irish woman with great intelligence and potential…and no political affiliations. The type of person Seamus thought we could easily control to keep our ventures under wraps. With everyone vanquished from Tweed's office, Kelly rebuilt with new faces, including mine. It didn't take long for us to come to the conclusion that 'openness and honesty' were not going to bring us voters or any sort of power over the people and politics that fuel New York. Kelly turned a blind eye to allow us to expand on our own terms, and we did just that."

This news did not shock her in the slightest. "So Kelly has no idea what you're doing, then?"

"Officially, no he does not. O'Neill is an old friend of his, one who would do anything to see Kelly thrive. When I came to him with the proposition of making Kelly a great success, he was on board, and I initiated running the unsanctioned portion of the Tammany campaign out his back door."

"So Mary ran the money and started to have reservations about her…or rather, your work, I should say."

Croker scoffed mockingly. "Oh, she didn't just handle the money, Madame, though that information is known by only a select few. But yes, I guess you could say she was becoming ill at ease with our operation, and rather than come to us, she did the one thing we asked her not to."

It was worse than she originally assumed. "And the store O'Neill runs is…?"

"Moderately profitable, but that, as you can probably assume, is no interest to me. We meet and operate through the private rooms of his place. No one has any idea what it covers for, and I plan on keeping it that way. We had one small request, and yet she had to break her promise to us. A shame really."

The flame of the Madame's temper lit. "It wasn't as if she went screaming into the fucking streets, Mr. Croker. She told a friend, a personal confidant—"

"On the contrary, Madame," he barked in response. "You should not challenge me when you yourself are not privy to the truth."

"And just what truth is that?"

Croker shook his head, as if her questions were childish and not worth his time. "Do you know what that 'confidant' of hers was going to do, Madame? Do you? No, of course you don't…Mary would never tell you the real purpose behind her being at the bar with him that night. And I'm sure she never happened to mention this was not the first time the two had met to discuss the Hall."

The Madame shifted in her seat. "I was unaware of that."

"The real purpose, or rather, the purpose of her meeting with Harry, was meant to try and obtain the ledger along with numerous other documents she alone had access to in order to bring our enterprise down. Mary was by no means meeting her 'confidant' to get some work bullshit off her chest. After spending some time interrogating her, Mary divulged that she was actually meeting both Harry and Pinkerton in a repeated fashion, who told her what she needed to steal and how to do it. Harry and this man made rapid progress, all of which was miraculously able to be undone in the aftermath. Mary's intentions were not as innocent as she tried to make you believe, Madame. Otherwise, do you think I would have gone to all this trouble for one measly, drunk conversation? I think we've all been there a time or two."

The Madame was baffled, not wanting to believe a word of it, though her gut told her it was no lie. That disbelief became irritation with herself for not perceiving what was directly under her nose for months. Albeit Mary had indeed conspired against Croker and Tammany, the Madame couldn't give into him so readily; if Mary were dead and they wanted to scare her, Croker wouldn't be meeting her on such unstable terms. There was something else he wanted, some other purpose for involving her, and she had a feeling she wasn't going to like it.

"You're telling me Mary was conspiring against the Hall, and that's why she went to Harry? Not because they were lifelong friends, and not because he was one of the few people she trusted, but because she was a part of a scheme to strike against her own people?"

"You find it so hard to believe?"

"I do, actually. I find it hard to believe she wouldn't fucking tell me any of this, when I am the one person who would–"

"Try to sway her otherwise," Croker finished. "She didn't want to be swayed, Madame. She had already made up her mind. You would have only convinced her not to do it, and she didn't want that."

The Madame went quiet for a moment. "So you took care of it," she thought aloud.

"Yes, we cleaned up her mess. The man Harry found to go after us is long gone. So is Harry, thanks to your personal hitman's expertise. Now, I believe, we come to the subject at hand: Mary."

"What the hell have you done to her?"

Croker was enjoying the anger on her face "Mary is under my jurisdiction. To you, she might as well be dead. No substantial harm has come to her; however, after an incident like this one, for the sake of Tammany, she will be kept hidden until I deem it is appropriate for her to be back with the public."

"And just who the fuck do you think you are to give and take people's lives away?!" she shot back.

Abruptly, Croker's eyes flashed red, and in a split second he snatched her arm in his hand and held it an excruciating, steel-tight grip.

"You are not in the position to be bargaining. You will do exactly what I tell you and pray that I find the mercy to let you live, and eventually, let Mary loose. If you disobey me, I will personally see to it that Mary suffers greatly before a long and drawn out death. And if you want to live and thrive in my city, you will do what I tell you, or I guarantee you will watch as everything you've built from the ground up burns to ashes."

The Madame spat in his face. "You think you're the first son of a bitch to threaten me with destruction?" she posed, yanking her arm away. "You can go fuck yourself, you bastard."

There was a pause. Croker acted as if he didn't hear what she'd said, giving no indication of hostility. He slowly pulled a handkerchief from his inside jacket pocket to wipe the spit from his skin. Then, without warning, Croker pocketed the fabric and struck her hard across the face with the backside of his hand. The hit felt like an explosion. Her eyes burned as the pain seared throughout the entire right side of her cheek, and she moved a few feet away impulsively in case he came at her for another round. Shielding herself and clutching where he had hit her, the Madame wanted nothing more than to draw the pocket pistol tucked away neatly in her dress pocket, or unsheathe her blade tied to her right thigh – but instinct told her she shouldn't. Tears involuntarily streamed from her eyes as Croker glared at her, unmoving. Then all at once, he burst into laughter, holding his hand to his chest as if some version of the situation might have been funny, and the Madame remained where she was, her guard rising.

73

"Madame, you misunderstand. I don't threaten. I am your reckoning." Casually, as if the strike were forgotten, he slid to her and examined closely where he'd struck her with mild concern. "You had better put some cold meat on that when you arrive home. Bad for business."

Filled with nothing but disgust and contempt, her hand twitched, wanting again to pull the pistol from her pocket and shoot Croker dead where he sat; this, alas, would only backfire. If he and Tammany were making the progress he bragged on, killing him would only ruin her and everything she'd spent a lifetime building. The rest of her days on earth would be spent running, and cowardice simply wasn't in her blood. If he wanted to play these political games, she would play them too. And if Mary really had done the things Croker claimed, then Mary had made her bed and she had to lie in it. There was too much for the Madame to lose, and Thomas…she needed to protect Thomas above anything else. He was all she had left.

"I apologize," she mumbled, her cheek screaming in agony. "I would like to get this settled between us with no…no negative repercussions. You know I had no knowledge of Mary's involvement in this scheme, and if I did, I would have put a stop to it."

"I do, Madame, I most certainly do," he agreed, his demeanor softening. "And I would like that as well. I have a proposition for you. In turn, I will tell you what I've done with Mary, but that information will stay with you, and you alone, and if it is pursued the agreements made tonight will be null and void. Can you accept my offer?"

"I had better hear a proposition before I agree to your offer," she countered.

Croker nodded. "That sounds more like the notorious Madame I've heard so much about."

Twisting away from her, he moved to the end of the pew and got to his feet, snatching something from the row in front of them. Circling around to her again, he held up what seemed to be a heavy, leather bag in his hand and then tossed it to her, and it weighed so much the Madame nearly dropped it. Inside, she found enough gold

74

to buy an entire plot on Fifth Avenue and understood exactly the terms he was setting. It was contracted blood money.

"Silence is only part of the bargain," Croker went on. "I want to make an investment in you. My aspirations stretch high, and when I do finally rise to power, unlike Tweed I will not fall."

"And John Kelly is…"

"John is a reformer, and he is what Tammany needs to get the Irish vote and support. Once that is secured, they won't need him anymore, and they will need me. They will want strength, power, and unwavering confidence. This is only the beginning of a long road, Madame, and I am going to build the Irish up so that this city can at last get a taste of what we are capable of, and we will run this city the way we should have from the start."

Her fingers traced over the gold. "What do you want me to do, Croker?"

He resumed his seat on the pew. "I want to build a system, Madame. Not politicians and their bullshit, but a network...like streams and creeks filtering into a river and rivers filling into the ocean. We are a part of the same water. I need people like you to be my eyes and ears, and that is what you are best at. You've been manipulating and blackmailing your way to the top since the day you made your business your own. I need those skills. I need to know that when I am on the rise, I can call on you to work with me, and not against me. That is my proposition. And you cannot leave this church alive unless you take it." He paused, and before she could retort, Croker had her by the throat, cutting off her breath straight away.

"You have less than thirty seconds until you pass out, Madame, and then only minutes until you die. I know your goon is outside, and this is the only way I know I'll get a real answer, binding you for good. My offer...yes or no…?"

Sheer panic set in – there was no way to fight him and no escape. The edges of her sight began to darken while she struggled to make him stop. Croker's grip was so forceful on her windpipe...maybe he'd been planning to kill her...maybe he was wanting to scare her...she kept trying to speak and couldn't get the words out...then, a horrendous thought struck her: the thought of Thomas alone... defenseless...in danger and at risk of walking into a trap. She should have shot Croker when she had the chance. As everything faded out a new fervor rose in her chest. If she died in that moment, she would be leaving Thomas to the same fate as his mother...to perish when he had a full life to live. She couldn't allow that to happen. Using her might, her arms wrestled with Croker's grasp. She hit him over and over with all the strength she had left in her muscles until at last he released just enough, and her lungs expelled a nearly inaudible "yes."

Immediately, Croker let go. The Madame fell over onto the pew gulping in air and coughing hysterically.

"If you want to live in my world, you had better be ready to fight for it," he said, matter-of-factly. "I have no sympathy for weakness."

"I...am not...weak...you fucking bastard," she gasped, pushing herself upright. The Madame clutched her throat protectively, glowering at Croker, "I'll do...I'll do it...but where...where is she?"

"Locked away," he informed her, scooting toward the aisle and standing up. "And she will be there for some time. I am glad we've come to an arrangement, and I will be in touch in due course. It's been a pleasure, Madame." Croker whipped around and strolled to the church doors, halting just as his hand touched the handle. "Oh, and make sure that boy has given up his hunt for her as well, or I'll send Seamus to see him."

The doors slammed shut as he left, and the Madame's eyes fell down to the gold in her lap, the pain in her neck and cheek throbbing worse than any she'd felt in years. The night had definitely not gone how she'd anticipated, mainly because Mary's problems were greater than the Madame originally assumed. With the political involvement of Tammany Hall, there was no hope left. Mary would stay locked up in an institution and never be let out again. Any attempt the Madame might make in searching for her would only kill her and Thomas, solely due to Mary's ridiculous efforts to take out Richard Croker and the Hall. She had to salvage what little she could from the wreckage and keep Thomas out of harm's way. There was only one option for them if they wanted to survive.

Gradually the Madame got to her feet, her brain finding it hard to focus with a bruised windpipe and a swollen cheek. It was time to get back to The Palace and start from the ground up – there were plans to be devised, money to be made, and she needed to put something cold on her God damn face or it would be horrendous by the following morning. Shuffling from the pew, the Madame followed Croker's route of departure, wanting to get the hell out of St. Michael's and the Points. While her hand reached out for the knob, she was greeted by Louis bursting through the entryway with a concentrated frown, his expression frazzled at the sight of her.

"I saw him leave from the church and began to worry," he conveyed, his jaw dropping as he saw her injuries. "What in God's name did he do to you? Why in the hell didn't you shoot him?!"

The Madame tried to clear her throat and grimaced. "Fucking bastard. I had to let him. He needs to think he's the only one in charge." Her voice was scratchy and her neck felt as if it were on fire. "I need you to get me home, Louis. Fast."

"The carriage is waiting out just three blocks," he replied, opening his jacket and motioning toward a flask in his pocket. "And I have whiskey in my jacket."

She smirked. "Good. We'll have to hurry or I'm going to look like a battered whore tomorrow."

Louis handed her the whiskey. "I don't know who you are trying to fool. You are a battered whore." The Madame scowled at him as she snatched the silver flask and took a sip. Louis couldn't hide his grin. "Stay here. I'll go get the coach."

The pair exited the church and Louis set out, leaving the Madame on St. Michael's steps where she gazed up and was greeted by a majestically starry sky – the rainy clouds receded from above and the moon shone down brightly, illuminating the streets and thus making her feel somewhat secure in her vulnerable condition. In this light, not a soul could sneak up on her, and she had a pistol ready for any idiot that might test her. The cobblestone under her feet was soaked from the excessively wet day, and while it was slick and would be a challenge for the horses, she admired how the road seemed to glisten. Mercifully, the Points was currently deserted: no one up to any good was ever out in that place after dark, and she despised Croker for making her go so far only to hear him preach about the Hall. He loved the sound of his own voice, that pompous prick. On the other hand, it did bother her, that he was so relaxed in the worst part of the city, and she wondered how many of her old enemies might be his friends.

Then, an even worse thought struck her. Perhaps there was a reason the Points was abandoned…perhaps there was a reason she hadn't seen a single person since her and Louis' arrival…and what if Croker had arranged it that way? In haste, she peered from right to left, pacing around the front of St. Michael's with no one to be found in plain sight.

Her stomach knotted. She needed whiskey.

The coach flew around the nearest corner and trotted straight for her. Louis leapt out and assisted her inside, then went to give their driver instructions for the ride home. The Madame was shaken and consumed in her thoughts, the bigger picture becoming more and more visible: Croker wasn't full of shit. She didn't know how, but he'd managed to claim the Points, or at least had enough power over the right people to execute a few hours of quiet and peace. He'd outdone her, climbing the political ranks the old fashioned way and securing his own people first. It was a factor the Madame didn't take into account, and one she fucking should have.

Sure, the night hadn't been a complete disaster – no one had died, and no one was hurt except for her. But it hadn't exactly been encouraging either. Croker didn't have to say outright where he'd put Mary — she could read between the lines. There was only one place a woman could be incarcerated without a lawful mandate in New York, and that was a mad house. There were a few in the area, and only God knew which one he'd thrown her in. With everything at stake, saving Mary was a ship that sailed the day she disappeared. Saving Thomas was all that mattered, and the only way to do that was to kill his mother…hypothetically speaking, of course.

Like everything, she had a plan for that.

Louis jumped back into the carriage and the driver headed northwest in the direction of The Palace. Staying silent, Louis' scrutiny fell out one of their small windows to watch for anything suspicious, allowing the Madame to get lost in her memories of what their life had been. As a boy, Thomas grew up during one of the most treacherous times for New York: the war, the riots, the political upheaval, not to mention the battle between the fucking immigrants all thrown together like animals in the ghettos. Mary did her best to raise him right, and the Madame kept a close eye on them, guarding and sheltering mother and son when they were not conscious of her participation. It was the only way she knew they were safe without getting too close…she couldn't afford any liabilities with her track record. As Thomas reached adolescence, he became headstrong like his father, and rather than accepting the Madame's multiple offers, found his own work without her permission. On the surface she was furious, but on the inside she couldn't help but feel a little proud of his independence — if there was one thing the Madame despised, it was a parasite that couldn't think for itself, and Thomas was far from it. He was better than her…better than Mary…a fucking genuine that she hoped wouldn't be ruined by his family's mistakes. Hit with a sudden chill, she wrapped her arms around her chest and shivered.

"Cold?" Louis asked, checking on her.

"I'm not made of fucking lace," she quipped. "I'll be fine. We still clear?"

"Rolling out of the Bowery now. All clear."

The Madame exhaled, relieved. "Just get me home."

"I didn't want to bring this up earlier...but Thomas...how was he?"

"Enraged, as you might expect. By the end of our talk I think I was at least making some sense in that thick skull of his. I doubt he'll ever forgive me for it."

Louis' eyes floated back to the window. "You did what you thought was necessary."

The way Louis spoke was skeptical, and the Madame couldn't let it go. "Do you have something else you'd like to say to me?"

"Edward was a good man. How do you know he wouldn't want to know he had a son? I would want to know."

"You also aren't a Lord of England, if I fucking remember correctly," she spat.

Louis raised his two hands. "I am sorry. That was unnecessary. This is your call, as it should be, not mine."

The Madame turned away from him, irritated. Edward...that bastard had made her life a nightmare. Her initial interference in Mary's letters was with the best intentions, believing with every ounce of her being that Edward's family would force an end to their romance or he would give her up at their influence and suggestion. And with a child...a child born out of wedlock...there was no way Mary would ever be accepted. After she'd already begun hiding Edward's correspondence, a letter arrived telling Mary of Edward's brother's misfortune along with the passing of his father, leaving only the mother and Edward left to carry on the Turner name. The Madame shivered again. No, Thomas was right, it hadn't been fair. Yet not a single part of her regretted it. The pride in her veins prevented her at every opportune moment to own up, despite the dozens of times she called on Mary for that reason and that reason alone. No one second-guessed Edward's absence until Thomas... he was the only one clever enough, or rather desperate enough, to solve the mystery, though his primary goal had nothing to do with finding his father. Without warning, a smile formed the Madame's face – all his time around her perhaps shaped Thomas more than he comprehended. New York was filled with young gangs roaming the streets and causing nothing but bloodshed; Thomas, on the other hand, she was pleased to say hadn't ever been that type of boy. The tiniest sliver of her heart felt sorry for him for growing up the way he had, devoid of any father figure; and alternatively, in her own masochistic way, the Madame also hated herself for having any remorse in the first place.

It was a strange human dichotomy.

"Madame…" Louis whispered, seated across from her, his expression alarmed.

"What is it, Louis?"

"You're bleeding, Madame." He pointed toward her cheek and sure enough, a cut from the ring on Croker's middle finger happened to slice her. Her fingers were painted red.

"God dammit," she swore. "That fucking son of a bitch. Tell the driver faster. I can't let this go untreated much longer or I'm going to fucking swell like a river corpse. Hope better be ready to mend me."

Louis snorted. "And what if she's with a client?"

"Go to hell."

Laughing, Louis yelled to their coachman to pick up the pace. "Are you going to tell me anything, or do we have to wait until we reach home?"

"About tonight?"

"Yes. What happened in your meeting? Did we find her?"

"Not exactly. There's nothing we could have done. She barked up the wrong fucking tree this time."

"You can't get her out of it?" Louis beseeched her, clearly not persuaded.

"Not even if I used every resource at my disposal, Louis."

The carriage hit a pothole and lurched, nearly sending them both to the floor. "And this is all because of her boss?"

"More. Much more."

"More?"

She stared at him. "The Hall was involved, and she was conspiring with Harry and others to bring them down."

"Do you think they might have been...?"

"Pinkertons? Yeah, I'd assume so."

Louis' eyes opened wide. "Christ. And the Hall didn't kill her?"

"Might as well have. They put her in a fucking nut house."

"But she's alive."

"I can only assume at this point."

"There's always a chance, Madame. Not now, but later...these new recruits rise and fall every day with Tammany."

"It's a chance we can't take right now," she told him, holding up the gold. "Until we get this figured out, we let it go for all our sakes. Is that understood?"

If it was possible, his eyes opened wider. "Yes, Madame. What about Thomas?"

"I have a few ideas. I'm going to need you and Ellis."

Louis nodded. "We should tell him, Madame."

"You know damned well we can't."

"I know. But we should."

"He wouldn't understand. There is no way he would ever understand."

"Not yet," he concurred. "But someday, Madame, he will."

She didn't respond. For the remaining duration of their ride, neither of them spoke. While Louis resumed scouring the road, the Madame's wits were gradually restored while she meticulously did what she did best: plot. She'd dealt with men like Croker before – men who craved power and were willing to cut down anyone in their path to get ahead; and though they weren't the most dangerous she'd taken down, they were by far the most challenging. What unnerved her was the inescapable setback, one that was different than the others. Unlike the greedy pricks who were Croker's predecessors, he was in a position that ostensibly outranked hers. His destruction couldn't be completed with just money and some dirty secrets; it would need serious exploration, time, and most notably, exploitation. Her first priority was neutralizing the threat to Thomas, because if he didn't stop pushing, there would be a push back by the Hall, and not one that would end well. The Madame, too, would naturally be punished with him, and those consequences were not a viable option.

When they finally arrived at The Palace, the Madame hastily made her way inside and up the stairs to her rooms, not wishing to be spotted by anyone before her injuries could be disguised. She could never appear hurt or defeated in front of her girls, otherwise their respect might dwindle, and with that came obstinacy. The Madame bolted the doors to her office shut. Louis would soon follow with Hope, who she prayed had some sort of remedy to mend her bruised face, and Danny would not be far behind them. Hope was a miracle worker whose skills topped that of most doctors, and she hadn't only fixed injuries at The Palace – on numerous occasions she'd saved lives, and became absolutely irreplaceable to the Madame's staff. Danny, in contrast, was different than the rest. Like the Madame, she was tough as nails, and more importantly could read when to keep her mouth shut, earning her special privileges with the Madame in times like these.

Once she was secluded, the Madame stripped down, tossing her damp, mist-worn layers onto the floor and rushed to her secondary wardrobe, grabbing something clean and dry to put on. Peeking down, she noticed her arm was already bruising where Croker savagely seized her, and decidedly threw the dress in her hands back inside and found another with longer sleeves. She slipped it on and, with great, acquired skill, the Madame pulled the corset laces tight behind her and tied them herself. Seconds later, a knock on the door signaled her team had arrived at last, and with a slow roll of her shoulders along with a deep breath, the Madame strutted to the entryway and opened the doors wide, putting on a tickled expression.

There stood Danny, Hope, and Louis, and a look of horror came over both the girls when they saw the Madame's face. Hope gasped, her hand flying to cover her mouth, whereas Danny's alarm subsided as she studied the Madame.

"What the fuck did you do to yourself?" she blurted out, making Louis burst out into laughter.

The Madame rolled her eyes. "Doesn't matter. Son of a bitch will get it in the end. Hope, can you lessen the swelling?"

"Yes, Madame." Hope rushed inside, pulling things from the knapsack hanging off her shoulder, and the Madame trailed her.

"Ah! A him, then?" Danny went on, tagging along inside. "You always did like things rough."

Beyond annoyed, the Madame turned to slap her, and immediately Hope grabbed her wrist, thrusting the Madame down into an empty chair.

"Sit your ass down and let me put you back together, or you'll look like a rabbit by morning. You already look like you've spent five rounds in the ring, for Christ's sake!"

The Madame stayed motionless, unflinching as Hope worked her magic, and Louis got her another glass of whiskey. All the same, it didn't stop her from berating Danny for half an hour, almost enjoying herself, though she couldn't stop from thinking the one thing that could make it better would be if Mary were there laughing along with them.

Thomas arrived early the next morning just as the Madame was finishing her whiskey breakfast, and she made sure to have coffee prepared for him. As he trudged into her office, it was evident he hadn't slept after her visit the previous evening, and she had a feeling this one wouldn't be much better. There was only so much the Madame could do to prime herself for breaking Thomas' heart and hopes. In her fashion, she would stretch the truth, yes, but there was no other fucking choice. It was the only way to keep Thomas out of danger.

The Madame never took chances when she knew she couldn't win.

Silently, he came through the doorway, his body language indicating he already predicted bad news. Walking over, he sat in one of the two chairs facing her desk, his eyes wandering up to find hers, and for a few moments, neither of them spoke.

"You look exhausted, Thomas. I've got some coffee for you on the table if you'd like. We have a visitor joining us shortly."

"A visitor?"

"Yes, Thomas. One to give you some insight. Last night, my meeting brought to light the reality of Mary's fate. I discovered from our source that Mary is...well, she's dead, Thomas. She was murdered. I really...I really can't believe it..." Her voice cracked faintly and trailed off.

Thomas' head fell. "I prayed all night we would find her. I knew it was a lost cause." He fought to hide his emotions and stay composed. "I guess it's good she's in a better place. A much better place than here."

"That's for fucking sure," the Madame assented. "Your mother was the best woman I've ever known, and I'm sorry we...I'm sorry I couldn't...save her." The Madame got to her feet and made her way around the desk, placing herself in the chair at Thomas' side.

He was struggling, and she felt an involuntary tug at her heart. "What did you learn?" he managed to muster up. "Did they tell you anything?"

"My meeting last night was not what we expected," she admitted. "Or at least, not what I had. The law is involved, and they've already solved the case."

"So they...they know how she died, then..."

"There was a dispute between Mary and one of O'Neill's employees who was working for him. I think Smith was his name? O'Neill confronted them both and accused one of them of stealing. Your mother denied it and so did he, but O'Neill knew your mother would never take what wasn't hers. Smith got thrown out and apparently went after Mary that night after her shift in a drunken rage. He killed her, Thomas. No one suspected him except O'Neill, and O'Neill couldn't find him for days. He eventually did, and turned that asshole into the coppers. He's to hang next week and gave a full confession to the crimes."

Thomas listened, his gaze fixated on the floor. "And…the body?"

"He says he…he threw it in the Hudson. The coppers are searching for it…no guarantees with the river, though. You know that."

Like clockwork, Louis knocked entered the Madame's office. "Your guest has arrived, Madame," he announced, rotating around to motion the newcomer inside.

Ellis strode into the Madame's office, a courteous but stern half smile on his face. He took off his hat and went directly to Thomas, holding out his hand in salutation.

"Hello, Thomas. I am Detective Ellis. My partner was the main investigator on your mother's case. He could not join us this morning. I wanted to be here to answer any questions you might have."

Ellis had been a copper first, and speedily ascended the ranks to detective with his sharp aptitude in piecing together what others might call unsolvable cases. He and the Madame had known each other for many years, and since she used her influence and connections to aid in his ambitions, he was her man whenever she needed a favor. A note was brought to him that morning with exact instructions of his task, and Ellis sent word back with Louis he would willingly gratify her request. The key was to make this as easy as possible for Thomas, to make him move on from his mother with definitive resolve with the help of someone other than herself. A detective would do the trick, someone who could provide a clean cut with nothing left undone and without tarnishing Mary's reputation in the eyes of her son. The Madame was nervous and did her best to hide it, her cheek and throat still aching though coated with enough powder and a touch of rouge that seemed to evade the suspicions of Thomas' distracted state. And Ellis…she sincerely hoped he could pull this off, or there would be hell to pay.

Thomas shook his hand, bewildered. "T-thank you, Detective Ellis. It means so much to me that you…you took the time to be here. I…I am happy to hear what happened. In your own opinion, sir."

Ellis nodded and remained standing, pacing back and forth in front of him. "From what I can tell, a man by the name of Smith was fired the morning before your mother disappeared, and her employer Mr. William O'Neill confirmed that with us. We are still working out the details, however we do believe Smith was stealing under the table from O'Neill, and in the beginning Smith went to O'Neill and tried to blame Mary. It was only a matter of time until the truth was found out. When it did surface, O'Neill got rid of him, and Smith then spent six hours at a Sonny's Pub a few blocks down…I can see from your face you've heard of it. Around eight and in a drunken stupor he went back to the shop, we can only assume to pick a fight with O'Neill, and encountered Mary instead. From there, you don't need to hear the particulars…it was gruesome, Thomas, she fought hard for her life. We searched high and low with no luck for days, and then O'Neill took matters into his own hands and brought Smith into the precinct at gunpoint. It wasn't pretty."

The Madame was impressed with Ellis' acting, and her apprehension evaporated.

"And he's to hang?" Thomas went on, his voice filled with rage.

"If we get the judge I want, a week or so tops. It'll be a speedy trial with the full confession Smith gave us."

The Madame watched Thomas closely and he believed every word of it – the poor boy was attempting to stay poised and collected in Ellis' presence, and it was taking every ounce of his self-control to do so.

"Are you all right, Thomas?" she asked softly.

"Fine," he said too quickly. "I'm fine." Abruptly, Thomas rose. "Thank you for the coffee, Madame. And thank you Detective Ellis, for making the time to speak with me today. I...I am late for work. I appreciate you...both of you...being so helpful. Detective, if anything comes up..."

"We know where to find you," Ellis assured him. "It was a pleasure, Thomas."

Thomas gave a curt nod and turned on his heels, marching out with his shoulders hunched from taking such a blow. They waited until his footsteps were heard echoing down the steps, and Ellis let out a small whistle, staring at her.

"I don't know what exactly you've got me involved in, but I'm pretty sure I just wrecked some poor kid's life."

"Thank you for your assistance. It was necessary, I promise you," she explained, discounting his comments.

"Right. Well, am I overstepping my bounds if I ask what in God's name happened to your face? Who the hell did you let hit you?" His tone was filled with more of an entertained air than worry.

The Madame shrugged nonchalantly, getting up and sitting down behind her desk. "A dispute, nothing more. It's been handled. Now if you please, I have business to attend to."

"Well, pardon my saying so, but you shouldn't be lying to that boy. Especially if she really is alive somewhere."

"Fuck you, Samuel," she snapped, inclining forward and slamming twenty paper dollars on the edge of her desk. "For your troubles – this morning never happened. Now get out."

Ellis grinned coyly, but did not move. "I don't want your damn money. Your secret is safe with me." He marched around her desk, leaning over her and pulling her in closer to him. She tried to shove him off of her, but it only enticed him further, and Ellis began gently kissing her neck and rubbing her chest, drawing her body into his. The Madame could feel the heat rising from her body, and before she could second-guess herself, her hands brought him in tighter and felt his own arousal. For a second, she considered stopping herself, but it had been weeks since their last rendezvous, and the smell of his skin was so intoxicating, it completely clouded her judgment.

Without warning, his grip around her waist tensed. "You know what I really want," he murmured in her ear, picking her up and laying her back over her desk. He thrust his hand up her dress and with his touch, she let out a sigh of anticipation. She couldn't resist. The contents of the Madame's desk scattered all over the floor while Ellis climbed on top of her, and they kissed furiously as she felt him inside her. She needed this. And she let him have her. Twice.

IV.

The sunrise blazed a deep red as it peeked over the distant rolling hills, causing the dew soaked trees and grass to sparkle as the summer heat began to die away. A storm was coming in the distance, one that was still far off in the early morning hours but would roll in as the sun dropped to the west. Until then, a beautiful day lay ahead, and Edward planned to enjoy the little time of peace and quiet he had alone at dawn. He swiftly kicked his horse up and into a strong canter, streaming like a shooting star through the wet field ahead of him, smiling as the cool breeze caused his eyes to water. The warm sun trickled down onto his face, and he watched as the land around him brightened from the gleam of daybreak.

Hiroaki would not be long behind, and Edward chose not to wait. He treasured these moments more than anything else – it was a brief memory of freedom, one he had loved during his time out on the open seas and now greatly missed. His everyday duties were like a condemnation, a sentence he felt he had to serve and whilst he realized it was delusional, Edward felt taking on this responsibility was the one way to make things right after his family's misfortune. Only on his horse and in the peace of his own mind he could escape, and only there did he feel like the man he used to be…the man he wished he still was. Edward squeezed his legs tighter around his mare, and she eagerly picked up speed. She delighted in their rides together as much as Edward did, both basking in the overwhelming sensation of release.

"Whoa!" he called a few minutes later, approaching familiar ground and giving a slight pull in the reins. His young horse obeyed, slowing her stride to a walk as her ears perked up, letting out a snort to tell Edward she would rather keep going than stop. Instead, they moved forward and halted only a few steps behind a descending bluff above his property. Edward stared out over the vast stretch of land that lay before him: Amberleigh sat at the end of a long, gravel road, surrounded by ancient, thick-trunked green trees and terrain in an area he thought to be the most gorgeous part of southern England. The landscape held a sense of the natural, and it was minimally maintained and designed with that goal in mind. Edward preferred the pastoral, the innate beauty of the earth to that of manmade construction, though he was certain if his brother saw the changes Edward made since his death, he would roll over in his grave.

Centuries ago, one of Edward's many great grandfathers constructed their indestructible Stuart mansion-house, and the sight of it never ceased to fill Edward with immense pride. Its thick brick and stone walls were laid perfectly to fit, giving it a stoic, intimidating exterior. On each corner of the house and on their front doors, the Turner family crest was carved in great detail, and not one of them had faded throughout the years of bad English weather. The distinguished, large square windows flashed bright in the sunlight, lined in heavy copper trim, and though the home was only three floors it possessed enough rooms to house an entire militia. In spite of his family's marked tragedy, Edward had never found any place that felt more like home.

"Enjoying your morning ride?" Hiroaki called from a few yards back, startling Edward.

"Christ!" Edward exclaimed and then laughed, shaking his head.

"How is it you can still sneak up on me? And on a horse for God's sake. It doesn't seem right."

"After all of our hard work and all of my lessons, I must say as a teacher I am highly disappointed in your aptitude for knowing your surroundings. As your friend, however, I can admit I am glad to remain having an advantage."

"I think it is one skill you will always master over me, Hiro."

He smirked. "I hope so, for my own safety."

Hiroaki's gelding reached Edward's mare, and the two men rested in silence for a few minutes side by side, taking in the magnificent view. As it happened on nearly all of his morning rides, Edward's thoughts drifted from his home, to his family, and then to her. His heart had never been able to evade her constant grasp. Her beautiful grey eyes found him at every corner of the earth, and as he took a deep breath, Edward prayed she could see him at this moment, to feel how much he missed her every day. Mary was taken from him many years ago, along with almost everyone else he had loved, and since that fateful day Edward swore to bide his time until they would meet again in another life. Sometimes, he imagined he could feel her warmth in the sun, smell her perfume in the flowers, even hear her laughter in the wind whenever it blew by his ears in the fields. This fantasy was entirely in his mind, or at least he did his best to persuade himself that it was – Mary's memory haunted Edward, but on no account did he ever want it to wither away. Oddly, it made him feel comforted, unlike the majority of other flashes into Edward's past.

Soon, he could feel Hiroaki's eyes watching him. "How is she today?" he asked.

"Sad," Edward answered. "Something is...something is much different, like it has been for days. How can a soul in heaven feel sadness, Hiro?"

"A soul can feel just as we do in the afterlife. That's where they look over the ones they leave behind."

Edward frowned. "It all seems incredibly nonsensical...she's long gone and left this world. I need to get out of my own bloody head and stop inventing things that don't exist."

"These things do exist, whether you believe or not," Hiroaki retorted. "It's not in your head. It's in here." He took both reins in one hand and tapped his chest where his heart lay with the other. "Listen to me, Edward. You have so much time left in your life. There is something else for you, something greater than you can see. I tell you this so often, I know you cannot hear the words, but I won't give up. It is time you went forward and sought out more purpose, for your own sake."

"What would you have me do, Hiro? I'm doing what my father would have wanted. The business is thriving, and that always was his priority. What else could I do? More of our missions?"

"Anything, Edward. Anything but stay here and slowly waste away."

"And leave you with all this?" he remarked sarcastically. "Are you trying to steal my land, Hiro?"

Hiroaki tried to hide another grin. "You know I will follow you wherever you desire. And your cousin inherits this land at your deathbed, not I."

"It's true. You can thank my brother for that." Edward glanced back toward the house, trying to force Mary from his mind. "Ah, what I would give to fix it...to go back and change it..."

"A man's life never follows the path he sets out upon," his friend reminded him. "We must expect the unexpected, so to speak."

A rush of resentment hit Edward's gut, though he instantly let it die rather than stewing at Hiroaki's response. It wasn't that Edward hadn't been granted the opportunity for a fresh start; his heart simply would not allow it. For years he loved one woman with every fiber of his being, and that had not changed since the day he met her in New York. That love, like Edward, was stubborn, and while Hiroaki's words were true, they did not matter. His feet were stuck to the ground, unable to move on from the heartbreak and damages to his spirit. Yes, his life did feel incomplete. The blame was placed on the numerous losses he sustained over the years: his father, his brother and his family, too many of his own men, and on top of that, the love of his life. In the end, those losses shattered a part of him he couldn't get back, and Edward consistently struggled, failing to pull himself back together.

"Remember the day you found me, Edward?" Hiroaki pressed, breaking Edward's train of thought.

"Yes of course I do."

"When you found me, like you I was convinced my path had ended. We had nowhere to go and nothing to live for. And yet there you stood on the beach, offering us another way. That day was my salvation, Edward. We live multiple lives throughout our many years…and those lives shift as our circumstances change. You need to find your next life. Something is calling to you, and you've chosen to ignore it. It is time you heard her, Edward. She's trying to tell you something. All you must do is listen."

Edward shifted in his saddle, his mare's hoofs stirring. "I don't know how to listen. I don't know what she's telling me."

"Try harder," he directed, pointing to his heart again. "But in here."

They rode home together at an even pace, and when they arrived at the stables, Edward handed his horse to Hiroaki and rapidly hiked through the gardens to the main house. He had a long morning ahead engaged with business constituents, most of which were in town from London conducting an entirely new set of trade contracts. In the meantime, Hiroaki would be off to attend to the property and livestock, which he preferred above any other occupation Edward attempted to offer him. Hiro was a man who found peace in that simplicity following a life of war, violence, and death – his existence was littered with misfortune like Edward's, though somehow Hiro vanquished his demons and was doing everything in his power to help Edward vanquish his. After thirteen years of friendship, Edward was beyond grateful for his friend's presence, and not just for his own mental and physical health. Without their chance meeting, they both would have been long dead, and Edward found solace in the knowledge they had rescued each other…in more ways than one.

Edward took the entire kitchen staff by surprise as he walked inside, and in a flurry they set out to accommodate him to the best of their abilities. He pleaded with them to not go to any trouble, and announced while he stole an apple from one of the baskets that the remainder of the day and evening would be at their own disposal following his guests' departure. Every servant in his household had been working hard that week to keep his lawyers, business partners, and associates happy, and Edward knew a break was well deserved. Cheers of gratitude rang out in response, and he blithely danced up the back stairs with his apple and a hunk of ham shoved into his hand by the head cook. Edward treated his staff like family, and only requested they uphold the formality of employee in the presence of his guests. While not all of the staff openly agreed with this policy, in their hearts they loved him for the respect he showed them on a daily basis. Particularly when so many others didn't.

Another two hours later, Edward met with his partners for breakfast and, passing quickly through small talk, jumped into the last of their negotiations. It was a tedious morning, but considering it was their last day Edward found enough motivation to remain attentive as the investors and lawyers battled it out for him. Five days of discussions had passed, regarding trade options and oversea growth, and their final deliberations proved to be a success. That evening, Edward would happily write to his cousin in New York with good news: their push to increase trade production across the Atlantic was fundable, and the two would reunite in a few months time to create a new business plan for the American expansion. It had been years since Edward had seen his cousin William, and while Edward was more than pleased to be reunited with him, he was slightly apprehensive at the thought of returning to the city he had deliberately avoided for so long. Edward grappled to suppress that anxiety with the thought of what this deal would do for Turner S & D – there was no rhyme or reason he should let his fretfulness over New York overrun a future his father and brother could have only dreamed of.

As soon as the contracts were officially signed and dated, Edward brought out the champagne to celebrate and he and his twelve colleagues spent the afternoon toasting to their new venture. His guests were gradually ushered home, and as the last carriage left on the long gravel road from Amberleigh, Edward noticed the storm clouds at last funneling on the horizon. He sincerely hoped everyone would make it to either the port town of Southampton or down to the village prior to being soaked.

He intended to retire to his den with a great sense of satisfaction, and most of his senior staff checked in with him as they cleared out of the house and to the village for the evening in the wake of the others. Edward granted a few nights of freedom to his servants a month, mainly because he relished in the opportunity to not have others waiting on him hand and foot. Edward's dignity from his years in the Royal Navy wouldn't allow him to ever be content having a person by his side constantly doing his bidding, particularly when he was capable of handling it himself. And for the rest of the night, there were letters he needed to read, one in particular he needed to write to William, and a bottle of wine that required solitude and tranquility for gratification.

By the time Edward reached the den, the first low growl of thunder resonated through the walls. As predicted, a pile of letters sat unopened at his desk, along with a large plate of fruit and cheese left by his master of household, who markedly foresaw Edward's evening agenda. There were more than enough correspondences to read following the last few days he'd spent occupied by business, as he had no occasion to break away, and Edward sighed as he dove into his task, opening the bottle of Bordeaux. His den was small and comfortable, just the way he liked it – he refused to take over his father's or his brother's offices after their deaths, and this space had previously been a reading room for his mother when she resided at Amberleigh. Edward took to calling it the Mahogany Room: there were dark red wooden shelves covering the walls fully lined with books, and it provided him with an instant sense of ease. Ignoring his mother's suggestions, he furnished it with brown leather couches and armchairs, a thick, medieval-looking rug he'd discovered stowed away in one of the attics, and his grandfather's desk, it's stained wood matching the shelves perfectly. The oil lamps flickered low on the walls, and a small fire burned from the fireplace to keep him warm as the nights in England became colder. Edward snatched the letters off the desk's surface and fell into his favorite leather armchair, pouring himself a large glass of wine to take the edge off. If his father was still alive, this would be the proudest he'd ever been of his second son, and it caused Edward to beam from ear to ear. He may not have done everything right, but Edward would see to it that the Turner legacy lived on, and to his late father, the business was more important than anything else. That notion was what kept Edward going, especially on the worst of days.

Time went by in a flash, and soon Edward noticed he was nearly through his Bordeaux. Stretching his arms long overhead, he was about to get to his feet when one of the last few letters on the side table caught his attention. The parchment was unlike any of the others – it was heavily weathered and marked with an excessive amount of postage from America. The only mail he ever received from the States was from his cousin, and this was clearly not from William. He picked it up and held it in his hands, scrutinizing it closely, noting there was an unfamiliar return address. Edward picked up his glass and finished the Bordeaux at the bottom, then opened the letter, wondering what on earth it could possibly be.

What was transcribed on that piece of paper was not at all what Edward could have conceived. In truth, he could barely comprehend what he read. Going over it again and again, analyzing every detail…every word and phrase…none of it made any difference. A portion of his brain decided it wasn't possible…or did Edward not want to believe it was possible? A son of Mary's claiming he might be the father? There was no plausible way – it was bloody preposterous. Mary would have told him she was with child…wouldn't she? In addition, this boy swore Mary had been alive all these years. He was seventeen years old, and the math added together with his story; the worst of the letter revealed one fact that Edward couldn't let go of…that Mary was…or had been…alive for almost two decades and he had never known.

Hundreds of scenarios played through Edward's mind, and each conclusion became more eccentric than the last. A swindling grab at his family's fortune could be the only authentic reason, yet so few knew of his time in New York with Mary. Why wait so many years if it was a ploy for money? Edward traced back in his mind, trying to recall how it had happened…her letters stopped just as he set home from China, and then he was overcome with malaria for months, unable to write more than a handful of times through his page. And then he received the last letter from…from…

A knock on the door gave him pause. "Come in!" he yelled, knowing it could only be one person. Hiroaki entered the den and stopped right where he stood when he caught sight of an extremely distraught Edward.

"Edward, what's going on?"

"Come here and look at this, Hiro," Edward replied, holding up the letter. "I don't know what the bloody hell to think about it."

Hiroaki walked over and took the letter from his hands, sitting down onto the couch across from Edward. When he finished, his eyes slowly crept up from the page.

"Well, Edward, do you have any ideas?"

Not sure how to answer, he stood up, needing the bottle of Bordeaux from his desk. "I have some, most of which are damned insanity."

"Tell me."

"I want to hear yours first…I can't think straight." He yanked the cork from the bottle and poured a glass for Hiroaki and another for himself.

"All right, if that's what you wish." Hiroaki leaned back, hand stroking his moustache. "My first assumption based only on my logic would of course be this boy is lying in an attempt to receive money. However, my personal opinion is much different than that."

Edward expected this. "How so?"

"Honestly, Edward…I do believe him. Something tells me he's your son."

He tensed – this wasn't what he wanted to hear, and he could feel the disappointment rising in his chest. He made his way back over and handed Hiro his glass, retreating to his own chair.

Trying to remain unruffled, Edward spoke softly: "You're saying it's all been a lie? My misery has been for nothing?"

"Our paths are never for nothing, Edward," Hiroaki remarked, taking a sip of wine. "Don't let your emotions overrule your head. The most straightforward explanation tends to be the correct one."

Edward gulped down his own drink and took a deep breath. "Continue, Hiro."

"Consider this from an alternative perspective. There are many reasons she would decide to not tell you about the child, ones I will not speculate over considering since I am a man and do not understand how mothers operate. There is, however, one piece of evidence that ties this together. One circumstance and, giving it away, one person in particular you're forgetting."

It took a few seconds before Edward realized what Hiroaki was saying, and he could feel his blood begin to boil. "The initial messenger."

"Yes, the Madame," Hiroaki affirmed. "She was Mary's guardian for most of her life, and I am sure the one person Mary turned to in times of need. You were not there to help her, Edward, and the woman your beloved trusted unconditionally just happened to be someone who never cared for you and wanted you gone." Hiroaki inclined forward and peered deep into Edward's eyes. "You're English nobility, Edward, do not forget this. She did what she thought was best. She did not know you, she did not like you, and I can only suspect she wanted to protect Mary from heartbreak and rejection."

Edward battled to wrap his head around it, straining to find a reasonable objection or at least a counter argument. But as his thoughts continued to churn, there was no denying Hiroaki's point. It was true…it had to be…

Overcome with anger, suddenly Edward couldn't control himself. He shot up to his feet and threw his glass into the fireplace as hard as he could, fighting the urge to tear the den apart. Pacing back and forth, he tried to get a grip on his temper the way Hiroaki taught him; unfortunately, his efforts were in vain. The unbearable perception of betrayal…deceit…devastation…his adult life squandered away by something as small as a letter when all he needed to do from the start was go and find Mary on his own. If it was real… if it wasn't a lie…the thought killed him, like a knife straight to his chest. She had been there the whole time and he hadn't known…and now she was gone…stolen from the tips of his fingers once again, and he was powerless…absolutely powerless…

Hiroaki stayed motionless, letting Edward's mind work for a quarter of an hour, until at last Edward turned to him with tears in his eyes, more confused than angry. "What do I do, Hiro?"

Hiroaki handed Edward his own glass of wine along with the letter. "You know what to do, Edward."

"No I don't, my friend."

"Yes you do. Do what she would do. It's what she's been trying to tell you these last few weeks."

Edward revolved back to face the fire, gathering himself and straightening up. There was only one way to know for certain.

"You will be master of the household in my stead. I'll be back before the winter storms, and I want my horse ready to ride at first light."

Hiroaki nodded and stood, bowing deeply. "Safe travels, Lord Turner. I look forward to your return. And Edward?"

"Yes, Hiro?"

"You have your path…and you may very well have your something to live for now. If this goes well, bring your son home where he belongs. And do tell your cousin and Tony hello for me."

It was nearly dawn before the storms began to dissipate the next morning, and the moment the skies cleared Edward set out in a fury despite the soaked, muddy roads. If he rode hard, he could reach the port in time to set sail to Liverpool later that morning. He packed lightly, with the impression he could buy any suits or clothing he needed once he was aboard the steamship and headed to New York. His heart had been murderous the night prior, wanting nothing more than to find the Madame and make her pay for what she'd done to him; yet as the hours passed, Hiroaki's words sank in deeper. The only reason the boy found him was because his mother was dead, and his first priority must be to credit or discredit the boy's claim and rectify the situation. If his story proved true, Edward would take Mary's son…his son…home to Amberleigh. He owed her that at the very least.

His mare was fresh in the crisp morning air, galloping at a pace that pushed even Edward's comfort level. Hiroaki would be by later the next day to collect her from the port stables – she would need a good day's rest after this twenty-mile expedition they were out upon, sprinting hard south. Amberleigh was situated between Andover and Winchester, making the distance to the Southampton port a few hours ride. From Southampton, he would cruise the coastline to the northwest town of Liverpool, then onto Queenstown in Ireland, and finally make his way to New York. Liverpool was over a two hundred-mile journey from Amberleigh by carriage, and much too slow for his taste. While Edward could take one of the new transport ferries up to Liverpool, he'd come across an idea the night before, one he was doubtful might work but was well worth a shot, and hoped to God his timing would be right. Otherwise it could be days of sitting and waiting for departure, and that thought made Edward's skin crawl.

The pair blew into town and went straight for the stables, where Edward saw to it his mare would be fed and boarded for the next two days. Afterwards, his real search commenced. The sleepy port of Southampton was only just stirring in the later morning hours, and Edward went straight for the docks, hunting for the familiar P & O flag he knew so well. Their distributorship had a regular stopping point at Southampton between London and the Iberian Peninsula, and he had a friend in their service who owed him a favor. Several, in fact.

Edward kept his head low, desiring to go unnoticed and not wanting to be recognized. It took him a half hour of hunting until Edward was ultimately saved by a familiar voice that snuck up behind him.

"Eddie! Eddie! Is that you?!"

Edward halted, smiling. He flipped around to see his longtime friend Captain Connor O'Brian running down the dock to greet him, looking mystified.

"Eddie! What in God's name are you doin' here?" Connor was weathered, appearing nearly ten years older than he actually was from his time on the open water, but Edward could recognize his loud, boisterous voice anywhere. That voice matched his large, burly frame, with bright red hair and a beard besieged with blonde and a hint of grey. His eyes were bright with laughter, and it was obvious up close Connor was extremely happy to see his old friend, though also a little perplexed.

"Connor!" Edward chuckled, embracing his friend. "I am so glad to see you. I hoped to find you here. How are things with P & O? When do you set out today?"

"About an hour, I reckon," he said, taking a step back to analyze Edward. "What in the hell are ya doin' here, Eddie? You look a mess."

Edward happened to be of the same opinion. "I am a bloody mess."

"What's your quarrel? How can I help ya? Do I need to round up a few of the lads?"

"If I tell you, can you promise me to at least consider an offer I have to make? I need a favor, Connor. A big one."

"Pretty damned sure ya know ya can have whatever ya need, Eddie."

With a quick glimpse left and right, Edward lead Connor away from where he feared he might find familiar company. The two men walked the abandoned docks further down the harbor as Edward described what had transpired the previous evening, and while Connor had heard of Mary, the news his friend might have a son took him by greater disbelief than it had Edward. Years ago, Connor and Edward served together in the navy during the Opium War in the South Pacific, where they tended to keep each other out of trouble. Connor, who notoriously had a short fuse after a few drinks, found himself backed into corners on a more regular basis than Edward; still, it never bothered Edward when he was called on for a little assistance, and sometimes he found it to be a good distraction when things became repressively stagnant. It wasn't until years after the war that Connor bit off more than he could chew and got dangerously tangled up – he was in gambling debt beyond his means, and with his life at stake, Connor sought out Edward, knowing it was his only shot of making it out in one piece. Without any hesitation, Edward went straight to Liverpool and paid Connor's debtors, and subsequently dragged what was left of his friend back to Amberleigh. He dried Connor out of whiskey for half a year, and as his health and wits came around, Edward found him work in London at P & O, a company he traded with on a constant basis. They had kept in touch through letters, and after seven years, it was a relief to see his endeavors had not been a waste.

"Jesus Christ, Eddie. This is fuckin' nuts!" Connor exclaimed, hands thrown in the air. "What are ya going to do, then? Seek him out?"

Edward shrugged. "What other choice do I have?"

"You leave it the fuck alone," he retorted. "Don't ya think she would have told ya? She loved you!"

"I know, and I never thought she would keep something like this hidden, but it's for her that I've got to see this through. And it's also precisely why I need your help, Connor."

"What do ya need?" he asked readily. "I am at yer service, and ya know I'm insulted ya asked politely."

Edward smirked, shaking his head and pointed toward Connor's boat. "I need you to give me a lift to Liverpool."

"Shit," he whispered under his breath, taking a look out to his boat. "I'll have to give my guys in London one hell of a good reason. That's two days out of transit."

He'd come prepared for this. "I'll give you fifty pounds right now. And another fifty when we arrive."

Connor's head whipped around, his jaw dropping. Just to further convince him he was being honest, Edward grabbed for his satchel and shuffled through his bag for the money, and Connor grabbed onto Edward's hands to stop him.

"Oh to hell with you! I am not takin' yer God damned money, Eddie. Stupid bastard. If this little prick isn't your son, I'll go to America and kill him meself."

"So...we can call it even, then?"

Connor let go of Edward's bag and slapped him on the back, smiling. "Of course not! Never will be, Eddie. But for now, get yer shit together. I gotta get my crew outta port before I can actually tell 'em where the fuck we're goin'. All prickly sons of bitches. I won't hear the end of this one."

Connor collected his men without delay, and as they sauntered out of the harbor, the updates regarding their journey were announced on deck. Mercifully, Edward noted that not one of them seemed to mind, mainly because Connor swore he would personally buy their first rounds when they reached Liverpool. Edward attempted to avoid their stares; they all were curious as to who he might be, but after a while their interest died, and their talk inevitably turned to gambling, work, and whiskey. Gaining speed as the boat barreled up the western coastline, Connor stationed Edward in his personal quarters for their trip. Their passage would take most of the day, but they would arrive later that evening in Liverpool, and Connor brought out biscuits and brandy for breakfast in his tiny living space. They sat at his two-man table, maps and log book in one corner and Connor's cot in the other. Edward felt very much at home, realizing how much he missed this.

"Just remembered, and you'll be happy to hear it!" Connor revealed, eating a biscuit and drowning it in brandy. "There is a White Star headed out of Liverpool first thing tomorrow. You're a lucky man...sometimes it pays to be impulsive, eh?"

"Ridiculously impulsive," Edward corrected him, pouring himself a brandy. "How can you be sure it hasn't set out yet? I thought the Atlantic steam liners only left on weekends."

"Ah! There's the funny thing! I grabbed a drink with another transporter like meself last night who came in from Liverpool. Said they'd fucked up a rudder that needed repairs and delayed for a day...people stranded and overcrowdin' the local joints longer than expected. Business was boomin', and he spent most of the night whinin' all the good whores were bein' used up."

He couldn't believe his good fortune. "You're right, Connor. I am pretty damned lucky."

"That ya are, Eddie. You holdin' together all right?"

"Barely," he chuckled. "If I think about it too much it's…well it's just overwhelming, and I can't sit still. You know me…that won't change until I figure this out."

"Damned right I do," Connor granted. "And like I said, if it turns out this little bastard is a liar, I'll take care of it if ya bring him back here to me. How's the Chinaman? I miss that crazy bastard…"

They talked a bit more, catching up on the time that had passed since they last saw one another, and after an hour Connor departed to check on the engine and crew. Connor left Edward another full bottle of brandy and some salted meats to keep him from getting 'too pissed.' Now idle and relaxed, Edward's head swam with recollections of the last few hours while his adrenaline waned, and he wondered if he had truly made the right call. The letter…his son… it could be a farce, put together by someone quite clever and with a lot of time on their hands; on the other hand, he wouldn't be alone. His cousin William and his wife Lucy were in New York, and they were the two people he cared for most aside from Hiroaki and his wife, Akemi. The odds didn't need to be in Edward's favor – what he did need was closure. And somehow, in that desolate city, Edward knew he would find it in one way or another. This wasn't just for Mary…it was for his own peace of mind.

Edward opened the other bottle of brandy and continued to nibble on his biscuit and salted pork, reminiscing on the time following the war – his whole world had been turned upside down. When Mary's letters stopped, Edward was suspicious as to what might be the cause. At first he thought it could have been out of anger and irritation…maybe out of heartbreak from his ongoing absence… or, worst of all, perhaps she had found someone else. To him, it didn't matter – he had to see her, and planned to set out for New York upon his arrival from the war in Liverpool, even prior to returning to Amberleigh. Then came an avalanche of unforeseen circumstances. His brother Arthur, along with Arthur's wife and son,

had died together in a chaise crash while out for a leisurely afternoon ride, and a month later Edward's father was gone as well; fur-
thermore, the one factor that altered his fate on a greater scale was
the sickness. Edward contracted malaria so badly he was isolated in
confinement for months. Nearly an entire year had gone by with Edward indisposed, and when at last he did recover from the disease,
his physical strength was so depleted the doctors forbade him from
extensive travel. Being the sole heir to his father's empire, Edward
was left with no option. The moment he was able, Edward wrote
to Mary, promising to come for her as soon as he could. It was two
months later when he'd almost recovered that the Madame wrote
to him with news of Mary's death, and Edward's future plans were
crushed. Edward's life from that day forward had felt so meaningless.

It took years, but Edward was able to make the pain bearable.
His lessons in the art of the warfare and his missions with Hiroaki to
aid others in need brought what was left of his soul back to life. As
soon as his illness subsided, Edward devoted himself to his father's
business. He would never forget the life he'd dreamed of in his youth
– becoming an admiral in the Royal Navy, taking Mary to live with
him at Amberleigh, and most notably, growing old with a family he
loved. Time went on, and his heart became easier to distract from
the tribulations. The placation of routine made his everyday a fog,
easy to get lost inside, and Edward took those dreams and swept them
under a rug, hoping they would rot away. His dedication to Turner
S & D was the only thing that kept him going, that and his morning
rides where he swore Mary lingered in the air, waiting for him. Edward felt his throat tighten. If only he'd known she was really alive.

A sharp drop in the boat snapped Edward into the present moment, and the calls from the crew confirmed it was nothing to worry over. He got to his feet, shook off his sentiments, and sauntered
out onto the deck to cure his ills with a little fresh air. The sun temporarily blinded him as he stepped outside Connor's quarters, and
then came the cool ocean breeze against his face, bringing about

an involuntary smile. He made his way to the rail and leaned over, resting his forearms on the top wooden beam as he looked out over the endless blue sea. Since he had been a young boy, Edward loved the ocean more than anyplace else; he found serenity on the water, no matter how calm the seas or treacherous the storm. Somehow, it seemed to steady his mind and alleviate his nerves better than the best bottles of wine. He shuddered, recalling the last time he had been on the water – it was when the malaria had overtaken him half-way home from the war. If he had abandoned Hiroaki and his wife in China, Edward would have been dead. They were the only ones who held onto hope when Edward's crew thought he was a curse, and they both fought diligently to save him. It was the most terrifying experience he'd had in all his time as a sailor, and he had been certain he wouldn't live to set foot on England's soil again.

For the nearly four years Edward spent in the South Pacific, the Royal Navy sat and waited – the British made tactless moves in an effort to pacify the Orientals, and to no avail. Each legion sat inert, doing nothing but growing fat and bored. In the end, a battle rang out in Beijing: the English and French artillery pummeled through the Chinese without mercy, as they were completely unaware of the odds stacked against them. Seeing thousands of men, most forced to fight unwillingly by the Chinese, fall and die at his orders still haunted Edward from time to time. Two weeks after the final push, the Convention brought peace, and Edward prepared his men for their journey home. That was when he found Hiroaki…or rather, Hiroaki found him.

"Eddie!" Connor shouted from the deck above. "You all right down there?"

"Perfectly well, Captain," he called, yawning. "Do you mind if I shut my eyes for a bit? Wake me when we are approaching Liverpool?"

"You bet, ya old bastard! Over half way, shouldn't be too long now!"

Edward turned starboard to see the deep cliffs of the coastline, the waves crashing hard against them with the water luminous in the sunlight. The one thing Edward knew he needed most was rest. His eyes were barely able to stay open despite it being midday, and he gave in, ambling back toward the cabin. There was so much to think over, but no solutions would be found on Connor's boat. It would have to wait until Liverpool, and then New York. And at that point, there would be no return.

When he woke they were already docked, and Connor argued for a time with the harbormaster until he got his way, though the man forced Connor to pay double his normal rate to anchor the ship for the night unscheduled. His men dispersed keenly with their whiskey money, each one in a different direction without a word otherwise, and Connor lead Edward to a local pub just off the water.

"White Star is closed, and I can guarantee yer shit outta luck tryin' to get a ticket at this hour," Connor notified him. "I got an old buddy from Queenstown that's worked the line for ages. Let's see if he can help ya get out on that boat tomorrow, eh Eddie?"

"Thank you, Connor."

They approached a small, dimly lit bar called The Dusky Cat, and at first sight Edward could have sworn it was condemned. His skepticism vanished as soon as the doors flew open, and he was immediately engulfed in a roar of commotion. Overcome with the stink of rotting beer and fish, Connor thrust Edward through the packed crowd and toward the back of the pub. Edward attempted to be courteous and not knock anyone over – he could barely get his bearings on where to step, yet Connor knew exactly where to go and stepped ahead of Edward, guiding him between the swarm of drunken sailors which thinned as they reached the rear tables.

"Knucky!" Connor yelled out. A man who appeared to be sitting alone raised his head to see who shouted for him and, recognizing Connor, waved them over. When Edward was within five feet of him, it was clear their host hadn't bathed in the last few days, as his hair was dirtily matted under his cap, and he reeked of whiskey, tobacco, and a few other odors, which Edward chose to pretend he didn't smell. Knucky had a scruffy beard covering his face, brown eyes, with a hooked nose, and the prickly wool sweater he wore was a clear indication he spent most of his time in Ireland rather than in the Queen's country. Edward could only hope Connor's source was reliable, because from where he stood, he couldn't help but doubt the man's competence for any sort of task. "Captain," Knucky said as Connor and Edward lowered down in two empty chairs. "I didn't expect to see you around here for a few weeks." He snapped his fingers and straightaway a bar maid was at his side. "Let's get a bottle of scotch for the table. On my tab, Netty." The bar maid rolled her eyes and said something vulgar under her breath before she ran off, leaving the smell of cheap perfume behind her. "So what do I owe the honor, Captain?"

Connor tilted forward with his elbows resting on the table. "Knuck, my boy Eddie here needs to get onto the White Star to New York tomorrow morning. First class. Is there any chance we can make that happen?"

Astonishingly, as Connor finished, Netty instantly returned with their bottle and three glasses, pouring them each a more than generous portion.

Knucky didn't hesitate, and locked eyes with Edward. "I don't mean to be a bastard. But who in the hell are you? First class on a bloody whim? Not a cheap ticket, boyo."

Connor peered at Edward with a helpless expression, meaning it was time for Edward to take the helm, which he did reluctantly.

"Name is Edward Turner. I run a shipping business—"

"Stop."

"Excuse me?"

"You…you're tryin' to tell me you are Lord Turner of Turner S & D?" Knucky studied him closely, and his gaze flickered over to Connor, who nodded. "Christ Almighty." Knucky shot back his

111

scotch. "What in the fuck are ya doin' with this asshole over here?" he asked, pointing at Connor.

Edward mirrored him, the cheap liquor burning the entire way down to his stomach. "We were in the Royal Navy together. He's doing me one hell of a big favor."

"A much deserved favor," Connor added. "And I'm not an asshole, ya prick. Watch it or I'll beat you in front of Netty."

Knucky laughed. "Fuck you, ya bastard." He poured another round for the three of them. "All right, Lord Turner. I can get you on the bloody boat. But it's gonna cost you quite a bit."

Edward tossed Knucky a wad of cash, which he counted, his eyes nearly bulging out of his head. "This is two hundred pounds!" he whispered, leaning toward him emphatically.

"Get me on that ship," Edward replied, snatching the money back out of Knucky's hands. "I want a guarantee I am on that boat. You will take me there in the morning. Understood?"

Knucky threw back another round of scotch. "Meet me outside of this bar, tomorrow mornin' seven o'clock sharp. If you're late, deal is off."

"He'll be there," Connor countered. "Thanks, Knuck."

"Anytime, Connor, as long as ya keep bringin' bastards who pay this well. I'll make the arrangements." He tipped his hat at Edward. "Lord Turner." Knucky stood up and strutted off, disappearing into the crowd.

"Where in the hell did you find him?" Edward inquired, resting back into his chair.

"Fuck if I know – but well connected, that one. All I can say is that bastard needs to clean himself up if he ever wants to get under Netty's dress again. She's a wild one, but even she won't fuck a dirty fish."

Despite Knucky's departure, Connor and Edward went on to finish their bottle of scotch merrily, carrying on until the early morning hours. After the bar threw them out, they took to strolling the docks like they had earlier the previous morning, reliving their time in the

Navy and where their lives had gone in the years that followed. It wasn't long until the two old friends knew the time had come to part ways. Connor escorted Edward to the bar to meet Knucky, leaving him with a bear hug and a melancholic laugh.

"I really hope ya find what yer lookin' for, Eddie," he said quietly. "You deserve to be happy."

"Thank you, Connor. I couldn't have done this without you."

Connor nodded. "Take care, ya hear me? And bring that boy of yours to see me sometime! If he's anything like you, he'll be one fiery bastard. You know those are my favorite kind of people."

When Connor left them heading in the direction of his ship, Knucky guided Edward down toward the main section of the harbor, not bothering to say much and took mainly to just motioning for him to keep up. Rather than staying on the docks, Knucky took him in toward the town and through a few narrow alleyways, away from the majority of foot traffic. Out of the blue, a loud horn from the ship sounded, and Knucky finally spoke up, explaining the alert signified the boarding process had begun, and they'd better hurry. Every few steps, Knucky checked over his shoulder to be assured Edward was right behind him, and urged him along speedily. They took a sharp turn around an old inn and right away, Edward saw why Knucky had chosen their route. A sea of people lay between them and the ship, and it was absolute madness. It seemed like everyone in Liverpool was fighting to get on board from every possible direction, and there was no end to the masses in sight.

Knucky took Edward's arm and dove in, weaving through hundreds of passengers as they pushed ahead to board, crammed so close together Edward thought he might suffocate. Peering over the crowd, Edward let out a groan of annoyance when he saw the line of people waiting for the inspection area.

"This is a bloody catastrophe!" Edward exclaimed, desperately trying to stay at Knucky's tempo. "That line will take me hours at best."

Knucky kept dragging Edward ahead. "Hah! Don't ya worry

113

yourself, Lord Turner. Ya won't be goin' through inspections. This way, and watch out for all these damned pigs everywhere."

Edward was puzzled. "But Knucky, they won't let me on board if I haven't been inspected, right?"

Knucky apparently didn't share Edward's apprehension. "One of the many advantages you gentlemen have in first class is if it's prearranged, you can be inspected in your cabins. Nice fuckin' perk, if I do say so meself. Ah there he is! Randall! Randall!"

A man in a White Star uniform with his back to them spun around and spotted Knucky, gesturing for them to advance. "This is my buddy Randall, Lord Turner. He will be takin' you from here. First class boardin' is the next ramp down."

Randall held out his hand in welcome. "Lord Turner, it is a pleasure to have you on board, sir. All we require is payment for your travels and I can take you up to your suite."

Edward leaned over and whispered in Knucky's ear. "How much did you bargain for my ticket?"

"A hundred, since it was last minute and all," Knucky replied, turning to face Edward so Randall couldn't hear. "You got the last suite, Lord Turner."

"And what's your fee?"

Knucky sighed. "For a man such as yourself, I'll charge ya five. Normally, it'd be double that for someone of your station. But since ya know Connor, I'll give ya a deal."

Edward nodded and took the cash from his bag, handing it to Randall without any further negotiations. Randall thanked him and fled momentarily to obtain Edward's ticket.

"Well, this is where I leave ya, sir," Knucky notified him. "Randall will come back with your ticket, and you're on your way to bloody America."

"How long is the journey?" Edward asked. "Two weeks?"

"Eight days! You're on a bloody steamer now, Lord Turner, you'll be there before you know it!"

Edward thrust ten pounds in his hand. "For your troubles," he thanked him. "I appreciate all of your help, Knucky."

Knucky grinned. "Anytime, Lord Turner. You know where to find me. God be with ya." He tipped his hat, disappearing the way they'd come and into the mob of people. Edward watched the hoard, almost in disbelief. The entire port was packed to the brim with immigrants. Hundreds battled to get on board and through inspections, scrambling up the ramps and into the ship like mice. Thinking back, Edward couldn't remember a time he was in a thicker crowd other than during the final battle in China. He wondered if all these people would survive the journey, or better yet, how many would make it past Ellis Island or face getting shipped home where they came from. It was startling…the roar of voices, yells, and orders almost deafening in the crisp morning air. Knucky was right. His inheritance did have great perks, and he wondered if Knucky had any clue the man he just helped was actually worth more than half of southern England. Edward figured most likely not.

Randall eventually returned with Edward's ticket and showed him along to the first class boarding ramp, where Edward took his time ascending, the reality of his situation ultimately sinking in. For a second, he considered fleeing the scene – no one would be the wiser, and he could be home at Amberleigh in a few days if he desired it. Then a breeze hit him, an abnormally warm gust from the west, and he glanced out toward the water. His reluctance drained from his body, and instead Edward was filled with an odd sort of excitement. For years, he'd sat and done nothing…he'd let himself age into adulthood without believing he could change his stars. Yet like the sea, his tide had changed, and he had to swim along with the current.

"Lord Turner, are you all right?" Randall beseeched him from a few paces ahead, his expression concerned.

Edward gripped his ticket tighter and threw his knapsack over his shoulder. "My apologies. Just some old memories." Edward started up the ramp, feeling somehow his whole life had lead him to this.

This was what he was meant to do...like Hiroaki said, this was when his new life began...

When he reached the top of the platform, Edward handed two nervous ushers his ticket, and he chortled sensing it was his appearance that made them uneasy.

"Good morning," he greeted. "My name is Lord Edward Turner. I am sorry, gentlemen, I left in quite a rush. Please do me great favor and make an appointment with your on-board tailor this afternoon, if you don't mind."

They both broke into grins at his account. "Of course, Lord Turner. We have your suite prepared on the top deck, with a balcony overlooking the port side of the ship. The Captain has also asked if he could have the honor of dining with you tonight."

"With pleasure! Who is your captain?"

"Bennett, Lord Turner. He always enjoys treating a fellow sailor when possible. This way, I will take you upstairs."

Edward nodded, recognizing whom it must be – Bennett's son was an old Navy rival of Edward's, and meeting his father would be entertaining at the very least. It took some time, but the usher brought Edward to what he could only assume was one of the finest suites on the ship. He was left to sit in the parlor room with the promise of morning tea and breakfast on the way, as well as the tailor within the hour. Edward thanked the boy and tipped him nicely – God knows what they thought of him in his dirtied clothes and bag almost entirely full of cash. William would have quite a laugh over it when he told him about it in just over one week's time.

To that day, it still astonished Edward how well known his family had become. With the death of Edward's brother and their father so shortly thereafter, news has spread like wildfire that Arthur Turner's second son, the naval officer, would be the next in line. He hadn't the slightest inclination regarding anything about the business; magnificently, Edward discovered that somehow the family's genetic code of trade must have run in their blood, and he promptly adapted to his change of profession. Currently, business was better than it had ever been under any Turner before him. For a while, he was the ever-invited guest everyone in the noble class wanted at their parties or gatherings, all eager for him to share his heartbreaking yet lucrative story. It made him sick, and Edward denied their intrigue and invitations over an extended period of time, slowly allowing their interest to dwindle. Only when it was absolutely necessary and unavoidable did Edward did indulge those around him, but that did not change his general distaste for high society.

Exhaustion set in following another sleepless night, and Edward sank down into an armchair, pulling out the letter he'd received two days prior from the boy claiming to be his son. He read it over and over again, memorizing every word on the page, when a thought occurred to him: if Thomas was Mary's son, the Madame would surely know he had discovered the truth by the time Edward arrived in New York. If she happened to be anything like the woman he remembered, Thomas took a great risk to reach out to Edward for answers, a risk not many would be able to stomach. Thomas mentioned in his letter Mary was missing, and missing meant dead in this day and age. The boy had acted rashly, desperately, with no other means to an end, and as he deliberated, Edward determined he was actually impressed with the boy's bravery. He went over the letter and it's details again, tracing every possibility Thomas' letter was a lie, and no alternative could parallel or challenge the boy's plea. He didn't threaten Edward or ask him to send money, all he wanted was to meet his father, to see him with his own eyes. If Thomas was real, then it was all real, and Edward had a son on the other side of the Atlantic waiting for him.

There was a knock on the door, and a breakfast spread big enough for five was paraded into Edward's sitting area. He folded the letter and placed it back into his pocket, a revitalized sense of purpose running through his body. He would find his son. He would make right the many wrongs the Madame had created years ago. And most importantly, he would show that vile woman she picked the wrong bastard to try to ruin, and bring Thomas home where he belonged.

V.

In the early morning hours, Mary was jolted awake by the sharp crash of thunder outside, so loud it was like a whip cracking in her ear. Rain poured deafeningly against the shingled rooftop, and little droplets sprinkled down through the ceiling, leaking into their cell and forming puddles on the floor. As the storm accumulated, the wind howled through the great stone walls, which kept everything in that dismal place damp, dark, and cold. So cold, she hadn't felt her toes since she arrived, and when she did, it was as if millions of needles were piercing her flesh. Her whole body ached, longing for a mattress instead of the hard ground she slept upon. She didn't even have the ability to stand up for a moment without her legs giving way to weakness.

The hardest part for Mary hadn't been the tortuous screams in the middle of the night, or the eerie scratching of rats while they wandered the insides of the walls and sometimes even the ground where she sat. It wasn't the unshakeable chill, the constant physical and verbal abuse by the nurses and tenants, or even that the days had begun to blur together into a memory she yearned to forget. No, the hardest part was waking up after being lost in the mindlessness of her dreams and knowing her reality had become the nightmare, and her sleep the only source of freedom she had left.

Mary's left wrist had been chained to one of the cell walls in the dungeon, a place of punishment that was obviously used for prisoners in another time. There were four other women with her, all in the same drifting state of consciousness, forced to rely on their caretakers in order to not perish in their gruesome confinement. Like Mary, these women were put here for the "sickness" of lunacy: trapped and held hostage for the sole reason of their very existence. Mary had been thrown into a mad house for attempting to do what she considered her moral obligation, and she quickly found out how easy it was for men of power to take away her liberties with their accusations and money. She tried to hold onto the little autonomy she had left, and to the ignorance of the nursing staff, deliberately hadn't taken her "medicine" for two days. After failing numerous times, Mary at last discovered a way to stimulate swallowing the pills by hiding them on the undersurface of her tongue, only to spit them out the moment the nurse turned her back. Tonight would be her final attempt of escape. She could only hope if she didn't succeed, she would find a way to take her own life instead of being thrown back into the perpetual hell of her incarceration.

With every guard, caretaker, and nurse believing her to be drugged, it would be an easy break from the dungeon; the trickiest part would be getting out of Blackwell's front door. In her first few attempts to flee, Mary was caught swiftly; however, she learned something new each time, reaching just a bit further in every endeavor. In her head she'd gone over every try a thousand times, not wanting to make the same mistake twice. During the two days she'd managed to stay sober, Mary diligently sharpened a splint of stone she found loose and dug out from a crack in the floor with her bare hands. The fingers on her right hand were bloodied and scraped, and her nails brutally torn up, but she carefully hid her wounds for the duration of her daily physical inspections. She planned on cutting down anyone standing in her path, regardless of who it was, and considering the manner in which the majority of the staff treated their patients, she didn't give a shit about any one of them. On her previous attempt, Mary nearly made it outside, only to be ambushed in her last steps at the front door with the guards' truncheons. All that was needed was a greater head start, and this time, she would have it.

Another blast of thunder outside caused her to jump. She glanced down at what had once been her favorite cream-colored dress, now covered in human filth and soot, and while she no longer noticed the smell, Mary knew her odor closely resembled a bay of pigs. The last time she was bathed had been over a week ago, and her greasy hair was beginning to knot together in what was left of her long braid. The beating she sustained from the guards and their clubs left her body covered in bruises, and she was in a state of constant, throbbing pain. Her chained wrist was covered in dried blood and scabs from both the voluntary and involuntary tugging of her arm against the metal, and her legs felt as if they were on fire whenever she tried to stir from being kept sedentary. The desperation she felt was so overpowering it pushed her closer and closer to her breaking point…she had to get out of the dungeon before it destroyed her. If she couldn't get out, or if she felt at any point her escape was a lost cause, that stone she'd been sharpening would take her to her judgment day.

Death, in this case, was better than life on Blackwell's Island.

The stone floor began to vibrate dully under her with a pattern of footsteps, and Mary's ears perked up. It was much too early for their morning force-feeding of gruel, and no other noises had come from the outside in the last few hours to make her suspect anyone stirred up trouble. She crawled as far as she could until the chain clinked at full length, sending an excruciating shot of pain down her arm and to her torso. Trying to block it out, she pressed her ear to the wall, hoping to hear an echo of voices that might give some hint of what was about to ensue, or worst of all, if they were coming to her cell. There was nothing but the drumming of swift moving feet, and as they drew closer, Mary felt a familiar, intuitive pit form in her stomach.

It couldn't be…

A click of lock and key turning in their door caught the attention of the other four women as well, fear spreading thick into the air. The sound of anyone approaching caused absolute panic in every patient despite their drugged state. They were all aware of what came next: no visitor was ever kind, and the only time any other living creature entered the dungeon was for gruel, discipline, or to drag one of them back to the more 'civilized' wing of the institution. Except in Mary's case, of course. She'd had the same visitor a few times, and she preferred the staff to him tenfold. As the lock released, the door creaked open, and Mary shielded her eyes from the blinding, bright light streaming into their dark prison. Footsteps approached her as she tried to focus and make out the figure looming over her, hoping with every fiber of her being it wasn't him. When her sight did adjust, it was with horror Mary looked up and saw the man who had put her there kneeling down next to her with a cigar in his mouth, not bothering to hide his disgust.

"Leave us!" he called back toward the doorway, and the guards complied, closing Croker inside. Mary's nerves were getting the better of her, and she found it increasingly more difficult to contain the emotions running through her head. Most importantly, she had to feign numbness…pretend she was inept and absentminded…or he would know. He always did. She worked so hard to get this time right, and already it seemed as if her efforts were for nothing. Croker was her Satan, and the dungeon her desert, but for Mary and unlike Christ, there was no ending to her time in the desert.

Croker studied her and took a long drag of his cigar before he casually blew the smoke into Mary's face. There was no empathy.

"How long have you been skipping your medications?" he asked bluntly.

For a second she couldn't breathe. "I…I don't…understand…" she mumbled.

"I can see it in your eyes, Mary. How long?"

Her eyes cast downward. "T-t-two days. I don't like the drugs… they make me lose track of everything."

"They're meant to ease the pain of this fucking torture chamber you're in," he snapped, standing up. "But by all means, enjoy it if you like."

"Mr. Croker, I just…when can I go home?" she raised, angry tears welling in her eyes. "I told you I'll do whatever you ask. Please let me go home."

Another cloud of smoke. "Damn, this place is filthy," he went on, pretending not to hear her, "It's like a fucking zoo."

"Please, Mr. Croker," she begged. "Please…my son…"

"Do you have any idea how long you've been in here, Mary?"

Mary stared at him blankly, realizing she didn't. "No…"

"Well I don't suppose you would, being in and out of a comatose state. You've been in this place well over a month, Mary. Everyone in the city thinks you're dead." He rested against the same stone pillar her chained wrist was attached to, puffing away carelessly. "Multiple escape attempts these last few weeks, or so I'm told…tsk tsk." Before she could think of what to say in her defense, Croker kicked the middle of the chain with his foot, sending another agonizing shot of pain through her limb, and she nearly screamed out in agony. "If you want that thing to come off, you had better pull yourself together. You want to die in here of a fever chained against a wall? Lose that arm, perhaps? Or do you want to see your son again?"

Mary felt her face grow hot with rage. "Stop it," she said louder than she intended. "I want to go home. I don't deserve to be here. You know I don't deserve to be here."

Croker laughed aloud, skipping over her comments once again. "Mary, you act so innocent I almost believe you. On another note, your beloved Madame sends her regards," he relayed. "And no, she had no part in this. She does know you're alive and is frantically scrambling to do whatever she can to cover it up since your son just couldn't let it go. She saved him, you know. If he kept digging any further he would have been digging his own six-foot hole in the ground."

"Don't you dare touch my son," she shot back.

"I won't. Not yet at least. He's moving on. For the time being, he will be left alone. As I told you earlier, he thinks you are long dead anyhow."

Mary's strength dissipated. "Dead? How could anyone believe it without a body?"

"Well, the Madame set it up quite nicely…I must give credit where credit's due. I wish I had the option to get rid of you all, but no one likes to clean up that big of a mess. And ironically enough, I need your beloved Madame and her resources."

"So I'm…I'm not getting out of here, am I?"

"Not any time soon." He took a final drag and tossed his cigar to the ground, putting out the burning tobacco with the heel of his shoe. "Morality is a curse in my world, Mary. It's for the weak and the powerless…for those who are meek and retain a false sense of optimism regarding human nature. We are violent, greedy, and cruel creatures, and anyone who tries to prove otherwise is either ignorant or in denial. The way to rule the mob is through money and fear – without those, you have no respect, no jurisdiction, and no power. You were a threat to my cause, and threats are eliminated the second they rise."

"Then why didn't you just kill me? Why did you put me in here?" she bellowed, slamming her good fist down onto the floor in frustration. "I would rather die than spend my life locked away!"

Croker leaned down toward her once more. "Be careful what you wish for, Mary." Lurching forward, he wrapped his hand around her throat and thrust Mary against the stone pillar as if she were only a rag doll. She choked, gasping for air, unable to retaliate with such a weakened frame. "I am keeping you with the hopes I will break you, like a young stallion that just needs to be taught his place. I need to be certain you haven't lied to me, you stupid bitch, and I will find out soon enough. Or I will make you watch as I kill everyone that you love before you can change your mind."

Just as Mary felt herself losing consciousness, Croker dropped her to the floor in a heap. She coughed, her whole body retching and her throat and chest burning for air. After a minute or so, she finally was able to compose herself, and she glanced up to see Croker at the door, knocking for his exit.

"You just let me know when you're ready to talk. Oh and one last bit of information for you. Harry and Al are dead. Harry, however, you can thank the Madame for." The door pulled open. "Good day, Mary."

Croker stepped out, leaving without another word. The moment the door slammed shut behind him, Mary's head lowered to the ground, and her whole world went black.

Everything stayed dark for so long Mary almost felt peaceful. When she came to, there was nothing but the sensation that she was weightless…in a dream, yet still quite present in her mind. Her eyes gradually fluttered open, her body floating on the surface of a calm sea, the water warm on her skin. With her back in the water, Mary waved her arms up and down at her sides and gently kicked with her feet, enjoying the ethereal feel of her physical state, her mind calmer and more restful than it had been in weeks. The sun shone mutely down from a clear blue sky as she glimpsed up into the abyss, alone… boundless…the air above filled with small, wispy clouds. There was no pain…no more thoughts…it was only her and the water. Nothing but blue all around her…nothing but the blue and the light…

All at once, Mary was being violently pulled deep underneath the sea. She couldn't breathe, sucking in the water wholly engulfing her, and Mary reached and tried to swim as hard as she could for the surface, combating whatever force that had a hold on her. It was dragging her down…down into darkness again from whence she came. She gulped in helplessly, fighting to find air…her lungs coveting for breath…

She was back in her cell, still unable to breathe, her entire body unmoving.

"Hold still! Hold her down! There we go. It's okay, Mary, drink. Drink!" She was sitting up with a pair of arms tightly wrapped around her shoulders and chest. An iron-gripped hand was holding Mary's mouth open and attempting to pour something down her throat. She choked and spat it out, realizing what it was they were trying to make her swallow. The potion was water laced with an immense amount of opium to cause her to be completely subdued. Battling to free herself, Mary exerted any energy she had left in her muscles; yet she found she couldn't free a single one of her limbs. There were shadows of people hovering around her, blurring together, causing the room spin and making her extremely nauseated.

They came at her again, and this time there were two hands: one holding her mouth open and another to restrain her tongue, thus it became impossible to spit any of it back out as they dumped the potion down. She felt it trickle down the back of her throat and burn as it reached her stomach, the effects almost immediate. The hands then speedily clamped her mouth shut, not wanting to take any chances. The arms held her for a few seconds in arrest, and Mary groaned, the potion taking its course, the consequences becoming inescapable. Eventually, her strength died away, and she ceased to tussle. She was released to the cold stone floor, and abruptly her left wrist was locked back into its shackle, not that it mattered anyhow. Everything around her grew hazy and vague, and gradually the opium ran thick into her veins. Mary rolled onto her stomach in misery as the shadows remained silent, rising to leave. She wanted to fight it…she tried to tell herself she could toughen through it and stay present, but the chemically-induced slumber would always win.

Before she was ready, Mary gave in and drifted off, away to another world once more.

She was standing in a thick, dissipating cloud of fog. For a time, Mary stood squinting hard to try to make out anything in her surroundings, and then slowly everything around her became distinguishable in spite of the limited visibility. Looking back and forth, Mary recognized just where she was: she was in the city, a few blocks above Greenwich where the barbershop apartment was, but the streets were completely empty. Alone and with no light save for the dim night lamps overhead flickering in the breeze, she peered down at herself and saw she was dressed the same way she had been the day she was taken by Seamus Murphy. Her befouled cream dress was perfectly clean, and her usual scent of rosewater crept up into her nostrils. Mary instinctively reached up and felt her hair, so clean it must have just been washed. Around her shoulders rested her favorite tan shawl and on her feet were her leather lace up boots, surprisingly without a speck of dirt on them. Why she was here, Mary couldn't say, but it was more real than any of her other hallucinations, and therefore, it made her much more nervous. She decided to walk down the abandoned cobblestone road, with no hint as to what she might find or why her mind took her there.

"Hello?" she yelled. "Hello? Can anyone hear me?"

There was no sound, not even the swish of her dress or her feet skimming underneath her. She could only hear her own voice, and everything else was mute. Her thoughts were so clear and so present, Mary was having a hard time believing she was in a dream. When there came no reply to her shouts, she kept moving, and after two blocks she still had not encountered a single living creature. Her confusion became fear, and with each step her heart pounded louder in her ears. Was this death? Was she abandoned in purgatory, or was this some sort of test? She whispered a quick Lord's Prayer in a vague attempt to keep a level head, and it steadied her breathing.

As Mary rounded the following corner, she stopped dead. Ahead, there were three patrolmen with their backs to her, none of which gave any indication of hearing her approach. Mary took a moment to observe, and she noticed they were immersed in something happening down a secluded alleyway. Mary kept her distance, though she knew it would be no use; curiosity always got the better of her. Cautiously, she took a few paces to the right, placing herself behind a lamp post where she surveyed the coppers closely, wondering if they could see her. They turned around every so often, never looking directly at her, and she assumed it was to make sure they weren't being spied on. When it was clear they had no notion of her attendance, Mary moved closer, jogging out of the street and to a corner building on the opposite side of the block. Again, the one on the far right looked over his shoulder, as if sensing her movement, yet as his eyes found her the patrolman glared right through her.

Out of the blue, Croker appeared gliding their way them from the alley, and in his wake was a dark and ferocious man with glasses, the sheer sight of him sending chills down Mary's spine. Croker was angered by something as the man with the glasses handed a bloodied blade to the copper on the far left and proceeded to wipe his hands on the officer's sleeve. Without speaking, Croker and the man took off together down the road and into the fog, disappearing. The knife was pocketed by the patrolman, and like ghosts, the coppers seemed to evaporate into thin air, as if they'd never been there at all.

Mary took a deep breath in, on her own again and not sure of what to do next, and her eyes drifted to the alley. Was there something more she needed to see…something down in the darkness? And why could nobody see her? With fleeting glances to and fro every few steps, Mary inched toward the alley and tiptoed between the two brick buildings. As she drew in the way Croker and his accomplice had left, she gasped, her hands flying to her mouth: about ten yards away from where she stood, a man was in a bloodied heap on the ground, and from his heavy, raspy breathing, he was only minutes from death. Impulsively she ran to him, unable to speculate as to why she could presently hear sound when before there was nothing except silence. The man was curled up the opposite direction, and Mary observed what must be a fatal stab wound in his back, his white shirt drenched a deep red with blood. Carefully and tenderly, she flipped him over to see his face.

"No…no it can't be…" Her stomach dropped so fast she felt as if she'd fallen from the sky. "No…no no no no no…Edward…please no!" She pulled him tightly into her arms and held him close, tapping his cheek to try to bring him back to consciousness. "Edward, look at me…please…it's me…"

He was coughing and spitting up blood, barely able to stay alive, and at last his eyes found her.

"Mary…" he whispered, staring up at her. His body began to shake, his skin as cold as ice, and Mary burst into a sob.

"Please don't go…please…" she cried, tears streaming down her face. "Please don't leave me…I don't…I don't know what to do, I'm so confused…Edward please…"

He raised his bloodied, trembling hand to her cheek, a small smile forming in the corner of his mouth. "My Mary…my love…" He held his hand there, his eyes sparkling with a sad sort of happiness. "I…love you…"

Mary wept hard and pressed his hand to her cheek with her own. "I love you, Edward…I love you…" His smile grew big, and Mary watched as one long tear traveled down his face. She clung to him until she saw the light leave his eyes, and the strength of his hand regress to nothing. Mary's chest heaved, unable to contain her suffering, and she pulled Edward into her even closer, not wanting to let him go.

It wasn't real…she kept repeating that to herself over and over in her mind as she held him, feeling as though God sent her there to suffer…to see him die as some sort of penance by the hand of her own captor…her Satan. She wanted nothing more than to die with him in that moment, and Mary collapsed onto Edward's lifeless body crying harder than she had in years. Eventually releasing him, she screamed up to the sky, aware that no one…not even God…could hear her pain.

What felt like weeks later, Mary woke on the stone floor, an orange gleam of light trickling through the barred window above while the day transformed to dusk. The amount of potion forced down her throat must have knocked her out for the whole day rather than just the typical few hours, and the effects of the dosage took their usual toll on her physically. Mentally, however, this induced slumber was much different. Her hair and face were soaked with sweat and tears, her heart broken from the tortures her own soul inflicted. All her regrets and her fears funneled together into one and lashed out, an experience she'd never had when forced the potion on previous occasions. Usually she rarely dreamed, and if she did, Mary saw little Esther or Thomas, reliving a memory from their happiest days. This dream, on the other hand, felt so genuine…so unlike the haziness of the others…and she couldn't deny it truly felt as if Edward died in her arms.

Her suffering growing too hard to tolerate, Mary pushed herself upright and took a deep breath, leaning back against the stone pillar that restrained her. She reminded herself Edward had been dead for years…lost on his way home to her…but it felt so real and left her emotionally raw. It was in her head…it had to be in her head… or was it? The questions fueled Mary's resentment and her anger at her helplessness. Croker…he couldn't win this way…she wouldn't let him control her…she wouldn't let any of them control her.

Her eyes skimmed the prison where she sat. The other four chained women remained numb to Mary's existence despite the fact that re-dosing time was not far off. Each one of them was locked there for two weeks after what the ward called a "violent incident." Most of these were attempted escapes, but on occasion, some of the women did attack the nurses and caretakers, either out of actual lunacy or the lunacy they found themselves in when being treated like a caged animal. It had taken Mary a week of being in the dungeon to figure out the horrendous and cruel way Blackwell's system operated – their methods were meant to break them down so there was no soul left…to make them cooperate willingly. They were given frequent beatings in the dungeon, two meals of gruel a day with their "medication," and when they acted out, the potion was poured down their throats to "calm the nerves." Two weeks of this would make anyone in their right mind breach insanity, and when they were removed from the dungeon and placed back in the regular wards of the asylum, the women were constantly man-handled by a nursing staff that was less empathetic than the devil himself. There was no way out unless the doctors cleared an individual as fit for society, and that occurred following extensive interviews and tests. For Mary, it would never be possible. Croker would in all likelihood kill her first.

The reasons no longer mattered…he had put her there to watch her rot and die in the worst possible way, eaten up by her own demons. He was too much a coward to kill her himself and instead wanted her to wither away like a flower without water. Her anger started to rise. She couldn't allow this to go on – she had to go through with her plan, and if she didn't make it, Mary would make sure she wouldn't see another day in that God-forsaken place.

The brightness of the orange light outside mulled into red meal time was growing closer now. A few days prior, Mary had lifted a hair pin from one of the other women as she was brought in and chained, which Mary concealed along with her sharpened stone in the crack on the floor. Discreetly, she scooted over to her hiding spot, eyeing the other four women for signs of movement, and found them still sedated. Digging out the pointed stone, Mary carefully placed it down in her bosom, not wanting the staff to notice it when they came into the dungeon. Then she picked up the pin, pulling the legs of it apart with her teeth and gripped it tightly in her right hand. She had to hurry. The light was growing fainter…any minute would be the ring of the dinner bell. She shook her head hard three times, trying to bring clarity to her brain…she had to be ready. It was the only chance she would have.

Clanging loud and right on schedule, the bell rang out, and the tremor of footsteps beneath her indicated their gruel would arrive shortly. Immediately, Mary set to work picking the lock on her left wrist, just the way the Madame taught her. Seconds passed, and she toiled, fumbling it with her sliced up fingertips. Faster…she had to go faster…please God…help me…Edward help me…I have to get out of this hell or I will lose my mind…

With a tiny click, the cuff released, and her numb arm dropped to the floor. She squeezed her fist tight, rubbing her screaming muscles to try and restore sensation. When she heard voices outside the door, Mary placed her arm back up hastily, leaving the unlocked cuff around her wrist to camouflage her free arm from any staff. The door swung open, and in came one guard and one of the caretakers, a giant tray of their meal bowls lifted in his hands. The two spoke inaudibly back and forth to one another, not wanting to disturb the patients who were considered to be the most hostile, especially at a time when their drugs would be fading. Just as Mary hoped, they approached her first. Spotting that she was awake, the caretaker avoided eye contact and quickly set her bowl on the ground, motioning for her to eat first and he would come back with her medication. They moved on to the next patient quickly, and Mary ate a little of her gruel, watching them. The timing had to be exact.

When they went on from the second patient to the woman in the back corner, Mary planned to throw the chain from her wrist, jump to her feet, and flee out of the door. Protocol required the doors to be locked when the staff visited patients, but in the case of the dungeon, Mary took note that their nightly dinner delivery crew never followed those restrictions. The door was always propped open for a quick exit in case one of the women lost it completely and attacked, with the keys remaining in the door on the outside. Their mistake would buy her a small amount of time to get a head start, or possibly not be detected until she left her floor, and that was all she needed.

The caretaker got to his feet again and made his way to the back corner. He squatted down, checking the vitals of the unconscious patient as the guard suspiciously eyed the others. Mary waited…he would turn as the caretaker asked for him to be handed the bowl… turn…turn you bastard…!

He turned, bowl in hand, and Mary bolted. Her legs roared in pain. She heard shouts as she reached the hallway and, with a desperate heave, drove the heavy door closed behind her. She locked it and took the guard's keys from the door, gripping them tightly in her fist. Not a second later there was banging on the door and yells for her to open it. Mary paused, slowly retreating a few steps while the gravity of what she'd done sank in. When no one broke through after her, she took off down the hallway at full speed, trying to block out the hurt in her legs and her body the best she could. Her bare footsteps were muffled against the freezing ground, and her ears listened intently when she reached the end of the corridor. With no sounds amiss, Mary unlocked the next door with the guard's keys and descended the stairs three at a time, pushing to reach the first floor ahead of those who might pursue her. Just as she made it to the ground floor, she grabbed for her weapon still tucked away in her dress, telling herself to be prepared…a part of her hopeful she might actually make it this time.

Mary hit the bottom of the stairs and raced out the door, running harder. She was so close now…all that was left was to reach the end of the hallway, make a left, and out the front door. She bypassed all the checkpoints…avoided all the unknown locked doors and gates…the stairs she used were the guards' stairs, meant to be used for emergencies only in the case of an escaped patient. No one other than the staff was supposed to know of their existence. In her previous attempt, she'd discovered that was the way they consistently stayed one step ahead. This time around, however, that would not be the case.

Adrenaline poured through her veins. She would get off the island, perhaps swim if she had to, and get out into the city streets – they would never find her in the masses. She would find her son, find Esther, and they would run west like they'd been planning for months. Mary was down the hall and made the turn left, and at last shouts began to ring out close behind her. The front doors were in her sights ahead…she could taste the fresh air…the freedom!

Out of the corner of her eye, a nurse ran toward the doors and threw herself in front of them, panting and out of breath. "Don't Mary," she said. "Please. You'll only make it worse. He will never let you out."

Mary did not hesitate and held up the sharpened stone threateningly. "Move. Now."

The nurse stood her ground until Mary rushed with a loud, savage yell, which caused the terrified nurse to timidly flee out of the way. Her heart racing, Mary propelled the final key into the lock and shoved double doors open, running out into the sunlight at a full sprint.

On the outside, there were scattered tall trees ahead and in the far distance on the other side of the river sat the buildings she'd been longing for; but as her eyes took it in, Mary's heart sank. The gravel drive under her feet led to an eight-foot-tall iron fence surrounding her, the smoke and smog of the city drifting above and up into the sky. A few gardeners outside working gaped at her, motionless, and Mary understood that her escape to the river was naïve and poorly planned. Croker locked her in a place she could never break free of, and without a second thought Mary's choice was made – if she had to stay on Blackwell's Island, she might as well be dead.

"Mary!" she heard a voice from behind her. A strong gust of

wind blew from the west, sending the fall leaves spiraling through the air, and strangely everything around her seemed to decelerate at once. Mary looked to the sky and saw the orange and pink sun setting on the far horizon of Manhattan, and the thought of Edward dying in her arms came back, suddenly causing everything to pull together. Her dream was a premonition…a reminder that he was waiting for her in the next life. This was her end. The Madame would protect Thomas better than Mary knew she ever could. This was the end…after all her torment, this was the end…

She spun to face her captors. There were eight guards standing behind the nurse who had confronted her at the doors, and as a group they advanced toward her.

"Mary! Please!" She could barely hear the nurse over the deafening wind. "Put it down! Come back inside, Mary! It's okay! Come to me." The nurse looked at her with pleading eyes and open arms, but no sympathy mattered. She remembered how the Madame coached her many years ago to defend herself with a blade, recalling instantly what was and wasn't fatal.

With the stone dagger in both hands, Mary held it high above her head. "One…swift…motion…" she told herself quietly, closing her eyes.

"No!" the nurse screamed, but it was too late. Mary plunged the blade down into her chest with every ounce of her might. The pain was unlike anything she had ever experienced, and her feet staggered underneath her before she collapsed onto the ground. Blood wet her chest, and she couldn't breathe, hearing nothing but the rush of the wind. It was severe, so horrible she prayed to God to make it end and take her…everything grew cold…her head felt as though it might explode, and she was choking…choking without end. The pain was all-consuming, and Mary didn't know how long she could take it, until abruptly it stopped. All she could see was the pink and orange sky above, the leaves spinning in the air, and Mary knew she was nearly gone.

"Edward…" she mumbled, feeling herself smile one last time, "I'm coming, Edward…"

The last thing Mary saw was the nurse's face, her dress covered in Mary's blood, shouting out her name…

Mary felt her eyes close.

VI.

Thomas' fists clenched in anger as he walked through the streets, his fury on the brink of explosion. Nobody seemed to believe he could take care of himself without Mary, like he was some kind of rash, foolhardy child, and the more he thought on it the more infuriated he became. Trying to restrain his temper, Thomas plowed through the crowded city. The afternoon was finally coming to a close, and he wanted nothing more than to strike the very next thing that happened to cross his path. It had been one of the longest days he'd endured since his mother vanished over a month ago, and while the sun began to descend from the sky, Thomas remembered the only one with his best interests at heart was himself.

That morning, he helped Esther pack her things and brought her to her new home at the Hiltmores', wishing to see her settled comfortably at the residence before he begrudgingly left her there for good. Three and a half weeks ago, Esther dropped the news that she would be moving into the Hiltmores' mansion as a ward of their family at their suggestion, and Thomas attempted to hide not only the shock he felt, but also the general loathing he had for Catherine Hiltmore. Esther wasn't naïve. She, too, shared his distaste for such a conceited and self-righteous person; however, without Mary or another female to keep a proper household, Thomas couldn't deny she would have a better chance at the mercy of the Hiltmores than with him. But he was devastated to let her go.

Before Thomas could make his way out of the Hiltmores' and flee to the fire and metal with Lawrence, Mrs. Hiltmore ambushed him in the front hall, forcing him into an interrogation of his own future plans. He wanted nothing more than to tell her to fuck off, yet he restrained himself for Esther's sake. She didn't need that cloud hanging over her head just after moving in.

"Thomas, you cannot seriously think you will be a blacksmith your entire life," she prattled on, blocking his escape down the hallway. "Please. Douglas could use a new clerk, and you're perfect for the job. Why don't you consider going into business, a field you can actually capitalize in!"

He was finding it difficult to remain polite. "I appreciate the offer, Mrs. Hiltmore—"

"Please, Thomas. Douglas and I hate the idea of you being out there without any family to turn to. You know we care for you as much as we do Esther."

Thomas could see through the angle immediately. "I'm assuming the Madame has been by to see you in the past few days," he replied coolly, and immediately Catherine's cheeks flushed red with embarrassment. Thomas continued: "I appreciate your offer, Mrs. Hiltmore, but as you can tell, I know how this operation works pretty well. Please don't think I am purposefully being arrogant toward you. I mean no offense. It's just not where I see myself down the road. Business has never been an interest of mine. I prefer 'the hell pit,' as you call it."

"I'd say you just proved how business savvy you are with that kind of intuition. Thomas, dearest, you can't tell me you don't like making good money, and you also can't convince me you make anything working for that smelly German."

"Money is money. I'd rather be doing something I like and making less."

"And how do you know you wouldn't like business?" She crossed her arms over her chest, determined and unmoving. "Take the job. I'll make certain Douglas pays you triple what you make now."

"Mrs. Hiltmore—"

"You aren't leaving this house until you agree. I won't have it."

Thomas' eyes narrowed. "You mean she won't have it?"

"No," Mrs. Hiltmore asserted, her tone on edge. "We both thought it was best for you this way. You start next week. I suggest you tell your beloved Master today you won't be returning after the weekend. Or I'll personally see to it that French goon tans your hide."

Seeing an argument would get him nowhere, Thomas consented to think on her proposal, which she took as a yes. She pestered him further on his salary to prove her point, and when he did break down and disclose that information, Catherine nearly laughed out loud and rested her hand on his shoulder condescendingly.

"I'll send word to Douglas. He'll be happy to hear you're on board," she sang, escorting him to the door and waving enthusiastically as he went on his way.

He despised her. She embodied everything he hated about the people who considered themselves "high society," and the worst of it was he was stuck in her calculating web with no way out. It wasn't that Thomas had much more to learn from Lawrence – he was close to being as fine a craftsman as his Master; he simply loved working in the fire, wielding the metal to his own satisfaction and developing something dull and lifeless into a piece of art. Working as a clerk for the Hiltmores would be nothing in comparison, but he was tired of fighting everyone, tired of hiding his frustration and pretending everything was fine. Because for Thomas, nothing was fine: his heart was utterly torn apart. Luckily, what the others could not guess was that soon enough, Thomas would be leaving New York anyhow, and once he was gone he would never look back.

Presently, Thomas continued treading along heavily as the sun went down, and his frenzied anger transformed into a melancholic sadness. Only a few more weeks to wait and he would leave New York. He had grown discouraged after sending the man he thought to be his father a letter, unsure if it would even arrive to him in England, yet he made a promise to stay two months and he planned to see it through. There was just under a month left, and he had to admit his real aggravation was in his inability to save Esther from the clutches of Catherine Hiltmore. Thomas didn't blame her for taking the opportunity, and would have done whatever he could to convince her to take it if she had hesitated in the slightest. She was seven years his junior, and Esther was offered what every orphaned girl in that city dreamed of: a family, and not just any family, but a wealthy family who sincerely wished to take her in. Allowing Esther to give up a chance to live without worry or frugality seemed absurd, even to him. His only fear was without his presence, Thomas would be unable to protect her from the frauds, both visible and hidden. Nevertheless, he couldn't afford to think that way any longer. Esther needed to learn the ways of the world on her own without Thomas there to hold her hand every step of the way. The time for that was long passed.

Lawrence was distraught when he heard Thomas was offered a job as a clerk, though he refused to let Thomas pass it by, claiming that from that day forward he was fired from his job. This made Thomas grin. Then, he watched the poor man choke up as he confessed Thomas had become like a son to him over their years together. Of the numerous blacksmiths in New York, Lawrence was the most sought out for his gift with metal, and Thomas loved being there more than any place else. With a respectful nod, Thomas told Lawrence the long days working for him had been some of the best times he'd had. He promised he would be back to visit him whenever he could, but only under the condition that Lawrence swore to bathe first, which caused him to roar with laughter and wrap Thomas up into a bear hug.

Lawrence was a tall, beefy German man with dark, coarse hair and a long beard that constantly singed in the tall flames of the fire. He wore the same dark slacks every day, the same tanned boots, and the same buttoned cotton shirt, all hidden under his thick leather apron. Even during the coldest winter months, Lawrence never once put on anything more, and Thomas concluded that working by the fire for most of his life must have altered his normal body temperature. Lawrence's most prominent attribute was his stench, which consisted of old blood sausage, beer, and sweat…and it was one Thomas had come to love, or at least gotten used to with all the hours they spent side by side, and he often questioned whether he took that smell home with him after a long day. Oddly, it would be that smell he missed most as he grew older.

"Before you go, Tommy, I have something for you," Lawrence announced, releasing his student from his hefty embrace. "Don't go anywhere."

Thomas acquiesced, and Lawrence trotted off behind the fire pit, digging in an old chest of scraps he always told Thomas were his experimental works. Shuffling diligently for a few seconds, Lawrence found what he was looking for, and he made his way over toward Thomas, handing him something wrapped in a linen cloth.

Thomas held it, weighing it in his hands. "Lawrence…you really don't need to give me anything…"

"Oh hush your mouth and open it," he ordered, taking a step back and resting his giant hands on his hips, his eyes sparkling. Thomas unraveled the object and was absolutely speechless when he saw what it was: a sheathed dagger made from the finest steel Thomas had ever seen, and on its hilt Mary's initials were engraved.

"It was…well, it was meant to be an eighteenth birthday present next spring," Lawrence explained. "I…er…figured you would like having something to protect yourself with…almost like she was protecting you, in her own way."

"I…I don't know what to say, Lawrence. This is so wonderful

and it's much more than I deserve…a real piece of mastery. Thank you so much!"

"You like it then?"

"I love it! How on earth did you make it?"

Lawrence grinned, reaching for the knife and taking it from its scabbard. "It's actually one of my own design! A smaller version of those Confederate blades they used to slash the shit out of the Yanks…fucking heathens. See the blade here? Spine is straight but it has a curved, keen point and is double edged. About eight inches long and slightly weighted so your strike will have power. And see here? The clip point on the top of the blade…that'll give you a little more control of the knife. Just keep that damned handle polished and clean. It's a hardwood…a leftover maple I got off a guy selling goods the street, so it'll last some time."

"This is incredible, Lawrence. I am so…so honored. Thank you."

"Promise me one thing, Tommy."

"Anything, Lawrence."

He gripped Thomas' shoulders with his hands, staring straight into his eyes. "Don't go looking for trouble with this. It's to protect yourself with, not to pick a fight with. You're a damned smart boy and know better than to do anything stupid. But with Mary gone, I just…I just want to be sure…"

"I promise," Thomas assured him. "You know my battle with that is over. There's no one left to fight. I'm putting it behind me."

"Good. And you come by any time, all right? Don't be a stranger. I'll let you work the fire on your own time whenever you want."

Lawrence hugged him once more and sent him on his way, his eyes reddening as he watched Thomas depart. It was hard for Thomas to leave the workshop he had spent so many days and hours in, sweating through his clothes, burning his skin, and suffocating on the black, billowing smoke. What would have maddened other laborers Thomas enjoyed the most – he never felt better than after a long afternoon of beating the metal into submission. The work and the challenges he faced with Lawrence were tough, and it was far earlier than he'd wanted to say his inevitable goodbye. He did genuinely hope to keep his oath and one day come back to find Lawrence there with a smile, holding Thomas' apron up, telling him they had a bitch of a day ahead and to get to work. He vowed someday he would make that happen.

Rather than going home after his farewell to Lawrence, Thomas was angrily hiking the streets north until he hit Central Park. The thought of being at the empty apartment alone without Mary and now Esther pained him, and he wanted to postpone the unavoidable state of whiskey intoxication that would later arise for as long as he could. Weaving down one of the gravel paths, Thomas found his favorite bench a minute later unoccupied, and he sat down to observe the sun melting beyond the New York City skyline. The leaves in the trees were beginning to change color and fall to the ground, and their rich, dark hues foretold of a long winter fast approaching. Only three weeks were left to wait and hear from Lord Turner, and there were no reasons to be caught up with false hope. In the end, the likelihood he would go west on his own was much higher, and Thomas knew if he stayed any longer in New York once that time had run out, it would become harder and harder to leave.

There had been a few instances when Thomas wasn't sure if he had made a mistake not telling the Madame of writing to England, only because the idea of lying to anyone made him edgy. She took it upon herself to look after Thomas for the last month, and this caught him by surprise. The sudden pique of her interest in his well-being and the new, more personal relationship between them was what triggered his guilty conscience, a part of him liking the idea of them becoming something like friends. However, then he would remind himself of the numerous times he felt betrayed by her, recognizing this golden age was a temporary commodity. Things would go back to normal, they always did, and when that happened Thomas would resume his old role as her "nephew," as

143

she often called him, always implying he was family but also a giant pain in her ass.

No, there was nothing to regret. Not in his mind, anyway.

"Need one of these?" came a familiar voice from behind Thomas' bench. He turned to see Louis standing there smiling, a cigarette outstretched in his hand to Thomas.

"God yes," he replied, taking it from Louis and grabbing the timber from his jacket pocket to light it.

"Mind if I sit?"

"Feel free." Thomas motioned for Louis to take the open space next to him, inhaling a long drag, his irritation from the day calming instantly.

"The Madame wouldn't be happy with me for giving you that," Louis confessed to him with a smirk, leaning back against the bench as he smoked his own.

"Yeah well. Not like it's my first one."

Louis scoffed. "I guess that's true. Still, do me a little favor and don't tell her I'm encouraging it."

"Not a problem."

They sat for a moment, watching people stroll by. "So what brings you up here? I thought you worked during the weekdays."

"Hah! Funny. I quit with Lawrence today. Apparently the Madame and Mrs. Hiltmore have other plans for my future."

Louis went quiet, then shook his head. "She is a stubborn bitch, that one. She wants what's best for you though, Tommy. We all do."

"I know that," he said, tilting his head back and letting out smoke toward the sky. "I had a good thing going, though. I just wanted something that was mine. Something no one could touch."

"That is a luxury most people cannot afford, Tommy," Louis responded.

"Yeah…yeah you're right."

"How are you doing with the execution over?"

Thomas had an inkling Louis would bring this up. "About the

best I can. Bastard is dead, that's what matters, and Mary can rest in peace."

Louis tossed his own cigarette to the ground and stood, putting it out with his foot. "Head back to the barber shop soon, it'll get dark fast. She'll be by to see you in a couple hours."

"Tell her I'll probably be piss drunk by then."

"I think she knows that already, but I'll pass it along."

"Thanks, Louis."

"Things will keep getting better," Louis remarked. "Just do me a favor, Tommy, make sure you keep that new knife sheathed on your way home. I don't want you hurting yourself."

The cigarette fell from Thomas' hand. "How…how did you…?"

Louis chuckled. "It's my job to know these things." Nonchalantly, he spun around and strode out of the park. Thomas picked up and finished his cigarette, admittedly a little intimidated, though more amazed. Prior to leaving Lawrence's, he had tied the sheathed dagger to the outside of his right calf, which was the leg opposite where Louis sat. How was it even possible Louis had noticed it?

The thought made Thomas uneasy.

Louis hadn't been exaggerating. Sunset had come and gone by the time Thomas neared the apartment, and as he rounded a corner only a few blocks away, a massive crowd stood blocking the entire street. From the monstrous cloud of billowing smoke towering above the buildings, it was clear there was one hell of a fire burning, and the looters and onlookers were swarming the spot. Off in the distance, Thomas could hear the clanging of the fire brigade pummeling their direction, and any minute the coppers would be there to take their own share and then go about "restoring order." Since there was no other way for him to go, Thomas would have to find a way through the rabble, and he cringed. It was not going to be fun.

Picking up his pace, Thomas plunged in toward the back and pushed himself through the bodies, so tightly packed he marveled at how anyone could possibly breathe. With every step he grew increasingly more frustrated: no one would let him pass without trouble, and with each person he climbed by he was either hit hard, spat upon, or came away with some sort of filth on him, which he didn't care for in the slightest. His annoyance was becoming a fiery resentment. He despised this city – it was like a pack of rats caged together, fighting to get a crumb of cheese and not caring who or what they suffocated in the process. Thomas tripped over something on the ground and simultaneously was checked in his shoulder by a man who might as well have been a tub of lard, staying on his feet only because there was nowhere for him to fall. His temper escalated higher and higher as he shoved through until he couldn't stand it, and Thomas charged like a bull, no longer concerned whom he hit or knocked down. It didn't make a difference – he didn't really matter to anyone anymore, and frankly, he didn't give a damn about any of them either. No one would care if he drowned in the mob…and he was drowning…drowning in that awful city he couldn't wait to be free of.

He wouldn't do this any longer – not sure what he was really fighting against, Thomas pushed harder and harder, combating with all of his strength until suddenly he broke free of the pack of people, catapulting himself down to the cobblestone road not ten feet from the barber shop. He braced for impact and crashed hard, bloodying his lip and bruising his forearms on the unforgiving road, the breath knocked clean out of his lungs. Thomas rolled over in agony and lay where he collapsed sucking wind, listening as jeers from the edge of the crowd temporarily followed him, although they eventually died away. It wasn't just the day. It was Esther…Lawrence… and it was his mother's looming absence like a giant hole in his chest. The people he loved were ripped from his grasp, and this left him broken and dejected.

In under a month, his whole life had been distorted into some sort of twisted version of what it used to be. Nothing was as he'd planned or imagined it would turn out, and Thomas couldn't figure out where it went from here. He could stay on the ground, beaten down and bloodied, or he could get up and go on. Mary would have wanted him to get up…to follow through on their plans…to make their dream his reality. If he could get through those next few weeks, he would begin again. It was that small hope that kept his sanity intact.

Thomas gradually pressed himself up and off the ground with his arms, and in that moment noticed something he hadn't been aware of when he fell: it was his own thick, protruding shadow, one much too dark for the dingy street lamps overhead. Understanding what it meant, his head snapped up to see a few lights glimmering in his apartment, and Thomas' mangled body went tense. He had not once left a candlestick burning in his adult life – Mary taught him better than that. Or rather, threatened it into a habit.

"The Madame," he assumed aloud to no one in particular. There was no other explanation. Their nightly visits were a ritual: every evening since the execution, the Madame made a point to come by for at least one drink and to discuss his day. He knew there must be an ulterior motive to keep her calls so consistent; still, Thomas did feel a small part of her casual meetings were purely out of worry. Her behavior toward him had changed drastically. During those weeks she spent with him at the apartment, the Madame listened to what he had to say with an unnatural sense of attentiveness…unnatural for her at least. She remembered details she never bothered to in the past, brushing away every one of her other matters the second she crossed the threshold and made Thomas her priority…something extremely out of her character. Regardless, tonight Thomas was going to give her a piece of his mind. She failed to mention the previous night of her involvement conspiring with Mrs. Hiltmore to find him a new job, one he didn't ask for or want, and at that thought he was riled up all over again. He got to his feet, dusting what mud and grime he could from his clothes, and hobbled over to and up the back stairs.

It wasn't until Thomas was halfway to the top that he realized something was wrong. By that moment, he should have encountered Louis, who refused to let the Madame travel by herself at night, no exceptions. Hesitating, he delayed to see if perhaps Louis had gone to investigate something suspicious or check out the fire with the mob, but when he didn't return after a few minutes, Thomas realized it couldn't be the Madame upstairs. His hair stood on end, readying himself to draw Lawrence's blade if necessary.

Thomas lightly tiptoed the remaining stairs, speculating who or what exactly he might find inside, or better yet, who had the audacity to make themselves right at home in his apartment. With his legs ready to run, Thomas coyly pushed the unlocked door open and hastily slid inside hoping to throw off the intruder. Instead, as his eyes found the uninvited visitor, Thomas' heart stopped.

Had he hit his head in his fall as well?

A man was sitting at his kitchen table, a quarter of the way through a bottle of Thomas' whiskey. Their eyes locked, and neither said a word to the other – they just stared. Without needing to guess, Thomas knew who this man was. They were nearly identical in spite of their respective ages. He had broad shoulders and sat tall in his chair, giving the appearance of a military man and years of trained mannerisms. Like Thomas, he had a strong jaw line scruffed from lack of shave, and his hair was nearly black with a touch of grey at his temple. Their facial features matched exactly, from the shape of their noses to the furrow in their brows, and most remarkable of all were their indistinguishable aqua blue eyes. Thomas didn't know what to do next, and it must have been two or three minutes of him standing motionless in the doorway before his father spoke to him.

"I...I apologize for breaking in and entering your home without your consent, along with helping myself to your whiskey. Will you...will you sit?"

Thomas was almost unable to comply, but somehow managed

to stumble over his feet to the open chair, wrestling with something to say. Edward poured him a bit of whiskey into the other empty glass and smiled kindly.

"I thought we could use a little…well…a little encouragement for our first…encounter."

Thomas' brain was frozen. He took a sip of his drink hoping it might loosen him up.

"Do you know who I am, Thomas?"

Thomas nodded and set the glass back on the table. It was difficult not to gape at Edward. Without thinking, Thomas picked up his glass again and threw back the rest of his whiskey in one gulp before rescinding into his chair. Edward's eyebrows lifted, and then to Thomas' astonishment, he laughed and filled the glass again. It was Thomas' laugh: a deep, low chuckle from the bottom of his belly, and the sound of it was completely overwhelming.

"Well, as you can see, I received your letter," Edward resumed. "The very next day I left England to seek you out. I won't lie to you. At first I had my doubts whether this was some sort of play at my estate, but I think we can both see with our own eyes that is not the case."

Thomas smirked, rotating the glass nervously in his hand. "I…I never wanted any money. It was a whim…all of it was a whim. I found your letters to my mother…and I just thought…I never really expected…" His voice trailed off, not capable of finding the right words.

"You thought I would want to know, because from those letters it was obvious I did not know of your existence. Something I would have very much liked to ask Mary about."

"I would have too," Thomas chimed in. "Christ. I am…I am sorry to tell you this…her killer was brought forth not a day after I sent the letter to you. He's already met with the end of the noose, and they haven't found the body, but she's…she's no longer considered missing."

Edward finished his whiskey. "I mean, I had hopes. But anyone missing for more than a few days…there was no possibility. I only wish that somehow we could have found each other sooner."

The room went silent again, and Thomas chose to change the subject. "Where are you staying?" he asked.

"With my cousin, William. He and his wife Lucy have lived in New York for many years, and he's made a life here for the two of them through our business ventures. Before your letter arrived, I had actually planned a trip to New York to see him. I think he was much happier to have the news delivered in person…it's been years since we've seen one another…half a decade, I think…although I have yet to tell him about you. I thought if things went well we could tell him together. If that's all right with you, of course."

"I…I would like that…I think…," Thomas mumbled. "I'm sorry, I am still trying to take this in. I just…I didn't think you'd come."

"Why ever not?"

He didn't see a reason to hold back. "Don't you have a new family?"

"A new family?" Edward was puzzled.

"Yeah. A new life in England? I thought hearing from a bastard son would only ruin that or…or make you relive things you wanted to forget after all this time." They were the Madame's words, but Thomas had to hear the truth.

Edward's face grew serious. "Actually, Thomas, your mother was the only woman I've ever loved. So no, there is no other family, no other life, nothing of that nature. I've had a number of things happen to me that have made me despise the thought of normalcy, purely because it would require me to disregard those incidents. Those tragedies have made me who I am, and my disposition will not permit me to forget, no matter how many years have passed."

A strain rose between them. "I apologize. I didn't mean to offend you," Thomas empathized. "I wasn't sure what to assume. I've only known you existed for a few weeks."

"Please, do not be sorry. I don't blame you, Thomas. How

could you know? And you have been through your own ordeal at a very young age. It's a cause and effect reaction, I've come to comprehend. You look back at who you were prior to the change, and you look at who you are after, and appreciate you can never be who you once were. When you accept that, every day gets a little bit easier."

"Do you mind if I ask a personal question?"

"Not at all."

"What...what were you like before?"

"Before?"

"Before the war, before all of it."

Edward shifted in his chair and leaned back, a grin forming as he remembered. "Ahh...life before the war. It was so wonderful when I think about it now. The life of a second son is not anything glamorous; but, I can assure you there is an immense level of freedom when your responsibilities are so much less than your eldest brother.

"My father was one of the wealthiest men in England, and though he was cordial with my brother and myself, he was never warm with either of us, and that caused Arthur and I to find solace in one another. I loved him dearly...we were in constant jest, always pushing one another to our limits. When I chose to enter the navy, I don't think he could have been much prouder. The last time I saw him was just prior to my trip to New York, where I attended my cousin's wedding...and also consequently met Mary.

"But yes, the early days...I grew up an outdoorsman. I loved riding horses, fishing, and hiking the grounds of our property even during the worst rainstorms. But the one thing I loved above all else was the ocean. I spent many summers by the water, and grew to respect its power and abilities. When given the opportunity to spend my life on the open sea, I did not think twice. I was a natural, some said. I was happy then. I think right as I left New York for China, I was the happiest I've ever been."

"Sounds like something you'd read in a fairy tale," Thomas uttered. "I can't say I know much other than how to use a hammer."

Edward then ushered him to go on. "Why don't you tell me about your life here? Your childhood?"

"There isn't much to say, really."

"Oh, be fair. I'm sure you can elaborate for my sake."

Thomas reached over and poured himself more whiskey, almost embarrassed at how his father's story compared to his own. "When I was young, my mother would take me to the Madame every day and from her I learned to read, write, and do math. After reaching ten and tired of being sheltered, I went behind both of their backs and found an apprenticeship with a blacksmith–"

Edward held up his hand to stop him. "You found your own work in this city at age ten?"

"Well...yeah."

"At ten?"

Thomas couldn't resist feeling proud. "I had two women making every decision for me and watching everything I did like hawks. I wanted to make my own way, I guess."

"How did you even find someone to hire you?"

"A friend of my mother's helped me...a man that tried to be there for me when...well..."

"When you needed a father," Edward finished, a little disheartened.

"Yes. Harry did whatever he could to keep me on the straight and narrow. He saw I was ready. My mother and the Madame were furious, but they got over it when I started making money for us."

"Didn't you have friends your own age?"

"A few here and there, never for long. A couple tried to get me to fall in with the younger gangs, but I was taught better. Most of the boys my age joined, either out of fear or boredom. I found Lawrence instead...he was said to be the best blacksmith in the whole city, and I begged him for nearly a week to let me work under him.

Eventually he gave in. Like you were with water, I was a natural with fire, or so he told me…said I had an aptitude for it. I've worked with him ever since." Thomas didn't feel the need to tell Edward about his day. Even now he was contemplating whether or not he was delirious after his hard fall.

"And Mary…what did she do?"

"She was a bookkeeper."

"Really?"

"Mary was damned good with numbers. She never made much, but between the two of us we made enough to get by without any problems."

Thomas went on to tell his father the whole story, from Esther's unanticipated arrival to the man who murdered Mary the previous month. Edward listened attentively, and when the details of Mary's death came up Thomas could see the despair in his face. As he went on, Thomas gradually sensed why his father was so upset – he traveled to meet Thomas in New York clinging to the smallest hope Mary might still be alive. Then something else occurred to him. What if Edward had only come for her? He'd found Thomas, uncovered the facts about the woman he loved…why would he stick around for a son he didn't know when Thomas was already of age? There was no reason to, not when Thomas could quite easily take care of himself. A pang of impatience built up. He could see where this was going. Edward would, because of his upbringing, try to financially assist Thomas, maybe even try to get to know him while he stayed in New York, yet not long after the time would come for Edward to leave and sail across the pond on home. Maybe his father might feel obligated to look after him, but Thomas didn't want that. He wasn't raised to be the type of man who lived off the goodwill of a father he'd never known until this night. Before Thomas could transfer his sentiments to words, his father cut in, taking him off guard.

"So…what did you do when she disappeared?"

"What do you mean?" Thomas asked.

"When you didn't know quite yet that she was murdered? Did you search for her? Or did the police officers take over and help?"

Thomas instantly went on the defensive. "Look, I did everything I could to find her. You don't know what it's like, all right? To be the only one who gives a shit about her and have no one believe she didn't just abandon us and move on for herself."

"Whoa, Thomas, I wasn't accusing you of not trying!" Edward exclaimed leaning forward, alarmed by his sudden outburst.

"What did you expect me to do, avenge her myself?"

"That's not what I'm—"

Thomas ignored him, and he slammed his fist on the table. "Stop pretending to care! About me…about any of it. She's gone, and you can go home now and forget about me. You have no idea what I've been through. All of my family just gone…stolen…and there's nothing I could do to change any it!"

Unexpectedly, Edward grew just as heated as Thomas was. "You think I haven't lived through the same heartbreaks?" his father yelled, taking Thomas aback. "I've lost my family too, Thomas. Every one of them! Quit acting like a bloody adolescent or that's how I'll treat you. I journeyed one hell of a long way to find you because you sought me out—"

"What about her?! If it weren't for her—"

"If it weren't for her, you wouldn't be sitting in that chair trying to patronize your own God damn father!"

"Then why are you here?! Why come all this way if she's dead?!"

Edward clenched his teeth in an effort to restrain his tone. "Because you're my son, and we are all each other has left. Or do you not understand that yet?"

Thomas glared at him, the words resonating as he took a few deep breaths. Edward was, of course, right on point. Earlier that day Thomas spent hours dwelling on the idea he was alone in the world, wrestling with his anger and sadness. This was the one thing he had wanted…to be needed again by someone who needed him just as badly…to feel like he mattered. Thomas shook off a lingering tear and reached into his pocket to grab a cigarette, attempting to thrust his emotions back down below the surface.

"Jesus. Your temper is as bad as mine," Edward observed, sliding a box of matches to him from across the table. "And you better have two of those bloody things," he added, pointing at Thomas' hand.

Thomas handed his extra one to him. "It's…it's just been a day…a month really." He waited for Edward to light his tobacco. "I just can't think straight about anything."

"If it's any consolation, I haven't been able to think straight either, particularly since you walked through that door. I mean, look at us. It's…uncanny."

They stared at each other again. "Yeah, it really is," Thomas responded.

"Look, Thomas, I am not asking you to trust me or like me much for that matter. All I want is a chance to be a part of your life. To get to know you, assist you when I can, and be someone you can rely on."

Thomas paused. "Because we're all we have?"

"In a way, yes that's a big part of it. It doesn't matter how much time has passed…days, weeks, years… Thomas, you're my son. That's the only motive I'll ever have, and I hope someday you see that."

Thomas took a drink of his whiskey. "Everyone I've ever trusted has lied to me."

"Mary never would have lied to you," Edward retorted.

"She lied to me about you."

"Yes, persuaded by the lovely Madame, I can only presume. Like I said, just a chance, Thomas. That's the only thing I want from you. Just give me a chance to be a father."

"No lies," Thomas emphasized.

"No lies. I promise."

They sat wordlessly for a few seconds. "What was she like when she was young?"

Edward let out a cloud of smoke. "Mary?"

"Yeah. When you met."

Edward smiled, his eyes going somewhere else. "She was special...like nothing I'd ever seen."

"How did you meet her?"

"Well, I was here for William's wedding, and a few days prior to the ceremony I was out for a stroll in the morning. As you can imagine, not being from here I got a little...lost. One wrong turn lead to another, and then I was in a part of town where I was begging to be robbed. Four men began to follow and haggle me for money, and before I could lose them there she was, telling them off by name with the filthiest language I'd ever heard a woman speak...I couldn't even understand half of it. I'm English, after all."

Thomas chuckled. "That sounds like her. So what happened next?"

"I tried to repeatedly thank her like a half-witted ass until she very vividly told me off as well and was on her way. It didn't matter – I followed her for a time to see where she went. Honestly, when I saw her go into the Madame's "Palace," knowing what it was, I was...well...discouraged would be one way to put it. But something about her...something told me not to give up.

"After that moment I was besotted. I couldn't stop thinking about her. She was so beautiful...I couldn't understand why she would associate with a place like that. A week or so passed and I finally convinced myself to venture back and find her, and I did. Boy, was I shocked to find out how well educated she truly was...there was much more there than just a pretty face. After convincing her to take a walk with me, we spent the afternoon discussing books, politics, even the war that was fast approaching. When I found the courage to actually confront Mary about her profession, she became infuriated with me..."insult to injury" was how she put it...and stormed off in the middle of our conversation. I was left standing in the middle of the road like a bloody fool with everyone laughing at me."

"Wait. What do you mean her profession?"

Edward's cheeks flushed a bit. "You…you didn't know?"

"You're not saying she was a…a…my mother wasn't…she would never…"

"She was young, Thomas, and for her it was easy money," Edward rationalized, failing to make it any better.

It was a big blow to Thomas. "She actually worked for the Madame?"

"For a time, yes. It was a very short-lived endeavor, I can assure you."

"How could they not tell me?!" Thomas was horror-stricken, and also feeling extremely nauseated.

"Why would they? There is no reason to tax you with her past. And like I said, it was short lived. Very short lived. No more than a few months."

Thomas' stomach couldn't handle the thought. "Jesus Christ," he said under his breath, trying to pretend he hadn't heard Edward in the first place. "Well go on then I guess…then what happened?"

"The next morning a letter was delivered to my cousin's house for me with a long apology from Mary, asking me to meet her again if I accepted her apology. I did, and from there, everything fell into place."

"So she…she…stopped? How did you manage to work this around the Madame?"

"Like I said, Mary had only been working a few months at the time. She had a very small and elite client list. I went to the Madame and told her I would give her what they all paid combined under the condition Mary was free to do what she pleased. Of course, the Madame didn't mind as long as she was paid her dues, believing whatever random inclination I had for Mary would die out. Well it obviously didn't, and we planned to marry and move back to England the following spring."

Thomas filled their glasses impulsively, finishing the rest of the bottle. "And then you went to China."

"I was called away rapidly. I appealed to her over and over to go to my home and stay with my family, but she refused, wanting to remain in New York until my return. I left her every bit of money I had and promised I would come back for her when the conflict resolved. And that...that was the last time I ever saw her."

Edward's words trailed off. Thomas struggled with what to say or how to console his father, yet there was nothing he could do. Edward was right: they did only have each other. There was so much to learn, and so many things to take in, but somehow they had been brought together when they needed each other most. And for the first time in a long time, Thomas felt something in his veins, something he hadn't felt in what seemed like ages. He felt hope.

A sound from the outside gave them both a start. Someone was climbing the back stairs, and Thomas' heart skipped. His eyes darted to his father, whose confused expression transformed into a snort, as he was apparently able to read Thomas' mind.

"She has no idea, does she?" he whispered, and Thomas shook his head. "Well, I'll be God damned. This should be entertaining."

There were two knocks and the door flew open. "I brought over wine tonight, Thomas, because I swear to God if I have to drink whiskey again..." The Madame stopped on Thomas' threshold, her eyes wide as they travelled from father to son, and the Madame's face grew as white as a ghost.

Edward took the lead, clearing his throat. "Good evening, Madame. It has been quite some time, I daresay. We have only just run out of whiskey, and a bottle of wine would do just the trick. Won't you join us?"

The Madame didn't say a word. Thomas could see she was stupefied at what was in front of her, and warily she made her way forward to an open chair at the table and sat. She was unable to make eye contact with either of them and only frowned down at the table, trying to figure out how in the world she missed it. Edward was visibly delighted at this, and Thomas leapt up to uncork the wine and grab new glasses. The awkward tension only got worse, and Thomas filled her glass to the brim. Expecting her to chug it down, Thomas stayed beside her, ready to refill, but instead the Madame didn't bother to take an initial sip. He could sense her wrath – she could barely restrain from tearing Thomas to shreds.

"I…uh…was just catching up with Lord Turner," Thomas blurted out, resuming his own spot at the table, pouring wine for himself and his father. "He was telling me about how he and Mary met. I'd always thought my father died in the Civil War, and now here he is…English nobility. It's fascinating, really."

Immediately the Madame straightened and causally picked up her glass of wine, taking a small, lady-like taste. "And how has your stay been in our glorious city, Lord Turner?" Her demeanor was so lackadaisical, Thomas became a little worried for their safety.

"I arrived just this morning. I am staying indefinitely with William, who I am sure you remember, and his wonderful wife Lucy. Thomas told me the news of Mary's death. Also fascinating, as I was under the impression she had died years ago."

The Madame did not drop her eyes. "It's very unfortunate such tragedies occur. We all must do what we can to make the best of these unfortunate events." Her gaze shifted onto Thomas, and it was filled with spite. "I am sorry to tell you I cannot stay. I have a busy night ahead, darling."

"Yes! I understand. Thank you for bringing the wine over."

"You will be by to see me first thing in the morning," she declared, getting to her feet. It was a statement, not a question.

"I will come by first thing."

She paused in the doorway. "Enjoy your evening, gentlemen. Lord Turner, it was a pleasure to see you in such good health. I will send a call card for dinner later in the week, if you would oblige me."

Edward stood and bowed courteously. "I would be very happy to join you. Goodnight, Madame."

The Madame gave Thomas one last piercing glimpse and then

was gone, the door slamming behind her. They stayed quiet until her steps disappeared, and subsequently both Edward and Thomas burst into laughter. Thomas had never seen the Madame so entirely blindsided, especially at their direct references to her scheming. She hadn't anticipated Thomas would do anything without her blessing, and considering how close they had become these passing few weeks he did feel a twinge of guilt in his gut. On the other hand, he reminded himself of her more recent ruse with Mrs. Hiltmore behind his back, and also that he had not lied to her – he withheld information, which the Madame did to him on a daily basis. Tomorrow, Thomas knew he would get an earful, but from the lightness he felt, it didn't seem to matter. With his father by his side, Thomas was beginning to feel his lost confidence return.

"I had better be off too, Thomas," Edward announced, draining his own wine. "The hour is late and William will be up waiting for me to return. Do you work tomorrow? Is there any way I can convince you to take the day off?"

"Well…no I don't have to work. But I will explain that to you later."

"All right." Edward rose and walked to the door, grabbing his coat and hat. Thomas had not been aware until that moment how finely Edward was dressed despite spending the entire night with him. He wore professionally stitched and tailored black trousers, a waistcoat and cravat, patent leather shoes, as well as a clean white shirt and a shining gold pocket watch, the chain dangling freely at his chest. The realization started to settle in that Edward, his father, was no ordinary man, and in turn, neither was Thomas. He, too, was English nobility by birthright.

"I will be by tomorrow around ten or so after your meeting with the Madame, and we can discuss whatever you'd like," he offered, putting on his hat and rotating around, "I know this is overwhelming, Thomas, and if it's too much you just need to be honest with me. If you need time—"

"It's not too much. It's…it's what I wanted when I wrote to you. It's exactly what I wanted. Maybe that's why I am so…so in shock."

"Whatever you need, I am here," Edward remarked with a pat on Thomas' arm. "And when you are ready, I would like for you to meet William and Lucy, since they are now your relatives as well."

"I would like that," Thomas said. "And…well…I just…I'm glad you're here. And I'm sorry I was short with you."

"You have no reason to apologize, Thomas. Honestly, where do you think you got that temper from in the first place?" Edward grinned, pulling his arms through his coat. "Until tomorrow."

"Until tomorrow," Thomas repeated, opening the door for him.

Edward took a few paces out and froze, turning around again. "Be careful with the Madame in the morning. Now that she knows I'm in the city, things will change, and that worries me a great deal."

Thomas shrugged. "Don't worry. I know her. I'll get a lecture and maybe a slap, but that'll be the end of it. She wouldn't do anything to purposefully hurt me after what we've been through together. She's just losing her nerve."

Edward let out a sigh. "That's what concerns me. Your mother said the same thing."

VII.

It was a God damn catastrophe. Just when the Madame thought she had everything under control, the rug was ripped out from underneath her feet. The peaceful calm following Mary's disappearance was evidently only the eye of the storm, and an arcane dread began to set in that, in all likelihood, the second hit of this tempest would be much more detrimental than the first.

After leaving Thomas' in a mad rush, the Madame and Louis returned to The Palace where she locked herself away, leaving Louis and George in charge. She didn't sleep. Instead, the Madame sat in her desk chair, gaping out the huge windows behind her desk, her third bottle of wine nearly drained as dawn crept over the eastern skyline. Earlier in the night, her horror-stricken face had worried Louis on their ride home from the barbershop, and when she explained in detail the confrontation upstairs, he quickly understood. They went back and forth, battling over how to approach the situation at hand, and neither could discern what action, if any, to take next. There were too many hypotheticals for the Madame's liking.

Edward was a presumable threat to Thomas and to her, mainly because he could unravel all of the hard work she'd endured to tie every loose end closed around Mary. If anyone aside from her or Louis discovered Edward's connection to Thomas…who he was…why he was here…Croker would find out in a matter of days, and then come after her and accuse her of plotting against him. It wouldn't just be her ruination, it would be her end, and Thomas' fate wouldn't be any different. She had to fix this, and fix it fast.

The Madame downed the last of the wine and set the bottle on the floor, pushing back in her chair while her mind raced a thousand different directions. The only assumption she could make was the obvious: Thomas believed Mary to be dead, as he had witnessed her "assailant's" execution firsthand, and he seemed to be moving forward more and more each day. She dropped in on him every night just to be cautious, and he had shown no signs at holding onto his mother's death; if anything, she was impressed at how tough he'd been the last few weeks. In order to lessen some of his hardships, the Madame had gone to great lengths and convinced Douglas Hiltmore to find a place for him as a clerk at one of his businesses. Thomas' future was set up perfectly without him having to lift a finger, and while he might have begrudged her for it in the beginning, she told herself in the end he might see her reasoning, perhaps possibly thank her for what she'd done for him. But that delusion vanished in a flash with the arrival of an unforeseen guest, one that none but her realized threatened their very existence.

She had gone to great lengths and sacrificed everything to make Edward disappear forever, and nearly twenty years later he reemerged from the abyss. If he decided to investigate Mary's death on his own terms, and there was a striking possibility he would, the Madame could only hope Ellis' evidence was as bulletproof as he claimed it to be. She was furious with Thomas for betraying her, for fucking stabbing her in the back, but how could she really blame him? It wasn't his choice to lose Mary, and if the Madame were in his place she would have done the same. Thomas was the last bit of happiness she had left – the last piece of Mary that existed. Losing him now would be her worst failure. This fiasco was spinning out of her control, and she tried to think through the fog of the wine. There had to be a way...she just needed to see all the angles.

Then, it came to her in an instant, and the Madame couldn't believe she hadn't thought of it before. No, there was nothing she could do personally, but maybe that was the key to winning the battle: where her hands might be tied, others were free to execute the bigger picture. Her goal above any other was to keep Thomas out of Croker's reach and save her own fucking skin in the process. Edward could be those hands—he could remove Thomas from the equation entirely. As a result, she would lose Thomas from her everyday life; however, it would mean he was safe somewhere far away from Croker, somewhere that bastard couldn't touch him. If Thomas stayed in New York...if somehow the truth about Mary surfaced...neither father nor son would sit idle, and they would both be killed by the Hall. The Hall never hesitated. The risk was too great, even for the God damn British aristocrat.

Her plan was a simple one – she needed to make Edward a proposal he couldn't refuse, or that he couldn't deny was the best course of action for him and Thomas. Perhaps it was time Lord Turner learned the truth about the dire straits his son faced, and maybe in the end, the truth could play to her advantage. He would hate her, maybe more than he already did, yet she really didn't give a shit. Too much was at stake. For once, the Madame was fighting a battle she knew she couldn't win. Not yet, at least.

A sense of determination blossomed, her purpose clear. She leapt up from her chair, consequently standing too abruptly and causing her vision to spot black as the room spun. Falling forward, the Madame reached for her desk and clung to it.

"Louis! Louis, God dammit! Water! And I...Jesus I need a fucking bath...God damned wine..."

It took some time, but a few hours into the late morning the Madame had sobered up enough to feel almost like her normal self. Her brain worked its magic, and the plan had come together nicely, though she was painfully aware there was only a small window of opportunity to act. To set things in motion, she sent Louis out to deliver an invitation to Mr. Seamus Murphy for a meeting around lunchtime. There could be no doubt in the eyes of Croker or the Hall that she was unwaveringly their ally, despite the involvement of Thomas. If the Irish believed she was more apt to assist them than aid Thomas, she could rescue him from the wrath of Croker and his thugs. And with the expectation that Thomas and Edward would soon be gone, it would build a strong bond of trust with the most powerful organization in New York, one she coveted and would need to keep her own business booming.

She finished dressing for the day after Louis left to make the delivery. Stunning, yet conservative was her angle, with the knowledge that any man directly faced with a pair of breasts would be incapable to comprehend anything else. There were only two dresses in her closet cut without her infamous plunging neckline, and one of which was her black, mourning attire, so green satin it would be to match the Irish spirit, even if the color did her little justice. The Madame called in Caroline, one of her girls, to help her lace the bodice, as Caroline did most of the on-hand and emergency tailoring at The Palace. They didn't speak more than a few words to one another, however she could see the look of confusion on Caroline's face when the girl realized the Madame wasn't fibbing about putting on the gown.

Caroline finally couldn't resist. "You can't tell me you're seriously going to wear this ancient, ugly thing? At a meeting?"

The Madame gave her a cold stare. "Do I look like I'm fucking kidding?"

Taking the hint, Caroline helped her into it, shaking her head. "All I'm saying is, if you want to impress, you have at least thirty other gowns that do the trick. This thing is hideous. The fabric washes you out."

"I don't remember asking for your opinion, Caroline," the Madame spat. "Lace it and shut your mouth."

"Fine," Caroline retorted, pulling the strings tight. "Sorry for trying to help."

From the offended expression on Caroline's face, the Madame felt she owed her more than that. She wasn't angry with her – she just fucking hated the dress.

"Trust me, darling, if I wanted to impress anyone, I wouldn't have this dress out to begin with. This is for emergencies only, if you catch my drift."

"Well, I'll be honest, Madame. No one will want to fuck you in this dress."

The moment Caroline was gone, the Madame chuckled to herself: the girls would certainly have some gossip for the morning, and just from her short conjecture with Caroline, the Madame was reminded how much she loved being surrounded by a group of eccentric women just like her.

Another hour and a whiskey later, Louis returned and to her relief, delegated that the invitation was positively received. He also announced Thomas had arrived, and as Thomas strutted into her office, it was apparent whatever confidence he'd lost with Mary's passing had come back stronger than before. Edward's unexpected presence changed Thomas' entire demeanor, which could pass as almost brash, and she was surprised to find she liked him this way – at least, she liked it better than the depression and anger he'd been grappling with for weeks. This transformation following just one night with his father was proof enough her idea might succeed, and possibly benefit her more than she initially predicted. Thomas was, after all, now the heir to one of the biggest fortunes in Western Europe, and friends like those were hard to come by. But she didn't want to get carried away just yet. First there were some words that needed to be had – Thomas needed a small reminder that just because his exceedingly rich father had come to town didn't mean their relationship had changed. As far as she was concerned, she still owned his ass.

"Good morning, Thomas. Won't you sit?" She nonchalantly gestured to the vacant chair, with a coffee in her right hand and her legs propped on up her desktop. The Madame's voice was smooth and melodic, wanting to hide the fact she was about to strike hard. A verbal disembowelment was in his near future, and once he'd taken it and risen his white flag, things would resume to their normal state. Thomas sat, attempting to appear unruffled and calm; he knew what was coming, much to the Madame's delight.

Her left eyebrow rose. "So your father has arrived, as I came to find out late last evening. Do you want to tell me about it?"

His self-assuredness dwindled. "I…well I found the letters in your safe, as you know," he sputtered. "But before you came to the house that night to confront me, I had already written him asking him to meet me. Edward read my letter and set out the next day for New York. And now he's…"

"And now he's here."

"Yes."

"And just when the fuck were you going to decide to tell me the whole story, Thomas? Hmm? You went behind my God damned back and lied to my face after I've spent weeks trying to help you recover!"

"Look, I didn't lie to you! I never lied about any of it–"

She got to her feet and leaned over her desk menacingly. "Just because you chose not to tell me doesn't mean it's not deception, Thomas. Why in the hell would you keep a secret like this from me? And for over a fucking month!"

Thomas' face hardened. "By the time you asked me not to write him I already had. I chose not to tell you because it's not like you have a right to know everything I do. I have been around you long enough, Aunt, to know how to protect myself and work things to my own advantage. I learned from the best."

The Madame couldn't believe what she'd heard. She wasn't sure if he'd let it slip, or if he'd done it on purpose to try and dishevel her composure; either way, it worked, and while it infuriated her it also filled her with a strange kind of warmth. The last time Thomas had called her Aunt, he was around eleven or twelve, right before his adolescence struck hard and their bond changed. "Aunt" was the name given to her by Mary for Thomas' ears, and he took to it without question until the fateful day came when he outgrew it. He wanted to hit her where it hurt…and it did sting a little, especially since she knew it was only to make his point and get her to back off.

She couldn't help but smirk, and she stood straight again, placing her hands on her hips. "Darling, I can't say I'm not sincerely impressed." She walked around her desk toward him. "Yet you seem to have forgotten a slight factor." She swiftly bent down and locked both of her hands on Thomas' armrests, causing him to jump back in his chair with their noses only inches apart. "I don't give a fuck what you think is best for you. I have done everything in my power to keep your ass from the bottom of the Hudson, do you understand? If it weren't for me you'd be dead, Thomas! Dead as a fucking doornail! So yes, you should have fucking told me about the letter!"

"Go to hell!" Thomas yelled, pushing her back, his strength startling her. "I am not a child for you to bully anymore. Not everyone wants to be a part of your constant scheming. I will be better off on my own without you and without all this bullshit!" His cheeks were scarlet with rage and his fests clenched as he scowled at her. She had to let him get it out, and stayed right where she was. "This has nothing to do with me or what I've done. If you had never hid my father from me, or from my mother, we wouldn't even be having this conversation. This has all been your doing, and I'm tired of you ruining the little good I have in my life!"

"Oh for Christ's sake. It's all my fault, is it? I'm the bitch, then? The woman who has gone out of her way to protect and keep you and your mother afloat since you were born?"

"I am not saying I don't appreciate what you've done for me, but if it weren't for you, Mary might still be here."

"Well Thomas, if it weren't for me, you wouldn't be here. And if your fucking mother had listened to me and not taken that job with those bastards she would be here sitting with us, too. If you want to fight over theoretical scenarios, you can talk yourself in circles all you want. The fact of the matter is we are the only two here, and there is nothing you can do to change it. Accept that and grow the fuck up."

Thomas didn't respond. His gaze fell from the Madame's eyes to the floor, and she could see her argument was well made – he was furious at her, but deep down he also knew she was right. Blaming her for everything was a cop out, a way to not feel responsible for his mother – Mary's death wasn't on him, though clearly he hadn't quite come to grips with it.

The Madame reverted to her chair without another word and lowered down, tarrying to see if Thomas had any fight left. When it was clear he had nothing more to add, she went on to the next phase, the most important: rebuilding the foundation.

"Thomas, I don't know what it's going to take for you to forgive me and let this be the past. What I did to you and your mother is inexcusable and heinous. I was fucking selfish, all right? And I am sorry for how it's affected you…and how it affected her…but for my sake I don't want us to be at odds with each other. Especially with your father here."

Thomas shook his head. "What do you want me to say? Thank you? That it's all better now that you've apologized?"

"I just don't want you to cut me out of your life, Thomas. That's all."

"Cutting you out was never my intention," he replied, his tone easing, "but I'm tired of this. I've outgrown the whole only telling me what I need to know crap. No more games with me. No more games with Edward. I don't want to keep wondering what you're hiding form me. I want you to be honest for once! Is that so much to ask?"

"No, no I suppose it's not," she sighed. "I swear to you I will be upfront from this day forward. No excuses."

Thomas' eyes narrowed. "If you are playing me…"

"I'm not fucking playing you. I'm dead serious. You'd just better be ready for it."

"What do you mean?"

The Madame's expression grew stern. "Not everything that you'll hear from me you're going to like. This world is an ugly fucking place, Thomas. What I didn't tell you in the beginning wasn't for my own amusement. It was because I didn't want you to see how much of a hell this place is."

"I can handle it," he said. "Or at least I need to learn to."

"We have a deal then."

Thomas paused. "Are you really inviting him to dinner?" he asked.

"Yes."

"All right. Just don't…scare him off again."

"I don't think I could if I wanted to, Thomas. Now quit using up all my time and get out. I have work to do."

Thomas agreed and got to his feet, heading toward the office doors. "Tomorrow night?"

"Tomorrow night."

He smiled, closing the doors slowly. "Nice dress, by the way."

When she was alone, she couldn't help but let out a slight laugh. He had learned well from her. Through the years, she didn't realize Thomas was watching…listening…learning how it was she did what she did. There would come a time when the Madame would have to stop underestimating Thomas. He was much smarter than he ever let on, and someday he might beat her at her own game if she wasn't vigilant. But that day was not today.

At half past one Seamus Murphy turned up right on schedule, and with him came O'Reilly, another of Croker's underlings. Since Thomas' departure, the Madame spent her time mentally grooming her mannerisms, appreciating that the role of strength and intimidation would have to be toned down. In order to create the illusion she was reliable, the Madame needed to eliminate herself as a threat to the Hall and hopefully, this would give her the advantage. It was an easy trick with men – they hated being outdone, particularly by a person they considered to be subordinate. Their fragile fucking egos had a hard time coping with defeat, so instead she would portray the overpowered, weak, emotional woman, yearning to fix whatever difficulties she created. It was her most recurring character in these type of scenarios, and one she'd learned to fully master.

When Murphy and O'Reilly reached The Palace, Louis brought them upstairs and into her office, where she pretended to be buried in paperwork upon their entry. As if taken off guard, the Madame overcompensated with apologies for not meeting them at the door herself, asking to be excused for her poor behavior, and then politely, she ushered both to sit away from her desk in the lounging area and took her own spot on one of the floral armchairs by the fireplace.

"Thank you so much for coming to see me on such short notice, gentlemen. I hope it was not an inconvenience." She snapped her fingers. "Louis, could you grab us some tea? Is tea all right, gentlemen?"

Murphy and O'Neill remained motionless, their faces a little bewildered as she watched them try to figure out what was happening – the last time these two goons visited the Madame, she was staring at them from behind a pistol. Clearly, friendliness and hospitality were not quite what they expected.

"Tea is fine, thank you," Mr. Murphy replied at last. "We planned on visiting you sometime in the next few days, Madame. To see how things were going with the boy. We just…we just weren't thinking we would get a warm welcome."

She nodded encouragingly. "I understand completely. And I want to take this opportunity to explain my actions. I was a desperate woman, and as you two know, desperate women have a tendency to act…well, just a little irrationally…" she let her voice trail off with a light laugh, guiding Mr. Murphy and Mr. O'Reilly out of their tension as they chuckled along with her. "It was impulsive and rash! I was completely distraught and I acted when I shouldn't have. So please do accept my apology. It was merely my…well I guess you could say it was my female emotions leading those actions."

"We appreciate your words, Madame," O'Reilly told her. "It has been a mess for all of us. We are just happy to resolve it."

"Wonderful!" she exclaimed, clapping her hands together. Louis knocked and strolled inside with their tea prepared, pouring them each a cup as if he were her butler instead of her hired gun. "Now, I do believe you gentlemen came here to discuss the young Thomas? Mary's son?"

Murphy took the lead once again. "We only want to make sure there is nothing you're hiding. The boy does believe his mother was murdered by Smith?"

"Oh, yes. To the core," she assured them. "He even attended the hanging of the man accused in the very front of the crowd. He's still mourning but by no means is he speculating anything."

"And his behavior has been…relatively normal considering the circumstances?"

"Absolutely."

"We did notice you had been going to see him every night since the hanging," O'Reilly interjected. "Which was one of the reasons we haven't been here sooner. We assumed you were just taking care of our job for us."

The Madame grinned – she predicted they'd be watching her every move, and she was thrilled to ascertain she already secured a certain level of trust. "I love Thomas. I want him to live a great life, and I know dwelling on this incident will not help him in any way. I have been trying to usher him along…to help him move on." Her tone was purposefully shaky, as if she might tear up, and she could see the sympathy forming in their eyes. The eyes of the fucking bastards who had Mary locked away somewhere and threw away the key.

"And his job?" Murphy asked.

"What of it?"

"Our tail said he quit yesterday."

The Madame grew a little nervous…they still had a tail on Thomas? "He did. He wanted a change, and will be starting work as a clerk next week for the Hiltmore family. You've heard of Douglas Hiltmore I presume? It will be a great starting point in a new world for him."

Mr. Murphy glanced at Mr. O'Reilly, and the pair visibly came to an internal, silent agreement. "Croker wanted us to pass along his regards," O'Reilly disclosed. "And also to tell you we have no reason to follow your boy anymore. We were sent to…uh…clarify our facts, and frankly Madame, our plates are so damned full right now, I think we can let you handle this on your own."

"The boy seems fine and he is no longer a threat," Murphy added. "Croker will be happy to hear how compliant you have been. And cordial. Here." He handed her an envelope, a giant red wax C sealing it closed. "You're instructed to read it after we've gone. And our…our employer also wanted us to pass along he will be by to check in sometime soon."

Benignly, she took the envelope from his hands. "Thank you, gentlemen. I am so glad our first meeting, of what I am sure will be many, went so well. Can I offer you anything else before you leave? More tea? Perhaps a bit of whiskey?"

"Oh no, that is…that's not necessary…" Mr. Murphy protested.

The Madame shook her head. "Nonsense. I have a bottle and glasses right here. Just one, as a token of my appreciation. I insist."

She sat with the two men for over an hour, observing closely as they drained almost four times the amount of whiskey she did. Discreetly, the Madame put forth a few carefully worded questions, wanting to get a feel for their individual roles in Croker's developing political machine. From what she could gather, Murphy worked directly under Croker and was O'Reilly's boss. They were more or less his errand boys, making sure deals were made and impending issues were taken care of. O'Neill, she'd come to learn from Croker, ran the books and the muscle from the back of his store to keep operations confidential and discreet – Kelly was truly a puppet, only for the public eye to swoon over. The Madame pressed them interestedly, wanting to know how deep Croker's roots already stemmed, but they held their own despite the whiskey, and when she knew she couldn't uncover more, let it drop. Alas, she was limited in how she could pursue her cause, and didn't want to push her luck too far just yet. This wouldn't be their last meeting, and now time was mercifully on her side.

As soon as they were gone, the Madame's enthusiasm faded, and after escorting them out, she retreated to her office riddled in frustration. She plopped down in her chair, swinging her legs up onto the desk top once more and grabbed for her own bottle of whiskey from the drawer along with a new, clean glass. Pulling the cork out with her teeth, the Madame's focus went to the envelope Croker had his men hand deliver. Rather than pour, she took a swig of whiskey from the bottle and picked the envelope up, speculating what sort of bullshit this message might bring. The man wasn't even in charge of Tammany and he seemed to have men everywhere at his disposal. How was it even possible? The Madame thought back on the glory days of Tweed. She wasn't sure why, but the Madame sensed this was much, much bigger than anything that slimy bastard could have dreamed up. For the time being, she was in Croker's good graces, and planned on keeping it that way until the tides changed. There was only one thing that stood in her way, and then everything would fall into place easily.

She snatched her letter opener and tore the envelope open. Inside she found a small piece of paper…and the sterling silver locket she'd given Mary the day Thomas was born.

For safe keeping. Don't disappoint me.

Her jaw clenched, and the Madame could feel her whole body tense with a hatred she couldn't describe. She lifted the necklace from the envelope and squeezed the locket tight in her hand, hoping with all of her might she'd have the privilege of killing Croker herself. She wouldn't disappoint him. Nonetheless, that didn't mean in the end she wouldn't get her revenge.

She would see him to his grave before she too went to burn in hell.

"Madame? Madame, are you all right?" Her eyes shot open to see Louis standing over her, a look of trepidation on his face. As she came to, the Madame had no idea where she was or how she'd gotten there.

"What time is it?"

"Nearly five."

She sat up, glimpsing around as she came to the realization she'd fallen asleep on one of her couches. "Fucking Christ. All right I'm up. Get me some coffee and whiskey, and I'll change for the night. Get Caroline."

Louis handed the Madame her drink hot and ready, always one step ahead of her. She stretched, yawning, and felt a sharp pain hitting her ribs.

"Dammit! You'd think I would have had the fucking sense to at least loosen this fucking corset…"

"How? You were barely coherent a few hours ago." The Madame glared at Louis, but saw he had more to say, and he didn't seem pleased. "I also received word we are having some special guests this evening."

She drank a bit of coffee. "And who might these special guests be?"

"You're not going to be happy about it."

"Who, Louis?"

"It's the young Mr. Adams, Madame. Him and friends."

She stopped dead. "As in the Adams from Virginia?"

"Yes, I'm afraid so, Madame."

"When?"

"They said ten o'clock."

"Fuck. And the details?"

Louis sighed. "Celebrating his nineteenth birthday. They're coming to our establishment at the recommendation of…well… of his father."

She rubbed her forehead, pained. "How much are we making?" she asked, dreading to hear the number.

"He's doubling what his father paid on his last visit."

She nearly dropped her coffee cup. "Doubling?!"

"Obviously he doesn't want to be refused."

"Well…Christ. Get Danny for me, Louis, and some wine. She's going to need it. And Hope. How many boys are there?"

"Three. All his age."

"Three boys and an Adams…"

"Danny and Hope can handle the four of them, Madame," Louis promised her. "They're all so young, if anything were to get out of hand…"

"I know, Louis. I know. This is just the last God damned thing I need right now."

The boy's father was Mr. Charles Adams, a wealthy business-man, well-known capitalist, and loved philanthropist from Charleston who often visited The Palace whenever he found himself in New York. He was an incredibly handsome and charming man, which made it nearly impossible for anyone to see his true nature. While most men were along for the ride and enjoyed the services her girls provided, Adams had specific tastes, desiring nothing more than the violent domination of his partners during sex, and while he disgusted the Madame, the amount Charles paid her to keep it quiet more than compensated for it. On those nights, she paid her girl in full, refusing to take any commission for herself, and made sure they were treated to a new dress and a week without work. She never forced one of them − they all volunteered, and each understood exactly what sort of situation they were getting themselves into. There was no way to turn away a man of such high social standing, and as long as she had girls to take him, she wouldn't say no to that amount of money. Being the professional she was, the Madame wouldn't allow her institution to be branded as a place that wouldn't satisfy the needs of one of her biggest contributors, and considering Adams' price for one night had consequently furnished most of her office, it proved to be worth the sour taste in her mouth.

Louis brought Danny and Hope to her office just as they started to dress for the night, half made up and clothed only in their robes. They were her two strongest girls, both long and lean and no older than twenty, one with a heart of gold and the other like a lion. Together, a few years prior, they had shown up at her front door asking for jobs, almost blue from the cold winter night, and from just one glance the Madame hired them on the spot. A perfect ying and yang, Danny was exotic and olive skinned with dark hair and eyes, while Hope was fair, with deep blue eyes and straw colored hair. They were fifteen when they found the Madame, each orphaned and left to fend for themselves on the streets. Somehow, they found solace in one another and never parted, and they survived by undertaking a number of low-level cons and juvenile thievery throughout the years. Their relationship was one the Madame didn't quite understand, noting that the girls were far more than just friends. But as long as they did their jobs and did them well, she didn't give a fuck if they were lovers or not, and they proved themselves to be viable assets. Now, as they pranced in arm in arm wearing happy smiles, Louis gently shut the door behind them with a confident nod her direction as he departed.

"Ladies, have a seat," she ordered, uncorking a bottle of wine and pouring out three glasses. "We need to discuss tonight."

Danny and Hope looked at her confused, sinking down into the nearest loveseat. "What's tonight? Different than our scheduled regulars?" Hope asked.

178

Danny's eyes narrowed. "Something's up, I can tell. She got the good wine out. What's going on, Madame?"

The Madame made her way over to them and handed each girl a glass of wine, dropping down next to them. "Our favorite client's son is making a visit," she explained. "Tonight."

Their smiles vanished, and the color drained from Danny's face. Hope grabbed for her hand and held it tight, and her eyes fell toward the floor as she took a large swig of wine.

"H-his son?" Danny stammered.

"Yes. Apparently he does have one of those."

"But not him?" Hope posed.

"Not him. His nineteen-year-old son and some friends. I don't know what to fucking expect Danny, but from what has been sent ahead with their reservation, I have a hunch the apple might not fall too far from the tree."

Hope looked at Danny intently. "You can do this, Danny. It's not him."

"Yeah, and what if his son comes back to try and finish me off?"

The Madame rolled her eyes. "Don't be so fucking dramatic. He didn't want to kill you. He wanted to get off. It just required you seeing spots and losing good lung tissue. And don't forget, Danny, you volunteered for that asshole. Therefore, you accepted the consequences."

Danny downed her wine and took a deep breath. "Fuck that bastard."

"This isn't a vendetta, Danny. This is about money. If you can't do it—"

"What other girls should I prepare?" she shot back.

The Madame had some of her wine. "Three others to accompany you two. Be sure to get them a little drunk ahead of time so everyone is loose."

"And there are how many clients?" Hope pressed.

"Four total. I need you two to have your heads on straight tonight. I need you to be ready for any fucking thing that happens, and if shit gets out of hand, we will handle it like we always do. All right? Safe word red, and if it's beyond repair, I'll sick Louis on their asses. We will get through this without any hiccups, understood?"

Abruptly, Danny grabbed the bottle of wine and refilled her glass.

"Danny..." Hope voiced gently. "Danny, it's not him. It's going to be fine."

While the Madame empathized, she hated this kind of feebleness. "If you don't want the money, Danny, half the girls in this house would take a fucking beating for it. So you tell me. I'm giving it to you firsthand because I know you can hold it together. Am I making a mistake?"

She shook her head, her eyes somewhere else. "This is ridiculous," she spat. "I don't understand why I have to just...to just take it! Why we all have to kiss his fucking ass and not gut him for what he does to us!"

"Because you're a fucking whore, Danny," the Madame replied matter-of-factly. "You're paid to sleep with men and to do whatever they want, even if that means degrading yourself. We fuck the unfuckable as long as they pay. Get your head out of your ass. You will earn your damned living and you will smile as you do it, or I will really give you something to be upset about."

Danny recoiled like a struck puppy, but the fire didn't die just yet. "I want the same rewards as last time."

The Madame smirked – the girl had a level of pride that rivaled hers. "If you're beaten to shit again, you'll get the same rewards."

"But–"

"But nothing. You'll have four others in there with you, Hope included. It's not like I'm sending you in without any damned back up. And Louis will be guarding the outside of the door. There will be no issues, darling. These bastards are young enough to be managed and handled, regardless who the boy's father is." She leaned forward and stared straight into her eyes. "What did I promise you last time?"

"You'd always protect me."

"Yes, I did. Have I broken that promise?"

"No."

"Right. Until that promise is broken, you do as I fucking ask and don't question it."

"Yes, Madame."

Hope got to her feet, dragging Danny with her. "We better finish getting ready, Danny. How long do we have?"

"A few hours," the Madame informed her. "The others are for your choosing. Get them and everything else ready in the India room. I expect these Virginia boys will be trying to enjoy every fucking second of their money. I'll send George to help you."

Walking out the door, Hope wrapped her arm around Danny's waist, leaning her head onto Danny's shoulder. They were a perfect pair, one calm disposition to balance out the other's tumultuous nature, and Danny and Hope weren't the only girls at The Palace with bizarre idiosyncrasies. They were all beautiful, all outrageously eccentric, and all different, working hard and motivated to earn their keep. No two were the same, and the Madame purposefully saw to it that each girl prospered in her individuality – it gave her a diverse menu for her clientele. And while she did have her favorites, the Madame was fond of every one of them.

She stood up and went to pour herself more wine when Louis' head popped in through the doors. "Madame…"

"What now, Louis? I need to fucking bathe again, for God's sake."

"There is a Miss Esther is here to see you."

She halted, wine bottle in hand. "As in ten-year-old Esther?"

Louis couldn't hide his grin. "Yes, Madame."

This was certainly something new. "Send her in, Louis."

He opened the doors wide and Esther trotted inside, nervously looking to and fro before halting in the middle of the room, her gaze locking on the Madame. She had never been to The Palace on her own without Thomas or Mary by her side, and the Madame couldn't help but wonder why she'd ventured across town alone to see her. Or, better yet, how she managed to get herself out of the Hiltmore household without an interrogation as to where she was going at this hour. But inexplicably, there she stood, beautiful little Esther with eyes that could cut like a knife.

Esther spoke first. "I hope this is not a bad time."

Slightly amazed at her alacrity, the Madame smiled. "Of course not, darling. Sit down, I don't have long. What can I do for you?"

Esther didn't move. "I want to talk about Thomas. I...I feel like I made a mistake...and he didn't come to see me this morning like he promised." Her voice trembled slightly, and the Madame could tell she was doing her damndest to appear strong and not cry in front of her.

Two plausible outcomes ran through the Madame's head as she closely scrutinized the girl, tossed right into her lap for no particular rhyme or reason. She could coddle her, comfort her, make her some tea...tell her the world would be right as rain...assure her Thomas loved her and was only busy with his own troubles, and that he would be by soon. Or there was always the truth. With the truth, the Madame saw another opportunity...one she had been desperately seeking...an opportunity to infiltrate her influence and control over the Hiltmores. And not just the Hiltmores. The Madame studied Esther from head to toe – she would grow to be a beauty beyond measure soon enough. Now that she was a ward of Douglas and Catherine, the odds of her marrying someone rich and powerful were much higher than only a few weeks ago, thanks to the Madame's own maneuvering and connection with Douglas. Her reach could only expand if she bonded with the girl. Here in front of her sat a gift, and unexpected gifts were always the most appreciated.

"Come here, Esther," she said. After a few seconds, Esther warily walked forward, stopping when she drew close. "I will make you a deal. I will treat you like a young lady and tell you the truth if you promise to behave like one. Is that fair?" Esther nodded, her eyes filled with curiosity. "All right, darling. This will not be easy to hear, so please do your best to stay calm. Thomas was not by to see you this morning, and he may not be back to see you for quite some time."

A look of horror brushed her face, and Esther tried to submerge it. "What do you mean? Not ever?"

The Madame moved to her and crouched down so they were level. "You chose a life that does not include Thomas, darling. You went to live with the Hiltmores, as you should have, because it was what was best for you. You left him to find his own path, and he has. But think on your own actions. The blame does not rest on Thomas for not visiting you. You are the one that moved out, am I not correct?"

Esther had tears welling in her eyes. "Well I just...I had to... otherwise...I..." she choked up a bit, beginning to understand. "I guess I did. It's all my fault..."

"Oh, hush," the Madame proclaimed, ushering her over to a chair to relax. "You listen to me. There is nothing wrong with what you've done, darling. Nothing at all. I want you to listen to what I tell you here today, because it will be the most important concept you grasp as you transform into a young woman. You must always put yourself first. There is not one human being in this city that will care as much about you as you do. Thomas will not be here much longer, and I am certain he will be by to give his regards before his departure; however, the moment you chose to move into the Hiltmores was the moment you decided you were going to stand on your own two feet. Things will never be the same, and we have worked very hard to get you to where you are. Do I make myself clear?"

She sat motionless for a few seconds, absorbing what the Madame had said. "I...yes...I just...he's leaving?"

"I would expect so. His father has come to claim him."

Esther was shocked. "So he is...real?"

"Apparently. I do not know any specifics as of yet, but I will tell you as soon as I find out."

"I just...I feel so alone."

The Madame pounced on the opening she'd been waiting for,

and gracefully took Esther's hands in hers. "You are not alone, darling. I will always be here to guide you. You have a glorious future ahead of you!"

"I am just afraid."

"What are you afraid of?"

"I don't have anyone to…to talk to. Celeste is my best friend, but…"

The Madame nodded along. "But you are afraid she will tell Catherine and they will judge you. And afraid they might throw you out."

"Yes," Esther confided, "I don't want to ruin it. And without Thomas…no one will tell me what's right or wrong."

It was so simple, the Madame couldn't believe her luck. "That's why you have me, Esther. There will be things that happen in your life you will need someone to advise you on, someone you can trust. I want you to come to me with these questions, no matter how small or silly they might seem. Rather than confide in the Hiltmores or even Celeste, I want you to talk with me first. For your own protection. Does that make sense to you?"

"My protection?"

She sighed and shook her head, appearing aggrieved. "Not everyone is as sincere as they might seem," she remarked, rising. "I want to help you Esther, like I always have. I have done a good job of that so far, haven't I?"

"Yes!" she exclaimed, as if grasping it for the first time. "Yes you have!"

"Good. Then it's settled. Now, I have a busy night ahead. Let's make Sundays our day to meet. I will send one of the girls or Louis to fetch you in the morning from the Hiltmores' after you attend church. All you need to do is tell them you are meeting with me."

"And they won't mind?"

"Cross my heart," the Madame pledged, making the motion over her chest. "I swear they won't mind in the slightest."

"Okay," Esther said, standing up as well, "Thank you, Madame."

"Darling, call me Aunt. Please. Madame is much too formal. And tell Louis on your way out to grab my red satin gown and bring it upstairs as soon as possible."

The Madame was seated at her vanity putting the finishing touches of rouge on her cheeks when Louis came in to inform her that the evening had begun smoothly. The usual customers were present to start the night, and liquor and wine were flowing heartily with no muss or fuss. The five girls including Hope and Danny were setting up the finishing touches in the India room, and the Adams party was to arrive shortly. So far, everything was running according to plan. All she could do was hope it fucking stayed that way.

"Can you deliver a quick letter for me, Louis?" she asked, holding an envelope over her head as she masterfully lined her lips.

"Certainly, Madame," he replied, striding forward. "Whom am I taking this to?"

"The Turner residence across the park."

Louis took the letter from her hand and studied her in the reflection of her mirror. "Dinner invitation?"

"Tomorrow night."

"The angle?"

"Saving Thomas' life. We both know he can't stay, Louis. Croker will find out about his father."

"Are you going to tell Edward?"

"I can't decide."

"We should tell him," Louis declared. "But there's no way we'll be able to gauge his reaction."

"He has a fucking son to worry about. Do you think he'd risk that when he knows he could kill them both?"

185

"I don't know…I just don't know. Edward is his own man, always has been. You better be at your best, Madame. You're the only one who could convince him."

"Yes. The one God damn person in the world he despises, and I have to get him to listen me. Say some fucking prayers, Louis."

He went out with the letter, and after a few more minutes she resolved she was ready both mentally and physically for the evening. Locking her office up behind her, the Madame descended down into the already buzzing first floor, greeting those she knew and checking in with George to make sure he kept an eye on the newcomers. The downstairs was laid out in a fashion that spoke both privacy and class: once through the front hall dominated by the great staircase and chandelier, visitors were escorted into the cocktail room on their right, where they could play a game of cards, gamble, socialize, or drink and smoke cigars to their heart's delight as they awaited their respective entertainers. There were four differently decorated rooms for business on the first floor, each with a specific mood and setting. There, clients could spend time with their temptress, or temptresses depending on the size of their wallet, doing whatever they pleased ahead of being taken upstairs for the final act. Once their time was spent, customers could stay for as long as they wished in the cocktail room until close. With very few exceptions, all appointments were by reservation only, and this was done in an effort to weed out anyone who couldn't afford her price range or was there for the wrong reasons. There had been very few incidents during the Madame's many years, and she went to great lengths to keep it that way.

The India room was ablaze with red and gold tones as she went inside. Wine was uncorked and ready to pour along with hookah coals ablaze, the lamps ready to be smoked. The girls had done a magnificent job – incense burned at every corner, pillows and drapes covered the floors and walls, and a feast of food lay out in the center of the room for whoever might need sustenance. What was special about this room were the separated cabanas, three along each wall, making it wholly unnecessary for the girls to take their guests back to their own space – here, everyone could be satisfied behind their own curtains, which proved to be ideal when safety was a concern or clients enjoyed sharing. In the center, the girls rested on the floor laughing merrily and perched up on pillows, smoking and drinking to their fancy. They were scantily clothed, donning colorful, exotic negligees and their eyes charcoaled dark: five magnificent temptresses, seductively awaiting their prey.

"Almost time," she announced from the threshold. "They should be here shortly. The room looks wonderful, ladies."

They lifted their glasses in salute, the five smiling save for Danny, though it didn't worry her the way any other girl would. Danny never failed her and had a way of coming through in the end, especially when the stakes were high. The Madame left them and returned to the cocktail room just as Louis showed the Adams party inside. As she expected, they were slightly rambunctious, but the boys at least attempted to behave like perfect gentlemen despite being some years away from it. The boldest of Mr. Adams' young friends stepped forward with their overly handsome payment for the night, which she counted in one single flicker of her eyes, and signaled to Louis everything was in order. Falling right into character, the Madame welcomed them with open arms and gave them her usual introductory speech, discreetly studying the young Mr. Timothy Adams in the hopes of being wrong in her instincts. In comparison to his friends, however, Timothy was composed, neutral, and discerning of his surroundings, displaying a general sense of excitement only when called upon by the others. Like father, like son – clearly not keen on showing any hint of what he was thinking. This was not something the Madame wished on her girls, Danny in particular, yet the money was all there. There was only one thing to do: every one of them would need to be ready for damage control.

Following a quick bodily search by Louis, which she informed the boys was only precautionary, she escorted them back to the India room where the girls beckoned them inside. The Madame made sure not to linger, as it wasn't in her repertoire: she wished them a fabulous night and was off, posting Louis directly outside the door. Reluctantly, she knew if any of those little pricks even came close to acting out, Danny would kill them herself, and the Madame couldn't blame her. After enduring a gruesomely brutal strangling by Timothy's father during the heat of sex on his last visit, Danny wouldn't give a second thought to his son if she believed he'd hurt her, too. Either way, the Madame was in for a long, anxious night.

She needed whiskey. A lot of it.

Another hour passed, then two, and then three. The Madame took on her customary rounds with great poise, and even made a few cocktails for some of her favorite guests, laughing at the Chief of Police's idiotic and overplayed jokes as she served. To her astonishment, she was actually enjoying her evening when the storm clouds rolled in. There was a sudden, loud slam of the door from the hallway near the cocktail room immediately catching her attention, and she sent George with the snap of her fingers to investigate. Swiftly, she called out for a free round of whiskey shots to every man at the bar to keep her clientele distracted, and George returned to the room out of breath and mouthed the one word she did not want to hear: "Red."

Keeping her cool, the Madame motioned for George to resume his post at the bar beside Claire. "Keep them drinking," she whispered and slipped away, rushing down the hallway. She had to fight her better impulses to run, and the Madame rapidly drew her pistol from underneath her dress and cocked it. When she got there, the doorway to the India room was abandoned and no noise came from inside. Assuming Louis was already ahead of her, the Madame burst in with her gun out and ready, her eyes instantly assessing the situation that lay in front of her.

It wasn't pretty.

Adams' three friends, half naked and with their hands in the air, were all being held hostage against the wall by a completely naked

188

Caroline, who tightly gripped onto Louis' pistol. Louis was on the ground, trying to revive an unconscious…Hope…? Searching, the Madame's eyes flew to find Danny a few feet away, holding Timothy Adams in a bind from behind with her legs and arms wrapped tight around him; a long dagger rested against his throat and she held his hair with the other. She had a black eye and a bloodied lip, despite obviously winning whatever battle ensued, and the Madame tried not to appear thrilled. The rest of the girls stayed near Caroline, watching the boys closely. Danny had the deviant, or rather the whole room, under her control.

"Louis, what the fuck happened?" the Madame demanded, uncocking her pistol and placing it back in the holster on her thigh.

Louis made a grab for something in his pocket, and she saw him pull out the smelling salts he carried in his pocket. "He choked this one out, Madame."

"Danny?" she called across the room.

Danny flicked her head to get the hair out of her eyes. "By the time we heard her muffled screams, he'd almost suffocated her. So I ripped him off of her." She was breathing hard but stayed collected, her knuckles white gripping on the knife at Adams' jugular.

Louis held a variation of smelling salts to Hope's nose, and within seconds she was on her side, coughing violently. The Madame breathed a sigh of reprieve, and walked over to Caroline, easing her aim downward with the touch of her hand on the girl's shoulder. Gratefully, Danny's head was on straight, and at the sight of the Madame taking over the chaos, she released Timothy Adams with a hard kick, pushing him toward his friends. Louis picked up the disoriented Hope and carried her out the door, and the Madame sent the other girls trailing behind him. As they shuffled out, she stopped Danny, motioning for her to wait until they were ahead.

"A fucking knife?"

Danny shrugged, like nothing out of the ordinary had happened. "What did you expect?"

The Madame had to turn away from the boys to hide her smirk. "We need to fucking clean this up so no one knows what in the hell happened. In ten minutes, I need you to send down five new girls. Understood?"

Danny's temper became vicious. "What? Why…why the fuck would you do that?"

The Madame held up her hand to silence her. "Will you fucking listen?" she spat, trying to keep her voice down. "I also need Marcy to bring me the blend…the strongest she can make it. Got it?"

Danny's anger disappeared, and she smiled. "Got it. Sorry for…well, sorry I questioned you. Do you want the wine or whiskey blend?"

"Wine. Now go."

"Of course, Madame. More girls right away," she pronounced loudly. "Whatever you desire for our guests."

The boys then moved toward the Madame as Danny exited, deeming their troubles were over; conversely, the Madame slammed the door and turned on them, ready to slash each of their egos to pieces.

"Mr. Adams, I am considering you to be the leader of your party. What the hell do you think gives you the right to come into my institution and choke one of my girls senseless?" For a few seconds they were all petrified and motionless, and no one dared to say a word. The Madame continued: "I would like a fucking answer to my question!"

The other three were scared and cowered back, but Timothy wasn't even flustered. "They're just whores. They don't even matter," he decreed, no fear or shame in his voice. His friends gaped at him, shocked at the words that came out of his mouth.

The Madame tilted her head with a look of scorn, arms crossing over her chest. "And did your father tell you that, Mr. Adams?" At once, his cheeks flushed, but he didn't respond to her taunting. "I thought so. Well regardless of what your father tells you, darling, allow me to teach you a few lessons about how these things operate since from what I've seen, every one of you is an amateur. I don't give two shits what your father tells you, Mr. Adams. This is my place of business. And you better hope for your own sake I don't go tell the Mayor or the Chief of Police what the fuck you've done, considering they're both only a few rooms down!"

"You're bluffing," Adams retorted, though clearly his air of confidence was fading.

"The Chief of Police has been one of my clients since I was eighteen, Mr. Adams. And the Mayor? Yes well, he just adores the girl who held you in a headlock because she can do things to him his wife never dreamed of. No, I am not bluffing, and you can go down and take a fucking gander if you please. You aren't in Virginia where your daddy can save you this time. So sit your pompous ass down or I will show you how honest a woman I am."

Leaping forward and shoving Timothy aside, the one who paid her stepped forward. "Please," he pleaded. "Let's come to an arrangement. We can pay you whatever you ask. It's all just a misunderstanding. We had too much to drink and too much to smoke… just got a little carried away is all."

"There's a difference between carried away and nearly killing someone, darling."

His face went white, but he didn't let up. "Look, Tim just made a mistake. Everyone makes mistakes. We can make an arrangement! I swear to you we will do whatever you ask."

"Good," she replied. "Gentlemen, let me explain how this works, now. From this day forward, if you have a particular fantasy, something you enjoy that is different than just a regular fuck, you are to report that to me when you make your reservation. We can gratify almost any request. I only ask to know ahead of time so our girls can be prepared…so things like this little incident do not happen.

"For the trouble you've caused me, and the money it'll cost taking one of my best girls out of commission, you are to pay me double what was asked for tonight, and this also includes my silence to

191

the authorities and to your families, all of which I have direct contact with. Yes, that's right, I know who each and every one of you are: Mr. Adams, you're already well aware your father is a regular at The Palace. Carl Wolchester," the Madame glowered right at him, "your arrogant father operates the largest fucking bank on Fifth Avenue and steals about three times what he should. He'll get caught soon enough, and you can tell him I said so. You, Matthew, the squirrelly one, yes your mother inherited all her wealth from her father…and we all know which bastard of a Senator he is. And last, you who seem to think you're the fucking ring leader…Richard Bomeister, nothing other than new money made off of the God damned good graces of the South with a carpet-bagging father milking them for everything they're worth. Satisfied, you ignorant little pricks?"

They were dumbfounded.

"Like I said earlier, I don't care what your father has told you about whores and their station, Mr. Adams, these are my fucking whores and I decide what is or isn't to be done with them. Not you. And not him, either. He has known those rules for many years and respects them, and if things do get out of hand he is more than happy to compensate me for it. I think he would be ashamed to see his son wasn't well-versed in such matters."

A knock on the door caused the four boys to jump, and Marcy strolled inside carrying a large tray with a bottle of wine and four glasses already poured. With a wink, Marcy handed over the tray and took her place by the door. The Madame went over to the boys, handed them each a glass, and set the bottle on the floor. It was hard not to laugh at their bewildered demeanor.

"Gentlemen, here is my peace offering. Please, drink your wine and relax a moment while I acquire a few other ladies to accompany you for the night. I will expect the remainder of my money upon their arrival to this room."

"You're…you're sending more whores?" Matthew asked. "After what happened?"

"Why of course I am!" she exclaimed. "That's my job! However, I will, of course, warn you. If a hair on any of their heads is harmed I will kill each of you myself. You know the rules now, and I expect those rules to be obeyed."

This did not sit well with Mr. Adams, who got to his feet and paced forward, a finger outstretched and pointed her direction. "You have the nerve to threaten us? You have no right. You're a whore just like them! I ought to—"

Suddenly his words ran out, and Timothy's face went a ghastly white. The Madame heard another pistol cock by her ear. Marcy was armed and ready right behind her, the barrel pointing directly at Mr. Adams' skull.

"Yes, Mr. Adams. I can more than afford to threaten you and your three measly friends. You nearly killed one of my top-earning girls tonight, which I do not allow in my house. I am a close friend to the majority of powerful men in this city, none of which would dare to double cross me to rescue a fucking nobody from out of town. That's right – you're a fucking nobody. Take my offer or leave it, but do understand. If you leave it, none of you will be welcomed back here again, and I will ruin your reputations, as I have demonstrated already the breadth of my knowledge regarding who you are and where you come from. So do not push me."

Another knock, and Marcy put away her gun as the door behind them opened. The other girls entered gaily, instantly fawning over the boys and alleviating much of the negative tension.

"Enjoy the rest of your night, gentlemen," the Madame called, turning to face Marcy. The other girls could take it from here. "Keep Claire behind the bar and have George take Louis' post. Don't let him leave until all four of them are out cold, and make sure you get the fucking money from them as soon as I am gone. When they wake, they shouldn't remember a damned thing about any of it. How much did you use?"

"More than enough," she whispered. "They'll be lucky if they remember what they had for lunch."

"Good."

With one last glance, the Madame paraded out of the room, aggravated with herself despite the undeniable inclination from the start this was inevitable. These nights, like so many others, had to go on, even with the worst of hiccups. It was like a dichotomous curse to be in her station: so much power, yet such an inability to use it when she desired. The Madame wanted nothing more in that moment than to beat the life out of that arrogant prick, just to show him how afraid of her he fucking should be. And if he ever slipped up again, she vowed the young Mr. Adams wouldn't have the benefit of a second chance. She would make sure of it.

As soon as she was out of plain sight, the Madame picked up her skirts and ran up the stairs to Danny's room, suspecting that to be where Hope was harbored. Skipping them two at a time, she was out of breath when she got to the top and down the hall. Throwing the door open, the Madame found Danny hovering at the bedside with the Doc, and Louis following protocol on guard by the doorway. Hope was sitting up and conscious, a wet towel to her forehead and a large, cold steak around her neck to ease the burning. If Danny hadn't been there, the Madame was certain Hope would have been dead when they found her. She looked like hell warmed over.

"That steak better still be good when you're done with it," she teased mockingly. "You all right, darling?"

"Never better," she stated hoarsely with a grin.

The Madame shook her head, leaning against the doorway. "Doc?"

"She has serious bruising and contusions around her neck, but fortunately that's the only place he got her," he elucidated, pushing the spectacles back into his long grey hair and wiping his eyes, "And the odd part is there are no signs of forced penetration."

"Meaning what exactly?" the Madame pressed.

The Doc glimpsed at Hope, then back at the Madame. "I mean that he wasn't having intercourse with her. Only choking her."

This disturbed the Madame greatly, but she tried to put it out of her mind. "What do we need to do?"

"I want to keep an eye on it for a day or two to make sure there's no serious internal bleeding. Cosmetically…you ladies probably know how to handle this better than I do. My best guess is it'll be a few weeks at the very least before the bruising fades."

The Madame scoffed. "We can fix it much sooner than that. Not that we need to. Hope, you have your week off. Danny, too. You both have fucking earned it." She reached into her skirt pocket and pulled out a wad of cash, tossing it to Danny. When she counted the money, Danny was stunned when she realized how much was in her hands.

"This is…"

"Double, yes. For both of you. In an hour when they're unconscious I need you to go downstairs and help Marcy rearrange the India room. We dosed those assholes. They won't remember a fucking thing. Make sure it's done right. Now, I am going to have a bottle of wine and a cigar. Unless the house is burning down, I don't want to hear a God damned thing. Louis, with me."

"Madame!" Danny shouted to her as she reached the door.

The Madame rotated around. "What?"

"I…I just…thank you."

"Don't thank me yet. Doc, see to it she's in no pain. Louis? Let's go."

"What do you need me to do?" Louis asked once they reached the hallway and were alone.

"Keep an eye on everything. Report to me every hour. I want everyone out by five. Make sure those idiots downstairs are out and then follow normal protocol in the morning. Tell them about how fucking amazing their night was, and they'll all believe it. Keep Danny and Hope out of sight."

Louis nodded. "Do you need anything?"

"I've got wine and a cigar in my office?"

"Yes."

"Then no. That's all I need right now. And some fucking quiet."

"Of course."

"Oh, and tell Marcy to never aim by my fucking ear again or I'll do the very same to her. Last thing I need is to blow another God damned eardrum…"

She broke away at last to privacy, convinced her people could handle their part without her incessant badgering. With a heave, the Madame closed the large doors to her office and bolted them shut, immersing herself in cool darkness. It was the most relaxed she'd been the entire night. As she straightened up and spun around, an odd sensation hit her. At first the Madame couldn't figure out what it was, and then she felt the hairs on the back of her neck stand.

She wasn't the only person in her office.

"Hello, Madame. I don't believe we've had the pleasure."

A match sparked and lit the candle at her desk, showing her chair to already be occupied. The flickering shadows and dim light made it hard for her to see; nonetheless, she observed from one once over she had never encountered this man before in her life. He was young, and he had black hair that was greased backward, making his broad face seemed formed from stone. His daunting features rested behind a pair of rounded spectacles, which reflected the flame of the fire. It didn't matter that he was seated – the Madame could size him up from where she stood, and physically, she easily ascertained this man was someone who could give Louis a run for his money, and that notion by itself was alarming. There were scars covering his hands and arms, which were a clear indication he'd seen his own fair share of battles, though from what the Madame couldn't say. There was something in his indifference that she did not like, and a very rare feeling swept over the Madame, one that caught her off guard and she could not stifle.

It was fear.

"Who the fuck are you and how did you get into my office?" she asserted, trying to keep her wits.

"Ah! Now that is a secret, I am sorry to say, as most things about me are." He leaned back into her chair, unfazed, and she watched his eyes flick toward a revolver loaded and ready, lying on her desk. The gun wasn't hers.

"Who in the hell are you?"

"You can call me Mr. Walsh."

"Well, Mr. Walsh, why don't you tell me what the fuck you want before I reach for my pistol and shoot you dead. I'm a quick draw."

His lips formed a sinister smile. "While I do enjoy a challenge, Madame, I can guarantee that would end quite badly for you. And in a very twisted way, you ought to be charming me for my approval at our first meeting. Fight much longer, and you'll have bigger problems than just me."

She swallowed hard. "Tell me who you are and what the fuck is going on."

"I know Lord Turner is here, Madame. And that your handsome, young nephew as you endearingly call him spent nearly an entire day with him today. I know where they sleep. I know where they eat. I know everything they do, all day, every day." His voice trailed off, as if waiting for her to react, and then went on. "They don't know the danger yet, do they?"

"Neither of them do. They don't know she's alive." Her heart was pounding so hard she thought it might explode.

"Are you so certain? Because uncertainty…nobody likes uncertainty…"

"Croker sent you."

Walsh got to his feet and picked up the gun in his left hand, the candle in his right. "If your plan doesn't work, and if they don't leave, I can promise you our next visit will not be nearly as pleasant."

Her eyes grew wide. "How…how did you know about that?"

"That is not your concern." He pointed the gun her way. "Now, sleep well, Madame. And let us hope we don't see each other again. But just remember…I'll be watching. Closer than you'll ever know."

He blew out the candle and the room went black. Without any delay, the Madame ran to the nearest of her side tables, desperately seeking the free candle and timber at its side. When she found it, she hastily lit the match and put it to the wick, scanning the room with her eyes: it was empty, and yet there had been no sound of movement other than her own shuffling around. The Madame whipped around to find the doors still bolted shut, and every window closed; her office was locked like a fucking fortress, and somehow, that bastard got in and out as if he were a ghost. The Madame's head started to spin, and she lowered herself to the ground.

She'd fucked up. From the very start, she'd miscalculated how far Croker's pull extended, and there was no room for error any longer.

Her cigar would have to wait. She had work to do.

VIII.

Edward couldn't resist basking in the overpowering sense of happiness he felt as he strolled home down the gravel walkway of Fifth Avenue. He spent an entire day with his son, the first of countless more, he hoped, and while at first they got off to an awkward start, it only took an hour or two to break the ice. By the end of the day, Edward and Thomas found they got along like two old schoolmates catching up after years of being apart, filling in the holes and cracks as they swapped stories, progressively coming to understand each other. Where Edward thought their interactions might be difficult, he found he was dead wrong: seeing Mary in Thomas made his heart feel lighter, though it was obvious Thomas was _his_ son. Even with their strikingly similar appearances put aside, Thomas' overall character and demeanor matched that of Edward's when he was around twenty, almost to a point that made Edward wonder how on earth it could be so. It was like staring into a looking glass, and Edward couldn't get enough of it.

Home for the time being was on Upper Fifth Avenue, and Edward had a hard time trying not to notice the residence was even more outrageous than the last one William and Lucy occupied. After the second great war with America in 1812, William and Edward's grandfather had fallen in love with New York for reasons that were never specified, and the family continued to have at least one home there ever since. Edward's father despised America and refused to take his children across the Atlantic; William's, on the other hand, made his family spend most of their time in New York, only returning to Amberleigh during the horrible heat of the summer months every few years. Thinking back, Edward often wished their fathers could see all the good he and William had done together – they were both blindly thrown onto the front lines of a business they had otherwise been excluded from, following what William referred to as 'the dark period' in their family's history. William's eldest brother had been outcasted by the Turners for his plentiful number of indiscretions not a month prior to Arthur's death, and very suddenly the entire Turner industry was at stake. Neither Edward nor William expected to be the stronghold of the Turner name, and yet here they were, the only two living sons left to uphold its legacy…until now.

Dinner was just a few hours off, and Edward had quite a bit to catch William up on in that short amount of time or risk giving his cousin a stroke. Edward landed just the day before in total disarray, and following a brief and emotional reunion with his cousin, Edward called a tailor to the house while William attended a social dinner with Lucy, which Edward refused to let them cancel at the last minute. He had plans of his own, after all. Edward then took off in pursuit of Thomas with great luck, and when he did return home later that night William and Lucy had already retired to bed. The next morning the three of them breakfasted together, glossing over the emerging business particulars with Turner's new contracts, and the moment Lucy began her inevitable cross-examination of his random visit, Edward excused himself with the promise of an explanation later that day. Rather than make assumptions, Edward wanted to be sure Thomas was ready to be introduced as a part of the family, not wanting to push his son too far too fast. Everything was developing so rapidly, Edward was afraid he might scare Thomas off; conversely, after their day together, Edward grew increasingly self-assured that he and his son were both prepared for it, and could only be optimistic that having Thomas to dinner was the right move.

When he did at last reach William's new mansion-house, Edward could hear Lucy and his cousin enjoying tea and laughing together as he walked through the front door. Quickly, he dropped his hat and coat to join them, skipping down the hallway to the parlor room. It was clear from his reception they were awaiting his homecoming, welcoming Edward with a smile and a place already set for him. He marched to their table and obliged his hosts, pouring himself a cup of tea in anticipation of an assortment of probing questions from Lucy.

"My dearest Edward," William jumped in, "I am begging you… will you please tell us the real reason as to why in the hell you are here? Lucy and I have both already made bets, and I am really not in the mood to lose any more pounds today."

"Don't you mean dollars?" Lucy teased. "Or rather, soon to be my dollars."

"Lose more, William?" Edward asked. "It's only tea time!"

"I don't want to bloody hear it."

"Ah, so there are high stakes already?" Edward chuckled, taking a sip of his tea. "I am so sorry. I have been meaning to tell you both since I showed up on your doorstep and rudely took advantage of your hospitality. It's…well it's complicated, but it will be a little easier to explain to the two of you since you are aware of my history with New York, and of course with Mary."

William and Lucy's respective manners changed at the sound of her name, and their playful banter evaporated along with their smiles.

"Mary…yes of course we do, Edward," Lucy said unsteadily. "We didn't realize you'd…well pardon my saying so, but I didn't realize she was an…an offered conversation piece, if you know what I mean."

William and Lucy had met Mary a handful of times before Edward was sent to war, and not long after Edward's departure William and Lucy were forced to travel back to England to deal with William's brother's grievances, closely followed by Arthur's accident. By the time they made it back to New York a few years later, Mary was presumed dead. In spite of his reassurances, Edward saw Lucy held some of that responsibility on herself, as Mary was seemingly abandoned without any of the new friends and family she thought would engross the rest of her life. Edward often forgot it was a hard time for all of them, not just for himself.

He went on to divulge what he had learned concerning Mary in the past few weeks, highlighting the most crucial point: Mary had, in fact, been alive, neither of them having any idea they'd been lied to by the Madame, and it was only in the last few weeks she had truly died under suspicious circumstances.

After hearing him out, William's expression grew confused. "Excuse my interruption, Edward, but how in the world did you find out about this in the first place? I didn't realize you kept in touch with anyone else in New York other than myself, let alone someone who knew the Madame or Mary."

"That, my dear cousin, is…at least in my opinion…the best part. The very sudden need for my departure to see you and Lucy was no mere whim. I received a letter from my estranged son, Thomas, beckoning for me to come to New York as soon as I could."

Lucy gasped, dropping her teacup, which shattered when it hit the floor. "A son?"

"Yes, Mary's son. He found the letters I'd written to Mary, which the Madame had been hiding over the years, and managed to track me down."

"But Edward, how can you be sure he's…" Lucy's voice trailed off.

"Mine?" Edward smirked. "Well, if I were any younger, you'd have a very difficult time telling us apart, Luce. He looks just like me. It's quite…strange. And hard to get used to."

Lucy was frozen, unable to speak, and William stood up awkwardly. "I…well then…you…you have a son," he reiterated aloud, pacing back and forth. "Jesus, Eddie. I don't know how to…I…I think we all need some brandy. Tea isn't going to do us any favors."

The next hour was spent discussing the story again from start to finish, this time with every detail thoroughly hammered out, along with everything he and Thomas talked of just that afternoon. William and Lucy could barely comprehend what Edward told them, and William couldn't seem to wipe the grin off of his face. Sadly, he and Lucy were never able to have children, and William had made a point in encouraging Edward to reproduce, if only to keep the Turner legacy alive. With no progress in his cause over the years, he eventually gave up hope. What seemed like a permanently lost effort turned out not to be the case, and while the brandy flowed, his cousin and his wife did nothing to mask their eagerness to meet Thomas.

When Lucy left the men to dress for dinner, William watched her depart, then took a more serious tone. "So what is your real plan, Eddie?"

Edward took a sip of his brandy. "What do you mean?"

"I mean, what is your real plan? I know you. And I understand you are…infinitely contented to have found your son. But I read through the lines the moment you told us Mary's body was never found. I know you better than you think." William poured another drink and set the bottle down on the table, flopping heavily back down into his chair.

"I…I hadn't even realized that's the word I used…"

"Oh bullshit, Eddie. What of it?"

As usual, William could call his bluff. Edward scarcely allowed himself to think about Mary throughout day, fighting off every one of his impulses so he could make the most of the time he had with Thomas. Still, his cousin's perception was right on mark. Edward heard Thomas' account of Mary's death and in all honesty, didn't believe a word of it. Thomas wasn't lying to him – he certainly did think his mother was dead. Somewhere in Edward came a voice that told him there was something else to it. Thomas went to wit-

203

ness her 'killer's' hanging and found his closure; however, with his own analytical mind combined with the skills Hiroaki taught him, Edward was convinced her fate was too simple. Naturally he concealed his true feelings from Thomas during the day to save him any more pain, markedly if he happened to be wrong, but Edward wouldn't be able to let it rest until he found more solid evidence to relieve his theories.

"Eddie?"

William was staring at him, and Edward realized he'd gotten lost in his own train of thought.

"I am just going to do a little digging, William, that's all."

"A little digging? There's no such thing as a little digging with you."

Edward waved him off. "You don't understand, William. You don't see the angles the way I do. And you didn't know her."

"I'd say I knew Mary quite bloody well—"

"No. Not her. The Madame. It's always deeper than she lets on. That woman has more skeletons in her closet than all the royal families put together."

"Eddie, they hung the guy, for Christ's sake! The courts got a full confession."

Edward took a gulp of his brandy. "And we've never seen innocent people convicted of another's crimes, have we?"

William shook his head. "This is different, Eddie. We aren't in England where half the country has heard of you. We're in America, where they don't give a shit who you are or what your rights are. This place has spent it's first century tearing itself to shreds, and it still is! If you go sniffing where you don't belong—"

"We both know I can take care of myself, William."

"It's not about that. It's about you getting yourself killed chasing a ghost that doesn't exist."

Edward felt a small pang of offense. "I thought you of all people would understand why I need to do this. To see it through."

"No, I bloody don't," William didn't let up. "Dammit, Eddie. Think about it. You have a son now. A son. You have a whole other reason to live. What I am trying to say is, even if you're right and there is more to it, then whoever did this is smart enough to cover their tracks to a faultless degree. And whoever killed Mary wouldn't think twice of eliminating you from the equation. Or Thomas. How do you not see that?"

It was hard to discount that William's advice mirrored Hiroaki's. "I know what I'm doing, William," he asserted stubbornly. "I can handle this discreetly."

William leapt up, his back to Edward, and the room went silent. Edward was a little hurt by William's words; he had gone into their conversation expecting nothing but unrelenting validation, and it would seem he read William completely wrong. He should have known better. Children had been William's Achilles heel since he and Lucy discovered they would never be able to bear one of their own, and as a consequence, Thomas would be his first priority. As far as William was concerned, Edward's biggest hindrances were his skepticism and his restlessness, unaware these qualities were not something Edward could simply turn on or off at any given time. After the countless jobs he and Hiroaki had undertaken throughout Europe, Edward saw the world through a whole new perspective, one that was vastly different than the average man. In reality, every instinct and hunch inside him did think Mary was dead, but Edward wanted definitive resolution, and maybe then he could put Mary's passing to rest permanently.

"You're going to do it anyway, aren't you?" William beseeched him.

Edward chose to ignore the question. "How would you feel about starting to train Thomas on trade distribution?"

"Eddie…"

"Yes, William, I am."

William sighed, rotating around to face him. "Just be careful.

I know the Japper has taught you more than I could ever understand, and I don't want to know. Really, I don't. But just...just don't do anything stupid."

"There's no reason for you to think I would. I only have a few days, and no one knows who I am or why I am here as long as it's kept quiet. I have a sneaking suspicion if there is something to be found, it won't be as difficult a task as you imagine. You can train Thomas during the day while I am out. And William?"

"Hm?"

"He is absolutely never to know what I'm doing, or anything to do with my adventures with Hiroaki. Those days come to an end once this is over. Understood?"

"Yes, without a doubt. You're too old to be gallivanting around trying to save everyone, Eddie. As for Thomas, I'll happily take him on. If he's really been a blacksmith the majority of his life, he's going to need some sharpening around the edges. And might I suggest an ethics tutor when you return to Amberleigh so he doesn't turn out like his father?"

Edward laughed. "I'll take it into consideration," he replied, leaning toward his cousin and holding out his empty glass for another refill.

William accommodated him. "There is one thing I can't seem to settle on."

"Which is?"

"Do you really think he is ready to leave his home behind? This is all he's ever known. It's going to be a bloody challenging transition at best. He is just willing to pack up and follow you home across an ocean?"

Edward thought for a moment. "I think he has been ready for quite a long time. From what I can tell, he's a lot like me. Lost. Discontented. Angry at the things beyond his control. I feel like Thomas and I have both been waiting for our next lives to begin...we just had to find each other first."

A very nervous Thomas reached the Turner house for dinner a little early that night, his eyes wide as he nearly tripped over the front threshold, absorbing his surroundings. Tony, William's butler, escorted him to the study where Edward met him alone to put him at ease. Thomas dressed in a white shirt, black slacks, newly polished shoes, and a jacket he had undoubtedly spent most of his early evening trying to clean, and Edward was proud of the noble effort he'd made to look his best with the little money his son had at his disposal. Tactfully, after years of practice, he had sized Thomas up that morning and found an older dinner suit of William's that might do the trick if his son wanted to change, and he'd had it cleaned for him; at the last minute, Edward decided against offering it. The last thing he wanted was to give Thomas the impression he wanted him to change into someone he wasn't – Thomas was perfect in his own way, and the bigger test of his disposition was yet to come. Surviving dinner with William and Lucy was no easy feat.

"Whiskey?" Edward greeted as Thomas sauntered slowly inside, mesmerized.

"Yes, thank you."

This study was similar to Edward's in England, covered wall to wall in books and decorated in dark, neutral colors. Hanging from the tall ceiling was an antique, medieval chandelier made of nothing but wood and iron, which William brought over to the states with him on his last trip. He was a enthusiast of all things from that time period, and while Edward loved William dearly, he cringed at his cousin's tastes, especially the damned suits of armor he bought impulsively at an auction and insisted be kept in the halls at Amberleigh. Nevertheless, Edward was thankful the chandelier in New York was his only reminder of this. Every other piece of furniture was handmade, created from tanned leather and oak to match the sizeable desk Edward took over following his arrival. The fireplace was the largest in the household, wide enough to swallow a man whole, and William often retreated there with Lucy during the winter for warmth and relaxation. The walls were decorated with some of William's favorite paintings, which he'd acquired over decades of travel, and each landscape had the central theme of the wilderness and countryside. William's own offices were upstairs and much larger, but here, Edward knew his cousin felt the most comfortable and at home – like they were together back at Amberleigh. It made Edward smile: William obviously grew tired of the urban lifestyle at times, and escaped here to try and remember the rolling hills and open air of England.

Thomas took a seat in an empty chair by the fire, and Edward watched him closely, pouring them each a drink. "I know it's a lot to absorb."

"A lot would be an understatement," Thomas quipped with a grin. "I feel so out of place. Like a bull in a China shop."

"I think with a little time, you'll see that most of this is a façade. William and I inherited this life in a similar fashion to how you will. We grew up with the notion of being a family burden and in our futures, having a much more modest career path than both of our brothers. It has made us appreciate our station more than most." He handed Thomas his glass and sat in the chair opposing his. "You won't find two better people than William and Lucy. And I can't tell you how ecstatic they are to meet you."

Thomas nodded, staring into the bottom of his glass. "I guess I am still taking this in. It doesn't feel real to me." He glanced up at Edward. "You don't feel real to me. It's like this is a dream I'm going to wake up from."

Edward had an inkling he might bring this subject up. "Well, I can tell you right now you aren't dreaming, although if it's any consolation I feel the same. We have only known each other a day, and yet it seems so much has already changed because of it."

"Yeah…yeah it has." Thomas took a drink of his whiskey. "I just need to say something, and then we can move on with the night."

"All right. What is it?"

Thomas took a deep breath, holding their eye contact despite his difficulty in speaking. "I don't want to force you into this, and I definitely don't want to be some charity case. I am…happy to be here with you. But if you decide you can't do this, I need you to do it soon, because I don't want to get my hopes up."

"You aren't a charity case, Thomas. You're my son."

"That doesn't mean you want me, Edward."

A little astonished at Thomas' directness, Edward took a sip of his own drink to gather the right words together, wanting nothing more than to reassure him this was not the case.

"If I didn't want your presence to be a permanent one, I would have never come back to New York in the first place. To be frank, I hate this city almost as much as I hate London. It took a miracle to get me back here, and that miracle was you."

From the look on Thomas' face, Edward knew he had said it just right, and their talk moved on. "This is probably the best whiskey I've ever had," Thomas declared. "What is it?"

"It's Scotch whiskey. William's favorite, which I am sure you will hear all about over dinner."

Thomas leisurely tilted back into his chair, a sly smile forming from ear to ear. "Scotch whiskey. I could get use to this flavor." His eyes traced the walls of the study in awe. "I've never seen anything like this place."

Edward smirked. "Just wait, there's much more to come," he stated, finishing his drink and rising to his feet. "We'd better be getting upstairs or Lucy will have a fit that we're down here enjoying ourselves without her."

Thomas took the hint and did the same, placing his empty glass on his father's desk and then stopping abruptly. "Do I…er…look appropriate?" he inquired uncertainly, standing up straight. "I got my shoes shined for the third time in my life. And I don't think my shirt has ever been scrubbed this clean. I have no idea what to wear for this sort of thing."

"What you have on is great," Edward comforted him. "They wouldn't care if you were covered in filth. Like I said, William and Lucy are thrilled you're here."

"Well I guess we shouldn't keep them waiting, should we?"

Edward nodded and extended his arm out to shake his son's hand, fighting every impulse to embrace him. "Welcome home, Thomas."

Thomas didn't waver and took it, beaming. "Thank you, Edward."

Dinner went smoother than Edward could have hoped: William and Lucy spent the entire meal in full force interrogation, not remotely realizing their intensity as they drilled Thomas about his life in New York. Edward found it hard not to laugh as he sat back and observed, a little amazed with how steadily Thomas handled the pair. It was like everything Edward conveyed earlier was completely forgotten, and the more in depth their talks became, the more Thomas seemed to flourish, and Edward could sense this was the start of something special. There was no discomfiture or judgment on anyone's behalf, only a hunger to make up for the missing time they'd spent apart...a true family, the way Edward remembered it from his childhood.

Just as they finished their entrée course, Tony appeared in the doorway, his expression agitated. "Excuse me, Lord Turner, but there is an urgent message here for you, and the carrier is insisting on delivering it himself. I am so sorry to interrupt dinner, sir, I did not have a choice."

William, Lucy, and Thomas were immediately silent, their eyes pointedly on Edward.

"Well, who is it, Tony?" Edward requested.

"He wouldn't say," Tony affirmed, yet Edward swore his face gave a different answer. "Like I said, he was insistent on seeing you, and only you."

Edward conceded, standing up from the table. "Thank you, Tony. Sorry everyone, I will just be a moment." He attempted to avoid eye contact with the others, having no explanation to offer them. Rigidly, Edward stepped out of the dining room and walked down the front hallway, wondering who on earth would call at such a late hour, or better yet, who possibly could have known other than his family and the Madame he was even in New York City.

When he reached the lobby, Edward paused. The room was poorly lit from where he stood to the threshold, and he was barely able to make out a familiar figure waiting at the front door, his back to Edward. This man he had by no means forgotten, after believing for many years they would never meet again. As the man turned and the two were face to face, Edward noted he was much larger and far more muscular than the last time they'd encountered each other. He remained stationary, his arms resting lightly at his sides with a pistol visible on his belt just inches from his fingertips. The darkness was meant to mask him, though not well enough. Earlier than Edward could move or speak, the man held up a hand for him to stop where he was, and casually lay a letter down on the side table by the door.

"An invitation. No reply is necessary, Lord Turner. She will expect your attendance."

The man moved to leave, apparently having accomplished what was needed, as Edward looked on, stunned. He still worked for her, still remained loyal regardless of their own personal history…after all the horrendous things she'd done…Edward felt his blood boil and paced forward aggressively in protest.

"She expects my attendance?" he answered, a slight rise in his tone. "You cannot be bloody serious. I'll be damned if that woman—"

Without flinching, the man spun around, the pistol now in his hand pointing straight for Edward's forehead, and Edward halted, slowly raising his hands up into the air in surrender.

"Louis…for God's sake, you're in my cousin's house…"

Louis kept his weapon aimed, undauntedly. "Lord Turner, as my own personal request, keep your son under a watchful eye. I officially withdrew the Madame's protection from him this morning, knowing you could more than handle it on your own. His safety is in your hands, and as you already know, fate can change in the blink of an eye."

Edward stayed where he was, only bowing his head forward to allude he understood the instructions given. Louis uncocked and holstered his pistol, making his way toward the front door, where he stopped.

"Take care of Thomas, Eddie," he whispered quietly.

The Frenchman then thrust himself out the door and into the night. Edward didn't chase him – he knew better than that, and let Louis slip away. This time, at least. Grasping that he might not get another chance for privacy, Edward decided there was no reason to delay reading the Madame's message. He moved forward, grabbing the letter from the side table, and tore it open.

Lord Turner,

Would you please be so kind and join me for dinner tomorrow evening? We have a few items of importance – or rather – just one in particular that need to be discussed. Certain events have unfolded following your arrival that need to be addressed as soon as possible.

Seven thirty sharp.

Burn this note after reading.

After reading it a second time, Edward went into the great room and tossed the letter into the fireplace, watching as the paper dissolved to ash. He hated doing anything she asked of him, though he felt for the sake of William, Lucy, and Thomas, it would be best to keep his contact with the Madame secret. She certainly wasted no time in her pursuit to control every person around her, and shamelessly had the audacity to assume that applied to Edward as well. To him, her moves had grown predictable, making him contemplate whether the outcome of a private dinner would truthfully be beneficial or hurtful in the long run. Both, he gathered, yet probably leaning toward the latter. While the flames engulfed the last of the Madame's paper, the one thing Edward could not get a grip on was the presence of Louis, and how despite all these years and all they had endured, Louis continued to be a part of her giant, ever-spinning web. Seeing his old friend made the rush of the passing few days a full force reality, and perhaps for the first time, Edward saw that everything about him and his future on this earth had drastically been altered. He had a son, a son from the woman he'd loved his entire life, who had been trapped alone in the world he fought so hard to forget. If only he'd come sooner…if only Mary were here to get him through this…Edward felt his throat tighten and his eyes water, unable to control the abundance of emotions swirling in his chest.

"It was her, wasn't it?" William's voice echoed loudly from Edward's left, startling him. His cousin stood leaning against the doorway. When William saw Edward had tears in his eyes, his countenance softened, and he marched toward Edward, concerned. "Eddie? What's happened?"

Edward forced a chuckle. "I'm fine. Really. I think it is just exhaustion."

"Oh fuck off. Did she threaten you? Us?"

"No, nothing like that. Just a dinner invitation, no threat to anyone. I do think you're right about one thing, William. I don't know what sort of mess Mary was tangled up in, but clearly it's not the story we've heard. And it worries me I don't know more."

William's head tilted to the side. "And this has sprung out of your imagination following a two-minute interaction with the Madame?"

"That's the thing. It wasn't the Madame" Edward told him, his gaze moving back to the fire. "It was Louis."

William's eyes grew wide. "Christ…you cannot be serious. Louis?"

Edward nodded, and William mumbled something under his breath, his hands running back through his hair – a practiced habit when he was stressed.

"Eddie, can't you see this is something you can't fix? I know you loved her. We all did, and the proof she loved you just as much is sitting in the next room eating cake with my wife. This is the one thing our family has been needing…this is our missing piece. If you must, tread lightly. But if you start digging, you put every one of the Turners at risk. Not just yourself. And I don't know about you, but I want to die old and fat in my bed."

Edward had nothing to say and grew quiet, reflecting on his cousin's words and adjusting his dinner coat in an attempt to straighten up. The idea of being fully responsible for another human being, and that his own pursuits could put Thomas' life in danger as well as William and Lucy's made his stomach turn. Not a month ago he was sitting on his horse with Hiroaki, watching the sunrise over his home at Amberleigh, utterly ignorant of his own flesh and blood's existence. He needed to think it over later that night when he could be alone to grapple with his own demons without the influence of anything external. For now, however, his and William's absence would be suspiciously noted if they delayed rejoining their party any longer.

"We have an understanding?" Edward pressed.

William let out a heavy exhale, shaking his head. "You have tomorrow. After that, my blessing and my patience will be gone." Edward acquiesced and gave a curt nod to William, heading back the direction of the dining room, his cousin right at his heels.

They returned to the dining room just in time to find Thomas finishing the last of his dessert and Lucy ordering a bottle of champagne to be opened in the great room to celebrate his homecoming, thankfully not aware of how long William and Edward had been gone. Retreating to the comfortable sofas by the fireplace where the Madame's letter was now ash, Tony brought them each a filled flute to toast. The four Turners stood in salutation and clinked their glasses, and as the evening went on, another bottle of champagne and two more bottles of wine were heartily consumed and gone fast. Edward was slightly lackadaisical in conversation, melancholic that the Madame had cast a shadow over what he considered one of the best days of his adult life. Instead of gaily laughing along with the others, he was burdened with agitation, trying hard to mask it at the sight of Thomas' smile. A sideways peek from William followed, one that told him to get over it and contribute to the festivities. William was only doing what he thought best for the family, and Edward held no animosity against him for that. The difficulty was that William would not ever be able to comprehend the way Edward was wired and what made him tick. Nothing would be discussed about what he might uncover the next day or so, not out of spite but out of courtesy to William. He couldn't handle seeing the world the way Edward did: he was too good a man with a heart of gold and a soul that could be saved. As Edward observed the three of them, going back and forth with formalities long forgotten, the previously absent paternal instincts formed thickly in his heart. This was his family. It wasn't perfect, but it was his. It was his duty to protect them, even if they never knew the extent of what that might entail.

The final hour of their night centered on the days ahead, and William was pleased to hear Thomas' enthusiasm to learn about the Turner trade industry. Lucy repeatedly pushed for Thomas to move into their residence, which he resisted politely with their first few rounds of wine. To her delight, as the drinks began to set in, it became clear his defiance was waning, and Lucy, with cunning grace, knew how to pounce when her prey was weak.

215

"Thomas, you cannot possibly think we are going to let you leave tonight. You have to be here at the house with William in the morning for your first day of training anyhow! It's ludicrous, just ludicrous. I'll have Tony make up the guest bed for you straight away."

Thomas again attempted to protest. "Please, I've told you I don't want to impose. Really!"

"It is not an imposition!" she asserted. "You are one of us now, whether you like it or not. You will stay with the family. Tony! Another fill of wine and have the Blue Room prepared upstairs!"

"Of course, Mrs. Turner," he complied, coming out of his statuesque position in the corner and adding a splash to everyone's glass.

"Edward, will you be joining us tomorrow?" Thomas asked, taking a sip to try and mask his exhilaration.

"Unfortunately, I will not. I have a few other matters to see to tomorrow during the daytime, and dinner plans with an old friend. You will be at the mercy of these two degenerates if that is all right with you."

Thomas' faced dropped, looking a little disappointed, and mercifully William came to Edward's aid.

"Don't worry, Thomas. I will make sure you don't even notice he's gone, and the four of us can catch up over brandy after dinner tomorrow. Lucy and I had been thinking of dining out for some steak, so the three of us can make a night of it. How does that sound?"

"It sounds incredible!" Thomas cried, his grievance instantly gone. "I just…I don't have any of my things…and what's worse is I don't know if I have anything appropriate to wear."

Lucy grinned warmly. "I know there is something in this house we can find for you to wear! You aren't quite as tall as your father yet, but I think you'll fit nicely in to one of William's old suits."

"And Tony can have two or three of the lad's help you move whatever belongings you need tomorrow," William added. "You just give them the address."

"I don't know…" Thomas started again, his gaze finding his father's eyes, and Edward sensed the reason for his hesitation: his son simply wanted Edward's reassurance this was approved by him, too.

"Why don't you sleep on it, and let us know first thing in the morning at breakfast?" William suggested, to which Thomas consented with a grin.

"Well, I love you boys, but I am headed to bed," Lucy yawned, stretching her arms long as she got to her feet. "William?"

"Yes, you're right," he chimed in, following her lead. "Goodnight you two."

"Goodnight," Edward and Thomas responded in unison. Thomas' cheeks turned red self-consciously, and Edward smirked, sinking back against the sofa with his drink.

"I guess we should get used to things like that," Edward professed.

Thomas took a drink of wine. "I don't know if I'll ever get used to this. It's all happened so...so..."

"Quickly?"

"Yeah."

"Thomas, if this is too much for you, I will not be offended. Lucy and William are...well they are enthused to have you here because you are my son and they have always wanted me to have a family. But it is also because they cannot have children of their own, and now that you are here, they want nothing more than to make you feel at home. I don't want you to feel like you need to give up everything to be here with us. I know that's what it may seem like...but I can promise you it's not my intention. I just want you to feel relaxed."

"I want to be here," Thomas declared. "I just can't...I can't believe I'm here. It's like I said earlier. This doesn't seem real to me."

"It doesn't seem real to me, either. We have a lot to learn from each other, and it's going to take some time to make the adjustment."

"It's not that. I...I guess what is bothering me is it feels too good to be true. Every part of my life was terrible until you showed up, and then this?"

Edward leaned forward, his face serious. "First lesson from me: a life of privilege has wonderful advantages, but it will never make you happy. People are what make you happy. And while yes, out of the blue you have a father and his two crazy cousins who already adore you to fill in the gaps, you will still grapple with the loss of your mother. And that...that won't go away. For either of us."

"Shit. I...I keep forgetting..." His eyes fell with shame. "God, I feel like an asshole. Why do I keep forgetting?"

"Don't feel guilty. It's because there is so much to take in, it's hard to keep track of things. Don't punish yourself for that. She wouldn't want you to feel that way. You haven't forgotten her, Thomas. You never will."

Thomas swallowed down his emotions with another gulp of wine. "Where are you really going tomorrow?"

"Truthfully?" Thomas gave him a look that almost made Edward laugh aloud. "I am going to meet with the Madame for dinner. We have some unfinished business to work through."

Thomas didn't move an inch. "Unfinished business?"

"Well, if I can put it lightly, let's just say we have some things to work through for your benefit, otherwise I won't be held accountable for my actions. She betrayed me too, Thomas. So yes, I'd say we have some unfinished business. Let's just hope we get through it and one of us doesn't kill the other out of spite."

Thomas' frown broke to a chuckle, and Edward went on, intending to finalize their plans. "You're moving in for good. I will let the Madame know tomorrow her old apartment is once again vacant."

"You're sure?"

Thomas' question was meant to aim deeper than the move – for him, the question was meant to parallel Thomas' existence in his father's world. Permanently. From here there would be no going back, and Thomas wanted to believe Edward was just as ready as he was to leap off the edge.

"I am absolutely sure, Thomas," he told him, smiling.

At dawn, Edward woke with the sun and clambered out of bed to dress before the others were up. Half asleep and groggy from too much wine the night prior, Edward fumbled to get on a pair of slacks and shirt, dressing carefully to match, as best he could, Thomas' more casual attire from the previous night. He needed to fit in if he was going to do this right, and blending in would give him the advantage of being forgettable to the average man on the street.

Before he went to bed, Edward sat up in his rooms, contemplating what he should do about the entire situation, if anything at all. He thought on what he had been told in accordance with his own assumptions, trying to piece together any sort of explanation, yet he kept going back to the same concept, one Edward couldn't ignore. The Madame may have never been fond of Edward, but she loved and adored Mary more than anyone…except herself, of course. If there had been a cover up, whoever saw it through got to the Madame in a matter of days and must have made it abundantly clear there would be no retaliation. Someone so far above her own connections, there was no other option other than to concede, and if there was no evading this for the Madame, Edward's chances wouldn't be any better no matter who he was on the other side of the Atlantic. He chose to write to Hiroaki, describing in great detail his plans for the next day with the promise of another letter to follow the next night unless something went awry. Edward eventually went to bed though he barely slept, tossing and turning for most of the night with impatience.

When he was finally dressed and ready to depart, Edward took Hiroaki's letter from the nightstand and tiptoed silently toward his door. It was then he noticed a small piece of folded paper on the floor that must have been slipped under his door while he slept. He picked it up, glancing it over curiously and opened it. It wasn't sealed.

Watch your back. I am sending a friend to look after your exploits today. You won't ever see him, but he will make sure no one follows.

Be careful, Eddie.

L

Edward knew it was pointless, but he ran to the door and threw it open, the hallway deserted and dark at such an early hour. Tony wouldn't dream of delivering the post under his door…this had to be distributed by Louis' own hand…and from inside their house when it was supposed to be locked for the night. A little startled, Edward also struggled with the thought that Louis knew his moves prior to Edward even choosing to make them. Edward shut the door and, like the note he received the previous night from the Madame, cast it into the fire. Chills tingled down his spine and his heart pounded loudly in his ears with the thrill of a challenge. He'd misjudged how deep this might go, or Louis never would have taken such drastic measures to get to him. Keeping in mind the safety of his family and his agreement with William, Edward granted himself one day and one day only to investigate Mary's murder, and by nightfall he would call it quits and take whatever he uncovered to the Madame at their dinner. Otherwise, no matter how lightly he stepped, he would leave a trail of suspicion behind. Not to mention Edward had a small inclination that if Louis knew his strategy, the Madame did too, and she would be earnestly awaiting to hear what he had to tell her.

This is what he lived for. He was a fixer, solving and executing the things most people saw as impossible. For Edward, impossibility didn't exist.

With a new rush of exploit, Edward retied his boots tighter and grabbed his coat, making his way out of the mansion. He was relieved to note he was the first one awake in the house by a few hours and therefore snuck out without any distraction. When he reached the street outside a light rain was falling, with shadowy clouds giving the day a dismal and grey atmosphere. Edward hailed a coach another block down the road, knowing Yorkville would be more than just a tiny stroll from Fifth Avenue. His discussions with Thomas gave Edward a few hints on where to start, and obviously beginning with her employer might set off alarm bells if there was foul play. When he heard from Thomas about Mary's close friend, Harry, who also happened to mysteriously be killed the same week, Edward chose to seek out the man's family for their perspective, if there were any members left to find. Thomas briefly described where Harry lived, and Edward hoped with those directions and a few helpful neighbors he could find where he needed to go without drawing too much attention.

His approach would be basic. Edward planned to tell them he was an old friend of Harry's there to pay his respects and give his condolences, nothing more. Ultimately, Edward thought it wise to not involve or mention Mary's name, not certain what exactly he was walking into. As a stranger to the family, they might be more inclined to share their feelings if he was unfamiliar, particularly since Edward wasn't from around these parts. After a time, the carriage came to an abrupt halt, and the driver bellowed at Edward they'd arrived and to pay up, twenty cents more than the original charge. He popped out and purposefully overpaid the coachman to get rid of him, which worked quite well and he disappeared as soon as he counted the money in his hand. Edward watched him ride off and turned around, his hawk-like gaze closely studying the layout from the corner where he stood.

For a few seconds, there were no sign of life except a snoring drunkard passed out on the edge of the curb. Edward strolled down to the end of the road and, just as he was about to knock on a random door, he spotted movement. Catty corner from Edward, a young woman donning a black dress was heading inside one of the apartment buildings with a pail, having just pumped water from one of the wells in the alley. He thanked God for his good luck and trailed her inside, staying a few paces behind. Taking no notice of Edward, the woman strolled into one of the first floor apartments, and following a quick count to ten in his head, Edward approached, lightly rapping on the door.

"Who is it?" the woman's voice called instantly.

Edward cleared his throat. "Uh…I am looking for the family of a man named Harry…an old friend. I've come to pay my respects."

The young woman cracked open the door, showing only a sliver of her face. "How can I help you, sir?" She was very plain, with mousy brown hair and brown eyes, yet her cheeks glowed bright, and Edward soon saw why. She was well on her way with child.

"Pardon my intrusion Miss, but I was told this had been the home of Harry. He was a dear old business acquaintance of mine, and after hearing of his passing I came to pay my respects to his family."

She nodded sadly and opened the door the rest of the way, allowing him inside. "Come on in. My husband was one of Harry's sons…the older one. His younger brother is out, but I know Harold will be happy to meet you. Haven't been more than ten or twelve people that have come by, and I know it's broken Harold's heart. You can have a seat wherever you like."

There was not much to their small home, and Edward took one of the few empty spots at their kitchen table. They had a small cast iron stove against the left wall, no doubt their only source of heat during the winter, with a few scattered shelves holding the limited amount of plates, pots, and pans they owned. Edward sat at the tiny wooden table, with four like chairs to match, and a tattered, brown spun rug lay underneath them. There were no photos to look at, no stitching to admire, and not much warmth provided by the bland décor that occupied the space. Edward considered her words, amazed at the lack of mourners to visit Harry's family, and also speculated if that might be for a reason.

The woman went to the stove. "Would you care for some coffee and toast, sir?"

"That would be lovely, thank you," Edward replied.

"I'm Molly, by the way."

"It's lovely to meet you, Molly."

The room went quiet as she worked, but it didn't take long. She served him a hot and ready fried egg on fresh bread with a cup of some of the strongest coffee Edward had ever consumed, almost too difficult for him to stomach. With a pleased look and a wipe of her hands on her apron, the woman receded for a few minutes back through a small hallway to his right, leaving Edward to finish his breakfast. As he ate the last of his toast, footsteps soon echoed Edward's direction, and Harold and his wife reentered the kitchen. Edward's misgivings regarding whether or not he would be welcomed were placated, as Harold walked directly to him and held out his hand in greeting.

"Thank you, sir, for coming by. I know it would have meant a lot to my father, God rest him. What is your name?"

Edward got to his feet and shook the man's hand. "Billy Turner. It has been many years since I saw your father, but he was always in good spirits, and I had a lot of respect for him."

Harold's face lit up, though clearly still shadowed with grief. "Thank you, Mr. Turner, that means more than I can tell you. He was taken too early, but I guess we can't argue with God's will."

Edward resumed his seat and Harold joined him, and the two men talked for some time as Molly resumed cooking some breakfast for Harold. Their conversation was easy, despite Edward having to consistently wrack his brain to remember the details Thomas shared with him about Harry the previous afternoon. To his relief, the answers Edward gave in response to Harold's questions seemed to more than satisfy him that 'Billy' and Harry were longtime friends. Edward also made sure to describe how he and Harry met in a pub years ago, the same one Thomas revealed was Mary's favorite, and that whenever he happened to be in the country for work he and Harry often grabbed a drink. Gradually their dialogue grew from a more reserved nature to fluidity, and rather than spend the entire morning with Harry's kin, Edward knew the time had come to dive in headfirst.

"Do you mind if I ask how he died? I was never given any particulars other than he was traveling outside the city."

Harold paused, his eyes browsing over toward his wife. "Molly, would you leave me and the gentleman for a minute?" Compliantly, Molly left the kitchen at her husband's request, and Harold continued. "Sorry, just don't want to stress her any more with the baby almost here. Doctor says it's taken a toll on her…" Edward nodded sympathetically. "They found his body about twenty miles outside of New York. Said he'd been robbed and was readily packed to join the frontiersmen." He stopped again, evidently battling with what to do or say next.

"Is everything all right, Harold?" Edward pressed, trying to thrust him further.

"I just…I apologize, Mr. Turner, but how did you find out about my father…you know…dying and such?"

"The barman," Edward lied. "I just got into town yesterday and went to our usual spot. He told me just last night. He also mentioned…well, he mentioned something wasn't quite right about it."

Harold studied Edward, then leaned closer to him. "He's right," Harold whispered. "I don't think my father was robbed, Mr. Turner. I think he was murdered."

Edward matched his tone to Harold's skepticism. "Tell me."

"I…I haven't told anyone this…there's been no one to tell, really. But mainly because I'm afraid for me and Molly. You see, he told me something a few days before he…before he died. Something that makes me think the coppers are all lying bastards."

"They are all lying bastards," Edward agreed. "But what did he tell you, Harold?"

Harold took a sip of coffee. "He came home drunk one night, three sheets to the wind, and starts talking about some new friend of his named Al stirring up trouble. Said he was trying to set up some politicians in the papers. He'd been going to a new place, not the usual pub, and staying out later and later."

"What was the name of this pub?"

He shook his head. "I couldn't tell you. It was underneath some jewelry store just north of Germantown…mentioned something about a hidden flight of stairs I think… It's all a big blur now, Mr. Turner, up until a few days before it…it happened. He was odd… gave me some money, you see, and told me to get out of the city. Told me to take Molly and our baby someplace else. Didn't mention anything about him leaving town…I'm his son, he would have told his own son! I think he was losing it…not right in the head, yeah? It's the only thing that makes sense to me."

Edward tried to appear compassionate. "Did you try to find his friend Al? See what could have been going on?"

"I thought it was just my father's bullshit at first," Harold made clear. "He…he had a habit of exaggerating. Always did, especially when he'd been drinking. Then, another close friend of his, a woman…I come to find out, you see, she was killed the same day. The very same day! That's when I start to think something isn't on the up and up, yeah?"

"It could have all been a coincidence, couldn't it?" Edward posed.

"I would have thought that. I would have…except every night that week when he would come home drunk, she would walk him home," Harold confessed, beginning to choke up. "She was such a good lady. Always took care of my father…walking him home and taking care of him, you see. But I knew she was with him at that bar all those nights, she had to know what was going on…right? And now they're both just…just dead…"

Edward felt his stomach drop. "Has anybody else been by to see you?"

Harold thought a moment. "A few of my dad's friends from the neighborhood. There was one guy, like you. Never met him before, but knew Harry."

"Did he ask you the same things I did?"

"Come to think of it, yeah he did. He gave me an…unsettling feeling, you see. Not someone I could have seen dad with. Really… hard-looking, you know what I mean? Glasses too…and slicked back hair. He was really interested about what Harry told me."

"And did you tell him anything?" Edward went on, glancing out the small window behind Harold.

"Nah, not to the extent I did you. Said he might come by later this week though and to expect a visit. You all right, sir? You're pale."

Edward's mind raced. "Harold, listen to me," he pleaded urgently. "You need to get out of this city. Do what your father told you. Do you have any friends any place else you can stay with? Any family?"

Harold rapidly became concerned. "Molly's family is in Philadelphia."

Edward got to his feet, pulling Harold up with him. "Go pack your bags. Get out of here today and don't come back, do you understand me?"

"But my brother…"

"Wait for him. And if he's not back by dusk, to hell with him," Edward replied, his voice hardening.

Harold didn't move a muscle. "Sir, I can't. I…I don't even know you!"

"If you stay here any longer, you're putting your family in grave danger. Do I look like I'm playing you?"

"Who would do that? Who…?"

Edward sighed, irritated that Harold couldn't see the bigger picture. "I don't know, Harold. All I know is two people are dead, and you know things you probably shouldn't. Don't be stupid. Think of your wife and your unborn child."

His eyes narrowed, but Edward could tell from Harold's body language he believed him. "Your name isn't Billy Turner, is it, sir?"

"No, no it's not."

"Are Molly and I really in danger?"

Edward put his hand on Harold's shoulder. "The same people that killed your father and Mary will come for you if they even think there is a possibility you know anything. Do you want to bet on that, Harold?"

He shook his head. "I'll get my brother and get out. Tonight. Wait…how do you…how did you know her name was Mary? I never said her name."

"Because a long time ago…Mary was my wife," Edward acknowledged, resisting the urge to think on it further. "I know what it means to lose my family, Harold. You don't want that. You need to get Molly and your brother and head for Philadelphia."

"And what about you, sir? What's your role in all this?"

"I hope nothing more than saving innocent lives." He released Harold and shook his hand. "God speed, Harold."

After a brief goodbye, Edward departed while Harold and Molly hurried to get their things together, and Edward hoped for all of their sakes they would never meet again. It was mind-blowing that William's exaggerated yet plausible scenario was actually spot on accurate from what Edward could gather so far. Somehow, whatever it was Mary and Harry were doing died along with them, except for one name: Al. Al was the only piece of the puzzle Edward could pursue, and he knew just the place to seek him out.

Fiercely, Edward marched north, trying to keep an even of a pace with the crowd, or at least as even of a pace as his intrigue would allow. His hunch regarding Harry's family was better serving than he'd hoped, and Edward was beyond grateful he sought them out at the start. Harold was clueless, unable to comprehend his entire world was at stake because of the mistakes his father made. Whoever the man with the glasses might be, Edward had a feeling he visited Harold for the exact opposite reason he had: he wanted the information to decide if the man was a liability that needed to be terminated, and if that was the case, Harold's family would die along with him. The only thing Edward could do was pray Harold heeded his advice and got out of the city unscathed. There was nothing more to be done.

A half of a mile outside of Yorkville, Edward had passed and counted three jewelry stores; he turned around, retracing his steps back the same direction he'd come. The first was definitely not the place. It was managed by a cranky, older Jewish man who would only talk with Edward if it had to do with buying a fake gold pocket watch he repeatedly shoved in his face, trying to barter a 'reasonable' price. Edward left wearily, almost having to push the man off of him, and checked behind the store, happy to see no basement or underground existed. The second store was run down with half of the windows boarded up, and he didn't even bother to try the inside; from the look of it, this place hadn't had any customers for months, and the only sign of life belonged to a few feisty feral cats.

On approach to the third, Edward immediately knew he had found it. The store was not luxurious or over the top, though it had a sense of legitimacy about it...a perfect camouflage. It was a small wooden building with glass windows intact, locked display cases, and a painted sign over the door, which read "Hudson's Fine Jewelry & Watches." Cautiously, Edward walked inside to find a woman sitting hard at work behind one of the numerous counters, inspecting a small diamond necklace with a microscopic eyeglass. Upon seeing Edward, she set her tools and the necklace aside and stood, making her way over to him with an almost threatening expression. His uncertainty was erased – if this were in fact a real store, any clerk would be welcoming him with open arms. Clearly that was not the case at this establishment...here customers weren't welcome, and that could only mean one thing.

"Good day, sir. How can I be of assistance?" she asked, her tone off-setting. "Jewelry shopping?" The woman stared at him long and hard.

"Actually, I am here on another errand. I'm looking for the bar. Downstairs, if I am not mistaken?"

The woman's arms crossed defensively over her chest. "I am afraid I don't have any idea what you're talking about, sir. There is nothing downstairs but storage."

"Ah, I see," Edward retorted, taking a step toward her. "And if I told you I was a friend of Al and Harry's, what would you say to that?"

"Don't know them," she snapped, but the flash of alarmed recognition in her eyes was just what Edward wanted.

"And Mary? Did you not know her either?"

She moved backward to counter his advance. "Who are you? What do you want?"

"Where is Al?"

"Al doesn't come around here anymore."

"Was he murdered too then?"

She nervously glanced around, as if to be certain they were alone, then pressed her index finger to her lips. Before Edward could respond, the woman scurried to the front door and locked it, turning the sign from Open to Closed. When she turned back around to face him, a Colt pocket revolver was pointed in Edward's direction.

"Down the stairs behind the ring counter. If you aren't supposed to be here, I'll have you shot. Got it?"

Edward nodded, hands raised, and edged to the back of the room, finding a spiraled staircase down into the darkness. It took most of his concentration to keep a level head despite having been in situations like these countless times. Unchartered territory, he called it, where he was straddling the thin line of life and death. Still, Edward had a feeling in his gut it wouldn't take him long to find what he was seeking. He was the unknown element in their midst. They would come to him, sniffing him out like hound dogs. With a deep breath, he descended downward, preparing for anything that might surprise him below.

At the bottom, Edward could make out a small, dimly lit bar, with a bartender behind the counter cleaning glasses as he talked with two well-spirited customers. The air was dense, without a window or door in sight, and with only candles illuminating the scene Edward could barely see the ground or his feet. To the right, a table of five men sat playing a game of cards at one of the tables, and at another sat two scantily clad women splitting a cigarette and fixing one another's hair. The other three tables sat empty...all but one, occupied by a lone man in the back corner making his way through a large bottle of whiskey. The brim of his derby hat shadowed his face, giving the impression he didn't want to be bothered.

To his amazement, the bartender waved Edward over, and as Edward pulled out one of the stools, the man poured him a shot and smiled. "First time in?" he greeted.

"Yes it is. Thank you." It was hard to tell what sort of place he'd stumbled into, especially since no one seemed to take any particular notice of his coming. Edward threw back the shot of whiskey and kindly asked for another. The two men a few places down were ignorant of his presence and continued their loud, amicable conversation, making the whole scene feel as if Edward had just stumbled into a regular pub with nothing special about it. He hadn't known what exactly to expect, but he hadn't quite expected this. The woman upstairs had been so overtly aggressive...and yet down at the bar, he found an almost friendly atmosphere. It was illogical, and it made Edward's guard go up even more than it normally might.

The bartender poured them each another round and pulled up his own stool, evidently desiring to have a chat with his new guest. He was a handsome man, with a clean-shaven face and shoulder-length blonde hair tied back into a ponytail. In his usual fashion, Edward had already sized him up: the barman was a bit smaller than he, as most were, although from the way he carried himself Edward could tell when he fought, he rarely lost. He had the advantage, being younger and probably a bit stronger than Edward; however, with all Hiroaki's lessons and his own personal experience, Edward was confident it would take only three or four moves to lay him out.

"How did you find us?" the bartender posed, starting conversation. "We do our best to keep a low profile, as I am sure you found out upstairs. Trying to keep the...the unwanted riff raff out, if you know what I mean."

"I can respect that," Edward answered, sipping his whiskey. "I was told about this place by an old friend of mine killed a few weeks ago. A man named Harry. Did you happen to know him?"

The bartender's countenance grew solemn. "Ah, yes. I was so sad to hear about Harry. He spent a lot of time in this place, and I got to know him well."

"Did anyone else here get to know him well?"

His new friend picked up on the insinuation. "Why do you ask?"

"Like I said, Harry was an old friend. I was only told yesterday of his passing. I guess you could say I am...seeking woeful company."

The bartender stood, taking Edward's empty glass, not angered but a little unnerved. "I don't think you'll find that in here today. Most of these regulars never met Harry, and if they did, there wasn't much time spent."

"And what about Al?" Edward threw his direction, hoping to gauge a reaction.

He stopped instantly. "Al hasn't been in for weeks, actually." Casually, he leaned over and whispered, so close that only Edward could hear. "Listen to me, I don't know who you are, but you need to settle down with the fucking questions or get out of my bar. Is that understood?"

He made a mistake, just as Edward hoped. In those few seconds of confrontation, the bartender's eyes had quickly flickered over to the man in the corner during his reprimand, and that was all the incentive Edward needed. He nodded, agreeing he would regress and ordered another whiskey. Then, as the bartender gave him his filled shot glass, Edward grabbed it and went to the lone man's table, taking a seat straight across from him. Edward was never one to take too kindly to a scolding. The man at the table pretended his new guest did not exist, and persisted to sit in silence with his head cast downward.

Edward cleared his throat. "Excuse me, sir, can I have a moment of your time?"

The man was motionless, and Edward could feel his neck burning. All eyes in the room were now on them.

"Sir?" he asked again, and again there came no response, and Edward's frustration grew. "If you don't answer me willingly," he murmured. "I will make you answer forcibly, and I can promise you won't like it."

The man's gaze crept up to find Edward's, and he spat tobacco into the tin on his left. "Fuck you, you English prick."

Edward bit his lip, trying with all his might to restrain the impulse to strike first. "You want to tell me what happened to Harry, then, or do I have to make you, you arsehole?"

"He's fucking dead."

"I know. But where in the bloody hell is Al, then?"

Without warning, the man was on his feet and lunged at Edward. His aggressor moved faster than most after whiskey, attempting to catch Edward off guard by throwing a right hook at his cheekbone from across the table.

Unfortunately for this poor bastard, Edward was more than ready for him. Like clockwork, Hiroaki's training and practiced instincts naturally took over. Edward's own hand seized the man's fist in midair, and with all his might, Edward slammed it into the table below as the man let out a groan of agony. His momentum carried him into a spin over his left shoulder, and Edward's elbow found and shattered the man's septal cartilage in one blow. Immediately, he released the man's broken hand and, in one swift motion, grasped the back of the man's skull and thrust his opponent's head against the table. With a loud crack, the table broke, sending the man to the ground, and Edward disarmed him of the Colt from his right hip holster, cocking it as he held the muzzle against the man's temple. The entire scuffle had lasted less than five seconds, and Edward kept the man pinned to the floor while he bellowed painfully. The audience stared at him, terrified and unable to move a muscle.

The bartender was predictably the first to react. "Everyone get the fuck out, the bar is officially closed!" he yelled. "Now!"

There was no need to ask twice. The gamblers, whores, and two men at the bar fled the scene without a second thought, scrambling up the stairs as fast as their legs would take them. Edward was steady, watching them scamper out. The woman guarding the upstairs came rushing down from the store, gun out, and stopped at the bottom of the staircase when she saw Edward.

"Who are you?!" she demanded, taking her own aim at Edward's forehead. "Tell me who you work for, because I know you aren't a damned copper. What are you doing here and why the hell do you want to find Al?"

"Tell me where he is, and I'll tell you why I need him."

"Al is dead!" she screamed.

The bartender, with a shotgun in his own grips, took the opportunity and threw himself between them. "Wait…Sally wait. Look at him. I knew he looked familiar I just…"

"What the hell are you talking about?" she bellowed in return.

"Look at him, Sally! Just look!"

Sally rolled her eyes back to Edward and after a few seconds, something took her aback. "Jesus Christ. He…he looks just…just like…"

"Thomas," the bartender said aloud.

Edward could feel his heart race, and tensed his grip on his captive's gun. "How do you know my son?"

"Mary," Sally told him, her tone less heated. "But you're… you're supposed dead."

"Obviously, Sally, he is not," the bartender interrupted, almost laughing at the irony, "The bigger question is, how in the hell did you find this place?"

"I was told Mary was dead," Edward explained. "Thomas found me when she disappeared."

The bartender set his shotgun on one of the vacant tables and turned to Edward while Sally lowered the Colt to her side.

"Well…Jesus, this is something, isn't it?" he exhaled warily, motioning to the man at the floor. "Let poor Edward go. Yes, that's right, the bastard you're holding down is named Edward, too. He's a decoy. I am not Al, but I think I am the man you are looking for."

Edward didn't move. "How do you know my name? And my son?"

"Like Sally said, from Mary." The bartender sighed. "Sally, grab us a bottle of wine. This man and I have some personal matters to discuss. It is going to be quite the afternoon."

The story Edward heard from the barman made him queasy. Both Mary and Harry had known Sally for a number of years, and when trouble began at Mary's job, Sally brought them to her underground bar where they could openly discuss the issue at hand. The bar originally was a meeting place for the Underground Railroad, where the abolitionists would plan raids as well as where to hide the newly freed slaves, and this was primarily run by Sally's father. She kept it open as a place where people could come with their own misfortunes and hire help if necessary, and for Mary, it began with small things until one day she uncovered illegal activity that was far worse than anyone could have predicted. To Edward's shock, Al and the bartender were previously Pinkertons, and when Harry drunkenly confessed his worries over Mary's safety, the pair put together a plan to bring the corrupt to justice. Then, without any warning, Mary, Harry, and Albert evaporated into thin air. Harry's body was found outside the city, as Edward already knew, but what he did not know was that Al's body had also been discovered and deemed to be a gang killing by the police. There was no trace of Mary with the exception of her 'killer's' spotty confession.

"How are you still alive?" Edward solicited.

"Would you believe me if I told you I had no idea?"

Edward's brow furrowed. "Something doesn't add up."

"No it doesn't. I have no idea why I am alive, how they didn't find me, or if they even know I exist. I can only assume somehow I was spared because someone's confession was misunderstood. I am going to push forward though, Edward. Mary had the evidence – she knew where all of it was hidden, and we lost her because of that. But I'm going to rebuild, and I will ring every one of these animals' necks if it's the last thing I do." He stopped and took a drink of wine. "Al was my best friend."

"You cannot expect to do this on your own. Not with their resources."

"There are others like me," he assured Edward. "This scheme runs vast and dangerous, and someone with a lot of power is trying to hide it. But that's the glorious thing about justice. There are always those who won't stop until it is served, even if it means risking their own lives. These bastards are everywhere, Edward. They've infiltrated everything. They have ears and eyes where you would least expect, and power in political offices and in their numbers with the gangs."

"Can I do anything? Help in any way?" Edward inquired. "I have certain skills that can be put to good use."

The bartender threw back his drink, his face giving away his response. "Edward, these men have no bounds for their brutality. I am fortunate because I am off their grid. Thomas and your family are not. If you want to help me, just know there may be a day when I might call on you for your statement. I've worked cases like these before, and one of the worst aspects is they require patience. And lots of it. If we act rashly, we have nothing."

Edward saw he was right, and the conviction he'd brought with him into the bar turned into a bitter acknowledgement of the circumstances. If he kept going, it would mean the end. Thomas might die. He might die. It would have been for nothing. There was no trail to follow, no scent to pursue. She was gone. Remarkably in all that tragedy, he had gained a son, and with his family whole again, Edward needed to preserve and protect the little he had left.

With a heavy heart, Edward got up, realizing it was nearly time for dinner with the Madame. "I think, in the end, these were the answers I needed to let Mary go, and let her go for good. Thank you for your assistance Mr....oh how rude of me. I don't think I ever got your name."

The bartender smiled and held out his hand. "It's John. John Erving. And Edward?"

"Yes?"

"I swear, for the three of them, I will see this through."

Edward tipped his head and saluted John. With his load now much lighter, he ascended up the stairs and back to reality, feeling after so many years of misery and unhappiness, he would find closure through the one thing he hadn't been searching for.

Thomas.

"And will you plan on ever coming back?" the Madame asked.

Edward's eyes were lost in the great fireplace, the wine going to his head. "If it were up to me personally? No. Not if I can help it."

"But what about Thomas, Edward?"

"He'll be safe for now, and that's all that matters to me."

She had a sip of whiskey, eyeing him closely. "He will want to come back one day. You and I both know this."

"I realize that," Edward admitted. "But I'll handle that when the time comes. I'm not sure New York will ever be safe again. Not for me, not for him, not for any of us."

A smirk came to the Madame's face. "What makes you think it was ever safe to begin with?"

It wasn't until Edward was halfway home that the Madame's words sank in, and he counted his lucky stars that unlike the Madame, he had a means of escape from the treacherous streets of New York.

For the Madame, there never would be a way out. And Edward couldn't decide if she liked it that way, or if she simply didn't have another choice.

IX.

The last of the lingering summer heat seemed at last to have dissipated, and Thomas welcomed the brisk morning breeze that brought a hint of chill to his cheeks. Hiking southward, he quickened his stride, pulling one of William's secondhand frock coats tighter around his waist. He kept his head down in an effort to avoid anyone he might know, or rather, just one person in particular, Catherine Hiltmore. His path downtown to the barbershop lead right by the Hiltmore residence, and considering he would be by to wish Esther farewell in a few hours, Thomas deemed one visit with Catherine more than enough for today. Despite Lucy's badgering at breakfast, Thomas refused to take a coach home to collect the last of his personal effects. There hadn't been more than a few moments of solitude for him in the last few days, and a long walk through the city streets would give him enough time to clear his head and mull over the new world being constructed around him.

Chapel bells clanged loudly to signal the ten o'clock hour, making him feel more and more exhausted with each step. Thomas tried to distract himself with reflecting on the big adjustments ahead, disregarding the want of sleep as best he could. The night prior, Edward arrived home just as Thomas, Lucy, and William were planning to go to bed, and what had been foreseen as an early night went into the premature hours of the morning. Thomas was already worn out after a day of following William through his role at Turner S & D; however, when Edward enlightened them to the real reasons behind his extended absence, Thomas caught an immediate second wind.

Edward sat them down and told them what he discovered during his afternoon and evening exploits. Thomas was blown away – he thought his father had been extremely candid on the subject Mary's death, yet obviously this had been a façade, and Thomas was both angry at being left in the dark and impressed with his father's diligence and dexterity. From start to finish, Edward relayed his long conversation with Harry's family and some of their friends, and he confessed now he did firmly believe Mary to be dead and the right man executed for the charges. A part of Thomas felt relieved what Edward uncovered was in full support of what the Madame and Detective Ellis relayed to him a few weeks ago, though what he couldn't quite figure out was how his father was able to implement such a search autonomously; the only story Edward heard was Thomas', and he definitely hadn't provided Edward with large scale details.

Needless to say, that hadn't stopped his father. "Every single person I met with told me the same story," Edward illuminated. "The man who killed her was a total bastard, and it was entirely work related."

"So you're saying there was no conspiracy? No cover up of illicit activity?" raised William.

"Cover up?" Thomas questioned aloud, to which William recoiled as if he'd made a mistake, and looked to Edward for a response.

Edward sighed, staring blankly in the bottom of his glass. "No. It was a lost hope from the start."

Lucy, who was sitting next to Thomas, was never one to let things slide. "Oh Thomas don't worry. It was something completely silly William concocted up in that great big imagination of his. Ridiculous really, but I'm glad to hear everything checks out."

Thomas stayed quiet, and Edward took note. "Thomas? Are you all right?"

"Fine," he replied too fast.

"Thomas, what is it?" Lucy posed. "Tell us."

All three had their eyes upon him, William's expression filled with guilt, and Thomas had no option other than to be frank.

He turned to his father. "You didn't even tell me you had doubts. That's all."

Edward's countenance grew solemn. "It's not that I had doubts in you, Thomas. I just wanted to be sure."

"Sure of what?" he retorted, irritated. "That she's dead?"

William and Lucy grimaced at his words, but Edward was stoic. "Yes, Thomas. Because I've been lied to before, and I didn't want to go back to England not knowing everything. Is that so much to ask?"

Thomas' frustration died as swiftly as it had risen. "I'm sorry. That was out of line. You have every right to ask questions."

"Wait a moment," Lucy interrupted, holding up her hand to stop them. "What is this about England? Edward...you're leaving us so soon? You've only just gotten here! And what about Thomas?"

In the heat of his aggravation, Thomas missed his father's small mention of returning home, and his heart sank. Edward, on the other hand, sat across from them beaming.

"We are all going back to England. Together," he announced. "I will make all the necessary arrangements tomorrow. But yes, to answer your question Lucy, we are all going back to Amberleigh. Where we belong."

William shook his head. "Edward...the contracts...I can't possibly leave New York with our new clients in America. Lucy and I will have to stay."

"You will do no such thing," Edward ordered. "There are plenty of good men here to oversee our business, William, men that have earned our trust over many years of fine service and loyalty. You're coming back with me and my son, and that's the end of it."

Before anyone could react, Lucy clapped her hands together and squealed with delight, startling the three men and sending her into a fit of laughter.

"I am so sorry, boys…really I just can't behave myself…I am so, so excited!" The three men chuckled. Lucy clearly had a gift for changing even the sourest of circumstances, and it was a trait Thomas greatly envied.

With Edward's news of their departure, Thomas felt the residual tension between them disappear, and his mood rapidly lightened with the knowledge that he would finally be saying his farewells to New York. When their night concluded, Thomas had gone to bed subdued though still somewhat upset with Edward. Deep down, he felt slightly betrayed that his father would conduct an investigation behind his back, especially when it had to do with Thomas' mother.

Currently, however, as he continued trudging through the streets with the cool wind refreshing his spirits, Thomas was able to let go of that offense, and for the first time, felt he really understood his father. What he had done wasn't out of pride or disillusion, it was out of an intrinsic notion that the truth needed to be heard with Edward's own ears, and only then would it be real. It was the same drive that gave Thomas the courage to search when no one else would, to push harder for answers when there were none to be found, and it was a trait running thick in both of their bloodstreams. Father and son were extraordinarily similar, and Thomas found himself smiling as that thought came to his mind.

In typical fashion for a nice, crisp morning, the barbershop was overly crowded when Thomas arrived to the apartment, and he was grateful the noises from the last of his packing would not be noticed. This would help him evade a confrontation with the barber, along with an unrelenting inquisition of where he was going next and Thomas having to assure him the Madame would once again be paying for the space. He skipped up the stairs and slid inside, bolting the door shut behind him. As he spun in to face the kitchen and complete the task at hand, his jaw dropped. William had not been lying when he told Thomas he would send "a few lads" to pack the majority of his belongings: nearly everything was boxed and ready for the mule cart, which would be there in a few hours to collect the load. It wasn't that Thomas had much needing to be packed, and he laughed seeing the majority of his and Mary's things fit easily into four wooden crates. The problem was Thomas wasn't sure how much of his old life he wanted to take with him, and above all, what of his mother's he should take for Edward.

He walked over to the crates, running his fingers along the smooth wooden paneling, and was happy to see the boxes had yet to be nailed shut. Carefully, Thomas pulled the lid off the first and inspected the contents, letting out a snort of amusement: it was, more or less, his entire bedroom, and it included his clothes, shoes, bed sheets, a few pieces of metal work, and, right on top of the pile, rested the knife Lawrence had given him. Thomas reached down and picked up the knife, enveloped up in it's linen cloth, feeling the weight of it in his hands as he began to slowly unwrap it. The beauty of Lawrence's work made Thomas' heart soar with appreciation and gratitude, recognizing it must have taken his old master more time than he would ever let on to finish such a piece.

The blade was a symbol of his past – a life that was so plain and uncomplicated, with the primary goal to survive each day and make enough money to put food on the table. That, Thomas realized, would never be the case again, and it was odd for him knowing his old self already had evolved into something far more complex. He held the knife to his chest and vowed to wear it every day if only to remember who he really was in his heart whilst everything around him transformed. There was nothing wrong with living in the world of the wealthy – he just didn't want to become like them. Edward, William, and Lucy were wonderful people, and very unlike most of their cohorts in the upper class; however, Thomas was divided, and would probably stay divided on where his real place was for most of his life. Strangely, he was content with that.

Gently tossing the linen aside and propping his leg on the crate, Thomas wrapped the blade in it's scabbard underneath his trousers and around his calf. Thomas could barely feel it's presence as he stood tall, making him feel secure in the way he assumed Lawrence intended it to. Tracing his thoughts back to two nights ago, Thomas recalled Edward's warning – he would only find real happiness in the people around him, and never in the riches their family possessed. His father's counsel seemed more applicable now as he soaked in the last of the barbershop, ruminating on the moments both good and bad that shaped his early years. This would make him an outsider… this part of him that remembered what it meant to be hungry, to spend every day from dawn until dusk working until he couldn't lift the hammer anymore. He liked it better that way, and in his heart, he felt Mary would have liked it better that way, too.

Her crate was the next he explored, and while none of her things were rich or fine, Thomas enjoyed looking through them and reminiscing over the incredible woman she was. Underneath her meticulously enveloped jewelry was one of her favorite possessions, and Thomas picked it up, studying the antique Georgian hair comb in his hands melancholically. One night, just after Esther was brought to their home years ago, Mary had bathed her, done her hair, powdered her face and rouged her cheeks and lips to make her smile. Esther struggled those first few nights, unable to sleep and desperate for her mother's warmth, but Mary had saved the day as she always did. Once Esther's makeup was complete, Mary proceeded to put Esther in one of her nicest dresses and, last but not least, placed the Georgian comb in Esther's long, beautiful, dark hair. With an evident change of heart, Esther haughtily trotted around with her nose in the air, pretending to play the part of a snotty, wealthy woman from Fifth Avenue, and the three of them spent the whole night laughing and teasing one another, truly feeling like a family for the first time. On occasion, when she thought no one was watching, Esther would often go into Mary's room and sit at her vanity, putting the comb in her hair and dabbling a bit of rouge on her lips, making faces in the mirror and practicing her French. Thomas sighed. This memory in particular was one of the reasons he passively let Esther go to the Hiltmores…her mocking portrayal gradually became a desired fantasy, much to his disdain. Esther wanted to be a lady, like Celeste and Catherine Hiltmore, and he hated to admit it was the right course for her to take. With her wit and smarts, Thomas expected Esther would surpass her friend's accomplishments in due course, and that had never been what worried him. What worried him was that when she saw what the Hiltmores' world was really like and who those people she aspired to resemble really were, her spark would die out, and she'd fall right into line with the others. He got to his feet and tucked the comb in his jacket pocket, wondering if after their goodbye he might ever see her again.

Thomas checked the other two boxes, finding nothing of sentimental value, and reminded himself there was only one place left to empty.

The floorboard was easy to pull up, and after prying it open Thomas removed the paper dollars, the letters, and the Madame's Griswold. He had no reason to keep the money, knowing full and well he would be taken care of, and resolved he would sleep better at night leaving the money with Esther in case she ever wanted for anything. Thomas thought it best to keep the letters for his father, and set them aside to put in his crate with the idea that Edward would either cherish them or burn them, of which he couldn't be certain. What he could not figure out was what to do with the Griswold. He had taken it from the Madame in a spur of the moment, yet something inside of Thomas told him not to let it go. It was heavy and would be burdensome to carry, not to mention concealing it was completely out of the question unless he fashioned a special holster for the inside of a jacket. As it rested in his hands, Thomas stared at it, the gold trimmed grip reflecting brightly in the light, and he drew back the hammer to aim the unloaded gun across the room and at the doorway. With a quick pull of the trigger, the blank release sent a rush through his limbs, making him grin. He pushed the floorboard back into place and packed the Griswold and his father's letters in his crate, then tucked the money into William's jacket beside Mary's comb.

Not an hour later, Thomas heard the thunder of wheels on the cobblestone street outside the apartment, telling him the cart had arrived to collect the wooden crates. The drivers swiftly loaded everything and, with a tip of their hats, took off in the direction of William's residence. Thomas was left to lock up the apartment and spend the afternoon saying his farewells to friends and family, of which he had very few. His mother's close friends, some of whom he was quite familiar, he seriously considered going to see; in spite of that, the last thing Thomas really wanted to do was spend his afternoon awkwardly attempting to explain his glorious change in circumstance, especially to those who were barely making enough money to get by. His intentions would be pure, but the bulk of responses would be spiteful at best, so he decided against it. Trotting down the back stairs with the keys jingling in his hand, a familiar figure caught Thomas' eye across the street. Louis smiled and took a drag of the cigarette in his hand, and Thomas took that as an invitation to approach.

"All packed?" he asked as Thomas reached his side, exhaling a cloud of smoke.

"Yeah, just about," Thomas conveyed. "They've already left with everything."

"Good." Louis continued to leisurely smoke and said nothing further.

"What are you doing here, Louis? Does she need something? I'll be stopping by The Palace soon enough."

Louis pulled another hand-rolled cigarette out of his pocket, lit it, and handed it to Thomas. "Go on. It'll take the edge off," he told him, and after a slight hesitation Thomas complied with Louis' request. "I am here watching you. Not on her request. On my own time."

Thomas had taken a long inhale and struggled not to cough up one of his lungs at Louis' words. "W-What? Your own time? Well hell, Louis, you could have at least helped me pack!"

He laughed. "That's not exactly in my repertoire. But you're ready to leave this shit hole at last, eh?"

"More or less. I've got to see Esther and the Madame, then I think I will be."

"You will love England, Tommy. It is…much different than here."

"You've been?"

"Many lifetimes ago, yes."

Thomas had another drag. "I think I might actually miss this place," he said, glancing out into the dirty, hectic streets.

Louis' gaze followed Thomas', peering out into the masses. "I have no doubt you'll be back soon enough. No matter what your father will try to convince you of."

A sudden insight hit Thomas. "You're here for my protection, aren't you, Louis?"

"Yes I am."

"And why exactly do I need protection?" Thomas knew protocol, having to abide by it many times.

"Because it's still not safe, Tommy."

Thomas scoffed. "She really needs to lighten up, Louis. It's over. It's been over for weeks. If it's so dangerous, how could you leave her side?"

"I left George with her."

"Oh, Christ. You know she hates George protecting her. Might as well be Claire, even if she is only fifteen."

"It wasn't up to her, Tommy. She didn't send me. I made other arrangements to keep an eye on you."

"I don't understand," Thomas confessed, more than a little perplexed.

"Your father asked me to watch you."

The cigarette fell from Thomas' hand. "My...what?"

Louis pulled another from his jacket pocket, again lighting it for Thomas. "Your father asked me to watch you."

"How...why? How do you two even...?"

"You think I didn't know your father, being with the Madame all these years?" He handed the cigarette over to him.

Thomas' head was spinning. "But...why would Edward be worried about my safety?"

"Some things are better left unexplained, Tommy. And this is not a conversation for us to have today."

"But—"

"Come along. It's nearing the lunch hour, and you have two important stops to make."

Louis' tone was firm, and Thomas did not want to push his temper. He knew better than that. The two sauntered along in silence for a while, while speculations and suspicions danced in Thomas' head. He felt foolish for not making that connection before – of course Louis and his father had met. Nonetheless, the idea that there was some sort of muted friendship between them that miraculously trumped the Madame's authority was...pretty baffling to Thomas. He had known Louis since he could remember, without any perception of how deeply intertwined their lives were, and Thomas was almost embarrassed to admit for someone who cared so much for him and his family, he knew so little of the real Louis. Every time he mustered up the boldness to say something, the next second it was shot down by his insecurity of not wanting to pursue an unwelcome subject. After a few minutes of battling back and forth, he regressed to saying nothing at all – if Louis wanted to discuss anything he would speak on his own accord.

They reached the Hiltmore house, and Thomas was received in a much different fashion than he had been previously accustomed.

248

Louis insisted he would wait for him outside, and Thomas marched in to be surprisingly greeted with smiles and formality, as if he were one of the many high society friends he'd seen the Hiltmores have to their home over the years. They had a new butler, and he stiffly escorted Thomas to the sitting room for tea and he insisted he would inform the Hiltmores of Thomas' visit. The moment the butler was gone, a maid came through the serving door with a tray of fresh tea and biscuits. She kept her eyes down as she poured two cups, and without any acknowledgement of Thomas, quickly retreated the way she came. Peering around to be sure he was alone, Thomas took some deep breaths wanting to appear at ease though on the inside he was squirming. He hated this sort of conventional treatment the wealthy imposed upon one other, and to his dismay, he had a hunch regarding who that second cup of tea was for. And it wasn't Esther.

"Thomas!" came the singing voice of Catherine Hiltmore, floating in through the doorway to see him, her arms spread wide in welcome. She was dressed in a bright, canary yellow gown, and it made her blue eyes sparkle as if she truly were enchanted to see her guest. Thomas tried not to vomit.

"Good day, Mrs. Hiltmore," he said in return, standing and taking a slight bow of his head. William had taught him a few general English courtesies the day before, which Thomas had whole-heartedly taken on and perfected in under an hour.

If it was possible, Catherine's eyes grew wider at Thomas' gesture, and she curtseyed lightly in reciprocation. "So it is true," she replied under her breath.

"What do you mean?" Thomas asked, taunting her.

She giggled and glided toward the sofa to sit, motioning for Thomas to do the same. "Don't play these games with me, Thomas. I know them better than you do. The rumors are spreading through town like wildfire that some sort of British nobleman has landed in New York to claim his son...and with what I could pester out of the Madame...it's you, isn't it?"

"My father is here, yes," Thomas admitted, trying to stay neutral and act unfazed, annoyed that apparently no one in New York City's upper class had anything better to do than gossip about one another.

His face must have given him away, because Catherine's formed an almost patronizing smile. "Oh dearest, you had better get used to being talked about. The building of rumors is a common thing among the women in our station, or women in general I should say, particularly when there is anyone or anything new to discuss. And this is new and exciting! Now, tell me everything. Your father is a nobleman? How did we never know this before? How did you find him and what are your plans?"

"I came today, Mrs. Hiltmore, to say goodbye to your family and to Esther," Thomas declared, reiterating the words he had gone over with Lucy multiple times that morning. "My father is taking me to see his home in England and I will be subjected to a bit of education and travel. I hope then to return to New York to run our newest venture of shipping and distribution on the coast."

Whatever answer Catherine Hiltmore had been expecting, this was not it, and her enthusiasm faded. "You will be leaving us so soon? How long until your return?"

"A few years, I would expect."

This improved her mood. "Perfect," she gushed. "We will have a massive celebration on your return home, I can assure you of that. Please promise to keep me and Douglas informed on your journey? Write as much as you can?"

Lucy warned him about this conversation, seeing through the motives of Catherine Hiltmore without even meeting her. "She'll want you to marry her daughter," Lucy clarified. "She will want you to write, to stay close, because having an ally like you will only increase her self-worth. You have to indulge her, Thomas, it's an obligation that goes with the lifestyle." Thomas protested, wanting nothing more than to tell Catherine Hiltmore she and her ridiculous scheming could go to hell, but Lucy was right. For Esther's sake, he could put on a smile.

"I wouldn't dream of losing touch," Thomas assured her. "I also plan to write to Esther to check on her, and would like your permission to do so."

"Of course!" she exclaimed. "You have our address, yes?" Thomas nodded, taking a sip of his now cold tea. She went on, "Good. It's settled then. I will go and fetch Esther for you. I hope you will accept Douglas' deepest regrets for not being here to bid you farewell. He had urgent business in Virginia and ran off just last night."

"Please thank him for all he's done for Esther and me, and on my return I will find a way to repay you both." Lucy's words were meant to tantalize Catherine, and she ate them right up. She got to her feet and Thomas followed suit, once again calling on his lessons from William and ushering her to the door. As she released his arm, Catherine turned to face Thomas, looking him up and down.

"I always knew you could have done better," she said, and with a mischievous grin, left him and skipped off down the hall.

"Es, are you even going to look at me?"

Esther sat in a chair across from Thomas, glaring intently down at her hands, which were folded neatly in her lap. Thomas told his story little by little with the hope she might be as happy for him as he was for her. To his disappointment, Esther sat down and avoided eye contact with Thomas, treating their final goodbye like it was an encumbrance. Catherine must have told her his situation prior to his visit that day, and he was becoming more and more aggravated with the passing minutes.

"Look, Es, I came here to wish you nothing but the best. I'm leaving for England with my father and I wanted to say goodbye. If you aren't even going to talk to me, then I'll be on my way."

At last she glimpsed up, and Thomas noticed her bottom lip trembling. "For how long?"

"I don't know, Es. But it won't be a short trip."

Esther sniffed, her eyes leaving Thomas again and moving to the windows on her right. "You're leaving me…" she whispered, one large tear trickling down her cheek. At first, Thomas thought she might be manipulating him, and his mood once again grew heated. But after a few seconds, he saw it wasn't so: Esther was a terrible liar, and he could tell from the expression on her face she was devastated to lose him.

"I did this," she cried, still looking out the window. "It's because I left. If I hadn't left, then you wouldn't have to go."

Thomas got up and went to her side. "Please don't cry, Es. I will come back, I promise. I need to go and make a new life for myself. You won't even notice I'm gone." He comforted her as best he could, taking her hand in his and squeezing tightly. "Look at us. We've both had so much good fortune these past few months. There is nothing to be upset about."

To Thomas' relief, Esther squeezed back. "I just…I already miss you, Tommy. I don't want you to go…"

"I promise I will write you every week. Every day, if I need to. You know you won't be alone − you have Celeste and her family who love you like you are their own daughter. And if you ever need anything, the Madame will take care of it. We…" Thomas paused, feeling a catch in his own throat. "This is what's best for both of us."

He swallowed hard, trying to restrain his own tears and be strong. It hadn't occurred to him their parting would pull at his heartstrings, and as he took in their final moments, Thomas felt something he hadn't foreseen: pain. The rapidness of the alterations to his lifestyle had been so fast, he had no time to emotionally prepare himself to leave not just the city, but the few people who had made him what he was, and Esther was one of them despite being a few years his junior. His transition had been easy up to that very second, and leaving her in New York became one of the hardest things he'd ever done.

With his time limited, Thomas released her hand and reached into his jacket pocket to take out Mary's old comb. He placed it in her open hand and closed her fingers around it with a smile, squeezing again and then letting go.

"This was your favorite thing of hers, wasn't it?" he asked, wishing he could have a picture of her flabbergasted expression. Esther nodded, speechless, and on the brink of a full out sob. Thomas continued, "She would have wanted you to have it. She always swore you'd grow up to be one of the most beautiful girls in New York."

Esther let loose her grip and studied the comb longingly. "I miss her, too. So much. I…didn't realize until I was here how…how much she did for me…for us."

"She was a wonderful woman. We were lucky to have her, and you know she'll watch out for you from a better place. And when you need her, she's right in here," he said, tapping his finger on his chest where his heart lay. "But Es, there is something else I need to give you," he murmured, lowering his voice. "This needs to stay between us, all right?"

She set the comb aside, giving Thomas her full attention. "What is it?"

Thomas removed the money concealed in the jacket and set it on the table in front of Esther, who froze in place when she saw what it was.

"Tommy…"

"Take it, Es. It's…well it was our life savings."

"Tommy, I can't…"

"Yes you can, and you will. I am giving this to you because I don't need it anymore, and this is for you and only you in case you ever are in trouble or need something. Hide it where no one will find it, understand? I just…" The catch in his throat returned, and his words cracked as he spoke. "I just want to know you'll be all right without me here."

For an instant, Esther simply stared at the money on the table.

Then, she leapt up and jumped into Thomas' arms, hugging him tight. They held each other, and Thomas hated that this was the only thing he could do for her. Together they had made it through so much strife and found happiness in one another, and it seemed too soon they were separating, headed two very different directions. He wasn't sure how they'd gotten so lucky, how after living without a penny to their names they had both been thrown into a life of privilege. Their hardships would never compare to most, or so he could only hope. If they played their cards right, they would be set for the rest of their lives. And that thought, while exhilarating, scared him.

When they finally broke apart, Esther had Thomas fashion the comb into her hair and tucked the money away under her dress, making him turn the other way as she did so. He chuckled, promising her again he'd write every day until she told him otherwise, and in return she swore to write him with every detail she could scribble down. In the end, Esther took his hand and walked with him toward the front hallway, where Catherine and Celeste joined them to say farewell to Thomas one last time. After general courtesies, he exited the front door, catching sight of Louis still smoking like a chimney across the busy roadway. Thomas turned around and looked back at Esther one last time, trying to imagine the lady she would be the next time they met.

"How did it go?" Louis called as he neared.

"Fine. She'll be all right, I think."

"The Madame will see to it she is taken care of," Louis vowed. "Just as she took care of you."

Thomas scoffed. "I don't know if I like the sound of that."

"Well would you rather have her only at the mercy of Catherine Hiltmore?"

"Point taken, Louis. Although I can't even begin to think how Esther will turn out with those two women helming her future."

"She's smart, that one, and I have a feeling she will take their musings lightly. Otherwise, she'll turn out to be a beautiful, wealthy, devious little monster like them, eh?"

"Thanks for the consolation, Louis."

They were welcomed to The Palace by an overly frantic George, who the Madame had obviously relished in torturing with impossible tasks and expectations the entire day. As they made their way inside, Louis took George aside and sent Thomas upstairs to meet the Madame in her offices. Thomas leisurely climbed the steps, his gaze floating to and fro, hoping that The Palace might stay this way forever. The Madame had worked, sweated, bled, and fought by the skin of her teeth to make her establishment flawless, and Thomas found despite their personal issues, he had a great sense of admiration for the Madame. She truly was indestructible in his eyes, and her resilience was something he respected and feared, though he would never admit it to her. He only wondered if all the Madame created and earned was really worth the crosses she had to bear in the process, and if one day, that weight might get too heavy for her to stay on her two feet.

She sat perched on her throne, anticipating his arrival, but by no means her typical self. For the first time in his life, Thomas was witness to the Madame's more human, vulnerable character: her hair was amiss, half of it falling long past her shoulders, with only a slip dress on barely concealing her loosened corset. There was no makeup on her face, no jewelry on her body – it was her, in her basest form, looking back at him with nothing to accessorize herself other than the chilled glass of whiskey in her elevated hand, and the only sounds to note were the cold, thudding drips of condensation as they splashed against her desktop.

Thomas was tempted to shield his eyes and turn his head, but thought better. "Is this a…a bad time?"

An arbitrary smirk came to her face, and without warning, she began to laugh – it wasn't malicious or sardonic, it was a genuine, honest laugh at something Thomas ostensibly did not understand.

255

She shook her head, and it became apparent the Madame was actually ridiculing herself. With effortlessness, she set her whiskey on the table and got up to get a glass for Thomas, as was the norm, not losing her humor as she poured it from the bottle.

"Well, I hoped you'd be delayed a bit longer, and I'm sorry you're forced to see me in my fucking lingerie," she asserted as Thomas made an effort to avert his eyes from the completely sheer fabric covering her black undergarments. "I haven't slept in two damned days trying to solve the mystery of how the fuck an intruder broke into my office two nights ago."

"Some guy going after one of the girls?" Thomas suggested.

"Not exactly, Thomas." She marched toward him, thrusting the drink into his hand and then resumed her original spot. "Someone came in to threaten me."

"Was it a client?"

"No. We shoot clients on sight if that happens. You know that."

Thomas' brow furrowed. "Business associate?"

The Madame rolled her eyes. "Business associate?"

He took a sip of his drink. "Is there a reason you're avoiding telling me what happened?"

"Yes. A fucking big one."

"And you can't tell me or won't?"

The Madame thought about it. "I can't. Yet."

"So I should expect an explanation…"

The Madame put her glass down once more and crossed her arms, tilting back in her chair. "If you ever come back here with the intention to stay, I will tell you. Because then you'll need to know."

Thomas knew he should have expected some sort of stunt from her on his last visit. "Well I am glad you're all right."

"Thomas, I want to say something." The Madame hesitated again, and he allowed her time to find the words, unable to guess what she had to say to him after the passing weeks. Somewhere underneath her armor, there was a part of her that cared for him, although she did her damndest not to show it. For him, it was hard to have any kind of faith in a woman who spent most of her life dancing a fine line between honesty and lies, and he was saddened because oddly, this was the one thing he would miss most of all. He didn't understand it, but seeing the Madame and saying goodbye turned out to be harder for him than his parting with Esther. They were both a mess, yet both too stubborn to concede their sides.

"This isn't easy for me to get out," she went on, taking a swig of whiskey from her glass. "It's…it's something I hope you will give a shit about one day in the future, when perhaps you've forgiven me. I am sorry I lied to you. And to your mother and father. I know I told you I don't have regrets, but I…I do fucking regret it. All I wanted was to keep you safe, and I wish things could be different…there are so many damned things I would change, and I can't."

"Please—"

"Don't interrupt me, dammit. Just listen. I want you to go. Go to England and be happy. Become the man I know you're supposed to be, and be your father's son…but then…then you come home where you belong. I don't give a shit what they tell you. This is your fucking home, and its where you will be needed most."

The Madame's words struck Thomas, not just in their context but also in how she said them. His gaze fell to the whiskey cup in his hands – what she said meant so much to him, and he could never tell her that. The Madame really was a walking contradiction, a friend who would both stab him in the back and then kill for him with the same blow. She caused him so much agony and conversely she had done so much to protect him, Thomas couldn't decide if his resentment or his gratitude would ever win out over the other. In his heart, he knew with her he would never win, but he would also never lose. He wanted to think he wouldn't come back to New York once he'd left – he'd tried so hard to convince himself it would be a waste. And then came Louis' tidings echoing through his mind, along with the Madame's: this was his home, no matter what he became or whose bloodline he was, and that was the only truth he needed to hear.

Thomas glimpsed back up, locking eyes with the Madame, who sat patiently for a reaction. Without uttering a syllable, she seemed to appreciate how he felt and what he meant to say in return. Tipping her head forward once, the Madame's reaction mollified Thomas, ensuring that there was nothing else left to say.

"Will you watch Es for me?" he requested.

"I absolutely will."

"Without ruining her?"

The Madame gasped, feigning offense. "Ruin her?"

He didn't change his tone. "I mean it. Don't."

"You have my word," she replied, instantly shedding her sarcasm.

"Thank you, Aunt." Thomas dumped the last of his drink down his throat and stood, making ready to pace toward the door.

"Wait," she demanded, rising to her feet behind her desk, her eyes a little red. "Promise me you'll come back to us. Promise me right now. It doesn't have to be soon...years for Christ's sake, I don't care. But I want to fucking hear it.

"I promise I will come back," he articulated, a smile creeping onto his face.

The Madame's entire demeanor changed, her armor instantly placed back on, and she lowered into her chair. "Well, that's settled then. Now get out of here, God damn you. I have work to do."

"All right," he countered, grinning when he spotted something... something that had never struck him before. "Madame...your eyes... they look just like Mary's. The hazel and the grey...it's...almost the same."

Her whole body tensed, and it was clear she was taken a little off guard. "Yes we...we used to always joke about it...in the early days. Before your father when we could still pass for sisters."

Thomas nodded. "I just hadn't really seen the similarity. It's... it's nice. To remember that. To remember her."

The Madame cleared her throat, easing up. "Don't forget her, Thomas. And like I said, remember at the end of the day where you came from. They may tell you different, but you'll never be one of those bastards. You know that better than anyone else. Now go so I can put a fucking dress on. I'm freezing my ass off."

It had been two long weeks of travel when at last their stagecoach turned down the gravel drive to Amberleigh Manor, and while Edward heartily enjoyed his time on the open ocean, Thomas found it absolutely terrifying after a lifetime on solid ground. It took all of his manners and strength not to throw himself on the earth and kiss it when they'd finally made it to London. Now, as Thomas gawked out his window in awe of the endless miles of green, rolling hills, he recognized how little he knew of the expanse of the world, never having left New York City in his life. There was no industrial smoke, no filth, no endless streets of buildings stretching high to the sky with dirty people crowding every corner; there was fresh air, trees, and wildlife, with estates so large they made Thomas' eyes cross. Edward sat across from him, smiling ear to ear at Thomas' enthusiasm, pointing out various landmarks and properties they passed by on the bumpy road. When they reached the front of the great house, a line of servants awaited them at the end, and the second their carriage came to a halt, the door of the passenger car was thrown open to a sea of friendly faces. Thomas was given a hand and stepped out into the light, nearly falling back as he soaked the whole scene in. A brief introduction followed, but Thomas couldn't concentrate on anything except his new, remarkable surroundings. Edward's home was one of the largest residences Thomas had ever seen, solidly made of stone and brick, and behind it sat a lake sparkling in the sunshine enveloped by a rainbow of blooming gardens. In the distance lay more rolling hills trickled with rock and bluffs, rising out of the ground like gods among men.

As he took his bows with the staff, two figures in Thomas' peripheral vision caught his attention, and he turned to find the two people he was the most eager to meet. The couple was strikingly different than the others, both "Jappers" as Thomas had been told by William, and though Hiroaki remained passive, his beautiful wife Akemi glowed with joy at Thomas from her husband's side. Edward went to greet his longtime friend and Thomas followed directly behind him, stopping a few feet away and taking a deep bow as a sign of respect. When he rose up, Edward had a look of pride on his face, as did Hiroaki and his wife.

"Astonishing..." was the only word that escaped Hiroaki's lips as he studied Thomas' features from head to foot.

Then unexpectedly, Edward took a step toward Thomas, and for the first time since they had met all those weeks ago, he hugged his son. "Welcome home, Thomas," he whispered in his ear. "Welcome home."

And with twenty eyes upon them, Thomas openly embraced his father in return, marveling at what the world would bring next.

PART 2:
SOUTHERN ENGLAND, 1883

X.

The showers of spring were relentless as they drenched the English countryside. It had been a dark start to the year with an array of constant, shadowing clouds, keeping everyone's spirits downtrodden despite the beautiful shades of deep green stretching as far as the eye could see. In his youth, Edward grew to love the rain; every morning he woke feeling revitalized with a clean slate, as if yesterday and all it's worries were washed away. His son, on the other hand, was having a bit of difficulty adapting to the dramatic change in climate, as this was only the second spring the two hadn't spent abroad traveling the cities of Europe or found themselves in London on business. It was Thomas' eighth year residing in England, and while he was a much different man than he'd been when he'd arrived, he was still Thomas, and Edward couldn't be more grateful for that.

Time was beginning to pass so swiftly, and Edward found he often stared at his reflection in the mirror, wondering when the wrinkles around his eyes became so prominent, or when his black hair began to sprout grey. For those eight years he had watched Thomas transform, and transform he had. Their bond had grown so strong in those years that, oftentimes, the two would be able to communicate in just a single glance. It made business a greater pleasure for

Edward, not to mention more entertaining, and together Thomas and Edward were a dynamic team. In the last two years alone, Turner's profits had doubled, in large part to Thomas' diligence and hard work, and he earned himself a partnership alongside William and Edward. Thomas was a natural at selling and a great reader of people – something Edward imagined he acquired during his years on the streets of New York City or, more likely, in the teachings of the illustrious Madame. Either way, William and Edward were growing more satisfied each passing day with the notion that, when the time came, their company's legacy would be left in the right hands, and they could both easily retire without compunction.

When Thomas was first put into practice at Turner S & D, Edward did not hesitate to challenge Thomas' abilities, and his son had welcomed the push, making it apparent he had an aptitude for numerous other skills. Within a year, his math tutor requested a private interview with Edward, confessing he could do nothing more to help Thomas – reluctantly, the poor man explained that Edward's son was already surpassing his tutor's own expertise. On the other hand, Thomas did initially struggle with languages; but after an extensive amount of trekking the continent with Edward, he managed to master French, Spanish, Italian, and a little German, not to mention he could comprehend the accents of the Scots and Irish, which at best were unintelligible to Edward. It was a marvel, and one William and Edward took full advantage of as soon as Thomas was ready. The only one of them who appeared to be unfazed by Thomas' rapid progression was Lucy, and she always swore after her third glass of wine she knew from the first time they spoke he would outshine all of the other men in the family. Her biased vindication would always come later – Lucy was half American like Thomas, and to the groans of both her husband and Edward, she was never unwilling to remind them that she and Thomas were far superior because of it.

The Turners' new business trade came easily, as tension between

Britain and America had at last subsided and thus eased the way to obtaining prosperous customers out of the mangled Southern states. With only three years of training, Thomas went with his father to meet a few wealthy sellers from South Carolina in London, and Edward spent most of their journey brainstorming methods to convince their potential clients Turner S & D could take their distribution to new and innovative levels on a global scale. The South was still rebuilding after the disastrous Civil War, and with new interstate tariffs being implemented, foreign import and export was taking off exponentially to avoid the extra cost of buying and selling to the North. Without a word and much to Edward's surprise, Thomas took the reins as the bidding war began, stepping ahead of Edward to introduce himself and his father, making sure to repeatedly emphasize that he was an American. Adding to Edward's horror, Thomas did not stop there, proceeding with a few snide remarks regarding "the Union" and Lincoln; yet Edward instantly saw the overwhelming relief in the three men's faces as they relaxed, and he found it hard to suppress his shock in their reactions. Within minutes, his son had all three confidently laughing with him and practically eating out of the palm of his hand. Thomas made his moves patiently, and when the time was right, dove right into logistics, and the deal was signed and completed by teatime. Realizing he was merely an observer, Edward added a few short remarks regarding numbers and ports of call, but the rest was Thomas' own careful planning. It was on that trip Edward recognized his son had a gift, one that exceeded any hopes he and William premeditated by a landslide.

In their leisure time, Edward and Thomas would hunt, ride horses, discuss books, and entertain, with Lucy insisting she needed female companionship. Edward knew better – Lucy took full charge of finding a wife for Thomas, and it was hilariously more challenging than she was prepared for. Thomas was always polite and gracious with their guests, though regardless of Lucy's constant reprimanding and persuasive efforts, there was never a definitive spark with any young lady she endorsed. Much to Edward and William's amusement, this did not keep Thomas from having a bit of fun with her. He tormented Lucy by simulating interest in a different girl each month, and his pretend attraction would always fade followed by a number of petty excuses and exaggerated reasoning. This capriciousness drove her mad, and after a few years of torment, Lucy gave up her quest and informed Thomas he could find a companion on his own. In that moment, Edward was quite certain he had never seen his son happier.

Their third winter together in England was one of the coldest Edward could remember, and the Turners spent the majority of their days huddled by the nearest fireplace. One bitter morning, Edward woke much earlier than usual, the sun still far from rising, and went to check on Thomas down the hall, as neither of them slept more than a few hours each night. After finding his son's room empty, Edward skipped down the back stairs to the kitchen, assuming Thomas may have woken before him and gone down for breakfast. Descending down toward the light, he was welcomed by the strong scent of cooked onions and potatoes, with laughter echoing off the great stone walls. Edward's staff was already active and preparing their morning meal, and when he pushed through the small door, everyone but his page Robert looked startled to see him.

"Good morning, Lord Turner!" bellowed Maximus, his head cook, who was as hearty as the beef stew he made every Thursday evening. "Would you like some bread and bacon sir? Breakfast can be ready in just short of an hour, if you'd prefer it early!" He was wearing a large white apron covered in what Edward assumed was blood from butchering, and he felt his appetite immediately subside.

"No, but thank you, Max. Has anyone seen my son?"

A few peered to one another, as if afraid to answer, but Robert got to his feet as his teeth crunched through the apple in his hand.

"This way, sir," he answered mid chew, beckoning Edward to follow. Edward noticed knowing looks and sideways glances while they passed, and it was clear every person in the kitchen was aware of something about Thomas that Edward wasn't.

Robert led him down through the servants' passage toward the main part of the house with a candlestick in hand, and then took a hard left at a fork where the path to the right went upstairs to the dining room. Soon, Edward saw he was being taken toward the place his grandfather hauntingly called "the cells," in a voice to imply they were still, in fact, used for holding. If Edward ever misbehaved, he was threatened with being dragged down through the lower levels and locked in the chains where prisoners had once been detained – to this day Edward hated being below the regular floors of Amberleigh and feeling the cool, dank air against his skin.

With a small whish of a breeze, the candle abruptly went out, and Edward stopped dead. A few seconds passed, and his eyes adjusted just enough to make out the figure of his page. Edward motioned for him to keep going, and Robert made another hard left at the end of the hallway, leading Edward down a stone spiral staircase into further darkness. Thankfully as they neared the bottom, they were saved by the flickering of a few lit torches on the walls. Apart from "the cells," the house had been completely modernized; as a tribute to his grandfather and his heritage, Edward pledged it was the one part of his home he would never change. That did not, however, make it any more appealing, and he could feel chills ringing down his arms and legs as he kept up with Robert, who remained utterly unfazed.

His page stepped lightly, turning back with a large grin on his face. "He's been coming down here for almost two years, sir, every morning he could. I think he feels happy with the work. Seems to clear his mind."

If it was possible, the air grew icier as they walked down the last few stairs. Edward shuddered, annoyed with himself partially for not putting on more than his robe during the coldest part of the winter, and also because his fortitude wavered over such a minimal temperature change.

"What do you mean, Robert?" he asked at last, clenching his teeth to keep them from chattering.

At the bottom, the pair turned the final corner into the old armory, and a sudden blast of heat and light from the blaze of the fire made Edward take a step back. There, with his back to them, was Thomas covered in black soot and sweat, holding a long piece of steel into the flames as it began to turn red hot. Edward could see a few burn scars on his arms as he struck the metal over and over, so loud it was almost deafening, and sending a mist of sparks skyward. A heavy apron was tied around his front and a mask in front of his face, giving him a daunting appearance – it was a version of Thomas Edward had never witnessed, one that made his respect for his son magnify despite the pedestal he already had Thomas upon. Robert started to go forward but Edward grabbed his arm, gesturing for him to stay at his side. Respectfully, Robert nodded and settled where he was, and Edward observed his son for half an hour in awe, astounded with every passing second at Thomas' skill and dedication to his practice. Not once did he happen to turn around or take notice of his father and Robert only a few feet behind him, and Edward admired Thomas for being so lost in his craft. Finally, when he thought his nose could no longer take the smell of burning iron or his tongue the taste of metal, Edward and Robert regressed back the way they came. Edward waited until they emerged from "the cells" to speak. "Thank you for showing me that, Robert."

"Of course, sir. I didn't realize you were…unaware."

"I had no idea," Edward disclosed. "If you don't mind, let's just keep this between the two of us. I'd rather have Thomas not know that I know. I want him to feel at home, and that he has free reign to do whatever he wishes on his own time. Can you do that for me?"

"Whatever you think is best, sir."

Edward reflected on the last time he and Hiroaki had been in "the cells" for training, and a thought struck him.

"Robert, how did Thomas get the resources for all that? I know we've kept certain weapons and things down there for years but I never knew we had blacksmithing tools."

"The jap–" Robert started, then paused, his cheeks flushing. "I'm sorry sir, forgive me. Hiroaki was the one who helped him set up everything."

"When?"

"It's been some time, sir. Like I mentioned earlier, around two years."

A little baffled, Edward left it at that, never broaching the subject with either of them. He went down only a handful of other times to watch Thomas work, always in the earliest hours of the day. Without fail, Thomas would be there, hammering metal to masterpiece, and no indications ever arose that Thomas identified he had an audience. His skill was something so effortless for him, so pure – Edward did not want to sully the one thing Thomas held on to from his past life in New York, and he let him have it completely to himself, the way it should be.

The low rumble of thunder in the distance brought Edward back to present, and he stood up and stretched. He glanced out his bedroom window, the pane glistening with water, and rung the bell for his morning tea. After rekindling the burn in his fireplace, he moved to an empty armchair, scanning through the last letter he'd received from Louis in New York. There was no news, and nothing of significance to report other than business as usual at The Palace. William and Lucy were safe and happy, and any possible fallback from Mary's death years prior appeared to be long gone. In conclusion, however, Louis warned Edward the Madame would be pushing for Thomas to return home, and to prepare himself for it.

"She wants to see him, Eddie,' he wrote. *'Don't you think it's time we at the very least allow her that? If only for a few weeks, I'm begging you. She's becoming unbearable about it."*

Trying not to overreact, Edward tossed the letter in the fire. The day he had been running from had inevitably been reached.

"They want us to come back," Edward said aloud. "I promised myself I wouldn't do that again. I promised you I wouldn't do that to Thomas."

Edward knew what she might say, as if she were sitting right next to him. "What's there to worry over if the danger is gone?"

"I don't want to risk it, Mary. What if it isn't gone? What if they find out who we are?"

Then the real question formed in his mind: "What are you really afraid of?"

"Nothing."

"Eddie…"

"I…I don't want to go back and remember it all again. We are so happy here the two of us. And what if they're wrong? I promised to keep him safe."

"Don't punish Thomas. Don't keep dwelling on the past. Take him home."

"He is home."

A short silence. "Is he, Edward?"

A soft knock on the door caused the back-and-forth conversation to fade away, signaling Liza was there with Edward's tea. "Come in!" he instructed. His maid quietly opened and closed the door, setting the tray on the side table by Edward's armchair.

"Good morning, Lord Turner, can I get you anything else?" she asked.

Edward didn't take his eyes off the glow of flames, the last pieces of Louis' letter simmering.

"That will be all, Liza, thank you."

He sat brooding for a few minutes over the harsh reality his subconscious never failed to spell out. Edward knew whatever voice was speaking to him was spot-on, and hated to admit they had been gone so long for his own selfish reasoning. Even William and Lucy returned to New York almost a year ago, though Thomas didn't press the matter, choosing to stay in England no doubt out of the love he had for his father. Nonetheless, Edward couldn't keep punishing his son out of his own self-pity. Perhaps it was time to start considering an alternative, though he just wasn't sure New York was the right answer.

After his tea had cooled, along with his mood, Edward turned for the cup at his side and became aware of another letter there beside it, addressed to Thomas in the Madame's writing. Edward kept a formal correspondence with her as well, without many details except the usual semantics and sometimes-sneering comments. He wasn't sure why the letter had come to him, but out of his own nosiness, Edward was overcome with an impulse to open it. Louis' caution of what was to come made Edward long to know what he was in for, and better yet, the true feelings Thomas had regarding New York.

Thomas,

I am so glad to hear your trip to Paris was a success – however I wish you would have ventured to any one of the brothels I mentioned to spy for me. Your moral standards get in the way too often, darling.

Esther is doing well. I tried again to confront her about writing you, but being the pain in my ass she is, she continually changes subjects and I eventually chose not to push it any further. She's eighteen now, and more beautiful than any one of us could have guessed. She has taken note from me and is secretive, but I never thought she would be with you. Things have grown better for her, particularly after Celeste married. The bastard that girl married, however, will only be trouble and I hope Esther is out of their household and married herself within the next year. She has a number of prospects chasing her around, and while she denies it, I know a few have come close to winning her over.

Whenever I mention your name she is eager to hear of your whereabouts, and Esther has been quite helpful in assisting me on the social forefront. I can't decide whether she does it because she adores me or hates the arrogant pricks she's surrounded by, but the number of favors I'm owed because of the knowledge she's acquired have put us higher on the food chain than ever. She is an interesting one, our little Esther.

I will only ask one last time – it's beneath me, you know. Please come back to New York. You are missed here, and you know all you need to do is tell your father you would like to be home for summer. He would send you in a heartbeat if he knew how badly you wished it – especially since William and Lucy are back and in a new residence on 5th. Just ask, darling. You two can't hide away in England forever.

Write soon.

Yours & etc.,

M

Edward put the letter down. He hadn't heard a word out of Thomas about this, not even the slightest suggestion he might want to return to New York, and it puzzled him as to why. The way the Madame wrote to his son indicated it was a topic that had been discussed between them on several occasions, one that Thomas wanted to pursue, and yet he had not mentioned it in passing. After another sip of tea, the truth became clear: out of what he could only guess was both pity and respect, Thomas would never request to go back, feeling it would hurt Edward immensely, and instead Thomas opted to live with his own pain rather than injuring Edward. He was aware his son felt indebted to him for the new life he had been given, and Edward's frustration mounted for being so wrapped up in his own devices to not piece it together. There must have been signs he missed, little things Thomas said in passing that meant more than he let on. Louis' warning was justified, and reading the Madame's letter cut right through the shield of Edward's denial, making him feel selfish and out of touch with reality.

It was both devotion and appreciation that kept Thomas quiet, and Edward wouldn't let his son sit in exile any longer. Every fiber in his being despised the idea of going to New York, particularly since he swore they would stay away as long as humanly possible. Still, with William and Lucy already there and a white flag seemingly raised by whatever threat previously existed, he resolved on a solution. For Thomas, Edward would go this one last time to see him settled and confirm Louis' report. If he'd learned one thing in all his years, it was that life was too bloody short for personal politics, and Edward had already allowed his to reign over his willpower for far too long.

"Good morning, father," Thomas greeted Edward as he strolled into the dining room for breakfast.

Edward set down his paper. "Good morning. How did you sleep? The storms were a bit heavy from the south."

"You could say that again," Thomas agreed, taking a seat across from Edward at the table. "So. What's next? Are we heading up to London to check on tobacco shipments? We could always head back to Paris for the summer…it just gets so damn hot…"

Edward sighed, leaning back into his chair as he prepared what he had to say. "Thomas, we have a…a different trip to discuss."

"A different trip?" he asked while Liza brought him a plate filled with eggs, bacon, and toast. "God please don't take me back to Italy. Once was more than enough."

"Missing Rome, then?" Edward chuckled, the memory of it stinging more than Thomas actually grasped. "No, I definitely have no intention of returning to Rome anytime soon. I…well…I did something you won't be happy about, and I apologize for my lack of…propriety."

Thomas' left eyebrow raised, his fork stopping halfway to his lips. "What do you mean…?"

Edward pulled the letter from the Madame out of his jacket pocket and slid it across the table to his son. "Please don't be angry with me."

Thomas stared at the letter, and his eyes didn't leave it as he spoke: "So we're going to New York, then?"

"Yes. Are you upset with me?"

Thomas went back to eating. "Not really, considering I paid Robert to leave it on your tray." He casually glimpsed up with a quick smirk. "I also apologize for being deceptive. But in light of your honesty, I thought I would be honest too."

"I...I don't...why?"

"I couldn't wait any longer, Father. It's been eight years. And I knew you needed to make the decision on your own terms."

Dead silence followed, and before he could stop himself, Edward burst into a fit of laughter. "For Christ's sake, Thomas! Did you plot this on your own?"

He could see a wave of delight hit Thomas as he spoke. "Don't forget whose shadow I was raised in," he reminded Edward coyly.

"Ah. So it was her idea then?"

"Of course it was. Let's face it, she can never do anything like a normal person."

The two continued their breakfast merrily, talking over their options and the length of their stay, each of their transgressions forgiven and forgotten instantly. They would remain in New York through the fall in an effort to avoid the storm season and be home just prior to Christmas, hoping to convince William and Lucy to come home with them for the following winter months. Edward made certain to emphasize that, while it was an extended visit for them, their number one priority would be business expansion, and if Thomas did well in New York he could make his excursions back and forth from England more frequent. From the expression on his son's face, Edward could tell this was a welcome prospect, and Thomas accepted his father's proposition with a grin. It was a good play for Edward to keep Thomas' business sense working with a set goal in mind, and with any luck, it might keep him out of trouble.

"I will write to the White Star Line today," Edward declared, jotting down a few notes as he sipped the last of his tea. "I think they are sending ships once every two weeks, so my estimate for our departure would be the third week of May."

Thomas nodded. "You know, we should really go to London and make sure everything is in order before we leave. I trust our contacts there, but a personal touch should keep them in line until we are back."

"All right. Off tomorrow, then?" Edward posed.

Another nod. "And we'll head to Liverpool from London?"

"Exactly."

"Well. Better say our goodbyes today, then," he responded, without any hint of remorse.

"Charlotte's should only be an hour ride, even with the rain. You could make that easily in the coach," Edward offered, already anticipating his son's response. Thomas had been courting a young girl named Charlotte for weeks while she was staying with their neighbors, the Hartfords. She was young, beautiful, and witty, and her family spent most of the year in London with the occasional summer in Bath, living off their long-standing family inheritance. Edward could tell Thomas did not love her, and that it was more the enjoyment of her company he sought rather than a long-term obligation; at any rate, Edward was happy to see him in pursuit, as the idea of grandchildren and family began to have a larger presence in his mind despite being years away.

Thomas tossed his napkin on the table. "Christ. I...I haven't told you. I told Charlotte last week we would only be friends, and like you would expect, she did not take it well. Serves me right, I suppose. It's not like I promised her anything."

"If you weren't going to marry her, there was no reason to lead her on," Edward imparted. "The right one will come along eventually."

"Eventually," Thomas repeated. "After the last few, I think a little break would do me some good. They've all been a little..."

"Eccentric?" Edward suggested. The string of young girls Thomas spent his time chasing were the life of every party, and as a result, exhaustingly extroverted...to a fault. Edward wouldn't let Thomas off the hook either, and teased him about it every chance he got.

Thomas scoffed. "The only women I've ever been around have been eccentric!"

"Well let's hope you can find one that doesn't drive us too mad."

"I'll do my best. But I'm not making any promises."

Sometime later when their planning had ended, Edward went out to find Hiroaki and let him know of his resolution in spending the summer away. Since Thomas came to England, Hiroaki and his wife, Akemi, had grown close with Thomas, treating him like their own son whenever he would take the time to visit with them. Their origins, however, they kept secret, only confiding in Thomas that they had once been refugees Edward smuggled away from China, which was at least a small portion of the truth. Akemi worked mainly in the kitchens and gardens, and while she got along well with the other female staff, she kept quietly to herself, staying separate from the household gossip and drama. Edward never pressed Hiroaki for any specifics regarding what the Chinese did to Akemi while she was in captivity – he had noticed on numerous occasions that she always wore long sleeves and pants despite the rising temperatures of the long summer days. One excruciatingly hot afternoon, her tunic was rolled up by chance during her harvest of the garden, and Edward saw thick, weaving scars on her arms, scars that were reminiscent of the hundreds of healed burns he'd witnessed throughout his time in the Royal Navy. Edward could only assume from what he saw that the tortures Akemi suffered were far beyond what most men could withstand, and it was a humbling reminder he wasn't the only soul on Earth taxed with tragedy.

He found Hiroaki in the stables tending to one of Edward's geldings, which had gone lame after slipping out in the drenched, muddy fields a few weeks before. Because of Hiroaki's great aptitude with horses, the gelding was miraculously a few days away from perfect health when he was originally expected to be put down for such a traumatic injury. The amount of useful knowledge in Hiroaki's brain recurrently fascinated Edward, and often made him contemplate what his friend was like prior to the devastations the war brought upon his family.

Edward stood outside the stall with a smirk, watching Hiroaki massage the tension from the horses back leg, sensing his friend could perceive his company without an introduction.

"Good morning, Edward," Hiroaki said, without even a peek his direction.

"And just how did you know it was me?" he demanded, crossing his arms and leaning against the stall door.

"I just do. Your spirit feels lighter this morning. What news do you have for me?"

"I am going to take Thomas back, Hiro. For the summer."

Hiroaki's hands left the horse's thigh and he turned to look at Edward. "To New York, I assume you mean?"

"Yes, to New York, and I would like you and Akemi to assume the household in our absence to keep everything in order."

"I would be honored, Edward," he answered, though his countenance remained solemn "My only concern is for you, and whether or not you are mentally prepared for the journey ahead."

Somewhat offended, Edward wasn't able respond for a few seconds. "Mentally prepared? What are you getting at?"

"You told me that the risk would always be too great for both of you to allow Thomas a homecoming."

Edward went on to digress Louis' letter. "I trust him, Hiro. He would not break my confidence. Not for the Madame's sake."

"This man who works for the woman who betrayed you? Multiple times?"

"He did not always work for her, you know."

"This is so much trust for someone who has been absent from your life for many years. How could you ever be sure?"

Hiroaki was testing him, and Edward felt his fists unintentionally clench. "I am unquestionably sure," he declared through gritted teeth. "Louis is not that type of man, don't forget that."

Hiroaki's gaze did not break. "I can feel your frustration all the way over here, Edward. I am only asking to help prepare you. What is this stemming from? Fear?"

"And where is this verbal assault on my person stemming from?" Edward shot back. "I am only doing what is best for my son."

"Are you sure you believe that?" Hiroaki rose and moved toward him. "Or are you hoping for something more? I'm the only one who knows what really happened on that day, Edward. The only one save for the Madame. You left to protect Thomas from things beyond your control. Who is to say this fire has not died out?"

"If Louis says it is safe, it is safe."

Hiroaki's head tilted to the side. "Are you so certain? I want you to see every angle, Edward. This is how I've been trained, and how I have trained you. I am not implying your choice to go to New York is the wrong one, I am only wanting you to see the bigger picture."

"There is no bigger picture!" Edward growled. "There is nothing to be ready for, Hiro. Can't you see that? It's over. It's bloody over. I came here with happy, positive news and you trample all over it with your own God damn hypocrisy. I won't have it! Quit trying to drag me under the water with you – I am done drowning in my own misery. It's time for me to breathe again."

Without another word, he stormed out of the stables, wanting nothing more than to hit Hiroaki as hard as he could; however, before Edward was even ten yards out, a strong hand took hold of his arm, and Hiroaki spun Edward around so that they were chest to chest with a strength that was more tremendous than Edward recalled.

"Don't misunderstand, me," his friend whispered under his breath, their faces only inches apart. "I just want you to know your enemy, as I have taught you so many times. And the hardest enemy we often have to face is ourselves."

"You seem to have lost your touch with reading people, my friend," Edward argued. "You have read me quite wrong. I have moved on. Thomas is my only priority, and he will remain my only priority. Now, get your bloody hands off me."

Edward yanked his arm free, cheeks hot with rage, and he left Hiroaki standing in his wake. "We leave tomorrow!" he yelled back as he ambled up toward the house, more and more insecure with each step whether Hiroaki had actually lost his intuition, or if Edward was ignorant of his own susceptibility.

Hours later, while burying his frustrations at the bottom of a bottle, Edward could no longer ignore the growing elephant in the room. He had already written to the Madame and to William of their approaching trip and their plan to stay until the frost came in. Five months in New York seemed a sufficient amount of time for now, and he informed the Madame that Thomas' trips would be a regular commodity with the prerequisite being she kept her business, and all her bullshit, to herself. Edward smirked – he had a feeling that would not go over very well, and with Thomas' company as a hostage, it had the potential to backfire on him. But for the time being, he thought it best to make the Madame understand his son was his and his alone, and her powers of persuasion no longer had the same effects they did when he was a boy.

The lingering reflection of his fight with Hiroaki persisted in taking over his thoughts, and Edward blamed the wine for his inability to suppress it. Hiroaki made his points well – he was the only one who knew about John, about the bar, the murders, and that the conspiracy was as much a reality as the rain falling outside. The bottom line, which Edward spent many nights convincing his heart of, was that Mary was dead. There was no reason to assume the worst, and despite the fact that he respected John's oath, justice was not something Edward sought in this matter. Hiroaki did not, and would not ever understand. Edward had his son. And that, he learned in the last eight years, was more than enough to keep him content.

Hiroaki was his master, the one man he could count on to mentally and physically push him and to further facilitate his self-introspection. A selfless, devoted teacher with no incentive other than Edward's welfare. Bearing those things in mind, his anger toward his friend began to die down. When Edward was stagnant, Hiroaki made his path for him, not allowing him the choice of regression and thus forcing him to use his talents to help others. They'd never had a mission go awry, though an accidental mishap in Rome on his trip with Thomas came close. Here Edward sat, distrusting the one person who in all their years together was steadfast at his side, prepared for whatever storm might come. Arguing was useless – neither would win, and it would only deepen the rift Edward now felt expanding between them. He needed Hiroaki, steady and resolute, to be his guide, even if he had given up their missions to be a better father.

Edward rang for Robert, and at once his page came into the den. "Will you do me a favor?" he asked. "Will you go and find Hiroaki and bring him to me?"

Robert hesitated. "Now? Right now?"

"Robert…"

"Of course, sir. Right away." He left hastily, tripping over his own feet as he scampered through the doorway. It took the better part of an hour, which Edward guessed was partially because Robert was both intimidated and slightly terrified by Hiroaki's company. Somehow, however, Robert managed to fulfill Edward's request, and eventually Hiroaki made his way into the den.

"Please, do sit down," Edward offered, and his friend complied, taking the glass of wine Edward gave him. "I owe you an apology, Hiro. I know what you said today was only out of worry, but please, trust me when I tell you I know what I am doing."

Hiro, too, was seeking forgiveness. "I was irrational and impulsive with my remarks, Edward. Please accept my apology as well. You are right – I am often hypocritical in what I say to you because of what I have lost, and what I endured following my daughter's death. I know what Thomas means to you, and I know you would not put him in harm's way." He took a sip of wine. "That does not mean, however, you do not need to work on governing your emotions. We will work on this when you return in the winter."

Edward was grateful Hiroaki never held a grudge. "Always teaching. A true master."

His friend bowed his head slightly. "The need for lessons never fades. For any of us."

"Well, I am certainly happy we came to such a quick resolution." Edward rested into his chair, at ease after a long and stressful day. "For the sake of our reputations at the household I think we should tell everyone there were at least a few punches involved."

Hiroaki smiled from behind his wine glass. "Because the staff needs more of a reason to fear us?"

He overlooked Hiroaki's protestation. "I mean, everyone saw our little scuffle on the lawn today. Might as well keep the rumors swirling for our benefit…"

"Edward, I am not sure that would be as beneficial as you think. Robert can barely look me in the eyes."

"Damn him, I thought he was improving. Did he cry again?"

"No, I think that phase has finally passed," Hiroaki conceded, then leaned closer with more to say. "There is something else I would like to discuss with you. Something in regards to Thomas which we have not brought up in some time."

"What is it, my friend?"

Taking a deep breath, Hiroaki set his wine glass gently on the side table next to his chair. "I would like to ask again for your permission to train Thomas."

Edward's defenses rose. "No, Hiroaki. My thoughts on that matter have not changed."

"Edward, New York is a war zone. Anything I teach him would only be for his benefit and protection. Nothing more."

"My son grew up on those streets Hiroaki," Edward said, aggravated. "He knows them better than anyone. I don't want him seeking out conflicts, and I know Thomas can take care of himself. Do you not remember the episode in Rome that almost got us killed? My answer is, and always will be, no."

Hiroaki was attempting to play the disaster down. "The debauchery you refer to is a repercussion of a prior mission. Thomas' safety was at risk, and you recovered without incident. It was only for a moment, Edward, and if he does have the skills we do, it would have never been so catastrophic in the first place."

"In that process, Hiro, my son was nearly murdered in the street! Or have you forgotten? It's a blessing he hasn't asked any questions about it after the half-hearted explanation we botched coming up with."

"And you suppose a man who is nearing twenty-six years old cannot make the decision on his own? Is this really your choice to make?"

Edward slammed his fist on his desk. "It is my God damned decision, Hiroaki! He is my son, not yours! Why are you pushing this so bloody hard with me again?"

"My traditions are not purely violent, Edward, they are there for better human understanding. It is a physical, mental, and spiritual unison. He has the potential to use the lessons in life I have to offer and do great things, just as you have."

"Hiro, you are not that man anymore. You haven't been that man for two decades."

Hiroaki exhaled, defeated. "Edward, I will be that man until the day I die. It's a code of ethics I live by, not something you can follow when the time is suitable. You yourself have lost track of much of the education I've provided you with because you lack that comprehension."

"I won't deny that," Edward stated. "And it has been a blessing to have your wisdom and your words to guide me when I am lost. But please, Hiro, respect my decision, for our friendship's sake. I don't want to open that world to Thomas. I want to have the hope that he will live his life without any more hostility. If we show him, and you teach him as you've taught me, his world will never be the same. And like me, he won't be able to sit in the shadows. You know Thomas, and you know I am right."

"Then maybe it is his destiny to do so. Would you really want to stand in his way if he could help others? If he could improve the world around him?"

"I am his father," Edward asserted. "It is my right to determine these things. Now please, this discussion is over. Let's stop our rowing and talk through these summer months. We have a lot to go over before our departure, and my temper is on the verge of exploding."

Seeing he would get nowhere, Hiroaki dropped the subject at Edward's request, and dutifully obliged him in running through the necessities of Amberleigh Manor in Edward's absence. Though he tried to put it out of his mind, Edward felt increasingly wary. He couldn't remember a time when he and Hiroaki were so severe with one another, and the visit to New York had been a catalyst for what he could only assume was years of apprehension. For the first time in a long time, Edward deemed that Hiroaki's arguments were extremely unreasonable and out of the blue – desperate even. It wasn't like him to throw things at Edward after being politely asked not to, and Edward hoped whatever was going on underneath, his friend could let it go by morning.

Edward wandered back upstairs to the library and found Thomas already there on the couch, sipping brandy and smoking a cigar by the fireplace. A poured glass sat on the side table next to his empty armchair, along with a cigar and matches. Edward grinned.

"Took you long enough," Thomas joked. "You and Hiroaki settle things?"

"I'd like to think so," Edward countered, sinking down into

his chair. "There are some issues we simply won't ever agree on. I think he is nervous we are leaving him here for such an extended period of time."

Thomas took a puff of his cigar. "Don't be so hard on him, father. Our culture is in such a contrast to theirs, I think he would lose his mind if he ever had to live in a city again…to deal with all the stench, dirt, and grime. It amazes me that Western culture thinks his people are the animals when clearly it's the other way around. What was the riff over? I can't think of another time seeing you two at each other's throats so much."

"The suddenness of our trip, that is all," Edward lied, having a sip of brandy. "He is nervous I'm going back. Apparently I'm a head case."

Thomas became serious. "Father, you are not a head case."

"The bigger issue, I think, is that he worries I am not letting you make your own decisions for your future."

"Well I think I can call bullshit on that one. I have not done anything in the past eight years I did not want to or felt was necessary to reach my goals."

Edward studied Thomas. "You're sure?"

"Don't be ridiculous," Thomas exclaimed. "You've never forced me to do anything! This has been entirely on my own, and it's been what I've wanted from the start."

"All right, all right," Edward replied, feeling better than he had all night. "How are you feeling about New York? Excited?"

"In a way, yes. And in other ways, I guess I can admit I'm a little on edge." Thomas inclined forward and rested his forearms on his legs, staring into the bottom of his glass as he swished the brandy around casually. It was the posture that had become a habit when he brought up a subject with Edward he was reluctant to talk about.

"Is this about Esther? And her stopping her letters?"

"I just don't understand. Two years and no response. And it's not as if she told me she didn't want to hear from me. Her letters got distant…formal, I should say, as if I were an acquaintance and not a friend. She used to be so willing and happy to tell me everything that went on, and after a few of her correspondences came in that manner they halted altogether."

Edward stood up and walked toward the fire, trying to hide his amusement. He had a few ideas as to what might be the cause, and one specifically that seemed the most plausible. It wasn't nearly as complex as Thomas made it out to be, and he had gone back and forth regarding the best guidance to give Thomas in such a situation. After delaying near the heat of the flames, Edward went over to grab the bottle of brandy from the drink cart and returned, filling Thomas' glass. Perhaps it was best that he let his son figure this one out on his own.

"My only advice to give you, Thomas, is to consider everything Esther has been through in such a short time," he put plainly. "She's lost her mother, Mary, and you, and had been transferred between three different households before she was a teenager. She's also eighteen, and probably does not think you will ever come back to New York, not to mention she will be married off as quickly as possible by Catherine Hiltmore. Do not take it to heart. Talk with her when you arrive, and I think you'll find your answer."

Thomas looked appeased by Edward's advice. "You're right. I'm getting ahead of myself." His voice immediately converted into a thick British accent. "I must be firm in my resolve and prosper on in America! Our invasion shall be a happy one, even if we did get our assess kicked by a bunch of farmers with pitch forks…"

"All right, that's enough of that," Edward ordered with a chuckle, holding up his hand. "You don't have Lucy here to protect you from the wrath of my British bloodlines."

Thomas laughed, shaking his head. "I know. I just couldn't help myself. Actually, father, can I ask you a favor?"

"Anything."

"Can I have a few days following our arrival to make my visits? I know we are going for work, but I could use a day or so to make my rounds. I haven't seen the Madame or Louis…or Esther in so long… there is a part of me that's…well…hopeful things may have changed. Maybe now, after I've been gone so long, she will be different."

"The she you're referring to being the Madame?"

"Yes."

"Well, I'd place a wager the vampire woman won't have aged a damn day," Edward affirmed, causing Thomas to almost snort brandy down his shirt. When he recovered, Edward went on in a more solemn tone: "Thomas, I don't want you to have unrealistic expectations. That woman hasn't changed in the slightest in the time I've known her. I don't want you to be disappointed."

Thomas' delight faded. "I know I shouldn't delude myself in hoping things are different. Sometimes, I just wish she were…"

"Normal?" Edward suggested.

"Yeah. Normal."

"Like you mentioned this morning, Thomas, she simply isn't normal. The Madame runs a whorehouse, launders money on the side, and has a life-long business built on bribery and extortion with the wealthy and powerful. The presumption that she might ever act normal is just a tad out of the question, don't you think?"

"Well you can't fault me for wanting the best in people," he said, his smirk returning as he held up his glass. "Here's to the un-conventional."

Edward held his up in salute. "Unconventional? I think the word you're actually looking for is nefarious. And that's being kind."

Edward couldn't sleep – he tossed and turned in his bed, unable to find comfort in body or mind. The evening had ended on a positive note, and he and Thomas parted after a long night of taunts and jests in great spirits. What bothered him were the words and opinions Hiroaki shared, not once but twice that day, hence making him rethink some of the biggest steps he'd taken over the years. This argumentative side of his friend was not one he was used to. Hiroaki saw something bigger in life than Edward did: a life centered on purpose and dignity, two of the key things Edward grappled with in the time before Thomas, and if he was candid, a few times after. Following his son's arrival at Amberleigh Manor, Edward let several of his teachings go, with his sole intention and desire aiming to facilitate a world for his son where Thomas could thrive on his own, in a world without Edward's ghosts constantly nipping at their ankles. Rome had been that wake up call. What Edward couldn't decipher was the aim behind Hiroaki's logic – his way of thinking was off course, including his mention of training Thomas when the two had settled that battle long ago. Something did not make sense, and as much as he wanted to forget about it, he could not allow it to slide. Edward resolved he would wake an hour before dawn and seek out Hiroaki, who in all likelihood would be awaiting his presence. His master knew Edward too well, and he had a hunch it was Hiroaki's intention to make Edward come to him.

Just as the sky started to lighten, Edward rose and dressed quickly, his mind spinning with presumptions. Once his boots were on, Edward silently snuck from his bedroom and down the back staircase, through the kitchen to the garden door of the eastern wing. It was drizzling outside in the thick morning air, and Edward cursed as he ambled down the dark path to Hiroaki's home, the stones slick from the unremitting all-night rainstorm. He caught himself almost falling three or four times, only building his eagerness, and he made a mental note to have every pathway on the property be redone come the fall season. On his approach to the cottage, Edward noticed a fire burning in the window, and the shadow of Akemi filtered through moving to and fro. It genuinely was Hiroaki's objective from the start to lure Edward in privately, and the plethora of his questions fused together in to one: what was it that made Hiroaki so fearful of his return to New York?

Then, for a brief moment, Edward seriously considered turning around and going back to the house. He had reached the gate and rested his hand lightly on the latch, deliberating on what good it might do him, or what harm, to hear what his friend had to say. There would be no placation in Hiroaki's words, as there hadn't been during their multiple disputes throughout the afternoon. Somehow, Edward came around with the realization that he needed the closure from Hiroaki; in their years together, the man had yet to steer him wrong, even when Edward couldn't see the true purpose behind it. Instead of disregarding the signs, he pushed the gate open and walked through, and as it swung shut behind him, the front door creaked open, illuminating the path in front of him.

Akemi stood in the doorway, a sad smile on her face, beckoning him inside. Edward paced down the entranceway and stepped over the threshold, taking his shoes off as he always did, and shut the door behind him. The koatsu was already heating tea, giving the room an aroma of ginger and lemon, and a pot of rice was reaching a boil next to the kettle. Looking around, Edward saw a fire blazing from the hearth in their sitting room down the hall, where Hiroaki most likely sat patiently in meditation. To his left was their tiny table, built low to the ground and meant for its diners to kneel in their places. The walls of the cottage were decorated with paintings, even more beautiful than the ones covering them through the winter months. Each piece was filled with color and brightness, portraying a different garden with a slew of flowers, trees, and Japanese pavilions. Akemi was their artist, and Edward marveled at their details, wondering if the scenes came from her imagination or from her memory. They made him feel as if he were in a dream.

"I told him you would come," Akemi murmured to Edward, checking the rice. "He is not so serene sometimes, you know this."

She had never been so direct with him. "Yes, I know what you mean. Shall I go to him?"

Akemi nodded. "Edward…try not to be angry. I made him do this. To protect you and Tommy."

"Why would I be angry?" he asked, startled.

"You will see. I will bring tea soon."

Edward crept down the hallway to find Hiroaki kneeling on the floor with his hands resting on his knees, eyes closed in concentration. Likewise, Edward sat on the ground beside him and tried to clear his mind, as he'd done a thousand times before, holding the stillness until his friend thought it best to speak. The warmth of the fire was a comfort from the damp cold outside, and with his master there with him, Edward's thoughts went blank in perfect harmony, focusing on nothing other than the moment he was in.

"I have hidden something from you," Hiroaki announced aloud with his eyes still closed.

"I could gather something was amiss. It is what has brought about your alarm with my leaving?" Edward inquired, also remaining at rest.

"Yes. I wanted to destroy it, but I know it would do you a great injustice if I did."

Edward rotated to face Hiroaki, and his friend's eyelids flickered open, locking Edward's gaze. Hiroaki turned around to grab something that lay behind him, and then placed it on the floor in front of Edward.

"Forgive me, my friend."

It was an envelope dispatched for Edward without any return address, and the wax seal had been broken. He picked it up and opened it, trying to remain calm despite his shaking hands:

Lord Turner,

I sought you out in New York and thankfully was given your residence address in England from your cousin, but have no fear he does not believe me to be any more than a friend. I wanted to reach you because I am once again trying to

build my case, and if you are still willing, your statement could assist us in our
cause. If you are up for the task, you know where to find me.
    J.E.

Edward read it in utter disbelief, empathetic as to why Hiroaki wanted to keep it secret, and also why he could not any longer. John was writing to tell him that somehow, after biding their time, his enterprise had rebuilt and found a way to uncover evidence, and possibly prosecute the people behind Mary's death. After all these years, John was summoning him for retribution, yet that wasn't what struck Edward hardest.

"This letter is eight months old," Edward contended heatedly. "You had no right to hide this from me. None whatsoever."

"Please, Edward. Do not be willing to throw yourself into the depths of hell when you have just climbed out. There is nothing in this that speaks of Mary, or that they have any solid evidence to put away her real killers."

"Hiro, stop—"

"No, I am not finished!" Hiroaki's tone escalated and was unyielding, forcing Edward to retreat and hold his tongue. "You are being tricked if you do not see what this will do. You left New York the first time to protect Thomas and your family. Even if what John has written is true, these people will be stronger and fight harder knowing they are cornered, just like a wild animal. I don't want you to endure what I have and watch your family die in your arms. You have the power to change that."

Hiroaki's lips pursed, his eyes like windows to an aching soul. Akemi remained motionless in the doorway, a tray of tea in her hands, the tension in the room thickening with each passing second. Edward did not know how to react — he had dropped John's letter onto the floor in front of him at the shock of hearing the uncharacteristic force in Hiroaki's voice. It took a few moments before Edward grasped it was a confused misinterpretation because he had

290

been too stubborn to share his own judgments with the one person who needed that affirmation. What his friend did not seem to have a handle on was Edward's own resolute attitude that no piece of paper might change. This was nothing but a taunt, a temptation that would have no happy ending for anyone involved. Edward's mind had been made up long ago, and it was obvious the person who did not need convincing was himself. It was Hiroaki he needed to reassure, his friend who cared for him more than he cared for his own well-being. He had been carrying this burden for months, a terrible dishonor Edward was well aware had been tearing him apart on the inside, only to shield Edward from the demons Hiroaki was unaware had already been vanquished.

Edward snatched up the letter into his hands and crumpled it into a ball, throwing it immediately into the fireplace. "Please listen to me," he pleaded, standing to address both husband and wife. "I will not make the same mistakes I made before. I made a vow no matter what the cost, Thomas' future and safety would trump any need or desire I have. I was only upset you did not come to me sooner and hid something from me. You have been punishing yourself for nothing, my friend. I go to New York for the last time with Thomas to guarantee his legacy, and then I will come home for good."

Hiroaki spoke first. "And if John comes to you? What will you do then?"

"I will tell him what I've told you. I'm too old for these dangerous games, even something as simple as a personal statement is too precarious. My son is the only thing that matters to me anymore."

Hiroaki's eyes watered as he looked at Edward, and after a moment they fell toward the floor. "I wish I had made the same choice when I had the opportunity, Edward." He paused, taking a moment to collect his final thoughts, and when he spoke his words were strong once again. "As your teacher, I have never been more proud of you, and I was wrong when I said you had lost the way of the warrior. You are more honorable and more dutiful to the cause than I could

291

perceive. I am sorry for my ill judgment, and I hope you will accept my apology. If you would so permit me, I will happily take my own life for this betrayal of trust, wanting nothing more than your forgiveness for my own humiliation and disgrace." He bowed his head in salute as Akemi came in and put down the tray of tea in front of them, Hiro's sheathed dagger beside the pot.

Edward hated when he did this. "I refuse to accept your offer, and you will remain alive at Amberleigh until I return. Your apology, however, is accepted wholeheartedly, and I do not want you to dwell any further on the matter."

"If that is what you wish, I will readily comply."

"It is what I wish. Damn you, Hiro, I told you not to ever ask that of me again."

"You have the full right to change your mind at any time."

"Like hell I will."

His friend had offered his own death as tribute, something Hiroaki was accustomed to yet Edward always had a difficulty understanding about his people. It was a perspective Edward understood little about, other than through the teachings Hiroaki provided. When they were young, Edward preyed on the topic of his master's youth many times only to be refused by Hiroaki, for reasons he would never specify. The only thing he ever confided in Edward was a history of his brother, who transformed from a life of goodness and virtue to treachery and greed. It was because of him Hiroaki was exiled and could never go home, and it was because of him Hiroaki's life was marked with sadness much like Edward's.

"Why do we do these things, knowing we are punishing ourselves?" Edward asked Hiroaki. "Why is it that one, small mistake can change the rest of our lives? I have spent so much time wanting to change something unchangeable. Only in Thomas have I at last found peace. Why is it so difficult to let go?"

Hiroaki set his cup of tea back on the tray. "Let me leave you with some words my own teacher used to say. Every cause has an effect. There are moments in our lives, whether we realize it or not, when we stumble to a fork in our path. From there, no matter which direction we choose, there is no return. This is what seals our fate, and our futures, with consequences that ripple out and touch others, even those we do not know. I chose my path, just as you have many times, and we must live with it believing it was a part of our destiny to do so."

"And how will I know when I have done what I am destined to do?"

Hiroaki picked up the kettle and poured Edward a cup of tea. "Every being is different. I cannot tell you for certain – you will feel it in your bones, an all-consuming sense of fulfillment. But first, you must make moves toward an inner purpose. What do you want from the rest of your life, Edward? That is the question you must answer."

"I am content with the idea that I will do everything to ensure Thomas' future," Edward proclaimed. "And as a father, I am quite sure that is all I could ever hope for."

Hiroaki smiled. "Then that, my old friend, is your destiny."

XI.

The great hallways of the Adams residence rang loudly with the howls of laughter echoing from the breakfast room. Esther and Celeste were just rising from a very late Saturday evening out on the town, joined by Celeste's new mother-in-law and sister-in-law. They ladies spent the entire night before at the Admiral's Ball, one of the biggest parties to kick off the summer months, and the four women slept in just enough to wear off a bit of the endless amount of champagne they consumed until the early morning hours. The kitchen staff dutifully prepared the ladies Celeste's usual favorite following a long evening out: strong coffee, lemon bread, and bacon. They had eagerly taken their fill and now sat reflecting on the exciting developments and gossip that had sprung from the ball, all trying to distract Celeste from what had been an embarrassing public argument with her husband, who had yet to return home. Only Esther and Celeste knew where he most likely was, and while Celeste had spiraled into a state of denial regarding her husband's antics, Esther was finding it harder than ever to hide her disgust.

Not six months prior, Celeste was married to the young and handsome Mr. Timothy Adams, and it was one of the most beautiful and extravagant weddings New York City had ever seen. Three weeks passed before the papers finished their reporting on the nuptials – Celeste and the inherently wealthy Timothy were a match years in the making, and Esther had never seen Mrs. Hiltmore more proud of her daughter. At Celeste's request, though much to the disdain of Catherine, Esther was in the wedding at her best friend's side. It didn't matter – Esther's heart broke with every passing second in anticipation of what was in store for her friend, and hating herself for not being able to warn her of what was to come next.

After a month or so of wedding bliss, Celeste begged Esther to join her at their new residence on Fifth Avenue under the false pretenses she missed her old bedmate and best friend. Esther was aware of the truth, as the Madame told her many times Timothy's real nature was in close comparison with his father. Celeste's husband was almost worse than Charles. He was a drunkard, an asshole, and enjoyed roughing his wife up after a night out with his bastard friends. His late nights were occasionally spent at The Palace, where the Madame would have to constantly drug him to keep him bearable for her services, otherwise her girls would leave the room bruised and battered. In this case, the apple clearly did not fall far from the tree. Esther implored the Madame repeatedly to refuse his attendance, but she rebuffed – it was good money, and his family had grown too powerful to refuse service, at least for the time being, and this frustrated Esther even more. Celeste was terrified and trapped in an abusive marriage, only finding solace in Esther and resolving not to tell anyone else her secret in fear for the reputation of herself and the Hiltmore family.

Then, four weeks ago, Esther's entire world changed, and her time of tolerating Timothy came to an abrupt and appalling end.

In the beginning, Timothy Adams never paid Esther any attention, scarcely acknowledging her presence in his household. Esther was there for months without even receiving a sideways glance from him; in spite of that and out of nowhere four weeks ago, Timothy snuck into her rooms and into her bed, overpowering her as she woke from slumber and nearly suffocated her to subdue Esther's screams for help. He'd torn away at her nightdress as he undid his trousers in a terrifyingly practiced fashion, and it was with dread that Esther understood what was actually happening. Timothy forced himself on top of her and inside her, holding Esther's mouth closed with one hand and her arms trapped above her head with his other, and Esther's struggle for breath weakened her battle against him. While she desperately tried to break free, writhing in his clutches, Esther felt some of the hair tear out of her head, caught in his grip on her wrists. A muted shriek escaped her lips which was stifled by Timothy's palm. Timothy didn't say a word: the only thing Esther could hear other than her muffled cries was Timothy's hot, panting breath in her ear. No matter how hard she battled, Timothy eventually won out, and in the aftermath as Esther lay on her bed battered and aching from head to toe, he rolled off her and stumbled out, slamming the door shut behind him.

The incident hadn't lasted long, and later the next morning after hours of shaking and sobbing in the corner of her bed, Esther spun into a state of denial. She swore it must have been some kind of horrifying nightmare, and after spending hours staring at the shredded remains of her nightdress piled in the middle of her floor, she eventually found the courage to burn what was left of the gown in her bedroom's small fireplace. The bruises on her wrists, breasts, and abdomen were a deep shade of blue amongst her porcelain skin, and far harder to hide from Celeste than a lost nightdress. Through careful disguises of her clothing, Esther concealed her wounded body from her friend as she healed, yet not without a few close calls with their maid, Laura, as Esther was being dressed in the mornings. Esther assured Laura repeatedly that the bruises were simply from falling out of the tub, and the maid didn't question her further.

At first, her excuse remained that the incident must have been a drunken mistake…that Timothy meant to be in Celeste's room and was incapable of telling the difference because of his inebri-ated state. Until a week later, when Timothy cornered Esther and threatened to kill her if she ever told a soul. He then proceeded to verbally terrorize Esther, insulting her in every possible way and re-minding her that she owed most of her newfound prosperity to him. Timothy had no misgivings reminding Esther that if word got out, with her innocence taken and without any money of her own, her value in an advantageous marriage had disappeared. It didn't mat-ter if he was the cause or not. She would be considered ruined and consequently, shunned from society.

Following this berating, Esther was so scared she hid in her room the rest of the day and that evening, wracking her brain for some means to run away or to erase that horrible night from her remem-brance, but she couldn't. The danger of her circumstances was so severe that Esther chose not to tell a soul until the risk subsided... if that day should ever come. What she couldn't come to grips with was why the occasion occurred in the first place.

As a consequence of Timothy's assault, Esther bolted her door shut every night since, incapable of sleep and listening intently with the slightest creak or blow of the wind to be certain it wasn't him coming back to take advantage of her again. It was hard to accept that she had been raped – she'd lost her virginity to a man she de-spised, who took that and her dignity away in an ungodly and bru-tal manner. What was worse was the notion that Esther could not escape Timothy or the prison she found herself trapped within. No one would believe her, and if Celeste or even the authorities chose to hear her out, it was her word against his, and Esther was afraid in this scenario her best friend would take her husband's side. The law definitely would. She would be homeless, abandoned on the streets without a penny to her name, other than what the Madame would give her out of mercy. However, four weeks had come and gone, and Esther was at last starting to find her fortitude. No...she would find a way to get rid of him on her own. This was her life, and she would take care of herself as she'd been taught. She was a fighter, like the Madame, and she would be damned if she let Timothy Adams have that kind of power over her.

Everyday life had become a sick routine, with Esther doing whatever she could to ease Celeste's pain after Timothy would come home belligerently intoxicated and both verbally and physically abuse her. Celeste would always have Esther prepare a steaming hot bath to ease away the bruises, and Esther used a remedy Hope mixed for her to help the breaks in the skin heal faster than anything a doctor could manage to concoct. When the trouble passed, Celeste would rise up again and be her usual self, cool and reserved enough to be sure no one suspected anything was wrong, and Esther followed suit. Timothy's attack of Esther made her see just what her friend lived through on a daily basis, and astonishingly as the weeks went on, Esther discovered no part of her felt victimized. Instead, somehow throughout her years of working with the Madame, Esther was ingrained with a fierce survivor mentality, and there was only one thing she now sought: revenge. She would see to it that bastard paid for what he did to her, and for what he'd done to Celeste. But until the moment presented itself, Esther found the one way she could stay sane was pretending it never happened, and that seemed to keep her temperament in it's normal state. Like the Madame taught her, she had to be resilient. And like the Madame, Esther swore to God she would get rid of him in one way or another.

"My dear Esther, why can we not find a suitable man for you?" Celeste's mother-in-law inquired, a mischievous grin on her face as she ate the last of her lemon bread. "You have had a number of attractive gentlemen seeking you out, or at least that is what Celeste has told us?"

Esther faked a gracious smile for being addressed. "There have been a few, Mrs. Adams, all wonderful gentlemen. I have just felt too young to be wed. I feel like I need more time to—"

"Nonsense," she interjected. "You are of an excellent age to be wed, and you cannot wait too long or you'll be deemed…well, let's put it kindly. People will think there is something the matter with you. No, I think we will set our sights on a husband for you next! Who was that handsome gentleman seeking your company last night? I believe he was a military man…"

"It was Captain Bernhardt!" Celeste exclaimed, jumping in with excitement. "He is so well-mannered…handsome…and he is very taken with Esther. He comes from a very wealthy American family in Vermont. A fantastic match for you, Es. I think he even said he would call on you later today, if I'm not mistaken?"

Esther could feel her cheeks flush, nodding in reply. Captain Bernhardt put forth a valiant effort to never leave Esther's side, and of the five dances she was obliged to undertake, four were with him. After Timothy's assault, Captain Bernhardt proved himself to be a valued distraction for Esther. They met at one of the Hiltmores' dinner parties, and since then Captain Bernhardt made certain to attend every social event she would, never taking his eyes off her. In the last year, Esther stomached a number of respectable young men competing for her attention, but there was something different in the way Captain Bernhardt spoke to her. Their discourse went beyond the typical small-talk and awkward chatter, and he sought to learn about her likes and dislikes rather than discussing his own qualifications, something not one of the others could understand would win her favor. It was endearing, and Esther had to admit she didn't mind his company or his interest. The only thing bothering her was the fact that she was wearing a mask, a mask she used to disguise herself amongst the upper class in New York, and she dreaded the thought of marrying a man who did not know who or what she really was underneath.

"Oh look at her, lost in thought, daydreaming about it," Mrs. Adam's daughter Henrietta squealed with a giggle. "Looks like we have some work to do, Mama."

"Oh no!" Esther protested. "It really was nothing, I can promise you. Just a silly inclination–"

"Esther, please," Celeste chimed in again. "I know that look. I have only seen you smitten with one other boy in your life, and this is exactly the same expression you wore last time."

Instantly, Celeste's lightheartedness subsided when she saw the look on Esther's horrified face, and her friend turned pink realizing her slip of the tongue. Henrietta and her mother were two of the loudest mouths in New York, and Celeste accidentally shared one of Esther's deepest secrets. She needed a recovery – a fast one.

"Well, well, well! I want to hear all about this other mystery man!" Mrs. Adams said with too much attentiveness. "Who was he, Esther?"

Esther discreetly eyed Celeste from across the table, giving her friend one unnoticeable shake of her head to indicate she personally would rescue the conversation. Celeste was mortified, and Esther sensed a storm of apologies would follow as soon as their company left. Internally, Esther was only upset with herself for trusting that information with anyone, hating that the Madame once again had been right.

Casually, Esther flicked her hair and rested back in her chair. "Oh years ago I was absolutely head over heels for one of Celeste's numerous potentials – she and I had a terrible fight over it one night, and then to our own shock, he was already married! Can you believe that? It was dreadful…and in the end, much more embarrassing than heartbreaking."

Across the table, Esther saw Celeste let out a tiny sigh of relief while the other two pressed further, Henrietta taking the lead. "And pray, tell us the name of this man from your love triangle?"

"We promised we would never tell," Celeste informed them. "Esther is so right. What a shameful scenario! And such an undeserving prick, if I do say so myself."

The Adams women gasped at hearing such a word escape Celeste's lips, and Esther couldn't help but laugh. "Very," she chuckled. "He was very undeserving."

With a smile, Celeste winked at her and changed the topic quickly to how hideously dressed the Mayor's wife was at the Ball, giving Esther time to recover as their customary gossip continued. She took a few deep breaths of reassurance, hoping Mrs. Adams and Henrietta would overlook Celeste's blunder as promptly as it had been brought up; and it only took minutes and the mention was long forgotten.

Not long after they finished breakfast, Henrietta and Mrs. Adams went out for the afternoon to join another group of ladies for a stroll to the boat house in Central Park. When they were gone, the girls retired to the sitting room, and Esther could see Celeste preparing an apology.

Immediately, Esther took her friend's hand in hers to stop it. "It's fine, Celeste. Really. There's no need."

"Yes there is, Es. I broke your trust and I am so sorry. I simply wasn't thinking and it just…slipped out!" she cried. "Please don't be angry with me."

"I am not angry in the slightest! Don't be ridiculous."

"You're sure?"

Esther gave her hand a small squeeze. "Of course I'm sure! Now, go play the piano while I paint. It helps me concentrate, and the new bundle of sheet music your father got for you is magnificent."

Cheerfully, Celeste did as she was told and floated toward the pianoforte, gracefully sitting herself on the bench as her fingers began to dance up and down the keys. Before she went to her easel at the window, Esther took a moment to watch her friend play, an odd sensation of grief flowing through her body. Everything had changed so much. Celeste was always the girl she wanted to be, the girl she had always been envious of and respected above anyone else – and those feelings disappeared when she discovered they were actually equals in inferiority. In her heart, Esther loved Celeste as if they were sisters, yet along with that love she felt immense pity. Celeste was betrothed to a brute, not realizing it until after their marriage was consummated, and spent most of her time with Timothy afraid of what he might do next. Regardless of having all the money in the world, Celeste lived in constant misery, and both she and Esther were shackled because of their gender. It was the life Catherine trained her for years to aspire toward; however currently, as she sat at the piano bench, Celeste was broken and falling apart to any person who would look close enough. The other basis for why Esther didn't want to marry was because she didn't want to be a prisoner, and that worry was enough to decline even the most generous offer. Witnessing Celeste stuck in this hell made Esther vow independence until the day she died – it was more of a comfort than to expect a future that could be vastly similar.

Heavy hearted, Esther got to her feet and went to her stool just a few feet from the piano, her painting half completed and begging her to be finished. She studied the landscape weeks in the making, a picture of endless rolling hills of green, bluffs jetting from the gradients, and a vast array of beautiful, brightly colored flowers. Whenever Esther painted, she included an immense amount of bold color where she could, wanting to pair the exotic with the everyday. The second she picked up her palette and brush, the world around her blurred to nothing, and Esther was able to put the trepidations of the previous few weeks out of her mind while she readied a perfect shade of molten scarlet.

She wasn't sure how long it'd been, but suddenly Esther was thrown from her dream-like fog with the fated slam of the front door, signaling the arrival of Timothy at home after his dramatic exit from last night's Ball. Celeste's face went white, her scared eyes finding Esther's, and slowly she pushed herself up to stand from the piano bench. After a moment, she hurriedly made her appearance more presentable, brushing off her skirts and impulsively fluffing her hair with a few well-rehearsed movements. Esther had to fight off a cringe, knowing her friend's radiance, notwithstanding how put together, wouldn't matter in the slightest to him.

"Husband? Is that you?" Celeste called sweetly, leaving Esther alone with her painting. There never came an answer, only the trudging of feet down the hallway and up the stairs, where Esther assumed he would pass out for the remainder of the day. Without warning, her memories flashed back to the agony of that night… the darkness…the fear and confusion. Chills ran down her skin as she pushed it away from her mind again, not wanting to ruin the best mood she'd been in since the incident.

Celeste trotted back in toward Esther. "I guess I should go upstairs and try to glaze this all over…perhaps it'd be best if you…"

"I am due for a visit with the Madame this afternoon," Esther declared, putting her paintbrush aside. "I hope it works out peacefully."

Celeste scoffed. "Hah! I doubt he will even be conscious." For a second, Celeste stayed motionless, so Esther did the same, ready for the lecture she'd grown accustomed to whenever she mentioned the Madame. "Es, please tell me why you are going to see her still? What could she possibly do to benefit you? Mother utterly despises that woman."

Not wanting to argue, Esther shrugged and took off toward the door to fetch her coat with Celeste disapprovingly behind her.

"Es, please. She is a bad influence. You have to see that!"

Esther rolled her eyes. "Don't forget that woman is the only reason you and I have each other, Celeste," Esther barked. "She's not bad, and she's been the only one aside from your family who gives a shit about me."

"Watch your language when you talk to me!" she exclaimed, then at once rescinded her temper. "Christ, I am sorry. I know she has been a great benefactor of yours, Es, but she is not…she is not of our station. You shouldn't confide in her or be spending so much time with her. It reflects badly on us, and she is not to be trusted."

"And your parents are so trustworthy?" Esther shot back harshly, turning to face her. "Where have either of your parents been since they dumped you with that fucking lunatic upstairs, Celeste?"

Celeste slapped her hard across the face. "Don't you dare question my parents after all they have done for you, Es."

Esther grabbed her cheek, trying to compose herself despite a fury rising in her chest. "I apologize...that was completely out of line. I did not mean it. I just...I don't like seeing what he does...to you. It's horrific, Celeste."

Feeling guilty for her brash actions, Celeste moved forward and wrapped her arms around Esther, pulling her in close. "I don't like it either. I can only hope he finds solace elsewhere, and that in a few years after I give him a few boys we can live completely separate lives. But until then, I have to deal with him. Go see the Madame but please be careful. And...well...I can only assume I will need a steam bath upon your return considering his mood. Should I at least get the carriage for you?"

"Don't say that..." Esther muttered. "And don't worry about the carriage. I think I could use a nice walk to the park. I'll be back soon. Stay strong...it'll be fine..."

A lie, but one Celeste needed to hear.

Celeste released her, her gaze on the floor while she mentally prepared for the worst. "I can take it. No different than any other day."

"No different," Esther repeated reassuringly, brushing the hair from Celeste's face. She gave Esther a half smile and shakily retreated the way Timothy had gone, and Esther painfully detected the small tremble in Celeste's hands at her sides as she went to see her husband.

Once outside in the warm sunlight, the air was buzzing as the high society of Fifth Avenue took to the streets on that exquisite summer morning. Being a Sunday, some were headed to mass, others out to mingle and socialize with friends, everyone chipper and happy to be about. Esther kept a brisk pace, giving polite hellos to a few acquaintances as she passed by, not in the particular humor to stop and talk over the glorious weather or the rumors already swirling after the Ball. To her, every conversation was the same bullshit, and that was followed by her customary excuse to exit and be on her way to confession when, on the contrary, Esther was headed to a whorehouse. Today, the irony of it was just a little much for her.

As she approached The Palace, Esther's eyes skimmed around to make sure no one saw her slip inside the front gate. On the exterior, it appeared like any other mansion-house close to Central Park. Beyond a first or second glance, however, it began to transform: the windows were oddly impenetrable by the human eye, and the new iron gates surrounding the front garden had spokes so sharp they could pierce the toughest of skin. No matter what, the front gate was closed and locked after nightfall, and a large French gentleman was the only regular resident to be seen on the premises keeping a careful eye out. At three stories tall, with a refined neoclassical style and being twice the width of the typical home on its block, The Palace was…unique. And while a woman might pass by and wonder what was hidden behind those walls, every wealthy man in New York with a taste for the publicly unsavory knew it was just the place to satisfy their cravings.

"Hello, Louis," Esther saluted as she pushed the front gate open. "Am I good?"

"No one for blocks," he replied. Esther could feel even from a distance that Louis was examining her still burning cheek from Celeste's slap, though thankfully he chose not to press her about it. "You look lovely this morning. She will be happy to see you."

Louis walked down the stoop and met Esther halfway, offering her his arm to escort her inside, which she took obligingly. After crossing the threshold, the entryway was abandoned, and Esther was certain the girls were sleeping after a busy Saturday night. Even while being overly familiar with the true nature of The Palace, Esther could never avoid an overwhelming sensation of enchantment as she made her way to the stairs, mainly with the knowledge that unlike most of its copycats, the décor in The Palace was in no way faux. Every piece was worth more than ten of her put together, from the artwork on the walls, to the hand sewn rugs covering the hardwood floors, to the glorious crystal chandelier that sparkled like the stars. A Palace… built for the luxury of royalty, and there really was no place like it.

Louis left her at the bottom of the staircase. "You will find her up in her office. She received some good news yesterday. It'll make you smile."

"Oh wonderful! From who, might I ask?"

"England," he conveyed emphatically. "Apparently we are having visitors soon."

Leaving it at that, Louis bowed graciously and returned to the front door, resuming his role of watchdog.

Esther was completely dumbfounded. She stood on the second stair, unable to move her legs, the shock of Louis' report more surprising than the slap she received from Celeste. It…it wasn't possible…it just couldn't be possible…

"Get up here, you stupid ninny," the Madame's voice boomed from upstairs. "I don't have all fucking day."

Snapping back, Esther rushed up the steps, not wanting the Madame to perceive the anxiety flooding through her body. The door to her office was cracked enough that Esther knew she had heard what Louis told her, and also most likely predicted Esther's reaction. Hurrying in, Esther closed the door behind her and went straight toward her usual armchair, flicking her hair out of her face to appear calm and lighthearted. The Madame sat at the adjacent loveseat on her right, a letter in one hand and a glass of wine in the other.

"Already started then?" Esther teased.

The Madame gave her a look that promptly shut Esther up. "There are glasses on the side table and a new bottle open. No is not a sufficient answer, darling."

"What's the occasion?" Instead of sitting, she sauntered over to pour herself a big glass of the Bordeaux, her confidence needing a boost.

"No occasion, really. I simply chose not to sleep last night."

"Ah! So avoiding the perpetual headache after a long Saturday night. Not a bad concept. I could use a drink myself after the Admiral's Ball last night." Esther guzzled half her glass and then refilled, and as she looked up she saw the Madame's left eyebrow raise high. "Don't judge me," Esther retorted. "The bastard came home to beat her right when I left. Was he here again last night?"

"Unfortunately, yes. Just bring that bottle over, darling, we might need another sooner rather than later." Esther complied, setting it on the side table, and then and lowered down into her spot, allowing the Madame to go on. "Now, first we need to discuss Mr. Adams. He was here again, and thankfully refrained from beating the shit out of another one of my girls, though he roughed her up a bit in the sack…what the hell is that face for?"

The burn of wine hit Esther's stomach, aiding in restraining her nausea. "I would really prefer not to hear the sexual ravings of that piece of shit, if you don't mind."

"You are such a prude," the Madame said, waving her off. "But we need to start deciding what to do about him, darling. I am one fucking night away from killing the man myself and I can't afford to have him here every other damn weekend with the kind of damage he inflicts. Before long he'll need to find a new place to whore and gamble in, and it won't be this one."

"So don't let him back!" Esther cried out. "I've been asking you that for years! What the hell could he possibly do to us?"

The Madame took a sip of her wine and stared at her hard. "He'll throw you out of the God damned house, Esther. That's what. And your friend will be forced to live her miserable existence without you, and I don't think she would last that fucking long. Or do you disagree with me?"

She couldn't. "No…no you're right," Esther sighed. "Christ, I don't think Celeste would make it for more than a night or two without me."

"You can't be seen as a problem by the Adams family and the Hiltmores, or you'll be excommunicated from society in a heartbeat. Neither of us want or can afford that, not with the substantial progress we've made together."

Esther shifted in her chair. "So what can we do?"

"Well you marrying would make life easier for everyone."

"Fuck off," Esther snapped. The Madame of all people understood her stance on that, and her suggestion of it was enough to set Esther off.

"I really hope you don't speak that way when you're around company, darling," the Madame mocked. "It's not proper for a lady to curse."

"Yes well, sadly enough the only time I can be myself is when I'm in the company of whores and criminals." The Madame didn't respond, though Esther thought she saw the hint of a smirk and carried on. "I always will do what you need me to do, but we've discussed this. Marriage is out of the question."

"Fine. Then realize your primary objective is to get Celeste knocked up as soon as possible."

Esther nearly choked on her wine. "I need to knock her up?! How in the hell can I do that? Nothing I can say or do would make that even a remote possibility!"

"When was the last time he fucked her?" the Madame posed.

"I don't know…a week? Ten days?"

"You said she had been telling you already it was what she was aiming for, and that it was her way out. So what's the fucking problem with adding a little encouragement?"

There wasn't enough alcohol in the world for Esther to suffer this. "And what if most of the time it's him raping her, Madame? I am supposed to encourage that?"

"It's your only option other than marrying yourself off."

The Madame wasn't being funny, and Esther again felt chills run down her spine. "How would she even survive a pregnancy with how he treats her?"

"I think you will find that once an heir to the family name is on the table, both your life and Celeste's will be a lot fucking easier," the Madame promised her. "Please, just have a little faith in me. I've had

309

an entire lifetime understanding how it is these people operate. Just do it, Esther. When Celeste is set and safe, I will give you what I pledged."

"My own apartments, and money to live on my own?"

The Madame nodded, rising and moving to her. "And an inheritance that will last until you're long gone from this world. However, until then, we have something else added to our agenda."

She tossed the letter from her hands into Esther's lap, and Esther froze as she recognized the handwriting.

"Oh, just fucking read it!" the Madame laughed aloud, taking Esther's glass out of her hands. "Here." She poured more wine into the cup, and Esther unfolded the letter warily.

Madame,

It is with great enthusiasm I am writing to tell you that I will be returning to New York City through the summer and fall, and your scheming, as always, worked magically. I should be arriving the fourth week of May and I realize this letter might not reach you until then, so expect a note or a visit promptly after we are settled back at William and Lucy's.

I hope you will send my warmest regards to Esther, who I also am looking forward to seeing. Please try to convince her I only mean well, and that after all we have been through together when we were young I just want to see her happy and smiling again.

Yours & etc.,

Thomas

P.S. I expect a big bottle of whiskey to be waiting for me. Especially after the fortune I spent shipping you that collection of paintings from Italy.

Cautiously minding her response, Esther handed back the letter and snatched her wine glass up once again – the Madame was correct in assuming she needed it.

"So he is coming home. Almost nine years later."

"Yes he is," the Madame countered.

Esther couldn't stop herself. "I don't really have any desire to see him."

"Why? Because you fell in love with him?"

"I...no...I did not..."

"Darling, everyone has fantasies. Yours just also happens to be a very fucking bizarre reality."

Esther flushed with chagrin. "It wasn't that...I...I fell in love with the idea of him. Nothing more, and that is long...long passed. I will be on my best behavior with Thomas home for a few months, but he will leave again at some point, and probably not come back."

The Madame snorted, amused. "So, you have this whole thing figured out, do you?"

"Yes. And, I have a very handsome gentleman in pursuit of me. He spent the entire ball following me around, waiting hand and foot. I think it's a good prospect. His name is Captain Bernhardt."

The Madame was intrigued. "Old money?"

"Yes. Apparently they are one of the most prominent families in Vermont."

"Well, I hope you have a heavy fur, because it's fucking cold up there," the Madame snickered, leaning against her desk. "And since that is settled and your heart is currently occupied by Captain Vermont, I supposed you wouldn't mind me telling you that Thomas has already arrived and is planning to visit us within the hour."

At the Madame's words, Esther lost a grip on her wine glass, spilling most of its contents on the floor.

"Fuck!" she squeaked. "An...an hour?"

"Hah!" the Madame cackled. "That's what I thought. Let me give you a piece of advice, Esther. If you want to appear aloof and carefree, you'd better learn to play the part better. You've always been a terrible liar, one of the many reasons I have you working behind the scenes where no one is aware of you spying. Take a few deep breaths, you look as if you're about to lose your fucking wine all over my furniture."

Esther couldn't pacify her panic. "Why in the hell did you not tell me he was already here?" she barked, her tone far too aggressive, and at once Esther recognized she'd made a big, big mistake.

The Madame's countenance hardened. "Pull yourself together. I don't know what your 'patrons' and 'friends' may tell you on the other side of town, but if you raise your voice at me again you will regret it. Your fucking privileged mindset is a sign of disrespect I will not tolerate, and I am the one who has put you where you are. And I can take it away any damned second. Is that understood?"

"I…I am so sorry. Yes…absolutely understood."

She glared at Esther a moment, then softened. "Life is full of surprises, darling. We need to work on your adaptability when it comes to your emotions." The Madame looked to the clock on the wall and sighed. "It's been long enough. Go home and take care of Celeste, and say a prayer she's not completely beat to shit. I'll tell Thomas you couldn't make it."

"But—"

"Don't fucking argue with me. Go."

Esther set down her wine glass on the Madame's desk and stood, flustered. "I am sorry, Aunt. I just…Christ I don't know what's wrong with me."

The Madame's stark gaze did not leave her. "You need to remember one thing. It doesn't matter what any man in New York or your dear friend Celeste promises. I think you've seen firsthand how much power she really has. You make one fucking mistake with any of these people, Esther, and you're out. You aren't one of them no matter what they fucking tell you, and they won't forgive as easily as I will."

Esther nodded, her hands trembling, and she sulked toward the door like a wounded animal. "I know. I'll be better," she articulated quietly, not sure if it was for the Madame to hear, or in an attempt to try to convince herself of it.

Not yet primed for what was waiting for her across the city, Esther resolved to take a walk and clear her mind before returning to clean up the mess. With a disheartened wave goodbye to Louis, Esther left in a stupor, irritated by her feelings and inability to handle the situation in front of her with dignity. The Madame put her to the ultimate test, and she failed miserably. With each step she grew more and more upset, trying to remind herself that she needed to forget Thomas and any remaining attachment she had to him. From the beginning, it was a ridiculous whim she devised in her immaturity, making her feel like nothing more than a stupid little girl. Celeste planted the idea in her mind upon witnessing Esther's enthused reactions to his letters and that suggestion grew like a weed, though after a while she realized how foolish she was for such a notion and broke contact. Just when Esther was moving on, when she'd finally found a prospect that didn't give her a headache, Thomas decided to force his way back into her life again. The whole thing didn't seem fair.

If it was possible, the streets were more crowded than when she'd originally set out from Fifth, and Esther crossed the street into Central Park to evade the bustling amount of traffic. The gravel path crunched under her feet as she wandered through the greenery and trees, her spirits lifting with each deep breath of fresh air, thoroughly enjoying the warm sun on her face. Today had been one giant overreaction. Not just that morning, but through the entire ordeal with Thomas. Sure, her embarrassment was the greater cause of Esther's resolution to cut him out of her life; however, she could at least admit the secondary motive was mistrust, and one that had been rightfully earned. How was she to know Thomas would ever set foot in New York City again? Empty promises had been something Esther endured her whole life, with a constant stream of people moving in and out without a care or concern otherwise. There was no reason to invest her heart into any person, particularly one so unstable. Her life, though it had its hiccups, was better than most, and the last thing she needed to do was ruin what she built on false hopes. She was smarter than that.

A few turns down the walkway, Esther found an empty bench overlooking one of the newer fountains and sat down to rest. Once again she fleetingly glimpsed around, hoping to avoid any familiar faces. Not caring that she had left her smoking wand in one of Celeste's rooms, Esther pulled out a cigarette and matches from her satin skirt pocket, desperately needing a release from the already stressful day. Louis would always pass on this small souvenir for Esther after every Sunday visit. The tobacco he smoked was better than any she'd ever tasted, and he made her promise to keep it their secret, which she contentedly obliged. Celeste had taken to smoking when out socially when she was seventeen, believing it gave her an edge in comparison to her other female competitors. It wasn't long before Esther, too, had taken to the habit, and now both girls had to keep their custom behind closed doors. Mrs. Adams hated "the stench," and if Catherine Hiltmore ever found out there would be hell to pay, as she firmly believed it was a habit of the "lesser-minded."

A few puffs later, taking pleasure in a buzz from the wine and tobacco, Esther felt relaxed as she reminisced on the many years of her naivety. The world she dreamed of as a child was an utter illusion, a façade that was kept up through counterfeited enthusiasm and lies. Everyone was a rival. Money and status reigned, and the frivolity lost its charm when she learned it came with a cost. She had no power other than her looks and her potential social climb in marriage, and those would only last so long. She lit another cigarette as her first burned out. Esther's spying for the Madame was the only leverage she would ever have, and even then the thought of blackmailing anyone terrified her. She did best in dark corners and stairwells, eavesdropping and listening when no one thought she was, passing on the information to someone who saw better how to use it in the right way. It wasn't glamorous, and it wasn't exactly decent – but it kept her balanced, as if she really did have a purpose in the grand scheme of things.

A young couple strolled by the fountain. By their clothes, Esther could quickly determine they were not wealthy, and after seeing the plain band on the woman's finger, her suspicions were confirmed. For a reason she couldn't quite put her finger on, Esther couldn't stop watching them. They sat on another bench not far from hers, giggling and holding hands as they sat close to each other, whispering back and forth. The woman leaned her head against the man's shoulder, beaming with happiness, and she heard the words "I love you" come out of her husband's mouth. Neither took notice of Esther, lost in their own universe, and she became sad, much too aware that what they had was a rarity. Being a firsthand bystander to her best friend's situation, helpless and trapped in a loveless marriage with a man who didn't have an affectionate bone in his body, made her cringe – it was all for the price of his last name, fortune, and title.

For so long, she thought it would be her fate as well, but if she could work with the Madame it didn't have to be so. Only a little more time and she could be free of such an outcome, and if she wanted, marry a man of her choosing. She thought of Captain Bernhardt. He had been the first man to make her truly laugh in years, somehow managing to gradually relieve the pain and the fear instilled in Esther after Timothy's attack, and not once had he tried to impress her with who he was. Unlike his predecessors, he asked her questions, only talking about himself when it fit into conversation, and his careful consideration of her was something Esther wasn't accustomed to as a young woman. Perhaps he would win her over in the end, though she wouldn't push the idea. There were still many months left to go of evading Thomas' company and working to get Celeste pregnant as fast as she could…and those would be hard enough tasks on their own.

Esther rose and put her the cigarette out with the toe of her heeled shoe, leaving the bench and the happy couple behind her. The prospect of Thomas in New York was bothering her more than it should, and Esther contemplated what the Madame would do in this sort of scenario to fix it. Maybe she ought to just confront the problem and send an invitation to Thomas that afternoon. They could have tea later in the week when she recalled both Mr. Adams and Celeste would be out at a benefit for the day, thus easing some of the awkwardness of their presence for such an encounter. Her best move would be to treat him for what he was – her long lost friend, coming to see her following years of separation. He could be engaged for all she knew, and for her own health she needed to bury the silly idea her sixteen-year-old self had dreamed up. It wouldn't be easy, yet Esther would explain to Thomas she was sorry for not writing and put herself at fault for being selfishly busy, wrapped up in her own day to day activities. With a bit of whiskey for encouragement, she'd get through it, and with that deliberation a little more pep came into her stride. Imagining the look on the Madame's face made her even more convinced she might just be able to pull it off. And perhaps, while Esther was sending invitations, she should also send a note to Captain Bernhardt and ask if he would be so kind as to join her along with the Celeste and Timothy in their suite at the theater for the weekly show that evening.

Esther had nearly reached the southeast edge of the park when it happened. The moment their eyes met, her whole body went numb, and Esther halted directly where she stood. Everything around her seemed to slow down, and an open path lay between them, making this chance meeting absolutely unavoidable. For a few seconds, Esther was incapable of believing what she was seeing. There he was, dressed in a three-piece grey suit, black necktie and top hat, with a clean-shaven face and his dark hair slicked back. A gold pocket watch hung from his vest, reflecting the sun like a beam of light, a cane in his right hand with a solid gold handle to match. He was taller than she remembered, and his blue eyes sparkled at the sight of her. From ear to ear he had a warm, doting smile, and Esther felt her knees practically give way. Everything she'd spent two years convincing herself of vanished in that instant, along with the fleeting self-assurances she'd only just begun to grasp. Esther couldn't breathe and watched like a spectator as Thomas strutted toward her, and she could only pray he wouldn't hear her heart exploding in her chest.

Thomas paused not a foot from her and took of his hat, stretching out his hand to hers which she took unsteadily.

"Hello, Esther," he greeted and bowed slightly, kissing her hand.

"Thomas," she met with a small curtsy, without a clue as to how she found the ability to use words.

"You look like you are doing quite well," he said, still grinning as he put his hat back on. "You've grown up to be more beautiful than any of us could have predicted. I am so happy to see you. Can I escort you somewhere? Are you heading toward the Adams residence?"

She tried to take a breath to subdue her nervousness. This was not the Thomas she'd known from their collective youth...and to her dismay, he was everything she'd ever dreamt he would be. When she didn't act, Thomas tilted his head, analyzing her silence.

"All right what is it? Do I really look that absurd? I've just grown used to it being around my father all the time."

Internally, Esther's emotions were screaming, and she tried to shut it out. "Oh...no! It's...well it's just such a shock to see you, that is all. I hadn't...I just hadn't expected it..."

"I did not have your new address, or the Hiltmores' new address after their move uptown to write and tell you of my visit and I apologize. I presumed the Madame would have told you by now." Not bothering to wait for permission, Thomas gracefully pulled her arm through his, which she later realized was the first time she hadn't flinched at a man's touch since Timothy's assault. Thomas began to lead her the direction of the Adamses', which was out of the park and down the street. Esther felt an electric shock of elation at his touch, and tried not to show it.

"From the look on your face, this was not exactly on your afternoon agenda," Thomas teased.

"No, not at the start, but the Madame told me this morning.

I just had…I had to be home to see to Celeste. I planned to invite you to tea later this week…at least, if that would be all right with you." She had to concentrate hard on putting one foot in front of the other, afraid she might trip over her now seemingly gigantic feet.

"Of course!" he replied. "I would love that. Now which way am I taking you? South on Fifth I presume?" Esther nodded, and they crossed the road. "And how are things with Celeste and her new husband?"

"It's going fine, I think. Still getting used to each other's…mannerisms…but fine."

"You are still happy staying with them then?" Thomas asked.

"Yes. You know how I adore Celeste…she enjoys having a companion around that is not…well that is not her new family."

Thomas smirked. "Not surprising. I am glad she has you for comfort. If only all of us could be so lucky." Her heart raced faster somehow, wondering if he was implying something, or if she was reading him too closely. "It's a beautiful day," he carried on. "Better than I expected for this time of year. The heat hasn't quite hit yet."

"Is it warm in England?" Esther inquired. She could handle small talk – it was second nature to her.

"Raining like crazy and then it will be blistering in no time," he told her. "Did you attend the Admiral's Ball last night?"

"I…yes I did. How did you know that?"

"Lucy Turner, my…well she's more or less a cousin I would say. She and her husband William went as well."

"I don't believe we have been introduced, but I've heard the name and seen them around town," she admitted. "I had no idea there was any relation to you."

"Yes. They were in England during my first few years and then returned to New York," Thomas explained. "They've been doing quite a bit of traveling, otherwise I am sure you would have met them by now."

"I see…" Esther tried to come up with something else to talk about, wanting to avoid an uncomfortable lack of dialogue.

"You…I mean…your hair looks beautiful by the way," he conveyed softly. Esther wasn't sure if she heard him correctly, and in a flash remembered Mary's comb was in her hair.

"I always wear it when I go to see the Madame. It means a lot to me. She meant a lot to me."

"You meant a lot to her. And to me." Thomas squeezed her arm amiably, and Esther felt her cheeks redden. "Can I ask you something?" he requested after a moment. Esther was tongue tied, hesitant in how to answer, and Thomas took her silence as a yes. "Es, why did you stop writing to me?"

Sooner than she could consider what to say, an answer poured out. "Well…I…I just was unsure if you would ever come back to the city. You had already been gone so long, I just didn't want to get my hopes up." Immediately she bit her tongue and cursed herself for her honesty. Thomas now did not speak, making her even more antsy. "I am sorry, Thomas. It was a childish thing to do. I was so busy and I figured you would be too, and why continue if we wouldn't see each other again?"

"You really thought we wouldn't see each other again?" His voice sounded let down.

"I guess I did," she blurted out again, wanting to get off the subject and avoid injuring him any further. Unfortunately for Esther's stress, Thomas proceeded not to say a word the last block and stopped at her request when they reached their destination.

He turned to face Esther, pointing southward down the street. "I live just a few blocks that direction on Fifth. William and Lucy's new home is spectacular, and I think you would really like it. Please feel free to come by whenever you like, and at any hour. I know my father would really like to meet you. If you aren't busy Friday evening perhaps you'd join us for dinner?"

"I would love to," she responded politely.

Thomas stared at her, as if he was trying to see what she was hiding. "Is that really why you stopped writing me, Es? That small reason, without even feeling the need to ask me about it?"

"I'm afraid so, Thomas, and I am so sorry. It was stupid, really, and I feel terrible about it now. I hope you can accept my apology."

He smiled despondently, took her hand in his and kissed it, bowing his head. "Thank you for the walk, Es. I'll send you a card for dinner." He let her hand go and left her in front of the house, pacing back the way they'd come, in no doubt going to see the Madame. Esther watched him walk away – he always knew when she lied, and what made her feel even worse was that she hated lying to him.

When she saw him disappear into Central Park, she went inside to find a merry Celeste, who had wine and tarts waiting for Esther in the drawing room.

"My dear Esther! Who was that incredibly handsome man who left you at the stoop? I want all of the details immediately!" Celeste sank down onto the French settee, plopping a tart into her mouth while her friend joined her.

Esther's suspicions rose quickly, not anticipating Celeste to be in such high spirits. "You are in quite a happy mood, Celeste. What's the occasion?"

She glanced at Esther with a clever grin. "I am late, Es. I didn't realize it until just after you left! Three weeks late, in fact."

It took a moment for Esther to soak in what her friend had just told her. "Oh my God, Celeste!" she exclaimed, running to her friend and hugging her. "This is such wonderful news I cannot believe it!" The paradox of her talk with the Madame not an hour ago made it more than a little difficult for Esther to accept this was truly happening, and rather than an expected feeling of relief, she was strangely overcome with concern.

"I can't believe I didn't notice!" Celeste persisted. "I am so ecstatic I could shout it from the rooftops.! It is still early so we will keep this between you and I, but another week and I think I will call the doctor."

For the time being, Esther put on an exhilarated smile for her friend. "Oh Celeste, I am so happy for you!"

"Let's just pray it's a boy. I think a girl might really send him over the edge," she quipped, yet Esther wondered if there was really some verity in that statement. Subsequently, at the thought of that monster harming Celeste or her child, Esther comprehended what was internally tearing at her following such great news. She wasn't sure if it was the sight of Celeste more pleased than she'd been in years, or her hatred of Timothy and what he'd done to them both, but something inside her snapped. It was the undeniable spark to make her take a stand, and her decision was made without further reflection. Esther no longer cared about any of the repercussions she might face, or the wrath of the Madame and her place in society. Protecting Celeste and her child was the only thing that mattered to Esther, even if it meant sacrificing her own self in the process.

"Actually, Celeste, I have one more quick errand to run, if you don't mind. I shouldn't be gone long, and then we can spend the rest of the day in celebration!"

Luckily, her friend's disappointment only lasted a few seconds, and Celeste exhaled heavily. "All right, go on. But no more than an hour or I'll be furious with you!"

"I promise no more than an hour," Esther swore, getting back to her feet, "I just forgot to pick up a hat from Miss Bell's."

When she got outside, Esther didn't bother to pause and search for a carriage. She knew exactly what she needed to do, her certainty growing more and more with each passing second. Esther was going to take that bastard out on her own and guarantee he never hurt them again. If she saw this through, maybe then Esther could at last feel free of her burdens and escape the black hole she'd been sucked into.

With Thomas home again, suddenly it seemed like anything was possible.

XII.

"All I'm saying is you look like a faggot," the Madame re-marked candidly, barely glancing Thomas' direction as he sat down in the armchair opposing her desk. She was settled with her feet rest-ing on her desk's surface, sporting a new set of spectacles and reading a piece of paper that apparently required her attention more than his first visit in almost a decade. Thomas chuckled to himself: noth-ing had changed in all the time he'd been gone. At least not with her.

"It's wonderful to see you too," he retorted with heavy sarcasm. "And when exactly did you say you started wearing glasses?" Eight years had gone by and the Madame was still flawless, appearing in-stead as if only a few months had trickled by. For Thomas, it was a bizarre sort of mystery how she remained imperviously exquisite, especially after watching his own father begin to grey and wrinkle over their time together.

The Madame didn't pay him any mind. "I hope you didn't come all this way to pick another God damned fight. You'll lose."

"Wow. I think I might have actually missed you."

"I can't blame you, darling, I would miss me too." At last, she peered up at him. "How is your father?"

Thomas ignored the question, his eyes searching around the

room. "I thought you were supposed to have a bottle of whiskey ready for me?"

Rather than respond, she pointed toward the drink cart where the crystal decanter was full of what he could only assume was Casper's, two empty glasses resting beside it. As he got up and went over, Thomas noticed the key to the safe he had once stolen resting back on the bottle. It was a deceivingly innocent decoration to anyone other than him. He poured himself a small glass of whiskey, and a much larger one for her.

"Father is great. He is not exceptionally thrilled to be here, but William and Lucy make it better. He had a hard time leaving Hiroaki behind – I don't think Edward will come back after this trip, but I do think you'll be seeing more of me."

"Happy to hear it. What goes on with him and the chink anyhow? Their friendship is not what I would call…ordinary…"

Thomas ambled over to her, discounting the Madame's inapt choice of words and handing over her cocktail. "They saved each other's lives. Hiraoki and his wife were refugees and Edward took them in. Akemi saved him when Edward nearly died from Malaria. That's grounds for a friendship, even if it's not ordinary, don't you think?"

"I wouldn't know. I don't have friends, as you may or may not have observed."

"What about Louis?"

"He's my employee," she said matter-of-factly. "There's a difference. And it's not as if your father could have taken them with you. They've banned all the fucking chinks from immigrating over, not that we need any more anyway. The ones in Chinatown can barely stay alive with all the nationalists and fucking gangs ransacking whatever they want. Not to mention they're more hated than the blacks are, and make half of their earnings." The Madame took off her spectacles and had a sip of her drink, leaning back in to her chair and putting down her papers. "Fucking class war is getting bad.

324

Stay out of the Points or you'll get clubbed to death. The Whyos are making a damned mess of it."

"I didn't realize it had gotten so bad. Killing people in open streets?"

"Coppers can't keep control of the mob anymore. Half of them are in on it, and the poor are fucking poorer than ever and live like filthy animals down there."

"Have you always been this crass? I was at least hoping for a few niceties this morning since it's been awhile."

She rolled her eyes at him and went on, clearly not caring for his input. He halfway listened to her complaints about rising prices and her incompetent staff for a quarter of an hour, allowing his own roaming thoughts to take precedent over her ranting. Thomas hadn't realized until he was back in the streets of New York how differently he saw the world – it was as if a new lens was cast in front of his eyes. When he had been younger, money was survival, food, and shelter. He'd owned so little and lived simply, pumping water from the communal well and baking his own bread at the start of each week. After Edward, money was no object, and his life revolved around it in an extremely altered fashion. The blade Lawrence gave him was, now and always, wrapped around his ankle, and meant to be his reminder of how fortunate he was to have such a drastic change in his stars. Regardless, until he had returned to New York with his feet back on the cobblestone and he smelled the stench of the city in his nostrils, Thomas hadn't understood how much of this new life he'd taken for granted. He could feel the chip on his shoulder burn shamefully.

"I saw Esther on my way here," he told her, interrupting the ongoing tirade. "She seemed well."

The Madame stopped mid sentence, apparently not minding a disruption. "How? I sent her home over an hour ago. It's not as if she's halfway across the fucking city."

Thomas shrugged. "Not sure. She was leaving the park. When did she start smoking? I could smell it from her dress."

"And just what were you doing so close to her dress?"

He scoffed. "Oh please. It's Esther, for Christ's sake."

"Whatever you say, darling. You can try and play dumb with me all you want but it's a load of bullshit. You know, she is nearly as striking as I was at that age."

"Modest of you," Thomas commented. "She is…well she is beautiful…"

"All grown up. And eighteen."

"Do you have another scheme I should know about?"

"Oh don't be so fucking smart. I know there is no way you didn't see that. I've put a lot of hard work into making her as fucking alluring as she can be."

"Can you please…just…not?" Thomas pleaded.

The Madame shrugged dismissively. "If you don't, someone else will sooner rather than later. That's all I'm saying."

"How is she doing? Are the Adamses treating her well?"

The Madame's devious grin weakened. "She's tough, Thomas, but it's not easy for her. Unlike you, money is not her birthright, and those rich bastards don't let her forget it. Not to mention she is trapped in Celeste's nightmare of a marriage that her own mother cast her into. So no, not everything is sunshine and rainbows like she thought it would be."

Thomas was perplexed. "Nightmare of a marriage?"

"He beats her when he's drunk. Sometimes it goes further. You don't need the gory details."

"He…he hasn't touched Esther, has he?"

"No," the Madame divulged. "But I honestly don't know how much longer that will last. Celeste has no control over her husband. He does what he pleases, even when he comes here, because he has more fucking money than most and can cover his tracks with it.."

"He comes here?!" Thomas exclaimed in disbelief. "You allow that?!"

"Yes I fucking allow it. This is not an easy business, Thomas, and not for the faint of heart. I tolerate him to maintain the leverage I have. And it keeps Esther's position there secured until the Hiltmores can marry her off."

Thomas felt his protectiveness increase. "Like you said, I don't see how that would be a problem."

The change of pitch in his voice gave him away. "Ah…a bit defensive are we?" she mocked, her smile returning.

Thomas lifted his glass to take a sip of whiskey and was annoyed to find it gone. "I would just like her to not end up getting beaten by her husband. I would like for her to be happy. Is that so much to ask?"

"Happiness is not something that comes standard in life, Thomas. Why do you care anyhow?"

"Because I care about her and her well-being. Though I can't say the same for her after our interaction in the park. I never imagined she would react so coldly to seeing me."

The Madame's eyes narrowed. "You really haven't figured it out yet, have you?"

"What do you mean?"

The Madame's feet found the floor as she went to the drink cart for more whiskey. "Don't worry about it, darling, I think everything will take care of itself in due course." She picked the decanter up nonchalantly and made her way back to him, refilling their glasses. "But enough about Esther. How is everything with you? Did you finally end things with that crazy bitch next door? Now she was a fucking disaster waiting to happen."

It was nearly two hours later that Louis' heavy knock rang through the Madame's office. He slipped inside and, from the shocked expression on his face as he entered, was not expecting to see Thomas in his new manifestation. With a huge grin, Thomas got to his feet to give the man a hug, noting that like the Madame, Louis appeared no different than when he left years prior. If it was possible,

Louis' grip had to be stronger, nearly causing Thomas to lose his breath with the tight embrace he received. When he stepped away, Louis fussed with his hair.

"Look at you!" he bellowed animatedly, "I am sorry I was not here to greet you, I was out on an errand." Casually, he walked over and handed a small sealed envelope to the Madame, not bothering to address it otherwise. "How was your journey?"

"Easy. Although we've only been here two days and Edward is already planning our departure."

"I'm surprised he made the trip at all," Louis answered flippantly. Thomas noted the overtly careless tone, and wondered if the Madame had any idea about the bizarre long-standing friendship between Louis and his father. He assumed probably not to the extent he did, and that Louis had gone above and beyond to keep it that way.

"Thomas, I need to take care of a few things," the Madame announced, her face stern as she put her spectacles back on, examining her inbound letter. "Why don't you come by later this week?"

"That would be great. Oh, before I forget, Edward wants you both to be at dinner Friday."

The room went stale at his mention of it. Both Louis and the Madame paused right where they were, their eyes meeting each other's in uncertainty.

"Oh come on," Thomas insisted. "Don't act so baffled. He wants to see everyone, and as much as he adores you, Madame, he really is uncomfortable coming here."

"Uncomfortable is an understatement," she grumbled, "Thomas I own a God damned whorehouse and a business that needs me here to operate it. Who is going to run this place on my busiest night of the week if I'm not here?"

"Hope and Danny would be fine I think," Louis uttered under his breath, and the Madame shot him a look of pure fury.

"It's settled then. I'll see you both Friday at eight."

He was halfway down the stairs when he felt a presence behind him, and turned around directly into Louis chest, his feet slipping off the step behind him. The Frenchman caught Thomas by his shoulders mid-fall and set him straight, not bothering to hide his hilarity.

Thomas brushed off the front of his suit, embarrassed. "Christ, Louis, are you trying to kill me?"

Louis slapped him on the back, continuing their descent. "I think we both know I wouldn't have to try. Come on. I'll see you home."

Thomas followed him, confused. "It's really not necessary, Louis—"

"I wasn't asking. Come along."

As would forever be the case with Louis, Thomas didn't argue and tagged along out of The Palace. He and Louis easily picked up right where they'd left off, and each burned through two of Louis' cigarettes before they got to the East Side. Louis clarified what the Madame described earlier, filling in Thomas on what he missed in his eight year absence, and as it turned out the city was more conflicted than when he'd left. The gangs went further than ever before, the violence more treacherous and gruesome in their targets, and the slums packed with more immigrants every day, dying at the same rate as they were born. The only safe place for anyone with money was moving near Central Park and the surrounding neighborhoods, and Louis advised him to count his lucky stars he was on the better end of things.

"The Irish are running everything," Louis conveyed to him quietly. "They started the right way, building up in the ghettos and now slowly dipping their fingers into every jar. If it hadn't been for your father, you'd be running money for Tammany like half the city is. Including the Madame."

Thomas took a deep inhale of smoke, halting under the shade of a nearby tree. "Was that why my mother got into trouble? She was a part of it in the beginning, right?"

Louis eyes went wide for a few seconds, then he nodded. "I was under the impression you still believed…well…you know…"

"I did, and I am glad I did because otherwise I wouldn't have gone to England. The truth came out four years ago. Lucy was never good at keeping secrets."

"And how did your father react?"

A little reluctant, Thomas' gaze fell. "Edward doesn't know. I care so much for my father, I didn't want to bring it up and do him that injustice. I was angry when I found out, and in time grew to understand why he did it. I don't know if it's worth telling him I know or letting him think it's long passed."

"Keep it that way, Tommy," Louis concurred with him. "Let the past stay in the past. Your father can't handle that again, not when it's a wound that opens and bleeds so violently in him." He dropped his cigarette to the ground, and killed the spark with the heel of his boot. "It's a dangerous world we live in. The Madame is right: stay out of the Points and the Bowery, or you won't come back, and you know quite well I can't save you from there."

"I'll take your word for it, Louis." The sun was beginning to drop in the blue sky, the heat of the day subsiding as the crowd in the park dissipated. "I'm two blocks out. I think I'll make it from here."

Louis nodded. "Plans for the night?"

"Lucy is making us go to the theater. Edward and William want to scout new business prospects, so they're putting me to work already." Thomas held out his hand, which his friend shook with a big smile. "Louis, it's been a pleasure."

"Likewise, Tommy. Until Friday."

Thomas took off from under the tree, his mood much darker than it had been when he first set out to The Palace. He endeavored not to think of his mother often – when Lucy accidentally mentioned to Thomas the conspiracy his father tried to unwind, it had only taken a few minutes to convince her to come clean with everything that occurred. She reluctantly gave in, all too aware if she didn't Thomas would go directly to Edward. Their conversation shattered the glass pedestal Thomas put his father upon, and angrily Thomas fled to the one thing that always made the pain recede, locking himself away in the heat and smoke of the fire. For the three days that followed, he spent every waking hour hammering away his feelings in the dungeons, wanting desperately to sail home and hear the truth for himself. He thought of confronting Edward and demanding an explanation, or simply leaving without a trace, never to come back or contact any of them again. In those three sleepless days, Thomas beat the steel harder than he had in his entire life, battling the rage and resentment piece by piece. Fortunately, William and Edward were out of the country, and though Lucy made multiple attempts to see him, he rebuffed her company and what he could only guess were her excuses. The last few years of his life felt like nothing more than a lie, like his father tricked him into a mold he wanted Thomas to fit. As the second day drew to a close, Thomas was nearly to the mindset of heading straight upstairs to pack his bags, when he had an uninvited visitor.

The cells were completely black save for the fire of his work and one flickering torch near the exit, and Hiroaki emerged as if out of thin air at his side. Thomas nearly leapt out of his skin at the sight of him and dropped his piece into the coals, letting out a slight yell of fright after thinking he'd been alone. Hiroaki's face and clothes were dirtied from the fire and ash, causing Thomas to consider just how long the man had been observing him before he came forward. Unlike the hardness of his expression, Hiroaki's soft eyes made Thomas ease up, though not enough to render his fury forgotten.

"You realize I could have killed you with that hot blade, don't you?" Thomas posed, holding his hand to his chest to steady his heartbeat and breath.

"Perhaps. There was a time I used to make my own steel as well. But that explanation is for another occasion. You know why I am here."

Thomas stood firm. "Not particularly, no."

A smirk crossed his face. "Lucy came to me. She's worried she's ruined everything."

"Hiro, none of this concerns you. This is between me and my father. I mean no disrespect, but there is nothing you can try to say to make it right."

"On the contrary, Thomas, I think it is my perspective you need now more than any other, and I think you would find your father a very poor choice for justification."

Thomas did not want to offend Hiroaki, but his ambush was crossing a line. "I think justification would be impossible for what he's done."

"What has he done, exactly?" Taking a step toward the fire, Hiroaki assumed the heavy mitts Thomas wore and pulled his smoldering work from the flames, thus not allowing it to ruin. "He brought you to safety, he gave you a new start at life, and he gave you a family that loves you. All these things you wanted."

"He lied to me to get me here."

"You think he did that on his own, Thomas?"

"What are you insinuating, Hiro?"

"There is no insinuation. William and Lucy, too, did not hear the full story until they were safe at Amberleigh, and I know from the letters I received from your father that they did this to protect you. That spectrum includes both your family here, and your family back in New York. Doesn't that speak volumes in your heart? Doesn't that demonstrate the level at which you are loved amongst those you care for?"

Thomas wasn't buying in. "Then they all can go to hell. They all lied."

Hiro peered intently at him. "And your mother didn't? What makes her the innocent victim here?" Hiroaki took the gloves off and set them aside. "Dispel your anger for a moment and hear what I am telling you. Your family did what they did because they didn't have another option. Your mother was lost to them, and rather than wreck the beautiful memories you have of her, they perpetuated the falsehood that was created to help you move on with your life. If those things are worth hating the people who would do anything and everything for you, then by all means, you have my leave to go before your father and William arrive home. However, you will lead a lonely life, Thomas. No one is perfect, and you will never find anyone that loves you as much as your father does. Not one. The choice is yours to make."

Hiroaki did not delay to hear Thomas' rejoinder; he left him with his thoughts and his hammer. In Hiroaki's own wise way, this left Thomas to see the truth of it through his own eyes rather than forcing his opinions and support of Edward's decisions. After a few minutes standing there in reflection, Thomas couldn't refute Hiroaki's arguments. They weren't wrong…indeed, they were completely accurate, and within a few hours, his thinking changed drastically.

It wasn't rational, yet Thomas was searching for someone to blame, and as the third day drew to a close, he had his answer. The only person he could rightfully blame was her. Mary knew the danger, and therefore put her family in danger with her. His father… the Madame…Louis…Lucy and William…they intended nothing more than to protect him from that knowledge, not wanting to spoil Thomas' sentiments toward the woman who raised him. On the third day, he finally laid the hammer down and the grief was gone. There was nothing he could have done to change her fate…nothing anyone could have done except Mary, and holding anyone else responsible for her actions was both wrong and unfair. Those three days revolutionized everything for Thomas, forcing him to let go of any lasting animosity, and from that time forward, his loyalty to Edward and the rest became indestructible.

From Central Park, he strolled those last two blocks at a leisurely pace, trying to put those memories aside. As he ruminated over the advice the Madame and Louis offered that Fifth Avenue was in its own bubble, isolated from the cruel realities of the city, Thomas be-

came a little forlorn. There was no going back to his old neighborhood, to his younger days when his primary objective was to make
enough money to eat and survive. It was hard for him to admit that
he'd transformed into a different man than he was eight years ago.
Many times he tried to dismiss the hindering indignity of his new status as the last of his boyhood childishness. It was no use. The smallest sliver of his heart would never let him forget it, and the privileges at his feet would forever remain a dichotomous two-sided coin,
one side a blessing and the other a curse.

The front gas lamps of the Turners' home were lit as dusk approached, and he grinned as he jogged up the front steps of the
stoop, happy to be home. Tony opened the front door with a delighted air, welcoming him inside where he was greeted with the smell of
a pig roasting in the kitchen, then followed closely by cigar smoke.

"They've been waiting for you, sir. Anxiously," Tony informed
him. "Better not keep them or you'll never hear the end of it."

"Thank you, Tony," he replied, handing over his jacket and hat
before heading straight for the sitting room.

"Thomas!" William's voice boomed as he came through the
doorway. "You're late! We've begun our brandy and cigar hour without you." Lucy was seated on her husband's lap, each with a glass
already half consumed in hand, and his father sat across from them
in front of the fire place puffing away at a cigar.

"I hope you saved one of those for me," he divulged, making
his way over to the couch beside Edward.

"I would consider myself a terrible father if I didn't," Edward
asserted, leaning over to hand Thomas an already cut cigar, "And
Lucy would love to grab you a glass of brandy." Upon hearing his
words, Lucy scoffed as if offended, but hopped up and did so anyway. "How did your visit go?" Edward asked.

"Which one?"

Edward was puzzled. "There was more than one? I thought you
were off to The Palace?"

Lucy begrudgingly brought Thomas his brandy, trying not to allow herself to smile. "Thank you Luce. I did, but on my way I ran into Esther."

William's ears perked up, ostensibly interested. "And? What happened?"

Thomas set his brandy aside and lit a match. "Nothing of any significance. She is coming to dinner Friday, father. But otherwise, it was oddly formal. I guess I didn't realize how different she might have become. It's been a long time, you know."

"Different how?!" Lucy was inclining frontward on her husband's lap. Thomas indulged her despite his growing concern behind their curiosity.

"Distant. Almost vexed to see me," he clarified, shaking his head. "It wasn't like her, or at least not like the Esther I used to know anyhow. I think after Friday I will give her some space…she actually seemed…nervous, now that I think about it."

Lucy sat upright and took a sip of her brandy, rotating to face her husband. "I think that's what…ten dollars you owe me?"

"For God's sake, woman, could this have not waited until later?" William scolded her, though he was struggling to suppress a chortle.

Thomas didn't know what to make of this, though he had a slight idea. "I'm a little lost. What bet did I miss, father?"

"You just had to make a stink about this, didn't you, Lucy?" Edward laughed.

Thomas eyed them carefully. "All right, someone tell me what's going on."

Edward put his arm around Thomas. "Lucy made a bet with William that Esther would fall in love with you when she saw you. It's been all they've talked about all day."

Reluctantly, William pulled the ten dollars from his pocketbook and Lucy snatched the money up greedily.

"Glad to see my romantic life is our family's continuing entertainment at happy hour," Thomas added, sitting back with his cigar.

"But I really think you are reading Esther wrong."

"I most certainly am not reading her wrong," Lucy exclaimed defiantly. "I think it's safe to say I know how someone of my own sex would act in this type of situation."

"Oh give it a rest," William groaned. "The poor boy doesn't need another one of your matchmaking schemes. And I thought you'd given up on that!"

"Tommy, you're twenty-six," Lucy went on, ignoring her husband. "I want you to be happy and find someone! For William's sake, I will digress until you decide to surrender bachelorhood, and I'll just keep making money off him. But I am not wrong about Esther, I can assure you of it."

"What makes you so certain?"

"Because everyone seems to know it except you. Would your father allow me to carry on like this if I were wrong?"

Thomas glanced at his father, whose expression gave it away instantly.

"Well, this should make things interesting," Thomas thought aloud, downing his brandy.

A few hours later, the four Turners were on their way to the Madison Square Theater for the evening. In his seat, Thomas shuffled around in his black suit, never quite growing secure with having such restrictive clothing on his body. The carriage bounced along the road as Lucy informed them of the latest Bronson Howard drama they would see, her enthusiasm greater than that of all three of the men put together. Thomas hated the theater almost as much as his father did and only went to get Lucy to stop lecturing them about staying in the house too much; if they ever chose not to go, she was intolerable for days on end.

"You all had better wipe those sour puss looks off your face before we arrive, or you'll pay for it later," she threatened, her gloved finger pointing at Edward and William. "We never get out, and I think it's high time we have a social presence in this city."

William sneered. "Social presence? Really, Lucy?"

She crossed her arms over her chest, agitated. "Don't start with me, William."

"At least we'll be able to get a bit of work done," Thomas cut in, trying to break the tension, "A man by the name of Bernard. He should be attending tonight."

"Who was it that gave you this tip?" Edward asked.

"The Fogarty boys from South Carolina," he explicated. "A letter from them was here when we got to New York. Apparently, Bernard is trying to revolutionize tobacco trade. He already does most of the land distribution in New York, Philadelphia, and Charleston."

"We already do tobacco," William verbalized indifferently. "Why is it we need him?"

"That's the key. We don't need him. We need his associate, a man named James Bonsack who lives in Virginia."

Edward's attention was growing with the complexity of Thomas' scheme. "Go on."

"Rumor has it he's invented a machine that can roll tobacco into paper automatically, and produce cigarettes at a much higher rate. Imagine the demand when people can buy tobacco in bulk rather than rolling their own. If we could land this, we could have the rights to distribute up and down the entire American coastline by sea and on to London. Our profits would be…unlike anything we ever dreamed."

As Thomas' rationalization sank in, William and Edward gaped at him, and when neither spoke in return, Lucy cut in. "And how did the Fogarty's know about this?"

"Alex went to school with Bonsack. They've been friends their whole lives."

The coach hit a pothole and lurched hard to the right, nearly casting everyone from their seats before it then came to a stop.

"Here!" the driver barked loudly.

"One moment!" William shouted back. "All right, what else did the Fogarty's say? Anything we can go on?"

Thomas eyed Lucy. "Well, there's something. But William isn't going to like it."

"What do you mean?" Edward asked.

"Lucy, we're going to need you as bait."

The inside of the theater was bustling with people, every guest dressed in their finest suits and gowns, drinking champagne and conversing at three times their normal volume to be heard above the crowd. Great, luminous crystal chandeliers hung down from the painted ceiling, and though no walls could be seen due to the density of theatergoers, a bright red carpet lay underneath their feet and up the staircases to the seats. Thomas searched the assembly for a man he had never seen, hoping his friend's literary illustrations would be enough to help him along. The Fogarty's gave great detail in describing Bernard, who had a taste for women half his age in spite of having a wife and family he willingly left at home in Virginia to pursue his capital. Lucy was a bit older than his usual pickings, and Thomas hoped that with her wit and smile she could win him over with nothing more than an innocent flirtation. Luckily, Lucy had truly outdone herself that night: her long, loosely curled hair was piled high on her head, drawing the attention unswervingly to her sparkling light brown eyes and elegantly bare shoulders. Her light green gown and laughter caused heads to turn as they walked through the masses, and Thomas knew if she succeeded in engaging him, an introduction would be incredibly easy for the Turners. To his relief, Thomas spotted Bernard within seconds of their arrival downing whiskey at the bar, in close conversation with a young woman who could have been younger than Esther. Thomas turned to Lucy and gestured to where Bernard stood, and without a word she glided off in his direction to get a glass of champagne.

"Not exactly the type of work you want your wife to be undertaking," William muttered quietly, deliberately looking away.

Edward put his hand on William's shoulder. "She took to that a bit more naturally than I expected, eh William?"

"Well at least it's for a good investment," Thomas remarked derisively.

"That's one way of putting it," Edward chuckled as they made their way up the stairs and to their box, William's face turning a harsh shade of purple.

Seconds before the play began, Lucy joined them with a sly smile. "Piece of cake," she whispered to Thomas, taking the vacant chair in front of him with her drink.

"We are going to have a talk about this when we get home," William notified her, still unnerved.

"Oh don't be jealous, William. When we are making more money than God you'll thank me."

The lights fell to a dim and the show started, much to Lucy's delight. Just as Thomas was starting to loosen up and take in the night, his eyes found the box across from theirs. To his astonishment, there sat a radiantly beautiful Esther along with a much older version of the Celeste he remembered and their two escorts, one of which Thomas assumed was Celeste's husband. The box to the right housed Mr. and Mrs. Hiltmore and another older couple he did not know, the group deeply engrossed in the show. As if she sensed it, Esther glanced away from the stage his direction, and her face showed she was just as startled to see Thomas as he had been her. Politely he nodded her direction and looked back toward the act, not wanting to appear as though he'd been staring her way long. A weird emotion came over him, one he couldn't quite describe, and he tried to forget it and concentrate on the performance. It was, in all likelihood, the alcohol along with the incessant suggestions from everyone around him, but he couldn't deny Esther was stunning, and he spent the whole first act trying to stifle whatever it was making his stomach flip.

At intermission, their preconceived strategy commenced. Lucy went to the bar alone once more and was almost immediately found by Bernard, while Thomas, William, and Edward loitered further off in the crowd as spectators. After giving them a minute or so to order a drink and begin their dialogue, Thomas took a deep breath and went over, identifying that this might be his only shot to get it right.

"Thomas!" Lucy called, waving him over when he drew close. "Come here and meet my wonderful new friend. Francis, I'd like you to meet my cousin, Thomas. Thomas, this is Francis Bernard!" She took a large gulp of champagne and revolved away from them casually, giving Thomas the floor.

"A pleasure, sir," Thomas addressed him, shaking Bernard's hand, as if it were actually a chance meeting. Francis Bernard was not altogether handsome, with a bald head that barely reached Thomas' shoulders and a slightly rounded waist. His face was bird like, with a long pointed nose and small but piercing eyes, as well as a dense handlebar mustache compensating for the hair he lacked on his head.

Bernard did not look quite as pleased, though he remained polite. "Pleasure," he mumbled. "Are you both enjoying the play thus far?"

"Drama bores me," Lucy merged back in. "I prefer something more entertaining! A comedy perhaps! The last thing I want to hear about is how immoral society has become. Thomas, what do you think?"

"Absolutely," Thomas agreed, reaching into his jacket pocket. "I hope you don't mind, Mr. Bernard, but I could use a break from morality. Smoke, sir?"

He nodded, warming a little. "A tobacco man…I like you already…" his voice trailed off as he smelled the cigarette. "You roll this yourself, son?"

"I did. Some of the finest tobacco you can buy in New York. Directly imported from North Carolina. Barman, another champagne for my cousin, and a whiskey for me and Mr. Bernard."

"Thank you, Thomas, was it?" Bernard pulled out a box of matches from his pocket, lighting his cigarette and then handing the matches to Thomas. "So many people lack the...well, the dedication these days to roll their own. I must say I am a little impressed, being a tobacco man myself."

Lucy strategically placed her hand lightly on Bernard's arm. "My cousin here is in trade and works with some of the best tobacco farmers in the business! He knows the ins and outs, I daresay. Isn't that right, Tommy?"

Thomas feigned discomfiture. "She loves to sing my praises," he said, taking a sip of his cocktail.

"And you are from New York?" Bernard raised, studying Thomas inquisitively.

"Born and raised, sir. I spent the better part of the last decade in England and have come home to try and expand business for my father's company. I just moved back onto Fifth Avenue."

"International?"

Thomas nodded. "Yes. We do importing and exporting of goods up and down the American coastline and over to London and Liverpool, Queenstown, even parts of France, Spain, and Portugal."

Bernard's tiny eyes grew a little wider. "I see. How old are you son? You can't be much older than my own boy back home."

"Twenty-six," Lucy told him. "He is the spitting image of his father. They run Turner S & D together along with my husband."

Somehow, Bernard had completely overlooked his pursuit of Lucy and centered in on his newfound adoration of Thomas. Francis put out his cigarette in what was left of his whiskey, set his glass on the bar, and rotated back to face Thomas, his demeanor becoming extraordinarily friendly.

"My son will be in town tomorrow. Perhaps you and your father would like to join us for brandy one evening? We run a similar campaign...perhaps a merger could be in the works."

Thomas handed Bernard his card, and took his in exchange.

"We would be thrilled. Let's say, Thursday night?"

"We will plan to see you then. And Thomas, might I get your father's name as well?"

"Ah of course, how rude of me. My father is Lord Edward Turner of Amberleigh, but please call him Edward. He hates the formality of his title."

Francis paused a moment, just then starting to recognize with whom he was speaking, and Thomas rejoiced in the idea that the man was utterly unprepared for this information. He could see Bernard piecing it together: Turner S & D, the fact that Thomas' father was longstanding British nobility, and that their enterprise was one of the leading traders in the business and had been for decades. It took Francis a few breaths, but eventually he remembered himself and nodded obligingly.

"Right. Until Thursday, then. Have a pleasant evening, Thomas, and pass on my good wishes to your father."

As Bernard lumbered away, seemingly shocked by the good fortune in his encounter, Lucy nearly exploded with exhilaration. "Flawless…flawless I tell you!" she voiced softly. "Your father and William have always been so…English in their operations and deals! I hate to say it, Thomas, but all that time with the Madame really has paid off!"

Thomas grinned, shrugging it off as he finished his whiskey and cigarette. Others may have found offense in Lucy's statement regarding his acquired skill set from the Madame; however, Thomas reveled in what he perceived as a compliment. What he'd learned from her had made him an eclectic and tactful businessman, bringing Thomas a sense of pride in that one of his greatest traits came directly as a result of his upbringing in New York. It made him feel untouchable amongst his competitors.

The lights flickered, signaling the end of the intermission. "Finish your drink and I'll meet you at the box," Lucy ordered. "I will run and find the boys."

"You've got it," Thomas approved. Lucy disappeared to his left, weaving in and out of those shuffling back toward the theater, and briefly, Thomas was so lost in his personal musings of the exceptional progress he'd just made, he didn't perceive Esther drawing near from the corner of his eye.

"Mr. Turner!" came Esther's voice to his right, nearly causing Thomas to drop his glass. He cursed under his breath and hastily put on his most dashing smile, which he fought to keep in place when he saw she had another gentleman with her.

"Miss Esther, how are you this evening?"

"Fine, thank you. This is my escort for the night, Captain Bernhardt. Captain, this is Thomas Turner, son of Lord Edward Turner."

He was an extremely handsome man, too pretty in Thomas' opinion, and their looks couldn't be more opposite. The Captain's hair was wavy and blonde, with brown eyes and a stature that resided a few inches shorter than Thomas'. The crooked smile the Captain wore could only come from a first generation after the Civil War, having to hear of the glorious blood baths, though never experiencing one himself, and carrying a small weight of animosity because of it. Thomas shook his hand. Thus far, it was the man's only saving grace: Edward instructed Thomas during his earliest days in the business he could tell everything about a man by his handshake, and Captain Bernhardt's was firm and resolute, leaving Thomas no choice but to have a certain level of esteem for him at first impression. Or at least enough willpower to tolerate him.

"A pleasure," Thomas said, finishing the whiskey and setting the glass on the bar. "Are you both enjoying the performance?"

"It's a little…difficult to get through…" Esther started, and to Thomas' surprise, both he and Captain Bernhardt laughed aloud at the same moment.

"It's pretty God damn terrible," the Captain replied. "If I may speak so bluntly."

Thomas hated that his fondness of the Captain was expanding.

343

"I couldn't agree more. I've had two whiskeys at the intermission just to make it through the second half."

"Hell, I've had three. Poor Esther here might be sending me home tonight in a carriage."

Thomas could intuitively sense that whatever interaction Esther expected between these two, this had not been it.

"Well, I just wanted to stop by quickly and say hello," she interjected. "Captain, we should be getting back."

"Right you are. Until next time, Mr. Turner."

"Captain," Thomas tipped his head. "Miss Esther, always lovely to see you."

She was distressed as she turned away, and when the pair reached the staircase he saw in her hair was Mary's pin, the one she'd told him she only wore to visit the Madame. Something hit him then, something he couldn't yet fathom, yet he could feel in that instant it was there…like it had been waiting for the right moment to surface and suddenly, that moment had arrived.

Thomas heard the orchestra start up and snapped to reality, making his way back to their box in a hurry through the already almost deserted lobby. Nevertheless, as he reached the bottom of the staircase, Thomas heard a muffled cry from somewhere in the distance. Halting where he stood, Thomas looked around to try to find it's source. Then, another cry, and a slap, someone's voice in a much lower tenor saying something Thomas couldn't quite make out.

"Thomas!" Edward's hushed call came from up the stairs. "What are you doing?"

Thomas motioned for his father to come down to him. "I heard someone cry out, and then I think I heard a slap."

His father considered this, his eyes never leaving Thomas. "And you were going to find it on your own?"

"Well…I didn't want to just leave…what if someone is in trouble?"

Edward shook his head and uttered something to himself, and

when Thomas tried to remonstrate, Edward held up a hand to silence him, clearly able to hear something his son couldn't. Then, without warning, Edward strode off at a healthy clip to their left and toward the other staircase, with Thomas trailing at his heels. They rounded the far side of the steps to find a man with a young woman cornered, shaking and crying, and Thomas was appalled to see it was Celeste and, he could only presume, her husband. The man had one hand on her shoulder restraining her where she was, the other right next to her nose with his finger pointed, clearly having been yelling at her for some time. Thomas was aghast.

"Excuse me, sir," Edward interrupted, his tone firm. "I'm going to have to ask you to move away from the young lady."

Celeste was terrified, though Thomas couldn't be sure if it was because of the man with her or because Thomas and his father had shown up and witnessed the scuffle. The man twisted around too violently, markedly more than a little drunk, knocking Celeste into the wall as she let out a little whimper of pain.

"You...you both fuck off...I can talk to...to my wife however I...I want..." He pointed his finger their direction, but his stumbling made it unclear whom exactly he was speaking to. Thomas had been in his own share of frays throughout the years; this, on the other hand, was something else entirely, and he let Edward take control of a situation that went way over his head. His father was unnaturally calm and collected, not an ounce of worry or panic in his countenance as he faced off with Timothy Adams.

"You will go home, sir, before you cause a scene," Edward advised him. "Shall I escort you outside to get a coach?"

"Do...do I need to repeat myself? Fuck off...you English prick..."

Celeste took a small step forward. "Timothy...please...let's just go..."

"Shut up, you stupid bitch!" he yelled, slapping her cheek and sending her backward again.

Thomas couldn't take it anymore. "All right, Mr. Adams, that's enough." He meant to move forward and intervene; however, it was not before his own father got to Timothy, moving so swiftly it was almost as if he were a blur. In a half second, Edward seized Timothy Adams by the throat and thrust him up against the wall next to his wife, his feet dangling two feet from the ground. Celeste gasped, her hand covering her mouth, and she fled toward where Thomas stood, cowering away behind him. Edward's grip was so strong, Timothy's face was as red as his wife's dress, though he struggled to fight back. It was no use – Edward was relentlessly unshakeable.

Edward's words were so muted, Thomas barely heard them: "If I ever catch you hitting your wife again, it will be the last thing you do upon this earth. I don't care who the hell you are. So you, in turn, sir, can fuck off." He gave it a few more seconds, fiercely glaring at Timothy as he pathetically kicked and squirmed, then released him. Timothy fell to the ground in a pile of drunken confusion, huffing for air and clutching his throat.

"Father…" Thomas began, unable to move.

"Mrs. Adams, are you all right?" Edward whipped around and went to her, disregarding Thomas.

Celeste's face was white, though the shock had somewhat subsided. "I…I think I'm all right." Remembering his manners, Thomas helped her to her feet, and she brushed off her dress in an effort to collect herself.

"Should I get you a carriage?" Thomas offered, anticipating there was no possible way they'd want to return to their box in such a disgruntled state.

"That would be wonderful, thank you."

Timothy was still on the floor, completely out of sorts, and Edward picked him up from under his arms as if he weighed nothing. Timothy didn't bother to try and dispute Edward physically – the point was well made that he was completely at Edward's disposal, whether he liked it or not. The four of them made their way through the lobby and outside, where Thomas helped Celeste up into a ready coach and Edward tossed her drunken husband in the empty one behind hers. Celeste did not speak, only nodded politely at Thomas as both carriages took off toward the Upper East Side.

Thomas watched them go, and then Edward took his arm. "We'd better get back," he told his son, ushering Thomas inside.

"Father, how did you…how did you know who they were?"

"It wasn't hard to figure out, Thomas. Especially given your account of their marriage this afternoon. Hurry, or Lucy will be furious."

Thomas went along with his father, dumbfounded, trying his best to comprehend what exactly he'd just beheld. They reached their box in no time and Edward shook off the interrogative looks from William and Lucy as if their absence was nothing to be concerned with. Thomas spent the remainder of the play staring at Edward, contemplating what other sort of talents the man had hidden from him all these years, and how well he truly knew his father.

"All right, one of you, please tell us what happened?" Lucy implored as the last of the actors took their bows. "Thomas looks like he's seen a ghost and Edward, well, you're tie has been undone since you returned. And your top two vest buttons." Lucy went to him and fixed Edward's ensemble, her brow furrowing with alarm.

"It was nothing. Just a mix up downstairs, that's all," Edward said, holding still for her.

William did not hide his irritation. "Eddie, what do you mean a mix up?"

Edward didn't budge. "Let's wait and divulge the details when we are back at home. All right, Thomas?"

"Yeah…sure. We can talk it over later."

"Well, can we go be social for an hour or so? Or would that kill you boys?" Lucy pressed, smiling from ear to ear. "Come on, I've got you out. Can you indulge me for just a bit?"

William sighed heavily. "All right. Just an hour, though, Luce." Their time ticked by slowly, and Thomas was introduced by Lucy and William to nearly twenty people whose names he would never remember. It was hopeless to think on anything other than their interaction with Mr. and Mrs. Adams, and Thomas' head swam with amazement over Edward's actions in the lobby...how fast his movements were...how relaxed his stature remained. The concept overwhelmed him so much, he was just about to excuse himself to go when he saw Esther again, and his mind cleared straightaway. She stood at the Captain's side smiling, a glass of champagne in her right hand and her left arm wrapped through his. They were talking with a few other military men, friends of the Captain he presumed, and Thomas observed her from afar, staying hidden within the crowd. Once her champagne was gone and she wandered in the direction of a refill, he took his opportunity, stepping lightly to make their meeting seem as coincidental as it was with Bernard.

"Well, hello again," he spoke to her, taking the empty glass out of her hand and turning to order them another round.

"Hi," she greeted, not quite as reserved and formal as she'd been before.

"Enjoying the night?" he asked, leaning against the bar.

"I am! I'm just a little worried. Celeste left at intermission and didn't tell me she was leaving. I expect she wasn't feeling well, but it's not like her."

The barman returned with her champagne and his whiskey. "Perhaps she was tired and knew you were in good company." He held up his glass. "Cheers!" Esther smiled and they clinked their glasses together. He tried not to gawk at her. "You look...incredible, by the way," he nearly stuttered, hoping his next sip would calm his nerves down – women had never made him anxious, yet apparently after the propaganda he'd been fed throughout day, Esther was becoming an exception.

She blushed, though she tried to hide it. "Thank you, Thomas."

"And Captain Bernhardt seems like a good man. Please feel free to invite him to dinner Friday, if you'd like."

His comment changed her body language, making it obvious the mention of her escort visibly aggravated her. "I will pass along the invitation," she remarked frigidly.

He pushed harder. "I'm sorry, did I upset you?"

"Not at all," she said indifferently. "It has just been a long night."

"I thought, since you seem to be on the brink of engagement, you would want him to attend with you. Selfishly, I'd rather have the opportunity to catch up with you without making him feel out of place, but that is your decision."

"Don't be ridiculous!" she cried. "We are not on the brink of engagement. We are just…"

"Friends?" Thomas finished her sentence, chuckling. "From the look on his face when you're together, I'd say that ship sailed long ago, Es."

Esther downed her champagne. "Is this a lecture on my conduct?"

"Of course not. Like I said, he seems like a good man. And I like him. I just don't want to see him getting hurt, that's all."

"What is that supposed to mean?"

Thomas looked directly into her eyes. "It means that perhaps you should ignore my efforts to be polite and not invite him Friday."

Stunned, Esther stayed quiet, and before she could say a word, Lucy appeared. "Ah! At last I get to meet Esther! My name is Lucy Turner, Thomas'…well, that's of no matter."

Thomas leisurely retreated, allowing Lucy to take charge and not wanting to ruin the seed he'd planted. Off in another corner, he spotted William and his father in an intense discussion and set out toward them. He was only a few feet away when Captain Bernhardt shifted into his path.

"Just the man I'm looking for," he beckoned merrily. "Can I ask you a favor, Mr. Turner?"

"Absolutely! What can I do for you Captain?"

He placed himself close to Thomas, not wanting anyone else to overhear him. "I have a few of my men in town that are planning on continuing their party elsewhere. I know you and Esther are like family. Do you mind seeing to it that she gets back to her residence? And that this…well, stays between us?"

"Happily," Thomas promised him. "Might I make a suggestion?"

"Suggestion?"

"There's a place on the west side called The Palace," Thomas clarified. "Have you heard of it?"

A slight blush crossed the Captain's cheeks. "Well, of course I have. It's the most expensive brothel in the city! But that's…well it's beyond the means of most of my men…"

"I understand. Tell the man at the door Thomas Turner sent you, and that I will gladly spot your bill for the night."

The Captain shook his head. "I…I don't know…I couldn't ask that…"

Thomas put his hand on the man's shoulder. "I insist, and I won't take no for an answer. Consider it a…a friendly hand out in the hopes we meet again soon."

"Really? You're sure?" The Captain's smile grew with each passing second.

"Go enjoy yourselves. I'll take care of Esther," he promised. "My family will be leaving shortly anyhow, and we're headed the same direction."

"Thank you, Mr. Turner. Thank you so much." The Captain vigorously shook Thomas' hand and trotted over to Esther and Lucy, illuminating that he would be leaving her with the Turners. Thomas didn't stick around to watch, not wanting to draw attention. The night was going remarkably in his favor.

By some means, Lucy engineered their rides home in order

that Esther and Thomas rode in their coach alone, and while Esther dissented Lucy put her objections to rest, claiming she wanted to give the long lost friends time to talk. With a wink, Lucy leapt into her own carriage where William and Edward already waited, giving Esther no choice but to comply. Their driver helped her inside and she sat opposite Thomas, refusing to make eye contact with him as he slid into the seat across. For a few moments they remained silent, and rather than forcing Esther into a useless banter, Thomas pulled two cigarettes out of his pocket and lit them both, handing one to her. Seconds later, the coach jumped forward, and they were on their way.

She held up her hand to decline. "No, thanks, I don't smoke."

"That's a total load of shit, Es. Take it."

Esther hesitated, then grabbed the cigarette and took a long drag. "Christ, I needed that." She inhaled again, staring at him. "How did you…?"

"I could smell it on you earlier. Takes one to know one, I suppose."

"I guess you're right…" Her voice trailed off, and Thomas gave her the time to put her words together. They did not disappoint. "I'm not going to marry him, Tommy."

His heart leapt at how she addressed him. "Captain Bernhardt?"

"It's just a…pleasant distraction for me. Dealing with Celeste and that monster she's married to is not exactly easy to bear…and recently it's…it's gotten…well worse. So much worse."

Seeing her distress, Thomas decided not to tell her about the incident he witnessed earlier, and changed the subject. "How long has he been courting you?" he entreated her, though he didn't really want to know the answer.

"A few weeks, I suppose. I don't know." She blew a cloud of smoke into the carriage. "He's the only man who ever had the decency to actually talk to me aside from you."

"Es, you don't need to justify anything to me. You are a grown woman and you will do what you want. It's been a long time since

I've had any sway in your decisions."

She laughed. "Now that is a total load of shit."

"Oh, don't deny it. I mean…Es…we haven't talked in two years…on your terms. You stopped writing to me, don't forget."

"And now you're back."

Thomas nodded. "Yes, I am, but I honestly want you to be happy. We aren't children anymore. Life can have detrimental consequences if we aren't vigilant."

Esther flicked her cigarette out the window. "Well if we're being honest, I want to know how you felt when you saw me tonight."

"What?"

"Tell me how you felt when you saw me tonight."

"Es, you've had a lot of champagne, maybe we should have this talk another time."

"And your comments about me coming alone Friday were what? Flirtatious or platonic?"

Thomas was stuck. "I'm not sure, if we're being honest. I'm trying to figure that out myself."

The coach went quiet again for the last few minutes, darkness swallowing both of them as Thomas let her mull over what was said. As the carriage halted outside the Adams residence, the coachman got out and opened the door for Esther, and she climbed down gracefully, not bothering to even glance at him or say goodbye. Just as Thomas started to believe he hadn't interpreted her statements or vibes correctly, Esther stopped and turned back, her face furious.

"You want to know why I stopped writing?" she shouted heatedly. "Because I got this idiotic idea in my head that I had feelings for you. And I dreamed up that you would come back and get me out of this God damned place and save me, like you always did. When I realized I was a total fool I broke off my letters. Because I couldn't handle it. And now here you are, messing my whole world up. Again!" Esther threw her arms up into the air and whipped around, storming off toward the door.

Thomas acted impulsively – her reaction was by no means the one he'd planned on. "Wait, Es!" he yelled, jumping out after her. However, Esther didn't stop, and he ran up to her and grabbed her arm, pulling her to face him. "Please don't run off so mad at me. I didn't mean–"

Esther spun around unpredictably and kissed Thomas hard. Caught in the rush, he kissed her back and then, realizing what was happening, Thomas pushed her away, astounded at his own behavior. A flood of emotions hit him at once, and he stood there, speechless, unable to articulate any of them. With his hands on her shoulders he held her at bay, staring into her eyes, unsure of how to act next.

Esther went first, her gaze falling to the ground. "I apologize. I shouldn't have done that."

"It's…it's all right…that was my fault," he managed to spit out.

"You're right. I…I've just had too much champagne. I need to…to go to bed." She broke free of his grasp. "I'll see you Friday," she muttered, walking up the stoop slowly.

Thomas didn't know why he said it, but the word came out before he could stop himself. He had to know.

"Alone?"

She peered down from the doorway, a smile creeping to her lips. "Alone."

Lucy was sitting by herself when Thomas made it home, though from the loud voices echoing from William's study, it was obvious as to why. She was drinking a glass of champagne, visibly strained though not wanting to leave before whatever was going on got resolved. When she saw Thomas she summoned him over, giggling at how ridiculous she appeared. Her shoes had been kicked off and lay on the ground under her feet, which were propped up on the coffee table, her body sunken down into the deep couch.

"They've been yelling since we've been home…I have no idea why, so I thought I'd try and stick it out. How was your carriage ride? Hmmm?"

Thomas lit another cigarette. "Thanks for that one, Luce. Way to make everything more complicated than it already is."

"Oh don't be that way," she retorted, swigging a sip of champagne. "You wouldn't have had a better opportunity to talk it over with her."

"I've only been home for three days!"

"Yes, but you don't have that kind of time, Tommy. You and Esther have had a special bond since you were young, something most couples never have, and that's friendship. She won't be on the free market much longer, and if it's not you, I can guarantee it'll be that Captain."

Thomas' head was swimming from the tobacco and whiskey – he told Lucy what happened on his ride home with Esther, and she listened attentively, shaking her head when he finished.

"You've just said it yourself. You've never felt this way about someone so quickly. What's the issue?"

Thomas was skeptical. "Is it because I really want Esther, or is it just something that will die out after actually spending time with her? I've always been fond of a chase, you know that. I mean, the bottom line is that I don't know who she is anymore. And I don't want to hurt her if it's not…right…does that make sense?"

"Just remember something, Tommy. Love doesn't make sense because it's not logical. It's raw emotion, and it's blind to everything else. From the moment I met William, I knew we would marry, and it wasn't a choice I made. It was just a feeling. Go see her tomorrow for tea. I think building up your meeting on Friday would only have a dissatisfying outcome, not to mention you'll be in some…well… rather odd company for that sort of thing."

"Won't that be…difficult…after tonight?" he beseeched her. A small part of him wanted to take some space and stay away, trying to sort through the reckless mess he'd made, but he knew Lucy wouldn't allow him to hide.

A loud bang of the study door followed by stomping footsteps alerted Lucy and Thomas that whatever argument was being had would not be settled that night. Neither of the cousins bothered to say goodnight, only trudged opposing directions to their respective bedrooms. With a roll of her eyes and a disapproving expression, Lucy left Thomas to deal with her husband, suggesting he try to cool off his father as well. Thomas considered it and made the determination that he wouldn't get involved, already a little flabbergasted at his father's random heroics hours prior. While dealing with Esther he'd buried the incident in his mind, and now, as he sat on his own watching the last of the fire burn out, Thomas dwelled on each detail with confusion. The strength...the speed...the accuracy... the excuse of naval training from almost thirty years ago didn't add up. Thomas didn't know what to think, but he couldn't deny he was fascinated. His father seemed to be an endless ocean of secrets, each passing wave bringing something new to the surface. There was no real way to confront Edward this time, though: he must be aware Thomas would want vindication, but he would let his father do it on his own time, and in his own way. That was just the way Edward was.

Strangely, the one factor bothering Thomas above the others was how helpless he had felt watching it unfold, and he never wanted to feel that way again. He could throw a punch or two, certainly, yet his father's actions were so exact and forceful enough to get his point across without further retaliation or incident. It was expeditious. And breathtaking, for both him and unfortunately for Mr. Adams.

The next morning, Edward and William were nowhere to be found, thus raising Lucy's anxieties, and she confided in Thomas that William hadn't told her anything about the argument, only went to sleep mad as a dog. Thomas took their morning meeting with Turner S & D's new American ship builders by himself, not minding having to take charge of the Turner enterprise. The new designs took on his father's personal suggestions as a former naval officer, and Thomas approved them after extensive review. The cost would almost double to build, but conversely their ships could take on harsher waters and sustain bigger loads, making the new fleet worth the increase of investment. He knew Edward and William would be a little irritated with him for not talking it over with them first; nevertheless, Thomas found he didn't have a guilty conscience. What was the point of him being a partner if he couldn't take certain responsibilities on his own?

Later that afternoon, Lucy stubbornly cast Thomas out of the house, telling him not to come back until he'd gone to see Esther. He conceded, despite having no idea what he might say to her on the subject. Following his arrival at the Adamses' home after pacing the block a few times, the maid informed Thomas that Mr. Adams, Celeste, and Esther were actually in the park for a birthday celebration, and wouldn't be returning until nightfall. A little relieved, Thomas thanked her and left. However, instead of venturing home, his feet took him into Central Park in the direction of the party. Maybe if he could just get a glimpse of her, it would help him sort through some of his feelings and determine his standpoint for the future. Thomas hoped it might even make him conclude that the night before had been a mistake, and take a step back from the slippery slope he was on. Deep down, he knew that wouldn't happen, and still he pushed onward, his logic once more resolving that the only things he'd felt were a result of the alcohol and the sway of those around him.

The party wasn't hard to miss – there were thirty or forty people, all clad in white scattered about, enjoying the gorgeous and sunny spring afternoon. Thomas kept his distance, standing in the shade of a tree, allowing his eyes to search for the one person he came to find. It didn't take him long, and unexpectedly, Thomas was swept away in rage, his whole body tensing.

She wasn't alone. Just as they'd been at the theater, Esther was arm in arm with the Captain, talking with another couple cheerfully. His blood boiled. Without a doubt, he had been deluded to think he would be the one to let her down easy; Esther was visibly just fine without him, and like reason suggested, consumed too much champagne. It must have been a farce, imagined because of their closeness as children, and played well by her. For all he knew, she could have done it to push up her engagement with the Captain by giving him a sense of competition. He was about to turn around when the Captain caught sight of him from yards away and waved merrily in salutation, causing Esther to look his direction. There was no reason for him to stay put. He tipped his hat to them with his best counterfeit smile and left, trying to keep the last of his cool.

His ego was bruised. Thomas assumed last night would throw the weight in his favor, and any rivalry would be squashed at his mention of an interest in Esther. Seeing her with the Captain firsthand, as if Thomas didn't matter, changed his mind – he didn't want a contest. The outside influences he swore wouldn't affect him had, and he would no longer listen to Lucy or the Madame again, least of all in these type of matters. There was a bottle of whiskey at home to drown his sorrows in, and he planned on doing just that. Then, out of the blue he felt a hand pull at his arm and, startled, Thomas whisked around to see Esther standing there almost as livid as he was.

"Thomas what are you doing here?" she inquired accusingly.

"Well, I live a short walk away, and I thought the park was public property," he snapped sarcastically. "Go back to your party, Es."

"So you just happened to be out by yourself walking by the party I'm attending?" She was trying to be coy, and it was only infuriating him further.

His polite filter dissolved. "No, actually I had gone by to see you and the maid sent me here. And I'm glad she did. It fulfilled the reservations I had. Now, if you don't mind, I'm going to head home, and you should get back to Captain Bernhardt."

Esther's face went as white as her lace dress, and her haughtiness died immediately. "You…went to see me?"

"Of course I did, for God's sake. To talk with you like normal people do after things happen that they don't understand. I understand now, and I can promise you things like last night won't happen again. I'm happy for you, Es, but don't think you can pull shit like last night and get away with it anymore. Not with me. I don't want to be involved in whatever games you're playing. I think I underestimated just how much the Hiltmores changed you." He spoke so brashly, those passing by ogled at them, and tears welled up in Esther's eyes. He stepped closer to her, taking his tone down. "Go back to your party, Es."

"Tommy, please…it's not—"

"I don't care what it isn't. I care about what it is. And it's not what I thought it was. Good day, Esther. I'll see you and Captain Bernhardt Friday."

Thomas spun around and left her there, a pang of remorse hitting him for leaving her in such a state publicly, though his anger outbid his worry for her. He let it pass and didn't look back, hoping he'd made himself quite clear.

It wasn't until he was out of the park he realized what he'd actually done. And Thomas knew it was too late to fix it.

XIII.

"I'm not going," Esther asserted. "The Captain is at home sick and there is no way I'm going without him."

The Madame sighed loudly from behind her room dividers. "And just what the fuck has happened to make you change your mind so drastically?" It had taken over an hour for her to find which dress suited the occasion perfectly – it had to be one that would be appropriate enough for the Upper East Side, but still emphasize the fact that she existed in a far different world than they did, and was proud of it. Conversely, Esther had only just shown up and rather than offering any reprieve, was making the Madame's trepidation rise.

"I told you. The Captain is sick and–"

"Esther please," she interjected, getting more and more pissed off. "My time is valuable. If you are going to keep fucking around, I don't have time for it. So why don't you fess up so we can get this over with."

The room went quiet for a moment. "I…sort of…kissed Thomas."

The Madame let out a loud laugh, emerging from the dividers and motioning for Esther to finish lacing her corseted dress.

"Oh darling, you thought this would surprise me? What else? There's got to be more to it."

She walked toward the Madame, finally making herself of some use. "He saw me the next day with Captain Bernhardt, then proceeded to embarrass me in the middle of Central Park before running off, and we haven't spoken since." Esther pulled the laces tighter, and the Madame exhaled all the air left in her lungs. With two hard tugs, she was ready to go, looking more ravishing than ever.

"Darling, you are going to dinner, otherwise it will permanently damage any social relationship you might want to have with the Turners in the future. You're already fucking dressed. I'm already fucking dressed. Don't blame Thomas for your own fickleness – you are the one who made the first move and then ran around with someone else. The next damn day, might I add."

Esther tried to dispute her. "I was not 'running around!'"

The Madame went to check her rouged lips in the mirror. "You were. Stop playing the victim. Thomas was right, you were wrong. You will go apologize tonight and we'll move forward."

"But–"

The Madame's face hardened. "Don't you dare fucking argue. This is how it's going to be. Now, go get Danny and Hope for me. I have a lecture prepared for them on running operations tonight."

"We're already here," Danny announced, waltzing through the doorway with Hope at her side.

The Madame waved them over and strode to her desk, picking up the reservations for the night.

"Here's the list of reservations made, all private clientele and the girls are already divided up. No switches or exceptions, got it? You know protocol if anything gets out of hand." The Madame gave Hope the list, and she studied it vigilantly while Danny tasked herself with adjusting Esther's current hairstyle. "And what are the two most important things?" the Madame pressed on.

"If shit gets ugly, send for you and Louis and don't kill anyone until you're back," Danny replied. "Esther, for God's sake hold still and let me fix it."

"And no matter what, keep business functional," Hope chimed in.

The Madame nodded. "You both memorized the list of bastards not allowed in our establishment."

"Georgie knows them all too," Hope appended. "We will make rounds, as you usually do, and he will stay posted at the front. Back doors bolted shut."

The Madame hated leaving The Palace under the jurisdiction of anyone other than herself, but tonight was the beginning of something she couldn't miss. Some scores took years to settle, and she had been patiently biding her time in the shadows, hoping the moment to strike would eventually be reached. The business would be in good hands – she'd been extremely scrupulous in preparing Danny and Hope, and Louis would be checking every lock and back alley prior to their departure. Trusting others in her stead was something the Madame would never master, no matter how hard she might try to make it otherwise.

Taking every available caution, she bent down and opened the bottom drawer of her desk, grabbing for two of her pocket pistols. "I want you each to have one," she said, handing them over. "You both are representing me tonight, and I'll be damned if someone tries to come after my business when I'm gone."

Both girls were wide eyed, staring at her blankly. "I…I've never shot a gun before," Hope remarked nervously.

"With any luck, you won't have to. Now take them and get out. You have less than two hours until the first party arrives."

Hope and Danny did as she asked. When they'd gone, the Madame changed her attentions back toward Esther, whose hair was now much improved being slightly more seductive than its previous style. A resistant pout remained on her face.

"All right. Enough of this. Get up."

"What? Why?"

"Because you need a fucking attitude adjustment."

When Esther didn't flinch, the Madame bolted to her and

grabbed her wrists, pulling Esther to her feet and making it known her behavior wouldn't be tolerated. "I don't care what you do in your personal life. However, you don't let it affect us when we are working. Got it?"

There was shame on her face. "Yes…Yes I've got it. I'm sorry."

The Madame glowered at her, then eased up. "If this happens again, I can promise you our next talk will not be pleasant." She released Esther's wrists, allowing her to sink down into the armchair like a scolded child. Instead of addressing her personal difficulties further, the Madame poured her a glass of wine and handed it to Esther. "Here is my advice, and this is the last time I will offer you any on the subject. Now, I don't know what the fuck is going on with you and the military goon, but if you want Thomas for yourself, you better patch this up fast."

She had a large gulp of wine, letting out a big breath. "I don't think I can patch it up."

"Oh don't be so dramatic, Esther. Fix it. I know you can."

"How?"

"He went to the fucking park to find you. There's something there for him too, and if you can't see that for yourself, then I've done a shitty job in developing your intelligence, and we both know that's not the case."

Louis' knock rang loudly through the office. "Come in!" the Madame yelled, pouring her own glass of wine.

He entered with a smile upon seeing Esther. "Ah, wine before the snake pit, I see?"

"Esther, darling, will you leave us for a few minutes? Have Claire take care of you at the bar and then head home to meet Celeste for the party." Instantly, Esther got to her feet and headed downstairs, and as the door closed behind her, the Madame pounced on another issue that had been clawing at her for some time.

"Louis, we need to talk."

"Yes, Madame?"

"I need you to stop going behind my back, and end whatever charade is going on with Edward Turner, do I make myself clear?"

"I don't understand."

Enraged, the Madame slammed her fist on her desk. "Don't bullshit me. I know somehow you two have remained friends, and I honestly don't fucking care, but you work for me, not for him. I have let this slide repeatedly. Not anymore. We have too much at stake now."

Louis sat down where Esther had been. "What are you planning?"

"It's time to get rid of the Hiltmores."

Louis shook his head. "We aren't ready. We don't have the magnitude of resources lined up to take them down."

"If we don't set this into motion now, we never will. We need to eliminate these four from the equation…they're keeping us stagnant. We take down Charles, Catherine, Douglas, and then the son-in-law. Esther will be safe and we can all get our hands out of the fucking mud and rid ourselves of two liabilities at once."

"Madame—"

"I'm not waiting any longer!" she nearly screamed. Louis was stunned at her reaction, and the Madame had a sip of wine to compose herself. "I can't wait," she told him. "It's been long enough. We're ready."

"You know I will do whatever you need me to. I just thought we agreed we would wait until we…we heard from our friend down south."

"The time is now. I will not sit idly by anymore, Louis. I can't fucking do it."

"And why now?"

The Madame set her glass down. "Because of Esther. Because of their fucking arrogance and disregard for everyone but themselves. That woman is a despicable, ladder-climbing hag who sold off her own daughter to the highest bidder, and under her control Douglas is no fucking better. Worse, if you take into account what we know

now. That boy is going to kill either Esther or Celeste, and I am not wasting the last eight years I've spent putting into Esther for the sake of walking on eggshells around the Hiltmores."

"And there's also the element of them betraying your deal."

The Madame's smirked. "You know I don't do well with rejection, Louis."

Louis' apprehension didn't fade. "And what are you going to do when the daughter comes looking to you for answers, eh? What then?"

"Tell her the truth about her parents."

Louis was bemused. "Why would you even take the time to deal with that? And what are you going to do when her family is gone? The remainder of her husband's family will devour her."

"No they won't, you can count on that. I will take her in."

Louis scoffed. "And what? Whore her out?"

"Please. I wouldn't dream of it."

"Then what?"

She finished her drink and glanced away. "That you will have to wait and see. I have big plans for our dear Celeste. I just need to figure out how exactly we're going to dispose of her damned husband once his father, Catherine, and Douglas are taken care of. That is going to be a challenge for me."

"You do better when you're challenged," Louis attributed, a small grin forming.

"Yes I do, Louis. Yes I do."

They were the last to arrive to the Turners', and Tony let them in with a skeptical look, showing them to the great room where the guests loitered with drinks and conversation. Esther came over and met them in the doorway, curtsying as if they met by chance and in the style of a formal greeting.

"We only just arrived before you did," she whispered, rising from her bow. "I've only been greeted by Lucy…Thomas has yet to appear."

The Madame nodded, a hidden indication that she could stay beside her and Louis for the time being. Every person there was dressed in their finest, the men sporting tuxedo dinner suits and the ladies in their summer ball gowns, though the Madame couldn't help but perceive there was an odd air about the group as a whole. In the far left corner were the Hiltmores and their daughter Celeste, who was without her husband on this occasion, and they did their best to ignore her entry by pretending to be consumed in a remark made by another bystander. Three couples she did not know, but clearly knew each other, laughed merrily to her right, completely oblivious to everyone else. Lucy Turner was talking with two men, most likely father and son, her back to the Madame, while William and Edward were deep in discussion with a handful of gentlemen, their wives tittering by the fireplace. As she took her mental notes, the Madame could feel Esther's nerves getting the better of her in spite of their talk, her eyes constantly searching the room for Thomas. The Madame paid her no mind – she was thoroughly enjoying the expression on every attendee's face as they spotted the final guests' entrance, and the conceit was tremendously evident.

"Ah, you've made it!" Thomas' familiar voice rang as he came up behind them. "I was afraid you might not show."

The Madame curtseyed ever so slightly. "We won't be here long. But I thought our attendance was necessary. For you of course, darling."

He smiled. "I should have guessed you'd only show up for cocktail hour."

"We were happy for the invitation," Louis jumped in. "Although I can't say we exactly blend in with your friends, Tommy."

"Everyone here is promoting their own business, in one way or another," Thomas elucidated, "I think both of you fit that category perfectly. And, since it was Edward's party, he's free to invite whomever he likes. I bet the majority of these gentlemen could learn a thing or two from you, Madame. Just as I have."

"I have no doubt about that," she sneered with pride.

Esther stayed quiet, and Thomas politely directed his attention her way next. "Esther, you look lovely this evening." His words were passive and without any hint of emotion. "I passed along an invitation to Captain Bernhardt and was sad to hear he couldn't make it."

"Yes he…he sends his regrets," she stammered, unable to meet Thomas' eyes.

"Well if you can excuse me for just a moment, I'll go grab Tony and have him bring you all a round of champagne before we start introductions."

When Thomas had trotted off to the other side of the room, the Madame turned to Esther. "You can do better than that," she hissed sharply.

"I'm trying, Madame."

"Esther, remember what's at stake. This is a lot bigger than you having a fucking tizzy over a boy."

Esther's mouth opened, as if she were about to protest, and then stopped as Thomas returned with a tray of full champagne flutes. They toasted to good health, and an array of greetings began, though the Hiltmores stayed as far away from the Madame as they could, sliding away to keep their distance anytime she drew close. Most of the party gave the Madame a courteous reception, some probably unaware of who she was or what her realm of employment included. One even inquired if Esther was her daughter, and the question nearly caused the Madame to strangle the woman for implying she looked old enough fill such a roll – the Madame never took any implications regarding her age lightly. It wasn't until her last stop where she met Francis Bernard and his son, Francis Bernard, Jr. that the party became fun, as Francis senior was utterly fascinated by her, Louis, and The Palace.

Predictably, Esther retreated to Celeste's side, keeping her eyes on Thomas from the other side of the room as he played his part of host along with Edward. A handful of times she came close to speaking up; however, in the end, her courage failed her. Thomas either didn't care or was doing a glorious job pretending as if he didn't, his social engagements maintaining his avoidance of being caught near her for too long. The entire scene was extremely juvenile to her, though the Madame did begin to wonder if perhaps Esther really did destroy whatever feelings Thomas might have had by continuing her relations with the Captain. It was either that, or he was by far one of the best actors the Madame had ever seen perform, and she thought the latter more likely. He'd been raised by her, after all.

Idle chatter consumed the hour she and Louis intended to spend, and as the actual dinner hour drew close, they excused themselves for the night, the real portion of their mission about to commence. Though she was already well aware of their plans, Esther was none too pleased to be left at the party with Celeste as her only comfort.

"You are quite literally abandoning me to the wolves," she expressed under her breath in the Madame's ear as they gave their farewells. "This night is going to change everything and I am stuck here with the people whose lives we are about to royally fuck up."

The Madame casually stepped back with a grin, keeping her voice low as well. "Just don't let them out of your sight." Louis wrapped her bejeweled shawl around her shoulders. "And whatever you do, don't forget to make sure you and Celeste take a separate cab home. Got it?"

"Consider it done."

"Good."

As she turned to leave, Esther piped back up. "Madame?"

"What is it, darling?"

"Just…just please be careful. I know how much this means to you. And what this means for us."

The Madame snorted. "Again, Esther, the dramatics are completely unnecessary. Now stop fucking stalling and get back to the party." Louis was already waiting with the door opened wide, and the Madame marched that way. "I'll see you in a few hours, darling."

Three hours later, the Madame sat in the backseat of a large coach, facing the opposing direction it was bound to travel, while Louis, donning a dusty brown overcoat and bowler hat, helmed the horses disguised as the driver of the carriage. It had taken her a bit to scout out their target, and the poor, terrified man would get his cab back at the end of the night, but until then, he was tied up, gagged, and blindfolded in the back alley of The Palace. She paid one of the Turners' maids handsomely to tip her when the party was coming to a close, and the girl proved to be a reliable resource, sending over one of the cook's girls to their hideaway when the time came. Louis wasn't fond of the idea, yet she persuaded him in the end, and he'd sulkily put on his false beard and sooted his face, no doubt cursing at her in his head. The Madame still wore the luminous, dark green gown from the party, and its embellishments flickered like stars from the street lamps illuminating each side of the road. The moment for redemption had finally come full swing. All she had to do was wait for the rest of the participants to arrive.

Fortunately, it was no more than a quarter of an hour. The calm street suddenly filled with laughter and jests as the Turners' guests made their way outside the residence and down the stoop, a little intoxicated from the party, and Louis joined the five other hired drivers as they marched forward to claim passengers. The Madame spied through her tiny window, masked by the surrounding darkness, to observe Louis approaching the Hiltmores and to her horror, Celeste was with them. Just as sheer panic was about to set in, Esther put her worries at ease:

"Celeste!" the Madame heard Esther call. "Could you wait just a minute for me and we'll leave together?"

With a quick goodbye to her parents, Celeste complied and strode away toward the front door. Louis took charge, hobbling over as if he had a limp in his left leg, and ushered the Hiltmores in the direction of their coach. There was no element of recognition in neither Douglas nor Catherine's face as to who their driver really was, and, like a gentleman, Louis escorted the Hiltmores to the small door of the car. He helped Catherine inside first by offering his hand, and she was closely followed by Douglas. At first, husband and wife settled themselves in their seats, unaware anyone else could possibly be in attendance. In the next second, they both were hit with a look of confusion when they felt her presence and uneasily glanced her direction, the dimness making it difficult to determine whom their third passenger might be. With the flick of Louis' reins the coach took off, and the Madame leaned forward so the Hiltmores could see her face.

"Lovely night, isn't it?" she asked, exhaling a cloud of smoke into their carriage from the cigar in her hand. Catherine and Douglas gaped at her in dismay, utterly speechless. "Oh come come now, you didn't think I'd want to pass on my regards? I was hurt to detect neither one of you was particularly pleased to see me. Such a shame after so many years of friendship!"

Douglas inched toward his wife, placing his arm in front of her, as if attempting to shield her from a blow. "What do you want, Madame?"

The Madame smiled savagely. "Want? Whatever could you mean?"

"You always want something, you insane bitch," Catherine spat before Douglas could stop her.

"We had an agreement that you refused to uphold."

"Oh for God's sake!" Douglas exclaimed. "You make good enough money to supply your whores with their own fabrics, don't you think?"

"No I don't," she answered blandly. "And you think you can hide behind the Adamses like a child behind their mother's God damned skirt. Really, it's despicable for both of you. The agreement was an easy one, and I don't see why you would argue considering what I have just uncovered about your southern operations."

Catherine's eyes were filled with fire. "Go to hell. We aren't going to be your puppets. You took advantage of us…from the beginning it was only about money!"

"You, of all people my darling Catherine, have always been only about money," the Madame shot back. "Money and muscle are the only things you have ever understood. Don't forget that without my help your shipments wouldn't be making their way up the coastline without the Union stopping them. I have allowed it to continue for the sole reason that I hoped you might see the light."

Douglas shook his head. "We've already found another way. And you have no proof against us. Blackmailing won't work anymore."

"And you think in a country that's still licking it's wounds from the war they wouldn't want to prosecute a racist pig who is still exploiting the work of negro women and men? You think they won't go investigate the brutality you subject them too?"

"Slavery is outlawed, they are employees who choose to stay," Catherine threw in. "They were given the chance to leave and did not."

"Yes, because you fucking threatened to hunt them down and kill them if they did. And every one of their children."

Douglas' face was turning red. "You can make accusatory suggestions all you want, Madame, the bottom line is it's your word against ours. And you're a whore who runs a business most people cringe when they hear of. The fact that the Turners' even had you present tonight is absolutely appalling and reprehensible, and you should consider yourself lucky they even allow Thomas to see you at all. So go ahead and get whatever it is off your chest. You're not changing my mind, and you will not be getting any more cotton shipments from me free of charge."

The Madame's head tilted sideways, challenging him. "Does your wife know the things you've done to those people?"

"What are you talking about?"

"I mean you murdering your own children."

Douglas' skin went pallid. "What do you...how....how could you..."

"How many have there been? Four? Five maybe?" she went on indifferently. "And you ordered them all fucking dead." The Madame spat at the floor where his feet were. "You think my establishment is filthy? Take a long fucking look in the mirror, Douglas. You're the real monster."

"Those were not legitimate children, and they were better lost rather than struggling through life," Catherine tried to defend. "I made that decision, not Douglas. They never would have fit in anywhere. Mixes are hated by both races. We all know this, even you Madame."

The Madame wasn't sure if she was shocked or just downright disgusted at the people that sat opposite her. So Catherine unmistakably had known her husband had a nasty habit of knocking up his "employees," and then she made sure the offspring never saw the light of day. For a moment, she wasn't certain how she wanted to proceed, recognizing that restoring her connection to free cotton was out of the question – the Hiltmores wouldn't budge, and even if they did, the small amount of conscience the Madame had left would never allow her to use their product.

When they had originally cut her off, the Madame sent Louis down to the plantations to investigate what was really going on and to see if there was any way to leverage the situation; what they found was so appalling the Madame eventually went herself to see it with her own eyes. It changed everything for her, and at last she found a reason to take down two of the people she despised most in the world.

"I have the proof," she informed them, relighting her cigar. "And I intend to use it unless you shut down your operations completely."

Douglas' mouth dropped open. "There is no possible way you have any proof. We've never documented anything."

Catherine fidgeted as the Madame twisted to her. "Actually, Douglas, your wife has done a few things without your knowledge. And she's fucked you over by trying to make the extra dime."

"What does that mean? What are you implying?" he implored, the nervousness escalating his tone.

"She's falsified everything. Inspection reports, tax statements, even Union approval for operations following the war as a certified business with the government. You're both fucked if I go public. Douglas will go to jail, and you, Mrs. Hiltmore, will have nothing left to your name. They'll take every penny." Again, neither of them said a word, and the carriage came to a halt outside their residence not thirty seconds later. "You have a week to get things in motion. And I'll know if you don't."

Louis swung the door open, his disguise gone and no hand offered to assist them out of the carriage. He simply stood back with his arms folded across his chest, his merciless eyes staring them down until the Hiltmores meekly climbed out of the cab and made their way to the front door of their home.

When they disappeared indoors, Louis quickly peeked inside, an almost nervous look on his face. "Verdict?"

"We're good."

He nodded, pleased. "You all right?"

"What do you think?"

"Why didn't you tell them you went and saw it for yourself?"

She sighed. "They never would have believed I made that trip."

"But…you did. You were disguised, but you did."

"That doesn't matter, Louis. They know that I know. The message has been delivered."

He paused. "You didn't tell them about Jeremiah."

The Madame couldn't resist a snigger. "Why spoil the grand finale when the festivities have just begun?"

It was Sunday evening before Esther showed up at The Palace, and she was in worse shape than the Madame beheld on Friday night. Under her beautiful green eyes were deep, dark circles from lack of sleep, and despite being already quite thin Esther seemed frail, as if she had not eaten in weeks. Misery was not a look she wore well, and her body language spoke of nothing but failure to mend whatever it was she had broken between her and Thomas. The second Louis closed the doors behind her, the poor girl bee lined for the Madame's drink cart and poured herself a tall glass of whiskey, downing it and then pouring another, not even bothering to address the Madame.

"What the fuck happened?" the Madame asked. "I…well, honestly I don't think I've ever even seen you drink hard liquor. How bad was it?"

"I tried. Twice Friday night and once yesterday. He wouldn't see me alone or speak to me." She had another sip of her whiskey and slinked over to her armchair. "I've ruined everything, haven't I?" The words choked in Esther's throat.

"Was he upset when you tried to confront him?"

Esther's head dropped. "Just…polite. He evaded the subject every time I brought it up or tried to question him, and always found an excuse to get away fast. When I went by yesterday, Tony told me he wasn't taking any visitors. It's a lost cause." She stifled down what the Madame could only assume was a sob and slumped back into her chair, absolutely crushed.

The Madame studied her closely. "And what of Captain Bernhardt?"

The mention of her other suitor didn't do much for her. "He's coming by tomorrow for tea, and then we're going to the park for some sort of festival. I don't know." Esther shook her head, trying to straighten up. "I don't want to talk about it. Have we heard anything from the Hiltmores? Any response? I tried to sneak away yesterday but I couldn't leave. Celeste had me cornered most of the afternoon and night. I thought you might send for me if anything happened."

"The message was delivered successfully," the Madame began, moving to sit beside her. "We need to have a chat, darling. You're not going to like what I have to say, but Louis and I think for your safety it's required sooner rather than later."

Their eyes met. "What do you mean?"

"For your own sake, I need you to get out of that house, as soon as humanly possible."

"I don't understand. Out of Celeste's house? Why?"

"Because Esther I don't want you caught in the fucking cross-fire. Things are going to be on edge for a little while. We have to be armed and ready now that the Hiltmores know I plan on using the evidence we have."

"But…but Aunt I can't. Celeste just found out she's pregnant! What's going to happen if he…who is going to keep her safe…?"

"I know, darling, but it can't be you. This isn't just about you or Celeste. In fact, it has nothing to do with either of you. If we don't do this right, you'll both be fucking collateral in the process."

If it was possible, Esther looked even more pained. "Please don't hurt Celeste. She's the innocent in this. She has no idea who her parents really are or any clue I've been involved."

"No, she doesn't. And if she did, it might make our plans run off the tracks prematurely."

"Can I ever tell her?"

"Tell her what?"

"That her parents only took me in because you blackmailed them? I'd probably be dead like half the other orphans in the Points if not for you."

The Madame rested her hand on Esther's knee reassuringly. "Not until it's over. She wouldn't fucking believe that in a million years otherwise. You have to let her witness this on her own, Esther.

Be there for her. Comfort her. She's going to need it. But you cannot under any circumstances be the one to break that news to Celeste. It would end your friendship."

"Right," Esther acquiesced. "So, where do we go from here?"

"We're moving onto the next phase," the Madame revealed. "And I will follow through with all I've promised you."

Esther's eyes lit up. "You mean…"

"Yes. You'll have your own place and sufficient income to carry on with your social engagements and uphold your status. You will, of course, continue working for me, but as far as the Hiltmores are concerned, you are sitting this one out for the remainder. I can't afford to have anything happen to you. It'd be too big of a fucking loss at this point."

"Is this your unofficial way of telling me you care about me, Madame?"

She scoffed. "This is my way of telling you you're an asset to my network and I need you."

"Ah, I see." Esther had a gulp of her drink. "Why is it I can't be happy with something simple? Why do I have to make everything so knotted up?"

"Only the weak are simple," the Madame countered. "You weren't meant to be a simple woman, darling, otherwise, you wouldn't be sitting next to me right now. And your life would be a hell of a lot more boring."

Esther laughed and, then her expression grew saddened. "You and Celeste are the only two people I trust. Everyone else is…is so dispensable. It scares me."

"Let me give you a piece of advice, Esther, and it's something I wished I learned at your age. All the acquaintances you have, no matter how many, will never be the same as having a real friend. Find the people who will kill for you and die for you, and don't let those ones go. I…well, I will try and be that for you, in my own way, just don't expect us to be braiding each other's hair anytime soon."

Esther set her glass aside and shifted forward to hug the Madame who, not particularly enjoying physical contact, lightly patted her arm and gave it a few seconds before she firmly separated them.

"That's about as much of that bullshit as I can take, darling. How about another whiskey and some dinner?"

Esther didn't have an opportunity to respond – she was cut off by the clamor of something breaking downstairs, causing her to jump in her seat. Shortly after came the sound of high pitch screams and loud voices, and the vibrations of a scuffle echoed up through the floorboards.

"What is going on?" Esther posed, turning to the Madame in alarm.

The Madame knew what it was. She expected it to happen yesterday, and had everyone on high alert. No one ever took kindly to being threatened, especially by the Madame. And Catherine Hiltmore was just shaken enough to have the fucking audacity to hire someone to kill her off.

"Whatever you do, you do not leave this room unless I say so," she ordered. "And you lock the fucking door the second I am outside. Both bolts."

A wave of fear hit Esther's face. "Is someone here? Someone bad?"

The Madame was already racing for her desk. "Explanations are best saved for later, darling. Stay dead silent. Don't move. Don't fucking breathe." She threw the second drawer open and pulled out her Colt revolver, grabbing an extra full cylinder as she swiftly ran out of her office and slammed the door behind her. By the fifth step down the staircase, she cocked the hammer, taking in the scene that lay below her.

To her left near the bar entrance were four of her girls, each clinging to one another and shrieking intermittently as they watched the battle. George was out cold on the floor in front of them, a trickle of blood leaking out from his posterior skull. The front door was wide open, her favorite painting of the Moulin Rouge windmill broken on the floor. At the bottom of the stair was Louis, barely able to restrain a man who was unmistakably heavily armed, and Louis was not.

"Louis!" she shouted at the top of her lungs. "Hold him, God dammit! Hold him!"

Skipping the remaining steps three at a time, the Madame picked up her speed as Louis readied his position. He twisted his arms around the man in such a way that the held the assailant's shoulders and head in a lock with his arms wrapped underneath the bastard's armpits, with Louis' hands holding the back of his head steady. The Madame uncocked her gun and flipped it in her right hand, holding the barrel with a firm grasp and the wooden grip exposed as her bludgeon. Struggling, Louis seized him tight as the man fought hard, sensing what was coming, but he was too late. In one motion, the Madame leapt down the last of the steps of the staircase and took two more bounding strides, striking the man as hard as she could across his temple and knocking him unconscious in Louis' arms, who then dropped him to the floor.

For a moment, no one moved. The Madame stood motionless, staring at the man on the floor. She'd never seen him before in her life. He was haggard, unshaven, and nearly bald, missing a few of his teeth and smelled worse than the pigs in Chinatown. It wasn't clear if he was Irish, but she made the assumption anyhow with over half the fucking people in New York currently stinking of rotting potatoes. She looked up to Louis while he tried to catch his breath and gave him one nod. The patter of bare feet running against the floor caught her attention, and she turned to see Danny and Hope standing in the doorway to the bar, aghast.

"Get the girls out of here," she ordered their direction, Louis carefully lifting George and carrying him out of sight. "Lock down the front room. Let any other customers we have out the back door – tell them they will all be refunded and have a free night on the house for the inconvenience. Go!"

377

Danny ran over and hustled the four terrified whores out of the room, yet the Madame held up her hand when Hope started to follow. "Let Danny take care of it. Get upstairs and check on Esther, and prepare my office for interrogation."

"W-W-Where should I put her? She…she can't see that, Madame…" Hope's voice trailed off shakily.

"Get her in the bar area where things are somewhat normal. And tell Claire to arm herself."

"But…but you want to… to arm Claire…?"

The Madame ignored her. "There is a shotgun loaded and hanging underneath the shelves. She knows how to use it."

While everyone proceeded to their separate tasks, Louis returned, his face twisted in slight trepidation. "Madame…this…this isn't right…"

"Well no shit, Louis."

"No, Madame," he countered, walking over to close the front door, though he left it unlocked. "This was too easy. It's not…it's not right. I've done this many times. No one would be this stupid to blindly come in swinging."

The Madame was anxious. "Talk me through it fast."

"He's the bait man, Madame. To get us ruffled, take our attention away and only focus on him. That's when the other comes in to finish the job."

"What do we do?"

Louis moved rapidly, checking to be sure every door connecting to the front room as locked. "It won't be long. The next one will come."

The Madame pointed to the unconscious man on the floor. "Get him upstairs and tie him up. Make sure everyone is secured."

Louis gazed at her, reading the Madame's mind. "Aim high. Don't stop shooting until he's dead on the ground."

"I won't."

Louis bent over and threw the intruder over his shoulder, sprinting upstairs. Without delay, the Madame readied herself, checking the bullets in her gun and then closed the cylinder. Quickly she assessed the room, deciding her best position would be behind the stair railing on the bastard's left as he entered, where he would least suspect anyone to be waiting. The stairs at the front of The Palace were widest at the bottom, making it an easy place for someone her size to hide. Through the bars lining the steps she watched, cocking her revolver and getting her grip steady, like a hunter stalking its prey.

Two minutes later, there were footsteps outside. The front door handle moved downward easily, and when it reached the end of its course, the door was slowly driven forward. In stepped a man gun first, wearing a dark brown suit and white cotton shirt, his hair almost exactly matching the color of the fabric, with a beard covering the lower half of his face. His eyes were focused and determined, examining the entryway with scrutiny like a hawk. Noiselessly, he shut the door behind him, and pressed onward unhurriedly. The Madame took a deep breath. She already had one motherfucker tied up in her office, and didn't need two to find out the truth. She exhaled.

One big lurch of her legs and she was plunging his direction, roaring out a bellow from the depths of her stomach as she began to pull the trigger over and over again, her adrenaline not allowing her to stop. Each bullet hit, sending the man's body staggering with every strike. When her gun wouldn't fire another bullet she stopped, and the man somehow remaining on his feet in front of her, his torso ridden with holes and blood. After a few seconds of suspense, he fell to his knees and flopped face down onto the ground, lifeless. The Madame reached into her left pocket and took out the final cylinder she'd saved. Her fingers were unsteady, yet she loaded it into the gun, rolling it to rest in the chamber. Glaring down at him, she took aim once more and fired a final shot into his head, blood spattering all over her dress. The heat of the gun steamed into the Madame's hand as she looked on until his right leg stop twitching. Then, he lay still with no signs of life about him.

It had been a long time since she'd killed anyone with her own hand, and the rush of it continued to run thick through her veins. The Madame didn't shift her gaze, wanting to be certain while he bled out onto the floor that the rotten prick wouldn't be getting back up. When she was satisfied he was long dead, she shoved the gun into her dress pocket, spinning around to call for assistance but, to her surprise, she came face to face with Esther.

Shaking, Esther's eyes were locked on the dead man, her white-knuckled hands clutching the bannister beside her, and at once the Madame grabbed the girl's shoulders to get her attention.

"Look at me Esther. Look at me."

Her focus went back and forth, from the body to the Madame many times, in absolute shock of what lay on the ground. Esther couldn't speak. She started to lower her body to the stairs she stood upon, resting down under legs that could no longer hold her. The Madame moved her hands gently to Esther's cheeks, kneeling down in front of her.

"Darling, look into my eyes. Please. It's going to be fine. Look at me, dammit, not at him!"

It took three or four shakes before Esther could say anything. "What...he was...he was..."

"He was going to kill us," the Madame informed her. "All of us. Breathe. It's going to be fine."

"You...you shot him..."

"Yes I did. He's dead, darling." The Madame pulled Esther into a tight embrace, holding her close.

Hope was immediately beside them, kneeling down. "I've got her," she stated, pulling Esther up underneath her arm.

"How the fuck did this happen, Hope?! You were supposed to secure her, God dammit!" the Madame chewed her out. "She could have been shot!"

"It's my fault, Madame," Esther declared, gently gesturing to Hope she could stand on her own. "I heard the gunfire and ran out. I thought you might be hurt and wanted to get to you and help. It was stupid, I know. I'm all right I…was…I've just never seen a dead body before…"

The Madame nodded, her dormant maternal instincts surfacing. "Darling, it's going to be fine. I'm alive and well, as you can see. Now get back upstairs with Hope. I've got work to do, and if you can't stomach this, there's no way in hell you'll be able to stomach what's coming up next."

Ester complied with her request and Hope accompanied her back the way she'd come. The Madame watched them go, knowing no explanation would be able to make Esther feel safe. Then, an idea came to mind.

"Claire!" she shouted. Her young barmaid came running, the shotgun braced in her hands, and stopped when she saw the lifeless body on the floor.

"Bar is…secure…" she murmured, remarkably not fazed by the corpse. "Are we expecting…more visitors?"

"No I don't think so. Is George awake, Claire?" the Madame inquired, gripping the banister with her left hand to help her stay up, the adrenaline waning.

"Yeah…I think he came to…"

"Get his ass in here to clean this up and give him your shotgun to protect the main hall. Then you'll go immediately to the Turner residence and get Thomas. Tell him I need him at The Palace and that it's an absolute emergency."

"The…the Turners, Madame? At this hour?"

"If you fucking question me again, you'll have to find employment elsewhere. Go. Now!"

Claire withdrew, and the Madame spun away from the corpse, shutting her eyes to restrain the emotions overrunning her. It was natural after taking a life, no matter how many times she'd been through it prior to that night. After another deep breath, the Madame counted to five aloud to steady herself, then made her way upstairs. With less than an hour to break the one man she had, she ought to do it fast.

Her confidence returning in full force, the Madame knocked the password on her office door and was let in by Danny. Louis was to the side of their prisoner standing guard, and the man had yet to wake. "Close the doors, Danny."

"Madame...should I...should I stay?"

The Madame rolled up her sleeves and pulled the revolver from her pocket, setting it on top of her desk. "That is entirely up to you, darling. Only if you can fucking handle it. Otherwise, get out. You know how this goes."

Danny closed the doors and remained in the office, taking out the pistol the Madame had given her earlier that week and stationing herself beside Louis.

"Wake him up, Louis," the Madame demanded.

"Yes, Madame."

One sniff of the smelling salts, and the intruder was wide awake, coughing and wheezing from the aroma. His eyes tried to concentrate on his surroundings, no real clue of how he'd gotten where he was. When he saw the Madame, a flicker of terror passed through his eyes. She grinned.

"We can do this one of two ways," she educated him. "The hard way, or my way."

"Go to hell," he retorted, his voice raspy. "I'm not telling you a damned thing." He coughed and twisted in his bindings, trying to loosen them.

The Madame pounced forward like a cat, their faces only inches apart. "Do you think I give a fuck what you say, you piece of shit? You're here under my God damned jurisdiction in my house. And there's no one coming to fucking save you now."

He turned his cheek to her, pretending not to hear. This offense the Madame would not tolerate, and she stood straight and slapped him as hard as she could without breaking her hand. Reaching for his chin and digging her nails in the man's jawbone, she pulled his head back around. She dismissed his groans of pain – this one was weak, but it would take more than empty threats to break him.

"You will talk, or I can promise you won't leave this room in one piece," she snarled – it was time for the real interrogation to commence. With a choreographed high kick, the Madame plunged the heel of her boot into the armrest of the chair where the bastard's right hand was tied, pushing it down firmly as he screamed out, then lifted her dress and drew the dagger she kept holstered on her thigh from its sheath. The veins in his neck bulged as he tried to tug his hand away, not realizing his pain had only just started. The moment his eyes caught sight of the blade they did not leave it, and she held it near his nose as it flickered brightly in the candlelight.

"You wouldn't..." he gasped.

She promptly flipped the knife in her hand like an old parlor trick and held it tight against his jugular, pressing so it cut him slightly. "I would...actually."

"Fuck you, you whore."

"You wish, darling," she chuckled. "I hope you're prepared to take your secrets to the grave, because I am going to take you apart limb by limb. And it will not be a fucking picnic."

He glowered at her, malice in his eyes. "Do your worst...I won't say a damn thing! You'll be dead soon anyhow...you filthy whore."

"Oh, you're talking about the bastard I just shot dead in my entryway?"

Any color left in the man's face drained away, a sudden, real panic settling in. "If you kill me, they'll send more," he said too fast, his tone changing. "They want you dead. It won't end."

A pounding on the door distracted her, and she motioned for Danny to go over and take care of it without delay.

"And who are they, exactly?" she posed nonchalantly, the blade pressing harder.

His gaze didn't waver. Before she could reiterate the question, he spat in her face, and the Madame shied backward, releasing him from the knife and her foot. She wiped it from her cheek leisurely, internally revolted by the gesture, and vengeful anger took over. This son of a bitch was there to kill her, and here she was, slapping him around when she should have already slit his throat.

The Madame turned toward him, and her assailant grinned. "Fucking woman. Like I said, do your worst. You don't have the balls."

Louis took a step her direction, but she waved him off. "You do know why they sent you in first, don't you?" she asked.

He grew confused. "It's a part of the hit."

"No. It's because you're the fucking amateur they don't care about getting killed. You're the fall guy, so if you die, they don't give a rat's ass about it. Maybe they will send more. But I'm still going to butcher you first." She grabbed his hand and held it steady against the armrest, as her heel had done before. "And just for you, since you asked so nicely, I will do my fucking worst." With one fleeting swipe, the Madame brought her blade down through the middle of the bastard's hand and left it there, the tip poking through the bottom of the wooden armrest. Screaming, he writhed back and forth hysterically, his other limbs frantically trying to break free. Blood dripped down to the floor, and she couldn't deny it made her feel a hell of a lot better.

"Now," she continued, ignoring his flailing movements. "If you decide to talk, I will remove the knife causing your suffering. If not, I will put one more through your other God damned hand…" She snapped her fingers and Louis sprung to her, grabbing the blade from his belt. He placed the handle in her open palm and resumed his former position. The Madame paused for just a second, looking her victim up and down with the blade raised high. "Another? Or are you ready to cooperate?"

"…fuck…you…whore…" he managed to muster out under his breath.

"Wrong answer, darling." An ungodly scream erupted as the second knife plunged through his other hand. The Madame took a retreating step as his struggle grew more violent, the pain sending him over the edge.

"The next limb will not be your legs. You have thirty seconds before I have Louis strip you of your trousers and I remove what little manhood you have underneath." Overwhelmed in suffering, the man couldn't make out words, so she went on. "Do you believe me yet, you piece of shit? Quit wasting my time." She leaned in close. "Who the fuck sent you?"

"Please I…I can't fucking think with these…these things in my hands…for Christ's sake!" Drool and snot began to pour from his nose and mouth. She was running out of time.

"The knives come out when I get a name."

"I don't know her name!" the man yelled. "Some fucking blonde cunt who set us up!"

"Was it Catherine Hiltmore?" she questioned placidly.

"Yes…fucking blonde…cunt…"

"Who was she after? Me?"

"Yes…and the girl…"

The Madame's stomach dropped. "The girl? Which girl, you bastard?"

The man glimpsed past her to the doors of her office. "The… that one…" Startled, the Madame whipped around to see Esther at Danny's side.

Sooner than the Madame could yell, Danny spoke up: "She wanted to be here, Madame. So I let her."

Esther took a step forward, her eyes on the man in the chair. "Catherine Hiltmore wanted me dead?"

Everyone looked back to the man in the chair, who was barely conscious. He nodded, and then his head bowed forward and he ceased to stir, passing out from the shock.

"D-D-D-Dead…she…she wanted me…" Esther's eyes blinked

hard and Danny ran to her just in time to catch her from falling to the floor, and then softly lowered her to the ground. "She…wanted me dead…" Esther couldn't stop repeating the words over and over again as Danny sat beside her, wrapping Esther in her arms.

The Madame grasped the blades and yanked them out of the man's hands, wiping them on her already bloodstained dress.

This changed everything.

"Louis, take him downstairs and get him cleaned up. If Hope can't handle it call the Doc. He's not to leave under any conditions."

"Yes, Madame."

"Danny, get her to a chair and find her some water."

The Madame set both blades on her desk next to her empty gun, giving Esther a few minutes to compose herself. Looking out the windows, the Madame tried to pacify the rage…a rage that had been woken up these last few days. It was one she hadn't felt in many years, and one that would only be put out by seeing this through to the bitter end. The Madame was certain that the last of Esther's naïve and uncorrupted youth was gone, stripped away by Catherine Hiltmore, and there was nothing that could be done to recover it. There would be no return to normalcy, no strength in her allegiance to Celeste – the Hiltmores made Esther choose a side without even allowing her an option as to which one.

"We need to wash your dress or we'll never get the blood out," Esther sniffed, breaking the silence in the room.

The Madame spun around, sitting back against her desk. "You should have never been in this room, Esther."

She wiped the tears from her eyes. "Why not?"

"Because there are things that go on here you don't need to see. That's fucking why."

"It's a little late for that, Madame."

The Madame couldn't read her. "Tell me what you're thinking."

Esther, while upset, was oddly composed. "I just don't understand why…why kill me? It doesn't make any sense! What could I have possibly…" Out of the blue, Esther stopped. An expression crossed her face, one the Madame couldn't quite make out. "Oh my God. Madame, I can't…I can't go back…he'll kill me…he… he knows…"

"I've already taken care of that," the Madame explained. "You also can't be alone either. You're going to be in shock. I don't want you hurting yourself."

Esther's head was in her hands, her voice muffled. "Fucking Christ, what have I done?"

Danny returned with a large carafe of water for Esther, who chugged it down the moment it reached her hands. Afterward, as the Madame predicted, she broke down sobbing uncontrollably, and Danny pulled her in close and held her once more, wiping the tears as they fell down her cheeks.

Louis reappeared for further instruction. "What do you need me to do?" he asked, paying no heed to Danny and Esther.

"Make sure this place is cleared out. Then we will discuss our next course of action."

"All right. Did we fetch Thomas?"

"Yes."

"Perhaps we should–"

"No, Louis. Not yet."

The Madame went to her drink cart and snatched up the decanter of whiskey. Any minute, Thomas would arrive with Claire. She poured two drinks worth into her glass and threw it back at once. The problem had grown too big, and with the threat stemming to someone else she cared for, the Madame took it personally. Her entire livelihood was at stake, and she was not ready to hand it over to a bunch of greedy and cowardly upper class sociopaths. The time had come for reprisal, if not for her sake then for Esther's, and nothing in all the world was going to stop her.

Ten minutes later, noises drifted up from the main hall, and the Madame instinctively got to her feet. Esther was calm, her head resting in Danny's lap as Danny stroked Esther's hair. The Madame signaled for her to stay put and made her way downstairs. Thomas waited at the bottom of the staircase for her, and when he comprehended what it was covering her dress, his irritated demeanor transformed into one of dread. When she reached him, she dismissed Claire with a quick nod, and motioned for Thomas to sit on the last step beside her. He didn't budge.

"Will someone tell me what the hell is going on?" he demanded. "And please tell me you aren't covered in blood?"

"Two men came here tonight to cause damage. One's been killed and the other detained. But Thomas…it's…it's not good."

"What do you mean?" he asked, lowering down. "Claire told me Esther was here and that it was an emergency."

"She has nowhere else to go. I need her to stay with your family. I thought I could keep her here but it's just not safe."

Thomas rolled his eyes. "It seems like everything here is clearly under control. If Esther isn't hurt and this is some sort of stupid little game you've concocted again–"

The Madame shook her head. "Thomas, those two men came here tonight not just for me. They came here to kill Esther, too."

Thomas gaped at her. "What do you mean they came here to kill her? Why would anyone want to kill Esther?"

"That's the fucking question now, isn't it?"

His concern grew. "Did you find out who sent them?"

"What do you think? Use your fucking head."

"Who?"

"It was the fucking Hiltmores."

"Why do they want you dead? And why in the hell would they want her dead? And please, can you tell me the God damned truth for once?"

"I honestly don't know, Thomas," she confessed. "There are a thousand fucking possibilities. They've hated that child since the moment she arrived. I got her there by blackmailing them, and our deal rotted out when they decided Celeste marrying gave them more power. And then...then I found out who they really were...and I went after them." She told Thomas everything she'd discovered in the south, about the night of their party, and that she had unknowingly been a piece of that giant machine and was using the evidence she acquired as retribution. When the Madame finished, the only thing Thomas could do was stare at her.

"But they...they wanted to kill Esther...why?"

"It's a mystery for now. My guess is because she knows about Timothy's issues, and they don't want any of that becoming public knowledge."

"And she saw..."

The Madame exhaled. "Everything, Thomas. Every fucking thing."

"Where is the man they sent now?"

"In the back. Doc will be seeing him soon enough."

"Thomas?" came a small voice from the top of the stairs.

They both looked up to see Esther standing there alone. Before anyone could say another word, Thomas rushed up the steps to her, and Esther began to cry once more. He picked her up in his arms and cradled her against his chest, sitting down onto the ground and kissing her forehead.

"Madame!" Hope called, appearing in the doorway of the bar room. "There's something I need to tell you."

"What is it?" the Madame stipulated, trying not to disturb Thomas or Esther.

Hope walked over and didn't speak until she was right next to the Madame. "He...the man who broke in...he told me something when he was in shock. The Doc had him all drugged up and he said something. I don't think he even knew he was saying it."

An involuntary shudder rushed over the Madame. "What did he say?" While Thomas was a floor above, the Madame could sense his ears perk up to listen in.

Hope peered around nervously. "It wasn't just Catherine Hiltmore that sent them. He had actually been hired by…well by the Hiltmore family and the Adams family, Madame. And you…well… you weren't the primary target."

"What the fuck do you mean I wasn't the primary target?"

Hope looked up at Thomas, then back at her. "It was Esther. She apparently filed a police report against Timothy Adams, and it leaked back to his family."

"A police report?" the Madame inquired, wondering why in the hell Esther hadn't told her about this before.

"Yes, Madame. I think the Adamses must have a friend in the department. But that's not the worst part." Hope paused, and the Madame saw there were tears welling up in her eyes. "She…she said he…he raped her, Madame…and she…Esther wanted to press charges…"

The Madame's teeth clenched and her fists balled up, feeling the furious storm inside her chest exploding with every heartbeat. The Madame's eyes drifted up toward Thomas, where they locked. His countenance was one of disbelief and outrage, his face contorting as he grimaced in pain at hearing of Esther's assault. Thomas glanced down at the woman weeping in his arms and pulled her in tighter.

"Take care of it, Aunt," he told her, standing up and bringing Esther cradled off the ground with him. "Whatever it fucking takes. Take care of it."

The Madame nodded as he disappeared with her into the office. "With pleasure, Thomas," she muttered without the intention of anyone hearing her. "With fucking pleasure, darling."

XIV.

It was a disturbingly quiet morning at the Inferno, and throughout the ward even the most fanatical of patients could sense it was bathing day. In the usual, rushed fashion, they were lined up after what many called breakfast despite it being no more than a small piece of bread and gruel that was composed mostly of water. No one said a word to one another, both out of fear of the nursing staff circling them like a pack of lions and also what awaited them at the end of the long, bitter-cold hallway. Hall C housed twenty-six women, together forming into a long line of pairs facing the bright light they trudged begrudgingly toward. Mary swore in all her time as an inmate on Blackwell, the chill that nipped at every inch of un-clothed skin never seemed to fade. There were a handful of times she'd come down with pneumonia, and one gruesome incident where she nearly starved to death after a long sentence in the dungeons, yet she counted herself blessed. She hadn't seen Croker in nearly six years, and prayed every day they never came face to face again.

Shivering now with dread and with cold, Mary took some deep breaths to prepare her psyche for the shock of the ice bath and violat-ing scrub that accompanied it. Sarah stood to her right, clinging des-perately to Mary's hand until one of the nurses caught sight of their closeness. Stomping furiously their direction, the nurse proceeded to berate Sarah at the top of her lungs, causing Sarah's lip to tremble and her hand to release from Mary's instantly. The comfort of Mary's being near was not worth the consequences of disobeying the nurses.

Nothing was worth that.

Sarah was young, no more than twenty-two, and ended up being institutionalized after suffering a series of emotional ups and downs following giving birth to twins. Her husband took her to see a doctor, though unfortunately, this doctor was not what they imagined. He diagnosed her as temporarily insane, sending her to Blackwell within days of testing, and her release would be pending solely on physician decision and her behavior in order to consider her recovered from her "affliction." Mary took the girl under her wing when she saw how weak Sarah had become, and subsequent to hearing her story, it was all Mary could do not to rejoice and thank God for mercy. Of the women Mary befriended during her incarceration, Sarah was the only one certain to get back out again. From what Sarah told her, Mary understood that Sarah's husband loved her dearly and was working to get her released by court order of a judge. Four months had passed, and Sarah claimed he was close – any day now – and Mary realized this was her one and only shot of reaching the outside world. She cared deeply for Sarah and her wellbeing, and did everything she could to help her survive her time locked up with them, but Mary was smart enough to see this was an opportunity she might never have again. If she could get a letter to Thomas or the Madame, they would find a way to get to her...there was no doubt in her mind about that. What worried her was the question that had been ailing her mind each and every day: were they even still alive?

For a time, she went back and forth, debating between whom she should reach out to; however, considering the numerous unfriendly eyes and ears hovering around The Palace and its constituents, Mary decided against sending a letter to the Madame. Even a message to Louis wouldn't be safe or secure. Over the years, the

Madame had done so much for Mary and Thomas. Therefore, putting the Madame's reputation and life in jeopardy because of Mary's own mistake was something she just could not stomach. Any denial of self-responsibility in being caught by Croker had long passed, and the little blame she previously bestowed on the Madame evaporated with that repudiation. On multiple occasions, the Madame warned Mary to get out and abandon whatever crusade she was on, and rather than listen to logic, Mary ignored her and paid the price. The concept of justice is a myth to those who have no power…she'd learned that the moment her freedom was taken away. As a result for uncovering secrets she had no right to, Mary was Croker's prisoner, and probably would be until the end of her days.

"Everyone stay in order!" a shout hollered from the end of the hallway. "If you get out of line, you will be forced back in and then be put into isolation after cleaning!"

With a sudden heave, the crowd moved forward at a faster pace, and the women shuffled along in a pack, trying not to trip over their feet or one another. The nurses kept them packed tight, not an inch to breathe fresh air, making sure no one acted out of turn. Any patient who had been in the Inferno for more than a few weeks wouldn't dare try to challenge this, and the ones who did were sent to isolation. Or worse, Hall B, from where most never returned.

Sarah reached for Mary's hand once more and squeezed it tight, and Mary quickly peeked toward her young companion with encouragement. "It will all be over fast," she whispered. "Just keep breathing steadily until they finish the scrub. Then hold your breath or you'll choke on the water." Sarah trembled and nodded as the light at the end of the hallway drew closer.

When Mary and Sarah reached the end, they were pushed through the doorway and into the sterilized room. Mary was temporarily blinded by the brightness. She released Sarah and the handlers thrust the two apart to opposing sides, causing Mary to nearly slip on the slick, tile floor that was completely coated with water.

Three sets of hands stripped her of her clothing from head to toe, and when Mary was exposed and naked, the handlers drove her toward her cleaning. There was a tub on each side of the room, one for each of the patients in the pair, and they were both filled with ice cold water only to be drained when it was so filthy the women were coming out dirtier than when they were thrown in. At each station was a nurse with a scrub brush and soap, along with more handlers to aid in keeping the patients steady for the duration. It was absolutely revolting, and Mary closed her eyes as they forcibly lifted her into the tub, trying to pretend she was anywhere else other than that room.

Unlike the others, Mary had a particular reason she was dreading this moment: a few days prior, Nurse Montell and a few of her followers managed to corner Mary and atrociously left her back in scabs and bruises. Mary didn't know why Nurse Montell despised her to such a drastic degree. Of the many nurses at Blackwell, she was the cruelest and most brutal with her patients, and those she singled out did not live for very long. Mary somehow managed to evade that fate thus far, yet as her scrub began, Mary could only expect an ungodly amount of pain in what was to come next. She stood after being rinsed with her fists clenched tight in the hopes of staying on her feet while being rubbed raw. To her relief, the brute of a woman with the brush left her back untouched and went on to soap her, lathering every surface of her skin and hair, including areas that were unexposed to the human eye. Soap stinging her eyes, Mary routinely sat and held her breath as three large buckets of even colder water were dumped over her head to rinse away the remaining dirt and grime. Once they finished, she was picked up and out of the tub and shoved toward an array of starched towels to dry herself and then change into a new set of clothes given over. Mary's hair dripped water down to the ground, matting to her head as she vigorously tried to get all the water off her body. When that was done, she hastily changed into her new dress, which was at best two sizes too big, and afterward was escorted to the "common" area to sit for the remainder of her day before dinner was announced.

On the way, Mary prayed for a day free of incidents. The screams and cries of the women courageous enough to act out or stand up for themselves were what haunted Mary most, especially since the majority of the women in her Hall were like her – sane and locked away for causing some kind of trouble. They weren't lunatics when they arrived. What made them delusional was the place they were imprisoned in like circus animals with no hopes of release. Every one of them was forced to endure things no human being should, and Mary often wondered how in the hell she hadn't lost her mind yet either. It was only a matter of time, she supposed.

The "common" room had the feel of being far larger than it was: the space was square, painted a dismal grey, and only two barred windows on the same wall that let in just enough light to not require candlesticks burning during daylight hours. Like most of the floors in Hall C, it was made of white tile to allow clean ups to be easier for the staff as a result of the "accidents" that happen to occur, though sanitary was not exactly a word Mary would use to describe its current condition. There were a few rows of benches nailed into the ground, a few tables as well, but if any patients lingered in one space or talked too long with one another, an onslaught from the nurses was inevitable. All twenty-six crammed into one small place, which was believed to help with socialization. In reality, it only provoked nuisances, although it was never amongst the patients. It was the one area where the nurses had open season to bully and harass the women to whatever degree they wished, prowling around, hungry at a chance to strike for any kind of reason they could come up with.

The benches were nearly full when Mary arrived, though she was thankful to spot her usual cohorts saving her a small spot as they talked timidly in the far corner. Sarah was among them, her eyes lost somewhere else as Bethany spoke to her softly, but after Mary joined them Sarah's awareness returned somewhat. Their group was small:

aside from Mary and Sarah, there were two others named Bethany and Grace. They found solace in their little pack, relying on each other for mental support and protection from the nurses, and their back stories were more impressive than Mary and Sarah's put together.

Bethany made the mistake of catching her prestigious husband in an affair, and to cover it up, he went to the police and had her arrested, telling them she was a threat to herself and society and that he had tried their entire marriage to cover up her episodic hallucinations. Two weeks later, he made this his legal argument for divorce, winning without any misgivings from the court, and Bethany was sentenced to confinement at Blackwell. The last she'd heard, her ex-husband remarried his mistress, and thus killed any dream of her being let outside these walls again.

Out of the four, Grace was, in fact, a little batty, but by no means was she insane. Mary and Bethany did their best to piece together her past, combining the rumors spread around amongst other patients and her vague mumbles in reply to their queries. What they could gather was simply that Grace's life was struck by tragedy. No account was overly convincing, though they did learn she was sent to Blackwell for the murder of her husband in the street outside their home, where she both brutally and publicly beat him to death with his own cane. Some claim Grace arrived to find her husband had killed their children in a drunken rage, as he apparently used to beat her as well, and a few claim it was Grace who killed them in her own madness. Never seeing a violent side to their friend, Bethany and Mary assumed the first tale was the more accurate one, however it did not make her any less intimidating. There had been other women who filtered in and out of their group of allies over the years, some staying longer than others. Regrettably over time they did lose their rationale and most were no longer alive…or worse than dead, locked up in Hall B.

"Grace, scoot closer to Sarah, we need to get her warmer," Bethany muttered, glancing at Mary with an expression of outrage,

"She said they held her out of the water and fucking laughed as she shook. Laughed. I swear to fucking God, Mary…"

"Shh. I know," Mary spoke quietly. "She'll be all right. Sarah, hold your arms in closer to your chest and cross them. There you go. Rub your arms and get some blood flowing." It took a few minutes for Sarah's teeth to finally stop chattering while her lips continued to hold their light shade of blue. Mary was content when a little pink returned to her cheeks, and motioned for Grace and Bethany to give her some space again.

"It's going to be fine, Sarah," Bethany cooed, trying to lift her spirits. "You'll be out of here soon. Stay strong."

Like Mary, Bethany understood if they didn't diligently care for Sarah, the probability of her dying within a few days rose exponentially. On the other hand, Mary also worried about Bethany's mental health in regards to dealing with Sarah's departure. It would not be easy to watch her go when there was no escape for them, and that notion alone had seriously damaging effects in the long term. There was also the nurses' maltreatment to maintain control of their patients, with the doctors never arguing otherwise, and Mary witnessed numerous deaths as a result of the abuse. A patient's death was unquestionably deemed the patient's fault without any of the medical staff being held responsible for the neglect.

This was the Inferno, and to Mary, it was far worse than Dante's journey through the nine circles.

As they continued to console Sarah, Dr. Hanley strolled into the "common" room, briefly saying hello to each patient but not bothering to really see to the patient's condition – a formality with no real intention other than to console his conscience. Grace gave a huff upon his approach to their bench, and the four discreetly scrambled to distance themselves just enough, not wanting to arise suspicions and be sent to isolation for a few days.

"Good morning, Grace, you are looking well. Hello, Miss Marshall…Miss Lincoln…Mary? How are you doing today?"

She glanced up from her feet. "Fine, thank you, Dr. Hanley."

To her dismay, he paused, his eyes scanning her up and down. "The night nurse informed me you haven't been sleeping again. Is that true?" he asked.

Mary gulped. "Just the last two nights, Dr. Hanley. I have a hard time sleeping because of my back, sir."

His head tilted in puzzlement. "What is wrong with your back, Mary?"

"It's just…just hurt, Dr. Hanley. It will be fine in another few days."

Dr. Hanley shook his head. "Injuries must be tended to. Come with me. We are going to see Dr. Sanford."

Mary's stomach dropped. "Please…Dr. Hanley…"

"Nurse Lewis, your assistance please!" he shouted out, taking Mary by the arm. Nurse Lewis trotted over and took Mary's other arm with a threatening glare: she was one of Nurse Montell's antagonizing clique, and Mary was sure the woman was to blame for four or five of the lashes currently scabbed on her back.

A few minutes later, Mary found herself in the examination room, sitting opposite Dr. Sanford and Dr. Hanley. In the place of Nurse Lewis behind them stood Nurse Finley, the woman who had saved Mary after her nearly successful suicide attempt on the grounds of Blackwell. It took months for Mary's health to recover, and in the process she and Nurse Finley formed a mutual respect for one another. Ironically because of this, Mary knew the three people in the examination room with her were well aware as to why exactly she was institutionalized, though not one of them could allow her departure without serious ramifications. She had no idea as to the extent of what Croker might have paid them or threatened them with, but oddly, each of them developed a slight fondness toward Mary, especially in observing how she would alleviate the transition for the newer arrivals. In a way, she felt they watched out for her when they could, and it was the only reprieve she had aside from Bethany, Grace, and

Sarah. A part of her wished she could forgive them for doing this to her, and she constantly tried to come to peace with her situation; in spite of that, Mary would never forget these people were her captors by choice. And she knew if the time ever presented itself once more, she would cut any of them down at the possibility of escape.

"Mary, can we take a look at your back?" Nurse Finley began. "Dr. Hanley says it has been keeping you awake at night?"

She didn't reply. The only way they could understand was seeing it firsthand. Mary stood up from the examination chair and turned from them. Unbuttoning her dress slowly, Mary's hand casually grazed the dreadful scar on her chest from eight years ago, causing an involuntary wince just as her dress fell down from her shoulders. Nurse Finley gasped loudly and Dr. Hanley cursed under his breath, while Dr. Sanford stepped forward and inspected her wounds closely.

"The deep bruising is much worse than the cuts...those are relatively superficial and should heal quickly with the right treatment. Mary, I am going to touch a few spots and I want you to give me a scale of your pain. Can you do that for me?"

"Yes, Dr. Sanford."

"Good. Try and remain relaxed."

Every spot was a ten. Mary lied and mixed the numbers up... an eight here, a six there...and her body tensed involuntarily as she tried not to flinch so hard at his touch. When Dr. Sanford finished, he rotated to face the other two and mouthed something inaudibly before leaving the room. Mary stayed where she was.

"Mary, Nurse Finley is going to clean and add ointment to your cuts to prevent infection, and it's going to sting pretty badly," Dr. Hanley explained, and she could hear him writing something on the clipboard in his hands. "Dr. Sanford would like to see you every day for the next two weeks, and I will send Nurse Finley to fetch you from the common room so there are no...problems. Is that understood?"

"Yes. Thank you, Dr. Hanley."

Nurse Finley came to her side and guided her back to the examination chair. Speedily, she prepared the gauze and reached for the peroxide, giving Mary an empathetic, fleeting glimpse. As she began to clean Mary's back, the pain was almost intolerable, causing Mary to let out an awful groan, and she fought against her impulses to leap away from Nurse Finley. Dr. Hanley exited the room, not saying another word to either of them, and Mary gritted her teeth to stop herself from screaming.

"I know it hurts, but I've got to clean this up to prevent an infection," Nurse Finley said. "I promise I am working as quickly as I can to get it over with."

"Mmm!" was the best Mary could do without losing her grip altogether. A few minutes went by and the pain subsided with the application of ointment to Mary's wounds, allowing her stress to reduce drastically.

"Mary...who did this to you?" Nurse Finley pressed. "Please tell me."

Mary took a deep breath. "Before I tell you anything, I need to know something. And you're the only one I trust enough to ask."

"Of course," she replied eagerly, applying the gauze to cover her injury. "What is it?"

"What has he done to you to keep me here?"

Nurse Finley's hand halted where it was. "I...I don't...I don't know what you mean, Mary..."

"Yes you do," she rejoined, a little anger rising. "Why do they allow me to be kept here when everyone knows the truth? What has he done to you...to the doctors?"

The room went still for a few seconds, and then Nurse Finley leaned forward so her mouth was only inches from Mary's ear. "You aren't the only hostage, Mary," she murmured. "It's extremely complicated and we've done our best to keep you in one piece."

"With the exception of Nurse Montell," Mary asserted quietly. "She's been out to get me since day one."

Nurse Finley kept her voice at a whisper. "Montell is his sister-in-law."

Mary's heart nearly stopped beating in her chest. "Jesus fucking Christ," she swore, the pain of this blow far exceeding that of her injured back.

"We're all trapped in this situation. I would get you out of here if I could. Don't doubt that."

Mary felt a lump rise in her throat, and pushed on with the next stage of her plan. "Can you get Sarah Lincoln out of here? For me? She is not ill and if she is here much longer, she won't survive. If you could do me that favor…please…it would mean so much to me since I…I can't…"

"You can pull your dress over your shoulders," Nurse Finley declared aloud as if someone might be eavesdropping, then dropped her tone just as Mary moved to get up. "I will get her out of here. Give me two days. Her husband has been advocating her release, but the order has to come from Dr. Peters."

"And you think you could convince him?"

Nurse Finley helped Mary to her feet and smiled. "It's not about convincing. We women…sometimes we do what's necessary to get what we want."

Mary stared at her, realizing the meaning behind her words. "I have a friend…a very dear friend that knows all about that. It's not…too horrible, is it?"

To her relief, Nurse Finley let out a small chuckle. "Not worse than most others." She lent a hand in getting Mary's arms through her sleeves. "Look Mary, Nurse Montell is trying to get a rise out of you. Don't fall for it. Despite her relation to…you know who…management is an inch away from letting her go, and after today I trust Dr. Hanley will push for her to be fired. She goes beyond what is necessary to keep this place in order, and it's getting out of control."

Mary buttoned her dress, frustrated. "You know I never provoke her. She willingly seeks me out, but at least I can say I finally know why."

"Please just be careful," Nurse Finley begged her. "Don't give her a reason, or she'll see to it you don't see the light of day again."

Rising to stand, Mary let out a heavy sigh. "Promise me you will do what you can for Sarah?"

"Of course I will."

"Then I'll make sure to keep to myself for as long as I can."

Mary could tell from the look on Nurse Finley's face she'd eased her friend's worry; nevertheless, Mary couldn't help speculating as to whether or not death would be considered a worse fate than the one she currently found herself enduring.

The remainder of the morning passed without further confrontation, and when Mary revisited the "common" room, her head was in a fog from her conversation with Nurse Finley. To her relief, the others assumed Mary was drained after her appointment with the doctors and let her be. She was badly shaken upon hearing the truth about Nurse Montell, though oddly not surprised, and she fought to set her distress aside to focus on the more important matter. The next step in her scheming to get Sarah released would prove to be the most difficult. Somehow, Mary needed to acquire a pen and paper, both of which were forbidden to patients, and her original idea of keeping this entirely to herself became impossible. There was only one person who could attain writing utensils for her in so short a time frame, and that was Grace.

Subsequent to her transfer to Blackwell, Grace was caught on multiple occasions roaming the hallways at night by the staff of the institution. Mary wasn't sure how, but over time, Grace managed to convince the doctors she had some sort of disorder called sleepwalking, and for security purposes she was therefore placed in an isolated room to sleep each night, the door tightly locked from the outside. Since then, in her own way, Grace indicated to Bethany and Mary her condition was absolutely fictitious, and oftentimes for sport she would leave little presents for them under their pillows, such as a small piece of ribbon or a hair pin. On other occasions, nurses who repeatedly singled her out seemed to lose personal belongings from their lockers soon after, never to be found again, thus sending a whirl of gossip around that a ghost haunted Hall C. Grace never confessed to them directly it was her doing, yet Mary was determined to find out if Grace lived up to her legend, or if perhaps she had dreamed it up as a way to make sense of the unexplainable.

A bell rang loudly, catapulting Mary to the present. "Line up!" the nurses bellowed. "Time for laundry duty! Line up! Let's go! We don't have all day, for Christ's sake!" The nurses hustled the pack of patients into order, proceeding to lead them out of the "common" room and down the steep stone staircase where at the bottom, an endless amount of dirty garments and linens awaited them. The smell of chemical bleach filled Mary's nostrils as she descended down, burning her nose and eyes. As she passed an attendant on her left, he handed over a cover for her nose and mouth, which she readily put on.

At the bottom, Bethany caught up to her. "I will keep an eye on Sarah, you keep an eye on Grace," she murmured. Mary agreed as they split from one another, Sarah and Bethany to the right to the folding and drying station, and Mary and Grace to the left to the bleaching and cleaning station. Another attendant posted closer to the giant pool of soapy purple water threw out aprons, and Mary snatched one out of the air and tied it around her waist while Grace did the same. With her friend in tow, Mary went to the furthest side of the station, which was the least patrolled by staff, wanting to be able to converse with Grace without drawing attention.

"Grace," she hissed, grabbing a handful of dirty clothes from the pile behind her and thrusting them into the pool. "I need your help with something. Something you can't tell the others."

Grace grinned. "Okay." Together they used their wooden paddles to dunk the clothes in and out, washing away whatever soil was left over.

"Sarah is going home soon, Grace, and I want to send something with her for my son. Something no one can know about. Do you understand what I'm saying?"

"Yes," she asserted definitively. "I know what a...a secret is."

"Right. A secret." Mary reached for the soaked clothing and pulled the lump out cautiously, setting it aside for pick up to be rinsed. "I need a pen and paper," she told her under her breath. "I can't get it by myself. Is there any way you can...you can steal it for me?"

Grace halted and turned, looking directly into Mary's eyes. "For you, I can get it...I will get it for you, Mary..."

Her gaze then went behind Mary, and as Mary rotated to see what it was Grace focused on. Indifferently, her friend took a few steps forward toward a sharp edge on the side of the tub.

"Call...help..." she mumbled, and in a flash, shifted over and sliced her arm open on the metal point, blood pouring out everywhere.

Mary was so taken aback she nearly fell over with astonishment. "Doctor!" Mary screamed, yanking the cover off her face. "We need a doctor! Quickly! Grace has cut her arm open!"

In a rush of footsteps, two attendants and a nurse pounced on them, the female attendant slapping Mary across the face to shut her up. "Keep your God damned voice down or you'll panic the others. What the hell happened here?!"

Clinging to her cheek, Mary tried to remain resolute. "We were just washing and she turned to get another sheet. That was it."

The nurse sighed heavily. "Johnson, take her up to see Dr. Sanford at once. She'll need stitches at the very least." Aggressively, she then seized Grace's face by her chin. "Be. More. Fucking. Careful," she spat, and when she let go, the attendant took Grace by the shoulders and forced her the way of the staircase. When Grace disappeared from sight, Mary took a few deep breaths, touching her chest for composure. It had happened so fast, there was no time to think, and Mary was overcome with shame for underestimating Grace's dedication to her as a friend. She would take care never to make that error of judgment again, and if the time ever came, Mary hoped she could find a way to repay her.

Hours later, Mary met Sarah and Bethany in their usual line-up for dinner. "Where is Grace?" Sarah asked, alarmed to see Mary by herself.

"She cut her arm while we were washing and had to be taken up to Dr. Sanford. It was a gruesome cut, but I think she will join us soon."

Mary was right. Just as the march forward began toward the dining hall, she caught sight of Grace a few pairs ahead of them with a freshly wrapped bandage on her arm. When they reached the hall, there was bread already set out on the rotting wooden tables, as well as boiled potatoes and a beef stew, most of which had gone cold an hour or two earlier and was attracting a small pack of flies. Food was swiftly vanishing in a sea of desperate arms and hands, and Mary fought hard to get a potato and some unbuttered bread – the Inferno tended to only use meat that was about to spoil to suspend their patients' hunger, and therefore beef stew was by no means on the top of Mary's list. Scrounging what she could, she promptly evaded the crowd and went to sit and eat at one of the further tables. The second she relaxed down on the bench, Grace was right beside her.

"Still...stay still..." she demanded. "Keep...keep eating..." Mary did as she was instructed and inconspicuously kept picking at her dinner. Mary felt Grace lift her dress up to her knees while she slipped something in between Mary's sock and boot. Then, casually, Grace placed the skirt down over Mary's legs again, the task successfully completed. Mary was speechless at first, trying to find a way to thank Grace. All she could muster was one word:

"How?"

Grace beamed from ear to ear. "A secret," she uttered, giving her a wink, and as if nothing happened, Grace proceeded to scarf down her bread.

That night, Mary lay down in her bed and found her back more tolerable than it had been for days, and she thanked God for Nurse Finley's compassion. The lights went out at curfew and the doors were locked closed – no one in or out except the night nurses until dawn. The night nurses came in three-hour shifts, and Mary decided to wait through the first shift before she wrote her plea to her son. For round one, she kept her eyes closed tight when she heard the keys in the door, feigning sleep as the light crept in from the hallway. Seconds trickled by in suspense until at last the door finally shut. After she heard the keys lock it, Mary still delayed until the deep resonance of sleep from her roommate could be heard. Convinced it was safe, she reached down and grasped the pen and paper from her sock, sitting upright warily. Once again certain she was the only one awake, Mary squinted hard, trying to see through the darkness of their tiny cell – it was the only time she would ever have alone, and she didn't have much of it.

Mary spent most of that afternoon after Grace's departure washing laundry and reflecting on what she should write to Thomas, and she had to admit she was frightened for both of their sakes. Doubts swirled in her mind about whether or not the risk was worth it…to put him in danger as well as Sarah…betraying Croker for damning her here. On the other hand, Mary knew if she didn't try, she might as well stab the pen into her neck and end it for good, because there would never be a next time. Focusing her eyes, Mary scrawled out a note, her handwriting only half legible after not using it for nearly a decade:

Thomas,

I am alive. They are keeping me on Blackwell's Island outside the city. I cannot escape and they will not let me leave. Please. Ask the Madame for help and get me out of this prison I am trapped in. You are my only hope.

I love you more than anything,

Mary

She folded the paper up and wrote the address of the barbershop on the outside –Sarah only needed to drop it there for her, nothing more. If Thomas was alive and in New York City, he would find her…she knew he would find her…

Immediately, Mary shoved the paper into her sock and hid the pen in the side of her mattress, making a puncture through the fabric and sliding it inside. In case she reached her breaking point, or in case things grew worse than they already were, Mary wanted the option of freeing herself from the Inferno, alive or dead.

Settling into bed, she heard the keys in the door. Instantly she closed her eyes and let her head fall to the side, mouth gaping open. The light lingered, pouring into their room for a little over a minute, and then it was gone as the door slammed shut. Mary managed to fade into a light slumber, remembering her son and imagining seeing his face and his smile again. Thomas was the splitting image of his father, and Mary's heart ached as her thoughts went to Edward for the first time in over a month. With all her heart, she prayed he was watching over her from heaven, and if not her than his son, who needed his guardianship more than she did.

"I'll be with you soon, Edward," she prayed inaudibly. "Soon we will be together again. Just keep Tommy safe from all this. Please keep him safe."

There was no news the next day or the day after until at last, allowing dinner, Nurse Anderson took a panicked Sarah away from the rest of the patients, her eyes searching her friends for help. Mary tried to encourage her with the knowledge that in a few minutes Sarah's troubles would fade away at the announcement of her release. Blackwell would send her off prior to breakfast, as was Inferno protocol, giving Mary only a small window to get the note to her, and it would not be easy.

Bethany cleared her throat. "I've been here six years and I've never seen them take anyone anywhere after dinner...unless..."

"Unless they're getting out," Mary completed for her. "She wouldn't have lasted much longer."

"She only lasted this long because you took care of her, Mary," Bethany complimented her. "All three of us know that. It's a God damn miracle, is what it is."

Mary blushed a little. "The strong are put here to protect the weak. Right?"

"Mmm," Grace grunted in agreement. The three women sat there in silence, sharing an internal moment of contented peace at the idea that together, they rescued at least one person from that miserable place.

"Guess we'd better keep our eyes out for a new victim then," Bethany added after a few minutes. "Otherwise I'm going to start planning how to kill the bitches who whipped Mary with that belt."

When Sarah returned, the color in her cheeks gave it away. "You'll never believe it," she squeaked as they hovered close to listen.

"You're going home, aren't you?" Bethany posed, astonishingly upbeat.

"Tomorrow morning. My husband...he must have gotten the court order! They said just after daybreak I'll be let out. Can you believe it?"

Bethany, Mary, Grace, and Sarah spent the next hour quietly gushing over their friend's discharge, and after a while came the nightly check of names called out by the nurses before they sent the patients off to bed. Coming to Mary's aid once more, Grace paired with Bethany and they went toward the doorway, leaving Mary just enough time to do what was needed.

Sarah moved to stand, but Mary touched her arm lightly. "Don't move," she said. "I will explain shortly. Keep smiling. Pretend nothing is happening." Sarah did so, though Mary could see she was extremely tense as she slid the note from her sock to Sarah's.

Mary straightened up and took Sarah's hand in hers. "What was that?" Sarah pressed anxiously. "Please don't get me in trouble, Mary…I'm…I'm leaving tomorrow, and–"

"Stay calm, I promise it's nothing. Just act as if everything is normal."

"But Mary–"

"Mary Dougherty and Sarah Lincoln!"

The two leapt to their feet and raced toward the line, the nurses eyeing them suspiciously for being the last two to join.

"Lincoln looks scared," Nurse Lewis observed, marching their way. "What's wrong Sarah? Afraid of the dark, then?"

Mary instinctively placed herself between Nurse Lewis and Sarah. "She is eager to get through the night. She leaves tomorrow morning, that's all." Mary kept her eyes on the floor and hoped Sarah was doing the same.

"Fucking pathetic," Nurse Lewis snorted. "Better watch out Sarah, or you'll be back here in no time!" She burst into vicious laughter and spat on Mary as she moved past, on to harass the next pair of patients. Mary wiped the spit from her neck and clenched her teeth hard, anger rising.

Halfway down the hall, Sarah spoke up: "Mary, tell me what's in my sock."

"It's a letter to my son. If you have the courage, would you do me the honor of delivering it to him?" When Sarah didn't respond, Mary suddenly grew frantic. "I am begging you, Sarah, please. Please just do this one thing for me."

"Stop! Stop here!"

The line halted. "What if they catch me with it?" she beseeched her. "What if they don't let me out?"

"You listen to me. You are leaving tomorrow, and you're never coming back to this fucking hell hole. Go and be happy. Live your life with your husband. You are lucky…I think very few that come into this place ever get out. Please. Just take my note to the address on the paper and leave it there. You remember me explaining where it was, right?" Sarah nodded, tears welling in her pretty blue eyes. "Good," Mary went on. "Just give it to the barber and tell him it's for Thomas. Don't stick around, just leave it and move on, and never think about it or me again."

"But Mary…"

"Everyone file into your cells! Last check is in three minutes! Three minutes!"

Mary pulled Sarah into a tight hug. "Be strong. Live for us. You are my only chance. Do me this favor, and the rest is in God's hands. It's all in God's way."

"What the hell is this?" came Nurse Montell's voice from behind Mary's shoulder.

Nurse Montell was not a big woman by any means. Being small of stature, she barely hit Mary at chin level, yet the woman made up for it in girth. Her waist was round, though not exactly fat, and her harsh facial features and general lack of femininity explained why she was an unmarried woman in her early forties. Unfortunately, she chose to take her own frustrations out on those who could not fight back, and her indistinguishable minions shared the same mentality as their leader. This woman had it in for Mary at the orders of her brother-in-law, Richard Croker, as if a giant target were painted on Mary's back. The initial beatings from Nurse Montell were more frequent but far less severe; nowadays, they were so extreme for the purpose of leaving a mark for months to remind Mary of her place as a prisoner. Mary was one strike away from isolation and the potion for a week, and she refused to allow that to happen, no matter what that bitch did to her.

Mary let go of Sarah and circled around. "Sarah leaves tomorrow. I was saying goodbye."

Nurse Montell scoffed, a spiteful smirk forming. "You know, any personal contact with an inmate is subject to punishment by the nurses in this staff. How would you feel about us taking another go at your back? Huh, Mary? Does that sound good to you? Since apparently, you are the one making all the new rules around here!" Her tone escalated from mildly aggressive to a full on shriek: she was provoking Mary, wanting any excuse to beat her to a pulp in front of the whole hall, or possibly to death. In a twisted way, Mary sensed she might have gained a bit of power in triggering such an emotive reaction from something so small as an embrace with her friend and fellow patient. She looked at Nurse Montell, keeping calm and her expression placid, vowing someday she would make it so that woman would never yell again, even if it was the last thing she did on this earth.

"I am sorry, Nurse Montell. It won't happen again."

Silence followed. "Get to your fucking rooms. Now!" she screamed at the entire line, and the patients scurried their separate directions. As Mary started to do the same, Nurse Montell grabbed her arm and held it so tight, Mary felt her fingers tingle after only a few seconds.

"I know you got that cunt out of here," she breathed so no one else could hear. "Just remember. Nurse Finley isn't always going to be around to save your ass." With that, Nurse Montell took off, dragging Mary with her down the hallway, and as they crossed the threshold to Mary's cell, Nurse Montell threw her inside and onto the floor. The ground was like hard ice on her bare skin, and as Mary got to her feet, Nurse Montell hurled the door shut, casting her into pitch-black darkness. Feeling around, Mary slipped into bed and underneath her stiff wool blanket in an effort to seek some kind of warmth. She wondered whether or not the lunatics weren't the inmates at all, and instead were the people who kept them locked up like animals. That notion alone seemed more real than Mary cared to admit.

For the first time in over a week, Mary slept until the sky began to lighten in the early morning hours. She woke to hear the shuffling of feet and low, hushed voices in the hallway. The time had come for Sarah's departure, and Mary listened intently, trying to catch any sounds she could. Unexpectedly, the clinking of keys in her door made Mary sit up in her bed, her roommate not stirring from her slumber, and as the door opened there stood Sarah with Nurse Finley, who held her finger to her lips to signal for Mary to remain quiet. Creeping out of bed, Mary tiptoed over to meet them in the hallway and Nurse Finley gently closed the door.

Marry wrapped her arms tight around Sarah, who broke down into tears. "I know it was you," she cried. "Nurse Finley told me you were the one who got me out. Mary…Mary, thank you. Thank you for all you've done for me. I will never forget it."

"You shouldn't have been here in the first place, Sarah. It's a crime what they've done to you."

"No…" she sobbed harder. "It's a crime what they've done to you."

Mary brushed her hair with her fingers, spotting Nurse Finley looking on with tears in her own eyes accompanied by a sad smile.

More footsteps came from the end of the hallway, and the three women glimpsed to see Dr. Peters, the head physician of Blackwell, and a handsome young man at his side.

"Donny…" Sarah uttered, her bottom lip quivering, and Mary took her friends hand for the last time and kissed it.

"Go home," she imparted. "You deserve to be home."

Sarah's face was drenched from crying, and she embraced Mary one last time, whispering in her ear. "I will deliver the letter, Mary. I swear on my life, I will. I wish there was more I could do."

Mary squeezed her hard and let go. "On your way, then," she urged, and Sarah ran off down the hallway to her husband and to her freedom. She leapt into his arms, and Mary felt her heart break as she watched them reunite with so much affection and love. The poor girl should never have been put in that wretched place, and while Mary was happy to see her getting out, the devastating concept hit that Sarah wasn't the only one falsely held captive. Including her.

With a sniff, she turned to Nurse Finley. "Thank you for what you did."

Nurse Finley inched closer to her. "Seeing this…seeing them together…that was all the repayment I needed. I wish…I wish I could do the same for you, Mary. I do with all my heart."

"The blame would be yours, and I couldn't live with myself knowing that. I know how he is. I know what he can do to people. I would never want that for you."

"Well, either way, this was well worth the cost," she replied with a sigh.

"How often do you have to?"

"Only when I need something. Or a favor. Repulsive, I realize."

"Not to me," Mary assured her. "You might find this strange, but I understand. More than you could know."

Dr. Peters strutted their direction and they stopped their conversation. "Nurse Finley, we are done for the morning. Please put Miss Dougherty back into her room and see me in my office. Mary, your back is healing?"

"Yes, Dr. Peters."

"Glad to hear it. Get some rest." He marched off the way he'd come, and when he was gone, Nurse Finley put a hand on Mary's shoulder.

"I'd better get you back before Nurse Montell does early checks."

"Do the nurses know why I'm here? Or is it only Nurse Montell?"

Nurse Finley got out her keys and unlocked the door to Mary's room. "She is it, as far as I've been informed. And she will do anything to put you in Hall B before the first frost. Watch yourself, you hear me? Don't fall for her stunts and I will make sure you are

413

safe. I've already got Sanford and Hanley on my side, it's making sure there's no repercussions for her dismissal from…well…you know who."

Mary didn't understand. "What do you mean repercussions?"

"I am fighting hard to keep you alive," Nurse Finley admitted, pulling the door open slightly. "If she provokes you, don't give in. All she needs is one reason or excuse. Just one. And then the only thing I can do is pray God takes you away from this place. Fast."

The next week was a blur, and Mary's hopes were high every day her son might appear and rescue her. Nurse Finley's warnings were also truer than Mary foresaw – Nurse Montell and her followers were coming at her from every angle, and Mary ignored their taunts and the occasional abrasive treatment as best she could.

Sunday morning, however, Nurse Montell didn't give her a choice.

It was cleaning day. Mary, Bethany, and Grace were assigned the dining area along with a few others and were diligently scrubbing the floors on their hands and knees when Nurse Montell boiled over. The day before, Dr. Sanford had publicly reprimanded her for not reporting certain injuries of the patients after interviewing them himself and informed her that following Monday, she would be on three weeks leave and docked pay. What Dr. Sanford failed to take into account was that Nurse Montell had one more day left with his injured patients, and on Sundays, most of the physicians were not present to enforce their orders, as they had the day off. Nurse Montell wanted to make someone pay for it, and sure enough, that one person just so happened to be Mary.

The three friends were covered in grime as they washed away the dirt beneath the main table when suddenly Nurse Montell burst into the room, tossing the doors wide open. One of the other nurses stood up and strode toward her in a vain attempt to pacify Nurse Montell's rage, and she was violently shoved aside as Nurse Montell stalked straight toward Mary. Her eyes popping from her head, Bethany stopped dead in panic, and Mary revolved around just in time to receive a blow to the face from Nurse Montell's foot. She collapsed down onto the ground, her nose spewing blood.

Everyone froze where they were, terrified.

"This is your fucking fault, you God damned cunt!" she screeched at the top of her lungs. "You did this! I know you fucking did!" Mary tried to push herself up and was kicked again, this time in the stomach, and she intuitively curled into a ball moaning in agony to try to shield herself. Through her watering eyes, Mary saw two nurses take off running from the dining hall to get help, while the others gathered up the patients from the scene, not one of them looking on with approval. A bloody grin grew on Mary's face – this would be the end for Nurse Montell at last.

"You like that, huh?! You stupid bitch! You deserve to be here, you fucking lunatic!" Nurse Montell kicked her over and over, and did not stop. First the shins, then her arms protectively covering her stomach and neck, followed by a few slaps to her head. Mary felt each blow to her body, and she rolled over in an attempt to shy away and immediately understood her mistake. One kick to her back, her back that was still deeply bruised and healing from Nurse Montell's previous tirade, and the pain was so immense the whole room went dark.

In an instant, Mary floated above her body, looking down as the scene unfolded below. The reluctant staff crowded by the door, their hands covering their mouths, unsure of what to do as the patients cowered on the opposite side, scared out of their wits. Mary noticed Bethany using every fiber of her muscle to restrain Grace, who was battling to get to Mary's side. Her own body was limp now, and she couldn't hear a sound, though she could see Nurse Montell shouting profanities as she kept kicking Mary repeatedly. She didn't know why, but Mary recognized she wasn't dead…she was somewhere in between, as if waiting to see if it was time for her to go or if she needed to stay behind…

Abruptly, Mary was back on the cold floor, staring up at a glare of light shining through the window, numb to every external element. The world surrounding her remained hushed as her head fell to the right and toward the door. Nurse Montell was being constrained by six of the hall attendants, her face beet red and her eyes filled with unshakeable wrath. A few nurses were over consoling the patients and escorting them out of the dining hall, with Grace and Bethany crying as they begged to go to her, and instead were forced out.

She felt a hand on her cheek…soft as it caressed her face, and like an angel in the bright sunlight, Mary beheld the Madame, looking down into her eyes. When she too tried to reach back, Mary found she could not lift her arm, and then without warning pain hit her like a tidal wave.

Her entire body was on fire, and Mary let out a piercing scream that resonated throughout the dining hall. She went in and out of consciousness, and at one point realized it was not the Madame who held her, but Nurse Finely. The yells of Nurse Montell echoed through the madness and noise as Mary felt her body start to shake uncontrollably.

"Can't…move…" she sputtered, choking on her own blood.

"For God's sake, where is Dr. Peters?!" Nurse Finley shouted, her voice cracking in desperation. "Mary…you aren't going anywhere, Mary. Don't you dare close your eyes. If you do, I can't save you. Keep your eyes on me. Stay with me." She stifled over her frenzied words.

"Can't…move…" Mary attempted to say again.

Nurse Finley swallowed hard. "She…she broke a few of your bones, Mary. Don't try to move, please…Dr. Peters! Dr. Peters!"

Mary wrestled with residing in the present until Dr. Peters dropped down at her side. "What in God's name happened? Jesus.

416

Look at her. We've got to get her to the hospital ward immediately and send for Dr. Sanford…"

"I want her gone, Henry. For God's sake, look at this!" Nurse Finley's eyes met Dr. Peter's, a ferocity in them Mary had yet to behold from her. Then, the darkness crept in and Mary was pulled down into a cloudy haze, lost to everyone and everything, and the last memory she thought of was Thomas and Esther together dancing in the living room…happy in their apartment above the barbershop…

She woke with a start and tried to sit up, no notion of where she might be or how long she'd been out. Thirst hit her hard as she gasped for water. Mary's whole body ached and hurt, and she nearly lost her breath at the clenching and use of her muscles. Steadily, her eyes adjusted to the dark room, and Mary struggled to concentrate on any of the shapes surrounding her. One of her legs was splinted, her left arm in a sling, and the dull pain coming from just under her breasts caused her to glance down. Evidently along with her limbs, multiple ribs were broken, and a bandage was wrapped around her torso for stabilization. The incident, whatever it had been, was shattered into bits and pieces…there was so much darkness…Mary couldn't remember what exactly had occurred. It was then she heard breathing…and then a hand on her own hand…

"Who's there?!" Mary drew back rapidly.

"Shh!" came a familiar, low voice. "They'll…they'll hear…"

"Grace?"

"Yes. Grace. You are hurt…hurt very badly. Thought you would…would die." Grace shoved a cup of water into her hands, and Mary downed it as Grace went on. "Dr. Sanford and Dr. Peters…worried. And you…you're awake!"

Mary let out a deep breath of relief, handing her back the cup. "I am so glad it's you, Grace. How long have I been…been out?"

417

She was starting to make out the shape of her friend, and could see she was counting on her fingers.

"Days. A few days."

"What happened? I can't...I can't remember. My head hurts too badly...well Christ, everything hurts."

"Wait," Grace ordered, and hobbled to the door, one of her own legs clearly injured, and opened it slightly. Mary was about to protest when Bethany appeared and ran to her bedside, more water in her hands.

"You're awake!" she exclaimed, gesturing for Mary to open her mouth and pouring the water in slowly herself. "Praise God. It's a fucking miracle."

"Bethany," Mary pleaded after taking quenching her thirst, "Please tell me what happened. I can't think straight. How are you two here? Where am I?"

"Grace, can you find any more morphine?" Bethany asked, and Grace nodded, going directly to one of the drawers of the cabinet by Mary's bed.

"Mary, you've been in and out of it for almost four days. After Nurse Montell beat you nearly to death, Nurse Finley and Dr. Sanford have been trying to bring you back. We...Grace and I...have been here every night to watch you. We wanted to be here in case you...you know...woke up. Grace has been sneaking me out with her. Did you know she could do that?"

She tried her best to appear shocked. "I had no idea!"

Bethany laughed. "She's full of tricks, that one. Ahh here it is! Don't worry, I used to be a nurse. Bet you didn't know that either."

Grace advanced to Mary's bedside with a needle and handed it to Bethany. "Hold...still..." Mary wasn't up for second-guessing, and soon the burn of morphine into her veins tamed the relentless pain scorching her body.

Bethany put the needle aside and took the hand of Mary's unbroken arm. "We had better go soon. Stay quiet, it's nearly dawn.

Nurse Finley will be so happy to see you and she'll give you another good dose of morphine later today." Bethany gave her a squeeze and got up, making her way over to the door. "Grace?"

Grace didn't budge. "Moment alone...alone please..."

Bethany left the room without an argument and went outside, shutting the door after her. It was easy to see the dynamic in their relationship had transformed in Mary's absence – Grace apparently earned a certain level of respect while she'd been gone, and Bethany was perfectly satisfied to follow suit.

Mary gestured to Grace's leg. "Why are you hurt?"

Grace took her hand this time. "I saved...I saved Bethany. She got...got caught. I took the blame."

"Caught? Doing what?"

"Trying to...to see you..."

Mary examined Grace's leg. "Does it hurt badly?"

"It's getting better." Her eyes didn't look away, her face twisted with sorrow. "I wanted...wanted to save you...I couldn't get to you...I'm sorry, Mary."

"Grace, don't be ridiculous. There was nothing Bethany or you could have done."

"Well I did something to...to make it up to you...to fix it."

Studying her, Mary could perceive something major had happened. "What do you mean you made it up to me, Grace?"

Grace smirked at her. "Montell won't hurt you...not ever again... never again, Mary."

The words took a moment to sink in. "Grace, what did you do?"

"Nobody...nobody hurts my friend. Nobody." Grace fought hard to string together the sentences, mixed with emotion and excitement. "She...she tripped down the...the long stairs. Late that night after she...she hurt you. Nobody saw me...and she...she got hurt even worse. She didn't get up...and she won't get up again... not ever again..."

419

XV.

"Esther?"

The door creaked open as Celeste tiptoed inside in an attempt not to wake her, though Esther had been awake for hours, endeavoring to avoid sleep. The mornings were the most difficult part of her day to get through since the incident at The Palace. Every night, Esther would have the same recurring nightmare: she stood alone, drenched in blood in the main lobby of The Palace, and circling around her lay everyone she'd ever cared for dead on the floor, their screams echoing as loud as a train in her ears. Six days had gone by, and she struggled to come to grips not particularly with the violence, but with the realization the Hiltmores and Adamses conspired together to see her permanently silenced after she tried to take Timothy down on her own. Her plan had been foiled, and if not for the Madame, Louis, and the girls, Esther knew the odds of her being alive were small at best. She remained hiding in the one place the Madame believed she was safe, and the Turners didn't bother to ask any questions, only graciously complied and made Esther feel right at home. Thomas saw her multiple times a day, intermittently between his business meetings, and he assured her that he only disclosed what had happened to his father because he had no other

421

choice. Edward came to see her briefly and promised until she was better, they would delay their assessment of what to do next.

Like Thomas, Celeste persistently visited her bedside, and during those times Esther guiltily pretended to sleep, not sure how to proceed with their friendship when her family evidently wanted Esther out of the picture. Two afternoons before, she overheard Lucy telling Celeste the doctor diagnosed it as a common illness that should pass in another few days, which thankfully her friend seemed to accept. Today, however, Esther had the inclination avoiding face-to-face confrontation with Celeste was utterly impossible, and prepared to put on the best mask she could to cover the lies that would pour from her lips. The Madame had been right – the thin ice Esther walked upon was cracking under her feet.

She felt the mattress below her shift as Celeste climbed into bed and under the covers next to her. Following a deep breath, Esther rolled over to see her longtime companion, whose air was full of concern.

"Hi," she whispered, taking Esther's hand. "I've been so worried about you, Es. I know you aren't sick. You haven't had a fever in days…I've been checking. And you're terrible at faking sleep."

Esther could tell Celeste was upset that she'd been evading her. "It was more of a mental thing, Celeste. I will be all right, I promise. I just needed a few days."

Her brow furrowed. "Did something happen? Why don't you come home and stay with me? I can care for you."

"Lucy won't let me leave until she's certain I'm cured," Esther vindicated, wanting to comfort her. "Just a few more days."

"Would you like some opium?" she asked, pulling a tiny bottle from her pocket, "It might help your nerves. It's helped with mine around Timothy."

"No, but thank you. Not just for that, but for being here to look after me."

"Well I'm not the only one. Captain Bernhardt has been here

every day as well. He and Thomas are becoming fast friends, which will only make this whole debacle harder."

Esther immediately was irritated with Thomas for hiding Captain Bernhardt's visits from her. "He's been here every day?"

Celeste nodded. "Every day. More worried than I was, I think. You have to tell him, Es. The sooner the better."

"What do you mean?"

"Oh, don't what me," Celeste giggled, squeezing her hand. "You're staying in Thomas' home, for Christ's sake, and his family all adore you and never want you to leave. I've watched him in this very room diligently taking care of you…I mean, you should see the way he looks at you. I think it's safe to say Captain Bernhardt has lost."

Her frustration with Thomas instantly vanished. "I…I didn't notice…I've been so out of sorts…"

"You'll see, I swear it. But never mind that. Right now, you need to get yourself out of bed and dressed. You bathed yesterday evening, correct?"

"Yes I…I did but why?"

Celeste released her hand and slipped out of bed, heading straight for the wardrobe. "Lucy and I decided a little socialization would help ease you out of whatever mess is in your head. So up you go. By the way I absolutely adore her."

Esther sat up in bed. For a few seconds, she seriously considered confessing everything to Celeste…she was her best friend, and had been her entire life. What good was she doing her by upholding the fallacy her parents painted and held right in front of her eyes? As she gazed on, observing Celeste's happy face as she dug through a few of the dresses she'd brought for Esther to wear, her momentary pang of courage passed. Dragging Esther to her feet, Celeste chattered on about the latest gossip around town, holding up the beige gown first, then the green one, and finally the red, oblivious to the argument occurring in Esther's head. The gorgeous glow in Celeste's cheeks from her pregnancy made her eyes sparkle even more than usual, and Esther's could sense her defensiveness of that happiness rise. The wheels in her head were turning, and a tiny voice inside her heart told Esther the time was not right. Not in this moment, with so much still at stake. She and the Madame had a plan to see through, and that plan came first.

After fussing over Esther's hair for nearly a quarter of an hour, Celeste deemed her fit for the remainder of the day and they ventured downstairs to meet Lucy. Celeste wrapped her arm through Esther's, making her wonder if perhaps during those years of leading a double life she had taken their friendship for granted. Maybe Esther hadn't given Celeste enough credit…maybe when she did discover the truth it wouldn't be nearly as hard for her as Esther imagined. There had never been other options for them to survive, and yet here they were, somehow able to subsist together. Esther could only hope that in the end, their bond might outlast the storm that was coming…otherwise, she knew it would irreparably tear them apart.

Tony was waiting for them before they reached the dining room, and announced that William, Edward, and Thomas would be late in joining them, as they were called away on a business matter. With a heartening smile at Esther, he opened the swinging door for them to enter, and immediately Esther was paralyzed with fear.

At the head of the table sat Lucy, unknowingly in happy conversation with Catherine Hiltmore, whose husband sat on her right. Across from them was none other than Timothy Adams, sipping wine and appearing sociable and utterly normal, as if nothing had happened. With a gentle push, Celeste helped her along, unaware of Esther's real reason of panic, and it took all the strength she had to not bolt from sight. Her mind raced, trying to gather her thoughts and assess the situation, the trepidation clouding her judgment and ability to overcome her emotions. They were trying to intimidate her, trying to show her she wasn't protected anywhere and frighten her more out of her wits than she already was. With each move toward the table, her bravery was fading, and when she grasped she couldn't resolve the problem, Esther used the one card she had left: what would the Madame do?

Suddenly, that same little voice that told her previously to keep her mouth shut with Celeste spoke up again, and it was quite a bit louder:

Turn the tables and show you aren't afraid of them. Make them sorry they ever believed they could succeed. Make them pay.

An odd sort of smile came onto Esther's face.

"Esther!" Lucy exclaimed, getting to her feet and striding to her. "I am so glad to see you are doing well." She wrapped her arms into a tight hug, which Esther wholeheartedly returned. "Come sit down. Are you up for a glass of wine? Some food?"

Show them you aren't afraid. Show them they are the ones who should be scared.

Esther took her seat jovially beside Douglas Hiltmore. "I am famished. Some wine and whatever food you've prepared would be wonderful, Lucy. Thank you."

Celeste made her way to sit by her husband on the other side of the table, and Tony magically appeared with a full glass of wine for each of them.

Catherine leaned forward and grinned her direction. "Happy to see you doing better, dearest," she said, though her tone wasn't entirely filled with it's normal level of confidence. As Esther was about to respond, she caught it. Douglas glimpsed up, his eyes meeting Timothy's directly, who glanced back only for a second with an air of unsteady apprehension that matched Catherine's words. If she had even blinked, Esther would have missed it, and that one fleeting glimpse gave her the edge she needed to keep the ball rolling.

"I am feeling so much better today!" she announced to the group, having a drink from her glass. "It has been so great to have Celeste here to take care of me. Thank you for sparing her, Timothy."

He was startled at being addressed. "I don't think any force on earth could have stopped her," he replied feebly.

Esther turned back to Lucy, who could sense something was

amiss and spoke up. "It was a horrible night. You were such a mess when you arrived, Esther! I was relieved Thomas was dispatched to get you from The Palace."

"You're so right, Lucy, it was a horrible night," Esther resumed. "It was sheer horror when the sickness broke out! I think mine was more…psychological from being a bystander to how ill the others were, but all the girls pulled through." She paused. *Turn the tables on them.* "Unfortunately, two of the men there that night didn't, which was so incredibly sad. They weren't regulars, so the Madame suspected they might have been the ones carrying whatever it was." Immediately, Catherine Hiltmore stifled a cough, choking on whatever she was ingesting. "Are you all right Mrs. Hiltmore?" Esther posed innocently. "You look pale!"

"I am…quite all right…thank you, Esther," she claimed, trying to mask her dismay at Esther's story.

"Well, I know the men of the house will be sorry to hear they've missed their guests!" Lucy proclaimed. "The Hiltmores came by with Celeste to check in on you and also invite us to their party this evening. Do you think you're ready to be out and about, Esther?"

All eyes were upon her – they wanted her to say no, and she wouldn't do them that justice.

"Absolutely! I would be delighted."

"Are you sure, dearest?" Catherine interposed. "It will be a very large party…lots of guests and I will presume very crowded. We wouldn't want you to overdo it and put yourself at risk."

"Of course I am sure, Mrs. Hiltmore. I wouldn't miss it for the world."

"Who is coming father?" Celeste chimed in.

"Most of New York, I should think," Douglas clarified, taking the forefront from a stupefied Catherine. "I think the mayor and his wife plan to attend, as well as the new chief of police and a few state representatives to go along with the usual group…oh, and the new fire commissioner. It should be an exciting gathering."

"Lovely!" Lucy's voice boomed. "Well Esther, why don't you plan on going to Celeste's early to dress so you can be back and see the boys before we attend? Would that be all right?"

"I think I would have to, considering most of my wardrobe is there!" she laughed, readying to make her final blow. "I will have Louis take me over after I see the Madame in an hour or so, and he will bring me back in time for the festivities to begin. That way, you know I am in good hands in case I feel the slightest bit ill."

Celeste beamed. "I cannot wait!"

Timothy and the Hiltmores, on the other hand, seemingly appeared as if they'd just eaten something far too sour.

When the visiting party excused themselves from the Turner residence, Lucy ordered wine and cheese to the sitting room, beckoning Esther to follow.

"I can't say they are my favorite lot," she declared, flopping down onto a couch by one of the large street side windows. "They like talking about how well-connected they are. It's incredibly boring."

"They've been like that since I can remember," Esther acknowledged, taking her place beside Lucy. "Thank you so much for housing me. I cannot begin to express my gratitude."

"Don't be silly. You are welcome here for as long as you wish. Can I ask, however, why in the world Thomas brought you straight here and not back to the Adamses' when you'd fallen ill? He hasn't been very…candid…about the whole affair, and Edward has been in a mood for days on end…William and I can pick up on when we're out of the loop on something, and in this case, I feel like there is something big we are missing."

Esther set down her wine glass. "Let's just say I do not see in the foreseeable future ever returning to that household, for a multitude of reasons, and I swear in time I will tell you what has happened. I love Celeste with all my heart. Her family is the problem."

Lucy nodded. "I just want you to know you can trust me. I realize we don't know each other well, but anyone Thomas cares for as much as he cares for you, I regard as a sister." She held her glass up to cheers with Esther. "Unfortunately, Catherine Hiltmore appears to be the type of woman who gives us ladies a bad name."

"I couldn't agree with you more, Lucy."

She smiled and moved on. "You've had a few visitors while you've been ill. One of them being a very handsome Captain." Esther blushed, not sure how to react, and instead took a sip of wine to allow Lucy to get whatever she needed to off her chest. "I think you are quite a catch, Esther. I like you and I like having you around. You make Thomas better...happier...but if you plan on breaking his heart, I'd much rather know about it now. Woman to woman."

"Lucy...I..."

"Just be honest with me. I only want what's best for him. You can understand that."

Esther sighed. "Lucy, I am not in love with Captain Bernhardt, nor do I have any intention to marry him."

"And what about Tommy?"

"What do you want me to say? That I'm in love with him?"

Lucy smirked. "Are you?"

"Christ...it's been a long few days, and I've had a lot of wine..."

"You do love him, don't you?"

"Well...I mean...yes," she blurted out, causing her free hand to fly up and cover her mouth. "Dammit!" she cursed, and then her eyes grew wider at her slip, causing Lucy to burst into giggles.

"Ah, Esther I think I like you more if that's possible."

"I'm so sorry, Lucy..." She was mortified at her blunder, especially in front of a woman she wanted so badly to impress.

"Don't be!" Lucy waved her off. "This is glorious, Esther! Glorious!"

"What do you mean, glorious? Please, you cannot tell Thomas!"

"All right, I will keep it to myself for now," she promised her. "Not forever though."

After a moment of quiet, Lucy's amusement seemed to continue to cultivate, and Esther's interest got the better of her. "Lucy, why are you smiling like that?"

"Oh, nothing of any significance. I've just won another bet, that's all. More wine?"

Esther hadn't seen the Madame since the night of the break in, and after an enjoyable lunch with Lucy, she prepared herself for a trip across Central Park. It wasn't just because she'd told the Hiltmores and Timothy her agenda, either; it was because the Hiltmores' party would draw the type of crowd the Madame always liked to keep eyes and ears on, and her duty and loyalty to the Madame outweighed any sort of enduring fear to prevent her from working. There was no plan for Louis to escort her – that was merely to impart the idea she would be guarded, though Esther would make sure he or Georgie went to the Adamses' with her in case any issues should arise. One quick stroll across the park and she'd be in safe hands…the only problem was, she had to get there first.

The sun and heat were blistering, and Esther grabbed her parasol, telling Lucy she would return in a few hours dressed and ready for the evening. Heading straight to The Palace, Esther only made it a block from the house when the all too familiar feeling of someone stalking close behind started to creep up. The bright sunlight caused her to squint her eyelids to definitively see anything, and sure enough, ten paces behind her was a man in a dark suit, a hat shadowing his face, and hands resting leisurely in his pockets, holding her tempo. Esther quickened her steps and, as she passed a group of elderly women tittering at one another, she dodged in front of a carriage heading into the park in the hopes of losing him. A few twists and turns down one of the gravel paths, Esther caught sight of him again in her peripheral vision and her heart raced faster. No matter what route she took or what speed she jumped to, the man was gaining on her, and nothing except breaking into a full on run could escape his progress. In one last effort to confuse her pursuer, she made an abrupt right down one of the more inconspicuous trails toward the fountain. The instant she turned the sharp corner, Esther was grabbed from somewhere in the brush and pulled behind a tree, one hand covering her mouth and the other arm around her waist, lifting her off her feet as if she were only a rag doll. Trying to resist, she hit at the man's arm, only to glance down and recognize the hand holding her tight, the familiar scent of tobacco reaching her nostrils.

"Shhh," Louis whispered. "Quiet."

Doing exactly what she was told, Esther went limp and didn't make a sound, trying not to even breathe aloud. Within seconds, she could hear the man in the dark suit sneak past the tree from the light crunch of gravel, searching around for wherever his victim might have disappeared to. Eventually, with a frustrated kick of the dirt, the man stormed off and Louis lowered her down to the ground, rotating her to face him.

"Bastard," Louis muttered, shaking his head. "I doubt he was going to kill you. He's been outside the Turners' off and on for a few days now, keeping an eye on things. He has no idea that, in reality, I've been watching him closely too. I think they are smart enough to know better than to get rid of you in broad daylight."

Esther found she was out of breath. "The...the Adamses sent him? Or the...the Hiltmores?"

"Either or both, I would assume." He motioned for her to walk over to the pathway. "I'll take you to The Palace. No more venturing out on your own unless I'm with you, or Thomas is, or Edward. Yeah?"

"Yeah." Esther looked down – her hands were shaking, and her throat began to tighten. The weight of it came rushing down over her like water. "Louis I...I can't..." Her vision went spotty, and right when she thought she might collapse he snatched her up and carried her to the nearest bench, sitting her down gently.

Louis gave her a moment to recover and then placed himself beside her, looking intently into her eyes. "If you despair now, you will not make it, Esther. The only way you're going to get through this is if you are brave and fight. You must fight this off, or you will die."

"I've never been a fighter, Louis. I've been a God damned spy. I can't defend myself like...like you can. They...they want to kill me, Louis...I don't know how to be brave when I'm this afraid."

"You pretend," he justified to her. "You pretend you are something until you become it. If you pretend you are brave enough, you will be, just as you did today in the dining room. I could see it in you...it's there, Esther, you just need to find it. To run away and hide...that is what they want you to do. It makes you an easier target. Now come along, or that son of a bitch will be back."

Louis held out his arm to her, and Esther took it, needing his support to put one foot in front of the other. "How many times have people tried to kill you, Louis?"

To her surprise, he grinned. "More times than I can count."

"How did you survive?"

"The only way I knew how to – fought when I must, and did whatever I could to seek them out and kill them first."

Esther's stomach knotted. "You...you killed them...all?" she entreated him, not sure she wanted to hear the answer.

"In most cases, I killed them first, yes" he reiterated, chuckling as he said it. "If someone wants you dead, Esther, there is no room for error. The problem can only be eliminated so many ways. And you are more fortunate than I."

"How is that?"

His free left hand went to hers, which was still clutching at his right forearm. "You have people who love you and will happily take care of the dirty work for you."

They spent the rest of their trip in silence, Esther brooding over Louis' words, and Louis keeping a sharp eye out for the man in the dark suit. Wandering by other cheery groups of people out in the park made Esther melancholic; the Madame's battle had also become hers much quicker than Esther could ever have anticipated, with a very firm line in the sand being drawn. She knew damn well which side she was on, and that wouldn't change under any circumstances, but she found what upset her most had nothing to do with a hit man chasing her through Central Park. It was the way Louis so callously depicted a world where life was kill or be killed…and that she was a member of it. There was no alternative – Esther would have to build her fortitude to a degree that outlasted the Hiltmores' and the Adamses' combined, or risk failure.

Upon entering The Palace, Esther was greeted with embraces and smiles from Danny and Hope, and their compassionate gesture gave her an undeniable lift in spirits. Being there amongst the people she regarded as her true family made her feel as if she wasn't in this alone, and after years of spending time there, reminded her of the resilience and strength every person in that place embodied. If there was a winning side, Esther decided she was on it: she would put her money on the members of The Palace over a small group of spineless aristocrats any day of the week. She would do anything for any one of them, and suddenly, Louis' words finally made sense.

The Madame reached the bottom of the staircase and dismissed Hope and Danny back to work, leaving only the Madame, Esther, and Louis remaining in the lobby. The three stood there for nearly a minute without speaking, the Madame's piercing stare scanning Esther up and down with her arms crossed over her chest.

"Did he follow her out of the house?" she asked Louis, her eyes not leaving Esther.

"Yes, just as we thought he would. I'm not sure he was armed to kill her…more to follow her and find out where exactly she was going. I honestly believe they will try and do this as quietly as they can."

"Hah! Quietly…we'll see about that. Come on, darling, follow me upstairs." The Madame spun around and ascended, Louis taking his cue of dismissal. "Are the doors secure?" she called to him.

"They were when I left, and I'm checking them again now."

"Good."

By the time they made it to her office, Louis was already there, and he shut and bolted the doors closed behind them. Esther noticed on his belt he wore both a pistol and a knife, and another pistol was holstered inside of his jacket. Looking from right to left, there were loaded shotguns and a few spare cartridges and cylinders in both corners by the doorway, and as her eyes traveled toward the Madame's desk, she watched as her mentor then proceeded to take seven different weapons off her person, each strategically concealed in places Esther presumed made sitting extremely unpleasant.

Sensing Esther's gaze, the Madame smiled at her. "We are well-prepared in case those bastards decide to stupidly try and attack again. Even if they sent in a small army, we'd blow those assholes to shit in less than ten minutes." When her proverbial strip of firearms and knives was complete and scattered over her desktop, she sank down into her chair with a long sigh, pointing toward Esther's for her to do the same. "Six fucking days, darling? You must have been doing a damn good load of soul searching."

"I wanted to come sooner," Esther divulged. "I was just... shocked. I needed some time to pull myself together. I was a fucking mess." Louis handed her a full glass of wine and set another in front of the Madame, who left it momentarily untouched.

"Why didn't you tell me that son of a bitch raped you?"

The question brought about the memory of that night Timothy took advantage of her, and Esther pinched her eyelids shut for a second to try to fend it off.

"I wanted to try and take care of it on my own. You have enough bullshit on your plate right now—"

"For God's sake, Esther, if somebody raped you I would want to fucking kill them myself! And what the hell were you thinking going to the coppers? What's the point of having someone like me around if you don't take advantage of my talents, darling? You should have told me, not let it brew until it fucking boiled over!" Esther couldn't decide if the Madame was upset with her for having such a monumental secret or simply upset at the idea of her being raped altogether, so she didn't respond and gulped down a bit of her wine.

The Madame picked up her glass. "How many times?"

"Just once."

"How long did you fucking wait before you went to the precinct?"

"A few weeks," she admitted. "I was in denial...and Timothy threatened to kill me. When I found out Celeste was pregnant a part of me snapped. I wanted him gone, so I did what I thought would... well...legally take care of that for good."

The Madame let out a cackle, amused. "I wish, darling. We can't take care of these motherfuckers legally. That was the mistake you made. They can pay their way out of anything."

"Then...what is it we need to do?"

The Madame leaned forward inquisitively. "We?"

Esther nodded. "I'm not sitting this one out. I want in. Since I was the primary hit, I want to have a say in what goes on."

Louis broke his stance by the doors and strolled forward to protest, but the Madame held up a hand to stop him. "It's her determination, Louis. Not ours."

"Madame, you can't possibly..."

"Do I need to fucking repeat myself?"

He turned toward Esther, his air distressed. "Please Esther, think of what you are doing," he begged, kneeling down beside her. "This is not something that will ever go away. Once you light this match, the fire will burn on no matter what you try to do to put it out."

Esther took his hand. "I've made my decision. I'm ready. I want to do this."

Louis' gaze fell to the floor, and the Madame spoke up: "You had better understand one thing, Esther. If you choose this, you choose your loyalty to us over anyone else, and on certain occasion, that may or may not include Thomas. There will be times when your reliability will be tested, and you will have no true friends on the outside of these fucking walls. This wonderful little life on the East Side of town you've put together will cease to exist. Are you ready for that?"

"I built that wonderful little life as a façade for us. It never existed, Madame."

"And what about Thomas?"

"There is no reason he would interfere in this," she replied blandly. "And it isn't about Thomas. This is about me taking back my life." Esther paused, grinning at the Madame. "The Hiltmores are having a party tonight, and I plan on attending in full force."

The Madame grinned. "Then let's get to work."

"Celeste, I can't possibly take this dress. It cost you a fortune!"

For the last hour and a half, Esther had been at the Adams residence, fortunately without the company of Timothy lurking around the house; in spite of that, Louis discreetly lingered on guard outside, standing across the street and nonchalantly smoking. The Madame insisted he would shadow her throughout the evening's festivities – Esther didn't have Louis' sixth sense of spotting a potential threat from a mile away, and in case the Hiltmores and Adamses did try anything in such a public setting, there was no room for negotiation. Now being laced into one of Celeste's finest silk gowns, Esther's protestations fell on deaf ears, the shade of green closely matching that of her eyes and therefore making Celeste firm in her stance that Esther should wear it. With her dark, curled hair piled on top of her head, Esther gawked at her reflection: it wasn't the first time she'd felt truly beautiful, nor would it be the last, yet it was the first time she was aware of how powerful that beauty made her.

"Beauty is your mask," she recalled the Madame advising her, "Underneath may be the real measure of your character, but what is on the surface is what will conceal your true intentions. If you veil it well, you will never find yourself in trouble."

For years, Esther spied for the Madame, listening in on conversations not meant for outside ears and handing over whatever she could to her for leverage. Tonight, and every night from this one forward would be different...there would be consequences and there were lives at stake, their fate resting in her hands.

Esther found it strangely exhilarating.

"You're taking that dress" Celeste retorted, from the other side of her room dividers. "I could never wear it anyhow, the color was not meant for me. Do you like this navy one?" She stepped out into Esther's line of sight in a gorgeous satin gown, dark navy with white lace trim, her face skeptical whether or not it was the right pick.

"Celeste...you are stunning!" Esther cried.

Instantly the doubt fell from her expression. "You really think so?" Celeste trotted over to view her reflection.

"Absolutely!" Out of the corner of her eye, Esther caught the time on the clock. "Damn, Celeste, I've got to be going, and you're going to be extremely late to dinner if you aren't in that coach in ten minutes. You told your parents you'd be arriving five minutes ago."

"Christ," she exclaimed, running to her vanity. "All right, I'll see you at 8:30, correct?"

"8:30 sharp," Esther fretted, shuffling to gather her own belongings.

Just as she was about to run out the door, Celeste stopped her. "Wait!" she ordered, picking something up from her bedside table and bringing it to Esther. "You left this in your room, and I thought you might want to wear it tonight." She opened her hands to reveal Mary's comb, and tenderly slid it into Esther's hair. "It goes perfectly with the dress. And it won't hurt your chances with Thomas."

"And here I thought you were rooting for the Captain," Esther teased, her heart warming.

Celeste shrugged. "I want you to be happy," she said, taking Esther's hand and kissing it. "Now go. We are both already late!"

Esther hurried downstairs, ecstatic to find Louis ahead of her with a carriage ready to take them to the Turners'. "You're a lifesaver, Louis," she declared, causing him to chuckle and help her inside.

"Tell me something I don't know," he remarked, taking the seat next to her and shouting for the driver to get a move on. They rode for a bit, the ride not being more than a few minutes, until out of nowhere Louis let out a long exhale, and Esther knew what was coming next. "Please don't do this. You don't have to. I can fix it."

"I know you can, Louis. I want to be the one to fix it."

"But look at you. Like this. This is the way you are supposed to be...I've never seen you more handsome in all the time I've known you. You want to give any enjoyment you have in this away? I just don't think you're ready. I don't think you understand where this road leads, Esther."

"Louis..." Esther fought to piece together what she wanted to say. "Do you know why I didn't tell the Madame right away about Timothy assaulting me?"

"No, I cannot say I do."

"No dress of Celeste's matters, no amount of makeup or jewelry or anything like that." Esther took Mary's comb out of her hair and held it in her hands, showing it to Louis. "This is what has mattered to me."

"That's Mary's old comb," Louis noted.

"Yes it is. Thomas gave it to me before he left for England," she recalled, gripping it tightly in her hands and holding it to her chest. "I've been unhappy for a long time, Louis, and it's because I let the entire world of Fifth Avenue swallow me whole. If I stay where I am, I want to do it to get rid of monsters like Timothy Adams who use their money and status to cover up their fucking messes. If I can do that, I will have done something worthwhile with my life. That's about all I can ask for."

437

"I understand the premise, Esther, but it's a double life, one filled with secrets and lies. One that won't end cheerfully."

She placed the comb back into her hair carefully. "I'm already leading a double life, Louis."

He studied her. "How is that?"

"I will never be one of them. I am one of you, I always have been. It's time to stop pretending to be something I'm not."

Louis put his hand on her cheek, and she could feel the roughened calluses. "You are still a little girl, Esther, unsullied in this."

"On the contrary, Louis, I am Helen of Troy. It's because of me this has escalated, and unlike her, I don't plan on cowering in the shadows."

"What about Thomas?"

Esther didn't quite grasp his insinuation. "What about Thomas?"

"He knows about everything that has happened. You two have yet to speak on the subject. What do you plan on telling him? He will accept...or rather, he has made it clear he wants the Madame to take action...are you so certain he would accept the same from you wanting to participate?"

"It won't change my intentions, Louis. I am what I am. Thomas knows that."

"Can I offer a bit of advice?"

"Of course."

The carriage came to a halt, and the coachman called out their arrived destination as he leapt down from the driver's seat.

"Don't lie to him about any of it. Hearing it will be difficult for him, but if you are dishonest, he will have an even harder time forgiving you."

She nodded. "I don't think you need to worry about that, Louis. I've always been a terrible liar. Especially to Thomas."

The driver opened the door and offered his hand out to her, which Esther took, and Louis barreled out after her. "I'll be here if you need me. You know the signal. With Lord Turner around, however, I don't really think you'll find yourself in any tight corners."

"Why? What does Lord Turner have to do with anything?"

Louis bowed, took her hand, and kissed it. "That story is for another time. Good evening, Miss Esther, you are a heavenly sight to behold. Good luck." Before she could press him further, Louis whirled around and sauntered off down the pathway, his parting leaving Esther a little mystified.

The front door of the Turners' swung open just as Esther reached to knock, and there stood Tony to allow her inside. "Good evening, Miss Esther. You are looking exceptionally lovely."

"Thank you, Tony." She strode across the threshold and Tony politely took her shawl, hanging it in their front closet. With impeccable civility, he ushered her to the sitting room where the rest of the Turners presumably waited when Esther heard someone loudly pacing their direction, and Thomas emerged from midway down the hall. He did not seem pleased.

"Sir, is everything all right?" Tony inquired, a little anxious.

"Leave us, Tony," Thomas instructed as he met them. "And don't tell them she's arrived yet. Just get the champagne." Tony complied and hastily trotted the way Thomas had come.

Esther was confused. "Thomas, what's the matter?"

Thomas impulsively grabbed her hand and, without warning, hauled Esther the opposite direction through the dining room and out the swinging door to the servant's hallway. He peeked here and there to ensure they were alone, and then released her hand, twisting around so they were facing each other. In that moment, Esther couldn't remember a time she'd seen him livider, and it made her increasingly uncomfortable.

"What in the hell do you think you're doing going out there by yourself?" he scolded her, his tone laden with exasperation. "Do you not remember what happened to you only a few fucking days ago? Are you trying to taunt these people?!"

439

Keeping her composure, Esther kept the volume of her answer as low as she could, though her defenses made it hard to remained unruffled.

"Clearly, since I am standing here right now, I am fine Thomas. How dare you yell at me like I'm some foolish little girl. Of course I know what happened. I was there, wasn't I? This is my problem, not yours, and I'm not going to be idle and allow everyone else to fight my battles for me."

"You made this my God damned problem, Esther. What exactly do you plan on doing, then? The coppers did a fine job of protecting you, didn't they? You're eighteen. You have no idea how big this problem is. And how could you?"

Esther's head was about to explode with anger. "I am not ten anymore, Thomas. I don't need you keep sheltering me. You've been gone for eight years, for Christ's sake."

"Then why was I the one sent for to come and get you? Why me?"

"Oh, Thomas, please just give it a rest!"

"No, I want a real answer. For once!" he shouted, apparently no longer caring who heard him. "Why not the Captain, or one of the other bastards you've been stringing along? What would they have done to help you?"

"Thomas–"

"Answer me!"

"Nothing, Thomas–"

"Then why me, Esther?"

"Because the Madame knows I fucking love you, all right?!" she yelled, falling backward slightly and reaching for the wall to steady herself, though she couldn't cease the word vomit from pouring out. "She sent for you because I was inconsolable and falling apart. You're the only person outside The Palace I actually trust, and she knew you'd take me in because she couldn't. That's why!" Her emotions were tangled up in her chest and she tried to catch her breath. "I don't have a home anymore, Thomas," she choked, the tears falling slowly. "And I am unbelievably grateful for your hospitality. I have never felt safer than when I am here. But I will not ask you to clean this up for me or make it your problem. It's for me to do on my own so you and your family are not involved. All right?"

Thomas stayed mute so long Esther began to worry she'd ruined everything with her confession. Then, at once he moved forward and pulled Esther toward him, cupping her face in his hands as he stared down into her eyes, their foreheads pressed together.

"I'm already involved," he told her. "And that is not going to change. I just don't want anything to happen to you, don't you see that?"

His hands brushed through her hair, and Esther's heart felt like it might explode. "I am just going to help move things along, that's it. Nothing I haven't done before, and nothing that will endanger me or anyone else. That's why I…we…have to go tonight."

Thomas squinted at her, trying to rationalize it. "You promise me? That is it? Nothing more than what you've already done for her?"

It wasn't a lie…it was a stretch of the truth, and Esther justified it by her intention to shield him from the outcome. "I swear, nothing more."

"Then just promise me one more thing."

"Anything."

He grinned slyly. "I want you to tell the Captain things are over. For good."

"I plan to—"

"Tonight," he insisted. "At the party. Or you'll never get another one of these." Thomas tilted downward and kissed her, not hard but with a definitive sense of urgency. Esther kissed him back, wrapping her arms around his neck, everything around them fading to a dull blur.

Seconds later, however, came the clearing of someone's throat to their left. Instantly, Esther and Thomas stopped and turned to see Lucy standing there beaming with two large glasses of brandy in each of her hands.

"William is going to be furious when he hears he owes me yet another five dollars," she quipped, winking at the pair and handing over their drinks, "Now, come join the rest of us. The boys are already suspicious, and I don't think I can handle one more talk about who owned a better something when they were younger... juveniles, I tell you..."

They were successfully delivered by carriage to the Hiltmore residence, one amongst the many in the mass of coaches. Esther's mouth gaped open, a little flabbergasted by what she saw: the Hiltmores had ostensibly invited everyone they'd ever known to this "little gathering" at their new residence, and as the crowd shuffled toward the front door, Esther realized she would have to be alert and far more guarded than she was accustomed. Everyone was dressed in the finest garments they owned. Men donned black, tailored suits, top hats, cravats, and canes; the ladies wore their most expensive jewelry piled on high, sparkling with each step they took, and the floor length gowns spoke a variety of colors and styles made from rare, if not impossible to find, fabric. It was then Esther saw through Celeste's insistence earlier in the day that she took the green dress, one that cost more than all of Esther's dresses combined, and she felt an immense sense of gratitude toward her friend. The last thing she wanted on a night like tonight with so much hanging in the balance was to stick out from the crowd and appear as if she didn't belong. Tonight was too important for mistakes.

"Do you think if we simply don't show up they'll even notice?" William joked, causing Lucy to hit his arm, and he let out a small moan of pain. "For Christ's sake, I was just kidding!"

"We all know William would turn this carriage around if Lucy would allow it," Edward teased. "Please excuse him, Esther, he was dropped as a child."

"Like hell I was!" William shot back. "I ought to tan your hide for that, Eddie."

Lucy rolled her eyes, glancing out the window on her right. "I honestly don't remember a time I've seen more people. Not even at one of the larger balls in England. Who are all these people?"

Esther shrugged. "Anyone who makes the Hiltmores feel as important as they think they are," she said sarcastically. "Along with a few others they are trying to win over."

"It's nights like these I wonder if the Madame has it all figured out," Edward chuckled. "How does she put this? Being fed to the wolves? Or was it the snake pit…"

Her stomach dropped, and Esther's eyes darted to meet Edward's. "Yes I…I do believe that's exactly how she puts it…"

Edward winked at her, and Esther tried not to seem out of sorts despite her mind being in a flurry during the slowly passing seconds Lord Turner held her gaze. No one except for her and Louis knew the Madame's code words regarding their operations…Esther's individual missions were designated as "being fed to the wolves" or "being tossed in the snake pit," and had been since the day she started. Hearing those exact words from Edward's mouth was extremely disconcerting, especially in the context of this night's importance to her and to the Madame. Then, in a flash, Esther remembered what Louis told her as he dropped her at the Turners…something about how with Edward around she wouldn't have to worry…and Esther wondered if there was more to his relationship with Louis and the Madame than any of them let on.

"All right, we're next!" Thomas announced, breaking Esther's thought process. A moment later, the coach door swung open and the gentlemen piled out first, followed closely by Lucy and Esther, and Edward took the lead as they made their way inside. Thomas pulled Esther's arm through his, not bothering to ask for permission, and she had to admit she liked that he didn't. The five of them waltzed through the entryway together, heading straight for the Hiltmores to greet them, a slew of whispers spreading as many turned to stare. Esther recognized the commanding attention they received had nothing to do with her: the Turners were considered a bit of a mystery, having yet to make their social presence known within much of high society in New York, which they were very much a part of even if they didn't act that way. Tonight would be one of their few public outings, and therefore, would be given special notice, much to William's dismay. This caused Esther to have another revelation, one that hadn't crossed her mind: her overtly close association with the Turners at the party provided her a blanket of protection, one she might need to survive the next few days, and if the Hiltmores or Adamses had anything planned for her that evening they would be meddling with one of the wealthiest families in the city. For the next few hours, Esther would be safe, and a few hours was all she needed.

"Welcome!" beckoned Douglas Hiltmore, shaking Edward's hand firmly. "We are so pleased you all could make it tonight, Lord Turner."

"We are delighted to be here," Edward replied. "Mrs. Hiltmore, you are looking radiant."

"Thank you, Lord Turner. It's an honor to have your entire family present! And Esther, too, of course."

Edward smiled politely, though anyone who knew him could see it took an exertion of effort. "Right, well actually Catherine, I think you can consider her a part of our family," Edward elucidated, becoming increasingly defensive, and Esther felt Thomas shift nervously beside her. "I doubt she will be going anywhere any time soon, so long as I have something to say about it—"

Thomas hastily left Esther's arm and stepped between Edward and the Hiltmores, interrupting his father. "Why don't you point us the direction of the wine, Douglas? I know I could use a glass."

Lucy and William gave their courtesies, and Esther gladly waited to be last, putting on a high level of charm to only baffle them further.

She curtsied low. "The party is incredible! So many people! Where will I find Celeste? Are there any acquaintances here I should make note to find, Mrs. Hiltmore?"

Catherine civilly took the bait as expected. "The Bernards are here somewhere…just follow the whiskey…the Abbotts, most of the Carringtons made it somehow…they must have taken three coaches…there are a few of Douglas' business associates from the Carolinas I believe you know, and then of course, Mr. and Mrs. Adams would love to see you, dearest."

Once again, Esther was blown away by how the Madame's prediction proved to be true, anticipating the moves the Hiltmores would make before they even put their hand on the chess piece. A last minute gathering at such a massive volume sang a song of desperation, as most of these parties took at least a few weeks in advance to plan for new gowns and suits to be made, caterers to be hired, and typically, over the top decorating of the household. When they failed to kill her and the Madame, the Hiltmores panicked, caring more about covering their tracks than finishing the task at hand, which would be much more difficult with one botched attempt under their belts. Those friends from the Carolinas Catherine spoke of were old runners from the southern plantations the Hiltmores still owned, and they'd been invited up to New York City for guarantees any evidence that could be used against them was destroyed. After tonight, the Hiltmores would pay them heftily and send them home to complete the charge. Esther knew what the Madame needed, and prepared to wrap up her end of their undertaking.

"I will be sure to give everyone my best," she assured them cheerily, curtseying another time and then gliding off to take Thomas' arm as he stood waiting for her.

"They have no idea what's coming, do they?" he asked, whispering in her ear.

This time, a real grin came to her face. "Not yet. They will soon enough."

"Just be careful. And don't forget our deal."

"Deal?"

"About the Captain…who is coming our way right now."

Esther barely had time to prepare herself when Captain Bernhardt emerged to her left from the sea of guests, taking a bow.

"Good evening, Mr. Turner! Miss Esther!"

"Captain!" Thomas exclaimed jovially. "It's an honor. Can I get you a glass of wine? Whiskey, perhaps?"

"A wine would suit me well, thank you." Thomas nodded and, with a squeeze of Esther's hand, sifted away from them toward one of the numerous servers filtering through the great room.

"Good evening, Captain," Esther greeted him. "I hope you're doing well!"

"I am just happy to see you out and about," he stated, his enthusiasm stinging her conscience. "I've been by to see you every day. Thomas has kept me company, but it doesn't compare to spending that time with you. All of us have been so worried."

The room was growing louder and louder, and Esther could hardly hear what he was saying. "Captain, can we go somewhere a little quieter to speak? There are some things I think we should discuss."

He agreed, and Esther turned around, heading toward the back hallway that lead to the dining room, hoping it would give them a bit of seclusion so their talk might be easier. She softly pushed one of the swinging doors open and peeked her head inside, relieved to find it completely deserted.

"In here," she insisted, and the Captain slipped in behind her, closing the door. Esther rotated back to face him, mustering up the courage to break his heart. "Captain, there's something I need to tell you. Something I haven't been honest about."

"Please," he said, holding up his hand to silence her and drawing a little too close. "Let me go first. I have something I need to say as well."

Esther had been dreading this. "Captain, I really think I should..."

He ignored her objections. "Esther, I've been in love with you since the day I saw you. I know you care for me, too. We haven't known each other an exceptional amount of time but...I figured, why the hell not?" Slowly, the Captain lowered down to one knee and opened his right hand. In his palm rested a ring, flickering bright in the candlelight, and Esther reclined back, terrified at his proposal.

"Captain...I don't...I don't know what to say...this was not what I was–"

"Say yes, Esther. You know my family. We will never be without anything we need or want. We can have our own place in the city, and one up in Vermont for the summers when it's too hot. The wedding can be wherever you like...I don't care, as long as I'm marrying you. Just think of it! We could have a family...children and a life that's all our own. Say yes, and make me the happiest man in the world."

A clamoring at the end of the hallway spooked them both, and a loud voice began to come closer. It was Celeste summoning Esther. Captain Bernhardt scrambled to his feet and placed the ring in Esther's hand as her friend's footsteps could be felt through the floor.

"I don't need an answer right away," he mumbled, trying not to be overheard. "Just think on it, Esther." The Captain caressed her cheek lightly with his hand, and then exited hastily through the door from which they came, leaving Esther standing alone to be found by Celeste, dumbfounded.

"Jesus, there you are!" cried Celeste, spotting her as she spun around the corner. "Where have you been? Thomas and I have been looking everywhere for you." Esther didn't know how to respond, and rather than use her words, she outstretched her hand and opened it, showing Celeste the ring.

She gasped. "Oh my God...that's...that's not from Thomas, is it..."

Esther shook her head. "He ran off before I could say no. He just told me to think about it and ran off. What am I supposed to do with this?!" She held up her fist, clenching it tightly. "I promised Thomas…I promised him I would end it. Now I'm going home with a fucking engagement ring?!"

"Shh! Put this away immediately!" Celeste instructed. "Don't tell a soul. Don't tell Thomas, not the Madame, not anyone. You give it back to him in a letter and explain to him your heart lies elsewhere. It will save him and you the public embarrassment."

"But Celeste, I promised Thomas it would be tonight! I don't know what to do!"

"So end it tonight! Write the letter the second you arrive back at the Turners'. The Captain won't be doting on you the entire evening, I can assure you of that. He has too many superiors here he needs to be winning over. Stay with Thomas and the Turners. And put this damned thing away before it blinds one of us! I think it might be bigger than mine."

Esther shoved the ring down into the corset of her dress – there really was nowhere else to put it. "Celeste I just…I just don't want to lie any more. Not to Thomas. This doesn't feel right."

Celeste grasped her shoulders and looked directly into her eyes. "Listen to me. This is how you take care of things in the proper way. Now, quit pouting. You look absolutely beautiful and the man you love is out there waiting for you with a glass of wine." Esther bit her lip and nodded, Celeste freeing her and taking her hand. "On the bright side, my bastard husband went home sick about twenty minutes ago, so I have the night free to stay by your side and try to keep the Captain away!" With a wink, she pushed the door open and they were swallowed by noise once more, but not before a smug smirk came to Esther's lips at the thought of scaring off Timothy Adams. She was already winning the night.

Celeste and Esther found the Turners without much delay, and they were joined by the Bernard's and a detective named Samuel Ellis, who Esther couldn't recall meeting though she swore she'd seen him before. On their approach Thomas beamed at her and handed her a glass of wine.

"And?" he asked her.

"I took care of it."

If it was possible, he grew even happier. "Good. No wonder he left in such a rush."

Esther's own spirits perked up. "He left in a rush?"

"Yeah. Said it was some sort of emergency...came by to give his best and was out the door. At least we won't have to worry about that awkward tension." He pulled her arm through his again and resumed his conversation with Detective Ellis about the general state of things in the southern parts of the city. Esther sighed deeply, taking a sip of her wine. With the Captain gone, the rest of her night would run smoothly.

An hour or so later and mid conversation with Muriel Abbott, the plan was set to commence. Esther strategically positioned herself to keep an eye on the Hiltmores and their whereabouts throughout the party, and from the corner of her eye, she spotted husband and wife climbing the main staircase with Mr. Adams in their wake. Her heart skipped a beat.

"Oh my goodness!" Esther giggled, clutching her waist and tilting toward Muriel so that only she could hear. "Muriel, you'll have to excuse me. I have to go and find one of the maids. I just felt one of my corset strings snap."

Muriel's hand came to her mouth to cover a laugh. "You are not serious!"

Esther pretended to be struggling with her gown. "I wish. Serves me right for trying to wear one of Celeste's! I'll be right back. Cover for me?"

"Consider it done," Muriel swore, and Esther took off toward the serving doors, hoping she had a clear path toward the maid's passage.

When she knew she was out of sight of the festivities, Esther slipped down the hall and took a left toward the small door, the staircase behind it leading up to Douglas Hiltmore's study. Glancing right and then left, Esther lingered until the hall was clear of people rushing about with food and drinks, too busy to take note of her, and soundlessly she cracked the door to the maid's stair and snuck inside. It was pitch black, and the size of her dress made climbing the steps a colossal challenge. There wasn't much time. She stepped cautiously, not wanting to make any noise or worse, trip over her own feet, and cursed for being so blinded by the darkness. Eventually she reached the top, and Esther could see a sliver of light from beneath the door, as well as the murmuring of voices. Slowly lowering down to the floor, she opened the hatch just a hair, and their muffled words became clear as day.

The first was Catherine: "...a miracle nothing else has happened yet. That little bitch is here parading around with my daughter, rubbing it in our faces!"

"Would you keep your God damned voice down?" Douglas Hiltmore commanded. "We don't need anyone else knowing about this, and this is your doing Catherine. You were the one who insisted they be killed. All I suggested was getting rid of the paper trail and look where we are now!"

"Timothy did too," she retorted, defending herself. "And Charles!"

"I only went in on this to keep the girl quiet. I did not ever specify to kill her," Charles maintained harshly. "You took those lengths on your own, and your stupidity is going to cost us dearly."

"It can be reversed," Catherine hissed. "The Madame is not going to the police like Esther did. She may have Detective Ellis, but she has no other friends amongst the officers, I can tell you that much. Otherwise they wouldn't have tipped us about the report, would they?"

"What do you propose, then?" Douglas asked.

"Our friends from the south are here to confirm anything incriminating us is burned and long gone. I will go to the police on my own terms, tell them she's been threatening our family…blackmailing us…the works. We pay them enough so they don't say no. The Madame will hang and burn in hell where she should be."

Charles wasn't convinced. "What about the girl?"

"She's your fucking problem, Charles. You think of something."

The room went quiet for a few seconds. "Take care of the Madame first. Then we destroy the girl."

"Destroy her?" Douglas questioned. "What do you mean?"

"Be creative. Stealing from my son, having men over to spend the night, anything that will ruin her. No one will want to be connected with her then, not even the Turners."

Esther couldn't be sure, however Douglas' tone sounded a little angered. "I don't think I could ever convince Celeste to betray her best friend, Charles. No matter what story I fed her."

"But you'd have her killed?" Charles snapped.

"If I had any idea Catherine was going to kill her I would have stopped it," Douglas snarled. "There has to be another way. Esther doesn't deserve that kind of humiliation."

"Douglas, let Charles and I take charge on this. You focus on making sure our slate is wiped clean."

"I agree with Catherine," Charles added menacingly. "And I would bet my son can be convincing enough. Enough to at least subdue her into passivity until it's taken care of and too late for her to do anything about it."

A swift hand wrapped tight around Esther's mouth, and strong arms drug her away from the door and against the sidewall. Just like when Louis had grabbed her earlier, Esther was lifted from her feet; yet the force of the grasp was beyond that of the Frenchman, and there was no room whatsoever for Esther to fight against him. Her body was immobile and locked, leaving her at the mercy of whoever found her in the passageway.

"Don't fight," Edward muttered into her ear. Esther was so shocked she could hardly believe this was real – somehow, Lord

Turner managed to inaudibly sneak up the staircase, which should have been impossible for any man taking into account how small the space was. Holding her, Edward descended the staircase backward, one step at a time without saying anything further and continuing to keep Esther off her feet, who didn't know what else to do other than comply. Instead of exiting the passage at the bottom of the stairs, Edward gently set Esther down and rotated her around so they could speak to one another.

"You heard what you needed to hear?" he posed. His expression, while she could barely make it out, was serious. She nodded.

"Esther, how long have you been doing this for the Madame, if you don't mind my asking?"

She swallowed. "Since Thomas left, Lord Turner."

"Since Thomas left..." he repeated, his hand running through his hair, seemingly vexed. "All right. We will head home, then, I think."

"Wait," Esther stopped him. "What...what was that? How did you...how did you know where I was? Or what I was doing? And how the hell did you sneak up on me?"

"In bed for six days, no illness to speak of after four doctors saw you...I've been in a war, Esther, and I've seen a lot of people die and the trauma that follows. I finally got my son to confess and went to the Madame to make a deal."

"You...you made a deal...with the Madame..."

"Yes. We will discuss the details later. Now is not the appropriate time. My son is very observant and will notice we have been gone for an extended period of time, and that will only make this more difficult."

"Of course, Lord Turner...I just...how did you do that? I didn't have any idea you were there and...well, not many people can do that to me. No one, actually."

She was pretty sure she saw a grin. "Practice, Esther. Lots of practice."

Edward sent her outside as he went to fetch the rest of the Turners, and Esther did as he requested, staying out of the main party room to avoid getting caught in another rudimentary dialogue. Her imagination sprung to life as she grappled with what just occurred in the maid's passage along with the ambiguity of Lord Turner's presence and apparent "deal" with the Madame. There was no way to justify it, no matter how hard she tried. As Esther reached the doorway to the outside, she realized Celeste would be furious with her for leaving without a goodbye, but she could make up for that later – Esther was so distracted by Lord Turner, acting as if nothing happened would be trickier than she had the patience for. With a quick check over her shoulder to be sure she wasn't spotted, Esther slid out of the Hiltmores' home, desperately craving a cigarette.

It wasn't until she was standing near the street Esther felt her shawl around her shoulders, and with a small, baffled guffaw, realized Edward somehow managed to sneak it there –Esther had been completely oblivious to it, and pulled the shawl tight around her arms. The labyrinth of people involved in her life ran deeper than she could have ever dreamed, so much so that she speculated how much the Madame was hiding from her to keep her shielded from perceived danger. There was Edward's awareness of the situation for starters, and that was, in all probability, the tip of the iceberg. Esther took out a cigarette from her dress pocket and lit it, taking a deep inhale as her body relaxed slightly.

"Excuse me, miss, I am sorry to bother you, but would you mind sparing me a bit of timber? I think I've used my last piece, damn me."

She spun around to see a man fancifully dressed, obviously trying to take his own break from the party. He looked as if he were a boxer, rounded in his shoulders and strong in stature. His hair and beard matched in a sand blonde hue, and his eyes were nearly as blue as Edward's. Despite being handsome in his features, Esther noted something in his disposition that left her guard on high, particularly after the last few days. Strangers were not exactly a welcome commodity in the current scheme of things.

"It would be my pleasure," she conveyed, digging up the last bit of charisma she had left over. Esther struck another match and held the flame up dutifully, and the man obliged with his cigar.

"Thank you kindly, and excuse my language. I'm afraid even the best training in manners never fully takes away my rough roots, no matter how much time has passed." He puffed out smoke like a chimney and smiled at her. "Might I get your name, miss? I'd be happy to learn who else is trying to escape from the nightmare of socializing with these lot, especially one so beautiful."

"Esther," she replied, studying the man as she politely dipped in salutation.

"Well, I greatly appreciate it, Miss Esther," he thanked her. "How are you so lucky to be leaving this soon? I wish I could be so fortunate."

Just as he asked, the Turners appeared at the top of the front stairs. "Ah Esther, there you are!" Lucy called out, making her way down. "Are you ready then, love?"

"That I am," she proclaimed as Lucy drew near. Esther's gaze went to the man next to her to bid him adieu, but his eyes were locked on the Turners as they descended their direction.

Lucy's consideration also went to Esther's new acquaintance. "How rude of me to interrupt your conversation," she went on, grabbing the cigarette from Esther's hand and having a drag herself. "My name is Lucy Turner, sir. I will be stealing this one away from you, if you don't mind. Another bottle of wine in a slightly... quieter environment is waiting for us."

"A pleasure, Lucy...Turner..." he bowed in reciprocation. "Your lovely friend was gracious enough to lend me a light for my cigar. You have my leave to take her back."

William and Edward went the opposite direction to hail a carriage and Thomas wandered over to hurry Esther and Lucy along behind them. Comically removing Lucy's grip on Esther, Thomas put his arm around her waist and gave her a quick squeeze.

"Time to go, girls. William is practically running to get the coach."

"You're such a spoiler, Thomas," Lucy scolded him, then seeing he was right, dropped the cigarette and put it out with her toe. "Christ, he is running. What an ass. Lovely to meet you, Mr....?"

"Richard Croker. The new Fire Commissioner for the city."

"Happy to have met you, Mr. Croker," Esther declared. "Have a pleasant rest of your evening."

Mr. Croker, however, did not appear to hear her. As Thomas hauled Esther away, Mr. Croker stared hard at Thomas, fixated in a strange sort of trance. His expression was stunned, like he had seen a ghost he didn't want to believe existed. Thomas took no notice of the man's interest, and by the time they were in the coach the Fire Commissioner's odd behavior at their departure was long forgotten.

Croker, on the other hand, would not forget.

XVI.

"*Are you ready?*"

"Yes, Madame."

"You know the importance of the assignment."

"It won't be difficult."

"Good. Because if you fuck it up, we're all dead."

"I am well aware, Madame."

She poured herself another glass of whiskey. "Watch your back, primarily once you get near the Points. It's going to be a rough fucking ride if you get caught down there alone."

"I'll only be in the area a few minutes to dump the body. Whyos won't have any clue I set foot across the boundaries, I can promise you that."

"And you have the documents ready to plant?"

"Right here." Louis opened his jacket and displayed the secured bundle of paperwork, which took them months to put together, wrapped neatly together in twine.

The Madame threw back her drink. "Well then, let's start the fucking battle."

It was the middle of August, and with the shorter days of fall fast approaching, the Madame decided it was time for their strike.

Throughout the previous weeks, Louis kept a watchful eye on Esther, and with the Turners officially moving her into their residence, the situation had placated drastically. This gave Louis and the Madame ample time to track down the Hiltmores' southern associates in attendance of their party, and when they did, it took no time at all to persuade the slimy bastards to hand over the evidence in their possession condemning Douglas Hiltmore, Catherine Hiltmore, and their franchise. Once the play was made, Douglas would be arrested and indicted on eight different counts of fraud and bribery, as well as treason for aiding the Confederacy and maintaining a slave plantation after it's official ban nationwide. In most cases, the upper class could evade their convictions through their money and powerful connections, yet in these circumstances, the Hiltmores would never survive: Louis and the Madame went above and beyond to stack the case against them high to the sky and their name, which they valued even more than the money, would be permanently tarnished.

The story was, in actuality, horrendous even for Louis to discover. Years ago, Douglas Hiltmore sold his soul to the devil for a shot at success. During and after the war, he made a name for himself in the northeast, claiming to be one of the sole manufacturers of non-slave labored cotton, something the abolitionist rich swooned over. Business was slow in the beginning, but in spite of that, in the course of the final eighteen months of the war when the hope for the South was lost, his capital took off radically. The secret to his business was that only one of his plantations was, in fact, slave-free, and this was the one used to show the investors and government inspectors. These representatives were neglectfully unaware that behind the veil of courteousness and hospitality bestowed on them, there were many other plantations under the Hiltmores' rule continuing slave labor. They had been blind, or rather, blindly trusted that there was no possibility of corruption amongst a name so highly regarded, and Catherine did a lot of nasty things in order to keep that information clandestine.

Aside from the evidence obtained through the Hiltmores' run-ners, Louis and the Madame also happened upon a star witness, a young man the Madame was now working extremely hard to hide for his own safety. Unbeknownst to Douglas, one of his illegitimate children, born half negro, managed to evade his perpetual death sentence and live on for twenty-two years. Understanding her son would be killed, his mother sent the boy to a different plantation in the arms of a young friend who had been sold, and therefore the mother's friend claimed the baby as her own. Eventually, the boy was freed, and with his adoptive mother, went to work on a legiti-mate, small farm in Virginia. Tracking him down was exception-ally problematic, and regardless of Louis' efforts, and it had taken the Madame making the trip to Virginia to see the mission through. With permission from his adoptive mother, the Madame and Lou-is told Jeremiah the story of the Hiltmores, his birth and origins, as well as the brutal death of his mother in later years. In the end, Jer-emiah vowed to do anything and everything to see the Hiltmores punished, and Louis swore to him it would be done.

Catherine's biggest mistake was the forgery. The Hiltmores' business associates and longtime investors found themselves tangled in a mess they didn't want to be a part of – not a single one would divulge what exactly their involvement entailed, and neither Louis nor the Madame forced the subject as long as they handed over ev-erything they had on Douglas and Catherine. Each of the narratives was the same: the partners had been threatened into submission for too long by Catherine, and they wanted out…to wipe their hands clean of it for the last time and not worry about the repercussions. Catherine ordered the men to destroy the evidence, when on the contrary, the men did the opposite and compiled it, hoping to use it as a bargaining chip with the Hiltmores for a hefty sum of cash and a quick exit. The emergence of the Madame changed their minds, and the moment she offered to pay them double what they original-ly expected, there was not much enthusiasm left for bargaining. The men took the Madame's money, gave over everything she asked for, and did not think twice. It was by far one of the easiest deals Louis and the Madame ever manufactured.

Louis got up from his chair to make his last round at The Palace before he left. "I'll be back when it's done," he told her, striding toward the doors of her office.

"Wait," she called, rising and walking to him. "Tell George on your way out I need him to go by my old apartment and pick up something the barber apparently has for me. Fucking Jewish bastard won't stop bothering me about it."

"It's not too far out of my way. I'll go by."

"I don't want you distracted. Send George."

"I don't want you and The Palace without muscle," Louis pushed back. "You can't send both of us out. I will take care of it."

Her eyes narrowed. "Watch it, Louis. I know this is just another fucking cakewalk for you, but let's not forget who is in charge. And it's not you."

"Yes, Madame," he agreed, and then turned to make his way out. He may have overstepped his bounds, but the Madame's safety was far more important to Louis than her ego.

Jumping in a carriage south, the direction of the barber shop, Louis observed the streets were more crowded than he typically liked to tolerate. On top of it being a Saturday, it was an unusually pleasant summer afternoon, a much needed break from the heat sweltering the city the last few weeks, and thus causing pedestrians and carriages to be rampant as citizens ventured out to enjoy the more tolerable weather. He was happy he'd hailed the coach. Being a man of his stature, it was these times when Louis stood out most in the masses, whereas he preferred the usual grain of working in the shadows of sunrise, sunset, and night. However, once he was a twenty blocks out of range from Central Park, he'd be in immigrant territory, where everyone was smart enough to not ask questions or stare for too long and invite unwanted provocation. When he did get that far, Louis paid the driver and set out, taking the remainder of the trip by foot.

The barber was with two customers, each having a shave when Louis arrived, and rather than stick around for a ranting about the Madame, Louis made it clear he was in a rush.

"What is it you have for her that required such urgency?"

Wiping his hands on his apron and setting aside his straight razor, the barber held up his hand for Louis to wait, going to his desk and taking an envelope out from one of the drawers.

"Came two weeks ago, delivered by a young girl I've never seen before." The barber handed the letter to Louis, heavily worn and directed to Thomas, without a return address or any hint as to where it originated. "For the boy who used to live upstairs. Not sure what's happened to him…figured the Madame might though."

"I'll take care of it," Louis assured him, handing over two dollars. "For your troubles. Have a good day."

Not wanting to be detained any longer, Louis spun on his heels and left, again grabbing the nearest coach he could find to take him uptown. He had half an hour to get to the higher end of Fifth and knew he needed to clear his head fully before he set to work. Lighting a cigarette as the coach thrust forward, Louis went over the play in his head, as he had almost a hundred times already. There had never been a time he disliked or minded his job for the Madame – after over two and a half decades of it, Louis found he was indifferent to taking a human life, particularly those poisonous to the world around him. It was something intrinsic in him, something that had been in his blood since he was very young, and while over the years his perfected skill set was put to use for a variety of good and bad reasons, he was content with the Madame and her ongoing agenda. The majority of those he eliminated were relatively horrible specimen, and those who weren't were on the verge of it – every single one of them died at his feet with the acknowledgement that somehow they'd earned that fate. Spite and darkness filled them, without any regard of the wrong they personally inflicted on those around them, and he certainly hoped they burned in the afterlife. His fate would be the same, yet that did not scare him off his path; Louis had a sense of purpose in what he did, ridding the earth of those it didn't want or need. Charles Adams was no different, and in a few hours, he too would meet the fiery gates of hell along with all the others.

The sun was creeping toward the skyline as Louis' coach delivered him to his destination, he hopped out, paying the driver and assuming his scouting position. Across the street from him sat Timothy Adams' residence, and Louis rested back against a tree, pretending to be reading the local paper and checking his pocket watch frequently. Father and son met almost every week on Saturday around five o'clock to go out for a brandy, talking over whatever business or family matters were prevalent at present. What Timothy did not realize was following each of these meetings, his father ventured to the "filthy" part of town for a quick fuck prior to heading home and seeing his obese wife and obnoxious daughter. Charles Adams' tastes had, if it was possible, grown worse. In the time Louis shadowed him, the bastard paid hefty sums of money to the Whyo-run whorehouses to cover his tracks, and they obliged him because the cash was far more valuable than the girls employed. Not wanting to be spotted, Charles stuck to the shady, smaller establishments on the south side of town and kept his reputation intact; he hadn't visited The Palace in over three years. Unlike the Madame, none of the Whyo johns gave a damn, either. With all the starving people in the Points, it didn't take long to find working girls who would do anything for a slice of bread and a roof over their heads.

A few minutes passed, and right on schedule, Charles and Timothy Adams strolled down the block, and neither seemed happy with the other. Outside the house they firmly shook hands and parted ways, son meandering indoors and father heading toward the edge of the road to signal a carriage, his expression harsh. When one stopped at last, Louis overheard Charles' order to the driver to head toward the Bowery. Louis paused long enough to see it rolling that direction, waited for a bit of traffic to pass to cover him, and then bolted across the street toward Park Avenue. Louis was already aware of the location Charles was heading and wanted to keep his distance to not arouse any sort of ill feeling or suspicion. Dodging traffic, glances fell on him as he ran, mainly due to the fact that he was disturbing what was normally a quiet neighborhood, but Louis had a very small opportunity he couldn't afford to miss. Hitting Park Avenue, to his left came the horse-bus perfectly on time, and Louis staged his jump onto the back, startling some of the passengers close by. He would ride the giant carriage until they got to the lower east side of Manhattan, and from there his journey would be on foot to Little Italy. The pursuit then continued on, consisting of abandoned back alleyways in order to avoid detection from the Whyos, who would recognize him on sight. Louis prayed to make it in and out of the Points before the gang caught him, otherwise he'd be belly deep in a blade at the very least.

The trek was long, yet once the trolley reached its final stop, Louis was on his feet again moving fast, keeping a close eye out for a tail stalking behind. There was nearly a half mile left for him to go, and he spent that dodging trash, human filth, and grime, remembering why all those years ago he sold out for a better piece of the pie. He hadn't even reached the outskirts of the Points, and it amazed him how the surrounding areas developed into a similarly abysmal slum, the armpit of New York with nothing to promise but misery and an early meeting of their maker. Charles Adams traveled all the way down from Fifth Avenue to this place because it was the only neighborhood wretched enough to sustain his fiendish habits, and reflecting on that small detail was one of the things that made Louis' job easier. No one would miss Charles, just like no one missed any of the others. And if they did, it's because they never knew his mark's true character.

Every one of them deserved it, in one way or another.

After narrowly avoiding a run in with two coppers inspecting a rotting corpse, Louis reached the rundown brothel, and within it Charles Adams surely lurked in anticipation of his prey. Silently, Louis revolved around and climbed the fire escape of the adjacent apartment structure up onto the roof, assuming the location he'd learned had the easiest access to the floor of the client's rooms not a week prior. In the eight times he'd followed Charles Adams, Louis took the opportunity to memorize every move…every twitch…every habit…every layout of his encounters and their outcomes. Like any intelligent gun, Louis went over each possible scenario repeatedly in his mind, able to give himself only a one in a thousand chance of failure, far lower than most, and that was thankfully because the Whyos drugged their whores so heavily not many of them appreciated what was going on in the first place. This establishment was only one of the dozens of brothels run by the Whyos, an extremely volatile gang that slowly managed to take over the Points and half the southern portion of Manhattan since the end of the war. They specialized in two things: prostitution and killing for hire, both available for the right price at any time, and any soul to cross them never stuck around for long.

A thunder of laughter ricocheted through the alleyway from the first floor, and Louis spotted Adams and two dirty looking Whyos in one of the downstairs windows with whiskey in hand, apparently amused by something he could not see. Then, out of the corner of the windowpane, a figure stepped into his vision that took Louis by surprise. It was Charles O'Reilly, one of Croker's house, a low intelligence goon who ran errands for Tammany and Croker. The friendliness and ease between the Whyos and O'Reilly made it clear this was not their first meeting, though Charles Adams remained stoic and markedly uncomfortable in their attendance. With a quick shake of hands, O'Reilly immediately disappeared into the background, as if he'd been some sort of mirage. A worry began to creep up Louis' spine – if Croker was conspiring with the Whyos, it would potentially be a serious problem for him and the Madame. He tried to put it aside. First thing was first, and the priority was getting rid of the bastard who wanted to kill Esther.

Ten minutes passed until Adams was beckoned upstairs by one of the girls, who was leaning hard against the banister as she trudged up the stairs, doped up no doubt with the premeditation of what her time with Charles Adams would bring. It was Louis' cue to move. From his hidden perch, Louis rescinded backward a few steps, squatting a few times to be certain his legs were ready, and took a big running start before leaping the five-foot gap across to the roof of the brothel. He landed hard and propelled forward into a somersault on the flat rooftop, spinning right back onto his feet. From there, he moved toward the edge of the roofline, dropped and dangled so he was hanging off the edge, and scaled down, the patchy and deteriorating brickwork making his descent from one floor window frame to the next easily. Two levels down, Louis would be on the same floor as Adams, and entered through a previously chosen window to a vacant room, one that was used for storage rather than whoring. Bracing his legs against the outside of the windowpane, Louis lifted the heavy window up and swiftly crouched inside, first his right foot to check the floorboards, and then he swung his torso through and subsequently his left leg. He leaned backward and, while still facing the room, slipped his palms upside down and under the window frame, cautiously squatting down to close it – he'd been caught once before with his back turned, and it nearly cost him his life. With the window shut, Louis held perfectly still, letting the vibrations tremor up through his feet, trying to get a sense of anything that might disturb his agenda. Suddenly his ears perked up…he could hear Adams two rooms down, prepping for his evening entertainment.

Instinctively, Louis reached for the pistol on the inside of his jacket, but halted just as his fingers grazed the handle and moved instead toward the stiletto dagger sheathed at his waist. Freeing it and securing the blade in his hand, Louis snuck to the door of the storage room and listened, waiting for his next signal. It came: a muffled cry from the girl, almost inaudible, and he tapped the door open as it let out a slight creak. Peeking ahead, there was nothing but closed doors and dust circulating the air. Louis pounced toward them, years of experiences allowing his feet to dance noiselessly on the hallway's wooden floor the direction of Adams' room. When he made it, Louis took a deep breath in, clearing his mind completely to the singular goal of this moment: he would go in, kill Adams, then get out as quickly as possible. With an exhale of that same breath after five long counts, Louis gently impelled the door open.

To his left was a chair holding Timothy's clothes and a small drink cart, two filled glasses of wine poised and ready on it's surface. Next was a cheap iron bed frame pushed against the wall lined with dirty beige sheets, the girl in it coiled up on her side with her face the opposing direction, naked save for a sheet covering from her hips to her knees. On Louis' right sat some sort of vanity – for show, he assumed – holding rouge, perfume, and opium, and the prostitute's dress draped over the stool. Adams had stripped himself down to bare skin with his back to Louis, and he stood there staring at the girl with an enormous erection, profanely declaring aloud everything he planned on doing to her despite her disinterested consciousness. Louis studied over the previous weeks and realized that Charles' sexual practice was done meticulously in the same fashion each time, and it was because of this that the hit would be so simple.

It was the part after that was tricky.

Guardedly trying to stay unnoticed, Louis bent sideways and picked up Adams' linen shirt from the chair to his left and held it around the handle of the dagger, wanting to keep the leaking of blood minimal and avoid the Whyos' suspicion of foul play. Louis eyed Adams, still enraptured in his trance-like chant, and in one fleeting motion Louis lunged forward and wrapped his hand seamlessly around Charles Adams' mouth, plunging the dagger into his lower stomach. He could have made it a quick death...he could have gone straight for the throat, heart or femoral like the professional he was, yet this hit was personal. Louis wanted this son of a bitch to suffer…to feel the pain…to know he was going to die, and nobody could save him.

Adams' body went stiff for a few seconds in absolute shock, and then the strength from his desire to live kicked in, and with his last few breaths managed to struggle in an attempt to break Louis' hold, biting at the hand over his mouth which was overpowering a scream. To Charles' dismay, Louis' grip was so fastidious and his hands so large he couldn't even open his jaw. The man's arms flailed at his sides, his strikes against Louis fading in their vigor with each passing blow. Not one would even leave a bruise. Holding the knife steady, Louis could feel the blood soaking through Charles' shirt, indicating his time was running thin. Finally, after almost a minute of resilience, Adams ceased to move, and Louis felt the life slip out of him at last as his body went limp.

Setting him down on the floor, Louis glanced at the girl on the bed. During the kill, she had turned to see what was going on, though her regard was not focused on Louis…it was somewhere in the distance, and while she'd watched the entirety of Charles Adams' murder, Louis could tell she was too drugged to be able to recall any of it later on. As planned, Louis left the money Adams owed the Whyos on the chair where his clothes had been to pay for the services rendered – as long as the Whyos got their money, they did not give a shit about much else. Hastily, Louis grabbed an extra sheet from the bed, the girl scarcely acknowledging his existence, and wrapped it around the gaping hole in Adams' gut, wiping a few drops of spilled blood from the floor. Next, he wrapped the body in the sheet along with the clothing Charles wore to the brothel, leaving the dagger in place to avoid a massive bleed out. Once he was finished, Louis picked up the body and retraced his steps exactly, wanting to leave the building as if he'd never been there in the first place.

They were only two floors off the ground. Tossing Adams down into a heap of trash below him, Louis climbed effortlessly down to the street, constantly surveying the alley for observers, of which there were none. The second his feet hit the ground, Louis threw Adams' body over his shoulder and took off in a full sprint, having four blocks to cover and very little time to do so. If anyone spotted him, there'd be hell to pay. He tactfully dodged in and out of doorways, back and forth between crates and stairwells, having a handful of close calls and narrowly avoiding every one. In time, Louis got to the drop point without incident and set to work with staging.

Adams would be positioned fifteen yards from the main roadway on a dead end street of grime-soaked cobblestone…a street no one in their right mind would venture down. Louis placed him behind a decaying old mule cart, the alleyway no more than seven feet wide, ominously dark and deserted while any lingering light faded away with the day. Hurrying, Louis yanked the dagger from Adams' stomach and began to dress the body, delicately planting the evidence against the Hiltmores in Charles' right jacket pocket. With his clothing neatly back on, Louis poked his head up, his eyes darting from left to right, evaluating his level of cover, and then with a heave, drug the body around to the front side of the wagon, arranging it in a way to draw enough notice so that the body would be found in hours, not days. The alley's shadows grew bigger, a warning the coppers would be out soon on their nightly patrols, and once he was satisfied with his work, Louis abandoned the scene without looking back, meandering out in search of a coach to take him by the Turners'.

With a high velocity of road congestion, it was an hour before Louis rolled up to the residence, and the duration of his ride was spent reflecting on the details of the hit. Happily, Louis was satisfied that every part had gone according to plan. If they succeeded, Douglas Hiltmore would be behind bars within days, and the Madame and Esther would be out of danger. Catherine Hiltmore would be cast out of society, penniless, and at the mercy of her daughter and unfortunate in-laws – more than likely, she would flee New York as soon as she could to try and escape the shame that would follow her.

The only one left to destroy was Timothy, and Louis had a feeling an answer to that question would present itself in due course. He was, after all, the one that mattered most. Louis couldn't allow Esther to take this on, regardless of what the Madame's decision might have been. He could only hope with her newfound love in Thomas, Esther's interest in pursuing it would die out.

As his thoughts drifted to Thomas, Louis' hand found its way into his jacket and grasped the letter he was to deliver, and he pulled it out to examining it. He wasn't sure why, but something about it felt familiar...something he couldn't quite put his finger on...

"Here sir!" came the voice of the driver just as the carriage came to a halt.

Louis opened the coach door and stepped down, paying the driver more than he should. Upon getting to the front door, Louis knocked and was greeted by Tony.

"I'm sorry to tell you, Louis, but regretfully, the ladies are already out for dinner this evening, and the three Turner gentlemen are in Virginia on business for the next few days."

"Ah, shit."

Tony stared at him. "Louis, what is it?"

Louis handed Tony the letter. "It's for Thomas. It was addressed to the barbershop and under his...well, his previous last name."

"Dougherty?" Tony asked, taking the letter and inspecting it in his fingertips.

"Odd, isn't it?"

Tony nodded. "I think I'll throw it in Edward's pile and let him sort it out."

"I'd say that's probably for the best," Louis granted, letting out a sigh. "You seem well, Tony. It's nice to see you."

"You too, Louis." He stopped. "It's been...too long."

They stood there in difficult quietness for a few seconds, neither wishing to leave, though neither wishing to stay much longer.

"They'd be proud of you," Louis said at last, a sad grin forming on his face abashedly. "And I'm proud of you."

Tony scoffed merrily in return. "They would be far more proud of you," he replied. "You always do more than you should." He paused. "Be careful, all right?"

"You know I am."

Again they lingered, and then with a hurried bow, Tony dismissed him and closed the front door.

"Pretty sure they wouldn't be proud after this afternoon," Louis chuckled pleasantly to himself, amused. Initially, he'd been let down by the Turners' absence, as he hadn't seen Edward or Thomas in weeks because of travel. However, his short visit with Tony raised his spirits, particularly because it was the first time in decades they had a real opportunity to speak.

"What we do for love…" Louis mumbled under his breath as he commenced trekking the direction of The Palace. "What we do for love…"

The Madame was eagerly awaiting news, and while she was thrilled for Louis' clean hit, her worries about the Whyos and Croker mirrored his own, along with their activities.

"What do you mean you saw O'Reilly?" she demanded, a bewildered expression on her face. "How is this the first time we've found out that Richard fucking Croker is involved in Whyo activity? And how the hell is Charles Adams…or, beg your pardon, how was that son of a bitch involved with the whole thing?"

"Was I wrong to push forward with the plan?" Louis pressed, pouring them each a glass of wine to calm her.

"Of course not!" she exclaimed, throwing her hands in the air. "I would have been fucking infuriated if you didn't! I just…ugh… Louis, this changes everything. We're fucked."

He handed her an overly full portion. "We don't know how deep it goes yet. Could be friendly dealings, we just need to find out."

"You know as well as I do, Louis, that if Croker is involved with any God damned Whyos he's running most of the Points. And right under Kelly's fucking nose." She took a gulp of wine. "The Whyos don't bow down to anyone...not the law...not the politicians...nobody. How in the fuck did he get an in with them?"

Louis sat in the armchair across from her desk. "I wish I knew. If they are working together, the Irish are running the underground with the help of Tammany. Meaning Croker has lived up to all he so modestly prophesized, and it's only a matter of time before we are involved as well."

The Madame sighed heavily. "He knows what he's doing. The bastard started in the damned ghettos, and now he'll slowly start creeping his way into the middle and upper classes with his fucking rhetoric and blue eyes. Smart...took care of the dirty work first..." Her voice trailed off a moment. "Fuck. We can't fight our way out of this one, can we?"

Louis' eyes locked on hers. "No, no we can't, Madame."

"Fuck!" she screamed, and in a rage, threw her glass across the room, shattering glass and spraying wine all over the wall and floor. The Madame's shoulders heaved up and down with her ragged breath, her face contorted up in fury as she cursed herself over and over again. "I am so tired of biding my fucking time. What more do I have to do? What?!"

Louis knew the question was not directed at him, and he stayed quiet, taking a sip of wine as the wheels in her head started turning. It was in times like these...the times when the Madame was backed into a corner...that she did her best work. Somehow, the anger seemed to perpetrate a deeper part of her intelligence, and her genius would find a way to shine through. The thought of those who slighted her fueled the fire in her eyes, and also attested as to why most of them were no longer around...or alive, for that matter.

Time went by, and eventually the Madame's hands dropped to her desk to support her weight, and she descended into her chair, downing the wine left in her glass.

"You're right. This is how it must be done. I'm going to have to learn to be a little more fucking patient."

"Madame, if this is as bad as we think…if Croker has gotten this much of a lead on us…you know we're going to need more than just me and George to keep us protected. We need to build the army… find our own people we trust, not just the ones we have in our back pocket. Croker is going to make enemies, and his enemies must become our friends. It's the only way we'll survive when we decide the time is right to cross him."

"Do you think…" she started, then shook her head, mad at herself.

"Do I think what, Madame?"

She fought with whatever it was on the tip of her tongue. "Do you think Edward would help us? If we told him what the situation was?"

Louis nearly dropped the wine from his hand, not remotely expecting this to come from the Madame. "I don't…I don't know… there would be a lot to discuss…Madame, you know if he was told the truth about who Croker was, he wouldn't hesitate."

"He's already come to us voluntarily and gotten involved with the Hiltmores and Adamses."

"Yes, but that was to protect Esther and help us bring these bastards down," Louis countered. "What you would be asking would require so much more than what he's already giving. Years of spying. Years of killing. A permanent residence in New York. A double life. And going back to doing things he stopped years ago to keep Thomas safe. I am not sure I could ever ask that of him when he's been through so much."

She nodded, though Louis could see she discounted every point he'd just made. "All right. Let's give this a few days. They should be finding Adams any second now, and a fucking hurricane will be in store for us. Let's just get through it in one piece. In the meantime, go grab another bottle from the cellar. We're going to fucking need it."

At promptly one in the morning, Esther showed up at The Palace, furiously rushing to see the Madame and Louis and wearing nothing more than her nightgown and one of Thomas' long jackets to cover her. The Palace's own night was winding down, and Louis alertly guarded his front door post, knowing who it was the moment the coach came to a stop in front of the iron fence. From the anxious yet triumphant appearance she wore, it was obvious the news of Charles Adams had been shared with her, and it made Louis smile.

"Is it true?" she called, nearly running from the gate. "I can't delay...I received word from Celeste not twenty minutes ago. Is it true?"

"It is. We've had a victory."

Her face lit up. "All right, I won't have much time to spare in between. I have to be at Celeste's as soon as possible."

"I believe she is waiting for you upstairs," he told her, motioning inside.

Rather than pass by him, Esther paused at Louis' side, and her eyes went to the ground, arms nervously crossing over her chest. "I'm ashamed that I'm...delighted by this. I feel like I might as well have been the one to kill him. Is that normal, Louis?"

"You have nothing to be ashamed of. I killed him, Esther, not you, and don't forget if not for that, you would probably not live to see Christmas." Seeing his words were not as soothing as he intended, Louis retracted. "You had no part in this. You only knew what was going to happen and chose yourself over that evil bastard. Not even Christ would have done otherwise."

She eased. "Right. You're right."

"George! Get the front door!" he bellowed, putting his arm around her and escorting her to the Madame. When they walked

473

in together, Louis followed protocol, shutting and locking the doors after them, not wanting to be disturbed or taken off guard on such an eerie night.

"Celeste sent me a note," Esther explained to the Madame as she found a chair, and Louis chose to keep his distance and monitor them from the doorway. Esther held it up in her hands. "Tears all over it, staining the ink. It's happened, hasn't it? We've killed Charles, and the Hiltmores are going to burn?"

The Madame didn't give any emotional response. "Fucking bastard is dead. The evidence was planted, and it will only be a matter of time before the coppers are at the Hiltmore residence arresting Douglas. She won't know about that yet, darling, so be sure not to burst the bubble and make yourself a suspect."

"What do you need me to do?" Esther pushed on readily.

"Feign ignorance. You don't know anything. Have tears ready and be her friend. If any irrational accusations come your way, you cower but don't break. Make them believe you are as distraught as Celeste is."

"That I can do," she stated. "But Madame...I can't help but think...Timothy is going to know I was involved. His family wanted me dead, for fuck's sake! How can I protect myself from him?"

"It wasn't his family, Esther, it was only him and his father, and the latter is lying dead as a God damned doornail in the police station. If that little shit comes after you, he knows he will be next. He's at your mercy, darling. You have the power and you should fucking act like it."

Esther's gaze went to the floor. "I'm...I'm just afraid..."

Straightaway, Louis paced to the drink cart, poured her a whiskey and took it to her – the Madame often forgot what this was like... being in fear for her life was something she dealt with every day. Esther, on the other hand, was not quite as accustomed, and that often required a little liquid courage.

"Make sure you leave by daybreak," he said, kneeling beside

her. "That is when the coppers will head to the Hiltmores, and from that point on all hell will break loose. I'll be close by if anything should happen."

"And," the Madame declared, trolling around her desk and holding out a pocket pistol. "You're taking this with you. And for God's sake, stay the fuck away from Timothy. Who knows what's going through his lunatic mind right now, and I don't want anything to happen to you. With this, you can keep him at bay until Louis arrives. Or kill him, he fucking deserves it. I may not have the patrolmen but I do have Ellis in my pocket, and self-defense is not murder, especially in this case."

Esther downed her whiskey, taking the gun from the Madame's outstretched hand and slipping it shakily into Thomas' jacket pocket.

"Esther."

"Yes, Madame?"

"You can do this."

Her big green eyes were worried, though she believed the Madame's assurance "I can, can't I?"

"It's no different than what you've been doing the last eight years," Louis promised her. "It's only a few hours. Then you'll be home free."

The Madame spotted the clock. "Time to go, darling. I'll be by in the morning for tea with you and Lucy. Louis will see you to the Adams residence."

Esther was silent the first few minutes of their ride. Louis had given her a cigarette and lit it for her, hoping to calm her nerves as much as possible. With each exhale of smoke, Louis saw her relax – Esther was not afraid of Timothy. Her greater fear was failing them, spoiling what was years of careful planning, ungodly amounts of money, and backhanded dealings. Vengeance was nearly had... their war against the Hiltmores almost won...and Esther was the final round. The pressure was surmounting on her shoulders, and

Louis was amazed as this awareness hit him how well Esther was coping with the responsibility.

"What about Timothy?"

"Just as the Madame said. Keep your distance and–"

"No Louis, that's not what I meant. I meant, when is it his turn to be eliminated?"

"Soon. As soon as we get this one wrapped up, he will be gone."

Esther took another drag. "I want to kill him, Louis. I put on this front...for Thomas, for Celeste, for everyone...all I can think about is killing him...hurting him as badly as he hurt me. I..." She shook her head, gathering her thoughts. "I feel like a monster. Like this can't be normal."

Louis shifted in his seat to move closer to her. "I think normal is not a word I would use to describe you anyhow, Esther. It's a perfectly human sensation to want to hurt someone who has hurt you. Timothy Adams assaulted you, took advantage of you in the worst possible way, and tried to kill you for it. I would be astonished if you didn't want to see him dead."

"That's not it, Louis."

"What is it, then?"

Esther's gaze went out the window to the passing street lamps. "Tell her I want to be the one to do it."

"Absolutely not!" Louis nearly shouted. "I won't allow it."

"It's not up to you. You tell her I want to do it."

"Esther please," he pleaded. "You don't want a man's blood on your hands. It's a burden you aren't prepared to carry. One you shouldn't carry! What would Thomas say if he heard this from you? He would never permit it, you and I both know that."

"This is my decision. That man...he attacked me, and I have to pretend every day like...like..." her voice trailed off, breaking with emotion. "If Thomas loves me, he will see past this, and you know damn well he's expecting the Madame to take care of it anyway." She finished her cigarette and tossed it outside as the coach came to an abrupt halt. "No one would ever have to know it was me. We can cover it up, and maybe then all these fucking nightmares will go away." Esther looked into his eyes intently. "Please, just take me into consideration for this."

They sat for a few seconds, Louis speechless, understanding nothing he could say would make amends. Then, as the driver came around, Esther got out of the car and went directly to the Adamses' front door. Louis watched her go, his heart breaking. As an aid, Esther had done exquisitely; however, as a primary, her emotions ran too thick. If she did take Timothy Adams' life, it would haunt her for the rest of her days. For the sake of the unborn child in her womb, Celeste would never forgive her friend, and Thomas' devotion would indisputably be tested...and possibly fail. Louis couldn't let her. He would find a way to do it sooner rather than later, even if it meant doing so without the Madame's permission and putting his own neck in the noose. Esther was like a daughter to him, and he cared too much for her to stand idly by when he could put an end to it on his own.

He stopped the driver two blocks later and got out, apologizing for the sudden change in plans. Strolling over to Central Park, Louis began to track back the direction of the Adams residence on the shrouded, deserted outer pathway. Throughout his later life, Louis had an inclination his end would come in a time like this – he wanted to die at war, to go out with dignity, fighting for a final cause he truly believed in. Killing Timothy Adams in the place of Esther might be just that, and if so, Louis' heart would be satisfied in protecting Esther from the overwhelming regret that would come. Yet somewhere deep in his gut, his instincts told him his undoing was still on the horizon. If there was one last battle Louis desired to win, it was to take down Richard Croker and die in the process...for the Madame...for Mary...and for Thomas and Edward. Revenge would be had, with the undeniable prospect of everyone he loved being massacred in the process. After years of living a lie to safeguard the ones he loved, Louis swore he wouldn't let it go to waste.

A bench ahead sat empty in the moonlight, and Louis took a rest off of his feet, leaning backwards to stare up at a sky full of stars, his memories tracking to another night so incredibly similar to this one. She'd found him by The Palace, beaming from ear to ear, her hazel-grey eyes sparkling as she implored with Louis to go with her for just an hour or two. At the time, Louis had started working for the Madame only weeks before, and didn't want to push his luck of abandoning duty without permission, but Mary was relentless. In spite of trying to uncover what was so urgent, Mary wouldn't say, and he'd gone with her hoping the Madame's wrath wouldn't be too unbearable. She dragged Louis through the streets, thanking him over and over again, making him vow never to tell a soul. They went southeast in a coach, and when they got to the tiny chapel, Louis understood why she so desperately needed him, and he laughed aloud.

The church was small, one that did not boast any large donations or important devotees, though it suited Mary in all of her euphoric splendor. When they entered the wooden doors at the entryway, Louis' breath caught in his lungs as he took in what lay before him. The gorgeously stained windows on opposing walls of the chapel made the room look like a dream, each biblical scene appearing as if it came alive. There were candles lit at the end of each row of pews all the way to the altar, where a grinning priest and an eager Edward waited. It was the most magical scene Louis had ever beheld, and he was the sole witness to their matrimony. Taking Louis' hand, Mary led him to the first row, where he sat the remainder of the ceremony, more honored than he'd ever felt in his life that they wanted him to be a part of it.

Mary could have been an angel, dressed in a long white dress and navy blue sash around her waist, her long, strawberry hair curled and cascading down her back. On her finger was a sapphire so beautiful it sparkled almost as extravagantly as her eyes. Edward wore his suit from the Royal Navy, elated to a degree Louis hadn't seen in the numerous years they'd known one another. As the priest commenced with their nuptials, Edward nodded to Louis and mouthed a thank you, taking Mary's hands in his.

Louis had never told the Madame. He'd never told anyone. And he never would.

All of a sudden, a twig snapped thirty feet behind the bench, and Louis spun around on his feet, pistol pulled and cocked, aiming at a dark, looming figure who leisurely raised his two hands in surrender.

"I'm only here to talk, Frog. So let's put that pistol down, shall we?"

His breath caught in his throat. Louis swore it couldn't be true – he hadn't heard that voice in over two decades.

"Come out of the shadows," he demanded. "Then I will make that decision."

"Fair enough. You're the one gettin' all riled up for nothin'." Slowly, the man stepped out into the light, a sheepish yet familiar smirk on his face. "Remember me now? Been a long time, eh brother?"

His blood went cold. Startled, Louis blinked hard a few times, then unhurriedly put the gun in it's holster. The man standing only a few feet away had to be a mirage or some sort of dream…and yet here stood Will Sweeny, alive and breathing, with the same grin and thick southern accent that made him seem deceptively more dawdling than he was in reality.

"So this means you aren't dead?"

Will shrugged. "Was dead. Had to be for a while, else I'd have been worse than hanged by the damn neck." Will then strutted to the bench and sat, tilting his head as he eyed Louis, waiting on a response.

"What do you want, Will?" Louis posed, unmoving, his hand persisting to rest on the grip of his gun. Will wasn't exactly a big man, but he wasn't small either. He was lean, strong, and could shift quicker than any thief Louis had met or heard of. His general appearance was rugged, while with his southern mannerisms and charm he had the uncanny ability to win over anyone he set his sights on. He had dark hair to his jaw line, scruff on his face to match, and light brown eyes that stood out amongst his high cheek bones. Apart from his good looks, Louis did notice Will had gained a few new scars on his pretty face since the last time they met, and he speculated as to what sort of trouble his old friend got into. "The Cat," as they'd all called him, earned his nickname for good reason: he had a nasty way of making his targets comfortable just before he'd strike: fast…sly…and deadly.

Will let out a chuckle. "What were ya doin' in the Points today? You know ya have a strict 'passin' through only' policy."

"I was gone in an hour," Louis remarked bluntly, angry at himself for not sensing someone biting at his heels, especially one he knew so well.

"Oh for God's sake, Louis, don' fuckin' lie to me about what you was doin'. You got a nice set up workin' how you do now, you got no reason goin' back there."

"Why exactly is it that you care about my time in the Points, Will? When did you start being my keeper again after being dead? Who is it you are running with?"

"I think we both know I don' run with nobody unless it'll pay off in my favor," he replied, straightening up. "Who was that rich bastard you did in? Fuckin' load he was. Can' say I was sorry to see him go."

"I asked you who, Will. I want an answer."

Their eyes met, causing Louis to flash back, thousands of memories stirring an array of emotions inside him as Will spoke. "I am runnin' some back end deals with them Irish pricks now. Not just a gang…real deal. Some asshole came and found me a few weeks after I got back from Texas…said his employer was interested."

"What man was this?"

"Some tough, young guy. Slicked back hair and glasses, with some nasty scars all up and down his arms…gave me the willies. They…well…they want me keepin' tabs on you, brother. Everythin' you're up to. Which blows my mind considerin' I've been home almost half a year and they never cared a lick about your ass until last month. You and your boss."

"What about my boss?"

"Not sure. They just wanna know what you're up to, and I didn' ask no further. Not my place, and not really a part of the job description to be askin' things like that. Sit down, would ya? You're makin' me nervous. I ain't here to kill you yet."

Louis let go of his pistol, taking the empty spot by his old friend. "Is the man you work for named Richard Croker?"

Will rotated his head away from Louis and spit tobacco on the ground. "I ain't supposed to say. And honestly, I ain't sure who is workin' for who half the time. They're all runnin' the Points with them Whyo bastards, who don' know how to get shit done other than pile up God damned bodies. Like the fuckin' war all over again down there. Glad I can stay the hell away and take care of the nonsense up here."

"They are just curious, then?"

"Far as I can tell."

Louis sighed. "I know you're here as a courtesy, Will. But I need to know if there's anyone I need to be worried about. I'd do the same for you."

Will genuinely smiled and looked at him. "Fuckin' stupid, we are…" He shook his head. "Yeah, I know ya would, brother. I know ya would." Pausing a second, he spit again. "One that came to find me? With them glasses? Scares the shit outta all the others, 'specially those Whyos. Only saw the fucker once since I been here. He's got a whole different set of orders, ya know what I'm sayin'?"

Louis recognized at once it must have been the mysterious Walsh who broke into The Palace years ago – he'd hoped the man would be long dead, though clearly Croker kept him around for what Louis could only assume were the more serious occasions.

"I haven't had the pleasure of his company, but the Madame certainly has."

"You're shittin' me. When?"

"Years ago," Louis informed him, resting against the back of the bench. "When I first became acquainted with Richard Croker and his people, I was worried, and following a lot of hard work we smoothed out the hiccup in our relationship. I believed we were on amicable terms, and I guess I was mistaken. Did it have to do with the man I killed today?"

"The sick one? Nah. Ain't nothin' like that. Like I said, I don' ask any questions I know I shouldn'…from what I can tell, they wanna make sure you ain't doin' nothin' they don' want. Catch my drift?"

"Yeah. Well…shit…" Louis scrambled to put a finger on anything definitive to explain why Croker was once again on their tail, but his attempts were in vain. Nothing added up…something was missing he couldn't quite see.

"Ya all right there, brother? You got pale. Guy I remember never used to get pale at nothin'."

"Yeah well, I'm not the guy you remember, Will."

"And jus' what's that supposed to mean?"

"I mean there is a lot at stake, things I don't want to lose."

Will peered at him quizzically. "Why would you care anyhow? You're just a hired hand for the head whore…can' be too difficult to abandon ship if the time comes."

Louis pulled out a cigarette, needing something to take the edge off. "It's not that simple, Will."

"How?"

"I've spent over twenty-seven years working for her. Walking away is not as easy as it sounds."

Will couldn't relate because he'd never held a job for more than a year. "Yeah well, she ain't the only one you was workin' for in the beginnin'. She know about that?"

"No, Will, she doesn't."

They sat in silence for a few minutes, Louis smoking his cigarette and Will chewing his tobacco, until finally Louis mustered up the courage to articulate the one thing that mattered most to him.

"Would you kill me if he asked you to?"

Will spit and defensively seemed to retract. "Don' ask me things like that," he uttered under his breath.

"Would you?" Louis pressed, not relenting.

His friend was pained. "Not sure I can make that call just yet."

It was the answer Louis expected. "Well, since I know where you stand, you should know if the ship goes down, I'm going with it. There's no out for me. She's all I got."

"The fuck she is!" Will shot back. "You could leave any day and get along just fine. Work for you would be easy to come by."

"I am not saying that. If I leave her, I will betray everything good that's left of me...everything I stand for...everyone I care about."

Will scoffed. "The point of what we do, brother, is that we don' stand for nothin'. We don' have no souls and the people we keep close die in our arms. That's the code we've always lived by."

"Many things changed after you decided to die, Will. You won't hear it, but I'm not the man I was when you left."

"Ah, to hell with that," Will snarled, standing up and thus indicating their reunion was coming to a close. "You watch your ass, got me? These bastards ain't fuckin' around no more. I'll be around. You know how to find me."

Without another word, he strode off into the darkness, his long jacket whipping out at his ankles. Louis stayed put, motionless for some time, lost in his thoughts. Oddly, he found he didn't care about Croker, or that he and the Madame might now have returned to his long list of enemies – that was inevitable. He was distracted... distracted to the point that his mind could only focus on Will. From their youths they were a duo, yet currently found themselves on opposing sides of the battle. One of them would have to kill the other if it stayed this way...they both knew that...or the other option was to run. Will might be a runner; however, Louis was not. He would rather die on his feet than in a hospital bed or spending the rest of his life looking over his shoulder.

There was something different in Will, something Louis detected from his appearance and his demeanor. He'd visibly been through anguish, sporting deep, new scars on his face and hands, not to mention the prominent wrinkles gaining traction around his eyes. On top of that, he'd acquired an ever so slight limp in his right leg that the average eye wouldn't catch, the damage ostensibly irreparable despite Will finding a way to recuperate most of his muscular strength. Louis always admired Will's unremitting toughness – it gave him an edge, one that allowed him to persevere when the odds were stacked against him, and it was more than likely the only reason he was still alive today.

But why had Will come back to New York? Was he running once again, or was it something else? Something he wanted to hide from Louis? Either way, Louis had gained a permanent shadow…one he had a feeling might do more harm than good to them both in the end.

He rose, making his way down the route toward the Adamses' household to keep an eye on Esther. As he reached the end of the park, he was aware that he was not alone: Will was resting against a lamppost stalking him forty yards away. Subtlety was never his strong suit. Wanting to prove he would not be maneuvered like a chess piece, Louis turned so that Will could see him clearly and took a deep bow, something they used to do as young men when they were celebrating a victory. Will watched, then mirrored Louis' movement, and Louis couldn't repress a grin as he marched to safeguard Esther. He was thankful he'd rolled almost a dozen new cigarettes that day – the rest of the upcoming early morning hours would be spent pacing the park and burning through every one in a vain attempt to find a solution to his impending problems.

The Madame had no knowledge of Will…there had never been much to tell. By the time they established a firm level of trust, his oldest friend was supposedly long dead. With the sun rising on the horizon, Louis couldn't make up his mind whether or not it would be a mistake to come clean, or if the bigger mistake was trying to keep one more secret to himself.

That would make three mysteries he'd hidden from her, all in retrospect of the three people he loved most in this world. And he wasn't sure he could handle more than the two already on his plate.

XVII.

After spending nearly a week in Richmond, negotiations were at last coming to a close, and with a great deal of help from Francis Bernard, the Turners secured the sole right to supply and distribute mechanically rolled cigarettes in every major eastern American city as well as London, Liverpool, and Queenstown. That level of circulation required Edward, William, and Thomas to completely rehash their current system of allocation, and while it would cost them a fortune, it was a small price to pay for what was coming. A man by the name of Duke bought out James Bonsack to the rights of his invention, aiding him in fixing a few of the mechanical mishaps Bonsack couldn't seem to iron out despite months of experimentation. In the end, "Buck," as Duke preferred to be called, resolved the final glitch and moved forward quickly, knowing that this instrument alone would change the face of American tobacco. From the moment Edward met Buck, any lingering doubt about the project's legitimacy vanished: having come from family money and an expansive history of tobacco farming, Buck understood the industry better than anyone, making Edward certain that their investment and partnership would provide decades upon decades of financial stability for his family.

James Bonsack enthusiastically showed the Turners his incredible machine during the second day of their visit in Virginia, and the three agreed it was beyond revolutionary. While on their tour Buck did most of the talking; however, when they were presented with the device that would make them all fabulously rich, Bonsack took over, describing every detail of how the tobacco was sorted and the cigarettes able to be rolled flawlessly. He was a soft-spoken man who kept mostly to himself in the Turners' company, yet there was no debating his intelligence. He saw mechanics and arithmetic in a way Edward couldn't dream of, and he found he admired that Bonsack put his heart and soul into something without any real intention of seeking notoriety or money.

"We are in the process of building more of these machines," Buck assured them that night over dinner. "And by the spring, their production will be one hundred times greater per unit than it would with one hundred and twenty-five people hand rolling cigarettes all day every day."

Prudence was easily overruled. Not one of the Turners could find a single thing to object to.

On their last day the contracts were signed, and Buck kindly invited the Turners to his estate in South Carolina for the hunting season ahead, which they accepted gratefully. Francis Bernard opted to stay in Richmond another week with his son and a few of the other investors, and thus the Turners returned to New York on their own, ready to celebrate their success upon their arrival; however, before the festivities could truly commence, Edward had something he needed to privately discuss with William, something he believed he and his cousin had both been internally contemplating.

The business side of Edward's life had never been one he enjoyed. It was only a necessity because for a time, he and William were the only two managing Turner S & D, William from New York and Edward from England. On top of that, New York was not a place Edward wanted to stay forever, and in his observations of Thomas,

Edward couldn't deny his son appeared infinitely happier here than at Amberleigh, though most of that he could attribute to Esther and their budding relationship. It wouldn't be long now before he asked her to marry him. Thomas broached the subject a handful of times with William and Edward, and already asked for a small company loan to purchase a ring. Together, Thomas and Esther made a great pair, and the Turners already accepted her as one of their own.

Wanting nothing more than for his son to be happy, Edward made a resolute decision: on his own accord, he involved himself in the Madame's planning a short time after the infamous night at the theater where he and Thomas beheld the abuse Celeste endured at the hands of her husband. Initially, Edward hoped that scaring the man would cause Timothy to rethink his behavior; and regrettably, Edward hadn't known then it was already too late. Esther's near death experience at The Palace and what unfolded in the aftermath made Edward resort to the one thing he did best. By aiding the Madame and Louis, principally in safeguarding Esther, Edward found the months he thought might be spent in misery became weeks of feeling more like himself than he had in years. Back came his training from Hiroaki, and he found those long hours meditating on purpose and honor began to flow through him once again like the current in a river.

Taking into account Thomas' future, Edward personally wanted to see to it that Esther survived the wrath of the Hiltmores and Adamses. When the tribulations passed, Edward would go home to England where he belonged and retire, leaving his seat to Thomas under the assumption that if he chose to remain in New York, he would be required to spend every other winter at Amberleigh. Edward would remain on the board as an investor, but would relinquish his partnership earnestly, and then he could go back to Hiroaki where they would resume their missions…as Edward realized it was the only thing either of them found sanity in. Thomas would be upset, Edward knew, yet it was both appropriate and logical for him to bow out. There was nothing here for him…nothing except the haunting memories of his past, the stiffening of his joints, and the boredom of day-to-day business meetings and deals. It wasn't who he was, and he didn't have to pretend any longer.

As the Turners boarded the train north, William and Thomas chatted eagerly of their next steps, allowing Edward to venture off in search of champagne from the dining car for an overdue celebratory toast. He effectively found the bar and, after a laugh with the bartender, acquired two bottles and three glasses, leaving the man a generous tip for his good humor. Flutes in one hand and the bottles tucked under his left arm, Edward ambled back through each of the passenger cars, trying hard not to smirk as a few fellow passengers fought hard to keep their balance moving about while he easily stayed firm on his feet.

Practice…lots of practice…

Two cars away from Thomas and William, Edward noticed a solemn, familiar face in one of the seats: it was Henrietta Adams, Timothy Adams' sister and Celeste's sister-in-law, and she was clad head to toe in black dress. At first she did not see Edward as he drew near, and Edward halted politely beside her row to inquire after her family in the hopes that perhaps the Madame had struck in the Turners' absence.

"Excuse me, Miss Adams, but do you by chance remember me? I am Lord Edward Turner, Thomas' father."

She smiled amicably. "How could I forget you, Lord Turner? It is a pleasure to see you again. I am…well, I wish we were meeting under better circumstances."

"I can see by your dress something terrible has happened. Is your family all right?"

"Unfortunately, no," Henrietta sniffed, pulling a handkerchief from her jacket pocket and dabbing her eyes, though Edward thought it was more for show than actual emotion. "I am on my way to New York to lay my father to rest. Mother is already there, caring for Celeste. Father was found robbed…stabbed in the street just a few days ago. Police have no leads…no one knows how or why, but all sorts of rumors are flying around…"

Edward did his best to appear appalled. "My God! I hadn't heard! My deepest condolences go out to you and your family, Miss Adams. I am so incredibly sorry for your loss. Please do not hesitate to ask if my family or I can do anything to ease your suffering."

"Thank you," she replied, her spirits offhandedly lifting, "I do know Esther has been at Celeste's side almost every day, and for that I know my family is grateful. Poor mother is in hysterics. And Celeste…it is such a shame what has happened to her father. Such a shame…I don't know if they'll ever recover."

Edward once again attempted to appear ignorant. "Whatever do you mean?"

Henrietta let out a slight gasp, taking her hand to her lips as if she'd just confessed something she shouldn't have. "You have not heard?"

"I can't say I have."

"Oh, Lord Turner, it is a horrible…horrible thing. From what the detectives found on…in my father's possession, my father was apparently in the midst of uncovering some sort of business indignity Douglas Hiltmore was involved in…fraud or something of the like…and the documents father had proved Douglas broke all sorts of laws." She leaned in closer, whispering so no one else could hear. "He's actually been put in jail! His sentencing is next week. When Timothy wrote me he said a minimum of eight to ten years! Celeste's mother…Catherine…you know her, I presume? She's gone into hiding. Humiliated. Won't even see her daughter. Celeste is distraught, poor thing. She has no one but us to care for her now. Except Esther, of course."

Edward acted awestruck by everything Henrietta told him. On the inside, however, he shamefully had to admit he was impressed. In one fleeting swoop, the Madame took out her greatest threat without any implication of foul play. Louis truly had not lost his touch.

The one person he felt truly sorry for was Celeste, cursed with a life of privilege in the worst possible sense, submersed in superficiality with no one caring what was in her heart…only in her pocketbook or the value in her connections. She still had so much more heartbreak to come, and Edward wondered what would happen the moment her reputation dwindled: he suspected her "friends" would abandon her, save for Esther, and he could guess many already had. Her family would be devoured by mortification, leaving her at the mercy of her in-laws, which Edward could see would not be easy for her. Like Esther once was, Celeste would now be a burden on another family, and she would get a taste for that hardship she witnessed growing up though never fully understanding it. Edward hoped with this heavy stress on her shoulders, Celeste's pregnancy would not be at risk. Without the baby, she would, in all probability, find herself on the streets.

After indulging Henrietta for a few more minutes of gossip and commiseration, which was an odd pairing for Edward, he made his way back to Thomas and William with a lot more to discuss than just their prospective business plan. He popped the champagne and relayed his encounter. William stared at him wide-eyed and conversely, Thomas was completely unperturbed by his father's report, either because with the Madame he expected it or because like Edward, Thomas knew firsthand something of this nature was coming.

"Was this…was this her?" William asked, looking back and forth from Thomas to Edward, who both remained silent and William took that silence as confirmation. "Christ. I hope to God I never piss off that woman. It's one thing to knock off the low lives and scum…another altogether to take out a prominent figure in high society. Or three, for that matter."

"You're trying to tell me Charles Adams isn't low level scum?" Thomas posed, in a tone that didn't want to be challenged.

William groaned. "That's not what I'm saying, Thomas. Everyone in this family hates that bastard and his son. All I'm saying is it's...eye opening. And you can trust that I'm not condemning her for what she did, because if I had the means I would have done him and his son in myself. So would you, and so would your father."

"So would Esther, I daresay," Edward countered, taking a swig of his drink. "The point is, we are lucky to have such a friend as the Madame, and what's done is done. Everything will unravel rapidly, and once it's passed, our lives will go on...as they always do."

William was not finished. "I was under the impression she would get rid of Timothy as well. Why leave the bigger culprit in the open if he's the true problem?"

For the first time in their relationship, William was actually soliciting Edward from his standpoint of expertise in this regard, and his son glanced at him intently, also wanting his input.

Following the night at the theater, Thomas pushed his father for an account of what exactly happened, and Edward swore to divulge it in due course. That lasted until the Hiltmores' party. William pressured him on a daily basis to share with Thomas the life he lived before his son, and that pressure had them bickering on and off like adolescents. In spite of this, Edward found he incessantly made excuses for a number of reasons, highest on that list being that he didn't want Thomas to seek out Hiroaki to be trained himself. It wasn't what Edward wanted for his son, and until he could find a way to tell his story in the right fashion, he would avoid that moment to the best of his abilities.

What troubled Edward was a little piece from the night of the Hiltmores' party he'd kept to himself: subsequent to pulling Esther from the stairwell, he discovered something extremely unnerving. What none of them knew...not the Madame...nor Louis...nor Esther ...was that there was a fourth party watching Esther. Someone that neither the Madame, Esther, nor the Hiltmores nor Adamses had any hint was there, a man hidden in the shadows on the outside balcony of Douglas' study. In haste and in fear for Esther's life, he'd gotten her out as quickly as he could. Since that day, Edward could feel this new character's presence lurking somewhere in the distance, and he made note to figure out that mystery prior to heading home to England. He needed to discern just whom this man was really watching: him, Esther, or the Hiltmores and Adamses.

"Eddie?"

Edward hadn't realized his response was so delayed. "Sorry... got lost there a moment. I think Timothy will be taken care of, in one way or another. The Madame doesn't leave loose ends, and she won't rest until the job is done."

Thomas' face formed a small smile of relief at his father's words. "She won't," he agreed, leaning back in his seat. "Well, how about a cheers, then? To a bright new future, in more ways than one?"

"I'll drink to that!" William joined in merrily, the three of their glasses coming together for a toast.

Thomas finished his flute, allowing Edward to pour him another, and reached into his pocket. He pulled out three machine-made cigarettes and set them on the table.

"And here's one for solidifying the Turner legacy."

Another cheers, and they each took one, lighting their tobacco with laugher. Both Thomas and William proceeded to gaily congratulate themselves over the next few hours, not bringing up the subject of what awaited them in New York again. Edward, steadfast as ever, spent most of his time filtering in and out of the celebration, his thoughts straying to Timothy Adams and the unknown spy from the party. There wouldn't be much time to delay when they got to the city in the morning. Edward would go to the Madame and Louis to hear their account of the days he'd missed, and possibly while he was there, offer his assistance once again to complete the mission.

They rolled into the Grand Central Depot earlier than any of them liked, with their heads hanging heavy from a night of little sleep and excessive consumption of champagne and tobacco. A carriage sat ready for them on the street as they stumbled out from the relatively deserted lobby of the station, and the three men rode in silence home, equally exhausted and ready to sleep off their trip. William fought desperately to keep his eyes open and Thomas' head fell back snoring before the coach even made it two blocks, causing Edward to suppress a laugh. He gazed out his window as the passing crowds grew larger with the rising sun, longing for the fresh, open air of England and wanting to get away from the endless mob of people. Edward looked at his son, unsure if one day he would follow his father and leave New York behind. He was by no means ready now...or...was he? The more Edward thought on it the more it occurred to him that with everything that ensued throughout the summer, why on Earth would Esther and Thomas wish to remain there? Perhaps for Celeste, or for the Madame...in Thomas' case, for the new tobacco contract. As he carried on in his internal conjecture, gradually Thomas started to come to, blinking his eyes hard and trying to focus on his surroundings. He grinned at his father, and Edward's curiosity got the better of him.

"Thomas?" Edward whispered. "Might I ask you something?"

He caught his son's attention despite the pending lethargy. "What is it, father?"

"I need you to be honest with me."

Thomas was instantly more alert. "Anything."

"Would you rather stay here...in New York...than come back to England with me in the fall?"

It was a query that caught Thomas off guard. "I...well..." he cleared his throat. "I'd be lying if I said I wanted to stay forever. Most of my earliest days were spent planning on leaving New York, and with Esther and everything that's happened, I don't see why we would want to stay."

"But you do want to stay for a little while?"

Thomas nodded. "I want to make sure the deal with Buck is solid, and I have a feeling Esther will want to be here for Celeste considering what's...recently come to light. I also wouldn't be surprised if Celeste and the child venture to England with us…if that is all right with you, of course."

"You know I have no objections to that," Edward told him.

"Those will be happy words for Esther," Thomas sighed, stretching. "A year at maximum, father. Then you can expect us at Amberleigh to start our lives new."

"And what of your notorious Aunt?"

"The Madame?"

"She is who I was referring to, yes."

Thomas chuckled. "She will be better off without me hanging around. And Esther. Business will go back to the way it was, no harm and no foul."

Edward didn't let up. "And what makes you so sure she would be pleased with your plans to go?"

"Well it's not up to her, is it?" Thomas retorted, a little too harsh, and realized his callousness. "I'm so sorry, father. That had nothing to do with you. It had to do with years of being under her jurisdiction."

"That's what I'm worried about Thomas," Edward remarked calmly. "You aren't the only one who has been a puppet…and unlike your situation son, Esther's was completely voluntary."

From the look on his face, that concept had yet to cross Thomas' mind. "Shit," he mumbled, shaking his head. "It worries me, you know. Every day. That she's going to do something about what that bastard…I mean I can't blame her, father, I want to kill him too…I just…I don't want her to do something stupid. The Madame has a way of putting bullshit ideas into people's heads…"

William had taken over Thomas' prior role and snored loudly, so Edward lowered his voice to keep it that way. "You need to be a source of constructive optimism for her, Thomas. Esther has been through an ordeal not one of us can really comprehend, and with the right amount of persuasion and anger, people are capable of anything. You need to be the anchor…to help her remember what life is really about. If there's any way to prevent a confrontation, that's

496

the only way you can do it without setting her off."

"Yeah…Yeah you're right…"

"You bought the ring, correct? The one you told me about?"

"Last week," Thomas reported. "She's going to love it."

Edward smiled. "Yes she will. It will change everything, just you wait and see."

"I hope you're right." He pulled out a cigarette. "Can I ask you something now father? A favor?"

"Whatever you need, Thomas."

Thomas hesitated as his match sparked, and he exhaled smoke. "I trust Louis, but I can't say I fully trust the Madame. Will you… will you keep an eye on Esther for me? I know Louis has…I would just feel one hell of a lot better knowing it was you instead."

"Would it surprise you if I told you I already had been?"

Thomas paused, cigarette an inch from his lips. "Well, shit, father, you could have told me!" Thomas exclaimed, much more amused than upset.

The noise woke William suddenly, who shot up and hit his head on the side of the coach window, causing him to plummet back down into his seat moaning in pain. Edward and Thomas burst out into laughter while the carriage jerked to a halt, and father and son got up to help William out of the coach, each supporting him from under an arm. As they forced their way into the sunlight, the driver grabbed their luggage and ran it to the top of the stoop as a flustered Tony rushed to William's assistance, taking Edward's spot opposite Thomas. Edward paid the coachman, still laughing, when he noticed the familiar figure of Louis standing across the roadway, smoking as he rested against a tree. Turning around, Edward checked that William, Thomas, and Tony found their way inside the house and then jogged over to meet him, clouds rolling in as a late summer storm started to form in the distance.

Louis put out his cigarette on the tree. "Contracts signed?"

"Signed. Should be easy from here. How have they been?"

Louis shrugged. "Nothing out of the ordinary. Esther has been fulfilling her end, spending time with Celeste and steering clear of Timothy."

Edward was pleased to hear it. "Any suspicions of her involvement?"

"Not in the slightest. Douglas Hiltmore is already behind bars, waiting on his sentencing hearing, and Catherine is holed up in her house in conniption. Charles Adams is on the record as being killed by an unknown criminal with an ongoing investigation into Douglas Hiltmore's enterprise. It's all done."

"How is the Hiltmore girl holding up?" Edward inquired, eyeing the surrounding street for eavesdroppers.

"Celeste? Devastated. Daddy's little girl is seeing the worst side of the world. Esther is making a difference…but I think the family has made it unmistakable, in their own way, that the baby is her only hope of staying an Adams permanently."

"Christ," Edward mumbled, amazed at such brutal disingenuousness. "Thank you, Louis. I'm planning a visit later this afternoon…there's some things I'd like to discuss with both of you, if that is all right?"

"She would like that," Louis communicated. Edward began to move the direction of the house when Louis grabbed his arm. "Eddie, wait. There's more."

He'd been afraid Louis might say that. "More?"

"Esther wants to be the one to kill Timothy. She won't take no for an answer. I think I'm going to take him out of the equation before she gets in over her head."

"Louis, no. You can't. The investigators will know something is amiss if the son is gone so fast after his father."

"I'll make it look like a suicide. Or better, an accident at The Palace."

Edward had to press him. "Does the Madame know about this?"

Louis rolled his eyes. "She says she's thinking on it, and to give her a few days." His cheeks reddened. "Fucking hell. First time in a long time I've really disagreed with her. Esther isn't ready. She's an aid, for Christ's sake, not a primary, and she's too emotionally invested."

"I agree."

Louis breathed in deep. "You know what I'm going to say next, don't you?"

"Yes," Edward responded, "And my answer is yes. But we can't tell her."

"I know."

Silence again. "We'll fix it, Louis," Edward assured him, resting a hand on his shoulder. "If anyone can, we can. Come by tomorrow, we'll put a plan together. I'll start thinking on it tonight."

"If you say so, Eddie," Louis rejoined, though he appeared content. "Last thing is…I had an unexpected visitor the other night… one that goes way back."

Edward's brow furrowed. "Who?"

Louis' eyes locked on his. "Will is alive, Eddie."

His stomach dropped. "Will…Will Sweeny?"

"The Cat himself."

"You've seen him? In the flesh?"

"He came to me, actually." Louis put another cigarette between his lips and lit it, and Edward couldn't help but notice the distraught expression his friend was trying to fight off. "Eddie, something isn't right. I don't know how but…come by The Palace later." His gaze flickered for a brief second toward the house, and when Edward nonchalantly rotated to investigate, it was Tony standing at the front door, his eyes focused on the two of them.

"How's he been?" Louis queried.

"Same as ever," Edward responded kindly. "On a very short list of men I trust, just like you." Louis didn't answer, but from the look on his face, Edward could see those words meant a lot to him. "Don't fret, Louis. We'll figure this out. For now, I need a little sleep to work through this headache."

499

He nodded. "Rest up," Louis dismissed. "Storm is coming in, and it's going to be a nasty one."

Thunder crackled overhead as dark, ominous clouds took over the sky; nonetheless, Edward knew Louis wasn't referring to the weather overhead. With a curt nod, they parted ways, Edward marching hastily toward Tony.

"We got William settled inside," the butler announced, watching Louis turn and walk west.

"My apologies, Tony. I saw Louis, so I went to check in and give my best."

"Of course, sir. Anything I need to be aware of?"

"Not as of yet, but I will keep you posted."

"Happy to hear it. Well then, I am just here to pass along Lucy's orders, as I was forced to do with the other two," he explained, a hint of annoyance in his tone that made Edward smirk. "You are to be as quiet as possible to let the girls sleep late. Esther has been taking care of Mrs. Adams diligently and until all hours of the evening, and they only went to bed just an hour before you gentlemen arrived. Dinner will be tonight at seven sharp, with a family gathering around five thirty."

"Happy to come home to a schedule," Edward said sarcastically.

"Well, you know how Mrs. Turner is, sir," Tony remarked, continuing on. "Your room is prepared for you upstairs, a hot bath as well before you sleep."

"Thank you, Tony." Edward slowly climbed up the stairs, seeking some clarity for his thoughts. He marveled at how somehow a fight always ended up on his doorstep no matter where he went. Yet as he sank into his bath, the other part of him...the voice that he presumed had to be hers, only posed one simple question:

"Are you sure it's not you who is always looking for the fight, Eddie?"

Edward slept until the early part of the afternoon. Rising for a strong cup of tea to try to rouse his senses, he planned on a quick stop at The Palace before the dinner and social hour began. He rang for his beverage and with it came a few letters that arrived in Edward's absence. Seeing there were very few, he decided to flip through them and make sure there was nothing pertinent needing his immediate consideration, thus allowing his tea to kick in prior to setting out. The first four were business letters, each pertaining to shipments and the like, the fifth from Hiroaki with updates on the estate and asking how everyone was doing in New York; however, the sixth and final letter was not for Edward. It was addressed to Thomas... Thomas Dougherty...and sent to the barber shop where Thomas had not lived in over eight years. There was no return address on the envelope to provide any hints, and the handwriting smudged to the point of being nearly illegible. Edward assumed whoever sent the letter was either in quite a hurry or did not write correspondence very often, and he was about to set it aside when something caught his eye: a detail, one that only he would recognize. The D in Daugherty – the curved way the pen finished on the paper – Edward had only known one person to use that signature, memorizing its character in the countless hours he'd spent rereading the letters she wrote during his stay in China.

Mary.

He didn't care that it wasn't for him. He didn't care he was betraying Thomas' trust. He didn't care that the reality might be this letter was so out of date it might not be relevant. Eight years of nothing...eight years of believing she was lost to him forever...

Edward tore the letter open.

"I need another fucking scotch," the Madame demanded after downing her double, and Louis went to pour her one.

Minutes after opening and reading Mary's letter, Edward sent for them, declaring it to be an emergency...a matter of life and death. It was the only way she'd come to him, and they arrived in under an hour, the Madame insisting on a justification for their attendance and Louis uneasy, understanding Edward would never command their presence unless it truly was something extraordinary. Edward retreated to his study after sending William's page, ordering Tony to keep everyone out and tell them he would be isolated for the remainder of the night on an urgent matter from Amberleigh, not wanting to rouse any misgivings from the others. As instructed from his brief note, Louis snuck himself and the Madame in through the back servants passage, Edward having warned them this matter required full disclosure, and he wouldn't have it otherwise. Now with the Madame and Louis in front of him, Edward found he could barely control his temper.

"I want you to explain this to me. I want you to explain how this is possible. You told me there was no way she was alive...you told me...you told me she was dead!"

The Madame was paler than her normal shade as she took a sip of her scotch. "What do you want me to fucking say, Edward? That I lied to you? That I knew all this time she'd been sitting somewhere rotting away?"

"You knew there was a chance and you lied to me!" he shouted, slamming his fist against his desk.

"I did not lie," she declared coolly. "I told you, Edward, that you had to choose. There was a one in a million chance she might still be alive, and if you went looking, you knew you and Thomas would be at the bottom of the fucking Hudson. The people who did this are more powerful than you remember. Don't let your God damned emotions cloud your judgment, you're better than that. You did this for Thomas' safety, or did you forget about your son and the fact that every fucking prick who worked for the people who took Mary wanted him dead?"

Edward got to his feet in a rage, meaning to go at her, but Louis defensively stepped between them. For a second no one moved, waiting for some kind of onslaught from one another; yet as the moment went by, Edward perceived the honesty in the Madame's words and he rescinded, flopping down into his chair.

"Who are these people?"

The Madame's face softened. "It's not so much people. It's one man, and everyone under him. And he has a lot of fucking followers."

"I asked who, Madame."

"I'm going to regret this," she remarked under her breath dejectedly. "His name is Richard Croker. He's the number two at Tammany Hall. And he's got half of New York in his pocket...technically, I even work for him..."

Edward's mouth fell open. "How...how could you?"

"I didn't have a choice, quite like you," the Madame admitted. "I don't respond kindly to threats, and the end game I had in mind is something I don't expect you to understand." She stopped to see if he wanted to interject, and when he didn't, she went on. "I got involved with the idea that in the end I'd be able to take this fucker out on my own. Repay him for what he's done to me and my family. Unfortunately, he's grown so influential...so dominating...I can't touch him. The opportune moment has yet to come, and probably won't until he makes a mistake."

"Which he hasn't yet," Edward finished, identifying with her perspective. "And probably won't for some time."

"Correct."

Louis' face lit up in dismay, as if something finally clicked. "Madame...I think I've figured it out. I can't believe I didn't see it before..."

They both stared at him. "What do you mean, Louis?" Edward queried, getting to his feet. "What is it?"

"Will. He told me that night Croker was watching us…you and me, Madame…we were back on his list even though it had nothing to do with the hit. Nothing at all! We've only ever posed one threat to him and that was when we were asking questions about Mary…and when Edward and Thomas left the first time that threat went away…"

The Madame's eyes grew wide. "He knows Thomas and Edward are back in New York."

Louis nodded. "He's watching us to make sure we aren't planning on resuming our search for her, which means he's…"

The Madame and Louis turned to Edward. "They've found you," the Madame informed him bluntly. "What's worse is, we have no fucking guarantee that letter also is not a plant to bait us out of hiding."

"It's Mary's handwriting," Edward retorted.

"It doesn't mean it's not years old, Eddie, and they kept it. I wouldn't put it past them," Louis stated. "Has Thomas read the letter?"

"No," Edward replied. "I opened it on my own accord."

Louis and the Madame shared a quick glimpse and she nodded. Without warning, Louis lurched forward and took the letter off Edward's desk, striding right for the fireplace. Before Edward could get to him Louis tossed the paper into the blazing fire where it burned down to ash, making it impossible to recover.

Edward stood in utter disbelief. "What in the bloody hell are you doing?!"

This time, the Madame inserted herself between them. "You think anything has changed from eight years ago, Edward? It hasn't. That bastard wouldn't give a second thought to killing me, Louis, you, Thomas…they don't give a shit! It's a fucking trap!"

"It is not a trap!" Edward snarled. "Mary is smart. She got this letter to Thomas by some miracle and we need to get her the hell off of Blackwell! How can you sit idly by and let her rot away in a place like that? She's your daughter, for Christ's sake!"

The tension in the room rose again, and the only sound was the rain against the windows from the storm outside. Not one of them was confident of what to do next. Edward shouldn't have said it, and now, he'd more or less confessed to knowing the Madame's biggest secret. It had never been confirmed or denied by her, though Edward saw it during his last visit to New York, when it was just the two of them resolving on what to do about Thomas. Their eyes were the same…the exact same mixture of honey and grey…and the loopholes in Mary's origin story suddenly made sense. It was the main reason he empathized with her wanting to see Thomas, and why he allowed it to happen all the same. From Louis' reaction, Edward couldn't tell if this was the first time he'd heard it, or if he was in such a state of shock that Edward discovered it and hadn't mentioned it previously. He'd thrown a giant elephant into the room with no regard for the consequences.

"I made a promise to myself that I would protect Thomas when I couldn't save her," the Madame persisted. "If Mary saw what was going on…if she knew what had happened, she would appreciate why I am doing what I'm doing. Unlike you, Edward, I am worried about everyone except my daughter because she was aware of the penalties that went along with her job in spite of my repetitive fucking warnings. I am doing what you should be doing and putting your family first. My family, mind you. You think those bastards wouldn't hang Lucy, William, or Esther from the rafters to make a point? You think they'd let Thomas live a single night if they thought he was out and at it again? No, Edward. I am doing what I have done my entire fucking life to survive, and that's prioritize. Because I am the only one who will make the hard choice. And since you can't see through your own fucking blindness, allow me to do it for you."

"You…you're just going to leave her there to die?"

The Madame finished her scotch. "I don't have a fucking army, Edward. Tammany does, and they have spies everywhere. You break her out, and we're all dead by the end of the week. And he'll make sure you and I die last so we have to fucking watch it happen."

Edward searched their faces in vain for compassion. "No one has to know. I can get her out."

"Eddie," Louis protested, "it's a state institution. He'll be the first to know. They let us live once, and they won't do that again."

"If neither of you will help me, I will find a way to do it myself without putting anyone at risk. I can't leave her. Not when I know she's alive." Spitefully, Edward pointed to the door. "Get out of my house."

Neither the Madame nor Louis budged. "Louis, don't leave his side," she commanded, her gaze not leaving Edward's. "No one knows we're here. You aren't going anywhere. I've got things to take care of and I'm not going to have you fucking up the safety net we've been struggling for years to build."

Edward almost laughed aloud. "What? You're going to have Louis kill me if I try to leave my own study?"

Her eyes blazed like the fire behind her. "It would be a favor considering what they'd do to you if they caught you," she responded, strolling toward the exit. "When I swore to do anything to protect Thomas, I fucking meant it. If you won't listen to reason, that does not exclude killing you, Edward. I don't care if you are his father." She opened the servant's door halfway. "And if you ever bring up that Mary is my daughter again without my say so, I will kill you myself." The Madame left them at that, the door swinging shut with a bang.

Edward glared at Louis who, to his astonishment, was reaching for the pistol in his jacket. "Louis, for Christ's sake. This is insanity. Think about this. We can save her!"

"It would require a lot more than just walking in and taking her out, Edward. It's common knowledge sometimes it takes weeks to get a patient released, and that's only if you have the money for it." He stepped so he was blockading Edward's path to the door. "How is it you are willing to put those you hold dear at risk for this, Eddie?"

"Because she's alive, Louis, and I have seen the proof."

"What's going to happen when you come home and everyone

here has their throat slit? How will you feel about it then?"

"We'll leave for Liverpool at first light and be gone. No one will know."

Louis cocked the pistol. "You haven't seen your wife in twenty-six years, Eddie. You can't see the bigger picture here. This is an impossible task and you aren't thinking straight." Pointing the gun at him, Louis motioned to the chair behind his desk. "Go sit down. We aren't going anywhere."

"Like hell I will." Edward stood his ground, crossing his arms over his chest. "You'll have to shoot me first."

"If I have to I will, Eddie."

"You'd kill me in cold blood in my own house?"

"Those are my orders, and considering what is happening, yes I would. You don't seem to grasp the gravity of our circumstances and who it is we're dealing with."

Analyzing Louis' aggression, Edward recoiled to his desk as instructed, keeping an eye on his friend to confirm he would holster his weapon. When Louis did, Edward instantly drew his own Colt from the top desk drawer, aiming it for Louis' forehead with his thumb resting lightly on the hammer.

"I am leaving this house," he revealed, words laden with angry determination. "And you cannot stop me."

Louis was baffled. "What happened to no guns?"

"We changed the code. We use them if there is no other way."

Louis leisurely lifted his hands into the air. "I think we both know you aren't going to shoot me."

Bit by bit, Edward inched closer until the nose of his gun was just inches from Louis' face. "Are you so sure?"

"I am willing to bet my life," he replied, unflinching. "I know you, Eddie, and what's more I know when you're lying. You and your son have the same tell. It's not in your code. It never has been."

"You're right," Edward conceded, and with a lightning fast jab, he struck Louis as hard as he could across the temple with the butt of his gun. For a few seconds Louis staggered, and then unconsciously, he fell to the floor, motionless.

Squatting down, Edward checked his friend's breathing and heartbeat – he would wake in under an hour…furious, though it was obvious Louis let him win. Edward was quicker, yes, but Louis was by no means slow, and Edward took the surrender to his hit as Louis' blessing to find Mary, covering his tracks for later with regards to the Madame. Sitting Louis upright, Edward scooted him rearward so that his back would rest against one of the walls. When he came around, Edward would be long gone, and just to give himself more of a head start he decided to lock Louis in his study. There was little time to see this through, and in case it went poorly, Edward scrawled a quick note to Hiroaki overseas, describing the situation and his plan to get Mary out. When he'd finished that, Edward wrote another to the White Star Line requesting to book passage on the next available boat across the Atlantic – if he could break Mary free from Blackwell and the Madame did not exaggerate the pending risk, Edward would need to get his family out of New York as soon as possible. He would offer passage to the Madame and to Louis if they so chose, and if they didn't, Edward really couldn't give a damn.

His two letters in hand, Edward left the office and locked the door behind him. He made it two or three paces and came face to face with Tony who seemed to be on his way to check on Edward and was startled.

"Tony!" Edward cried out in surprise, taking a step back after nearly running him over. "I apologize. I'm just headed out for a bit. All is well?"

"Yes, of course, sir. The others just left to go out for tea and I wanted to see if you needed anything. They should be home in another hour or two. Is…is everything all right, Lord Turner? You look flushed."

"Louis is locked in my study, Tony. He shouldn't wake until I return. If I am wrong, however, make sure he doesn't leave."

Tony nodded. "Not a problem. Should I be prepared, sir?"

Edward brushed off the front of his coat. "I shouldn't be long. Send these letters out, and if I'm not back by the time the family returns, get the house in lockdown."

"Of course, right away, sir." Tony took the letters from his hand and returned the way he'd come, allowing Edward a moment to collect himself and make his next move cautiously.

It was already late in the afternoon – it would not be an easy task to get on the island within the few daylight hours left, particularly since visitors were rarely allowed without notice ahead of time. Edward racked his brain. There was no way to get across by ferry alone. He would need someone else to assist him in case Mary happen to be in hysterics, and for a few seconds Edward wondered if he ought to find Thomas and take him along, though he promptly decided against it, not wanting his son to be put in any greater danger than he already was. Strangely, he kept going back to the same solution: involve the police. Sure, the department was corrupted, as most forms of law enforcement were nowadays; however, Edward's instincts told him as long as he was smart, it might be the only way to see it through. And if he had the money to pay them off, who's to say their favor wouldn't sway in his direction?

Fumbling for the keys, Edward turned and went back into his study, heading straight for the safe. A glance down at Louis reassured him his friend was still some time away from revival, and after casting the picture frame aside, gave a few small turns of the lock to retrieve enough cash to buy a fleet of carriages. He tucked it away in his billfold and set off again, this time making it through the residence without any confrontations. Grabbing his jacket off the front hook, he threw open the front door, more determined than ever he was doing the right thing. If this was how things in this city operated, he would accommodate his own tactics to match, no matter how shady they might be. Nothing else mattered to Edward anymore. Only Mary.

The closest precinct resided a few blocks away, and as he made his way inside the station, it was a buzzing with activity. To his left were what appeared to be offices and interrogation rooms, and to his right sat a few people impatiently waiting, with policemen hurrying to and fro. Straight ahead was a large counter, two men seated behind it, and while one was in conversation with a distraught-looking elderly woman, the other spotted Edward and waved for him to come forward. The officer had a friendly face, a strong build, and the remnants of a black eye fading from his cheek. From this second forward, there was no turning back, and Edward walked to him.

"Good afternoon. Is there somethin' I can help ya with, sir?" the officer asked politely, his Irish accent overpowering.

"Yes well...I could use a bit of help."

"What seems to be the trouble, then?" A request the man clearly used twenty times a day given the manner in which he said it.

Edward swallowed and leaned in close, whispering. "Look, I don't know how to say this, but I need to talk to someone on the higher end of jurisdiction. I've discovered a woman being wrongly held at Blackwell, and I need to have her released."

The officer studied him close. "You said on Blackwell, sir?" He rubbed his goatee, trying to determine how dire Edward's plight was.

"Yes. She's been there for...for far too long. She'd been missing and no one could find her."

"How are ya related to this woman?"

"I am her estranged husband. Upon my return to New York I was told of her situation and thought it best to go straight to the police. Is there any way you can help me? I have...plenty to compensate for the efforts," he added, with the hopes his incentive would be enticing.

"Christ," the officer muttered. "Legally speakin', as long as the state has not condemned her to Blackwell for any lawful reasonin', you can have her released with a sign off from the doc. What's her name, if ya don't mind me askin'?"

A rush of anticipation hit Edward. "Mary. Mary Dougherty."

"And what is your name, sir?" He grabbed for a piece of paper and wrote her name down, and Edward couldn't help but notice he scrawled a small dollar sign under her name.

"Edward Turner."

The officer wrote Edward's name next to Mary's, peering at him sympathetically. "Gimme a few minutes, Mr. Turner. I'm goin' to ask the Captain what he reckons about your statement. Why don't ya take a seat over there and I'll be back shortly?"

Edward did as he was told, and the man ran off through a door to the left, heading at a brisk tempo down the glass hallway. Closing his eyes, Edward tried to stay calm in spite of the flurry of potential scenarios he was overanalyzing in his brain. What the Madame failed to realize is that her status and enterprise earned her a reputation amongst the people of New York, and not all her business was legitimate, to say the very least. There were bad apples in every bunch, Edward learned that lesson many years ago, yet money had a way of making opposing sides come together. After eight years, he highly doubted the legitimacy of the threat the Madame and Louis spoke of in a city this big, especially with as many existing problems as there were amongst its people and politicians. The longer he thought on it, the more he presumed they were bullshitting him, and that was why Louis allowed him to get away. The Madame put herself first – she always had and always would, and Edward thought it wise of him to bear that in mind as the officer reemerged.

"Mr. Turner, this way please!" he beckoned Edward, his previously friendly expression now flustered.

Edward stood up to follow, and when he did, a familiar face appeared coming through the main entryway. "Good afternoon, Detective Ellis," Edward greeted him with a nod.

Samuel Ellis stopped dead in his tracks, gaping at Edward. "Lord Turner? What in God's name are you doing here?"

"Missin' persons," the officer who had been helping Edward explained, from Ellis' side. "We've got it under control, Detective. He's goin' to sit down with the Captain now."

Ellis wouldn't let it go. "I should sit in on this if he's meeting with the Captain."

"I don't think the Captain—"

"I insist." Ellis said it so firmly, there was no way for the officer to object.

Annoyed, the officer led the way. "We will only be takin' Mr.—"

"It's Lord Turner," Ellis corrected him, at Edward's side.

The officer turned around, though he did not pause. "Sorry. Lord Turner's statement is all we will be takin' tonight."

"Just my statement?" Edward posed, a little outraged as he followed the officer down the corridor. "We cannot retrieve her tonight?"

"Unfortunately sir, by the time we reach Blackwell, it will be too late. They close the damn ferry down in a quarter of an hour for safety reasons. The Captain will be sendin' an escort with you first thing in the mornin'."

Ellis was puzzled. "Wait. An escort where?"

"Blackwell," the officer told him. "His wife is bein' held there."

Any lasting color in Ellis' cheeks vanished. "Fucking hell…" he murmured under his breath, as the officer held open the door to the chief's office. He grabbed Edward's arm before allowing him to enter. "Do you know what you're doing, Lord Turner?" he beseeched him, so quietly only Edward could hear him.

Edward opened his jacket to display his billfold, stuffed with paper money. "We can't always do everything according to the Madame, my dear Detective. And I plan on getting my wife back."

A half hour later, Edward shook hands with the Captain, Sergeant O'Donnell, and Detective Ellis, with the promise of returning to the station in the morning and setting out for Blackwell in the company of the Sergeant and Detective, as well as a written order for Mary's release. The Captain wanted his staff to double check their records that evening to be certain Mary was not incarcerated for breaking any law, and if there was nothing to prove so, she would be let out into Edward's custody immediately. The Detective was shaken, and took off after seeing Edward to the door, not saying a word to him and only left with a polite goodbye. Edward had paid the Captain to keep the errand under wraps, and the Captain obligingly took his bribe with the pledge that not a soul other than the three in that room would know of what was to come.

Not the Madame nor Louis could stop this – not with police and money on his side. Edward debated over going himself once more, but his efforts would surely fail if he made the attempt on his own. No…tomorrow he would rescue Mary. In a few days, they would go home to England with William, Lucy, Thomas, and Esther. And this entire debacle would be left in the dust for good.

He opted to avoid heading home and felt a walk of fresh air might help him prepare to tell Thomas of what had occurred. This would be his greatest gift to his son, and Edward pondered over the way he would reveal to Thomas that very night he'd found their missing piece, excited to have his son at his side on their way to the island, and when they saw her for the first time in years. The Madame would be furious, and while eight years ago when she voiced her concerns Edward agreed wholeheartedly, since then the times had changed. The heat of their previous circumstances was long gone – no man, regardless of how powerful, had the ability to know and see everything going on around him consistently. This kick would be a swift one to the corrupted Tammany Hall, though without imposing threat. All Edward wanted was his wife without any kind of crusade against this Richard Croker and his people. He just wanted Mary, and he would leave in peace.

Realizing he took a wrong turn, Edward glanced around, checking the numbered streets and saw rather than being six blocks away from the park he was now twelve to the south, and with the sun setting in the distance, Edward knew it was time to make his way home. Quickly, he started to retrace his steps, keeping a lookout for a coach to hail the minute one came into view. A bottle of brandy and an intense conversation with Thomas lay ahead, and a wave of excitement flowed through him of all that was to come next.

Unexpectedly, the hair on Edward's neck stood on end. Casually, he peeked over his shoulder and spotted a man across the street, ten paces back and keeping an even rapidity with Edward's stride. Not a man who believed in coincidence, Edward led him a few more blocks and picked up his speed, then made a fleeting turn down the next narrow, darkening alleyway and waited patiently behind the corner of the brick building. Sure enough, the man followed and circled the same corner. In one swipe, Edward grabbed the man with both hands by the collar and flipped him around, pressing his tail hard into the brick wall, feet dangling in suspension off the ground. At once, Edward saw it was a friendly face: George, the Madame's number two man from The Palace.

"Put me down!" George yelled, struggling to break free. "Get your hands off me! I'm not here to fucking hurt you!"

Edward chose not to listen. "Why in the hell are you following me, George? Have you been on me since I left the house?"

The toughness drained, and George panicked. "She told me to, I swear it! She wanted me to keep an eye on you in case Louis didn't! What the fuck happened to him? Where is he?!"

"I knocked him unconscious and left him in the study," Edward revealed. "Why does she want you following me?"

"Because she knew he wouldn't fucking do it!" George spat out. "And I…I couldn't stop you in time! You were inside the station by the time I caught up to you. Christ, do you even know what you've done? We're all dead, Lord Turner. We're all fucking dead!"

Edward released George and slapped him hard across the

face. "Pull yourself together, you bloody imbecile. We are not dead. She's brainwashed you into her scheming, just like she has everybody else!"

George clung to his cheek, both physically and emotionally stricken. "You just don't fucking get it, do you? He's got eyes everywhere…doesn't matter how much money you have! He's going to find out. He's going to know you've gone to the coppers and then he's going to come for us."

"Who is? Croker?"

George was starting to break down. "He's…he's the only one she's ever…ever been afraid of, Lord Turner. She's not afraid of anybody…you know she's not afraid of anybody else…"

"All right, George, that's enough. Let's get you back to The Palace. There will be coaches another two or three blocks up."

Taking George's arm tightly in his grip, Edward turned, a little irritated and slightly unnerved by George's overwhelming terror. How was it possible the Madame could do so much damage to a man who had seen plenty of violence and death throughout the course of his life? However, the second Edward's eyes left George and were on the street, it finally began to sink in that he had made a grave mistake. There stood three patrolmen with their batons out in their hands blocking his and George's path, and not one of them was smiling. Edward took in a deep breath, recognizing exactly what this meant, and where this was heading.

The Madame had been right all along.

"Good evening, gentlemen, is something the matter?" one of their voices boomed, the patrolmen's appearances barely distinguishable, shadowed in the last of the daylight behind them.

"No, thank you officers," Edward responded calmly. "We were just on our way." They stepped closer, and as they did their faces came into full view. One of the three men was Sergeant O'Donnell, the other two Edward had never seen before, and their body language indicated their true intentions. George and Edward would not be going anywhere without their permission, though Edward knew he could handle these three without much exertion. Alas, it was then that five more men appeared in the wake of the officers from around the corner, and Edward's body went rigid.

"Heyya, Georgie," one from the new group shouted. "'Bout time you ran on home, I'd say, unless you want to end up in a bloody heap. Tell the whore she'll be gettin' her own special visit later."

George's eyes found Edward's, and there were tears forming in them. "Lord Turner...I...what should I..."

"Go George," Edward ordered, pulling him into an embrace so he could whisper in George's ear. "Get Louis from my study. Tony will help you, and go to the Madame. Tell Tony to go into lockdown and to get my family out of this city. Save them for me."

George stalled a moment longer and nodded, then ran off as fast as his legs would carry him, the band of assailants parting to let him pass and jeering all the while.

Edward was ashamed of himself. The Madame knew this city better than he ever could...knew it's workings, dealings, and loop-holes...and he'd ignored her at a time when he should have heed-ed her words. There truly had been eyes on them. They must have been waiting, anticipating something was bound to happen or, bet-ter yet, the odds that Mary's letter was a trap strengthened in Ed-ward's mind. He'd taken the bait, and suddenly the dream of find-ing Mary alive...the dream of bringing her home faded away like a distant memory, and was replaced by the fear that he put those he loved in jeopardy for his own selfish motivations.

Standing his ground firmly, Edward accepted this would most likely be a fight to his death. He was not afraid to die – being a sol-dier for so many years, he welcomed the idea of dying on his feet and taking out as many of these bastards as he could before he met his maker. Eight was simply too many for a man his age, namely one who was unarmed. All he could do was say a prayer the Ma-dame took care of his family for him – she'd predicted he'd go this far, and he hoped she'd planned enough ahead to prepare for Edward to selfishly betray them to the mercy of the Tammany Hall.

If there was anyone who could save them, it was her.

"Make it quick," Sergeant O'Donnell commanded, and the three of the patrolman rotated around so their backs were to the alley, assuming it did not make them complicit. The other five, gang members Edward assumed, filtered forward, though one in the back was much larger than Edward and towering over the others.

The boldest of the men cracked his knuckles and sneered, making his way to the head of the pack as the other three smaller ones formed a diamond shape behind him. Nonchalantly, Edward removed his jacked and hat, folding them up neatly and setting them aside on the ground as if unperturbed by their menacing glares.

"Right then, shall we get started?" he asked, coolly rolling up his sleeves.

With an angry yell, the first man pounced, his stance instantly indicating to Edward that while he may have won a few drunken brawls, he had little or no physical presence in a true standoff. Fist aimed at Edward's face, and with the simple bat from the back of his left hand, Edward deflected the blow and swung his right fist hard, striking the man remorselessly in the side of his temple. He toppled to the ground, groaning, undoubtedly seeing stars.

The second bound in, tackling Edward against the brick wall at his waist while the third hastily struck blows to Edward's face, neck, and chest. Edward gripped the man holding him steady and plummeted his knee into the man's stomach three times, and with the last his attacker released and fell over. Skittish from losing his partner, the third backed off, and Edward took advantage by delivering another massive blow to the man on the ground, kicking him in the face with all his strength.

Lights out, as Hiro called it.

Man number three drew a knife from his pocket, an ugly grin on his lips, but Edward could sense he was frightened. The man stepped forward, thrusting the knife at Edward in frantic, undisciplined jabs, coming close yet by no means near enough to pierce Edward's skin. Wanting to disarm him, Edward allowed the man to gain an extra foot and therefore, also an edge in confidence, and the man fell for the trick straightaway. He made a drive at Edward's left stomach just as Edward lifted his left arm and caught the assailant's wrist between his abdomen and upper arm. Without hesitation, Edward twisted his body forward and resiliently brought around his right elbow directly into the man's throat, wherein man number three dropped the knife instantly. He clutched at his throat, staggering backward and gasping at what Edward could only imagine was the agony of a severed windpipe. To add insult to injury, Edward marched forward and retorted with a hard kick to the groin, and watched amused as the fourth man cowardly retreated behind the now advancing giant.

His blood began to pump harder. Edward spat on the ground, taking a sideways step to assess his surroundings. The alley wasn't large enough to play much of a cat and mouse game, but Edward had one major advantage over the giant: being smaller gave him more room for action, whereas the giant was more prone to hitting walls as well as his target.

"You think just because you're larger you'll fight better than any of the others?" Edward quipped, his words oozing with condescension. "Your fourth man wouldn't even give me one more round!"

The giant stopped and smiled, some of his teeth missing. "Ain't gonna be much of a fight, old man."

Edward scoffed. "We'll see about that, you bloody bastard."

The giant's face hardened, and without warning he lunged at Edward. He led with a right hook, mustering the immense amount of velocity he had in his back and arm, and Edward made a quick dodge, the giant's fist missing Edward by only a few inches. The giant fell a few paces frontward, extremely off balance, and Edward whipped lightly around to attack from behind, hitting the giant's right kidney and then his left with as much force as his punches could offer. His opponent growled in pain and spun his direction, knocking Edward to the ground with the brute force of his left elbow to Edward's face, and Edward heard the snap as his jaw dislocated at the impact. Quickly he leapt up, hardly evading the grasp of the man's enormous hands and Edward kicked him in the diaphragm so hard the giant keeled over, unable to breathe. Lurching forward, Edward hit the giant directly in his nose, shattering the septum as blood spurted all over the brick walls.

The giant shied away in an attempt to shield his face, giving Edward the exact opportunity he needed to win. He jumped onto the man's back and wrapped his right forearm across the giant's windpipe, eliminating the little oxygen he was receiving from the newly perforated diaphragm. Edward was slammed repeatedly into the neighboring brick walls as the giant fought to reach him, straining to stay conscious. Two ribs...then three...then four were broken, yet Edward held on as the giant's thrusts grew weaker, his shoulder on the verge of dislocation. Ultimately, the man fell to his knees and Edward was able to stand and pull tighter to put him out. A few seconds later the giant went limp. Unable to hold his adversary because of his excessive weight, Edward dropped him to the ground with a massive thud.

For a moment, Edward had a rush of hope as he turned to face the final man and the police officers. Then, out of the blue, he felt a knife penetrate through his back, and his left lung collapsed. Blood rose up to his mouth, sending him into a fit of coughs and down onto his hands and knees. With a swift yank, the knife was removed in one pull, and Edward's lingering hope disappeared.

The giant...the others...it was a decoy.

It was a few seconds before a voice came from somewhere in the distance. "One of the things I learned over the years after growing up on the streets is that when a family comes to check the body, they never look at the backside," it said matter-of-factly. "Which means, while you are only about three to four minutes from your passing to the other side, these last few minutes will be some of the most painful you've ever experienced. Even worse than the malaria, Lord Turner."

Using the last of his residual drive, Edward managed to flip over to meet a man with dark, slicked back hair and round spectacles, with knife scars littered on the parts of his arms and hands that Edward could see. He wasn't a close comparison to the giant in size, yet something about this man's presence made him seem a lot larger and stronger than he really was. On the man's face was an ominous smile, lacking any kind of empathy, and Edward's blood stained the knife in his left hand.

"It's time," he hollered to the officers, and after a few seconds, the policemen moved aside to let a man down the alley in a formal suit with sandy blonde hair and a countenance that demanded respect. The blonde man, upon viewing Edward on the ground, glared at the one with the knife, wearing an expression of utter disdain, and then turned to Edward, crouching down beside him.

"You're dismissed, Mr. Walsh," Croker asserted, pointing for him to withdraw toward the officers, and the man complied with little reluctance.

"You're...you're him..." Edward wheezed, wishing he had the power to get to his feet for one last hit.

The man with the blonde hair nodded. "You are correct, Lord Turner. I am sorry for the nuisance, I just don't want our first and last exchange to be overheard by anyone. Considering your...current state, we have to make this look like an accident, and for the record I just would like you to know you are not a man I enjoy seeing to his end. It was my initial intention only to scare you and leave you in a bloody pulp, not to kill you. However, my man appears to have taken the reins into his own fucking hands in my absence, and for that I must improvise."

Edward felt as if he were drowning in his chest...he could barely breathe. "Just...let me die..."

The man with the knife started to take a step back their way, but Croker held up a hand to stop him. "Lord Turner, before you leave us, I need your word on something. As a man of honor, and to prevent harm to those who don't deserve it."

Edward laughed ironically through red teeth, then fell into another fit. "You're no…no man of honor, Croker…"

"Oh Christ no. And I won't ever claim to be one. You, however, are, and I need your word as a gentleman and a soldier, that your son was completely ignorant of Mary being held at Blackwell, and has had no idea there was a letter from her. That brute of a man over there with the knife is one of my eyes and ears, and he informed me it was only you, the Madame, and the goon who knew of the contents. Is this true?"

When Edward tried to speak, the only thing that came out was blood. He nodded.

"Praise the Lord for that," Croker bellowed, his hands clenching into triumphant fists. "No harm will come to Thomas, or the other members of your family. I am sorry it had to be like this, Lord Turner. I blame the Madame for her inability to let things rest. She just keeps stirring the pot and expects there won't be consequences! I can only hope the news of your death will get the Turners out of my city and keep them away from her, and therefore away from harm."

Edward swallowed hard.

"Is she…is she still…alive…?"

He knew his voice was pitiful, and from the look on Croker's face, it struck him on a personal level. His head bowed as he rose up, and he forfeited eye contact with Edward for his shoelaces, appearing remorseful.

"Not for long."

Edward crumpled over to his side, unable to hold himself up any longer, his entire body going into shock. "Just tell her I love her… tell her, please…"

"I apologize, I cannot," he expressed, "And I am sorry for this

521

upcoming bit of unpleasantry. It's to not draw suspicions when they find you, and I promise the pain will soon be over. Goodbye, Lord Turner, it's been a pleasure."

Croker snapped his fingers, and the police officers bound Edward's direction and began to finish him off, beating him to a pulp though he couldn't feel anything but the cold shiver of death. Slowly, his whole world faded to black, and the last thing he imagined was Mary, bending over him crying, holding him tight as he felt his body at last let go…

Louis' eyes shot open. He was lying on the ground of Edward's study, head throbbing so badly he could feel the pulse of every heartbeat like a hammer. It was night, and the only perceivable light came from one of the candles Edward left lit by the door. Aching all over, Louis pushed himself up to sit, blinking hard. He touched his temple and instantaneously flinched away from his fingers – Edward certainly made a point to knock him out. Much harder and the blow could have been fatal.

"'Bout time ya woke up, Froggie," came Will's voice from the darkness. "I was 'bout to leave myself. Just wanted to catch ya up 'fore you ran back to the boss across the park and found out."

Louis spun and saw Will sitting in Edward's chair at his desk, feet propped up on top comfortably, appearing much more at home than he should have been.

"How did you get in here?" asked Louis, getting to his feet and staggering to the nearest chair.

"Take it slow, brother. Window. You know I can get in and out of anywhere without makin' a racket. Unlike someone else I know," he remarked derisively. "Some shit has gone down while you've been takin' that nice long nap. Or at least…should be wrappin' up about now…"

Louis froze. "What are you talking about Will? What's going on?"

"Your good ol' pal Eddie tried to take a few matters into his own hands down with them coppers. Didn' go too well. Took thirty minutes 'fore my boss found out and made the call. Body will be at the morgue within the hour."

"He's…dead?"

"Sure as shit," Will went on, unfazed. "I told ya not to mess with these assholes, brother. I tried to warn ya. This here is somethin' y'all know they don' like, and they obviously aren' gonna play nice 'bout it."

Louis was overcome with disgrace and devastation. He allowed Edward to go, not really supposing the problem would escalate to such drastic measures…he let Edward march right into a trap and… die, when he alone could have stopped it. The Madame gave orders for a reason, and Louis felt all the blame rest on his shoulders as the doom of his decision set in.

It would be a miracle if they survived the night.

Sensing his friend's dread, Will pulled his feet from the desk top, his tone more grave. "Listen to me. They're goin' to see her. They aren' gonna kill her, but they're gonna make it known she's got one chance left. You'd better get your ass back over there in case she tries to do somethin' stupid, ya know what I'm sayin'?"

Abruptly, a desperate banging came from the door of Edward's study. "Louis! Louis! Wake up!" It was George. The knocking only grew louder along with his pleas, and Louis pointed toward the window.

"Get out of here, Will. Go! Hold on, George, dammit! I'm getting up!"

Will didn't need to be told twice; by the time Louis was to the door Will was halfway out the window. "Louis?"

"What?"

"I'm…I'm sorry about Eddie, brother. I know what he was to you." With that, Will dropped from the window and disappeared.

Gulping down his sadness, Louis threw the door open. "Calm the hell down, George. We've got to keep our wits about us and get back to The Palace now."

"Louis…" From the looks of it, George had been in hysterics. "They…they killed him, I know they did…"

"I know, George. Do the Turners know you're here?"

"Just Tony," George sputtered. "They're sitting down to dinner…waiting for…for…" His head sank, and Louis saw tears fall.

Suddenly there came the sound of footsteps, and both George and Louis peered up to see Tony approach. He didn't bother to address them, only looked to Louis, who foresaw what was coming.

"Tell me," Tony demanded. "What's the status? Do I still need to lock down the house?"

"Not necessary yet, Tony," Louis verified. "Edward left you instructions in the event of his death, correct?"

"Of course he did. But I can't very well protect the family if we don't lock down!"

George gawked at Tony, and then at Louis. "He's…he's in on this, too?"

"Shut up, George, we don't have time to explain," Louis declared. "They'll be fine as long as they're here. Stay armed and do sweeps every half hour. Keep every door and window bolted shut. No one in or out. We've got to get back now and clean this mess up before it's too late."

"Louis," George whispered, getting his and Tony's attention. "It's already too late. Don't you see? Lord Turner…he's…he's dead…"

XVIII.

"Just fucking listen to me George," the Madame demanded spinning around, a finger pointed harshly at his protesting nose. "If Edward leaves this house without Louis at his side, you stay right on his ass and try to stop him. I do not care what it takes or even if you have to cut him down to do it. Do you understand?"

George nodded and took her hand, assisting her up the small step and into the coach. As he closed the latch on the door, the Madame leaned out of the small window, her eyes filtering back toward the Turner residence, where they stayed for a moment.

"It won't be long, now."

It was unreasonable to expect Edward would take her words seriously – how could he? He hadn't seen what Croker and the Hall were capable of, and even with the threat of life to his family, nothing she'd said would penetrate his thick, stubborn skull because that's all they were: words. Edward hadn't witnessed the night Croker threatened her at the church, he hadn't experienced the foreboding condition of Walsh's negotiations, and more importantly, Edward hadn't lived through Tweed's reign as she had. Being English nobility, Edward never had to steal to prevent himself from starving, he never had to sell his body just to have a roof over his head, and he never was forced to kill in fear of death. She'd tried to instill the fear in him, the fear of losing the only real things that mattered; however, until Tammany decided to wreak havoc on Edward, her warnings would be scorned. And while the Madame hated the thought of it, she knew in her heart nothing would stop Edward except a hard dose of reality. There was no escaping it now – Mary's letter sealed their fates. She just hoped the Turners might survive unscathed.

George was sputtering again. "And how exactly do I stop him when I can't even match to Louis?"

Her temper was on edge. "I don't give a shit, George. But you only have a few minutes to make it so I suggest you fucking pull yourself together."

They'd met down a few blocks from the Turner mansion. She'd prayed for Mary to still be alive, that one day she might find her and make it right somehow. This, however, was not the way to go about it. Even if Mary were being held on Blackwell, the Madame learned long ago not to underestimate Croker – setting a trap was the sort of game he liked to play. It was too easy to march over there and demand her release. There were obstacles deliberately set by him… obstacles that were meant to catch those in the act of betrayal and have them sent to be slaughtered.

George took off the direction of the Turners' just as the driver approached the carriage.

"Madame? Where am I taking you? I forgot the exact address."

"Midtown. East. No address, I'll be going on foot. You will be paid to wait for my return."

He nodded and climbed up to his driver's seat. With a flip of the reins they set out, leisurely creeping across the city. Before an inevitably rough evening, there was one loose end the Madame wanted to tie up, one she was doing without the knowledge of any of her compatriots, and for the sake of two young girls who needed a fresh start. Catherine Hiltmore hadn't been seen for days, and according to Esther's account, she ceremonially threw out every domestic servant, maid, and butler following her husband's arrest, refusing to see anyone or allow anyone entry to her home. Her daughter tried repeatedly to visit her and wrote to Catherine in vain, and Celeste's health was beginning to suffer for it. Though Esther didn't realize it at the time, her report was proof enough that the Madame needed to take action and put an end to the theatrics for good. The pain of having a vindictive encumbrance was far greater than not having one, and she would liberate Celeste from her mother's clutches, while at the same time scratching off one more name on her long, long list.

The sky was painted a deep, dark violet as the coach came to a halt four blocks from the Hiltmores'. Not bothering to wait on the hand of her driver, the Madame stepped down gracefully taking in her surrounding environment.

"An hour," she requested, tipping him extra to not move an inch. It was the first time in ages she had done anything without Louis a few paces behind her, especially on a night like this. With so much ambiguity in the balance, the Madame found herself out of character, anxiously overanalyzing what was to come, and struggling to put Mary out of her thoughts. She didn't have the luxury of second-guessing herself. For the time being, the Madame's primary objective was to finish off the arrogant bitch who tried to kill her, to see her sunk down to the bottom of the barrel with nowhere else to go. With a wicked grin coming to her lips, the Madame greatly looked forward to standing over Catherine Hiltmore and beholding the expression on her face when she understood the Madame had won. After years of tolerating Catherine's bullshit, that vile bitch would finally pay her dues, and the Madame impatiently awaited sending her to her grave.

The house was completely dark when the Madame arrived, though there was one lone flickering light in the far upstairs window. It was obvious the grounds were left unattended to since the news of Douglas' arrest surfaced, and she could only assume the furnishings inside would be no different. With a deep breath, the Madame pushed open the unlatched gate and strolled toward the front door, tentative as to what she would find once they came face to face. At the front door she paused, turning around to be confident she was alone, unable to shake the feeling since meeting Walsh that someone was always watching her. Slowly turning the handle, the Madame's left eyebrow rose when she realized it was unlocked.

Catherine really must have gone mad.

Instinctively, the Madame slipped her hand into her dress pocket and cocked the small pistol she carried, her index finger readily resting outside the trigger frame. Lunacy did funny things to people, and the last thing the Madame wanted was to suffer at the hands of a deranged Catherine Hiltmore.

She pushed the door open and it creaked as it swung back, revealing a hauntingly shadowed entryway, the furniture covered in sheets as if the house were closed for the summer season. Warily, the Madame lightly tiptoed inside and tried to listen for the hint of a sound, yet there was only silence, and she moved on, closing the door quietly behind. Her eyes scanned every corner as she inched onward, and as she suspected, there was nothing on the first floor for her – what she sought was upstairs, where the light shone from the street. Progressing up the stairwell, the carpet helped to mute the Madame's heels, and each step she took with caution, not wanting to startle the madwoman somewhere at the top. The second floor was utter blackness gulping her in, but at the distant end of the hallway was a cracked door with a tiny beam of light striking through. Taking her time to not make a sound, the Madame inched toward the room and casually slipped in, a vengeful pulse coursing through her body.

There was Catherine Hiltmore in a raggedly torn and soiled light blue dress, her blonde hair askew and knotted into a rat's nest of an updo, soot smeared on her cheeks and chest. She was heaped onto the floor against the far wall of the room, two empty bottles of wine knocked over at her side while a third rested in her right hand. The Madame couldn't help but gawk at the things scattered everywhere, thrown about and broken in a rage: pictures, glass, clothing, chairs, side tables…as if a battle of some sort had taken place on that very spot. This was the wreckage of what Catherine had built, crumpled up onto the floor, now worth nothing more than garbage. Standing a few feet away, the Madame could sense Catherine knew she was there despite her eyes staying glazed over and off in the distance. The Madame moved closer, until Catherine could no longer ignore the visitor standing only two paces from where she sat.

"Get out…of my house…" she slurred, her words almost incomprehensible.

The Madame uncocked the gun in her pocket and peered around mockingly. "Well, I like what you've done with the place."

"D-d-did you not…hear me?!" Catherine bellowed. "Out! Out now!!" Ferociously she fought to get up and fell to her side on the ground, too drunk to stand on her own feet.

Not an ounce of pity lingered in the Madame's heart as she watched the woman tussle pathetically, trying hard not to laugh at the irony.

"A shame really," the Madame went on. "Such a beautiful house. Wasted. All for nothing." Catherine muttered something nonsensical, pushing herself back upright and taking a swig of wine from the bottle, some of which had spilled onto her dress. Suddenly, the Madame couldn't stop herself, and she shot forward to get directly into Catherine's face.

"You are a disgrace to your daughter," the Madame spat, their noses less than a foot apart. "Look at you. You have a fucking pregnant daughter that needs you and all you can do is wallow feeling so God damned sorry for yourself."

"You…you did this to me. To…to my family." Catherine couldn't look into her eyes, and threw the bottle aside, casting wine all over the floor. "You r-r-ruined us!"

"Oh for fuck's sake. You ruined yourself, you stupid cunt. You didn't have to cross me, betray me, and then try to kill me. But you fucking did." The Madame grabbed her chin hard so Catherine was

529

unable to avoid her gaze. "The devil doesn't sympathize with your kind, Catherine. Self-pity is weakness."

"P-p-pity?" Catherine sputtered, and then unexpectedly let out a shriek that even left the Madame uneasy. When she released her, Catherine made an effort to grab for her. "I...I will tear your...your eyes out, whore."

"What would your daughter say, if she saw you now? Would she be proud of you?" the Madame asked, playfully tilting her head to the side as she stood up. "How does it feel to know you've failed your daughter? All because you had to have more fucking money in your pocket. I know Douglas well enough to tell this was by no means his idea, Catherine. You wanted me dead. You wanted to cut our fucking deal off. You have only yourself to blame."

"Like you would...would know anything about it. I am not... not someone's charity...I won't be degraded...degrading..."

The Madame let out a cruel giggle, flippantly covering her mouth with her hand. "Degrading? Have you seen yourself, Catherine? You aren't worth more than the horse shit in your street. My station outranks yours, and I am nothing but a murdering, thieving whore. I think it's safe to say your so-called degradation has come and gone. Your husband will never see light of day again, if he even survives his first year of prison. You refuse anyone's offer to help–"

"I made this...this f-f-family," Catherine reacted, her eyes nearly popping out of her head. "I made it! You...you are nothing...you don't...you don't talk to me that way. I built this...this family..."

"And look how wonderfully everything has turned out."

Catherine tried to lunge at her once more, however the minute she charged she collapsed right to the ground, cursing the Madame and pandering on, blaming her for her family's misfortune under her breath. There was no saving Catherine: Celeste and her unborn grandchild were not enough. Greed and selfishness were the foundation of Catherine's being, and nothing else...not even the love of her daughter would suffice in its place. Any mark she would have on

Celeste's life would be detrimental if she went on like this. The Madame wouldn't have it: Celeste had the potential to do great things in her future, for herself and for their cause when the time came, and she wouldn't permit those plans to be ruined by the girl's poisonous mother.

"Either way, Catherine, the family you built no longer exists. There's nothing left of it. After Charles' funeral and the will is settled, they will move back to Virginia and not come back. Your daughter will leave you behind, the way she should have years ago." It was a lie, but it had the impact the Madame was going for.

"Celeste would never…would never leave me…"

"Well what did you expect?" she retorted, crossing her arms, "Look at you, for Christ's sake! You are worth nothing to anyone. The second that baby is born she won't give a damn about you or whatever catastrophe you and your husband brought her into…putting her into a marriage with a husband that rapes and beats her and her best friend…that's how you wanted her future, was it Catherine? At the mercy of some bastard whose only redeeming quality is that he'll hopefully die before she does? The best thing that could ever happen to Celeste would be to realize it was her mother's own fucked up view of the world that got her into this mess in the first place and leave you in the fucking dust to rot."

When Catherine didn't respond, the Madame recognized she had her. The truth that Catherine's world was destroyed couldn't be denied, and as she expected, the woman on the floor couldn't stand what she'd become. With an air of confidence, the Madame pulled the pistol out of her pocket and laid the gun on the floor in front of Catherine. For a brief moment, she wasn't sure if Catherine would pick it up and use it against her; but, that was the point of the exercise. For as much as Catherine hated the Madame, in that moment, she hated herself more.

"Do me the favor so I don't have to do it myself," the Madame muttered callously.

531

Not wanting to sit around and wait for what was inexorably to come, she spun on her heels and walked out of the room, taking the chance a bullet might go straight through her back. Fortunately, she reached the hallway unharmed, and the Madame halted for a second, letting out a shaky exhale of relief, resting against the wall. It had been a gamble…a big gamble, though a necessary one to prove her point. Once her heartbeat calmed to a normal pace, she took off down the stairs and through the entryway, not having any desire to be present for the final act. The Madame didn't bother to close the front door, and as she passed through the gate the way she'd come, a shot rang out from the house like cannon fire. Her feet instantly stopped moving and her eyelids fluttered closed, her fingers gripping her palms into tight, tense fists. Rotating around, the Madame opened her eyes, and every window in the house had gone black.

Victory at last.

The coach sat just where she'd left it, the driver finishing a cigarette as she approached and he ushered her inside.

"Thought I heard gunfire!" he exclaimed nervously, a little frightened. "Not a regular occurrence in these parts. Glad you made it back! Full moon tonight's got me jumpin' at everything…"

The Madame tried to appear offset by the driver's statement, instructing him to take her back to The Palace immediately, no other stops. He did as he was instructed, and the carriage rolled steadily northwest, bouncing here and there on the uneven road and sending the Madame into an ominous, reflective trance.

It was done. No matter what happened from that point forward, the Hiltmores had been grossly eliminated, and within a few weeks she would see to it the vile son of Charles Adams was disposed of as well. Her elation in her triumph didn't last long, remembering her night had, in all likelihood, only just started. There was no report of where Edward was now…and while she prayed he hadn't done the unthinkable, her gut told her otherwise. If only he had seen what she'd seen…known what she'd done to keep them safe…

It was no matter. Despite how ugly things might get, the Madame could never hold Edward responsible for any of his actions concerning Mary regardless of how impulsive or idiotic. The bulk of it came down to her – she'd separated them, she'd lied to them, and she'd tried to convince him not to save Mary after almost three decades of loving her. The minute Edward opened that letter, it was as if a switch had been flipped in his brain, one that could not be undone.

Half an hour later, the coach reached The Palace, where there was still no sign of Louis or George, and the Madame could feel it deep in her bones while leaping out of the carriage: something was really, terribly fucking wrong. Danny and Hope stood in the doorway, fear in their eyes as she sped toward them.

"Nothing?" she posed, not needing an answer.

"No, Madame," Danny answered, shaking her head. "We've closed down service for the night. Whoever is here finishes their time and we're shutting down."

The Madame ceased her strut in the doorway, glancing at them both intently. "This place needs to be locked up like a God damned fortress within the hour. Hell is coming and I can only imagine bringing friends. Come get pistols when you're ready."

They nodded. "Ellis is in your office," Hope informed her. "He wouldn't leave. He…he said it was something that couldn't wait…I tried to tell him…"

The Madame's stomach dropped, and she tried to remain composed. "Fuck him," she whispered to no one, shoving past the girls and sprinting upstairs to her office. "Fuck that stupid British bastard and the horse he fucking rode in on."

Ellis was sitting and waiting for her there, his face stricken as he rose to greet her. "Madame," he addressed her softly, his eyes speaking for him.

"Edward is dead, isn't he?"

Silence ensued before Ellis replied. "Yes."

533

There was no way to control the anger nor the sadness that pained the Madame as she felt what was left of her heart break, overcome with emotions so strong she sensed her body's impulse to cry for the first time in twenty years, and she gulped it down. Slowly, she walked around to the chair behind her desk, clutching it for support as her shaking legs nearly gave way. Unsure of what to do next, Ellis sat back down where he'd been when she entered the office, tolerantly allowing her a minute or so to collect herself. Unconsciously, the Madame went for the bottle in her drawer, pulling the cork out with her teeth and taking a swig, not bothering to search for a glass. Her anger transformed into fury, and then that fury into something more…something beyond rage she hadn't felt in a very long time. Eyeing her closely, Ellis got to his feet and went straight to the drink cart, grabbing them each a glass.

"When?" was all she managed to get out.

"Less than an hour ago. I came straight here when I saw him brought in…he was…he was beaten worse than I've seen in a long time. But it was unmistakable." Ellis placed the glasses in front of her, grappling with how to empathize with a woman who would only see it as a fault and not a virtue.

She filled both of their glasses. "Who brought him in?"

"Three patrolmen."

"Which?"

"Shouldn't…don't you want to tell Thomas? For God's sake, his father is dead. What if they get to him? What then?"

"If they were going to kill Thomas or any of the Turners, they would have done it at once. There's no fucking delays with hits, Samuel. One swoop and out. Now, who were the fucking bastards who brought in Edward's body?"

"All Irish and…all Croker's," Ellis disclosed. "I…Madame, I saw him before it happened. He came in and made a statement. I…I didn't know they were going to kill him and I sat through it to make it clear but…there was nothing else I could have done. It was

534

too late to delay him by the time he got to the Captain." He had a drink of his whiskey. "And the Captain gave the fucking order. I know he did. Edward sat with us for a half hour telling us about his...about Mary. Croker has the Captain and O'Donnell, the one Edward talked to...they're all working for him."

The Madame looked up at him, and put her hand on his. "No blame rests on you, Samuel. He brought this on himself." She picked up her own drink and downed its contents. "Can we use any of them?"

"You know as well as I do once he gets to them, there's no way they can be turned."

"I wasn't going to try and turn any one of those motherfuckers, Samuel."

"What do you mean, then?"

She poured more of the whiskey into her glass. "I think you know what I mean."

Ellis was deep in thought. "If we want to send a message we've got to get O'Donnell. He's the Captain's favorite. We use him, we make it clear we won't be pushed around."

"O'Donnell it is, then. What's the bullshit story they've concocted for Edward's...of the corpse's state?"

"They claim he was found trampled by a runaway carriage," Ellis explained, his words full of resentment. "There's two witnesses swearing they saw it all fucking happen. Body has been sent to the coroner but obviously he's probably under Croker's thumb, or at least under Tammany's like the others."

The Madame reclined into her chair. "So it begins. Bring me O'Donnell. I need him tonight."

Ellis didn't move. "I...I don't know if I..."

"Listen to me," she urged, irritated by his hesitation. "This is not the time for you to be getting a limp dick. I need that asshole, and just him, do you understand? Don't tell a soul what you are doing, and no one will know you had anything to fucking do with it. Take

Claire with you, tell her who that bastard is, and she'll get him to you from there. And tell her she'll make triple tonight."

"Why Claire?"

"Because that girl knows what it takes to get out of a tight spot. That's why."

Ellis finished the drink in his hand. "I'm in the stacks if they catch me. And I won't be any use to you anymore."

The Madame rolled her eyes. "Don't be so fucking dramatic. Do what I ask, and no one will know. You're no fool, Samuel, and I...I trust you."

"I'll have him here just after three," he acquiesced, setting down his glass and turning to go. Halfway to the door he halted mid stride and circled back, heading straight for her. Before she could speak, Ellis lifted her to her feet and kissed her hard for a few seconds. As he let her go, she could see a hint of fear in his face, and the Madame stayed quiet, wanting to remain detached though failing miserably as she found her hand caressing his cheek. "God damn you," he breathed, giving her hand a squeeze. "Don't do anything too stupid while I'm gone."

Ellis set out again and departed from her office, this time without returning. When he was gone, the Madame sank back into her chair, hating herself for the feelings she had for him and the indisputable sorrow she had for Edward. Then, her thoughts drifted to Thomas – his father's death would change him in ways she couldn't yet predict. He spent eight years living out the life the Turners handed to him, wanting to be his father's son and as a consequence, becoming a far better man than he would have in staying behind with her in New York. What worried her was Thomas learning the truth. Sure, he learned from Lucy what happened regarding Mary's treacherous fate, but he still believed her to be dead and that the responsibility rested in his mother's own decision to work for the wrong sort of people. If he ever discovered who Croker was, and that one man alone was responsible for his family's now tragic circumstances, he would be a ticking time bomb – unpredictable, violent, and more than likely, reckless. She couldn't have it. If she lost him, there would be nothing left for her to fight for. The time for revenge would take careful planning and circumstance, both of which a grieving human can never fully comprehend; nonetheless, she would give him the opportunity if he wanted it…that she could not and would not deny him. After what Thomas lost at the hands of Croker and the Hall, it was the least the Madame could offer. Until that day came, she would do what she did best. Prepare and plot.

The sound of footsteps approached her doors, and within seconds Danny and Hope burst through them, their faces troubled. "We're locked down, but Georgie and Louis still aren't back," Hope announced, a little manic. "Where are they? It's been hours!"

"Neither of them have returned?" the Madame pressed.

"Nope, both of them have fucking evaporated into thin air," Danny stated, pouring herself some whiskey into Ellis' leftover glass. "What do you need us to do?"

"Take these," she directed, pulling two pistols from the drawer and sliding them across her desk. "One of you take the back, the other take the front. Claire is leaving with Ellis, so you two, Caroline, and Aggie will have to be our muscle. I don't have any idea where those bastards are, so we are going to have to fucking take care of our own, all right?"

Hope wavered. "I don't…I don't understand where they could be…"

"Take the fucking gun, Hope," Danny demanded. "They could be…gone." She looked to the Madame. "Who was it that got killed?"

"Edward Turner," the Madame told them. "He was murdered, and they're probably coming here next. I've got to get a damned handle on the situation as fast as possible. Just do what I ask."

Danny finished her whiskey and picked up the pistol, grabbing an extra cylinder from the Madame's other drawer. "What's the order on shooting?"

"If anyone who isn't supposed to be in this house tries to get in, you fucking fire that gun until they're dead. Shoot first, ask questions later. And if George or Louis show up, you send them up to me immediately."

Hope and Danny dispersed without delay, with Hope reluctantly taking the other gun. The Madame grabbed for her own No. 3 revolver, fully loading it and then thrusting four extra cylinders into the pockets of her dress for safe measure. She wasn't certain what Croker might have in store for her tonight, and planned to prepare for a massive onslaught if necessary. A small trickle of foreboding loomed in her chest…one she ignored but couldn't suppress. It wasn't a band of Croker's thugs the Madame was afraid of…it was a visit from one man in particular….

And it was in that moment the Madame felt something that hit her like a speeding train.

With a pang of dread she turned, gaping at the giant windows behind her desk, feeling more in danger than she had in most of her life. Her eyes scanned each window. Every one of the panes was locked except the one on the far left side. It was the one she'd left open while smoking her cigar hours earlier when they received Edward's urgent beckoning. She hadn't locked it when she'd left, and had forgotten about it until she felt a small draft breeze against the bottom of her dress. There, on the floor just below it, she saw a hat, shoes, and jacket neatly folded into a pile, scrupulously fashioned by a professional who had done this many times before. He was in here already, and had been waiting somewhere in the room for her to arrive home. Walsh knew where she'd been. He'd known exactly when she arrived back at The Palace as well. He was her dark and deadly shadow, and knew just when she would send the girls out to shut business down, granting him enough time to strike and never be caught.

Still facing the windows, the Madame heard the bar slide against the doors from behind her, bolting them shut from the inside with no way out except the side stairwell, which he would never leave astray. Instead of peering his direction or saying a word to indicate his presence was perceived, the Madame cagily lowered down to her chair, which currently faced the windows, and placed the No. 3 Samuel gave her as a gift years ago into her lap. If Walsh wanted to kill her he would have done it already. Which only meant one thing: something worse was yet to come. The Madame clenched her teeth in preparation and flipped around to face her adversary.

"I was beginning to wonder if you would show," she stated, mustering as much confidence as she possibly could. "If you aren't here to fucking cut my throat, then what do you want?"

Walsh stood inert; the guise he sported was one the Madame recognized hid an agenda that was to be laid out for her. Unarmed, he appeared more dangerous than any man with a gun, knife, or bludgeon. His features she hadn't forgotten despite eight years of trying…the vacant eyes, the glasses, the dark hair, the horrendously scarred arms…but it wasn't until the moment he spoke the Madame realized it was the tenor of his voice that was the feature which truly haunted her.

"My dearest Madame, it has been too long." He strode forward and took a seat directly across from her, in a manner that to any outsider might seem friendly. "I do hope you aren't thinking of screaming."

She shook her head. "If things are as I think they are, then you already know both my guards are unaccounted for, and the only people here who could protect me are four whores who couldn't get into this fucking room if they tried. That is the whole point of the steel frame I had installed."

The smirk grew to a full-toothed smile. "Smart woman. And just so we are clear, I will kill you and anyone else who tries to intervene with our little…exercise."

"Exercise?"

"Oh, you will see."

539

"So what the fuck is it you want, then? I had no part in Lord Turner's antics tonight. In fact, I tried to stop it from happening. If you aren't going to kill me, why in the hell are you here? To physically harm me?"

The awful black eyes behind the small spectacles danced, like he was growing more excited hearing her frustrations. He sneered spitefully at her.

"First thing's first. Revolver on the desk and unload it."

Her hope that he wouldn't detect the gun scorned her, and she made a mistake delaying to comply. Walsh was clearly not there to play games. In the blink of an eye, he drew his own pistol from behind his waist and pointed it directly between her eyes, his left thumb leisurely cocking it. His smile was gone, along with his good humor.

"I will not ask again."

Wordlessly, she picked up the revolver and pushed the latch, spinning the cylinder out. With a few taps, it fell to the desktop and she laid the gun down, her hands resting and folded in her lap. There was no talking her way out of this one. Whatever Walsh had come to do, he would prevail in spite of any fight or distraction she threw his direction. Years ago he made the promise to her they would meet again, and the Madame did what she could to prolong it. No…not with this one. He'd been waiting for this chance a long time, thinking on it, envisioning it over and over. Mercy was something she wouldn't receive, and the Madame could only get through the next twenty minutes and endure the penalties of her past, or she would undoubtedly be dead.

When he was satisfied, Walsh relieved his aim and nestled the gun back on his belt. "Now then, I want you to tell me all you know about your son-in-law's involvement with the letter. Did he share it with his son…Thomas, is his name, am I not mistaken? Or the new Lord Turner…pardon my rudeness."

"Edward Turner was not my son-in-law."

"Come again?"

"Edward…my daughter and Edward Turner never married."

"Are you so sure about that?"

The Madame sighed, remembering her heated discussion with Edward and Louis earlier that day. "Any conversation you may have overheard was Edward speaking out of how he remembers her and thinks of her. I would have known years ago if my own fucking daughter were married to him."

Walsh's eyes lit up. "Would you, now? Mary does not even know she's your child, am I not mistaken?"

"No…no she does not. It was better for…for everyone that way."

"It amazes me how full of secrets your tiny family is!" he chortled. "Still, I hate to be the bearer of bad news, but I have a little something here that just might interest you."

Walsh drew a piece of paper from inside his vest pocket and got to his feet, striding toward the Madame's desk and placing an old, withering paper on her desk. Her eyes scanned the contents: a marriage certificate from the city of New York, dated September of 1856, and signed by four others. A priest whose name she didn't care about, Mary Daugherty, Edward Turner and…her heart nearly stopped. There amongst the others was Louis' mark, a large cursive L, nothing more to it. No…it couldn't be possible…they could not have hidden this from her. Was Walsh playing a trick on her? Was this certificate fraud, as perhaps the letter from earlier that day might have been?

"Anyone could have made one of these and falsified signatures," she shot back, tossing the paper aside. "Just like the fucking letter sent to Edward today. They're all fakes, aren't they? We were at peace, for Christ's sake! It's you, isn't it, you bastard? You're trying to kill us off piece by piece."

"Ahh, I am sorry to say that is not the case. I find it much more… entertaining…to use people's secrets against them. Not unlike yourself, I daresay. No, my dear Madame, this is real, and that also includes the letter from your daughter today. Somehow it slipped right through our fingers, but no matter. No one but you and your French goon now know it exists."

"So what then, you show up here just to tell me my daughter did something against my wishes? As if that's never fucking happened before."

Walsh was amused. "No...no. This was just for you. Croker doesn't even know about it, and out of respect for the deceased and your daughter's...condition...I will see to it no one knows unless I decide it's necessary. Sadly, the reason I am here with you today, Madame, is that I tried to warn you eight years ago. I told you if you lost control of your family and couldn't be in charge of this situation I would be here to remind you failure is unacceptable."

"Failure?" she laughed aloud. "How about the part where you fucking fail to keep her from contacting the outside? We believed she was dead until that letter showed up. If you're going to point a finger, point it the right fucking direction. I couldn't stop Edward."

"Yes, yes you could have. You could have killed him."

Her temper rose. "I gave the order. It wasn't carried out."

"You gave the order with the knowledge that Louis would never and could never complete such a task."

The Madame no longer cared what Walsh might do to her – this wasn't punishment, it was to send a message that she was Croker's pet, and he could do with her what he pleased. It didn't matter that the situation was beyond anyone's control or the effort she had put forward to keep the past at bay. Croker wanted this over with, to have any misgivings in his security eliminated, and the Madame began to worry that Edward's push to find Mary might have been her daughter's death sentence.

And maybe Walsh would kill her anyhow.

"The point, Madame," Walsh went on, starting to pace back and forth. "Is that I do not make these decisions. They are already made and set in stone. I do not negotiate. I only do what is asked. Now, because of our unfortunate time restriction, let's begin our little exercise."

542

After gesturing for her to stay right where she was, Walsh marched over to her room dividers, his steps more urgent than before. For a brief second he disappeared behind them, and then dragged something...or someone...out from behind it. He pulled a girl forcefully by her bound legs, dragging her directly in front of the Madame's desk and left her on the floor whimpering, unable to move as she was tightly roped and gagged. It was Mae, one of her newer girls who had only just turned seventeen two weeks prior. Tears streamed down her face as she looked to the Madame for reassurance, her eyes filled with fright.

The Madame moved to get up, but was stopped by Walsh raising a finger for her to go no further. "Sit. Back. Down. We are just beginning."

He hoisted Mae up so she sat on the floor against the loveseat, her long brown hair damp around her face from crying into it. Thenceforth, Walsh proceeded back to the room dividers and, to the Madame's horror, drug out another one of her girls by her scalp, this one struggling fiercely. It was Aggie, a beautiful negro girl she'd found in Virginia who wanted to get out of the South. With the heart of a lion, Aggie tried to fight back, the ropes visibly tearing into her skin. Unlike Mae, her eyes were filled with indignation, and Walsh threw Aggie on the ground next to Mae, her breath heavy from her continuous attempts to break free of her bindings. The Madame understood after a few seconds why he'd picked them – they were her two newest, and already two of her highest earning, and he wanted to strike at her not just to harm her financially, but also to hurt her pride. The Madame always took care of her own, to an extreme that made her girls loyal to a fault, done purposefully so that they would never betray her or anything that went on at The Palace. These two would have brought her in a fortune in the years to come, and they would never have faltered. Hardly able to believe what she was seeing, the probability that either of the girls would make it out alive was minimal at best.

543

"All right, everyone, the time for action has come." Walsh clapped his hands together lightheartedly and took out his gun once more, aiming again at the Madame and unsheathing a blade from his boot. "In front of you sit your two most recent additions, and might I daresay your finest yet, but they are both quite different from one another. One must die for your disobedience, and you will choose which one." Mae let out a slight squeak and twisted fretfully, whereas Aggie simply stared at the Madame, waiting for an answer.

The Madame needed to stall. She had to. If she could stall him another five or six minutes, someone might come.

"If one of them must die, why the theatrics? Why didn't you just bring one up here and kill her, rather than making me choose?" The Madame wished she could do something…anything to signal someone. Hope and Danny would notice Aggie was missing while trying to find her to do sweeps of The Palace. Alas, with Louis and George missing, if any of the girls tried to help her it would be a bloodbath. There was no way to save them unless Louis was still alive and decided to come home to do his fucking job.

"Ahhh forgive me, I was hoping you might ask. There is a reason this is your penance, Madame. Not only will you choose which one will die, but you will also be performing the execution."

The Madame felt bile rise in her throat. "You can't fucking make me kill one of my girls, you sick son of a bitch."

"Like I said before, there are no negotiations. You will pick and kill one, or I will kill both the girls, you, and your darling, devious little Esther, just for the irritation." He set the knife down on the desk in front of her.

This was too much for her to stomach. "Why not just kill me? If I am the one to be punished, just fucking kill me."

Walsh's grin reemerged. "Because Croker still needs you, Madame. When he doesn't, I will happily carry out your execution personally. But until then…" his voice trailed off, his eyes drifting toward the knife. "Stalling isn't in your favor, Madame."

544

She understood there was no other option at her disposal. Taking her own life would benefit none of them. Attacking Walsh would get the three of them killed, and possibly Esther. Screaming was a coward's way of saying they couldn't handle the game, and like the previous option, sacrificing their lives for nothing. Running The Palace had never been an easy business, and it had definitively hardened her over the passing years. She'd done worse…she'd done much worse…but gazing directly into the eyes of an innocent and sending them onto the next life was never something she liked. It was what kept her up almost every night, lost in the haze of the whiskey.

As she went to reach for her revolver, Walsh interrupted her. "No…no guns. You will use that blade sitting in front of you." Motioning toward the knife, he signaled for her to pick it up. When the woven gripped handle was clenched between her fingers, Walsh rescinded a few feet, his gun continuing to point toward her. "You have less than two minutes."

There was no reservation over whom she would save, and whom she would kill. Mae, though young and beautiful, was too fragile of heart to live through a circumstance like this one and not suffer long-term mental effects. Aggie was her only negro. She lived on a plantation most of her young life, a slave despite her given freedom, and was the toughest bitch she had aside from Danny. There was never a night when men came in and didn't want Aggie, though the Madame respectably gave her a certain level of discretion with which customers she took on. Sadly, Mae was replaceable…and the Madame wasn't so certain Aggie was. She took a step forward to Aggie, whose demeanor indicated she expected to be the one chosen to die. Closing her eyes, the Madame shook her head, and cut Aggie's bindings. Mae screamed from behind her gag.

The Madame turned to her, trying to keep a serene face. "Darling, please be quiet. I am sorry. You know I don't want to do this. Please hold still and it will all be over soon. Please."

Mae did no such thing, thrashing back and forth though her

ropes would not break. The Madame gestured to Aggie, who knew instinctively what to do. She scooted toward Mae and pulled the girl into her lap, wrapping her arms around her tenderly, as if to sooth her into passivity. Mae resisted for a few more seconds until her despair was fully realized, and she broke down into sobs. Aggie leaned forward and whispered something into her ear, stroking Mae's hair, which seemed to calm the panic into acceptance.

"Mae, I am going to do the throat," the Madame said softly, kneeling down in front of her. "I will do it quick, I promise there will be little pain." She held the knife just above the jugular at her neck, and her hand did not shake. With one last look into Mae's eyes, the Madame readied. "I am so sorry, Mae. God is waiting for you, darling." Mae nodded slowly, tears streaming down her face, and her eyes closed tight. With one swift slice, the undertaking was finished, and it did not take long for Mae to leave them. Aggie devotedly held her until the bitter end, her own dress soaking through in blood, not wanting to abandon Mae in her final moments.

The Madame stared at Aggie, whose stoic nature through the trauma filled the Madame with gratitude. However, before the Madame could process another thought, a gunshot blasted in her right eardrum, and she fell to the ground in agony. Everything was a blur, and the only thing she could hear was the high-pitched ringing from the explosion far too near to her head. Impulsively, the Madame held her hand to her ear to check for blood dripping, and said a prayer of thanks when it came back clean. Blinking hard a few times to try and focus, she straightened up, and what she saw made her body go cold. There lay Aggie shot dead in the chest, with Mae's lifeless body still in her comforting arms.

"Wh-what have you done?!" she roared, scrambling to her feet. "I did exactly what you fucking asked me to! Aggie didn't need to fucking die!"

Walsh was wiping the barrel of his gun on his sleeve. "Yes she did. My intention from the start was to kill them both."

Her hands clenched into fists. "You fucking bastard." The Madame picked the knife up off the ground and advanced Walsh's direction. "I should fucking gut you where you stand!"

"Ah, ah, ah!" he sang, cocking his gun again and forcing her to halt. "I do not think so. And if you come any closer, I will have no problem putting a hole through your chest too, Madame. I know how skilled you are with knives, but I can shoot faster than you can throw."

As a measure of defiance, the Madame threw the blade at his feet, and it struck into the ground less than an inch from the toe of his boot. "I swear to you I'll see to it someday that I cut your throat. And then you can fucking rot in hell."

"Someday, perhaps, my dear Madame, but not today or any time in the near future. Just remember, the next time you don't do what is requested, I will kill all of your girls in front of you one by one, slowly…painfully…and save you for last. And don't think I can't. With the resources Mr. Croker provides, anything is possible. Especially for me."

A clamoring was felt through the floor, rushing up the main stairs and in course of the Madame's office. She glared at Walsh, staying where she was, poised for whatever fastidiously planned words he wanted to part with.

Annoyed at being cut short, he sighed heavily. "I believe that is my cue to leave you. I am just the messenger, Madame, and I think now you finally see what we are capable of in our organization. Make sure the letter has only stayed between you, Edward, and Louis. If it hasn't, you will take care of it, or I will be seeing you again real soon. Good day, Madame."

Somehow, the moment Walsh whipped around to make his way toward the window every candle burning went out in an instant. The Madame was left in utter darkness, and any effort in chase was useless. Her knees gave out, and she tumbled down into nothingness, no longer giving a damn of who might possibly be coming to her aid. They were too late for anything that mattered. Mae was dead…Aggie was dead…how was she to keep order if any rat bastard could stroll in off the street and kill two of her girls without contest? She couldn't…control would be lost…

Control would be lost.

The thought sank into her brain, sending the Madame crawling toward the door on hands and knees. No one could know but Louis…and if Louis wasn't at her door, she would handle it herself. Propping her back against the frame, the Madame slid to stand, balancing the weight in her legs as she tried to be steady while still unable to see. A repeated banging on her doors ensued, and she could make out the voices of Danny and Hope desperately searching for Mae and Aggie, and then came George, claiming he and Louis barely made it back alive and needed to meet with her …the news was urgent…pressing. And then came the pound of Louis' fist against the door, so hard it nearly knocked the Madame back onto the floor.

"Stop!" she yelled at the top of her lungs, feeling for the bolt holding the door closed. "Send Louis in, and only Louis! The rest of you wait outside until I fucking say so!" Using all the strength she had, the Madame pushed hard and released the lock, then adjusted her posture. With a small tug, the door cracked open and light poured in, making her shy away for a second or two before she could confront the others.

"Louis, inside and find a light," she mumbled, blinking her eyes to get a glimpse of the other three. They stood there, petrified when she came into view. At first she didn't notice, but then she saw why: the Madame, like the dead girls on her office floor, was covered in blood. Louis didn't wait, pushing past the others and shoving his way inside. He slammed the door closed, the thrust yanking the Madame against the wall with her hand still hanging on the knob.

"Jesus, a little more fucking courtesy!" she snapped, though without a trace of candlelight she had no idea where he'd gone in the black abyss.

The hiss of a match caught her attention, and a stream of light blared through the dark as Louis lit a few of the candles around the room hastily. He didn't say a word, only proceeded to illuminate the whole scene to the best of his abilities, centering his attention on the actual problem. When he spotted Aggie and Mae lying together on the ground, his countenance transformed from being perplexed to outraged, and he circled around to face the Madame with a mystified look, wanting to hear an explanation.

The Madame, too, wanted a God damned explanation. "Walsh," she told him. "Bastard snuck in when I was gone, made me kill Mae, then he killed Aggie. I had no chance to fight back…no fucking chance. The bigger question is, where the fuck were you, Louis?" she demanded, her voice was laden with stress. "Where were you when these girls and I needed you?!"

Louis was frozen, not clear on how to answer her demands. It was the first time he had ever truly let her down, and the Madame couldn't afford to have it happen again.

"You are a fucking weak link in the chain, Louis, and it's because your allegiances have never rested solely with me. Deceit gets people killed. And your untrustworthiness almost got me killed, and now has two of my fucking girls dead on my fucking floor!"

"It won't happen again," he said softly. "I swear on my life it won't happen again." With his eyes downcast, Louis snatched the bottle of whiskey from her drink cart and walked back toward her. He took a swig from the bottle as he lowered down into the loveseat, still avoiding her gaze. The Madame had never seen him like this, and didn't know quite what to say. So she did what she did best – poured herself a glass of her own and went behind her desk where she belonged.

"Edward knocked me unconscious," he confessed to her after a moment. "I let him. I couldn't kill him, even though a small part of me knew I should. When I came to, the Cat was there. He told me…he told me Eddie was dead. And that they were coming to get you next. George and I made it back as fast as we could…and I can see now that it wasn't fast enough."

"No, it fucking wasn't," she snapped, taking a sip of her drink, her eyes staying on the bodies across the room. "Two are dead, Louis. Two of my best. You let Edward march to his own death, and as a result, Mary will most likely not make it through the night either. When I give you an order, you fucking do it for a reason."

Louis nodded. "I know, Madame. I know I failed you. I let my personal sentiments get in the way. And like I said, it won't happen again. I swear to you. Or you can shoot me dead."

"What in God's name was the Cat doing there? I thought he was dead."

"He's apparently working for Croker, Madame."

The room went quiet. With Edward gone, Louis would be true to his word, though her anger with him would not subside. What shockingly was sitting on her nerve was not Walsh, not Edward, not even Aggie and Mae…death was something she had dealt with her entire life on earth. It was that Louis had sat on information for almost three decades…information that would have changed the lives of everyone she knew.

"Why didn't you tell me they were married, Louis?"

He frowned at her, as if he knew it was coming, but his reaction surprised her. "Why didn't you tell her she was your daughter, Madame?"

"I want you to clarify to me how the fuck you kept a secret like this from me for twenty-seven years," she went on, ignoring his remarks.

Louis rested against the sofa, taking another drink. "Because I made a promise to her. And to Edward. And it was before I permanently signed on at The Palace."

"Just what the hell is that supposed to mean?"

"It means, this happened before you officially hired me."

The Madame began pieced together Louis' implications. "You… you started working for me that summer…"

550

"Yes."

"When Mary was already seeing Edward…"

"Yes."

She was flabbergasted at how she hadn't seen it sooner. "I want you to tell me everything from start to finish."

It took Louis forty-five minutes to get through his story, and when he was finished, the Madame could only laugh at her own blindness. She imagined his allegiance to the Turners was based on little merit, and it became plain she had severely misjudged Louis and his morality. In an odd way, she and Louis were one in the same, doing everything in their power to protect the few they really cared for without sinking their own ships, and it amazed the Madame their partnership went on this long with so much unsaid. A part of her was furious with him, yet also impressed he kept his past buried, especially now, with everything that made him who and what he was hanging in the balance. Time would be the only thing to heal their relationship, and the facts were so ironic it was almost comical. They actually were all tied together, in one way or another.

"So, what is the plan?" Louis pressed. "We don't have much time now and we've got to get rid of these bodies."

She couldn't agree more. "Get George and get them out of here. Make sure none of the girls see or they will fucking lose their minds. Then get one of them up here to clean all the damned blood…fucking Egyptian carpet is ruined beyond repair…"

"Then what?"

The mischievous smirk formed on her face. "We will be having our own visitor in a few hours. Send Caroline to deliver a note to Seamus Murphy. Tell him…tell him we need to have a peace meeting in the morning."

"A peace meeting?" There was indignation in Louis' tone.

"Yes. A peace meeting. To tell them we surrender, but also to send our own message that we won't be fucked with." She finished the last of her whiskey and slammed the glass against her desk. "Yesterday was the battle with the Hiltmores was finally put to rest. To-day, our God damned war begins."

"What do we need to do?"

"We do what we've been preparing for all these years. Let's start building the army."

Just after eight in the morning, Seamus Murphy strode into The Palace, still pissed from drinking at the bar the entire night and wondering what in the hell the head whore could want this early from him. Croker warned him she might be up to something after the organization took out Edward Turner yesterday; on the other hand, Croker promised there was nothing more to sweat, and that if anything the dumb bitch would probably be begging for forgiveness. As he strolled through the front doors of The Palace, cracking his neck left and then right, something didn't feel right to Seamus. It seemed too easy a win for them, and with the Madame, Seamus knew nothing came easy. She was a fucking crazy bitch, and that was on a good day.

The giant Frog eyed him closely and set off up the steps two paces ahead of Seamus. This woman was a fucking riot. Loved to be treated like royalty even though she herself was considered the filth of society. Peering around, Seamus couldn't help but notice no girls were anywhere to be seen, and he made the assumption they were sleeping at that early of an hour. No fucking matter. He'd be out of there in ten minutes, report to Croker, and go sleep of his own mind-splitting hangover.

When they reached the top of the stairs, the goon escorted him to the doors of the Madame's office and then casually pushed them open. Seamus sauntered inside and then stopped dead when he saw the manner in which he was being received. Before he could turn and get out, the Frog had a gun at the back of his his head, holding Seamus in place. The Madame sat patiently at her desk, and on either side of her stood one of her whores armed with shotguns aiming right at him. Standing behind her chair was another one of her bodyguard bastards, not as big as the Frog but damned well close enough, and in his hands was a revolver resting lightly with his arms crossed over his chest. Seamus nearly peed on himself, and cursed aloud, raising his hands into the air. Croker sent him right into a fucking trap. He'd be lucky to get out in one piece. Just then, the Madame waved them closer, and the bastard with a gun at Seamus' head lead him to the vacant chair directly in front of her desk.

"What's with the fucking hostility?" he exclaimed. "If I knew you were calling me here for this brazen bullshit, I wouldn't have come at all!"

The Madame's expression was ice. "My apologies, Mr. Murphy, it has been a long night for us," she said, motioning for the girls to lower their weapons. The dark haired girl on the right was unwilling to obey, though after a few seconds of suspension, did as she was ordered, glowering at Seamus. He could feel the heat of her anger from across the room, and his palms started to sweat. He should have listened to his fucking gut. Something wasn't right. The head whore was too calm.

"Well, what exactly is it you want to discuss so early, Madame?"

"I just have a small delivery for Mr. Croker," she responded politely. "One I am sure he will want right away. George? Would you be so kind?"

The guard behind her nodded and marched to Seamus' right, disappearing through a side door and out of the office. "As I said before, Seamus, it was a long night for us," the Madame carried on, drawing his attention back to her. "I lost two of my girls and an old friend in a terrible, terrible accident. We have been mourning our losses with heavy hearts. However, I think I can say with some certainty, these nights from here on out will come to an end."

Seamus shifted nervously. "Well, I think Mr. Croker will be glad to hear it. We both know he wants a solid partnership with you Madame. One based on trust and…um…goodwill I suppose."

"I couldn't agree more, Mr. Murphy. And please tell Mr. Croker that is exactly the aim of our little meeting. Ah, here is George!"

At first, Seamus couldn't believe what he was seeing. George grunted as he hobbled in, carrying what Seamus knew was a God damned corpse hoisted over his shoulder. The goon ambled over until he was not two feet from Seamus and threw the body on the ground, the sound echoing loudly and making him jump in his seat. George leaned over and pulled back the bloodied sheet covering the body, and Seamus let out a small yelp. What he saw horrified him. He was in over his head, and he should have never come alone. They should have known better with her. There was always a trick, always a turn of events…and without anybody else he had no way to gain any ground for Croker.

Fucking Sergeant O'Donnell, the poor bastard that tipped off Croker about the Brit's search for Mary, lay at his feet…he was sliced up…badly…worse than Seamus had ever seen anyone done in, and it made his stomach turn. The fuckers must have tortured him for hours, and the look on his dying face was one of absolute agony. How had they found him? Seamus tried to stand, but the Frog was right behind him and firmly sat him back in the chair, holding him there by his shoulders. This was a mistake, a big fucking mistake…

The Madame got to her feet and made her way around the desk casually, her face full of malevolence. "Such a shame, don't you think, Mr. Murphy?" she asked, her air aloof. He tried to get up once more and found the steel grip on his shoulders was unbreakable. The Madame strode to him and sat down on his lap, straddling Seamus with her legs and pulling out a knife from a hidden holster under her skirt, which she held candidly up to his throat.

"Deliver this message. For every life he takes from me, I will take one in turn. This son of the bitch on the floor is for Edward, and for my two girls, the two bastard Micks guarding O'Donnell are gutted and lying outside the back of the Hall for Croker to clean up. I am not to be fucked with or scared into submission. We do it on our own terms, or we don't do this at all." The blade pierced his skin slightly, and Seamus felt a trickle of blood run down his neck. If he moved an inch, he'd bleed out and to his death in seconds.

"Do I make myself clear, Mr. Murphy? Do you think you can convince Croker to back down?"

"Y-y-yes…yes I can…" Seamus mumbled through clenched teeth.

"You will emphasize this is a partnership of equality, not one he will bully me and this enterprise into?"

"Yes…of course, Madame…equal footing!"

"Good. Because if you don't, I'll make sure you're the one who's fucking next. And I can promise you by the time I am finished, you'll be begging me to die."

XIX.

Thomas' initial surprise at seeing Detective Ellis at William's doorstep was quickly overrun by grief. Edward had been missing most of the night, and the entire household anxiously waited up with the hopes he might stumble in and put their worries at bay. They weren't so lucky. William and Lucy only just retired to their bedroom about a half hour before the Detective's arrival, and Esther slept soundly on the sofa by the fireplace after Thomas dismissed the staff for the morning, telling them they earned some much needed time off in his father's usual fashion. It took a few moments to realize what the presence of Detective Ellis at his home truly meant, and as he listened to the policeman's account, Thomas was wracked with the news he would never see his father again.

Detective Ellis clarified what eyewitness accounts reported to police in the early hours of that morning: a drunk man at the helm of a coach had fallen off, spooking the horses he was driving and thus causing them to take off into an overcrowded street. Patrolmen claimed the scene was a massacre, four having died on impact and many more injured. Ellis went on, stating the story would absolutely make the front page of the newsstands that morning, and out of his respect for Thomas and his family, he wanted to get to them first.

Thomas could barely comprehend the words coming out of the Detective's mouth. His father was the integral heart and soul of their family, tying them together and without him…without him, Thomas wasn't sure what to do next.

As they stood on the stoop, Thomas battled to keep his emotions in check. "Thank you, Detective Ellis, for taking the time to see us yourself. I know you are a busy man, and it is greatly appreciated."

"Please, call me Samuel."

Thomas nodded, a lump rising in his throat. "I can't…I can't believe it. You are positive it's him?"

"I hate to say it, but yes. I saw the coroner personally."

"Fuck…" Thomas mumbled. "He didn't…suffer, did he?"

"No. We believe his death was relatively instantaneous." Detective Ellis rested a hand on Thomas' shoulder, his eyes filled with sadness. "I am so sorry for your loss, Thomas. Things like this… they're out of our hands. Shit happens and sometimes we just have to tolerate life's punches."

Thomas shook his head, tears forming. "My father was the best thing that ever happened to me," he choked, embarrassed at his fragility. "I only wish I could have told him one more time…" His voice faded out before he could finish.

"He knew, Thomas," Ellis reassured him. "He was a good man. One of the best I've ever met." Gradually, Ellis released his grip, his tone quieter. "Do you…do you want me to tell the rest of your family? I can't imagine it will be easy for you to do this on your own."

"No…no I will," Thomas replied. "They should hear it from me."

"Do what you think is best," he concurred wholeheartedly. "Now…I hate bringing this up but…well, you know you are the next of kin. You will need to come to the station and identify him when you feel up to it. Then, funeral arrangements are entirely up to you, though you're required to have him out of the morgue within the week."

"When do I need to go?"

"This afternoon, I would suggest, or straightaway tomorrow morning. The longer you wait, the harder it will be to do this. And I'll be there to assist you."

Thomas let out a shaky exhale. "I will be by this afternoon," he pledged, holding his hand out to shake Ellis'. "Thank you again, Samuel."

"Of course."

A few seconds of silence followed until Thomas spoke again. "Do you realize this is the second time we've had this conversation?"

Ellis' face fell. "I do. And I wish you knew how sorry I was to be the one to tell you. On both accounts." His eyes on the ground, Ellis turned around to take his leave.

"Does she know yet?"

Ellis paused. "I came to you right away. Would you like to be the one to tell her?"

"Not in the slightest, if you don't mind."

Ellis understood, and descended down the stoop. "I'll pay her a visit for you then. Anything else I ought to pass along?"

"Just my respects. Good day, Samuel."

"Good day, Lord Turner."

The last of the Detective's words hit Thomas so hard, he thought he'd taken a bullet.

Esther was still on the couch where Thomas had left her, sleeping quietly, her face relaxed and at peace. Resuming the spot he'd been in when he saw Ellis approach, Thomas sat down at her feet. He was struggling to fully comprehend what had just occurred. Not one of the Turners would take this lightly. Edward dying in such a startling way would throw them into a spin, and the plans they made together as a family were gone in a flash. Thomas watched

Esther, dreaming, happy in a far off place, and he wished he could be there with her…that the last fifteen minutes were some bizarre nightmare he would wake from. Nearly losing Esther was a scare too close for comfort, and in that moment, Thomas realized how much he loved her, and didn't ever want to live without her again. At his father's suggestion, Thomas even bought a ring, considering the option of dragging her back to England for the fall and winter to see Amberleigh, and return to New York next spring. The ring currently was nestled in Thomas' vest pocket, as he'd been waiting for the right time to ask.

"Tommy?" came Esther's distant voice to his right. He was completely lost in thought, his gaze somewhere in the flames of the fire, and tried to smile when he saw she was awake.

He took her hand in his. "Hi, Es."

"Who was that at the door?" she asked sleepily, propping herself upright.

"It was Detective Ellis."

"What in the world was Detective Ellis doing here?" she beseeched him, more alert.

"Es, I've got to tell you something…Christ…" Thomas felt the lump swelling in his throat again, "My father's…dead."

Esther's eyes grew wide. "He's…he's dead?" she cried. "How is that possible?!"

"It was an accident," he told her, trying to stick with the facts and keep from breaking down. "Carriage accident. He's one of four dead. It happened last night…must have been when he went out without us. I don't know, it's just so…insane…I just can't wrap my head around it…"

Esther leaned forward and wrapped her arms around him. "Thomas…I am so…so sorry…"

"I am, too." He felt a tear fall off his cheek.

They stayed that way for what felt like hours, until at last Esther broke the silence. "Your father lived a great life," Esther said,

560

holding him tighter. "And I think the happiest years for him were the ones he spent with you."

"I just wish I could have known…seen him one last time and told him how much he meant to me…how much all of this meant to me…"

Esther pulled back so they were face to face. "Thomas, Edward loved you. He knew how thankful you were to have him and he was beyond proud of you. It was written all over his face every time he even looked at you."

"I am beginning to feel like the curse of the Turner family is the incessant losses we sustain," he confided. "It's really…well, honestly it's pretty damn frightening when you think about it. We lost my mother, Edward lost his entire family…and it makes me worry if I'm not careful I might lose you, too."

"You will never lose me," Esther conveyed. "Even if everything went up in flames, you know I would do anything for you, Thomas."

He smiled and kissed her forehead, taking her hands in his. "The same goes for me."

Esther let him sit for a quarter of an hour in contemplation, and Thomas was thankful she understood him well enough to give him space to think; however, no matter what he tried to do to distract the notion, Thomas kept coming back to the same issue at hand.

"Es, how in the world am I going to break this to Lucy and William? I can barely hold myself together…they are going to be destroyed by this."

"I really don't know," she admitted. "But the best thing you can do is just get it over with so you three can deal with this together."

"They've just gone to bed. I should have a few hours before they're—"

At that second, William paced into the room to join them, wearing a robe over his nightclothes. "Couldn't sleep a bloody wink. Any word from Eddie yet? Wonder what in God's name he got into last night." When he sat in an armchair beside them, William finally saw both of their expressions, and stopped with the paper in his hands half unraveled.

"Oh no...Christ...don't tell me..."

"William–" Thomas started and then was cut off by William, who held up a hand to silence him, grasping the depth of the situation.

"Eddie's...Eddie's dead, isn't he?"

Thomas didn't know what to say, and clearly Esther didn't either – they were dumbfounded at how to respond to a confrontation neither was prepared for. William took their lack of response as affirmation and bit his lower lip hard.

"Tell me how," he demanded, setting the paper aside.

"It was a carriage accident," Esther reiterated. "He was one of four who died, according to Detective Ellis, who was here not too long ago."

William gaped at Thomas, his eyes watering uncontrollably, "Tommy...I can't...I can't believe this..."

"I know he meant the world to you, William," Thomas uttered, holding back a sob at seeing William so devastated. "He meant the world to me, too."

"He meant the world to all of us," William corrected him, getting to his feet and walking toward the fireplace. "Bloody hell... bloody fucking hell. What am I going to tell Lucy? This will...it will crush her..."

"I don't know, William, I didn't even know how to tell you, for God's sake. The Detective was here, and then he was gone, and now here we are, talking about my father in past tense..."

William punched the wall with his fist, breaking a hole in it as his knuckles cut and bled, though he didn't seem to give a damn in the slightest. Without another word, he strode out of the room, leaving Esther and Thomas and heading the direction of the whiskey in his study. Before either could say anything, they heard a knock at the front door, and speedily Thomas wiped his eyes and rose to see whom it could possibly be at such an hour.

Swinging the door open, Thomas found it was a young maid. "Good morning," he greeted unenthusiastically. "How can I help you?"

The maid was stunned. "Excuse me, Mr. Turner, why on earth are you answering your own door?"

Thomas exhaled loudly, annoyed. "It's not worth going into. What can I do for you, miss?"

"Is Miss Esther here?"

"Yes, Laura," Esther answered, who stood directly behind Thomas. "What is it?"

Laura's cheeks flushed pink. "I am so sorry to disturb you, but Mrs. Adams insisted I find you as fast as I could. She is very distraught, Miss Esther, and could use your consolation. Some more news has come about this morning regarding her parents."

Esther looked to Thomas, who nodded his approval of her departure. "All right. Tell Celeste I will arrive after I clean myself up a bit."

"Thank you, Miss Esther." Laura took a slight curtsey and ran off down the street. Just as Thomas went to close the door, he spotted Louis across the road, smoking a cigarette though notably not his typically poised self, and Thomas sensed he was waiting for him... and that he, too, must have heard about Edward.

"Go on in, Es, I'll be right back."

She was worried. "Where are you going?"

Thomas tipped his head Louis' way and, once Esther caught a glimpse of their mutual friend, dutifully left him to go find William. Skipping down the steps, Thomas jogged over to Louis, whose slightly haggard appearance made Thomas wonder what his friend's own night must have been like, or if the news of his father took that large of a toll on him. Not bothering with small talk, Louis held out a cigarette for him, which Thomas took willingly.

Thomas sparked the match and lit the tobacco, not realizing how much he needed it until that very second. "You know, then?"

Louis couldn't look at him. "I'm sorry, Tommy. I am so sorry."
He was crying, unabashed, and then Thomas felt himself crying too.

"Louis it…it was an accident…right?"

"As far as I can tell, yes."

"God damn him," Thomas blurted out angrily. "What the fuck
was he doing out by himself? I should have been with him!"

"What, and gotten killed alongside him?" Louis countered
through frustrated tears. "It was a fucking accident, Tommy. It's
nobody's fault, and especially not his."

It was the first time since Thomas' return Louis reprimanded
him, and rather than fight, Thomas recoiled sullenly. "I'm officially an orphan now."

"You should feel privileged to have had the time you did with
your parents. Most people your age haven't seen theirs since they
were young."

"Are you here to tell me I'm an ungrateful bastard or are you
here for a reason, Louis?" Thomas barked. "I just lost my father.
Forgive me if I'm upset over that."

"I'm here to tell you, Tommy, that you have shoes to fill." Louis
dropped his cigarette to the ground and put it out, then lit another.
"I'm envious because I wish I had more time with those I loved, the
way you did. I don't want you to be like your father and waste what
time and relationships you do have."

"Like with the Madame? Is that what is going on here? Did
she sent you to remind me I'm still hers? Or is this one of those offhand visits where you are here on 'your own terms,' as you put it?"

Louis did not try to hide the fact that he didn't appreciate Thomas' sarcasm. "Watch your mouth, Thomas. You may not see it now
but she would do anything to make you happy. She wants you to
come by and see her and give her condolences, that's all."

"For God's sake, Louis, it's only been a few hours!" Thomas
yelled. "She can do whatever the hell she wants with her condolences. It won't bring him back!"

Before Thomas could move, Louis was inches from him, unswervingly in his face. "You're not the only fucking person who lost someone last night, Thomas. Quit acting like a pampered rich asshole throwing a temper tantrum because life hasn't turned out the way you wanted!"

Thomas was unmoving, hurt and taken aback. "He was my father, Louis…"

"Yes, and long before he was your father, he was my friend."

"Friend? Because he had you protecting his family? That's your job, Louis. That doesn't qualify you, or the Madame, as my family."

Louis put his cigarette out on the tree next to them. "I know it's just your grief talking, but if your father heard you speaking right now, he would be ashamed of you."

"Fuck you. You didn't know my father."

Louis shook his head. "No, Thomas…on the contrary, you didn't know your father."

He spun around and took off through the park. "Oh, and be sure to tell Esther the Madame said it's done, and the rest will soon follow!" he shouted back, not bothering to turn around.

Thomas finished his cigarette, fuming as he watched Louis stroll off and away from him. The only thing Louis and Madame had ever brought Thomas in his years in New York was trouble – his real family, the people he knew best and who truly loved him sat in William's house twenty yards away, regardless of whatever bullshit Louis tried to feed him. He was wrong – if Edward really believed anyone at The Palace was his family, he would have never made him promise to live in England when the time came. Louis could say whatever he wanted…Thomas refused to let it get a rise out of him. It was her…all her…and Louis was just the God damned mouthpiece. He decided then and there he wouldn't allow them to ruin his father's memory – he would celebrate it the way Edward would have wanted: starting a life new at home in England, with the woman he loved and the little family he had left.

When the tobacco burned out, Thomas sauntered home, finding

Esther with a tray of coffee in the dining room, snacking on bread and cheese. "Everything all right with Louis?"

"It's fine," he replied, sitting down next to her, "Are you heading to see Celeste soon?"

"After I eat something, have a whiskey, and make sure you're all right. You, Lucy, and William come first, as far as I'm concerned. I can at least thank the Madame for helping me see the facts. I can't save Celeste. But I can save myself. And I'm tired of being scared."

This was music to Thomas' ears. "You don't feel a need to stay with her?"

"As of this morning, and after everything that's happened, no I do not," Esther went on. "She will move to Virginia with the Adams family and have her baby. A small part of me wanted revenge... wanted to see her husband die. I...Christ, Thomas, I even wanted to do it. But after your father being taken from us...all morning I've been thinking about it and that desire just completely vanished. I hate Timothy with every fiber of my being. I can't...it's...it's not for me to say if he lives or dies. I've got to trust it will work out and he'll get his in the end."

Thomas stared at her. "Do you love me, Es?"

Plopping a piece of cheese in her mouth, she rotated toward him. "You know I do."

Thomas reached into his vest pocket. "I know this is a lot. But... it's what he would have wanted." Slowly, Thomas lowered down to one knee in front of her, and from her face, Esther grasped what exactly was happening. "He wanted me to move back, to start my family in England and get out of this city. What better way to celebrate who my father was than with doing the one thing he wanted most from me?"

Thomas pulled out the ring and took Esther's left hand in his, sliding the ring onto her finger. "Es, will you marry me? Come back to England with me and we can begin again, the way Edward would have wanted it?"

Esther grinned, nodding her head up and down. "Yes...I...I will!"

Thomas lurched forward and kissed her hard, drawing her in close. Feeling the passion escalate rapidly, they pressed harder and harder into one another, until Thomas made them stop, laughing.

"Later," he told her, pulling her in close and causing her to laugh as well. "You're happy with this? You're sure?"

"Of course I'm fucking sure!" she squealed, her hand flying to cover her mouth the second the words left it. "Shit, I'm sorry," she mumbled. "I am just so...oh my God. I don't know what to say!"

Thomas beamed. "You already said the only thing that matters to me."

Gently his hand caressed her face, and Thomas felt in that moment everything made sense. This was what Edward wanted. The only thing he ever wanted from his son. And in his death, Thomas resolved that this was what was right. These last few months, Thomas was so consumed with building their empire and their legacy, he had completely brushed aside what mattered most to those around him, and what should have always mattered most to him.

Esther held out her hand and stared at the ring, sparkling on her finger. "Thomas...this ring is..."

"Fitting?" he suggested.

"Outrageous!" she declared. "I just...I don't know. Are you sure this is what you want? This is so much so fast...I don't want you doing this because of your father's wishes and regretting it later."

"Don't worry. I wouldn't have bought the ring in the first place if I didn't plan on proposing in the near future."

Esther smiled again, then grew solemn once more. "What time are you going to the precinct to...to see him?"

"In a few hours. I wanted to talk things over with William first...I just need to think of what to say and...well...I just need to get it over with."

"I understand," she stated, touching his cheek. "Do you need me to do anything?"

"Go see Celeste. Tell her about our plans, and be careful. You know my rule though."

"If he's there, I come home right away."

Thomas nodded and stood. "I'm going to go find some whiskey for me and William. You should go dress so we can have time together later."

"I look forward to it," she said flirtatiously, rising to leave the room and head upstairs, when Thomas remembered Louis' remark.

"Oh, Es I almost forgot. Louis told me to tell you the Madame said…it was done and the rest will soon follow? I have no idea what it means, and I'm sure you don't either."

Esther halted where she was. "He said it…it was done?"

"Yeah." Thomas studied her closely. "Do you know what he means?"

"I…"

Thomas saw her face had lost all color – she was terrible at lying. "You do know, don't you?"

Her eyes found his. "I do. Just let this go, please Thomas," Esther begged. "I want to start over, just like you do. I love you. When we leave New York, we leave this whole past behind us. Can you do that for me?"

"Does this have to do with Adams?" he questioned. "Is she going to kill him?"

"Do you really want to know the answer to that?"

"Yes."

"Then yes."

Flustered, he spun away from her: he had asked the Madame to do it. His brain told him to be angry with Esther for being involved with this scheme any further, but on the other hand, his heart knew her better, and understood why she felt she had to be. That bastard attacked her, violated her, threatened her, and made her live on as if nothing were wrong. An excuse of a drunken mistake was not something that sat lightly with Thomas. Esther was right – it didn't matter anymore. They'd be gone soon enough.

"Six feet under is where he belongs," Thomas admitted. "Please just…make this it. We need to get out of this mess, you and I."

"I will do what I can. I love you, Thomas. Please trust me, I wouldn't jeopardize what we have."

"I love you too, Es."

As he watched her go, Thomas couldn't deny a small fraction of him feared Esther was already in too deep, and despite her perpetual love for him, would not be able to be cleanly extracted from her life in New York City.

Sitting across from Thomas in a state of desolation, William downed a double of whiskey like it was nothing more than water, adrift in his own sorrows as Thomas tried to be a consolation. It was, needless to say, not going as well as he'd hoped.

"She won't bloody get out of bed," William confessed aloud, though his eyes were on his drink, "She's a mess, Tommy. A bloody mess. She keeps swearing she knew this would happen and I can't think of a damn thing to tell her that would make it better."

Thomas had yet to see Lucy, though William mentioned repeatedly Lucy was beyond brokenhearted upon hearing of Edward's death. The day hadn't been easy for any of them, predominantly William and Lucy: they had known and loved Edward for most of their lives, but with his passing, William's true sentiments toward Thomas' father started to surface and were compounding with the passing hours. There was no doubt in Thomas' mind that William loved Edward as if they were brothers, and if his words were not enough, it was evident in the unremitting break down he couldn't shake off; still, as they continued in their reflections, William's loving remarks held a tinge of bitterness Thomas couldn't quite fathom. Not jealousy, not competitiveness, not wealth or circumstance... Thomas attempted a handful of interjections and discovered he had no clue how to bring up a subject his father's cousin might find irrevocably offensive. Then, like a rising tide, it came pouring out.

Another glass was poured by William for each of them as he shook his head, eyes bloodshot from crying.

"I think you're doing the right thing. Get Esther out of this dump. It's a nasty place that never did a damn thing for either of you. And if it's what Eddie wanted...if it's what Eddie wanted, you should do it."

Thomas took a sip from his glass. "What will your plans be, William? Do you want to skate back over the Atlantic with us or ride out the rest of the year here? We have an empire to run, after all."

William smirked sadly. "I'm sorry Tommy, but I'll have to stop you there. The truth is, you have an empire to run. I...I have taken my leave from Turner S & D, at least from the business standpoint. I'm now just an investor. You're the one calling the shots."

A knot grew in Thomas' gut. "Wh-what?" he stammered in absolute shock. "You took your leave?! When were you going to tell me this?!"

"Eddie and I were going to sit you down in a few days and officially pass the company onto you," William clarified, "We both wanted out. We wanted to see this summer through...to set you up so the rest of your career would be a breeze. But you did it all yourself, and we saw our opportunity came earlier than expected. We were...we were so proud of you, Tommy..." Thomas could see the tears welling in his eyes again, and William sniffed hard trying to fight them off. "Bloody prick, leaving us like this. How could he be so reckless?"

Thomas' defensiveness of his father grew. "William, it was an accident. You can't blame Edward for this."

"Was it?" he posed, his voice growing louder. "I can't ever be sure with him. You are like your father, Tommy, in so many great ways, and I love him for instilling those in you. But don't be like him, Tommy, for God's sake. Be your own man."

Thomas was baffled. "What is so wrong with being like him?"

"He forgot…he forgot what it meant to live for so long. He cast us aside, and we all had to watch him drown for years…years until he found you! Eddie wanted to die, with no courage to do it himself, so he let his life rot away. You brought him back…you and you alone, Tommy. And now you're set…you're set without him. I saw the moods come back. I saw it in his eyes – he wasn't needed much longer, and it would go back to how it was before. It's a blessing…a blessing he was taken now. I wouldn't want you to see…the only one who could ever keep him sane was the God damned Samurai, for Christ's sake. What does that tell you!"

Thomas labored to make sense of William's drunken speech. "What in the hell are you talking about, William? Are you talking about Hiroaki?"

William's mouth snapped closed, and he looked at Thomas as if he'd just revealed information he shouldn't have. "You…you don't know about him?"

"Know about what?"

"Jesus fucking Christ, Eddie," William swore, slamming his fist on the table and getting to his feet. Thomas stayed quiet as William wandered around the room, scolding Edward from under his breath as if he were right next to him. "You know why your father saved them from China?" William nearly shouted from the other side of the room. When Thomas didn't reply, William came toward him and resumed his previous seat. "Because Hiroaki was a fugitive of Japan and Mongolia…the man was a captive assassin for the Chinese army, and those bastards made him fight in the God damned drug war by torturing his wife and murdering his daughter right in front of him. He was the best of the best, and he trained your father to pass the time they had at Amberleigh."

Thomas was appalled, reminiscing back. "The night at the theater...I couldn't...I couldn't fathom how Edward could move so fast...and he was so ambivalent about it..."

William went for yet another pour of whiskey. "Finally seeing the big picture now, Tommy?"

"Why the training? What was the purpose?"

"He 'helped people'. That was the way he put it. You can decide what bloody context to put that vague bullshit in. All I know is, Eddie traveled more than anyone in our family, and always alone."

Thomas leaned forward, resting his head in his hands and wiping his eyes, remembering what Louis cited just a few hours before.

"William, did I even know my father?"

"I am not sure any of us truly knew Edward, Thomas," William professed, shaking his head. "You knew the best of him, and I think we can be obliged for that. But that's all I can offer you...I myself speculate how much truth he really told me."

The grandfather clock in the hall struck two, and the final clang reminded Thomas he ought to be heading to the police station. With a quick goodbye to William, Thomas set out from the house, his head swimming as he grappled over how to handle the world around him rapidly whirling out of control. It was remarkable that so many things were now coming to light, as his father was no longer present to keep them hidden.

Out on the busy street, Thomas was hit with an unwelcome wave of heat from the scorching late summer sun, and within ten yards he was already sweating through his shirt. The stench of sewage filled his nostrils in spite of being on the best avenue in the city, and he cringed thinking what the Points would smell like on a day like today. His tempo stayed even, his thoughts scattered every possible direction, and his emotions were growing harder and harder to control. The bustle of people was relentless, with no room to breathe and no silence to feel alone – he wanted out of this place, and he wanted out fast. Being here held too many bad memories, like an unavoidable plague Thomas couldn't seem to run away from.

Nothing could have prepared Thomas for seeing his father lying there lifeless on the morgue table. Ellis kept his distance, standing in the doorway as Thomas pulled the white sheet back and cringed, the image burned into his brain forever. It was impossible to look on for more than a few seconds: Edward's face was nearly beyond recognition, his body bruised and beaten, and the sheer site of the man he loved so utterly damaged caused the bile to rise in his throat. Glancing away, he gripped the metal table to hold himself upright, his legs almost giving way with nausea.

"Jesus..." he exhaled, looking to Ellis. "It's...it's him, Detective. Fuck me." Thomas tried to walk away too soon, and every muscle in his legs screamed in protest, his vision darkening at the corners. Falling sideways, Thomas' torso rammed into a vacant metal table on the other side of his father just as Ellis reached him, who tucked under Thomas' arm and slowly lowered them both to the floor.

"It's all right, Thomas. Just stay with me. Try not to pass out, ok?"

"Yeah, I'm here." Everything was still black, though somehow Thomas hung onto consciousness.

Ellis remained silent and gradually, Thomas came to. "I'm sorry, Thomas. This is never easy for the people left behind."

All at once, Thomas could no longer ward off the sobs, and he found himself bawling then and there on the floor. Out of what Thomas could only assume was respect and sympathy, Ellis stayed beside him, an arm around his shoulders, allowing him to get it out of his system without offering any sort of desultory solace. A few minutes passed before Thomas gathered himself together. Wiping his eyes, his pride hurting slightly, he acknowledged to the Detective that his emotional outbreak was coming to a close.

"I'll send a mortician first thing tomorrow, and I'll have the body picked up."

"Where are you having him buried?"

"Home. Where he belongs."

"Home? As in England?"

"I can stand now, Detective."

"Samuel," he remedied, helping Thomas up. "Are you leaving soon?"

"As soon as we can, I suppose."

Ellis' tone changed unexpectedly, beseeching him. "You should go see her, you know. She doesn't know you're leaving."

Thomas brushed the dust from the floor off his trousers. "Samuel, I could never ask you to understand the relationship I have with the Madame. It's time we went our separate ways for a while. There are never-ending difficulties surrounding her, ones I don't want to be a part of any longer and neither does my fiancée. I have to do what's right for my family, and what's right is going home where we belong."

Not bothering to wait for a guilt-ridden response, Thomas tipped his hat and left Detective Ellis in the mortuary, not desiring to discuss it any further. The words he said were harsh, brutal even, but true, and when Samuel told them to her later she would understand. It was time for them to part, and perhaps one day he might see her again. For the time being, however, it was time to leave her and his past in New York, along with the indisputable steel grip she'd had on his life since he was a boy. After nearly a decade as a Turner, Thomas would make his own way, without any influence from her on whatever direction he took…the way Edward wanted it, he reminded himself. He left the station without remorse, a smirk forming on his face as he stepped outside.

"For you, father. For you."

Tony was at the door when he arrived at the house, clearly anticipating he would be home around that time. "Sir, there is some… time sensitive information I need to ask of you, but please pardon my question it's…well it's regarding your father."

"That's fine, Tony, what is it?" Thomas asked, handing over his hat.

"Well, your father had me look into travel options back to England before he…passed. There is a ship that leaves in two days. Would you like me to book passage for you in his stead?"

Thomas paused. "Yes, actually that would work perfectly. For myself, for Esther…William, and Lucy as well. Also ask for storage space for my father's casket down below."

"Of course, sir, right away," Tony assured him, withdrawing from the entryway.

"Tony?"

"Yes sir?"

"Don't call me sir. I'm not ready yet."

Tony smiled at him. "Yes you are, sir. But for you, you will remain Thomas the rest of the day."

"Thank you, Tony."

"Also, Miss Esther is having a glass of wine in the sitting room."

Thomas dismissed him and went to find Esther; seeing her would make his heart feel a little lighter. When he reached the sitting room, Esther was perched on the windowsill, a large glass of wine in her hand, staring outside at the people passing by, not aware of Thomas' presence in the doorway. Her eyes were tired, worried, her shoulders slumped, and he could only assume her afternoon with Celeste had been just as rough as his. For a moment he considered joining her, then decided she might need a little time alone after such an overwhelming day.

Down the hallway, Thomas heard the advance of footsteps and hushed voices, hoping it would possibly be Lucy and William. Instead, two of the day maids turned the corner in a hurry with anxious looks on their faces. Thomas moved toward them to see what their worry might be; oddly, when they glanced up and noticed it was him, they both turned bright red and halted where they stood.

Thomas was suspicious. "What's the matter, ladies?" he asked. "Can I help you with something?"

Nervously they exchanged glances. "We…we were just going to see Miss Esther, sir. Just something she…misplaced."

"Misplaced?"

The girl on the right then took the lead. "Something she left in the pocket of her dress, sir, and we found when we was washing it. It's nothing, really. We can put it in her room for her."

"Ah, no problem there. I'll take it to her. What is it?"

Neither of them budged an inch, clearly trying to hide whatever it was from him. "Just a small something, sir," the other one continued. "I…I'll just put it in her room…"

His annoyance drew through to his tone. "Please give me whatever it was you found that neither of you wants me to see."

The one on the left closed her eyes and sighed heavily. "Christ, forgive me." She put her hand into her apron and pulled out what seemed to be an engagement ring, and Thomas at once saw why they hesitated. It was not the ring he had given her only a few hours ago…and he had a good guess as to whom it was from. On the inside, his fears were affirmed when he saw the engraving:

JB

Thomas' anguish from the entire day boiled over. "Which dress?" His teeth were clenched, and his words almost inaudible.

"It was the dress she got from Mrs. Adams, sir. Miss Esther asked us to bring it back to her, and we was only trying to do a favor…taking it back clean and all."

Thomas snatched the ring out of the maid's hand and whipped around, his logic giving way to madness he had never experienced. Marching angrily, he made his way straight for Esther, no longer caring about giving her space. He had asked one thing of her… one thing, and she had gone behind his back and done the opposite. Every one of his emotions funneled into his rage, and as he sped through the doors to the sitting room, Thomas slammed them shut behind him, causing Esther to jump to her feet and spill wine all over the floor.

"For God's sake, Thomas, what is going on?! You scared me half to death!"

He advanced toward her and grabbed her hand, shoving the ring into it. "Explain this to me, Esther. Now!"

She opened her hand and stared down at it, her expression distressed. "Oh my God…no…Thomas…listen to me…this is a big misunderstanding—"

"There is no misunderstanding here!" he yelled. "You lied to me! I ask one damn thing of you, Esther, and you can't even follow through on it! An engagement ring? Are you engaged to both of us, then?!"

"Of course not! Thomas, it happened so fast, I was trying to tell him and then—"

"You were trying to tell him you loved me, not him, and that somehow that ended with him giving you a fucking engagement ring?!"

"I was trying to do him the justice of being polite!" she shouted back, her own temper growing. "And before I could tell him anything someone came and scared him off! I couldn't have done anything about it!"

"And have you written to him to tell him no since then?!"

Esther paused, the read on her face was one Thomas had witnessed many times: guilt. "I…I was going to, but—"

Thomas felt entirely betrayed. "There is no 'but' in this one, Esther," he spat. "You've had more than enough time to give him the ring back and say no, and you fucking haven't. And you took that ring from me today knowing damn well you were deceiving me and destroying everything we stood for!"

Unable to gather a retort, Esther sank down onto the windowsill and began to cry. Thomas stayed where he was, his blood pumping hard. She'd been under the influence of the Hiltmores and the Madame for too long, and became as conniving and secretive as they were. He lacked all compassion for her tears, astounding himself with the coldness of his heart, and set the Captain's ring on the side table.

577

"Thomas…p-p-please…" she sobbed. "I love you…don't do this to me."

"Don't do this…to you…? To you?!" He threw his hands into the air. "How can I marry you if I can't even trust you?!"

"Please, it was just this one thing," she pressed, getting to her feet and trying to take his hand. "Please, I made a mistake…"

"It's always something with you, Es," he rejoined harshly, withdrawing his hand from hers. "I need time to think."

"Thomas, talk to me. We can talk this out! Please!" She threw her arms around him, and the coldness melted away, causing Thomas to feel his heart shatter. Giving in, he cupped her chin in his hands and shook his head.

"I can't deal with this right now. I can't…" His voice cracked. "I can't trust you, Es…why…why would you do this to me? I loved you. You were all I wanted!" Tears fell, and Thomas let Esther go and took a step back from her. "I'm going home. I'm taking my father back to bury him."

She stared at him. "What…what about us?"

Thomas fought hard to not forget his composure, all of his losses setting in. "I don't know, Es. I don't have an answer for you."

Esther sank to the ground, numbly oblivious to the wine seeping through the bottom her dress, and Thomas couldn't stand it any longer. He took off and out of the sitting room, throwing the doors back open to find both maids listening at the door. Openly cursing at them, he strode down the hallway and up the stairs to his room. Not giving a damn who was around, he pushed to pass Tony in the upstairs corridor, ignoring the butler's concerned questions, on the brink of his sanity. When he finally reached his room, Thomas closed his bedroom door and locked it. Then, before he could stop himself, Thomas' whole world went red, and his grip on reality faded away. In a quarter of an hour, he had broken every piece of furniture in his room and shattered every shard of glass, belting out primal screams of agony that drowned out the incessant knocking and banging on his bedroom door. When there was nothing left to break or throw, Thomas collapsed in the middle of the disaster that now was his life, overcome by mental and physical exhaustion and plummeting down into darkness.

The pain was subdued only by the violence and the havoc his heart released, and slowly, dreadfully, everything faded away.

"You were in and out for almost twenty-four hours," William informed him at his bedside. "Fever, hallucinations, we thought you'd lost your mind altogether."

Thomas had just woken up without any clue as to where he was or why, and there was only one thing he wanted answered.

"Did...did I dream it, William?"

William's face twisted with agony. "No...no Tommy, you didn't."

Despite the prickles in his muscles, Thomas managed to push himself up, reaching over for a glass of water at his bedside table. William eyed him closely as he drank an entire cup and then refilled for another, feeling more revived with each sip.

"Esther's gone," William added.

Thomas nearly choked. "Gone?"

William handed Thomas an unsealed envelope. "She wouldn't tell us what happened, so I took liberties on my own, and I apologize. The girl refused to stay, even just to see you come around. The...the ring is in there too, Tommy."

The hurt came rushing back. He drew out a letter and, to his dismay, Esther's engagement ring lay below it, the beautiful ring he'd spent weeks trying to find for her because nothing else was good enough. With stumbling fingers, Thomas opened her last words to him, his heart breaking once again.

Thomas,

579

Please accept your ring back, along with my resignation from your life. I don't deserve you, I never have, and I never will. I will stay in New York, and I will miss you every day that you are gone. I am sorry for the pain I've caused you and your family, particularly in a time when you needed me most. I guess, after all this, I realize that I had it wrong. I've always been the one to walk away in spite of blaming you for it, and for your sake, I am going to regretfully do it one last time.

I love you.

Es

Thomas folded the letter back up and placed it in the envelope, leaning back against the headboard as his eyes painfully closed.

"If you don't mind my asking, what in God's name happened with you two?" William pressed. "You were a perfect match, Tommy. What was it that caused such a rift?"

"I wasn't the only man she'd accepted a ring from," Thomas mumbled, putting the note aside. "One of the maid's found an engagement ring in her dress. From the Captain, when she had told me it was over."

"But it was over. She said yes to you, didn't she?"

"Then tell me why the hell she still had it, William," Thomas shot back angrily.

William's scoffed. "Did you even hear her out, Tommy?"

"Hear what? Excuses? She promised me she had ended it weeks ago!"

"Well Christ," William withdrew. "When it rains, it pours, I suppose…."

Thomas flipped the envelope upside down, the ring falling into his palm. It sparkled in the dim lighting with an impressive luminosity. It would have to go – every time he looked at it, he would see Esther. He hadn't been sure what their future might be when Thomas confronted her about the Captain, and she went ahead to make the choice for them both: there wouldn't be one. Conversely, Esther, as it turned out, was the only girl he had ever felt anything for other than the need to satisfy his baser impulses. Accepting they would never be together was something he couldn't do. He didn't want to be without her…but the lies…the lies and the secrets were enough to stifle his forgiving nature. A part of him thought he might write to her when his father's affairs were in order, and the other part knew he never would. The one person whose advice he could use was long gone, and Thomas recognized any mistakes or decisions he made were his own now, with no one to blame or credit but himself. Edward was dead…his father was dead…and he wasn't coming back to save him.

"Why don't I put this somewhere safe for a while?" William suggested, taking the ring from Thomas before he could protest.

"We might as well take it back to the jeweler, William. There's no need to have it."

William ignored him, placing the ring in his robe pocket. "Come down and eat a little something if you have the strength. Otherwise I'll have Tony bring supper up for you." When he got to the door, William turned and smiled. "Home tomorrow, Tommy. Maybe then we can find a little peace in this."

Thomas nodded, his eyes tracing over to the fireplace. His head throbbed, and he sank back down into his…

It was then he noticed his surroundings: he was in his father's room, in his father's bed, wearing new nightclothes with his initials and family crest already stitched on the front breast pocket. Somehow, William put him in here, and he'd done it for two reasons: because Thomas had clearly ruined all of his own belongings during his rampage in his old room…the blue room…and also because he was not just Thomas any longer.

He was Lord Thomas Turner of Amberleigh.

PART 3:
FALL 1883, NEW YORK CITY

XX.

"Before I go ahead and close out our monthly meeting, I am going to give the floor to our Fire Commissioner, who would like to discuss some of the new zoning legislation that will hopefully put an end to some of these God damned street brawls. Richard?"

Croker politely smiled as John motioned for him to stand and take the lead from the head of the table. While not one of the others had the dexterity to detect it, Croker could distinctly make out the ever so slight tremor in John Kelly's voice. Normally, John wouldn't dare rescind his position as their discussion leader; he would talk through the issues of the day with no more than a consulting head nod or two from the others to affirm each of his points was correct.

The cough was coming back.

For months on end, John had been fighting an illness and be-lieved the summer heat might finally kill the last of whatever was lurking in his lungs. Of all the Hall members, only Croker knew it had returned with a vengeance, and was taking a hold of their boss faster than any doctor anticipated. He had a year, maybe two if he was lucky, and most of that remaining time would be spent coughing up blood. As Croker rose, even then taking note of his old friend's pallid color, it was difficult to repress the satisfaction he felt that soon

enough, the time he'd put in over the years would finally pay off…
and he would be the Grand Sachem of Tammany Hall.

"After careful persuasion, we've passed a motion to change each
zoning district to better accommodate the growing immigrant population and to keep each neighborhood focused on a particular eth-
nicity." He paused, allowing his words to sink in, and he was happy
to perceive approving glances and nods amongst his constituents.
"The fights amongst the fire brigades and police forces have become
a nuisance, and after the bad press we've dealt with all summer regarding this issue, I've taken it upon myself to see that this new law
will eliminate the problem altogether."

"And what about the Points and the Bowery?" Greyson asked
from a few chairs down. "It's already a fucking pigs den. Aren't we
just going to create more strife by solidifying the ghettos?"

Croker cleared his throat – fucking Greyson always had to be a
pain in his ass. "After discussing it with John and a few high ranking
members of our esteemed city government, we thought the benefits
of lessening the toll on our citizens outside the Points and the Bowery outweighed any risks in that area, Mr. Greyson."

"And do you mind my asking, with of course your permission,
Mr. Kelly, how they might know better than the rest of this board
what to do with the most violent neighborhood in America?"

"Maybe because the men I personally sought out to consult
had, at one time or another, lived in those ghettos, unlike you, Mr.
Greyson," Croker retorted icily. "So I would say that yes, they would
know a hell of a lot better than most."

"Easy, Richard," John interrupted, holding up hand. "Mr.
Greyson, I can assure you the research was done and the correct
choice has been made. We are trying to build a political base, gentlemen, one that goes beyond our Irish brothers and into the general population."

Greyson sank back in his chair, and Croker couldn't stop himself – he wanted to put an end to that bastard's constant doubts in

his judgment. Looking directly into the man's eyes, Croker's temper calmed and his tone took on a heightened intensity to ensure there would be no response from his opponent.

"Nobody at this fucking table should forget we are still fighting to reclaim our lost ground after Tweed. I've been tiptoeing around to build our reputation the right way, and with the exception of John, not one of you has a real clue what that takes. I will not let a few little pricks down at the papers keep us in hiding by associating the Hall with some stereotypical micks who don't know shit about running this city. We already do run it, and in time, everyone will know it. The next time anyone has any reservations about the way I do things, you can take it up with me personally and not waste this board's precious time."

Everyone's eyes went from Croker to Greyson and then back to Croker again, a somewhat shocked, nervous silence filling the room. Never had he been so direct with a member who was worth considerably more financially to Tammany than his own person, yet Croker didn't for a second regret his affront. They were all fluff, as far as he was concerned. When the end of the day came, these bastards needed him much more than he needed them – the Hall required one thing, and one thing alone from the men at that table: money. Everything else, Croker spent years to formulate, from connections in the Mayor's office to running brothels in the Points. He was the real future of Tammany because he had come from the bottom of the barrel, like all the Irish had. Without blinking an eye, he would win them the votes of the mob, and the mob mattered more than one or two easily replaceable investors.

The time had come to make it known this was his organization, not theirs.

John got to his feet and Croker sat back into his chair with the foresight of a public reprimand, as he was accustomed to receiving from John when he "overstepped." To Croker's amazement, however, John thanked everyone and dismissed the meeting, requesting that Croker stay behind for a few extra minutes. When the last man exited and closed the doors behind him, John pulled two cigars from his pocket and slid one across the table to Croker, along with a box of timber.

"Thought you shouldn't be smoking these anymore?" Croker posed, not truly that concerned as he lit his match.

"I'm not supposed to be," John confessed, lighting his own. "Fuck the doctors. I'm already dying, so I don't see the God damn point of depriving myself."

Croker almost choked on the smoke in his throat. "E-Excuse me?"

John sighed, taking a long drag. "You've known the illness is back, and I saw my physician two days ago. I've got a little time left, but not much."

"Jesus, John. Why didn't you tell me?"

"Like I said, I knew you knew. Your old man died of the same thing, you perceive the symptoms better than anyone." An enormous cloud of smoke escaped his lips. "Take it easy on Greyson, would you? He's just a fucking snake. His job is to undermine you and second guess, because if no one else does, then you take the fall if shit goes bad."

Croker shrugged, though he saw his point. "I didn't look at it that way. You are, of course, right." He released a small chortle. "Guess I can still learn a thing or two in the time we have."

"You're the new Fire Commissioner. You get this zoning policy implemented, and you get the numbers up and in our favor, I think you'll finally be ready, Richard."

"Ready?"

John laughed. "Don't play dumb with me, you sly son of a bitch. We both know you're getting my chair the second I can't run this circus any longer."

He smirked immodestly. "It's not that, John. I thought I'd still have a few years of moving up."

"The reason I got you this role is for the formality of your... grooming process," John explained. "You'll win the Irish because you are a mick, plain and simple. It's a fucking fairytale ending. But you've never been a public figure with a reputation to watch, and rely on others like I have on you. The time has come for that. And I hope you've found enough gutter dwellers to see that through."

"I think my men will suffice," Croker replied confidently.

"Good. Now, did you solve that problem with the head whore?"

"We are meeting face to face this afternoon."

"And the girl?"

Croker shrugged. "Off the grid. She hasn't been spotted for days, and I've had one of my best on her."

"Keep it up. The news cannot get out that the Adams family was contributing substantially to our organization, and I don't want to give the damn Swallowtails more ammo than they already have."

"What about a public trial to humiliate her?" Croker suggested. "Character assassination! It would completely ruin her societal status. Charles mentioned the idea to me before he...well... got nicked."

From the expression on John's face, Croker could see his mentor didn't like it. "I don't want it getting out about the rape – no one knows and it should stay that way. This mess has gotten big enough. Make sure it stays quiet or deal with it in person."

"Understood."

For a moment, neither of them spoke, both appreciating the silence and the density of smoke surrounding them. Then, John pressed on.

"The boy is gone, then?"

"Left a few weeks ago along with his cousins and his father's body."

"Make sure that stays quiet, too. Last thing I need right now is more Protestant assholes from across the pond breathing down my neck." He got to his feet and walked around to where Croker sat, resting his hip against the table, visibly disconcerted. "Did you really have to kill him, Richard? A member of the House of Lords? The press in England is losing their fucking minds over this."

Croker scooted his chair back, swinging his left leg over his right knee. He couldn't actually tell John the truth without giving him reservations in regards to Croker's competency, and in an effort to not put his future leadership position in jeopardy, thought it best to maintain the charade it was his plan the entire time.

"Keeping him alive would have exposed us. He wouldn't have stopped until Mary Dougherty was off Blackwell, and she knew about the double booking, where the background files were, everything. Even the dirt we have on our own guys, she kept track of it."

"What turned her?"

"Some fucking Pinkerton on his own mission."

"Ah," said John, remembering. "She's still in the asylum, then?"

"She won't be alive much longer. I am seeing to that." Croker flicked away the ash from the stub of his cigar. "The problem is solved, John. Don't worry yourself with it. Right now, the Swallowtails are the bastards we need to keep at bay, or we're looking at a bad election year, and that we definitely can't afford. Who have we got lined up?"

John grinned, content. "I'm glad you asked…"

"You're going to The Palace? Are you out of your God damned mind?!" Seamus Murphy exclaimed from the other side of Croker's office.

"If I had a choice, I would send you, Seamus. But the last time didn't go so well."

Seamus didn't respond, only threw back his glass of whiskey and took a begrudging seat. On Seamus' left sat Sullivan and to the right stood O'Reilly, with Will Sweeny loitering over near the door. They were downing drinks in celebration of Croker's next big step up in Tammany, and he'd called them together that afternoon to empha-size the need for absolute discretion with their errands and move-ments. The time had come to focus on camouflaging their true col-ors behind the walls of the Hall; nevertheless, there was still much to be done, and Croker wanted it done fast.

"You can' seriously be thinkin' of goin' alone, Richie?" Sulli-van piped up, "That bitch is crazy as shit. And the Frog could take ya out in one swipe. Me and two of the lads will go wit' ya. If your arse goes, we go, eh?"

Croker took a sip of his own cocktail and shook his head. "It's a gesture of good faith. And she knows damn well if anything happens to me she won't make it through the night in one piece. The Madame is smart – she wants a piece of the pie, like the rest of us. I have a feel-ing down the road she could be a major asset to the organization."

Seamus' anger was boiling over. "An asset?! She'd slit all our throats if she had the chance!"

"Just like we would slit hers," Croker added. "But we need her, and she needs us. The Madame is one of the best at what she does for a reason, and I plan on using that to our advantage. If your balls can't take that, Seamus, then get the fuck out of my office."

"All right, all right," O'Reilly cut in. "Look, we get the picture, Richie. Just been a bad few days is all. We're a little…worried."

"Only thing you boys should be worried about are the next or-ders I give you," Croker chastised them. "I don't pay you to worry. I pay you to do your fucking job. I've got this empire at my finger-tips and I'll have no qualms taking out each and every one of you if it slips away. Is that understood?"

Sullivan gulped down his drink. "What's next for these Swal-lowtail pricks then, eh?"

Croker grinned. "Their power and importance are dwindling. John's done one hell of a job healing the hemorrhaging of Tweed's open wounds. The Swallowtails had their purpose, and we only have a few nails left until the coffin is sealed shut."

"Orders?" O'Reilly reiterated.

"Seamus and Sullivan, you're headed to the Points. I want updates from the Whyos – all their fixings, raids, saloon incomes, everything. I want to make sure the money is pouring in and if not, plug whatever hole exists. O'Reilly, we need to keep the morale base up. Let's schedule a fundraising picnic in one of the parks closer to uptown in a few days. Free bread and beer for any hungry working man and his family, and a chance for our 'investors' to mingle with the common folk. Let's start pushing loyalties – we need the masses on our side. Think patronage above all else!"

"What the fuck is patronage?" Sullivan turned to ask O'Reilly quietly, utterly lost.

Croker could barely suppress his amusement. "Something your tiny brain will never understand, Sullivan, and that's why I like you. Now, finish your whiskey and get to work."

"What about the copper?" O'Reilly entreated him. "The one the Madame killed? And them guards she butchered?"

"Ah yes, I almost forgot. Detective Ellis should be waiting in the lobby. Send him in on your way out."

Sweeny peeked out through the window. "He looks mighty pissed off, Richie."

"I think I can change his mind." Taking their leave, the others filtered out, but Croker stopped Will in his tracks. "A moment, Mr. Sweeny. If you don't mind."

Will indifferently closed the door, pacing Croker's direction. "What can I do ya for, Richie?"

Croker lowered his tone. "I need you to do two things for me without letting the others in on it, understood?"

"Course. What is it?"

"Watch the Frog. I know you two have some weird, befuddled history, and frankly I don't give a shit. Watch him, and let me know where he stands. I have a feeling after everything pans out with his current employer, a crossover isn't something completely out of the question."

"Louis is faithful, Richie. Stupid son of a bitch would go to the grave for that woman, I think. I'll do my best, though. What's the other?"

He took a glance back toward the windows behind his desk and proceeded to take a few steps forward, gripping Will's arm tight as he whispered: "You need to keep an eye on Walsh."

From his reaction, it was clear Will was not pleased with his charge. "I don' want nothin' to do with that bastard, I told ya that at the beginnin'.'"

"This isn't a negotiation," Croker reminded him, trying to mask the unease in his voice. "I don't trust him. He's becoming more and more of a loose cannon, and I need to make sure he's following suit. Otherwise, you can find work elsewhere, but I can guarantee that won't come easy for a man such as yourself."

Will's gaze narrowed. "What the fuck is goin' on, Richie? What'd he do to ya, then?"

"It's not about what he's done. I just need to keep that bastard on a tight leash. Now, do what I ask and report back to me if anything comes up."

Will sauntered back toward the door to the hallway and paused. "He's gonna know I'm tailin' him, Richie."

"Most likely, yes."

"What am I supposed to do if he confronts me 'bout it?"

"He won't," Croker pledged.

"How're you so sure?"

Croker made his way to the chair behind his desk, sitting casually. "I'm not, but we're just going to have to find out," he told him, reaching over to pick up his whiskey. "Now, send in Detective Ellis. I want to get this headache over with."

Will swept out quickly, observably irritated with him, and within seconds Ellis stormed inside rampaging toward Croker's desk, only stopping when he reached it. He lunged toward Croker with a finger pointed at his chest accusingly.

"I am not playing this fucking game anymore, Croker! You keep me outside waiting for over an hour when I know you're in here gloating like I'm a God damned fool!"

"Detective," Croker started passively. "You will have respect for this office when you are here, even if you are in a bad state. Take a seat, and let's talk through whatever misgivings you might have."

Ellis didn't sit – his face was red with fury and his finger was still outstretched, pointing at Croker. "I covered for you and ruined some poor kid's life, and this is how you repay me? I'm fucking done. You can run your bullshit agenda on your own from now on, because I'm out!"

The door cracked open and Will peeked inside. "Everythin' all right in here?"

Croker nodded Will's direction. "Detective, you can either sit down and have a normal conversation with me, or I'll have Mr. Sweeny escort you off the premises, and I can guarantee he will not be…gentle about it."

Ellis whipped around and spotted Will, taking a few seconds to deliberate his options. Realizing he was defeated, Ellis descended down into one of the vacant chairs, not making eye contact with Croker. The man was exhausted, appearing as if he'd gone days without sleep: his slumped shoulders were an immediate sign he'd been deprived of rest, with dark circles running deep under drooping eyelids and a five o'clock shadow that was impossible to miss forming on his jaw. Croker poured the man a fresh glass and placed it on the edge of his desk, like an outstretched olive branch. At first, Ellis only stared at the whiskey blankly; eventually he gave in and leaned over to reluctantly pick up the drink.

"Now, what is it you're so upset about?"

"You know what the fuck I'm upset about."

"You have to be specific with me, Detective."

594

"About me covering up a murder, that's what!" Ellis drank his glass empty and slammed it back on Croker's desk, a crack spurring from the bottom. "It's taken everything I've got to keep this under wraps. And I can't do this shit. I won't do it, and if I don't my men won't either."

Instantly, Croker let out a loud laugh. "Your men, you say Detective? Your almost entirely Irish precinct? How funny. Don't think I haven't forgotten what you've done either, Detective. You brought one of your own in to be tortured and killed by that whore you've been fucking on the side. What do you think your boys will say when I tell them all about that little incident, eh? That you gave up a boy in blue for a piece of tail? I think you'd find yourself in a pretty fucking bad state."

"You can try to intimidate me all you want, you Irish prick. I don't give a damn. I came here to tell you I'm out, and nothing you say can change my mind."

"Please, Detective, please," Croker retorted, another mocking smirk growing on his face. "Let's take down the hostilities. I am a businessman, and a man of my word. If you uphold your end of the bargain, you can be guaranteed I will uphold mine. Is the statement release complete?"

Ellis' eyes were filled with hatred. "It's done."

"Good!"

Croker rose, shuffling leisurely to his right where the notorious Civil War painting of Gettysburg hung on his wall. "That was one hundred, along with the photographs, am I correct?"

Ellis didn't respond, only glowered at the floorboards under his muddied boots. As promised, Croker would pay the Detective handsomely for his services, along with a small token of his appreciation. Another Detective barely holding rank over Ellis in their precinct had a few nasty habits, and one of them happened to be young boys. Thanks to a little booze and a lot of opium, Croker brought Ellis what was necessary to be rid of the sick bastard, who thankfully had never been of much use to Tammany anyhow. Carefully, Croker lifted the painting from the wall with both hands and placed it on the ground. He plugged in the combination to his safe fastidiously, one only the best money could buy for a man hiding a great many horrible secrets. A few clicks here…two more to the right… and five left…with a light clink the door swung open, and Croker retrieved Ellis' envelope before promptly shutting the safe once more.

"Your promotion will put you in a very powerful, yet precarious situation, Detective. Why not wield that power? We could cultivate your advantage. Think of what we could accomplish together."

Without a response, Ellis got to his feet and proceeded on to Croker, grasping the opposite end of the envelope. "Like I said, I'm done. Do what you want with the boys. You can't buy me."

"I'm afraid, Detective, I already did once, as is evident from the envelope you're holding. Don't be so ungrateful. I'm providing you with the means to further your own cause without any hopes of promoting my own agenda."

Ellis rolled his eyes. "You're always promoting your own agenda, Croker."

Croker did not let the package go – instead he gave it a firm tug, pulling Ellis closer to him. "You're done when I fucking say you're done. Otherwise I'll see to it that your precious Madame is gutted right in front of you, and your life will come to its own bitter end. You're off the hook for now, but when the time comes I will call on you again, and you will do as I damn well ask. Or you will be very, very sorry." He freed the envelope, causing Ellis to take a hard step backward, his face not nearly as threatening as when he first arrived.

"You think your words will sway me to follow your orders? Thank you for the fair warning, but I'll take my chances."

"Hah! Like the Madame did? And how exactly did that work out for her?"

Ellis didn't bother to answer, and Croker was pleased to see his point had been taken. The Detective tucked the envelope under his arm and sulked out of Croker's office, slamming the door shut behind him.

Croker let out a sigh of annoyance and went back to his chair, lowering down to see the last of the fall sunlight began to fade away. Out of the blue, Croker's stomach rumbled from too much whiskey and not nearly enough sustenance following a long day of nothing but damage control. Lizzie and the children would be cooking dinner right about now back in Harrison, where he would go for a visit in a few days. She'd been more agitated than normal lately, one letter loving and doting and the next angry with him for being gone on business so often. The devastation of losing her sister, though they never were close, in addition to what Croker could only assume was a possible pregnancy with their fifth child, caused her mood swings to heighten. A new silk dress and a night on the town might make her smile, and Croker made a mental note to ask John what festivities were in store for the Hall that Saturday.

He would meet the Madame in just a few hours for the first time since their messy and unfortunate misunderstanding, which ended with more casualties than Croker originally intended to stack up. It infuriated him that after his hard work to build his foundations they very nearly came crumbling down, and because of some lower class, Irish bitch who evidently was worth more than Croker predicted. In the beginning, he'd repeatedly laughed knowing Mary lied to her family about the depth of her involvement, and why wouldn't she? The shame of it, storing someone else's dirty laundry…the recognition that what she held in her hands could destroy the lives of that person and everyone around them. She'd tried to sneak off with a majority of the files for the Pinkerton and was found out by Seamus, who caught her in the act just in time; giving her the code to the safe was the biggest mistake they'd made. And sure, initially Mary's life sentence might have been cruel, but it was earned by her and her alone, and Croker thought it far more righteous than dying in the sewers of that rotten city.

Yet Mary wouldn't be around much longer. Croker had recently just learned Lizzie's sister, Susan Montell, a nurse at Blackwell's Island, had died at Blackwell under suspicious circumstances, and apparently only hours after nearly beating Mary to death. Something wasn't right, he could feel it, and Croker would uncover the truth. He never liked Susan, and neither had his wife, but it was the excuse he'd been looking for to finally put Mary Daugherty in her grave, and he planned on capitalizing on that.

"Brian!" Croker shouted out to his aid. There was a shuffling of feet and after half a minute passed, the door to his office flew open.

"Yes, sir, Mr. Croker?" Brian asked. He was a young man, not yet twenty, and eager to work his way up the ladder. Loyalty was what Croker needed to ingrain in his pack, and Brian was already turning out to be more valuable than a damn good hunting dog.

"I want you to go find Edmond for me. I need to let off a little steam."

"Edmond…Edmond O'Connor, sir?"

Croker grabbed for another cigar from the humidor on his desk and lit it. "That's the one."

Brian nodded, seemingly unsure of himself. "I'll go to him, sir. Where should I expect he'll be?"

"Down at the docks, Brian. Tell him I want a challenge this time. Also grab Seamus. He should be at the pub in another two or three hours and tell him to meet me down there…and make sure he brings me a clean shirt."

"Of course, Mr. Croker. Right away. Also you have a note here dropped off by a rather…well…let's just say he didn't belong in these parts."

"What's it say, Brian?"

He opened the envelope carefully. "It's from the initials D.L. It says…oh Christ, sir. It says O'Neill has been stealing from him and if you don't take care of it…"

"Shit," Croker groaned under his breath. O'Neill had been stealing from the Whyos. After all these years, Billy finally got himself into a mess he couldn't get out of. It no longer mattered that he was one of John's oldest supporters. He would have to be taken care of, or the Whyos would blow this out of proportion.

"All right, burn the note. Thanks, Brian."

"Sir? For tonight…what about bandages? Wraps?"

Croker declined, rolling up his sleeves, desperately needing to let off steam. "No wraps. I think I'd rather bleed a little tonight."

It was the fourth round when Croker spotted Seamus' panicked face in the crowd – the sight of Croker at that moment he imagined might be a little staggering. The first had gone smoothly, as it always did for him, evading the blasts of the two hundred and fifty-pound pile of meat throwing punches uncontrollably and without any true form. Croker successfully knocked out five of the man's teeth, shattered his jaw, and badly bruised a few ribs, not to mention got one hit to his opponent's balls that would easily leave him childless for some time. The second round, however, commenced the same as the first, yet spotting a familiar figure shadowed in the masses distracted Croker for just enough time that the brute cold cocked him, nearly knocking Croker out completely. Staying on his feet was almost impossible – his steps were slower, his vision blurred and darkening at the corners, and the pain from the left side of his head was so substantial Croker thought that son of a bitch might actually have done some serious damage. Mercifully, after a few quick dodges, the round ended and gave him a break to collect himself, and that's when he noticed blood streaming down his shirt. Bastard had broken the skin…

Down at the docks, the boxing matches were a regular occurrence, and typically Croker found himself on the betting end rather than doing the fighting. Strictly Irish only, and allowed at the end of the day so the barge crews could finish work and provide first pickings of whiskey from the crates that happened to be "damaged" during shipment. The ring was right next to the water, on the outstretch of a dock that often found drunks, fools, or anyone unaware of their feet falling backwards for a cold, dirty swim. The dank air smelled of fish and sewage, and no matter what time of day, the obscurity of the water made it feel like this was a location where the sun never shined. It wasn't just a place of boxing: here, every single back-door dealing went down between the underground enterprises because it was one of the few spots in New York even the most crooked coppers wouldn't venture. From the start, Croker made a name for himself and formulated his empire on that very ground, earning a vast amount of respect and notoriety. When it wasn't his place of business, the docks ensured he could maintain that respect and more importantly, fear, markedly with the gangs from the Points. Only the big fights drew the higher end crowd, and that took a large level of promotion and sweat, though it always paid off with big money. Tonight, on the other hand, was amateur night, and Croker had some ground to make up.

The third round hadn't been his best, and the jeers echoing from the crowd only grew louder when they saw that a fight they thought wouldn't last more than a few minutes might be more evenly matched than expected. Bets were being made left and right, heightening the stakes and making Croker speculate how much money he would gross if he kept his head on straight. Edmond made him swear to draw the fight out as long as he could and allow his opponent at least a small glimmer of hope, and Croker had inadvertently done as he was asked. In the third he clambered to recover and did it sloppily, dodging potentially four broken ribs on his right side and a grab for a chokehold that would have ended the match then and there. How he evaded those was a mystery. Then, another blow to his head on the same side blinded Croker with a sting for nearly five seconds, and it was a miracle he did not pass out or sustain another in the process. His right wrist was also sprained from being caught and twisted behind his back, and he was fortunate had not snapped in the process. Stupidly, he'd head-butted the muscle man as hard as he could to escape, which he did, yet with the cost of knowing he'd need to see a doctor the following day. With the brute dazed, Croker pulled the man's head to him and kneed him hard in the diaphragm, ending the round and sending the man reeling to the ground in agony. As he stepped out for the fourth and saw Seamus, the time had come to end it and start the rest of his evening.

It took a tremendous left hook to the bastard's jaw and a knee to his face to send him down on all fours, barely able to stay off the ground. One last hit to the temple, courtesy of Croker's right foot, and the meat man was out for good. The crowd let out a deafening roar, both curses and praises ringing out, causing Croker to smile. This was what he did it for. The victory. And, of course, the money that followed.

Suddenly Seamus voice was in his ear. "What the hell happened to ya?"

Croker turned to face him, aggravated with his own blunder. "My fucking concentration got cut short," he vindicated, his eyes scanning through the horde of bodies. He'd seen Walsh, and whenever that asshole showed up, it was only because there was something he needed to deliberate with Croker over. Croker absolutely despised his random appearances. He wasn't there to dwell or to be a part of the "team"; and on top of that, he was impossible to find. He had to find you.

Seamus inspected his hairline. "Christ, Richie. You could use a stitching."

"I could use a lot of things," Croker uttered smugly, "I've got bigger fish to fry, Seamus. Now where is Edmond with my money?"

"Richie!" Edmond yelled off from somewhere to his left.

Seamus lifted to his tip toes and waved Edmond over to them as onlookers dispersed, many stopping to shake Croker's hand and congratulate him on his win. As Edmond reached the two men, he pulled the top hat from his head and yanked out a wad of paper money, hoisting it into Croker's hand with a happy laugh. Edmond was a tall, burly man, leaner than most professional boxers yet quick, agile, and above all, had a punch that felt like iron pummeling against the human body. He was missing a few teeth, with his hair cut short to make any injuries easier to sew back up, and he always had a shiner hanging over or under one of his eyes. Croker liked him immensely, apart from the fact that he constantly tried to cheat him out of his money.

"You took a thirty percent commission," Croker remarked, counting the bills once and then twice. He shoved the money in his pocket – there was no alternative with an audience still lingering. "I want what I was owed."

Edmond laughed again, slapping Seamus on the back as if Croker might be joking. When he saw his reaction met without reciprocation, Edmond cleared his throat and stood tall.

"Changed a few weeks back, Mr. Croker. Thirty percent, now. Thought you knew or I'd have told ya."

Keeping his mood under control, Croker glared at Edmond. "I don't give a shit what changed for you, Edmond. Our arrangement hasn't."

Edmond became visibly perturbed, taking a step back from Seamus and Croker. "Look, Mr. Croker, rules is rules. If you got a problem with that, you shoulda told me before. Just tryin' to run my business is all."

"You look here, you stupid bastard," Croker barked, lunging after Edmond and grabbing his cravat, pulling to cut off air supply. "Give me my damn money or I'll embarrass you in front of your friends, and you can forget about ever having a deal with the Hall. You got me?"

Croker didn't have to look over his shoulder to feel Seamus' nerves on end: in one swing, Edmond could take Croker out and put him in the hospital for weeks with no guaranteed recuperation. In the years they'd known one another, Croker had never gone so far with Edmond, whose face turned red yet made no sign of struggling to breathe. This was an effort to show that not all power is gained in brute strength. Everyone needed to be afraid of him and what he was capable of, regardless of who they might be.

Edmond's hand slipped down into his pants pocket and pulled out another fifty dollars, which he then unceremoniously handed over to Seamus. Immediately, Croker released his hold on the man's tie and held out his hand.

"Always a pleasure doing business, Edmond," he declared.

Edmond took a few wheezing breaths and after a moment, reluctantly shook Croker's hand in return without saying a word. He gave one glance to Seamus and took off toward the city, fixing his tie as he angrily paced away.

"Boss…"

Croker stayed silent, watching Edmond walk off, feeling a rush of power he hadn't in some time.

"Boss…"

"For God's sake, what is it Seamus?!"

Seamus wasn't looking at Croker. His eyes were on Walsh, who was cavalierly strutting toward them.

Croker nodded to Seamus. "Walsh."

"Quite a fight there, Mr. Croker," Walsh greeted with a baleful tone. "Let's have a chat tonight after your meeting with our lovely friend the Madame."

"You have updates for me, I assume?" Croker asked.

"In a matter of speaking, yes I do."

"Good. I can make that happen. Our usual spot?"

Walsh was about to correct him, as there was no usual spot: he usually just appeared out of thin air when Croker found himself alone; conversely, noting it was for appearances sake in front of Seamus, Walsh gave him an eerie smile.

"Of course, Mr. Croker. The usual spot. 'Til then." He tipped his head and followed in Edmond's tracks, along with what was left of the dissipating mob of onlookers. Croker made a grab for Seamus' sleeve, and wiped the sweat and blood from his face.

"Got my shirt, Seamus?"

Gawking after Walsh, Seamus handed over a perfectly white new button down, vest, tie, belt, and Croker's pocket watch that he had been carrying in his satchel. To Croker's surprise, Seamus then handed over his top hat and a tin of grease to slick back his hair, which was drenched in sweat.

"Boss?"

"Yeah, Seamus?" he asked, stripping off his soiled undershirt.

"You…you have a usual spot with Walsh? I just always thought he…he just showed up when the job was done."

"That's the way he works," he grunted, hating to do the buttons himself. "He shows up and we meet at the spot."

"That makes me feel a little better. I always thought that prick was like wild dog. Glad you've got him locked down, Boss."

Croker finished getting dressed, knowing the lie was necessary. There was no meeting place, and there never had been, hence Walsh's sardonic air. Walsh was, in actuality, what Seamus feared: a wild dog that would eat out of the hand that fed him only to bite it off the next second. He just couldn't let anyone other than himself know the truth.

A coach was waiting for them at the entrance to the harbor, and Croker lit a cigar before he and Seamus hopped in and took off toward The Palace. The meeting was scheduled as soon as the dead copper and his gutted protection officers showed up on Tammany's doorstep, and John ordered Croker to clean it up fast or there'd be serious hell to pay. All in all, he had to admit the Madame's play was a hard hit, and one he did not expect – impressive, yet impetuous. Croker wanted nothing more than to kill her and silence the problem for good, but unfortunately she was a potential friend he could use to his advantage. Her mind was a lockbox of information, things he would never be able to dig up on his own, and digging up secrets on both his enemies and contemporaries was something Croker took immense measures in doing. The only way to overpower someone who feels entitled and inherently better than the average human being is to expose their surreptitious habits. If there was one thing Croker had learned in his time doing what he did, it was that everyone lies and everyone has something to hide. There's always a weak spot, a chink in the chain…and like him, the Madame had a special talent of using that to promote her own wealth and power. Conversely, and unlike the Madame, Croker didn't care about the money. He only wanted the power.

"Think they'll have another body for us?" Seamus quipped nervously.

Croker let out a cloud of smoke. "Nah. She can see by now that she needs me as much as I need her. We are incontestably bound for the time being."

"So we should be expecting a warm welcome, then?"

"I'm going in alone."

Seamus scoffed. "Like hell you are. Boss, ain't no way I'm letting that happen."

"This is the way it is," Croker told him firmly. "I don't want anything to distract from me getting this arrangement locked in."

"How much we giving her under the table?"

"It's going to depend on how much she will give us. We will compensate her above and beyond if it's good."

Croker could tell from the look on Seamus' face he was skeptical. He took of his hat and slicked back his hair, the same move he always made when his disposition was shaky. Seamus had been with him since the start, a friend from the brutal days of public school who always had his back even if it meant getting his own head beaten in. His job with the Hall got his hands dirtier than Croker ever had, and while he was smart as a whip, Seamus wore his heart on his sleeve and would never rise higher than where he was now. It was a setback that had gotten them into some tight spots with Tammany, and one of the reasons both Croker and Seamus knew his rise up the ladder hadn't happened earlier. Regardless, Croker would never drop Seamus. Some bonds were worth the extra hassle, chiefly because Croker didn't trust anyone else around him.

"Where am I headin', then? When you go inside?"

"Get a telegram to Blackwell. Tell them to expect us in the morning, and that it is not going to be pretty."

"Time to get some justice for that sister-in-law of yours, then?"

"Something like that. Mainly, I just want to put this problem to rest and forget it ever happened. When you're done, go check on the boys at the pub and make sure there is no animosity – I want everyone on the same page. Got it?

"Course. What time you want the coach back to get you?"

"A half hour, no more than that. And do me a favor and go home and get some fucking sleep. You look like shit."

Seamus laughed. "Yeah well, that makes two of us. You're God damn head is swelling about as big as your ego."

The carriage came to a halt outside The Palace and Croker got out, throwing his cigar onto the road. "I want a full report on everyone tomorrow morning."

"Sure thing, Boss."

Croker sped off toward the front walkway, the giant, bald guard dog waiting for him on the other side of the gate. The smaller one sat at the door with a shotgun over his lap, their eyes locked on Croker and openly entertained that he decided to attend their meeting alone. Louis unlocked the iron bars and opened the gate slowly for him to enter, his body language suspicious and predatory. While he wasn't sure the origin of their connection, Will mentioned to Croker Louis was not someone to ever take lightly, and that he was just as, if not more deadly, than Will was himself. Croker believed bringing him onto their side would be a work in progress, and although neither Will nor Louis were still in their prime of life, he had yet to find anyone better at killing for their profession.

Other than Walsh, that is.

Louis closed and locked the gate as Croker passed. "She's expecting you."

"I'd certainly hoped she was," Croker countered, purposefully wanting to pry a little further. "Pity about your friend. I trust his son has gone?"

This hit a bad nerve in Louis. "Yes."

"A shame to lose both parents in such horrible circumstances," Croker went on. "I must say, to his own fortune, fate stepped in and certainly gave him a fair hand in the process." Louis didn't respond, so Croker pushed him again. "He doesn't know the truth, I assume?"

Louis cleared his throat. "If he had, Mr. Croker, I can assure you he wouldn't have rested until he put your corpse into the ground."

Croker chuckled, slapping Louis on the back. "That's the spirit. We're in a nasty business here. Cutting losses and moving on is the only way to keep going forward. Now, upstairs to the office I assume?"

Once more ignoring Croker's commentary, Louis took two strides ahead of him, leading through the front door and up the center staircase. The bar downstairs was busy with customers, multiple card games already rolling and whiskey flowing like water to whoever asked for it. A grin came to Croker's face: this place would be a goldmine for Tammany, specifically if they began to send their own high-ranking people that direction. Eight years ago when he first met the Madame, he'd avoided pushing his luck after their initial encounter, not quite strong enough to speak for the Hall on his own and not wanting to jeopardize the ground he'd made with some of the board. Since then, the forecast had changed drastically, and Croker was next in line for total takeover. No, he wasn't speaking for John any longer. Croker was Tammany Hall. What he ruled from that point forward might as well have been set in stone.

Louis threw the double doors open and showed him inside,

where the Madame sat behind her desk, a glass of whiskey in one hand, a cigar in the other, dressed in a deep plunging purple velvet gown and her hair pinned up on her head. The moment she saw Croker she beckoned him to sit in a nearby armchair, though she herself did not move from her contrived position of authority.

"Mr. Croker!" she sang out. "I've been expecting you. Please! I have a cigar ready for you and a bottle of my finest whiskey at your disposal."

Croker ambled over and grabbed a cigar and cutter from her desk as she went to the drink cart to pour him a whiskey. Sinking down into the chair she'd directed him to, Croker lit it and took a few puffs.

"We have a few things to discuss, I believe," she continued, ushering his drink over. "Business matters, am I correct?"

Her demeanor was too welcoming, but unlike Seamus, Croker was prepared not to fall into another one of the Madame's traps. Peeking over his shoulder to make sure they were by themselves, as he did not want to cause too much of a scene, he was glad to see Louis had left them to their own devices. Croker rotated back around, and for a brief moment they locked eyes tensely. With a swift lurch, he snatched her left wrist in his hand and she dropped his whiskey to the floor. He gave one hard twist, hoping to send her to the floor off balance and in pain, when instead the Madame maneuvered sideways, swiftly drawing a pistol from nowhere and pointing it at Croker's head with her free hand. Neither moved for a few seconds, and then suddenly Croker let out a loud, bellowing laugh and let her wrist go. She took a few steps toward her desk, keeping her pistol aimed, and Croker leisurely rose, picking the shards of glass from the floor.

"Relax, Madame, I just wanted to see what you were hiding," he justified, as if he'd done nothing irrational, and made his way to get a new glass. "Put the gun down and let's have a real discussion."

The clink of the pistol cocking was not exactly a reassuring sound. "Tell me why the fuck I shouldn't just shoot you now. After all the damage you've caused me and my family, I'd have every God damned right to end you."

He kept his back to her. "I won't deny you that. But you know better." When he'd finished pouring his new whiskey, Croker resumed his former seat, gun still aimed at his head. "Whether you would like to hear this or not, I am the next Grand Sachem of Tammany. My foundation is nearly complete, and to finish building, I could certainly use a friend like you. You've acquired a wealth of knowledge I want access to, and I will compensate you heartily for it."

The Madame uncocked the gun and set it on her desk. "How much?"

"For every new detail you give me, I'll pay double what your highest paying customer pays per night. And I'll be sending you a plethora of new clients, as well as a few new business propositions."

Mulling over his words, the Madame took a minute and went back to her chair, picking up her drink and taking a puff of her own cigar. "What do you need me to do aside from feed you everyone's dirty secrets?"

"I have a list here of gentlemen who have been in before. Some are friends, others I want specifically targeted, mainly Nationalist pricks and Swallows." Croker handed over a list of names from his jacket pocket, which she glanced over as he resumed. "When these bastards come in, I want to know about it, and I'll send instructions along for what is needed. If this goes well, I'll give you more autonomy, and more expansion opportunities." Then, from his vest pocket, Croker pulled out a large amount of paper money and tossed it on the Madame's desk.

Her eyebrow rose. "What's this?"

"Call it an act of goodwill. To reestablish a little trust, which will be needed for this to work smoothly."

The Madame went back to skimming the list. "I will do what you ask without any fucking argument as long as I'm paid what you say. If that arrangement is ever broken, or the moment that sick son of a bitch you keep sending here to try and frighten me into fuck-ing submission shows up, I will find you, and cut you apart piece by piece. I don't trust you, and I will never be stupid enough to trust you. But I'll make the deal."

"I can accept that," Croker voiced, ironically liking the Madame more this way than in her false enthusiasm, "Walsh will keep out."

"Wait," she said, her finger resting beside a name on the paper. "Why the fuck is Timothy Adams on this list?"

Croker had a feeling this issue might arise. "Charles Adams was a major contributor to Tammany Hall. One of our top investors these last few years. His son has vowed to continue this generosity and he has therefore become a friend of the Hall. May I remind you, Madame, this is business, and has nothing to do with the unprov-en indiscretions he has committed against your people in the past."

The Madame set the paper down on her desk, her demeanor dif-ferent than Croker expected. "What if I told you there was more to this piece of shit than just running the company for his dead father?"

"What do you mean?" Croker hated to admit he was a little intrigued.

"I mean what if I could provide you with the proof that this as-shole isn't who he says he is…someone even the Hall wouldn't want to associate with no matter how much of his God damned money he was dumping into the organization?"

"Give me the evidence and we will talk," he told her, wonder-ing what in the world the Madame could have possibly dug up that Tammany's vetting missed. "Before I go, however, I will make an-other suggestion."

"And that is?"

"You should have a talk with your darling Detective. He isn't exactly playing nice, and I can't guarantee his safety if he doesn't bet in with everyone else."

Any warmth left in the room vanished at the mention of Detective Ellis, and the Madame's wrath at his mention was far beyond what Croker saw coming.

"I don't speak for any person but myself," she snarled. "I'll be in touch regarding your list, Mr. Croker, as well as the evidence I have on Timothy Adams. When you see it with your own eyes, you will grant me permission to have him killed, though for the reputation of your precious Hall, I will see to it that the task is done in a disguisable fashion. And now, Mr. Croker, you can get the fuck out of my office."

Croker got to his feet and dropped his cigar onto her carpet, putting it out with his heel. "'Til then, Madame." He threw back the last sip of whiskey and set the glass on her desk, turning and pacing toward the door.

"Oh, one last item," he called out, stopping. "Mary is dead. So any idea of retaliation would be extremely unwise. This is the way it should have been from the start."

Hoping he'd made the impression he intended, Croker made his way down the stairs and out the front door, the eyes of everyone he passed burning a hole in the back of his skull, and he thoroughly enjoyed being that reviled. It meant he'd made his mark. It meant that, while they hated it, there was no denying that he owned them.

The coach was out front, and inside sat Walsh, cloaked in darkness save the reflection of the street lamp in his spectacles. The two men didn't say a word and waited until the driver was two blocks away before they spoke, and Walsh took the lead.

"And?"

Croker stared at him, unable to deliberate whether it was the bitter evening or Walsh giving him chills. "Stay out of The Palace, I've got the Madame under control for the present moment. I need you to watch Sweeny and that French bastard – their odd sort of

611

friendship is not exactly approved, if you get my drift. The number one priority is wrapping up the last of this bullshit with the Turners."

"Do you need me to make a trip to England?"

"No…just make sure they're gone and not planning on coming back. Ask around…the staff…friends…you know the drill. I am taking care of Mary Daugherty tomorrow. The one that worries me is the girl."

Walsh was interested. "Why the girl? The rape?"

"Not the rape. Just her. I know the type. She's got a rage in her like the head whore but no means of restraining what she does. It's only a matter of time. One spark and she'll blow."

"And this worries you? That is what we'd been hoping for, I presumed."

Croker leaned forward, resting his elbows on his knees and lowering his tone. "There is no way I am going to allow Tweed's illegitimate daughter to start stirring shit up. Not on my watch, and not when we've only just cleaned up his mess." Croker shook his head, almost unable to believe the twisted dynamic of it all. "No one has any idea who she really is, or that she even exists."

"Except the Madame?"

"After what Tweed did to the Madame, I doubt she would have ever taken that girl in if she knew who she really was."

"So you need me to monitor this from a distance…"

"Yes," Croker agreed. "Watch her closely. I want updates every day. Like I said, it's only a matter of time. She's grasping at straws."

"And what do I do if we can't keep it contained?"

"What you do best," Croker charged him. "Make it disappear."

XXI.

He had spent days watching Esther hoping for some sort
of turn around in her well-being, but Louis was skeptical whether or not emotional recovery was on the horizon. It wasn't just her
heartbreaking fallout with Thomas that set Esther spiraling downward so abruptly – it was a combination of the bad memories of
that summer pooling together into a giant, tornadic storm, tearing her apart. She'd been beaten and raped by the husband of her
best friend, left by the man she loved, and on top of that, been an
integral part of the offensive against the Hiltmores…a lot for a
girl who had barely reached nineteen. Every day since the Turners' departure she exhausted with Celeste, assisting her around the
house, packing up the last of her dearest friend's belongings before she took the train south to Virginia for the winter. When she
wasn't there, Esther stayed inside the apartments gifted to her by
the Madame, burying her sorrows at the bottom of the wine bottle and crying herself to sleep. Louis wished he could find a way
to placate her, yet he knew there was nothing he could say that
would change her circumstances. Instead, he was forced to observe
it from afar, praying she could find the strength to pull through it
given the right amount of time.

To Captain Bernhardt's credit, the man somehow managed to ascertain the location of Esther's new living arrangements and made a point of stopping by three to four times a week; there was never an answer to his calls and his letters went unrecognized, though he persisted, never giving up the faith that one day she might come down. Nevertheless, late one night, Louis spotted Esther had taken the ring out from the bottom of a drawer in her dresser and stared at it, and rather than a look of longing on her face, Esther's eyes would fill with abhorrence. The ring was what had destroyed her and Thomas, the constant reminder that she betrayed his trust, and in a peculiar way, this would cause Louis' empathy to lessen. Only he and the Madame were aware of how much she kept from Thomas, so much to try and shield him from what she truly was, and this only hurt him in return. All those years of being mentored by the Madame and upper class philosophy seemed to do Esther more harm than good – she might claim to be a terrible liar, but she was becoming talented in the same way the Madame was: a brilliant deceiver in the withholding of information.

Still, it was psychologically difficult for Louis to witness her misery.

Thirty-three times she'd written the same letter to Thomas, and each time Esther burned it without sending or showing any intention to send it. Louis couldn't be sure what exactly it said, though anyone with half a brain would discern it was, in all probability, an apology of some sort. Esther was fighting with an identity crisis, wherein she wanted to be something she knew she was not. It was hard for her to accept the dark side of her story, the part where she'd been a prisoner her entire life, living off the graces of others and doing everything she could to chameleon herself to the prearranged surroundings. To survive, she'd bargained and worked for the Madame to maintain her grip on what real life was like for most, and thus made her feel more isolated than ever. Louis understood that loneliness better than anyone: it was a notion he hadn't overcome in the entirety of his adult life, and sadly, it was something he feared Esther wouldn't be able to conquer either.

Louis was a firsthand spectator to Esther's depression regarding Thomas and their split, and he wondered why on earth she held onto Captain Bernhardt's ring and not the one given to her by Thomas. In an effort to identify with the sentiment, he mulled over the topic a few times and came to the conclusion that the Captain's ring not only reminded her that losing Thomas was her fault and hers alone, but also…that the ring was a failsafe she could run back to. Esther felt she didn't deserve Thomas, and frankly, Louis wasn't sure she was wrong in that regard. Louis had lost sleep over the way he and Thomas parted, angry with one another due to miscommunications concerning the unsettled elements of his father's life, elements Louis had the answers to and did not believe Thomas was ready to hear. In time he would be back, that much was certain, and until then Louis swore he would keep Esther safe for Thomas. What would happen in those years, Louis couldn't say, though he had an inclination the Thomas that left them would be a far different man upon his return.

For awhile, Louis broached the subject of Esther with the Madame, and each exchange ended in a similar manner: she vowed Esther would figure it out on her own, that it was a necessary mourning period for any young woman to endure, and eventually she would come to and be her normal self again. Her visits to The Palace had by no means ceased; however, it was plainly obvious any smiles or laughter were an act, forced in order to seem natural. And while the Madame never pressed Esther on her disposition or the state of her feelings, Louis could tell on the inside it bothered the Madame more than it did him, principally because the were going through almost double the bottles of whiskey they normally did.

And that was one hell of a lot of whiskey.

It was a Friday morning, cold and bitter with damp leaves on the ground. Louis sat outside her apartment, a cigarette ready for her and another already between his lips, the smoke rising toward a grey sky.

They hadn't spoken alone since the night in the carriage in spite of her stopping by The Palace to see the Madame. Maybe it was selfish, but Louis was tired of worrying, and unlike the Madame, he wasn't good at letting things go to ride out their own course. Esther needed some-thing…something he could only discover from a face-to-face interac-tion and, in all honesty, he missed her and the sincerity of her smile when she saw him. Mourning was one thing…self-pity was another.

At ten, Esther made her way outside, wrapped up in a fur lined coat she'd bought out with Celeste the week before, her hands shaky in the brisk air as she locked the building door. Fumbling with the keys, she accidentally dropped them to the ground and let out an audible sigh, one much more aggrieved than just the irritation of her clumsiness. Louis, who was leaning against the lamppost across from her stoop, shook his head and walked over to her.

"Need a hand?"

Esther must have noticed him prior to leaving her apartment, and did not pretend for a second his appearance was a surprise. "I've got it Louis, thank you."

He stood patiently, allowing her to retrieve the keys and de-scend down toward him. "Got one for you," he told her, holding out one of his own hand rolled. She took it with a small grin, mak-ing Louis' heart a little lighter as he struck a match for her. "How is the new place?"

Esther had a long drag before she spoke. "I think you know how miserable I am right now, Louis. I know you've been hanging around."

"You're the one making yourself that way, Esther," he pro-nounced bluntly, thinking perhaps a hard dose of reality was best. "What's done is done. The Turners are gone. And I would bet they don't come back for quite some time, if that. You can move on with your life as you please."

"Yeah, well what if that's not what I want?" she retorted ag-gressively.

"You've had plenty of time to change that and you haven't,"

he responded, not backing down. "If you wanted to talk to Thomas you should have sent the letter you've written countless times, or tried to see them the days before they left. Now, be an adult and deal with your own consequences like the rest of us."

Esther grew quiet and sank down, sitting on the stoop. Louis lowered down beside her and saw a tear falling down her cheek, which she wiped away at once. Without thinking, Louis impulses took over and he wrapped his arm around her, pulling her in close to his chest and holding her tight.

"I…I don't know what's wrong with me, Louis…" she sniffed, "I just don't' know what the fuck to do!"

"You chose your path. Now you must live with that choice."

"I don't want to be alone," she cried, "I feel so alone."

Louis released her and took her delicate hands in his. "We're all alone, Esther. You have been through so much. Don't become the victim. Be the conqueror of your fears…the way we've taught you since you were young."

Esther nodded, her eyes going out to the roadway. "Celeste is going back to Virginia for the winter."

"Just the winter?"

"Through having the baby. Then they'll be back in late spring. Apparently Timothy has taken quite a liking to New York despite his father being…"

Louis couldn't repress a little chortle. "I'm not ashamed. Charles Adams was a monster, just like his son."

Esther smiled again, this one indisputably real. "Must be genetic. I hope the other one goes soon as well."

Her words were meant as a joke, however Louis saw through them. "Promise me you won't do anything without telling me first," he articulated softly.

Esther scoffed. "I've dreamed of killing him a thousand times, Louis. Every fiber of me wants to do it. But I can't. I just can't." She put her cigarette out against the brick step to her right. "I know what it would do to Celeste, and I can't do that to her. He hasn't touched her since the pregnancy and I keep wondering if maybe the Madame was right. Maybe in the end, the baby will save her from destitution."

"I hope she is right, too, but what if she isn't, Esther? What then?"

"I don't know Louis…"

"You know, you just don't want to tell me."

Esther shook her head. "No, I don't. I would love to think getting rid of him would make it better. It won't. I know better now."

"And what will make it better?"

She sat silent for a few moments, not moving an inch. "Nothing, Louis. Nothing will make it the same again. Nothing will ever be the same again."

"An' just what in the hell kept you so long?"

The sight of Will was usually a welcome one to Louis. But today, after his morning with Esther, he was in no mood to deal with the typical semantics and bullshit. Their meet point was on the outskirts of Chinatown, near enough to keep the scent off their tracks but far enough from the Points to keep Louis out of trouble. It was the same routine every week: both men would have a drink and a smoke together on the porch of a house owned by a poor negro doctor, a man by the name of Washington. Will had known him for years and trusted him from his…for lack of a better word…rougher days. The doctor's wife would bring their whiskies out, with a smile and a small curtsey before she disappeared back to help her husband with his work. The one thing Louis couldn't stand about Chinatown was the smell – foul meat, ginger, and opium smoke seemed to pour from every direction, and no matter where he stepped Louis would nearly decimate a chink half his size. Needless to say, he avoided the area almost to the degree he avoided the Points.

As Louis trotted up the step, he chose not to react to Will's jibe, trying to shake off the foul mood he was in. His drink was already on the table, and a countenance of offense was forming on Will's face.

"Got a problem there, Frog?"

Louis pulled the chair out and sat down. "Not with you," he replied, grabbing his glass to have a sip.

"What is it?" Will asked, not one to give up.

"Nothing, Will. Let it go."

"Nope. Tell me what the fuck is goin' on," he demanded, leaning closer to him, "Somethin' come up?"

"Not like that. It's the girl. She's a God damned disaster, Will."

"How's that, then?"

"She's in a bad way of it," he put plainly. "I can't reach her. The Madame can't reach her. It's not pretty."

Will studied him closely. "Not goin' to be an issue, is it? For the Irish?"

"Just for me, I think." Louis reached into his jacket pocket for a cigarette. "I don't know why, Will, but I get this feeling like she's heading down a bad road. One I don't think anyone can pull her off of."

"Because of Tommy?"

"Thomas was a few strokes of the bigger painting. Esther's on hard times. It's not going to end well."

"You need to stop carin' so much. If ya can' change it, quit fightin', brother. It's a losin' battle! Long as she doesn' kill someone the Hall needs, you and I can keep her safe. I promise ya that. Deal?"

"What's your interest in her?" Louis pressed curiously.

"You care, I care," Will stated bluntly. "You oughta know that."

Louis concealed a grin. "Right. So what've you got for me, Will?"

Will shifted in his chair, pulling a sheet of paper from inside his left jacket pocket. "Got a list here, brother. A few Fridays from now, all set for The Palace an' on orders to be given whatever spoils necessary." He put the list on the table and slid it toward Louis. "No expense spared, ya hear? Most are potentials, people Tammany want for votes and backers. A few are union fellas, and those are the three

619

we need to win over above everybody else. Last, we've got two rats we wanna smoke out. They're the last two."

"I'll let the Madame know," Louis informed him, scanning the names and stopping when he read one that nearly set him off. "Timothy Adams is on this list."

"Yes."

"As a backer."

"For Christ's sake, Louis, the bastard inherited a fortune from his father, and that boy's daddy was throwin' money at the Hall like hot cakes! He wants more political involvement, and Tammany is givin' it to him as long as he gives back. Don' get all indignant with me. I didn' write the God damned list!"

Louis stuffed the paper in his vest. "Will, he's the one who raped Esther."

Unexpectedly, Will became upset. "You think I don' know that? You think it doesn' bother me some prick with money gets away with that shit? What bothers you bothers me, brother. But it ain't my call. It's Boss man's call. He pays the bills."

Just then, the doctor's wife returned with a bottle of whiskey and refilled both Will and Louis' glasses. Louis thanked her politely and she retreated inside again, though he made sure her footsteps were long gone when he spoke.

"I don't know if I can control Esther if she finds out about this," Louis whispered. "She's distraught. The Madame made her a deal not to let him back at The Palace again. If she knows the Madame is having him—"

"The only way she'll know is if you tell her," Will interrupted. "Don' be a fool. Keep her outta our shit. She's safe. Let's not shoot ourselves in the foot again, eh?"

Louis finished his whiskey, his irritation with the situation rising. "What else, Will? Time's running thin."

"All right, keep your damn pants on. Just wanted to tell ya with the Turners gone, everythin' is calmin' down a bit, but I've still got that nasty son of a bitch followin' me 'round the city. Shouldn' be a problem much longer. But hey, now that they're gone, we can breathe easy, brother. It's over."

"That's the difference between us, Will. You move from one to the next. Mine all link together. It's never over for me."

"Ya know, we could fix this. Walsh tailin' me, you gettin' out of the fuckin' mess you're in...all that."

"What are you talking about, Will?"

Will quickly scouted right and left, then scooted his chair closer to Louis. "Finish with the head whore. Come work with me. Croker wants ya, brother. Think of it, us workin' together again? We'd run the city in no time."

Louis locked eyes with Will. "Any man who employs Walsh will never be a boss of mine, Will. You know what he's done...you've seen it firsthand. Unlike you, I don't turn a blind eye to complete fucking brutality."

"And when did you get so sensitive, eh?" Will countered, "You ain't never apologized for a hit or for anythin' you done. And you're mad because some guy who's a little rougher than you is the same way?"

Louis was beginning to boil over. "He is nothing like me, Will. He's the devil if there was one. I wouldn't ever cross the lines he has. He is insane...deranged, even. It's not human."

Will let out a chuckle. "Shit we did in the beginnin' ain't nothin' to be proud of either, brother," he reminded him, getting to his feet, "Get another whiskey and get outta here. Whyos find out you're here with me havin' a drink you're a dead man. And we're just startin' to have fun again! Like old times..."

"Fuck you, Will. This isn't a game."

"If ya can' deal with it, get out, brother. Simple as that."

Louis didn't bother to answer, already sensing Will's aggravation with him. His friend got up, took three strides away from the porch and halted, spinning around and marching back Louis' direction.

"All the hell we been through, and you treat me like shit? This the way it is, brother? Is it?" His voice rose along with his bad humor. "You act like you're so fuckin' high and mighty. Don' forget the God damned fall I took for ya 'cause you were my friend, and I ain't ever held that over your head! Jus' like I said earlier, I'd do anythin' to help ya and here ya are, actin' like everythin' we had don' matter a lick to ya."

A pang of guilt hit Louis' stomach hard. "It was just a bad day, Will. You know it's not like that."

Will waved him off, but Louis couldn't stop himself. "It's hard enough seeing you alive, let alone that we're on different sides of the equation. If we were ever found out…if our past was ever found out…we'd be dead."

Will stared at him and lingered wordlessly for nearly a minute, the intensity between them growing.

"We'll never be on different sides, Louis. Ain't in my make up, and it ain't in yours either."

"Then what is this, Will? What the fuck are we doing?"

"We got each other's backs, like we shoulda had all along," Will affirmed. "Bosses don' need to know that."

"And if they do find out?" Louis queried.

"They won'."

Will whipped around and strode off toward Tammany to report back, peeking over his shoulder at Louis once or twice before he disappeared. In spite of their argument, from the few minutes he spent with Will, Louis felt more relieved than he had in weeks. Losing Edward triggered a small break in his self-assurance, and somehow, Louis found himself questioning every aspect of his life and purpose, his friendship with Will being no exception. Every time Louis had to watch him go he speculated whether or not it would be the last, never certain if one or both of them would make it through the night and on to dawn the next morning. After years of working alone, Will's presence was blurring his better judgment

and his loyalties, especially since the Madame's temporary new direction with Tammany was one with little need of him, other than
to throw out any aggressors at The Palace or to run her small errands. Of course, the Madame was by no means ready to lie down
and play nice with Croker; their provisional status as a partner to
that bastard was only to stay alive in anticipation of formulating a
new plan of attack. The part that worried him was how and when
they were going to make that happen.

Louis drained his whiskey and he abandoned the small table,
leaving a dollar underneath his glass for the wife. The ride back to
The Palace would be a long one, and he treaded a few blocks prior
to hopping on the horse trolley heading uptown. He avoided small
talk with his overly friendly neighbors, not even bothering to glance
their direction. Instead, he internalized, wanting desperately for his
head to be on straight for his talk with the Madame. Louis' thoughts
were all over the place, and growing steadily more pathetic by the
second. Losing Edward…seeing Thomas leave again…the emotions
took over his body like a disease. There was a substantial amount
of grief he'd been hiding, burying away from the outside world was
starting to bubble to the surface. So many secrets kept from the people he cared about most, and for what? To watch them die in the
street, unable to stop it? And Tommy…Tommy was gone, and if
he knew what was good for him, he wouldn't dare set foot in that
city again. Louis only wished he'd taken Esther with him; to his astonishment, she confessed to Louis that morning she had been the
one to break it off permanently. Her staying would bring no good
omens to any of them. There wasn't much he could do other than
attempt to be her confidant and friend, shielding her in any way possible. For her sake, Louis wanted to strangle the life out of Timothy
Adams, because without Thomas at her side, her strength wasn't
what it once was. On top of that, the bastard had become an asset
to Tammany, and unless he was truly ready to hang from the rope,
Louis couldn't lay a finger on him without repercussions. Finding

himself back where he'd been only a few weeks ago, his conscience couldn't decide whether or not taking the fall for Esther would be worth the sacrifice.

"Central Park!" the driver called through the car. "South entrance! Central Park!"

Louis hopped off. He grazed through the southeast entrance and sat down on a bench nearby, taking the list from his pocket with the intention of examining it closely. As he unfolded the paper, Louis shook his head when he realized Will hadn't just given him the list. There were two sheets folded together instead of one. Louis pocketed the list and read through the second note, a wave of shock hitting him more with each word.

Will's handwriting read:

Whyos will let you back in the Points if you take out O'Neill. They think he's been stealing from them. He'll be at the Dry Dollar by eight.

Croker will approve only if you agree to work with him over the Madame, but he wants you to keep your position with her for leverage.

Crossover job – easy for you to keep your loyalties.

I'll meet you there. No is the wrong answer, brother.

It was hard to believe it wasn't a set up, but Will would never lie to him about this. Immediately Louis made a judgment call: they needed a new angle, a new set of tactics to gain the advantage, and this was their chance.

It would probably be the only one they ever got.

He ran, and by the time he arrived at The Palace, she would be prepping and dressing for the night. Louis climbed up the steps as fast as he could without causing any alarm, knowing she wouldn't mind the interruption when she heard what was in store for the rest of his evening.

"Excuse me, Madame," he announced himself loudly, cracking the door and wedging his head in. "I need you for a moment."

624

"For fuck's sake, I'm trying to get dressed, Louis!" she yelled back "Can't this wait an hour? And can someone get me a God damned bottle of wine?!"

"Madame, I have news from Croker."

"Yes and that can fucking wait like I said!"

"No…no it can't." Louis took a deep breath and pushed through the doors, closing them shut.

The Madame, who was very visibly naked underneath her silk robe, was by no means amused by his boldness. "If it was anyone else, I would have you take them downstairs and beat the living hell out of them."

Louis pulled out the list and Will's letter. "I understand we need to meet with Danny and Hope about the prospective clients Friday. But there is something much more pressing. This…this is the key, Madame. It's more important than anything else right now."

"What is?"

Louis held out the letter. "Read."

With a glower his direction, the Madame snatched up Will's note and inspected it. Her eyes grew wide, along with a large smile.

"Please tell me this is real."

"Yes."

"Who gave it to you, Louis?"

"It's from Will. He hid it in with the list, and Will would never feed me false information."

"You're so sure of that?"

"Yes. This is real. It's the next step we've been searching for."

The Madame made her way over to her vanity and sat down, reading over it again. When she glanced up at him, he knew the wheels of her scheming mind were turning.

"Louis, this changes everything."

Louis sat down onto the sofa. "Does it?"

His contesting words set her off. "What do you mean, does it? Are you trying to imply something?"

625

"Madame, I am not trying to imply anything."

"I can see through that bullshit, Louis. What is it?"

Their eyes met. "The last few weeks have been more difficult for me than I could have predicted, and following your alliance with Croker and Mary's death, I want to make sure our original goal is still in order."

"You have so little faith in me to think I'd throw out my scheming against Croker? From a few minor setbacks?" She flipped around and began rouging her cheeks. "The plan has…and never will change. We can't play our best hand in the first round, Louis. We've been laying low, wanting to seem as harmless as we can while we slowly begin to sink our teeth into the grit of it."

"I am risking everything if we do this, Madame. Everything we've done together will be on the table."

She paused. "I know. But we don't have a choice. Or you wouldn't have shown me that letter."

Louis conceded. "If this deal goes through—"

"We can start working the Points again," she went on. "Is it doable?"

"It'll be the easiest hit I've done in fifteen years."

"Good," she reacted contentedly and started to make herself up once more, looking at him from the mirror's reflection. "Are you sure you're ready for this, Louis?"

He didn't quite comprehend what she was insinuating. "For the hit?"

"For infiltrating Tammany. For going behind the fucking enemy lines."

"Will wouldn't go behind my back. If Croker does start sniffing me out, I'd have a head start out of town."

The Madame wasn't satisfied with his answer. "It's not the Cat I'm worried about, Louis. It's…it's that sick son of a bitch Walsh… he knows things, Louis, things no one could possibly know…"

"Will thinks Walsh will disappear soon enough."

"Soon enough isn't soon enough."

"I'll take care of Walsh," he reassured her, "Trust me, Madame. Our prayers have finally been answered."

"Well it's about fucking time. Now for the love of God, go get a bottle of wine and the girls. This was a bit more information than I was fucking planning on for tonight, and I can't entertain when I'm overly distracted."

Louis got up and instinctively checked to see his gun was fully loaded. "I just hope the Danny's don't show up."

Again, she stopped in her process and revolved around, her character becoming sincere. "There's no reason Croker would directly involve the Whyos in a hit like this. He can barely control those mongrels as it is, and getting rid of his own man doesn't need fucking up. Fucking up is the only thing they're good at."

"Madame," Louis began, "if the Dannys or McGloin ever discover I took out Charles Adams in the 4th Ward without their permission, they'll kill me on sight regardless of Croker and his deal."

"I realize that."

"So I can only hope he's sobered them up long enough that they remember their end of the bargain, or that Will knows what the hell he's doing."

She was suddenly worried. "What if Will betrays you?"

"Then there's no question I'll be dead, but he wouldn't."

"But if he does…"

"You'll have to win this war on your own, I'm afraid."

"Well, I guess you'd better take a few extra bullets, then."

Will was two blocks from the Dry Dollar waiting for Louis at a quarter past eight, smoking a cigarette with his hat tipped low over his eyes – it was old protocol for them, meeting a safe distance from where the target was in order to prep and discuss their method of attack. Louis made his driver drop him in Little Italy and walked the rest of the way southward to the Points, and the closer he got to the Dry Dollar the darker the streets became, so dark that Louis could barely see his feet, as no one was brave enough to be out at night to keep the lampposts lit in that neighborhood. In the Points, not a soul ended up there by accident, and if they did, they wouldn't last long with the drunken, sadistic Whyos now in control of it.

For Louis, this was an incredibly steep gamble. He was officially crossing into enemy territory, lines that had been drawn out years ago for him and for the Madame that they crossed only under the most desperate of circumstances. Charles Adams' hit being one. On those occasions, Louis was in and out so hastily he was virtually undetectable; tonight, however, his presence would be felt in the Bowery…a place he purposefully hadn't ventured near in years, and the smell of the polluted water alone was enough to bring back the memories of his previous life. A rush hit his bloodstream. During the height of their youthful conquests, Will had been his most reliable friend and in a way, they became an invincible pair. That hadn't changed, no matter how much time passed since. The Whyos were vile…unpredictable… violent…there was no telling how the night would turn out, and Louis' senses were sharp as a blade, assessing every angle of the shadows, readying for what could possibly be a complete and utter disaster.

Will didn't make eye contact with Louis as he approached, just went on puffing his cigarette, his gaze locked on the saloon one hundred yards away.

"Got a bit of bad news, brother."

"What is it?"

"McGloin's with him. Well, not with him. O'Neill thinks he's with him, but really, prick's just watchin'…keepin' a close eye on him 'til our man showed up."

Disconcerted by this, Louis circled casually, surveying the street for onlookers. "The Danny's aren't there, are they?"

"Nah," Will assured him. "They'll be down at The Morgue.

This is Quinn's main hang out now, and Kitty hates Quinn even more than she hates you."

"Funny how hatred pours down a generation," Louis muttered. "Not a damn one of these children knows the real reason I've been outted."

"That's the way it goes, I'm 'fraid. You and I are the old bastards now. Gotta keep these young motherfuckers in check."

Louis smiled ironically. "That should go over well."

"Hell, we still alive, ain't we?"

"And how the hell did we stay alive so long?"

Will chuckled. "I'd say we're just a bit smarter than these young bastards who think they know what killin' is, and they don' know shit."

"Right then, let's get this over with."

"Whoa, hold it right there, brother," Will halted him, addressing him with a step Louis' direction. "What's the plan?"

"How we always used to do it with these pricks," Louis stated brusquely. "Clean sweep. River. Like the old days."

With a hesitating glance left and right, Will turned and moved closer so that he and Louis were only inches apart. "Stay careful, all right? Move fast. I've got my pistol if he tries to run, and extra cylinders if we have ourselves a confrontation."

Louis opened his jacket, showing both the dagger sheathed at his waist along with his revolver. "Just watch my back, Will."

Will regarded him for a long few seconds, then moved aside for Louis to take the lead to the Dry Dollar. Strutting ahead, Louis was pleasantly caught unawares by the sensation of excitement, one he hadn't experienced prior to a hit for years. Excitement was often a distraction, something to breathe through and concentrate on the kill ahead without inhibiting the unusual natural instincts of a murderous mindset. It wasn't because of O'Neill, either, or the Whyos, or the return to a place he never dreamed he'd set foot in again. It was Will: once again they were together again…partners.

The Dry Dollar was packed as Louis and Will drew closer, and with a quick reaffirming look over his shoulder, Louis went straight for the entrance. He pushed open the doors to the saloon and was immediately absorbed by the roar of the crowd: someone was pounding the keyboard on a piano from the balcony upstairs while an off tune tenor sang, glasses breaking, chairs and tables screeching against the wood floors, and on top of that the shouts of drunk customers wanting either another beer or to be taken upstairs for a night of pleasure. The low hanging chandeliers were dripping wax to the ground, and a distant staircase off in the corner led to the second floor, where the whores ran their operations and McGloin sold opium to the highest bidder. Cards and gambling to his right, topless women and the staircase lay ahead, and to the left was the bar, a sea of arms outstretched for more whiskey and beer. Louis knew O'Neill, though somehow he spotted McGloin first in spite of never seeing him in person before: he was at the far end of the bar, chatting idly with one of the bartenders, and he was exactly the way Louis imagined. Mike McGloin was short and squirrelly looking bastard, with yellow teeth and wide eyes that were just a little too close together at his nose. His Irish roots shone through his reddish brown hair, so filthy it was dreading on the sides, as well as the freckles that covered his forearms and face. McGloin's brown trousers and waistcoat were ordinary…dirty, but ordinary…and Louis had done enough of his own investigating to understand just how to handle a son of a bitch like him.

He and Will had killed plenty of McGloins during their own time running the Points.

At that point, the target presented himself. O'Neill saw Louis approach with Will, beckoning them over for a drink, while it was plain he had consumed more than enough for five on his own.

"Jusss…Will…what're'ya doin' bringin' the Frog around, eh? He'sssss…he killed a fuckin' copper, lad…one o' our boys…."

"Actually, he works for Croker," Will accounted cheerily, bellying up at the bar beside Louis. "All in the schemin', I'm afraid. Bartender! How's about a few whiskies down here? My treat, boys."

Sliding over, McGloin's eyes gave Louis the up and down, undoubtedly searching for weak spots that he would never be able to find.

"So you're the Frog?" McGloin snuffed as he joined the conversation, trying to appear unimpressed even if Louis was twice his size. "I thought you wasn't allowed down here no more."

"McGloin, quit your bitchin'," Will interjected, pouring four shots for them. "The Dannys know. Special deal was confirmed for tonight. And if you've got a problem, take it up with them, eh?"

McGloin didn't budge. "I was told the deal was pendin' the outcome. You know, followin' through on the deal first?"

Louis downed his whiskey and refilled his shot glass. "Hard to follow through on the deal when you're keeping him occupied all evening, isn't it?" Louis hissed under his breath, irritated.

McGloin didn't appreciate this. "I expect you oughta get outta my face, Frog, before I break it. Danny's said if I got there first I'd get paid and get to kill the infamous Frog. An' I'm just wonderin' if I might take them up on that instead."

Tired of messing around, Louis shifted and in the blink of an eye, grabbed McGloin so hard by the balls the man squeaked aloud, knocking his glass of whiskey aside just as his face began to turn blue. With a little twist, Louis then reached for McGloin's right arm, holding him steady where he was.

"This is the way it's going to be," he asserted, leaning forward to whisper in McGloin's ear. "And you couldn't break my face if you tried, you stupid little bastard. My skull would break every last bone in your hand. So take you're act somewhere else, and let me work. Got it?"

McGloin hesitated at first, and Louis gave one more tiny twist, sending his victim reeling. With an enthusiastic nod from McGloin to submit his surrender, Louis released him at once, causing him to slip down to the ground and roll into a ball of agony, cupping his testicles like they were crown jewels. Happy they hadn't caught the bartender's attention, Louis bent down and shoved something

631

in McGloin's pants pocket, then spun around to grab O'Neill. Will was close behind as they exited the Dry Dollar, not a single person noticing that anything unconventional had occurred.

Will hushed down O'Neill's protestations, constantly reiterating the lie that Croker wanted to see them all, and eventually Will's convincing voice had O'Neill compliantly stumbling along beside them, too drunk to ascertain that Louis was marching them for the wall by the river.

With O'Neill drunk and babbling on to himself, his words all slurring together, Will nonchalantly looked to Louis. "What did you put in McGloin's pocket?" he asked quietly, not wanting to rouse O'Neill's suspicions.

"A hundred dollars."

Will stopped dead in his tracks. "Are you fuckin' shittin' me, Louis?"

"Keep walking!" Louis directed punitively, keeping his voice down.

Following orders, Will skipped onward, steering O'Neill along. "You best tell me why the hell you wasted that God damned money for a guy who wanted to slit your fuckin' throat," Will murmured.

"For his fee."

"Fee? What fee? What the hell you talkin' about? Ain't no fee we owe those bastards for bein' here."

"I paid him the Whyo fee. What the Danny's would have paid him for taking me and…you know who…" he motioned toward O'Reilly. "For taking us both out tonight. It was meant to be a peace offering after I crushed his balls."

Will laughed aloud. "Still got some tricks up that sleeve, eh Frog?"

"Always."

Slowing his pace, Will flicked his head O'Neill's way. "Hudson is just around that corner. Pick an alleyway and get it over with."

"O'Neill!" Louis called, the man ten feet behind them taking a piss on one of the buildings. "This way. Croker is this way."

Staggering, O'Neill shuffled to them and followed Louis down a pitch black corridor that wreaked of feces, and for a brief second Louis thought he might pass out from the horrendous stench.

"Christ!" shouted O'Neill. "Do you…you smell that? Where the hell are you—"

In one hurried motion, Louis drew the pillowcase from his jacket and had it over O'Neill's head, pulling it tight and wrapping his hands around the man's head as he began to struggle in a fumbled attempt to fight back. With one hand he plugged O'Neill's nose and held his mouth shut, and with the other arm he held him stationary around his torso, sustaining a few blows to his abdomen that would leave minor bruises for a week or two. He counted, as he always did. It took fifty-six seconds of moaning and thrashing around the putrid darkness, and then O'Neill's body wilted in Louis' arms. Immediately, Will appeared as his secondary, grabbing the legs and cursing when he, too realized the stench they were engulfed in.

"Jesus fuckin' Christ, what the fuck is that, a shit street?! Come on, half a block then it's over…come on…"

They lugged the body down to the water's edge, perusing their environment circumspectly to be sure there were no witnesses, and tossed the lifeless corpse over the dark stone wall. What was once a man splashed into the Hudson, gradually resurfacing on the water and floating downstream toward the bridge off Manhattan. Louis took out a box of matches and lit the pillowcase on fire, dropping it to the ground while both men took the load off their feet on the ledge and watched the inconspicuous murder weapon burn away slowly.

"I'll give it three days 'til they find that bastard, and it'll be ruled a drownin'," Will thought aloud. "I forgot how brilliant the pillowcase was…"

"Or it'll be ruled a homicide with no leads and no evidence," Louis chimed in. "We've both done this enough to know the secrets of the game, Will. I can promise you I don't need any reassurances. No harm no foul."

"Yeah, I know. I…well I didn' think you'd do it, honestly."

Louis was shocked. "Why not?"

"Guess it's just one of those things. Been so long. Didn' know if you'd trust me, 'cause I definitely ain't earned it."

"It did bring back some memories, didn't it?"

"Sure as shit," Will granted, grinning. "I don' know, brother. I never liked killin' much, money was just always good. It was jus' different when we was together, eh? Easier, I reckon."

"Don't forget safer," Louis added. "And faster."

"Wasn' 'til we split we got into trouble. An' that was all my doin'." His head fell. "It really was all my doin'. I know that. I'm sorry, Louis. I wish ya knew how much I wish I could take it back, brother."

"Don't apologize to me. I haven't earned that either. You took the fall for me, Will. I won't ever forget that."

"Nah," Will waved him off. "I only took part of the blow," he crossed his arms, thinking back. "An' I got out, don' forget. Got a whole new life for a while 'til I ran that one to hell, too. You're the one that got exiled 'til about five minutes ago. Almost lost everythin' you had workin' to try and save us. I won' let you do that again…I wouldn' do that to you again…"

All of a sudden at the very same second, Louis and Will felt it – someone was advancing from their right, probably believing they were sneaky enough to catch the pair unawares. Louis and Will simultaneously reached for their guns and cocked them, and as one, leapt to their feet to face the intruders, both men taking full aim the direction of the disturbance. Neither faltered, but Louis felt his heart drop just a little when he saw ten young men, all presumably Whyos, on approach and headed right for them. Only three had pistols, while the others were armed with their own handmade weapons, some of which Louis imagined were of their own design. The group halted twenty-five feet away from where Louis and Will stood, and from the rear of the pack, Danny Driscoll pressed through his cohorts to the front, holding his hands into the air as if asking a question, a bloodied dagger held in his right hand.

"Well, what've we got here? The Cat and the Frog. Such an unlikely friendship, and somehow alliances again? I gotta say, boys, I didn't see that one comin'."

"You know the deal, Danny," Will insisted, his gun hand tensing as his finger edged toward the trigger. "We just wrapped up with Croker's orders, and we'll be on our merry way now if you don' mind."

"See, that's where you're wrong. Sure, Lyons tells Croker I am in on the agreement, but I never gave my official say…" his voice trailed off as he eyed Louis. "And I would certainly like to gut your friend here and feed him to my fishes."

"I hate to disappoint you, but I am not lowering my gun," Louis pronounced resolutely. "I've got a full barrel of rounds in and four more cylinders in my pocket that will take no more than a second to reload. I could take out half your party before they even got within arms reach."

Danny shrugged, looking back toward his boys. "Meh. All replaceable. All it takes is one and you're done, Frog. Just one."

"I ain't lowerin' mine either, Danny," Will adjoined, moving a half step closer to Louis. "You'd have a hell of a time takin' us both out, and even if you could manage that, you'll have one mad son of a bitch to deal with when Croker comes lookin' for ya, I can make that promise."

Danny let out a loud noise of scorn. "Do you think I give two shits about Tammany Hall? They can suck a cock for all I care. This is Danny Driscoll's turf. Their jurisdiction doesn't exist in the 4th Ward!"

For a moment, Louis thought the gang would ensue the battle, and he readied for what he could only assume would be a vicious and bloody fight. Then, came a voice from their left, startling the gang along with Will and Louis.

"Tammany's jurisdiction may not exist here, but mine certainly does."

Louis peered at Will as a man stepped out into the light, and when they saw who the new player was, it was by no means a relief.

He'd listened to the Madame describe his appearance dozens of times, yet nothing could have ever prepared Louis for the rage he felt when he first laid eyes on Walsh. It took every fiber of his being to not instantly turn and shoot him dead then and there. Deep down, something told him if he didn't, he'd regret not pulling the trigger in those few seconds. But he restrained under the assumption Walsh might be their only way out of this skirmish unscathed. Ignoring Louis and Will's shocked faces as he grazed by them, Walsh ambled toward Danny without any hint of wavering or nervousness, and strangely, Louis noted there was no weapon visible in his hands.

"Tsk, tsk, tsk," he scolded contemptuously, waving his finger back and forth, stopping a few steps away from the Whyos. Nothing but horror filled Danny Driscoll's face at the sight of Walsh. "You may not need Croker's sound off, but you should know by now that you need mine, Mr. Driscoll. I am...disappointed in you."

"Mr. Walsh," he greeted nervously, "I had...I had no idea these men were friends of yours. I was just goin' to take care of a few trespassers, that's all."

"That's all, is it?" The way Walsh spoke was sinister, and it made the hair on Louis' neck stand on end.

"Yes, I swear Mr. Walsh, that's all. You know I wouldn't go behind your back! All ya had to do was ask!"

A crooked smirk. "Sure, sure, Danny," he cooed. "I am sure that was the case." Walsh retreated backwards a few feet, and then uncrossed his arms, as if he were bracing for something. "Send one."

Danny lost all color in his cheeks. "S-S-Send one?"

"Send one of your lads forward to me, Danny."

"But...but Mr. Walsh..."

"Now!"

The roar of Walsh's raised voice was haunting, like the roar of a dragon, so loud it echoed through the alleys and streets around

636

them. Shuddering, Louis looked to Will who uncocked and holstered his gun, and getting Louis' eye, shook his head no: they were not to get involved.

Danny unhurriedly rotated around to his gang, every man standing silent with dread. With his index finger shaking, he pointed to a small boy, not even sixteen, the weakest of the litter Louis could only presume. With unquestionable devotion to the pack, the boy set down the wooden club in his hands, tears welling in his eyes as he wobbled on his trembling legs toward Walsh.

When he reached the dragon, Walsh stroked the boy's face gently, then forcefully turned him so he was facing the pack of perplexed Whyos.

"Go ahead and kneel down on the ground. For your own sake, this will be quick."

The boy shakily did as he was told, his back staying to Walsh as he lowered down onto his knees.

"Will, for Christ's sake, we should do something," Louis whispered.

"That boy would have killed you without a second thought, brother," Will snapped sharply. "This ain't our fight."

"Mr. Sweeney, please do keep your friend quiet," Walsh commanded loudly, still not bothering to physically acknowledge his or Louis' presence.

"Will, he's going to—"

Will gave a hard lurch and locked Louis gun arm underneath his own, and the men were chest to chest. "You say another word, we're dead too. I ain't kiddin'."

Louis could feel Will's breath on his face, and knew right away that whatever he'd seen of Walsh must have been far worse than anything the Madame experienced. He jerked free and straightened his coat, submitting.

"Fine."

"Now listen here!" Walsh bellowed out and drew a blade from his belt, his words aimed at Danny. "This boy is dying because of your insolence. You plan on taking anyone out…even petty intruders, you go through me first, is that understood?!"

No one spoke a word. They stared on, the boy already dead in their eyes.

In a rapid stroke with a glint of metal, the boy's throat was slit and he fell to the ground, twitching for half of a minute until he finally lay motionless in a pool of his own blood. Walsh wiped his knife on the boy's sleeve and sheathed it once more in his belt.

"Get rid of the body, Danny. And don't try to play me a fool again, or next time, it will be your blood on the ground."

Walsh didn't bother to turn; he simply strode through the pack of Whyos, who parted obligingly to allow him to pass. With a gentle push from Will, he and Louis pursued in Walsh's wake toward a coach parked under a distant street lamp at the end of the block. Louis kept his gaze at Walsh's back. It was unbelievable…so unbelievable, Louis had a hard time wrapping his head around it. Walsh… the Whyos…Croker…

Anxiety set in, as did the reality of the depths his enemy possessed. Any man with the right hunger who wasn't afraid to break a few backs could take Croker's spot – that was a given. There were always pricks with a power hungry agenda, not worrying about anyone or anything they crushed along their way to greatness…a part of life that would never change. Walsh, on the other hand, was a different sort of animal. Running Croker's uglier errands was one thing, yet being able to rule the Whyos without any kind of defiance was something else entirely. That gang answered to no one, not even the Hall, and they relished in their lack of affiliation and freedom to rob, kill, and rape whomever they liked.

Walsh had them trembling. He had all of them trembling… Croker, the Whyos, the Madame, even Will. And that scared the hell out of Louis.

XXII.

It was nearly four and the wind was picking up outside, the sound of it whistling in Esther's ears as she glanced out the window. Leaves were whirling, spinning up in great circles in the street as Celeste and Esther sat, each downing another glass of red wine to try to numb themselves from the painful anticipation of a hard winter ahead. For the first time in years, they would be separated and on their own to handle situations that they, by and large, tackled together for the majority of their lives. Celeste held Esther's hand tight, quiet after wiping away tears of frustration the two cried, with a more formal goodbye soon to come. The move was only a few days away, and it was becoming clearer to Esther her friend was not expecting to have an easy time without her by her side. Conversely, she knew Celeste worried about her – Esther locked herself away those first few days when she left the Turners, not seeing anyone and who included her best friend. To her surprise, Lucy had even come by before the Turners left and begged to be let in, but Esther's courage failed her, and she turned her away. Louis had been her saving grace, watching and protecting her when she never asked for it or deserved it, and now Esther was trying to be that for Celeste, who needed strength in their friendship, not another martyr. Soon enough it would be over,

639

and with the birth of the baby, Esther hoped Celeste would be able to find some peace in the chaos.

Their silent moment was interrupted abruptly by the fast approaching sound of footsteps down the hall, and Laura, one of Celeste's maids, appeared in the doorway, her hand flying to cover her mouth as spun her back to them, embarrassed.

"Oh, Ma'am I am so sorry," she apologized, moving away slowly. Celeste and Esther were doing their best to hide out in the library and have a bit of privacy, which was nearly impossible with people running to and fro, packing up the house for the winter. It hadn't lasted long, but Esther was thankful they had the short amount of time they did when it could be years until it happened again.

Celeste straightened up and let go of Esther's hand, a false yet welcoming smile coming to her face. She motioned for her maid to enter.

"It's fine, Laura. What is it?"

Laura stepped forward timidly. "I just needed to know if you wanted me to leave your summer gowns here since you plan on returning by the end of spring."

"Absolutely," she instructed. "And also do not forget the dresses I set aside are for Esther. You remember which ones I pointed out?"

"Yes, ma'am."

"Lovely. Please have them ready to send to her apartments first thing in the morning. Is that everything Laura?"

"Yes, Mrs. Adams," Laura consented with a nod, taking a quick curtsey and leaving the room.

"Dresses?" Esther inquired. "What dresses?"

Celeste's grin grew large, and was no longer artificial. "Just a few of my personal favorites I always knew you loved. I obviously won't be able to wear them, and after this boy finally decides to pop out I'll make Timothy buy me a new wardrobe." Esther set her wine glass aside, intending to protest, however Celeste hushed her dismissively. "I also set aside one of my heavy fur jackets along with the matching hat, muff, and leather gloves. I know the Madame is providing for you, I just wanted to contribute a little on my own. And you're going to need those if it's going to be as cold as they're predicting."

Esther was beyond touched. "Celeste, you really shouldn't have."

"Yes I should. You are the only reason I've gotten through these past months." She took a sip of wine, sighing heavily. "I don't know how I'm going to get through the last few weeks of this pregnancy without you. I really don't."

"You will do great," Esther comforted her. "Your mother-in-law and Henrietta will take good care of you…they love you like you're their own!" She swallowed, taking a moment to summon all the vigor she had left to say what Celeste needed to hear. "And Timothy will be a good father. I think he will warm to you when he finally gets his son."

Celeste saw through Esther's words, though she noticeably appreciated them nonetheless. "I don't know, Es. I don't think there's a warm bone in his body, but I'd like to think once the baby is here things might change."

"They haven't changed?"

"Not particularly, no."

Esther's defenses sprang up. "Celeste he…he hasn't hit you again, has he? I thought that stopped when he found out about the pregnancy!"

"No…no it hasn't been the way it was before," Celeste proclaimed, reaching for the bottle of wine on the coffee table. "That did change, thank God. Not that he has been a loving or doting husband, but he's been…respectful. Kept his distance from me I think to avoid an incident. In fact, we very rarely spend time in the same room for more than a few minutes, which has been somewhat of a relief I suppose. I just hope it's a boy and then there will be no reason to keep the charade up any longer."

"And then what?

Celeste filled both their glasses. "Separate living arrangements, perhaps? I don't know. Right now, the only thing I'm focusing on is having a healthy baby. Then we can figure out how to tolerate each other the rest of our lives."

While the thought of it made her cringe, a small part of Esther speculated whether Timothy might want to dispose of Celeste after she had their child. When the Madame suggested the idea, Esther promptly rejected it; nonetheless, after seeing the lack of remorse not only with the Hiltmore scandal, but also in the death of his own father, there was no way to deny it was an enormous possibility considering what he was capable of. Timothy's reaction to the news of Charles' murder was not normal by any means – there was no sentiment, no sadness, no feeling whatsoever. According to Celeste, it was received with a long stare and a few questions about his inheritance, then not spoken of again. He also made no effort to hide his contempt for Celeste's parents and their fall from society, causing Esther to worry that if Timothy saw Celeste as nothing more than a hindrance, he might try to lighten that load burdening his shoulders once they reached Virginia.

Celeste took her father's imprisonment and her mother's death hard, withdrawing from her typically overt social agenda and dates out with her friends. She was mortified by what occurred, and Timothy's antics were no help in the matter, causing Esther's hatred of him to escalate. There was no proof, though she was convinced Timothy was doing his wife no favors in rebuilding her reputation in their social circle, making life even harder for Celeste than it already was. She erroneously saw his distance as respectful...a kindness even: Esther saw it as a purposeful detachment, one that made others assume he did not want to be associated with his wife.

It was a perfect set up for that son of a bitch to start over again... to dispose of Celeste and find another rich, young society darling to marry. In the beginning, Esther prayed the Madame was wrong, but that woman repeatedly demonstrated over the years she had a nasty way of being on the mark about things like this.

"Are you sure there is nothing I can do to convince you to come away with me?" Celeste pressed, scooting closer to Esther and resting her head on her friend's shoulder, "I think it would do you some good to get away from all this…particularly from all the constant memories of Thomas. It's only for the winter, and it's not as if you're needed here for anything."

"I think it would do me some good to be on my own," Esther lied.

"Es. The thought of you being by yourself scares me a little."

"Why would that scare you? I'll be all right."

Celeste shook her head, sitting upright to look into Esther's eyes. "I know you haven't been sleeping. Every time you're here I know you've spent most of the night crying because your eyes are puffy and red. You barely eat and it's starting to show in your clothes, and you don't even bother with your hair. Tell me what I can do. Please. I'm miserable too, but I've got something that keeps me going. I'm afraid you're…I'm afraid you might snap and I won't be here to help you the way you've helped me."

"Well, I can assure you I am far too vain to do anything like that," Esther told her, patting her hand. "Celeste, I just need time. It'll be good for me to figure this out by myself. And when you and your family are back, I will be myself again and we will have so many happy things to celebrate."

"What about a visit? Maybe a week or two for Christmas? You can take the train down with Timothy."

Esther paused, trying to appear surprised at the information given. "With…with Timothy? What do you mean?"

"Oh Christ. Have I not told you? Timothy will be spending most of his time here. Back and forth a week here and a week there, but the company decided to push forward with opening a new manufacturing plant on Long Island. So a lot of his time will have to be in New York."

"Wow! I am just…well…I am only a little shocked because…I thought he would hate it here after what happened to his father…"

Celeste rolled her eyes. "Timothy hates just about everything in general, Es. Oddly enough, he seems to love it here now that Charles is gone. He's gotten on a few of the committees down at City Hall trying to meet a few more big fish and find investing opportunities for the company. I think he wants to sell it, but how would I know? I hear this from his mother and sister. You'd think this is the kind of thing he'd share with me."

"So he will be here?" she requested, wanting to confirm the rumors for the Madame. Recently she'd instructed Esther to gather as much as she could from Celeste concerning Timothy's whereabouts, especially the time he spent in Virginia. It gave Esther hope that the Madame was preparing to conclude the prearranged plan and kill Timothy since unfortunately Esther had lost the courage to fulfill that undertaking on her own.

"A lot of the time, yes. Are you ok, Es? You look a little ill all of a sudden. Was it something I said?"

"Oh no!" she asserted. "I'm fine, my stomach is just a little queasy. Grab me a lemon tart I think I've had too much wine."

Celeste grabbed one for Esther and then another for herself. "I also have something else I need to tell you."

"What is it?" Esther's tried to keep her attentions on Celeste as best she could, subduing the overwhelming thought of what the future would bring.

"Please promise me you won't be angry."

"I won't, I promise."

Celeste bit into her own tart. "I had a visitor the other day, one who was asking a lot about you."

Esther always grew faintly irritated when Celeste played this game, and she already knew the answer. "Who was it, Celeste?"

"Captain Bernhardt." For a few seconds, Celeste waited for a dramatic reaction or response, and when it didn't come, she carried on. "He said he had been stopping by and you refuse to let him in. He just wants to see you, Es. He cares about you. He wouldn't have come to me if he didn't."

"And what exactly did you tell him?"

"Es, I didn't have a choice…"

"Celeste, what did you tell him?"

"He loves you, all right?" she pronounced guiltily. "He knew something was wrong…knew there was someone else when you didn't say yes, and he chose to wait for you anyhow. I told him about what happened. About Thomas, everything falling through, and that you need time and space to heal. He doesn't mind any of that. In fact, he was so understanding it completely blew me away! He just wants to see you and to talk with you. He's worried, like I am."

Esther gaped at her. "Do you honestly expect me to take this well, Celeste?" she cried, withdrawing her hand. "I don't even know what to say to you right now."

"Es, you can't keep doing this to yourself," Celeste insisted, her tone lecturing. "Thomas is gone and he isn't coming back. It's over. You're almost nineteen and you're not getting any younger! There are hundreds of men in New York who would kill to have someone like you. Including Captain Bernhardt, who you were quite attached to before Thomas showed up."

"Yes, and then Thomas showed up and it changed," Esther stressed. "I can't see him. I don't want to see him."

"Are you sure it's that you can't? Or is it that you won't?" Celeste took her hand again. "I know you've put these giant walls up, Es, but sometimes it's ok to let them fall down. I'm not saying you need to marry anyone. I'm saying you need to stop hiding away, because it won't change anything. You're never going to move forward unless you start forgiving yourself."

"I'm not ready for this. It's only been a few weeks."

"I know. Just keep it in mind. That's all I'm saying."

"Fine."

"Are you angry with me?"

Esther was furious, and then Celeste's pouty expression softened her into a laugh. "I'll get over it, I suppose."

"Good. And you're coming down for Christmas, even if I have to write the Madame personally to ask."

Esther scoffed. "That'll go over well, I'm sure."

Celeste giggled and peeked out the window, becoming more serious when she realized the hour. "Sun is heading down. I better go upstairs and make sure Laura has everything prepared. Do you want to stay tonight?"

"No, that's completely unnecessary. I'll be by in the morning for our last goodbye." She squeezed her friend's hand and let it go, standing up first and then helping Celeste to her feet.

Celeste paused, holding onto her. "Es, we're going to be ok, right?" she asked softly, tears forming in her eyes. "We can get through this, can't we?"

Esther wrapped her arms around her friend. "We're going to be fine, I promise. As long as we stick together we can get through anything. Don't forget that, no matter what happens. I love you, Celeste."

Celeste drew tighter into their embrace, sobbing a little. "Christ I don't know what I'd do without you, Es. I'm sorry for what I did... telling the Captain...it's just because I care. You know it's just because I care."

"I know," Esther replied, stroking her hair. "Everything's all right. If we can make it through this, we can make it through anything. Only a few months apart, and it'll all be all right."

She and the Madame would have to start formulating their strategy. Esther would make sure that for Celeste's own survival and long-term happiness, by the time spring arrived, her husband was nothing more than a far distant memory.

The wind persisted to howl as Esther walked home. She pulled her arms in tight around her waist, the fingers of her right hand running over every button on her jacket to make sure they were fastened, and her left then moving to hold down her hat, desperately hoping not to lose it down the street in a gust as she plunged through the chill onward and home. Neither Celeste leaving for Virginia nor Thomas' departure to England were what had been plaguing her heart so heavily these last few days; ironically, Esther had been thinking of Captain Bernhardt more than usual, for no other reason than the unremitting hammering from Celeste and the Madame to consider giving him another chance at winning her over. She had yet to give up the ring…it served as a symbol of so much heartbreak, yet on the other hand, Esther realized this ring also gave her an out if she ever wanted it. They could be happy together…however the one factor she refused to gloss over was that she would never love him the way she loved Thomas, and she by no means wanted to subject Captain Bernhardt to feeling like a subordinate. With her own future hazy, Esther hated admitting she would have to let him go and send back the ring – she didn't want the responsibility or the consequences of the unfairness in leading him on just to comfort her shattered spirit. It was not fair to either of them.

Passing a group of young men, Esther kept her head down and ignored their catcalls, trotting away and hearing nothing save for the wail of blowing air by her ear. When she reached Midtown, she got off the main roadways and was able to escape the increasingly extreme weather. Minutes later, Esther relaxed as she passed by and waved to her butcher, who was outside rinsing the blood from his rubber boots and apron. A little further along she spotted the widow and two daughters who lived on the first floor of her building, who saluted Esther with a gracious curtsey. The notion of kinship in society was not one Esther had ever been used to living amongst the upper class, and she had to admit she appreciated it far more than the coldness of uptown.

Her neighborhood was extremely friendly and safe for New York's standards, and her furnishings more than accommodating thanks to the Madame; however, the one aspect Esther hadn't prepared herself for was what it was like to truly be on her own. It took Thomas' absence for her to realize how alone and traumatized she felt after a sincerely harrowing series of events that summer. Thomas helped alleviate the weight she carried each day as if it didn't exist, and in a classic Esther fashion, she pushed that respite away as hard and rapidly as she possibly could. The cost was more devastating than she could have ever premeditated.

Dozens of times she'd written him a letter, only to burn it in the fireplace. There was nothing she could say to fix it, nothing that would take back the hurt and pain no matter what excuses she made or what she pledged to him. Esther had broken Thomas' trust many times in their youth, and still this one she did not believe he would forgive her for, and she found she couldn't blame him. Prior to his proposal, a small voice in her head kept telling her he would change his mind as time went on and send her packing… that same voice was the part of her that feared abandonment more than anything else, one that hadn't left since Esther's childhood. The smartest thing she could have done was chosen to ignore it, but she hadn't; she allowed that fear to control her and in return, Esther lost the only man she'd ever loved. Each morning since, she hurt with the same intensity – he wasn't there, and it hadn't been a bad dream. It was real.

She stopped two blocks from her apartment, pulling out a cigarette and lighting it after a few fumbling tries. Taking a small break from her stroll, Esther leaned up against the side of a tailor's shop, watching the people walk to and fro in their own personal clouds, not taking any notice of her. An elderly woman and a young boy, who Esther assumed had to be her grandson, made their way along, passing by slowly. He had his arm wrapped securely through hers, assisting at every step with a smile on his face, not the least bit bitter of how he was spending his time. Next came a young family with three children, all rambunctious and running around their parents, who chided them and threatened to send them to an orphanage, causing Esther to laugh a little to herself. Another drag, and she spotted a young girl, barely an adolescent with wavy red hair that made her stand out and a band of freckles on her nose. She was dressed plain, and evidently on an errand as she strolled into the bakery and left with a large loaf of bread. The girl whisked by Esther the way she'd come in a hurry, though not without a short glance her way, a small grin forming in the corner of her mouth before she disappeared down the street. More people circled by as the minutes went on, and Esther couldn't help but observe the one thing each of them possessed that she was lacking: ease.

For most of her life, Esther had been afraid. Afraid of desertion, afraid of hurting the few people she held close, and in the last year, she'd discovered the fear of others harming her, a feeling she never thought she'd have to understand. It was a trepidation that had lost her Thomas on both accounts, the same that kept the Madame's judgment so harsh, and that first allowed Timothy to violate her and then send someone to kill her. Months had come and gone where the only thing Esther could do was listen to others on how to act the right way, on how to remain safe and secure…and where had it gotten her? Isolated in a lonely existence, torturing herself over what could have been. Esther didn't want to be afraid anymore… not of anyone or anything. It was time she stopped listening to everyone else and finally took her life into her own hands.

Esther put butt of the cigarette out on the side of the building and hiked through the bustling roadway to her place, the wind dying down as the temperature began to drop, along with the loitering light in the sky. She arrived at her stoop and got out her keys, preparing herself for the usual semantics with her landlady, a pleasant woman though intrusive in her questions and always sitting in the downstairs lobby. To her surprise, Esther found a casually dressed and distraught Captain Bernhardt standing at her door. Evidently by the flush of his cheeks, he had been waiting for her for quite some time in the brisk air, and there was no way to escape his company.

649

"Esther!" he exclaimed the moment he saw her, rushing down the steps. "Please, just talk to me. I am begging you."

A small part of her was glad to see him. "Hi, Captain. I apologize, I was just at Mrs. Adams' residence. She is leaving tomorrow for Charleston for the duration of the winter."

Remembering his formalities by her tone, the Captain straightened up. "Of course! I wished her good tidings earlier this week. Is she ready for a long train ride south?"

"I expect so," Esther responded, and then followed a slight awkward silence despite her knowing what he expected. "Would… would you like to come upstairs for a few minutes and warm up?" she asked politely.

His face lit up. "That would be wonderful, thank you."

Esther motioned for the Captain to follow her inside, nodding a hello to her landlady as they passed – there would be gossip in the building for the next month about her having male guests in her quarters, which would be somewhat amusing. Her apartment was the entire third floor, and she lead the Captain up the small, spiraling wooden staircase in the middle of the building, warning him to watch for wax leaking from the massive chandelier dangling from the ceiling at the top. She'd been burned three times in the short span she'd lived there, however there was no room for complaints. The Madame owned the top half of the building, and thus Esther's quarters were much larger than that of a normal family-sized home.

They made their way inside, where Esther escorted the Captain to her sitting room and to her reprieve, the landlady already had lit a nice fire for her to warm up with. She didn't have a good deal to decorate the room with: a loveseat, side table, coffee table, and two armchairs by the fire. There were a few shelves of books on the adjacent wall that towered over her small desk at the window, and one of the Madame's favorite red Persian rugs took up most of the floor space. A full rack of wine was gifted to her from the Madame's personal stash, along with a small station Louis had set up for her to roll her own cigarettes, which he stocked every few days.

The Captain strolled over to one of the empty armchairs and lowered down, taking in his surroundings as he rubbed his hands together for warmth.

Esther was already on her way over to open a bottle of wine to deal with her nerves. "Would you like a drink, Captain?"

"That would be great."

She poured them each a large share and made her way back over, seating herself across from him on the love seat. Rather than waste their time with small talk, Esther sensed she would only feel better to say the things that he came here to hear, and to, for once, be honest about it.

"Celeste told me you came to see her, and that she informed you of my…well, my situation to you," Esther initiated, sipping her wine.

The Captain nodded. "Well…yes, she did…at my request. I hadn't heard anything from you since the Hiltmores' party, and… considering the events that followed, I kept my distance for a time, wanting to give you space."

Esther had a gulp of wine. "I hope you know how sorry I am for hurting you, and for not telling you straight away. The summer was a…well it was a scary one, in a good and in a bad way. But I should have told you that night at the party my answer. Things would have been much different if I had."

Another quiet moment came about, and each self-consciously had another drink from their respective glasses. Esther wondered if she should say anything else to console him when the Captain spoke: "Do you really think they would be different, Esther?"

"What do you mean?"

"I mean do you think things would be different between you and Thomas?"

Troubled, she tried to come up with a dignified response to the Captain's directness. "I…I'm not sure why they wouldn't be…"

"I am not saying this to try and sway you one way or the other," he explained. "I'm saying this as…as an outsider. Celeste told me you broke off the engagement with Thomas, and that your relationship with…forgive me…with Lord Turner had been tumultuous from the start. I just wonder, do you really think it would have lasted?"

Esther was appalled. "Captain, I think you are stepping a little out of your jurisdiction," she retorted as steadily as she could. "My relationship with Thomas had its ups and downs in the beginning like any other, but that changed drastically once we had an…understanding of each other."

"Then why did you call off the engagement?" he beseeched her, puzzled. "I know you loved him, and he loved you."

She blushed. "If I hadn't called off the engagement, he would have."

"How do you know he wouldn't have forgiven something that was, in my opinion, his own fault?"

"It was not his fault, Captain. I kept the ring you gave me. And I should have never taken it from you in the first place."

Captain Bernhardt's eyes studied her closely. "If you were confident in your relationship, I don't think you would have," he said, sitting forward. "It's a man's job to make the woman he loves feel secure with the direction they are going."

"We did get engaged, Captain."

"For a day?" he posed. "Be honest, Es. You kept the ring I gave you because you weren't convinced it would go through. This is not just a silly mistake…you didn't have faith in him to follow through. You wanted to believe it would but somewhere in your heart you knew it was short term. And that's why you called off the engagement without trying to work through it."

"And where exactly have you come up with such wild theories?" she posed, her palms sweating.

"They're not theories, Es. You don't have to hide from me. I think we're long passed that."

652

Esther's throat tightened. "I think you should go," she squeaked, setting down her glass and rising abruptly to pace away toward the back window. Her eyes were welling up, her breath shortened, and it took all of her concentration to not immediately break down in front of the Captain. As her body weakened with wretchedness, she sank down to the windowsill and kept her gaze averted outside, because in seconds, she wouldn't be able to contain the sobs any longer.

Captain Bernhardt followed and kneeled down beside her, taking her hands in his. "Listen to me. I don't care about any of that. Don't you understand?"

"What are you talking about?" she sniffed. "I'm a fucking mess, Jonathan. Please go." She tried to pull her hands away, but he wouldn't budge. The tears poured out, and he moved to sit next to her, refusing to let go.

"Esther, I don't care about Thomas," he whispered. "I don't care about any of it. I love you, and I want to be here to do this. To hold you when you're sad and help you through it. You are the only thing that matters to me, and I don't expect anything in return. But you can't push me out now."

For a time, she resisted, yet eventually Esther's emotions overtook her, and she fell into Captain Bernhardt's arms, crying for quite some time as he hugged her close. There were so many emotions ripping at her heart, she couldn't decide what exactly the trigger was that lurched her over the edge. Esther's issues ran deeper than most, making her feel helpless – she was her own worst enemy, in almost every way imaginable, and despite sensing she would regret her momentary weakness, Esther let the Captain dry her tears.

In due course she pulled away, and he wiped her cheeks with the sleeve of his shirt, looking deep into her eyes. She wanted to get up and avoid the inevitable, but she couldn't, and she didn't try to stop it.

"Please…just let me…" he said, touching her face with his hand. Slowly he tilted forward and kissed her gently.

After a few seconds she drew away once more. "I'm sorry. It's too much. I…I just can't…I'm sorry, Jonathan."

Respectfully, Captain Bernhardt let her go and got to his feet. "Can I come and see you tomorrow? I promise, nothing will happen. Just to talk and to see you. That's what I want right now. I won't kiss you again until you are ready for it."

"I don't know…"

"All right, let's just say I'll be by around three. And if you let me up, we will go from there. How is that?"

Her spirit lifted slightly at his enthusiasm. "Sure. Three tomorrow."

The Captain beamed at her, and without another word, gave a small bow and left the apartment. Esther watched him skip down the front stoop, and when he was a block away, she got up from the windowsill with the bottle of wine and returned to the loveseat. Flopping down and filling her glass to the brim, Esther wanted nothing more than to be numb to absolutely everything around her. There were too many emotional streams taking over, guilt stabbing her the deepest. Esther enjoyed every second of the attention the Captain paid her even though she wished with her whole heart it had been Thomas and not him. Was she betraying Thomas again by allowing the Captain to calm her? Or did it even matter, when Esther firmly believed she and Thomas might never cross paths again?

A loud banging on her front door caused Esther to spill a few drops of wine on the Persian carpet, and she cursed loudly.

"Who is it?!" she yelled angrily, expecting to hear Louis' familiar tone.

"Miss Esther?" came the sound of a small female voice.

"Yes, who is it?" she yelled again.

The girl's words were panicked. "Miss Esther, it's Laura, the maid from the Adams residence. Please can you let me in? I am so sorry but it was Mrs. Adams that gave me your address. It's an emergency!"

Esther leapt up and bolted toward the door, her heart racing while she threw it open. "Please tell me everything is…is… oh God…"

There was blood on Laura's apron, her face twisted up in distress. "Please, we have to hurry. She told me to get you, but we need to get a doctor. No one can know, Miss Esther…she made me promise no one could know…"

"Laura…why is there blood on your apron?"

The girl's chin shook. "There…there was an accident. And I think she's losing the baby. We have to go, and we have to go now! The carriage is waiting."

"You tell her I don't give a fuck who is arriving in a half hour!" Esther screamed at the top of her lungs, hoping the Madame would hear her. She was standing at the front door of The Palace, a terrified Laura at her side, where she had been berating George for almost five minutes in an effort to get the attention of the staff. Girls were gathering behind George, donning fretful looks at the sight of Esther so frenzied.

"I need the God damn Doc, Georgie! Where the fuck is Louis?! And where is the Madame?!"

George, however, held his ground. "No one is allowed in tonight that's not on the list, not even you, Es. There are plenty of able docs down at the hospital. Now get lost before you get us both in serious shit. What the hell you need the Doc for anyhow?"

Esther glanced at Laura. "Look, I just…I have a friend who needs medical attention from someone with his…skill set."

"There are plenty of those down at the hospital."

"No, Georgie, you don't understand…please!"

"Ain't my job to babysit you, sweetie. And Louis is busy. Take your friend to the hospital and get a real, legitimate doc."

655

"George, I need a doctor that isn't going to open his fucking mouth. No one can know! Please, for God's sake, help me"

Seconds later, the Madame pushed through the expanding pack of girls, Hope and Danny trailing not far behind, her face livid.

"What the fuck is going on down here?!" she shouted, sending everyone that was not Hope, Danny, and George back to work. "Esther, why in the hell are you down here causing a commotion on a night when you know I have clients? I ought to fucking skin you alive."

"I need the Doc," she pleaded urgently. "Please just tell me where he is. I'll go and get him myself I just need to know how to find him."

Her eyes narrowed. "Who needs him, Es?"

"Celeste."

"Why?"

"He beat her bad, Ma'am," Laura interjected. "So bad I think she might lose the baby…you can see…" She gestured down to her blood covered apron.

To Esther's astonishment, the Madame actually seemed startled. "Fucking Christ," she mumbled. "Esther, he's north. Out of the city until Monday. Take her to the fucking hospital you don't have another choice. Don't be stupid or she'll die. Got it?"

Laura spoke up again: "Ma'am she…she won't go to the hospital…"

"Are you fucking with me?"

"N-n-no ma'am, she refuses to leave the house."

The Madame turned to Hope. "Go with them and get your ass back here before I even feel that you're gone. Damage control only, then get her to the fucking hospital, I don't care if that stupid bitch refuses to go, she's fucking going."

Hope instantly made her way to them. "How bad is it?" she asked Laura nervously, throwing Esther a fleeting look.

"Bad," Laura told her. "She's been bleeding a lot. I don't know if we can save her or the baby."

"Hope, go. Now," the Madame commanded. "Or she might be dead before you get there."

"Madame, that bastard is coming here tonight," Danny remarked angrily. "Why the fuck don't we just–" Whipping around, the Madame threw her a scowl, and immediately Danny realized her blunder.

Esther froze. "What do you mean he's coming here?"

The Madame closed her eyes, shaking her head. "Esther, he's on the list for tonight for a reason."

"You…you went behind my back…you promised me he would never be allowed back here!"

"Hope, get the maid in the carriage. Now!" Doing as they were told, the girls dashed off, and with a flick of her head, George too understood it was his time to get lost. The Madame pulled Esther out of the doorway and to the side of the staircase so they wouldn't be overheard. "God forgive me," she murmured. "Esther, he was on the list for tonight because we were going to fucking take care of him. Tonight. Everything is all set and ready for it. Louis will be back shortly and we already have a cover."

For a few seconds, Esther was speechless, her brain absorbing the information. "You said…you said we had to prep…"

"Yes, and I misled you on purpose, darling."

"Why?" she demanded, somewhat distraught.

Her voice lowered again. "Because I owe you this, Esther. And after careful consideration, Louis and I both agreed you were the most important, and that you would be better left untainted in this madness." Esther's gaze fell to the ground, and the Madame took her shoulders, shaking them. "Look at me, God dammit! I'm doing this for your own good. You don't want a life on your hands, Esther. It's a fucking curse that never leaves you…blood on your hands you can never wash off–"

"What if he's there? What if he's there when I get there?"

"He won't be."

Esther was infuriated. "I'm going to kill him if I see him, Madame."

The Madame sighed and grabbed something from under her skirt. "Here." She shoved a pocket pistol into Esther's hands. "If he's there, aim for the torso."

"This isn't over—"

"Shut up, Esther." Her tone might as well have been a slap, and Esther's protests ceased. "Take care of Celeste first. If your friend dies, you won't find any retribution in killing that son of a bitch. It will be for nothing. You got me?" Esther took a deep breath, nodding, and an expression of relief washed over the Madame's face. "Get the fuck out of here. You don't have much time, and she's going to need you."

The moment their driver halted the carriage, Esther, Hope, and Laura piled out, sprinting the direction of the house. Laura took the lead and opened the unlocked front door, running up the front steps two at a time and Hope chasing her closely. Grabbing the little cash she had on her, Esther paid the coachman, practically throwing the money at the driver, and followed, locking the door behind them. Rapidly, she did a lap of the first floor, wanting to double check that Timothy was no longer home, and she found the entire level deserted. Suddenly, yells and moans began to reverberate from the upstairs hallway, and Esther froze at the bottom of the staircase, the painful sounds of agony tearing at her like knives.

Then, out of the darkness, Celeste screamed for her, and Esther flew up the steps faster than she'd ever moved before. She made a hard right and took off down the hallway, internally reprimanding herself for being so selfish: she should have never moved out and left Celeste alone with that monster. She should have told her from the start he was a bad man to his very core, to leave him, and that no amount of abuse was worth the money regardless of what Celeste's mother brainwashed her with. Above all, Esther knew she should have told her friend about the night her husband snuck into her room and raped her, and what really happened when she tried to tell the police. Esther hated herself for the secrets she kept and for what had ensued because of those secrets – it hadn't just ruined her life, but the lives of everyone she cared about. And as Esther walked into the room and saw Celeste writhing in pain on her bed, there was no one left to blame but herself.

"Es," Hope grabbed her attention, drawing near at a low whisper. "It's not good. You need to ask her what happened…she doesn't know me and I don't want to pry, but it's the only way I can figure out how to help her."

Esther dashed to Celeste's bedside. "Celeste? Celeste, find my voice. Try to find my voice."

Celeste heard her and reached out, as if she were blind in her struggle to find her friend's support. Esther snatched her hand.

"Celeste…it's me, Celeste…that's my hand. Listen to me, okay? I know you're in a lot of pain. I need you to tell me what happened."

She let out a groan. "It hurts, Es…it hurts so much…" Her body was bruised nearly everywhere her skin was visible, and as Esther's eyes traced over her friend, they revealed Celeste's forehead and cheek bloodied along with her wrists, elbows, knees, and ankles. Paralyzed with dread, Esther hadn't the smallest clue what to make of it, yet the worst was the deepening purple color of her belly and the notion that the baby was already gone.

Hope swept over with a glass of wine, stirring something into the mix. "Drink this, Celeste. It will help ease the pain. Drink it fast, ok?"

Celeste did as she was instructed, finishing the wine and recoiling slightly, though managing to get every drop down. Without delay, Esther snatched the glass from her hand and set it aside, taking Celeste's hand once more.

"Celeste, look at me. Look in my eyes." Hope and Laura helped to prop her up. "Please tell me what happened, Celeste," Esther pleaded. "You have to tell me what he did to you. Try to think!"

For a moment, Esther thought Celeste might not respond. Thankfully, proving she still had her wits about her, Celeste surveyed the room to be sure it was only the four of them present, then blinked hard a few times.

"I told…I told him I wanted to…to stay…and he…he hit me twice…no…five…six times…kicked me on the ground, picked me up and…and then…he pushed me."

Instantly her pupils glazed over and Celeste lost consciousness, causing Esther to turn to Hope in terror.

Hope directed her query to Laura. "Where was she found?"

Laura was absolutely aghast at what she was witnessing, withdrawing step by step toward the corner. "I…I don't know…she was on the ground…"

"Where?!" Hope demanded. "Think!"

"The…the bottom of the main stairs!" Laura cried. "She was in a heap…I hadn't even heard the fight or her tumble down…I didn't know what to do…I didn't know what to do I just did what she told me…"

Hope was already moving. "Es, I need you to hold her steady in case she wakes. Got it?"

"All right," Esther complied. "How?"

"Sit behind her so your knees are supporting her ribs at her sides and wrap your arms around hers. The baby is gone, and if I don't get it out, she'll bleed internally and die right in front of us. It's… it's not going to be pretty…"

With a slight whimper, Laura passed out to the ground, neither Hope nor Esther paying her any mind. Esther went ahead and positioned herself behind Celeste to support her, even restrain her if need be. When she was in the correct stance, Hope took a deep breath in and threw Esther an exasperated glimpse; with a long exhale, Hope let her worry go, and thrust her hands inside of Celeste.

It took thirty-six minutes, a pair of scissors, a needle, and a lot of thread. Celeste amazingly did not wake thanks to whatever was in Hope's concoction, and Esther couldn't remember much after the fact except for the blood. The remnants of what had once been Celeste's future were wrapped in a sheet and tossed in the fire to burn, the smell something Esther would never forget. Wordlessly, she and Hope cleaned Celeste up the best they could with a rag and steaming hot water, waking Laura to grab a new set of sheets for the bed. Hope had done everything possible to try and save Celeste. She told Esther the only thing they could do now was pray for her, and Esther sent Hope off to bathe and clean herself up, her appearance like that of her butcher in Hell's Kitchen. When Hope returned some time later, she sat on the bed by Esther, who hadn't moved an inch, wiping the frightened sweat from Esther's forehead.

"You stop that right now."

Esther glanced at her. "Stop what?"

"I know you're blaming yourself."

"How could I not?" Esther attempted to smother an encroaching sob. "Hope, look at her…"

"Esther, don't think because you knew about him it's in any way your fault. She knew the risk of staying with a man like that."

Esther couldn't take her eyes off Celeste's weakened frame. "No, it's not just that, Hope. I should have told her the truth. About what he did to me…about what his family tried to do…"

"No, don't think that for a minute. If you told her, she never would have believed you. Her parents would never allow it. It was never bad enough for her to think that his assaulting you was even possible."

"And what about you?" Esther asked her candidly. "That son of a bitch almost killed you, and his father almost killed Danny. Why have we let this go on? What am I not seeing?"

Hope shook her head. "I trust the Madame. He's not the only client that takes certain liberties with the girls he shouldn't, but from what I can tell, he's paid a lot of people a lot of money to keep this quiet. The same way his father did. The Madame has been trying to piece together a plan for weeks, and she did. For tonight."

"Behind my back," Esther snapped, feeling both deceived and let down.

Hope smiled kindly. "So that you wouldn't have to live a life like she does. She doesn't want that for you, and neither does Louis."

"And how does he fit into all this?"

"Well, he was the one who insisted the Madame not let you kill him," Hope elucidated. "Like her, he knows what that does to a person. They want you to have a real life, Es."

Esther could feel warm tears on her face. "What if I don't want a real life anymore?"

Hope looked down at Celeste, then back to Esther. "Well, I don't think you'll have one of those either way. Neither of you will. But you need to be here for her if she makes it through."

"What...what do you mean if?"

She spoke too loudly, and Hope pressed her finger to her lips to keep quiet. "Any other doctor wouldn't have been able to save her. That's why I came with you."

Esther got to her feet and took Hope's hand, leading her away from Celeste's bedside. "I thought we saved her! I thought as long as we got the baby out, we would be able to keep her alive!"

"Esther, her husband was trying to kill her, and the internal damage done has to heal itself. At The Palace, if any of the girls have complications or need an abortion, I take care of it. I know how everything is interconnected for females after working with the Doc for years. It will be a miracle if Celeste makes it through the night. Her fever is going to spike any minute now, and she could be hemorrhaging somewhere else I couldn't find. There's no way of knowing for sure, and most doctors...they won't have anything to do with this stuff. Celeste was smarter than most and knew to get you. Can you imagine what would happen if this got out? No physician would want to be accused of killing a prominent young society man's child

662

and have the risk of being ruined. And that's probably exactly what Timothy Adams was aiming at."

For Esther, the bigger picture suddenly came into view. "He… he set it up…"

"Most likely, yes."

"He would say he came home and found her that way…no indication of why…she'd either be dead or he'd take her to the hospital where she'd die…"

"And he or the Hall would pay off the doc to take the hit."

Esther's ears perked up. "The Hall? Are you referring to Tammany Hall?"

"Of course," Hope countered. "That's the only reason the Madame couldn't say no to him being there tonight. So she and Louis planned around it."

"Since when does the Madame work for the them?" Esther posed, confused that this was the first time she'd even heard it brought up.

Seeing Esther's perplexity, Hope's eyes grew wide. "Jesus," she remarked, though not precisely at Esther, and she took a step away from her. "She really was trying to protect you…" Her voice trailed off, and just as Esther was going to speak up, Hope rotated back and continued. "The Madame has been working on and off with the Hall for quite some time, but that's something you need to discuss with her, not with me, and I don't know if you should mention that I–"

Celeste began to stir in her bed, and the two women looked at one another. "Go get Laura from the kitchen and send up a few sheets I can tear and use as bandages. Make sure her head is on straight and get rid of the rest of the staff. No one else needs to know what's going on here."

"Whatever you need."

"Es?"

She stopped in the doorway to the maid's passage. "What?"

"I need you to go to The Palace and let them know I won't be returning tonight. They should do just fine without me."

Esther's jaw nearly dropped. "But Hope, the Madame—"

"In this regard, fuck the Madame," Hope retorted, a smirk on her face. "This poor girl needs me more than she does. And I'd rather be here."

Esther descended down the tiny staircase to the kitchens, where she found Laura crying uncontrollably and the rest of the staff grilling her for information, though she was pleased to discover Laura withheld anything pertinent. Announcing they were dismissed for the evening, Esther went on to explain that Celeste had a terrible accident and needed only her and Laura's assistance, and that a doctor was currently at her side. They filtered out one by one, and after they'd gone, Esther cautioned Laura and sent her upstairs with everything Hope requested. Rather than head directly to The Palace, Esther stayed in the kitchen for a moment, taking the last cigarette from her jacket pocket. She lit it and took a long drag, removing the pistol the Madame had given her from her pocket and setting it on the table. All she could do was stare at it as she puffed as much stress away as she could, not sure as to what exactly she wanted to do next. The only thing on her mind was all the red...all the blood and all her friend's pain that Timothy alone caused, and what he'd taken away from Celeste. If Celeste didn't live through the night, Esther knew her remaining sanity would die along with her. In turn, the only thing that made her feel better was imagining Timothy's rattled, bloodied, and rotting corpse on the ground at her feet.

Suddenly, Esther felt the chemistry of her being change. Her sadness, the frailty of her mental state, the powerlessness she felt suddenly vanished. It was inexplicable, as if her compassion dissolved and that space was then filled with something else...something she couldn't quite describe, though it resembled a kind of overwhelming abhorrence for the world she lived in, and a self-justified aspiration of vengeance. She couldn't allow this masquerade to go on. Tossing her burning cigarette to the ground, she smothered it with her heel and drew out the Madame's pocket pistol from her pocket, headed directly for The Palace.

Louis emerged from the shadows as Esther exited the Adams residence at a fast pace from the servant's entranceway, and he hurried toward her. It wasn't until he was a few feet away he saw the pistol glimmering in her hand, and that her dress was covered in red.

"Esther!" he called, and she stopped in the middle of the street. Realizing it was him, Esther angrily sped to where he stood on the gravel walkway, and Louis seriously wondered for a few seconds if she might shoot him.

"Where the fuck have you been?" she demanded, her voice more aggressive than the hurt. "Do you know what's happened? Do you know how much I actually needed your help tonight?!"

"I was on an errand for the Madame, or I would have been there," he avowed. "Es...you are covered in blood. Why don't we find you a new gown to wear?"

She ignored Louis. "Is this an errand for the Hall?"

Louis felt himself tense, and he cleared his throat. "How do you know about our involvement with the Hall?"

"A little bird let it slip. And this is why that bastard is now at The Palace like he didn't just try to fucking murder his wife and unborn child?"

Louis was appalled. "Oh my God. Are they alive?"

Esther's eyes were full of rage, her intensity only growing. "She is...barely..."

"Christ," Louis groaned. "Esther, let me take you back inside. What are you doing out here anyway? You can't be in public with a gun."

"I'm going to The Palace."

"Like hell you are." He reached for her arm, but she yanked away before he could grasp it.

"Hope asked me to inform the Madame she's staying here tonight, and I will do that for her considering it's Hope that's saved Celeste."

"I will tell the Madame. You go back inside at once. Someone could see you and call the police, Esther."

"I honestly couldn't give a shit anymore." She tried to appear stagnant, but after almost a minute of glaring at Louis and the approach of a carriage, Esther slipped the pistol into her dress pocket.

"Thank you," he breathed, his anxiety alleviated. He tipped his hat to the driver, who mirrored his acknowledgment and kept moving.

"So you were going to kill him tonight?" she entreated Louis with the coach out of earshot. "That was the plan?"

Once more Louis was astonished, wondering how he'd missed so much in such a short time span. "Yes it is the plan. I am on my way there now to carry it out."

"Well, the plan has changed." Esther once again held up the gun, pointing it at Louis, her hand steady as she cocked the pistol.

Louis went silent, raising up his arms. "Please, Esther...try to think clearly..."

"You have no right..." she started, trying to put the words together. "You have no right to tell me what I can or can't do to that bastard. After what he's done to me....to Celeste...!"

It was too late – Louis saw her rationality was gone. "What do you want me to do? I can't let you leave here. I won't let you ruin your life and do something I know you'll regret. You'll have to shoot me if you want to get away."

Just then, three carriages turned the block corner, heading their direction. "I'm sorry, Louis," Esther declared. "This is not up to you. Or to her. This is my right, and for Celeste I am going to do this my way."

When the first coach was parallel with her, Esther took off behind it, spooking the horses pulling the second not more than four feet behind it's predecessor's wheels, and thus causing a distraction for her to get away. Louis cursed loudly, frantically steering them on and having to wait until the third carriage went past before running straight into the park. He'd gone fifty feet when he halted, head turning side to side as his eyes searched every direction for a sign of movement on the dark paths shooting five different directions. There was nothing, and there were far too many footsteps to determine which could be hers.

Esther was gone.

XXIII.

"It's been over and hour and she hasn't come back yet,"
Danny declared, nipping at the Madame's heels with each of her
steps up the front staircase. "We need her back for tonight! What in
the hell could possibly be taking so long?!"

The Madame was not exactly pleased by Danny's castigating.
"You do not need her, Danny. We will do just fine without her…in
fact, it's probably better she isn't fucking here." She stopped three
stairs from the top and spun around. "And what's taking so God
damn long is that she's trying to do the right thing, and I gave her
permission to leave for it. If you have a fucking problem with that
and can't do your job, then get out of my sight and send me Caroline so I can make sure we're prepared."

"You can't tell me this doesn't worry you," Danny bellowed on,
refusing to let up while ignoring the Madame's jibe. "Hope would
have sent someone by now to let us know she wouldn't come back.
You know she would have."

"Get a hold of yourself," the Madame snapped. She could feel
her cheeks turning red with irritation. "This type of behavior, particularly toward me, will not be tolerated. Especially by you. Just because your fucking girlfriend is on an errand for Esther doesn't give

you the right to badger me about it. Now back off before I really lose my God damn temper."

She climbed the rest of the way up and went straight to her office, hoping Danny would be off to get the girls ready and check the rooms. Of course, those hopes were in vain, as Danny followed her inside and shut the doors.

"Fine, then answer me this," Danny charged accusingly. "Why did you lie to Esther, when we both know Doc was in the back checking Selina's infection?"

The Madame had finally reached her breaking point. Instantly she pivoted to face Danny and grabbed the girl's wrists hard with both hands, digging her nails into Danny's skin. It wasn't enough to cut, though enough to get her point across to shut her damned mouth or be ripped to shreds.

"If you don't stop yelling at me this second," the Madame told her, observing the shaken expression on Danny's face become frightened. "I will tear the veins out of your arms without a second thought." With wide eyes, Danny nodded, and the Madame let go of her, then made her way over to her desk.

"I…I…" she started, and the Madame held up her hand to stop her.

"Pour us each a drink, Danny. I won't ask twice."

Danny complied timidly and brought the whiskey back to her, avoiding eye contact as she took a seat, her eyes fixated on the bottom of her glass. After a gulp or two of her drink, the Madame lit a cigar.

"If you ever come at me like that again, especially if it's in front of the house staff, I will personally see to your beating and then throw you in the fucking streets. Got it?"

"Madame, I just–"

"I am not finished!" she roared, causing Danny to uncharacteristically cower away from her. "Now, to answer your questions all in one, let me explain what happens when you have the ability to think quickly and not emotionally, something you need to fucking learn before it gets you into trouble. I knew why Esther was here. I knew that son of a bitch snapped, and knew the likelihood that the baby was already long dead and the mother wouldn't be far behind. Are you with me so far?"

"Yes, Madame."

"Good. Because we're going to do this one together," she remarked sarcastically, letting out an exhale of smoke. "Who at The Palace is our fixer for the girls?"

Danny finally met her gaze. "For babies? Hope."

"Right you are, Danny. She takes care of all the abortions, takes care of every issue we don't need the Doc for because it's free, isn't that right?"

She could sense it was coming together for her, and Danny had a sip of her whiskey. "Yes it is."

The Madame clapped her hands together. "Great! Now the second part. Who is coming here tonight that, per our history, and puts Hope at risk?"

A tiny smile took shape. "Timothy Adams."

"Right you are again! So, let's make this easy. I made the call to kill two birds with one stone: get Hope out of this fucking place before that bastard arrives, and also, send a girl I think is better than the Doc to help Esther."

Danny was both astonished and embarrassed. "I shouldn't have suspected you," she apologized after a moment. "I know better than that. I'm sorry for how I acted."

The Madame tilted back in her chair, propping her feet up on her desk. "Danny, I know why you're acting like a fucking lunatic. Trust me when I say that I'm a selfish cunt, but I do try to take care of my people."

"I just don't know what I'd do if...if anything happened to her. I can't live without her, Madame."

Finishing her whiskey, the Madame shook her head. "She's safer there than she ever would be here."

An idea struck Danny, and suddenly she was spiraling downward once more. "What if he goes home? What if he finds them together?!"

"I wouldn't worry about that," the Madame commented, getting to her feet to pour another whiskey.

"What do you mean?"

The Madame smirked as she grabbed the decanter and took it over to her desk. "If Timothy Adams is stupid enough to go home early, he will end up with a hole in his gut."

It took a few seconds for the Madame's words to sink in. "You gave Esther a gun?"

"Of course I did."

Danny's alarm didn't cease at this information. "Madame, how do you know she won't seek him out? You're actually going to let her do this?"

The burn of the whiskey was at last hitting her stomach. "Don't pretend to be so stunned, Danny. Esther has wanted to fucking kill that son of a bitch since the day he raped her. She even tried to do things the right way and because of that, nearly ended up killed in a hit sent by her best friend's parents...think about that. No, there won't be an opportunity for her to kill Adams because he will be arriving here in...oh...twenty minutes or so? So I'd say we have it covered. In the off chance he did back out, however, I wanted to make sure Esther and Hope had artillery. The plan is still a go – Louis is going to take care of him toward the end of the night, and it will be deemed an overdose. An easy play...partying too hard after so much loss...happens all the time, you know. And we can finally send that fucker to burn in hell with his Daddy."

Finishing her whiskey, Danny seemed pacified. "As long as you promise me Hope and Esther are fine, I'll believe you."

"They're fine. I wouldn't have let Hope or Esther leave here if I thought they'd be getting in over their heads."

"All right," Danny sighed. "So, who have we got coming in from Tammany to add to The Vault tonight?"

The Madame smiled. "Eight of the twelve. The other four are just investors…nothing but fucking idiots with checkbooks." From her pocket, the Madame drew out the list of names and slid it across her desk to Danny. "The ones that are starred are the ones I need everything we can get from. There's a brief description of their appearance and what specifically I need at the very fucking least. Make sure you match the girls accordingly with their particular expertise."

Danny grabbed the list and studied it. "Consider it done." Rising, she finished off her drink and set the glass on the Madame's desk, heading toward the door.

"Danny?"

"Yes, Madame?"

"Keep an eye on him. We only need a few hours."

"Don't worry," Danny declared. "You know I have no problem with maintaining order."

The Madame chuckled and filled her whiskey again as Danny left to finalize their arrangements, closing the doors of the office. When she was finally alone, the Madame slammed two whiskies in a row – she hadn't wanted anyone to see it, but every inch of her skin was crawling with anxiety. Tonight was her first night hosting Croker's constituents, and thus everything she worked for hung in the balance. And in addition to that, Louis would be discreetly sending Timothy Adams to his grave, which was a difficult assignment when there were multiple others in the room who needed to believe it was an accident.

The Madame originally believed convincing Croker of killing Timothy was out of the question; however, fate stepped in to offer her exactly what she needed to show the Hall Timothy's true colors. The excuse of business expansion that winter wasn't Timothy's only reason for not wanting to return to Virginia with his pregnant wife, and when she and Louis dug up what they needed in Virginia, the Madame went straight to Croker with it. To her amazement, Croker told the Madame to get rid of Timothy, and she and Louis went immediately into strategizing the best way to make it look like an unfortunate mishap.

Another whiskey later, the Madame gathered herself, as the time had come for her guests to be arriving, and she waltzed over to her room dividers and dressed in the gown and jewelry she'd already set aside for the evening. It was her usual cut, with lace sleeves and a plunging neckline, the dress a deep blue to fit the nights jewel-toned theme. Makeup on and hair perfectly curled and pinned half up, she made her way downstairs to ensure everyone was ready and in position. The Velvet Room held fifteen of her twenty girls for the gentlemen's entertainment, and the other five were hastily assisting with any oddities that might be requested at random by their guests – anything from a specific type of wine or a fix of opium from her friend in Chinatown was up for grabs, and the Madame wanted to see to it she demonstrated to Croker the power and depth she had at her fingertips.

As she entered the Velvet Room, the Madame couldn't hide the sly grin that came to her face. The scene was a tantalizing one: deep blue, red, and purple drapes hung from the ceiling, the diamond chandeliers were dimmed to create an almost dream-like atmosphere amongst the incense burning in each corner. Every pillar stood tall, painted a shimmering gold, centering around the lounging platform where the girls were enticingly situated, each donning goddess-inspired dresses made of a sheer, silky fabric that left nothing to the imagination. In their usual fashion, the girls were having their pre-guest round of wine and cigarettes, readying to be at the service of their clients and do whatever was requested of them.

Danny met her at the doorway, and with an approving nod, the Madame let her know everything was done to her approval. Like the others, Danny was clad in the same attire; however, the Madame informed her earlier that day she intended to put her in charge of the night's event as her second in authority. A cigarette hung form her lips and an almost empty glass of wine dangled from her hand: on the exterior, Danny was cool, calm, and collected, ready for business hours.

"You love it, don't you?" she posed to the Madame, one hand resting on her hip as she leaned against the door.

"It's fucking perfect. You've done a brilliant job, Danny."

"Girls are set to go, their rooms are made up and ready for privacy if the time presents itself."

The Madame gave it one last glimpse. "Then we're ready. They should be here any minute. Finish your wine and have the food and drink brought in."

"Of course, Madame," she consented. "Should I expect Louis to have the door, or will that be George?"

"George for now. Louis should be returning soon. He was going by after an errand to keep an eye on the Esther situation."

Danny's mouth fell open. "But you...you said..."

The Madame rolled her eyes, strutting back down the hallway.

"I told you I take care of my people Danny," she said over her shoulder. "Don't ever fucking doubt me again."

The gentlemen arrived late, and the Madame did her customary formal introduction before handing the reins to Danny for the evening, telling them if they needed anything at all or if any issues arose to ask for her immediately. Normally she would put on a bigger show for her guests; nonetheless, she lacked the usual desire to make them feel at home the way she would with her own, handpicked clientele. These men were Croker's friends, partners, and associates, and they were far more interested in the naked women in the Velvet Room than in her. With her girls well-versed in the tactics needed to extract intelligence, there was no further need of the Madame's attendance, and for her, this was only a temporary matter anyhow. Sure, she and Croker needed each other...that would change one day soon, and she determinedly refused to do anything extra for the man who ruined her family. When the opportunity arose, she would rid the earth of Croker and his band of monsters, most notably Mr. Walsh.

From time to time the Madame checked in on the general vibe of the night, ensuring every man in the room was more than happy with his arrangements and that their needs were being taken care of without delay. Hours ticked by, and the Madame eventually shut herself away in the office, feeling strangely not like herself, and also vexed as to why in the world Louis hadn't shown his face. If he missed his window, there would be no way to recover, and the true aim behind their scrupulous planning would be lost. The clock struck midnight, clanging loudly in the Madame's ears. Something was wrong. Then, as if her thoughts were actually being heard, there was the abrupt sound of boots on the wood floor climbing her back stairwell, and instinctively the Madame reached for her gun, pointing it at the door. Within seconds, Louis burst through, breathing hard and sweating, and the Madame gaped at him, stupefied.

"Louis, where the fuck have you been?!" she exclaimed, setting the gun down and standing up, "Is Hope all right? You were under strict instructions–"

Instead of hearing her out, Louis paced to her drink cart and poured himself a large drink, gulping down the entire thing before he said a word.

She stopped her lecture. "What's happened?"

"I lost Esther."

The Madame's stomach dropped. "You…you lost her? How in the hell did you lose her, for Christ's sake?!"

Louis poured more into his cup. "You think if I knew that I'd be here? I have no idea how she did it, but she evaded me. And we both know not many fucking people can do that, Madame. It's worse than we thought."

She made a grab for her own glass. "Go on," she breathed, though not sure she wanted to hear it.

"For starters, Hope is doing whatever she can to keep Celeste alive, but I am not sure she will make it to morning."

"I fail to see how this is the most pertinent issue of our evening," the Madame replied, crossing her arms. "She'll pull through, she's strong enough."

"It's not that," Louis clarified, taking the load off his feet in a vacant chair. "Esther ran off with your pistol, and she's out for blood. I don't know what's going to happen, Madame. I can guarantee you that bastard is going to die tonight, whether it's by my hand or hers." Resting for a few seconds, Louis shut his eyes tight, as if he were hurting in some kind of way. "The change…it happened right in front of me. She crossed over for good."

"Talk me through it."

"The sadness…that last bit of sweetness evaporated. It became an anger I've never seen in her. She pointed the gun right at me and I swear I thought she would pull the trigger if I didn't let her go. She's not afraid anymore, Madame, and she doesn't give a damn what happens to her as long as he's dead."

"We have to get to him first," the Madame asserted, marching to sit by him. "If we take him out now, we can stop this fucking catastrophe."

Louis listened, nodding along in agreement. "How do we make it work?"

"I want the doors checked and locked," she elaborated, rising up. "I'll notify Danny, you get George, and I will keep this place under lock and fucking key until we find her. They won't want to be leaving for another few hours. You will stick to what we've discussed and–"

He cut her short. "Maybe…"

"Maybe what, Louis?"

"Maybe we should let her do it."

She practically dropped the glass from her hand. "Excuse me?"

677

"We should let Esther kill him."

"Are you out of your fucking mind? We were given the go ahead as long as we made it look like a freak accident! Letting Esther unload that pistol into his chest will make it pretty fucking obvious it was a hit, Louis!"

Louis got to his feet. "And how are you going to respond when she never forgives us for this? I wanted to do it, to save her, but the more I think about it the more I'm not sure taking away the one thing left she wants to do with her life is the right move."

The Madame gaped at him. "I can't believe I'm hearing this…"

"Madame, she's…she's not Mary. She knows the consequences, and she's willing to face them anyway. She's not yours to save, nor mine."

Her hand went to her forehead. "We're going to lose her, Louis…"

He put his hand on her shoulder. "She's already gone, Madame. I saw it. You know that I of all people didn't want this for her. The only thing we can do now is attempt to keep the hit as clean as possible. Maybe we can actually get away with it…"

There was a moment of silence as she came to accept Esther's fate. "I'll go talk with Danny. Find George. Croker isn't going to be happy."

"And since when do we operate according to Croker's expectations?"

Louis' words hit her like a hammer, and the Madame assented. "You're right. We don't. We absolutely fucking don't."

They hurried downstairs together, each taking a different direction at the bottom of the stairs. After assuring a few of the girls things were perfectly normal, the Madame made her way to the Velvet Room and knocked five times, the only way the door would open. It cracked ever so slightly, allowing Marcy's head to pop out.

"Madame! I'm sorry, Danny is currently occupied. One of the gentlemen took quite a liking to her and wouldn't have anyone else. Is everything ok?"

"Do you remember which man it was, Marcy?" the Madame pressed urgently.

Her expression grew serious. "Not him, Madame. He just left."

The hair on her neck stood up. "He…he what?!"

"He left, Madame, along with a few of the others who had families they claimed they needed to be home for. Only a few minutes ago."

The Madame tried to appear normal. "What was his condition like, darling?"

"Drank himself silly," Marcy asserted. "Oddly, didn't want to touch any of the girls, just watched. I think after his…prior incidents…maybe he didn't want to come across as the bastard he is in front of his new friends. We've gotten a lot of dirt tonight, Madame, I think you're going to be quite happy about it!"

"Marcy, keep everyone distracted for as long as you can–"

Suddenly there was a rustling, and Danny was at Marcy's side, the space between the door and the frame widening. "Madame he's…he's not here…" She flipped around, checking again, desperately wanting to be wrong. "I didn't even realize I was with a…fucking hell what do we do…?"

Marcy was perplexed. "What do you mean, Danny? What's the…Madame, are you all right?!"

"Just do what I asked of you, Marcy," the Madame demanded, grabbing Danny by the arm and pulling her through the doorway, "Tell whatever son of a bitch that's been swooning over her Danny's taken ill and if you have to keep him quiet, drug him."

Marcy nodded, a bewildered look on her face, and closed the door. The Madame and Danny ran through the hallway and out to the lobby, and as they rounded the corner they spied Louis talking with a man by the front door…someone that wasn't George. When the two men heard them coming, they turned to address them, and right away the Madame identified whom the stranger was was.

"Spotted your man in a carriage just a few minutes ago," he reported. "Alone. Headin' home with the hope of findin' his wife

679

dead on the ground, I expect." Will glanced and Louis. "Little girl was hot on his tracks. She had a small pistol in her hands and was in pursuit. Reckon it was takin' her longer than she liked to hail her own coach, so she took off through the park fast as a rabbit, headin' toward Fifth. Hell, no way I could keep up with her, damn thing was fast as shit. But I can tell from the look on your face you already knew what I was gonna tell ya."

Danny clutched the Madame's arm. "No…no no no! Hope! She's alone there with…with Celeste…Madame she's completely fucking defenseless! And she has no idea he's coming!"

"She's right," Louis interposed. "And with carriages, traffic, and the elements of a weekend night, we'd be a lot faster on foot like Esther. That's why she ran. She knows what's at stake without her there."

"I agree," the Madame added. "Danny, upstairs and grab my extra loaded cylinders out of the top drawer of my desk. Put on my extra boots and jacket hanging at the door to cover." Danny let go of her and took off as fast as she could. "Are you both armed?" she asked Louis and Will.

Will gave the Madame a mocking smile. "Is that s'pose to be funny, Ma'am?"

She took a step toward him. "No, it's not supposed to be fucking funny."

Louis moved forward to stand between them. "Madame, please. We need to think about this. Danny cannot be allowed inside…it could be a bloodbath by the time we arrive."

"'Fraid so," Will agreed, "I'll keep an eye on the whore. You two clean up shop. But you oughta know…Croker don't care if this little prick meets his maker, but he ain't gonna be able to guarantee anyone's…innocence, if ya know what I'm sayin'. So we best be gettin' outta here sooner rather than later."

The Madame began to take off as many layers of her underskirt as possible, and upon seeing this, Louis and Will drew away, hiding their eyes.

"What in the hell are ya doin'?!" Will hollered.

"It's so I can run and keep up, you idiotic bastard," she retorted, tugging at her corset strings. "Danny!" she screamed. "We don't have any more fucking time!"

Within seconds, Danny was flying down toward them, leaping down the steps four at a time and shoving the cylinders into the Madame's hands as soon as she reached them.

No one spoke another word.

The four took off sprinting out the front door of The Palace one by one, the Madame last to lock the door and then the gate. Bolting in the tracks of the others across the street and into Central Park, the Madame held her dress up high, her heart pumping harder than it had in decades. They ran as fast as their legs could carry them through the darkness, sucking wind in the cold, damp air, their shoes crunching hard against the frosting dirt path as moonlight stretched out ahead, illuminating their path. Will was in the front followed closely by Louis, with Danny and the Madame keeping an even pace, though the only reason Danny wasn't ahead of the others was because of the little sobs everyone pretended they didn't hear. Every few strides Will would peek back and then push them to even greater speed, making the Madame's legs scream with resistance. There was no other option – a few crucial seconds could make the difference of life or death for every soul in that household, and her temporary ache would fade much faster than the guilt of losing any one of them. Peering to her right and left, she knew they were almost through, all of them panting hard, their breath a visible stream streaking behind them. The Madame looked ahead to the backs of Louis and Will, noticing how in sync they were, reading each other's minds before the other could say anything. And in a strange way, the Madame found herself envious of it.

"Two hundred yards!" Will called back. "Louis, take the front with the head whore. Girl, you follow me 'round the back. We've gotta move fast, I don't know if…if we're gonna make it in time…"

"Why do you…say…that?" the Madame riposted, barely able to make the words out while trying to breathe.

Louis answered for them: "He has the element…of surprise. And Esther…Esther is impulsive…"

Will gave a nod of agreement, and not a half second later they were out of the park, dashing toward the house without any regard for the traffic around them. Thankfully, there were no pedestrians on the roadway, and as they slowed upon reaching the Adams' darkened residence, Danny took the Madame's hand in hers, squeezing it tight as tears fell from her eyes.

"It's going to be fine," the Madame gasped. "We're going to get him." Danny swallowed hard, biting her lip as she let go to chase after Will.

Louis and the Madame jogged up the front stoop and found the front door faintly opened. They didn't stall – Louis pushed it open and concurrently he and the Madame drew and cocked their pistols. Their first few steps through the door completely noiseless. Listening intently, Louis headed for the staircase to the second floor, motioning for the Madame to keep up. Together, they ascended swiftly and quietly, the haunting silence of the pitch black house making the Madame increasingly uneasy.

Tilting his head to indicate for her to take the lead, the Madame inched onward, blinking hard to aid her eyes in adjusting to the lack of light. For the initial minute they were in the house, the only sound she could hear was her heart thumping in her chest from their sprint, fighting hard to steady her breath; yet when they got to the top of the spiral staircase, two feet came into view…then legs… and though she had to squint, the Madame saw it was the maid knocked out cold on the ground. Cautiously she circled around, her finger over her lips, and she advanced to where Laura lay. The Madame bent over to make sure the girl was still breathing, and when she felt the gentle pressure of air against her face, waved for Louis to follow her and keep going.

They pressed down the hall, a tiny glint of light up ahead from underneath one of the last of the closed doors. As their surroundings became more discernible, they crept toward the light, still hearing nothing. Then, out of the blue, a hand emerged from the adjacent door to her left and grasped the Madame's ankle. The Madame shied backward in surprise, and Louis ran to where she was, squatting to the floor.

"Fuck…" she heard him mutter, and peeking over his shoulder, she felt a catch in her throat.

It was Hope, covered in blood. Her dress had been torn to shreds and was barely covering her as she wheezed to try and stay alive.

The Madame dropped to her knees and clutched at Hope's mangled hand, setting her gun down. She was weeping raspily, choking on blood as a drop leaked from the corner of her mouth. Bowing over, the Madame stuck her ear to the girl's chest and listened: her heart rate was scattered and her lungs were drowning. Examining the girl's body, it took all the Madame's vigor not to wince at damage done. If she wasn't at a hospital in minutes, she would never make it. Hope had been beaten, conceivably raped, and beaten again… Timothy had gone to The Palace that night more than likely wanting her, and when he didn't get it he came home only to find her here, trying to save his wife. That must have sent him so far over the edge there was no going back.

Louis' hand came to her arm, and the Madame looked up to see Will and Louis at her side. Before she could give any instruction, Will swept Hope up into his arms gently and took off down the hallway. As he ran off, Will passed Danny standing at the top of the staircase, collapsed onto the floor in a heap, her knees pulled into her chests as she rocked back and forth. The Madame attempted to spare her composure and, turning back to Louis, he helped her to her feet, their final destination no more than ten feet further down the hall. Halting at the door, Louis drew his gun up ready at his shoulder, one sideways glance to the Madame to make sure she was ready. She nodded, and together, they kicked the door open.

On the bed to their right lay an unconscious Celeste, who had no hint of what was going on around her. To their left, apart from the wrecked furniture and broken décor on the floor was Esther. Timothy stood behind her holding a dagger to her throat, smiling as if he'd planned it this way the whole time. Esther's temple had a deep gash, dripping blood down from her hairline, her arms were battered and cut with defensive wounds, her right hand gripped on Timothy's forearm in an endeavor to pull the blade from her neck while the left was held at bay. Her right eye was already darkening, bruised after enduring a few hits from Timothy, and the Madame noticed he had scratches on his face and neck, and his shirt was torn in a few places, indisputably from the struggle with both Hope and Esther. Neither Louis nor the Madame moved – they waited to see if Timothy had anything to say, markedly feeling he was in charge of the situation. And his narcissistic disposition did not disappoint.

"You're a little late to my party," Timothy said to them contemptuously. "You shouldn't have sent the whore. It was like being sent a prize for having to suffer so long without...without any fun..."

"I'd say you've had plenty of fun for one fucking lifetime, you sick bastard," the Madame shot back. "What do you think you're going to do? Kill us and escape? Hah! Louis and I will shoot you dead if you move a God damned muscle."

Timothy continued to grin. "We'll see about that. You don't get it yet, do you? How could you...you're just a whore. I am invincible now. All it takes is money and poof! It's all gone. Even little Es' complaint to the police department went away with just the snap of my fingers, like it never happened." His grip on her tightened, and the knife was a hair away from slicing through her skin. "You may think you know what you're up against, Madame, but I can assure you with the connections I've made, I could kill each one of you and then walk away a free man!"

684

The Madame let out a scathing laugh. "Connections? Oh please, do go on. I would love to hear it."

His face grew red at being ridiculed. "I'm a Tammany Hall man, and Tammany protects their own, especially in consideration of how much money I am contributing. You're nothing but a worthless whore, and your sidekick is what? Some French dog that's your gun for hire? And these two…" he was snarling, his eyes going from Celeste to Esther. "I'd say they've earned this with the God damn antics they've carried on with for all these years."

Just as the Madame was about to speak, Louis cut in. "It's over, Timothy. The Police are on their way, and we've already dispatched a telegram to Virginia. The Pinkertons will be here to drag you back in chains to hang for what you've done."

Timothy's eye started to twitch, his expression firm. "The Pinkertons are a myth. They've been gone for years."

"They are still very much a running agency for anyone who will pay them what they require," the Madame informed him. "And there are plenty of rich fuckers in Virginia who want you at the end of a noose, Mr. Adams, men missing their lost sisters, wives, and daughters. Your Daddy won't be able to get you out of this one."

Timothy was trying to hide his distress. "How…how could you know about that?" his voice staggered.

"During a visit with an old friend from Virginia, I happen to hear about a man whose daughter had just been found brutally murdered. He explained to me that a young man was on the loose and apparently responsible for a series of murders, all women…all blonde…all with blue eyes and all killed in the same way: beaten repeatedly and raped. It was a mystery for quite some time because you could never be identified by a witness. However, the man who lost his daughter just so happens to be not only one of my clients, but also one of the state's congressmen, and one of the many now funding your capture via the Pinkerton Agency. At first I didn't want to believe it was true, but somehow one of the girls you tried to fucking kill on your last little vacation home survived, and she provided a sketch to the coppers who then handed it over to Louis." The Madame caught her breath a moment, watching him closely. "I gave it to the Pinkertons through an acquaintance of an old friend of mine…along with a little cash incentive. Even if you get away tonight, it won't be long before they catch you, you son of a bitch. And that will be over my fucking dead body."

The hand holding the knife at Esther's throat trembled. "You… you couldn't have…" He looked down at Esther. "I'll kill her and happily watch her die. You know I will."

"Celeste will get every penny," she went on, discounting his threats despite the notion that Esther's time was running thin. "There is no way you win in this. You're fucking done, do you hear me?"

"Mmm," came a sudden sound to their right. Celeste was rousing, though not yet fully awake, and the Madame could see the panic in Timothy escalate.

Everything then happened very quickly.

Timothy's eyes weren't on the Madame, Louis, or even Esther – they were focused on Celeste, and his drunken state was betraying him with slow reflexes and a serious lack of shrewdness. Somehow, Esther's gaze locked with the Madame's for a half of a second, and in that time an entire conversation was communicated between them. With a thrust of strength, Esther yanked her left hand free and propelled herself forward, pushing hard against Timothy's grip while her neck was cut and wounded severely by the blade. Amazingly, her plunge forward maneuvered out of his clutches. Taken entirely off guard, Timothy was motionless, unable to comprehend the situation unraveling in the room around him. Esther rolled onto the ground and away from Timothy, reaching first instinctively to her neck and, convinced the blood covering her hands wasn't fatal, allowed her rage to take over.

Seeing their fight escalate, Louis concurrently moved toward Celeste's bedside and picked her up, carrying her away from anything that might do her harm and shielding them both behind the Madame, who covered Louis' movements. Leaping to her feet, Esther went after Timothy who, following a few fleeting swipes with his dagger, managed to lacerate Esther's left arm while her right hand knocked the knife from him with a hard hit against his wrist. The Madame tried to aim her gun for the shot, though she couldn't get a clean one with Esther blocking her view of Timothy, and so she waited. Attempting to retreat, Timothy fell, tripping backwards over his own feet and hit the wall with a loud crash. Esther went after him, striking him over and over again until Timothy responded with one distinct backhanded blow to her cheekbone, sending Esther spiraling to the floor.

"Madame!" Louis yelled at her. "Do something!"

The Madame didn't flinch now. She was steady, her finger on the trigger of her pistol, knowing she could shoot Timothy dead. Timothy's interest went the direction of Louis' voice for just enough of an instant to allow Esther to recuperate, though not expeditiously enough. Grabbing the knife and diving at Esther again blade first, the Madame recognized the moment had come and she couldn't delay any longer. She took the shot, the blast of it rocketing Timothy backwards and away from Esther.

The bullet hit him at the left outer shoulder, blood spattering the wall behind him. It was just deep enough to not be a graze, but the shock of the hit sent Timothy to the ground, scooting frantically away to a dead end in the corner of the room. His blade was again on the floor, leaving Timothy defenseless, and Esther got to her feet, moving straight to the Madame.

"Do I have your permission?" she asked frankly, holding her hand out for the Madame's gun.

The Madame revolved around to see Louis, whose face was torn, making this entirely her call.

"Please!" Timothy pleaded, holding up his arms in surrender. "Please, I'll do anything you want! Anything! I'll give you as much money as you want!"

For a moment, the Madame hesitated, lowering her pistol. This wasn't the way. Esther would never get away with it.

"Es?" came Celeste's voice from Louis' arms. She had almost come around, the sight of her in such a debilitated and weakened state hard to bear. Then, without warning, Celeste broke into the present, her eyes finding Timothy cowering across the room and she stared viciously at him, a fiery hatred burning in her pupils. A quiet declaration came from Celeste's lips that did not resemble her own:

"Kill him."

Sooner than the Madame or Louis could take action, Esther snatched the gun from the Madame's hand and paced away, cocking the pistol as she aimed it at Timothy.

"Esther!" Louis bellowed.

On Esther's face was a look the Madame had never seen before. There were five bullets left in the gun, and Esther unloaded every single one into Timothy's chest. She kept firing, even with the cylinder empty, and then dropped the pistol to the floor. Turning toward them, she woefully smiled at her best friend that Louis held close, her eyes filling with tears.

"You're safe now," she assured Celeste, sinking down as her legs gave way. "The police should arrive any minute, and…and when they do, tell them they can find me up here and that I'll…I'll go quietly."

Ellis had to restrain the Madame in the downstairs library, though she fought him tooth and nail to stay at Esther's side as they loaded her into the paddy wagon. Every copper there wanted to take the Madame in for interrogation, to know just what in the hell had gone on at the Adams residence that night, but Ellis refused her immediate detainment, maintaining that because she was not a suspect she couldn't be put into questioning without a warrant. Trying to keep her out of the investigation area, Samuel barricaded them in Timothy's library, locking them inside until she got a grip on herself long enough to tell him the facts. The Madame, however, was not exactly cooperating.

According to Louis, Will had taken Hope to the nearest hospital and made sure a doctor saw to her injuries. When he'd left, Danny was at her bedside, and then he'd gone straight to the precinct to get any support he could find. No more than two minutes after Esther pulled the trigger, the house was swarming with blues, and the now awake Celeste was in a fit of hysterics from the general shockwave of the night's events. The time came when the police wanted to know where the shooter was, and not one of them could lie: Esther hadn't moved from the second floor bedroom, despite Celeste's desperate efforts to drag her away.

Louis battled to keep Celeste and the Madame from causing too much of a scene until Detective Ellis arrived at the house, and ultimately Samuel was able to drag the Madame away from Esther as Louis took Celeste back to The Palace. Now, standing between her and the door, Samuel was furious.

"I need you to tell me what in the hell happened here tonight! Before it goes to the God damned papers! I can't hide this one, don't you fucking get that? Everyone is going to know about what happened here!"

The Madame slapped him hard. "How dare you come after me like this is something I've fucking done to you! That son of a bitch was a rapist and a murderer! It's a blessing he was taken down before he killed his wife or anybody else!"

She went to hit him again, but Samuel caught her hand in mid air, forcing it down. "It doesn't matter what he is! Croker isn't going to let her go, Madame, don't you see? He's not going to do anything to help her. He's going to let her take the fall and cover this up so nothing leads back to the Hall."

"So what?! I've got three people including myself who will say it was in self-defense, and one of my girls barely clinging to fucking life at the hospital after he savagely beat and raped her!"

689

Samuel sighed. "You've got three witnesses Timothy's lawyers are going to use to their advantage and pin them as people who plainly saw Esther shoot Timothy Adams in cold blood."

Will's words of warning flickered back to the Madame's mind. "He's…Croker's going to make her the scapegoat? To cover up for that bastard just so he can keep the Hall's image clean?!"

"Yes."

"But…no…there must be a way…"

Ellis' firm hold on her hand loosened, and he pulled them to his lips, kissing her hands in sorrow. "Someone is going to have to hang for it. With every finger pointed at Esther, the only option you have is to send the Pinkertons to Croker to try and negotiate a deal of some kind."

The Madame pulled away from him, her emotions getting the better of her as the adrenaline wore off.

"I've killed Mary…and now Esther…" she said aloud to herself, the her eyes found Samuel's. "They were the only women who ever meant anything to me…what does that say about me?"

"They both were like you," Ellis contended. "Headstrong…so much so that you couldn't save them. They had their own plights, Madame, you only did what you thought you had to do to make them happy. You can't save those who don't want to be saved."

The Madame was distraught. "But Thomas…Thomas won't ever forgive me now…he'll never come back."

"Tell him before it's too late. Write to him—"

"I have been fucking writing to him. All of my letters have gone unanswered…unopened for all I know…"

"Madame, just tell him."

She fell heavily against the bookshelves on the wall, her head spinning, struggling to find an answer to the devastation around her.

"Get me a whiskey, Samuel," she said softly. "And get me home as soon as you possibly can. I just can't…I can't face it…"

"Louis?"

Will's voice felt so far away despite the fact that he was sitting right next to him.

"Louis…please…"

They were in Central Park and had been for hours, closely observing the faraway crowd currently dissipating from the area surrounding the Adams residence. Louis was at a loss, no longer able to clearly think, livid with himself for not stopping Esther from killing Timothy Adams. If only he had intervened sooner…if only Celeste hadn't spoken…Louis tortured himself tracing through the details of the incident over and over again. There was nothing he could do now…nothing he could do or say to change that Esther would surely hang for the murder, a murder he let happen right in front of him.

His chin drooped to his chest. He'd failed again to protect the ones he loved. Like Mary, Edward, and even Thomas, he'd failed Esther. They were the few most precious to him…the few he loved more than any other, and he'd let every one of them down and would have to live with that, bridled up in his own misery.

Giving him a start, Will took Louis' hand, forcing him to acknowledge Will's existence on the park bench beside him.

"I don'…I don' exactly know how to tell ya this, but I'm gonna do my damndest to try and make it easy for ya. Hope is…well…she's dead, brother. She was too far gone when I got her there. Danny got to say her goodbyes…it wasn' easy. I don' know how that one's gonna do without her other half. I reckon she's beyond fixin'…ya know I wouldn' say that if it wasn' true. I tried to tell her I knew how she felt but ya know, nobody knows the real story…" His words trailed off.

"They were like us," Louis murmured.

"Yeah…yeah they was."

Louis' fingers stretched around Will's. "Thank you for all you've done tonight. I don't know how I can ever thank you for it."

691

"What've I got myself into here, Louis? Eh?"

"What do you mean?"

"I mean, I'm fine takin' a life for my own reasons. Tonight…seein' this shit and havin' to live through it…fuckin' breaks up the little bit that's left of my corrupted soul, brother. I don' know how to deal with this…or with you…all over again like it was in the beginnin'."

Louis studied Will, unsure of what he wanted to say or how he wanted to say it. Their history was clouded by the tumultuous space between the present and the past; everything they had together Louis had put behind him years ago when Will was pronounced dead by the state. It wrecked him in a way he could never own up to anyone, and it took him over two decades to recover from losing Will in those circumstances. Then, out of the darkness, Will came back into his life like a ghost, as if he'd never been gone in the first place. From that moment they reunited in Central Park, there seemed to be a tangible agreement not to ever discuss or bring up what had once been between them. Tonight changed that. Will came to his aid without hesitation, when every lead had gone cold and there was nothing more he could do, going against all of Croker's orders to try and save someone that mattered to Louis – because Esther mattered to Louis, she mattered to Will. He'd taken Louis' hand, his reasoning was for solace and support yet Louis knew better. In another life, they'd meant so much to each other, never telling a soul the depths of their relationship though never caring what anyone thought either. Will abandoned him to save him…and now here he was, trying to do it once again.

Ignoring his doubts, Louis leaned over impulsively and kissed Will, his heart pumping faster and faster. The moment he felt Will kiss him back, Louis pulled away, appalled at himself, and got to his feet as he apprehensively paced back and forth in front of the bench.

"We can't do this…"

"Louis, stop."

"We can't, Will. If anybody knows…if Croker or the Madame finds out it will be out of our hands."

"Nobody will know!" Will cried out, standing up. "Nobody has ever known! What's the point of…of lovin' someone if you can't be near them? I left you once, I ain't doin' it again. Not when I know you need me and I need you. We can keep this secret, Louis. We always have!"

"It's not just Croker," Louis continued. "It's that other son of a bitch following our every move. You say you can't live without me, well I don't want to live without you either, and you can't for one fucking second tell me Walsh won't find this out."

"Well what in the hell are we s'pose to do then? Act like there ain't nothin' between us?" Will was truly suffering, Louis could see it in his eyes.

"That's not what I'm saying—"

"Then what are you sayin'?"

"I need time, Will!" Louis shouted, more aggravated than he initially recognized. "This has been a God damned massacre! I need to find a way to try and save Esther, for God's sake, or I've got nothing else to…to…" Like a lightning strike, an idea suddenly sparked in Louis' brain. "Will, if I work for Croker, could he do it?"

He crossed his arms. "What're ya talkin' 'bout now? You're goin' a million fuckin' miles a minute, brother."

"Save her," Louis pressed, grabbing onto Will's forearm. "I need you to tell Croker we need a meeting."

"You…you what? What the hell are ya talkin' 'bout? Tell Croker to meet you? After the hell that's been raised tonight?"

"Tell him it will just be me. Not the Madame. Me working for him as his man. Tell him after tonight the Madame and I are through, and I'll be his no matter what he asks of me. You tell him that."

Will shook his head. "Louis, are ya sure ya want to be doin' this right now? Why don' ya sleep on it and let me know tomorrow."

"Because if I waste any time, she'll be gone."

Will's gaze fell to the ground. "I'll arrange it. All right? I'll take care of it for ya."

693

"Thank you, Will."

Louis started to walk away, but Will wouldn't let him go that easy. "So you're just gonna leave like nothin' happened? Like this is nothin' to you?"

He stopped. "I have to go," Louis replied. "And you know it means more than anything to me. But that doesn't mean I can stay."

"And why's that?"

"Because I can't do this without you."

Louis marched onward, his heart swelling with overwhelming sadness and the undeniable rush he felt from being so close to Will. Shaking it off with the passing strides, he cleared his head, wanting to give his full attention to the task ahead.

This could be the first step to saving Esther, to find the redemption he sought.

He only hoped it would be worth the cost.

XXIV.

Winter was setting in quickly throughout southern England. The gusting winds were often so shockingly cold it felt as if a blade might be piercing Thomas' skin, and he swore he hadn't seen the sun peek through the clouds in over three weeks. Nothing but a bitter, sleeting rain fell from the grey sky, icing over the rolling hills he passed by in his carriage as far as the eye could see. Another hour or two further, and they would have to stop to warm up – Thomas' driver, Sal, was tough as nails, but even he couldn't fight off the frostbite for long with his jacket nearly soaked through. Miraculously, the horses were getting along fine at a nice, steady tempo, staying just warm enough in their muscles to keep the chill out of their bones. The entire traveling party could use some time to dry and warm up by the fire, including Thomas, who despised that he was stuck inside the carriage. There were only a few hours left until they reached Amberleigh, and in addition to his craving to be home, Thomas wanted to make sure they made it back without incident, even if that meant stopping more frequently than normal.

For weeks, he had been journeying back and forth from London settling Edward's estate. Thomas spent countless days held up in meetings with lawyers to be confirmed as Edward's next of kin, and therefore, considered the true and fortified heir. It was a ridiculously tedious process, but there was no other way around it. Once they finally settled the Turner estate, Thomas was forced to attend a small ceremony amongst the Peerage, where he was formally accepted into the House of Lords. He knew there would be speculation as to whether or not his assertion that he was truly Edward's son was valid or fabricated; however, whatever doubts existed toward Thomas' claim vanished the moment he met with his contemporaries. He was, now more than ever, the splitting image of his father, and after presenting the drafted out legal rights he possessed to Edward's seat, Thomas was welcomed to their group like an old friend.

Somehow without Thomas' knowledge, his father had already completed the necessary patent documentation with his lawyers on their last business outing in London, just days prior to their trip to New York. When Thomas first went to them, they were a little uneasy to open Edward's folder in front of Thomas, explaining that because he was not birthed through a legitimate marriage, his succession to his father's title would not be possible. William had already clarified most of this to Thomas, and while he realized it meant a lot to William for Thomas to be accepted into the House of Lords, Thomas honestly couldn't give a damn about politics or society. Then, as the lawyers started to sort through the contents, the entire room fell into a stunned silence when they discovered amongst the authenticated records was an unopened letter from a familiar address in New York, received only a week before Thomas' arrival. Since it was considered confidential and for Edward's eyes only, Thomas reached over and opened the seal, finding no contents except a marriage certificate, binding Mary Dougherty and Edward Turner to one another.

There was no note from the Madame. Only the piece of paper, signed by both his parents, a priest, and Louis as a witness. It was one of the most earth shattering moments Thomas experienced since he found the letters from his father in the Madame's safe, and it took most of his self-control to not completely lose his composure in front of the men holding the keys to his future as Lord Turner.

"Sal!" Thomas shouted out through the carriage window, attempting to shield his eyes from the fierce, pelting rain.

"Yes, Lord Turner?!"

"Time for a warm up, I think!"

"What?!"

"Time to warm up! Top of the next hill!"

"Sir, we're only two hours out! The horses and I can make it!" he argued, stubborn as an ox.

Thomas chuckled a little. "Don't be such a bastard! Top of the next hill! Otherwise I'll make you sit in here while I drive!"

"Fat chance!" Sal hollered, laughing and shaking his head. "All right, top of the next hill, Lord Turner!"

They reached the peak faster than Thomas predicted, and as he leapt out of his coach car, he was relieved to feel the dense humidity had warmed the air, though only to a minimal extent. Sadly, it would be nearly impossible to light a fire with the rain still pouring, and the low hanging, thick grey clouds muted all color from the sky which gave the feel of it being nearly night when it was just after lunchtime. In the distance, the rolling hills seemed to be infinite as the disappeared into the hazy distance, the grass dark blue with the shadows of the storm. Thomas pulled his coat tighter around his neck and pressed his hat firmly atop his head, jogging up toward the horses and feeling their chests to check their temperature, breathing a sigh of reprieve. Both geldings were moderately heated from their drive, though if it were to get much colder, traveling would be absolute lunacy.

Sal hopped out and down from the driver's seat. "Sir, I'm not sure we'll be able to get a fire going in this rain! Even with the cover, it's bloody dumping like a waterfall. If we don't keep the boys moving they'll freeze up in no time!"

"Sal, let me drive and you go warm yourself. I can handle

two hours, but I can't have my driver losing fingers and toes on my account."

"No offense, Lord Turner, but there is no way on God's green earth I would ever allow that. I've been through worse, and for a hell of a lot longer of drives. Boys doing all right?"

The wind began to howl in his ears. "Horses are good to go. You sure you can make it the rest of the way?"

"Yes, sir."

Thomas nodded, impressed by Sal's perseverance, and turned to trot back toward the passenger door when a rider from the south came cantering into view just down the road. A look of confusion came over Sal's face as he turned to Thomas for orders. Thomas on the other hand, broke into a smirk.

"Sir…? Do you know who that is?"

"Yes I do. It's my father's man, Sal. The one you've never been very fond of."

Sal instantly became irritated. "How in the bloody hell did that Celestial bastard know we was here, eh? How could he have possibly known? Jesus. We're the only bastards dumb enough to venture out in this God damned weather, that's why!"

Thomas tried to mask his amusement. "Hiro always knows, Sal. That's why he's one of a kind."

Within minutes, Hiroaki was at Thomas side, dismounting his horse and handing the reins nonchalantly to a hilariously enraged Sal, which he ignored, his attentions focused solely on Thomas.

"Lord Turner, please order your coachman to take my horse home immediately. I will drive you back in the carriage. You cannot stay out in this weather much longer or there is no way you will be capable of resisting a fever."

Sal opened his mouth to speak out in protest, yet immediately shut it, recognizing Hiroaki was saving him an hour of suffering in the miserable rain and wind.

"How is home?" Thomas asked.

"William is…well…irritable as he tends to get when it rains for days," Hiroaki conversed. "And Lucy is better, becoming much more like her old self. Akemi's teas have helped her strength."

This was music to Thomas' ears. "Is she eating meals yet?"

"Oh for Christ's sake, Sir!" Sal exclaimed, interrupting them. "If you two need to talk can you do it when I'm not freezing my arse off?"

Hiroaki whipped around swiftly, glaring at Sal. "Have a care how you speak to Lord Turner, or I will make it so that you can't say another word ever again. How does that sound to you?"

"Hiro…that's enough," Thomas interjected, once again trying to hide the merriment he found in their interactions. "Sal, take his horse. Go to the house and tell Akemi to prepare us each a hot bath, soup, and brandy for when we arrive. Understood?"

Sal already had one foot in the stirrup, hoping around to gain his balance and lunge up in the saddle. "You've got it, Lord Turner!" With one swift kick Sal took off over the hills the direction of Amberleigh, not bothering to delay any further.

"What is your primary objective of keeping that mouth around?" Hiroaki posed, crossing his arms while his gaze traced Sal's path.

Thomas put a hand on Hiroaki's shoulder. "He'll drive in any weather as long as I compensate him. Come on, now. We've got at least two hours of ground to cover in this shit, and I want to be indoors."

Hiroaki followed him to the carriage, and after they checked the horses one last time, Thomas hopped up behind him to the driver's booth to take a seat, much to Hiroaki's dismay.

"If you catch a fever, William will kill me. You know this."

"Hiro, I'm not going to catch a damn fever and die. Let's get going. No more questioning my motives."

"You're as obstinate as your father."

"Hah! You should have met Mary. She was even worse than Edward, and that was on her good days."

699

The screaming wind made it impossible for conversation, and instead of two hours it took nearly three for Hiroaki and Thomas to brave the storm back to Amberleigh. They steered the horses to the stables right away, where Hiroaki and one of the stable boys began to untack and disassemble the carriage, throwing blankets on the horses to help first absorb the water and sweat before removing it and throwing on another dry blanket for warmth. To Hiroaki and Thomas' surprise, both geldings continued to be in good temperament, and their hooves were happily not torn apart by the mud and rocks on the constantly flooded roadways from London. Once they were settled, Thomas departed toward the main house and Hiroaki returned to his cottage, promising in a few hours he would join Thomas in the study for some of his promised brandy.

Jogging lightly up the pathway through the back garden, Thomas was looking forward to his hot bath; he wanted nothing more than to get out of the heavy, sopping wet clothes clinging to him and thus making him feel as if he were at least two stones heavier. The smell of bread in the oven filled his nostrils just as he reached the door, making his mouth water and stomach rumble. Thrusting the door open, he was expecting to be greeted by the kitchen staff. However, as he stepped inside, there was only one man there, and he stood leaning back against the table in the middle of the kitchen eyeing him crossly. William, for one reason or another, was not pleased. In fact, Thomas was certain it was the angriest he'd seen William in quite some time, and instantly he racked his brain to try and think of a reason as to what could be the cause.

"Just what in the fuck do you think you're doing, Thomas? Huh? Driving the damned carriage back in this mess? Are you out of your mind?"

Thomas rolled his eyes – he could tell William had already consumed at least a glass or two of something while waiting for him to arrive and let his paternal instincts get the better of him. Rather than shake it off and apologize, Thomas decided to stand his ground, as he'd been trying to do more lately to establish a new pecking order for his family.

"I chose to return today," he asserted calmly. "It was my responsibility to get the carriage and Sal back."

"Hiro left here to do that for you. Then of course when I look out the window, I see both of you in the driver's seat. You aren't fifteen anymore, Thomas, you need to be more accountable with your health!"

"William, please. I don't need this right now."

"Well someone has to bloody well tell you when you're being a stupid bastard! If Edward ever saw you pulling stunts like this–"

"My father isn't here, William," Thomas cut him short, holding up a hand to silence him. "And while I appreciate your concern, my health is just fine. I'm not going to die because of a little bad weather."

William sighed. "You should have been in the passenger compartment, Thomas. You can't afford to be reckless." William moved forward and shoved a cup of hot tea into his hands, then threw a blanket around Thomas' shoulders, brushing his hands up and down his arms to warm him. "We are a small family now. And we need you. Just don't be so bloody careless, all right?"

"I know."

"I'm sorry for my verbal ambush."

"I know you care William. We can talk this over later. I need get out of these clothes." Thomas began to walk away, then paused just shy of leaving the kitchen. "I'm not going to abandon you, William, not for anything. I'm not my father. You should know that by now."

William smiled forlornly. That's not news to me, Tommy. Save it for later. Your bath is waiting in your rooms."

Thomas sipped his tea and made his way through the hallway to the back stair, climbing sluggishly up to his room. A day of hard riding in a harsh climate set in, taking a toll on his physical strength, and with each step up the staircase his muscles and bones ached more

701

and more. When he got to the top, Thomas proceeded to stumble down to his room, pushing the door open erratically and then closing it shut for privacy. Fatigue hit him harder than he was prepared for, and his muscles trembled as he undressed from the shock enduring the outside temperature. Thomas trudged slowly to his bath that smelled of roses, steam rising high above it, and stepped in, lowering into the water. The contrast of the heat against his cold body nearly caused him to black out, though he managed to resist, and after giving it a few seconds, his mind went blank and allowed the drama of his day to disappear. Glancing over at his cup, Thomas recognized it must be the tea…Akemi always had a way to rid the body of excess baggage, in ways that Thomas considered almost magical. Every element his adrenaline had been fighting off for the last few hours felt as if it were gradually seeping out and into his bath, and Thomas was consumed in the serenity of being home again.

Soaking in the heat, Thomas had an odd sense of déjà vu take over. He dozed off and on, letting his body relax, and each time he closed his eyes Thomas imagined he was back at the funeral, standing there watching his father's body being taken down into the ground. There had never been a time in his life, not even after losing Mary, that Thomas' heart broke more. Edward was his salvation… his new life and his new beginning…taken from him and propelling him into the unknown alone. The day his father had shown up at the apartment above the barber shop, Thomas went with him, expecting a journey with his father that would last far longer than it had. The day of the funeral, a part of Thomas was buried in the ground along with his father. There was no longer a safeguard of learning and experiencing life under the wing of the greatest man he'd ever known. All that was left was Thomas and the cruel world he'd been sprung into.

He'd never felt more lost.

Sure, as his father taught him, Thomas knew how to play the part. He could talk like the other Lords, keep up the necessary formalities, obtain the right kind of interests and, without difficulty, keep the business blossoming the way Edward and William wanted him to. In his chest, somewhere deep down inside, there was a hole in Thomas, growing bigger every day. A hole he didn't know how to fill, and one he could only guess he'd hoped Esther, children, and a different future might have brought him. His soul felt empty and wasted. For most of his adolescent life, money was his key to survival. Despite having more money than he could ever think of ways to spend, Thomas promptly discovered it was not what he'd imagined. With the dirt still loose around his father's grave, Thomas seriously contemplated doing what he'd meant to do almost ten years before and go west to the American frontier. He'd even packed his bag three...maybe four times, only to unpack again, his father's shame in this notion haunting him from the afterlife. If there was one question Thomas wished more than anything he could ask his father, it was what he should do next...because he was losing his mind trying to figure it out.

And there simply was no right answer.

Hours later, following his long bath and a large glass of brandy by the fire, Thomas was about to finish dressing for the evening when there was a soft knock on his door.

A knowing grin came to his face. "Come in, Lucy," he called to her, buttoning up his vest.

The handle on the door turned and Lucy crept inside, giving him a small hug and a kiss on the cheek to welcome him home. A few seconds passed as they stood in silence until Lucy went to the side table to pour her own brandy, and subsequently lowered down into a chair next to the fireside. Though it had taken months, she looked remarkably better than when Thomas initially left on his trip: the fragility of her body was beginning to subside, her cheeks were fuller and had a nice, pink hue, yet the one thing that struck Thomas was her eyes. They were no longer as vulnerable and vacant, which was how they'd been since she heard the news that Edward died. In reality, he was amazed to find their original sparkle and luster returning, the way they had been before their whole world fell apart. Seeing her in such a state lifted his own spirits, especially following his confrontation with William earlier that afternoon.

"Are you sure you want brandy?" he asked, trying not to sound patronizing. "Maybe some tea would be—"

"Sit down, Thomas," she commanded firmly. "And no, brandy will suit me just fine. I'm feeling like my old self again. So don't be an ass."

"Right." He walked over to the other empty armchair and sat, picking up his own glass from the coffee table. "What is it, Luce?"

Her eyes went from Thomas to her drink. "I need to ask a favor of you. One you won't like in the slightest."

"You know I would do just about anything to keep you happy. What is it?"

Lucy took a sip of brandy, avoiding eye contact. "I need you to just…just for one second forget everything that's happened and consider…"

"What is it?"

"I want you to write to Esther."

Thomas scoffed. "Oh Lucy, you've got to be kidding me."

"Please, Thomas," she insisted. "Please! Just hear me out and try not to immediately refuse."

"What good could possibly come of that?"

"The girl made a mistake…we all make mistakes, even you! She wouldn't even see me…before we left. I've written to her over and over…still I get no response. You didn't even tell her you were going so soon and I'm sure she's been torturing herself about it ever since!"

Thomas grew defensive. "Luce, how many times do we need to go over this. Esther ended it, not me. I was angry, yes. Hurt, yes.

Jealous…to a level I don't want to feel again. And yet I had no plans on ending anything. She gave the ring back, I didn't ask for it, and she fucking left us." He stood up again, reflecting on their final moment together in New York. "Like she always does when things get hard. Fleeing has always been what Esther is best at."

"Thomas…"

"No Lucy. That's my answer."

"Thomas, your father loved her," Lucy went on. "He loved you two together. He wanted her to be here with you!"

"Yeah and he's fucking gone too, Lucy!" Thomas yelled loudly, spinning away from the fire to face her. "I don't know how to explain this any better, but she chose to go. I didn't make her!"

Lucy glowered at him. "Do you want to grow into a miserable old bastard like your father? Alone in this house, rotting away because you sat writhing in self-pity rather than doing something with your life because you felt slighted and cheated out of happiness? Blaming it on anyone except yourself? Because if that's what you want, you're well on your way, Tommy."

Her words were meant to strike him hard and they did, hitting him like a ton of bricks. It was a punch to his stomach that left him utterly speechless. Lucy had never said a disrespectful word about his father, not even the tiniest slight when she thought no one might notice. To have her so abrasively criticize Edward to Thomas as if it were a commonality amongst them made him see how much Lucy had changed in her weeks of illness.

Impulsively, Thomas went over to his bedside table and opened the top drawer, pulling out a small velvet pouch and came back to his chair by the fire, staring at it as he tossed it back and forth between his fingers.

"What is that?" Lucy asked.

Thomas opened it carefully and tipped the pouch over, and Esther's engagement ring tumbled into his palm. "Every time I look at this, I want to write to her and tell her to come here," he confessed, his eyes fixated on the ring. "But I can't make her, Lucy. Writing a letter won't change anything."

"No, it might not," Lucy agreed, scooting forward and closing Thomas' hand around the ring. "But I think you need to forgive her so you can either have another chance or move on."

As his sentimentality vanished, Thomas tugged his hand away from her. "I'm sorry, Lucy. Esther has run out of chances with me, because running is all she's ever done. I'm not going to chase her anymore."

"But she loves you, Thomas," Lucy pleaded. "And I know you are upset because you love her too."

"Sometimes love isn't enough." Thomas slid the ring back in the pouch and handed it to her. "Get rid of this for me."

"But Thomas—"

"But nothing, Lucy. I don't care what you do with it. I just don't want to see it again, and we are not going to discuss Esther either. From this time onward, she is in our past. You want me to move on, so this is me moving on."

"You can't just shut these things out like they don't exist," Lucy declared, snatching the ring from Thomas. "You can't ignore these things and expect it to fade away. That's what your father did with your mother, and look how that one turned out."

Thomas' fist clenched in rage, and he turned toward the fire, unable to look at her. This wasn't the Lucy he loved. This was someone else entirely, and he'd had enough of people in his life telling him how to live it.

"Leave now, or I cannot guarantee I will be capable of restraining my anger."

"Someone has to be a mirror for you, Thomas, and I am not letting you become Edward. I can't...I can't let that happen again."

Thomas knew if he spoke he would regret everything he had to say. Instead he marched toward his door and flung it open, gesturing for her to exit. Lucy got to her feet perturbed, taking her glass of brandy yet leaving the ring on the side table. As she swept by, she paused and looked at him.

"I just want to help," she whispered, then continued on out of Thomas' rooms. He slammed the door behind her.

Heading over to brood by the fire, Thomas grabbed the entire bottle of brandy – it was going to take a hell of a lot more than one glass to ease him out of this mood. His gaze drifted to the ring, and for a moment, he seriously considered throwing it in the fire, wanting nothing more than to destroy it and everything it stood for. What Lucy failed to comprehend was the complex relationship Thomas had with Esther, and his motivations in not pursuing any further contact with her or anyone else in New York. In two different times in his life, Thomas needed her support when he'd felt the most alone, and in both circumstances she'd flown the other direction as fast as her legs would carry her. Twice he'd wanted to have faith in her reliability and she'd left, abandoning him to take steps on his own, first as a childhood friend and then as his fiancée. No, there was nothing more he had to say. Lucy might empathize with Esther but Thomas did not. The guilt Esther might be dealing with was well earned, and if she sought forgiveness, she knew where to find him.

And yet…he couldn't burn the ring.

Thomas opened the pouch again and studied the ring closely, a flawlessly cut diamond flickering light around the room from the blazing light of the fire. Flawless…like Esther's eyes whenever she looked into his. He wanted to hate her…wanted so badly to despise everything about Esther and not think of her ever again. She'd lied to him…hurt him…left him and in all probability, jumped back into the loving arms of Captain Bernhardt. Considering what she'd done, Thomas' best option was to write her off as another coquettish flirt who used him for his money and resources.

Nevertheless, that idea was a lie, plain and simple, and it was what hurt Thomas the most. Lucy was right – Esther did love him as much as he loved her, furiously and irrationally, and somewhere in that foolishness they both made bad judgments. With logic taking control, Thomas saw that accusing her of desertion did Esther's character no justice, and Thomas became livid with himself for tearing her down to make himself rise above it. Esther walked out of his life because she thought that was what he wanted, and he made no counter arguments or moves to sway her otherwise.

Straight away, the understanding came that Lucy had a point in this matter. He was acting just like his father and making excuses for not fixing something he could repair easily. It was as much Thomas' fault as it was Esther's, and if he didn't try to change it, he was no better than Edward had been with Mary. Did he really want to forget her, or was that just his immature way of admitting his pride had been hurt more than anything else? Gulping down more brandy, Thomas let out a deep exhale.

It was going to be a long night.

In under an hour, he was at his desk in the library, opening another new bottle of brandy with a pen in his hand, dripping dark ink onto the fresh white paper. Esther's ring sat next to his glass and Lucy's words echoed through his head as he wrote the letter he should have written months ago.

Esther,

I apologize it has taken me so long to write. Things have been hectic in the aftermath of my father's funeral, and I have been traveling for weeks back and forth to London in an effort to settle my father's estate. The greatest surprise of it all has been to find out my father and mother were actually married, at least according to a certificate the Madame happened to send to the lawyers in House of Lords upon my induction, thus making me officially Lord Turner in my father's stead. I can't say whether or not I believe it's real or falsified, but either way, I once again owe the Madame a great deal.

He stopped, wondering how to proceed further. Lucy said Esther wanted forgiveness, but Thomas was skeptical if forgiveness was what was necessary. Sure, it was what any woman would want, however Esther wasn't any woman. She was different. Thomas ruminated on the compilation of things she'd confided in him, over the wrongs they set right together, and then it struck him. When things were hard, Esther always told Thomas she needed him to keep her safe, needed him to love her and make her better. Somehow, Thomas couldn't recall a single time he'd ever told Esther he needed her. Not that he loved her...that he needed her...

I shouldn't have locked myself away that night. I should have told you what I've wanted to tell you since I saw you for the first time in New York last summer. I love you, and I need you and I do not want to live without you. If you can forgive me for being such a stupid bastard, or at least find it in your heart to try, please write to me and I will book your passage to England as soon as possible.

If you cannot forgive me, I will understand and leave you in peace.

I love you, Es.

Yours & etc,

Lord Thomas Turner

"Robert!" Thomas yelled, and within seconds the page was present.

"Yes, Sir?"

Thomas sealed the envelope and handed it over to him. "Get this to Tony, and see to it that the letter is sent out today."

Robert read the front of the envelope, and his eyes opened wide. "To the Madame's address, Sir?"

"Yes, Robert."

"Of course, sir, right away. Can I get you anything else?"

"No Robert, thank you."

"Of course, sir."

Robert left in a hurry and Thomas leaned back in his chair, pouring the new brandy in his glass, his frustration somewhat alleviated.

"May I join you?"

Hiroaki stood in the doorway of the library, his body language giving off a more serious vibe than earlier that afternoon.

"Brandy is waiting," Thomas answered, preparing himself for another reprimand. "What's got you so stern? I feel like perhaps I should have stayed in London with the reception I've gotten from everyone today."

"It is a difficult time for us. We are adjusting to the changes that have altered our lives, just as you are." He sat down across from Thomas. "Sending a letter to the Madame?"

"No," Thomas replied. "To Esther. There is only one person in New York who will know exactly where she is."

"Ah, but no letter for the woman who secured your title?"

Thomas shook his head. "I can't, Hiro. Not yet, at least." Wanting to change the subject, Thomas rose and went to grab Hiroaki a glass for brandy.

"You cannot or will not?"

"It's not that simple with her. It never is. It's just not the right time."

"And when will the time be right, Thomas?"

Hiroaki hadn't used Thomas' first name since they arrived from New York. "What do you mean?"

"I mean when will it be time for you to move forward?"

"What is it with everyone attacking me on this?" He set Hiroaki's glass in front of him and poured him some of the brandy. "Really, Hiro. I am in no mood for this from you, too. First it was William, then it was Lucy. Now you?"

"My intention is not to upset you, Thomas," Hiroaki countered. "My intention is to be your counsel and guide you, like I did with your father. That is the only reason I am here, and perhaps if you could set aside your irritation, you would take note that the three of us have breached the same subject for various reasons."

"Well maybe you can help me to try and understand why it is everyone thinks I am not 'moving on' with my life? What have I not been doing lately that is making you question my well-being?"

"Why don't you tell me why you think it is, and then I will share my own thoughts on my ideas?"

Thomas let out a heavy exhale. "I've been buried up to my eyes trying to get my Lordship taken care of these last few months, and on top of that, trying to be the head of this family. There has been little time for much else. William and Lucy are pestering me and making assumptions based on their own regrets and judgments. I am perfectly aware I need to work out on my own, but I have a hammer and fire to do that."

"I agree with you on those points," Hiroaki told him. "And I would say you have an astute sense of the issues William and Lucy have trouble with themselves. You've done a fine job separating their personal demons with your own."

"Why is it you are asking me when I am moving forward then?" Thomas went on. "You're trying to lead into something, aren't you?"

Hiroaki smiled broadly. "Actually yes, I am. You have a much keener sense of others than your father ever did, and you can thank the Madame for that." He had a drink of his brandy. "I want to talk with you about your father, and share with you some things I'm not sure you are aware of. But before I go further, I have one thing I would like for you to tell me."

"And that would be?"

"Is the life your father wanted for you the life you actually want to have? Or are you holding onto that dream because you loved your father and want to do what he thought was best for you?"

Almost automatically, Thomas nearly went with his gut reaction to say yes, of course he wanted the life Edward mapped for him; yet as he began to think about it in retrospect, he realized something was stopping him, and it was the same notion he'd been ruminating over earlier that afternoon – deep down, Thomas wasn't convinced Edward's fantasy life for him was really the path he ought to take. Something was missing, and it was not the prospect of a "happily ever after."

"I don't really know anymore," Thomas admitted, a little surprised he was only now just comprehending his true feelings. "It's like there is a void I can't fill, and it's one I'm not sure a wife, kids, and settling down would fill the void either. I'm a good businessman because it's in my blood…it's easy, like breathing air. I got a letter last week from Bernard informing me sales are taking off, shipments are increasing, and we'll be going overseas in no time at all." He gulped down a bit of brandy, and Hiroaki eyed him closely. "I have all this money, this house, this land…and none of it matters, or at least, not in the way I thought it would."

The room grew silent, and Thomas could see Hiroaki analyzing his words in his head. "What changed, Thomas?"

He thought for a moment. "After losing Edward, it's like the dream my father had for me left along with his existence in my life."

Hiroaki sank into his chair. "If I could offer you insight, insight that would dramatically change the way you see everything around you, is that something you would want?"

"What kind of insight?" Thomas posed inquisitively.

"It would…enlighten the little background information you've received about my relationship with your father."

Thomas nodded. "William told me that you were some kind of warrior and trained my father."

Setting his glass aside, Hiroaki leaned forward, elbows resting on his thighs. "This is far more than just that. This would…give you new purpose. If I tell you these things, I can never untell them to you, and your life will never be the same again. My recommendation would be to sleep on it and make sure that the life Edward wanted you to have is truly not what you want, and not what would make you happy."

Thomas' gaze narrowed. "Hiro, what's going on?"

"Thomas, you should really consider taking my advice and—"

"Tell me immediately," he demanded. "I can see it in your face. You're hiding something. I want to know what it is."

Hiroaki reluctantly pulled out a letter from his pocket, placed it on the surface of the coffee table, and slid it over to him slowly, his eyes not leaving Thomas'.

"Once you read this there is no going back. But it is not my place to hide it from you, either." Clearing his throat, he got up and took a step backward to give Thomas space. "Your father sent this to me the day he died."

Thomas snatched up the letter and opened it. He read it from top to bottom, his body going numb.

"This…this can't be real…" he mumbled, scanning it over again. "It's not possible, Hiro. It can't be."

"Why is it not possible?"

Setting the letter down, he looked up at his father's old mentor. "Why did you hide this from me?" Thomas demanded. "You would just let something like this sit idly? For months on end?! What the hell were you thinking?!"

"You needed to mourn your father," Hiroaki stated. "And what would you have done if you had seen it? Run back to the place you'd just left and die the way your father did?"

"This says my mother is alive and being held against her will in a God damned mental institution!" Thomas shouted heatedly. "You didn't think it was worth sharing that bit of information?!"

"No."

Thomas hadn't expected Hiroaki's response to be so definitive. "W-What? You cannot be serious!" His voice cracked, his emotions bridling in his throat. "My parents…my mother, Hiro…"

"Use your head, Thomas," Hiroaki ordered, his voice strident enough to give Thomas pause. "Try to keep your mind clear and not be so impulsive. Take a few deep breaths and consider the facts you know. Your father was strangely absent for most of an afternoon and an entire evening, only to be found run over by a carriage. Did you ever

713

see or meet any of the other families that lost loved ones in that accident? Did you see the injured parties and the damage done to them?"

"No...no I didn't..."

"The last word we have of your father is that he's found your mother and plans to retrieve her, correct?"

Thomas nodded, speechless and in shock, his eyes hypnotically fixated on his brandy glass.

"And he was going to the police station. Now also think back on the trouble your mother was in all those years ago...the corrupted people she worked for, her own cruel fate...leaving us with the belief she was long dead already. When you add all those aspects together, what is the most plausible explanation here?"

Thomas couldn't think straight; his thoughts were jumbling together into one chaotic mass as he struggled to understand what it was Hiroaki was telling him. Seeing Thomas was visibly toiling, Hiroaki persisted in his analysis.

"Your father was impeccably trained, Thomas, and he was murdered when he discovered your mother was still alive. That should show you the type of power whoever has your mother locked up possesses and, if I am being unconditionally honest with you, the odds after the skirmish with Edward that Mary is alive at this very moment are...small. Very, very small."

Thomas leapt up, marching back and forth. "I should go to New York...I should go back and figure this out...I can't just leave her there, Hiro! What if she isn't dead? I can save her!"

"She very well may not be dead," he conceded, not stirring despite Thomas' frenzied conduct. "But if you go to New York, I can guarantee you won't last more than a few hours on those streets. They will be waiting for you, Thomas. This is no ordinary group of thugs who took out your father – we are talking about a criminal enterprise, with roots deeper than you could ever imagine."

This was not what Thomas wanted to hear. "So what then?" he

cried in frustration, throwing his hands into the air. "I'm just supposed to burn the letter and pretend it never fucking existed?"

"No. I would never ask that of you."

"Well explain this to me, because you obviously already have it all worked out." He sat on the couch, the aggravation was building exponentially, and Thomas' inability to contain his strife was getting the better of him as anger seeped into his bloodstream like a drug, building with the passing seconds.

Hiroaki approached Thomas and sat beside him. "You have returned from a great loss, and it is obvious to those around you that you are on a strikingly similar path to that your father found after the malaria. You have no aspirations, no sense of drive, just going through the motions and letting them consume you entirely. I tried to give your father another path; however, I think I see now he was too far gone to retrieve in this life. You, Thomas, are not too far gone. I can provide you with tools and skills you can use for many purposes and make your own future a little…different."

"I don't want a fucking purpose. Do you know what it's like to hear your parents have been murdered? By the same…the same people?! And to know others have been lying to you about it? People you trusted?! Even you!"

Before Hiroaki could speak, Thomas reacted impetuously. With a clenched fist, he punched Hiroaki as hard as he could across the face. It didn't impact with the amount of ferocity Thomas felt, but it was enough to get his point across. To his amazement, Hiroaki barely flinched from the hit: a little blood trickled from his nose and his head shied sideways, though he lost no balance and remained sitting firmly planted where they'd been the whole time. Thomas staggeringly rose, his knuckles screaming in agony. All the same, he wasn't finished with Hiroaki just yet.

"You lied to me! You hid this from me for months when you had no right to do so!" Thomas roared at him. "On top of that, you think the Madame isn't aware of this? Or Louis? Hell, if we're

715

going that far, William and Lucy probably fucking know too! And you're going to stand there and tell me to be calm?! Bullshit! I am tired of being calm! I am tired of being passive! I have to do something! I have to—"

A loud popping noise, and Thomas stopped mid sentence, his jaw dropping when he saw Hiroaki had just snapped his own dislocated nose back into place.

Hiroaki stared at the now gaping Thomas. "If you had the option, would you want to do anything to avenge their deaths?"

Thomas was timid, not certain how to answer. "I…"

"Yes or no, Thomas."

"Well…yes."

"How far are you willing to go?"

"As far as it takes me."

"You would kill for them?"

"I would," Thomas said, meaning it with all his heart.

"Then you need to learn to use your anger in a more productive fashion," Hiroaki declared, crossing his arms over his chest. "I know the way to do this. You must be aware that if you do choose the path I give you, there's no going back."

"Back to what? How miserable I am right now?"

"I see." Hiroaki indicated for Thomas to have a seat again. "Please," he persisted. "I have a story you need to hear. It will give you some insight as to where I come from, and where I can take you in the future. A future where you will never again feel as helpless as you do at this moment."

Thomas frowned at him suspiciously, and then resumed his place. Hiroaki cleared his throat and began:

"I grew up in Japan many years ago, one of the last true tribes of Samurai still in existence in the mountains. My younger brother, a man known as Saito Hajime, grew up with my sister and I, learning in the ancient ways of Shinto, which trains mind, body, and soul to be a warrior of honor. I was never the fighter my broth-

716

er was, but my philosophy was strong in the ancient ways, whereas his started to corrupt along with the majority of Samurai culture. Late one night, my brother had too much sake…he was drunk and killed one of our Samurai elders for disciplining him and asking him to commit seppuku."

"Wait," Thomas interjected. "What is seppuku?"

"Suicide, for dishonoring his family and himself," Hiroaki revealed. "My brother refused this honor and killed him instead. To my misfortune, I found my brother trying to discard the body, and my brother told me if I did not leave our village, he would hunt me down and kill me and my family. At this time, Akemi and I had just been married, and had our daughter on the way. So my choices were limited."

"Your village wouldn't protect you?"

"Saito had already built a band of loyal followers, the majority of which were like him. Hot headed, sociopathic, and dangerous. We wouldn't have lasted through the night. Akemi and I ran far away to Mongolia, sneaking through the borders and settling into a small hunting village not far off the coastline. One day, our farm was attacked by looters, and in an effort to protect my family, I took down eleven of the men meaning to do us harm, and…it did not go unnoticed."

Again, Thomas' jaw dropped. "You…you killed eleven men?"

"I did," Hiroaki professed. "The koshun…our king…then called upon me to serve under him when the Qing emperor ordered Mongolia to aid them in the Second Opium War, and it was at that time I realized those looters were passing through to join the Mongolian army. It was the greatest mistake I've ever made. The koshun explained if I did not, he would kill my daughter and my wife. We were all trained in Shinto…all prepared to die in the name of honor; nonetheless, in a moment of weakness, I could not stand the thought of my daughter dying because of my lack of judgment. Much to Akemi's protests, we went."

Hiroaki grew silent. "And then?" Thomas pressed.

"I killed the koshun not long after arriving in Beijing, only to be recaptured by the Chinese and forced to continue fighting. My daughter was killed to keep me in line, and Akemi tortured savagely. Once the treaty was settled, I knew if we did not escape, Akemi and I would both be put to death. I had to kill many men, but we made it out alive. And that was when I found your father."

"This was when my father smuggled you on board...he knew you would die if he left you there."

"Yes. And in turn, when the malaria took him, Akemi and I saved Edward. We were bound to each other from that time on. Your father returned home to find his life in shambles, and I thought because Edward wished to be trained as I was, I could save him once more. So I taught him our ways the best I could, hoping to be proven correct."

Thomas remembered the incident with Timothy Adams at the theater. "My father attacked a young man assaulting a woman right in front of me. He moved faster than I'd ever seen any man move."

"In the early years, your father and I were what I would call employable vigilantes," Hiroaki described. "We took many trips, helped countless people, but it stopped when he found you. The only time I know since then he has used his physical training was that confrontation in Rome. That trip haunted him for weeks."

Thomas held up a hand. "Hold on...what happened in Rome that I don't know about?"

"You were unconscious in the carriage. I wouldn't expect you to know..." he shook his head, chuckling to himself. "There are so many things you'll learn now I wish you'd known before, but your father forbade it. An enemy of one of our old clients found out your father was in town and assaulted the carriage you two were in. He killed fourteen men that night, the largest number he'd ever killed at once."

The brandy glass fell from Thomas' hand. "He...he killed..."

"Fourteen men, yes. It was either that or your father understood you both would be killed, and Edward would never accept that."

Hiroaki got up and retrieved another glass for Thomas, bringing it over to him with a melancholic expression. "He loved you, Thomas. He wanted you to be the man he should have been. Considering the circumstances you are currently facing, I firmly believe that is unfeasible. Your family has been torn apart by something larger than yourself. I am offering the opportunity to do something about it."

Thomas had a large gulp of brandy. "You're telling me you can turn me into some kind of killing machine? Is that what this is? That I could go destroy the enterprise that murdered my parents?"

"Close, but not exactly. I am telling you I will give you a chance to be able to outsmart an organization that has proven to have the upper hand and has ruined far more lives than just yours and your family's. Your mother knew something, something someone with a lot of power and a lot of money did not want her to know. She was locked away in a prison for years for this reason, and these same people killed your father to keep it a secret. Perhaps it's time they had a challenger, someone to level the playing field and with any luck, save a few innocent lives in the process."

When Thomas remained speechless, still venturing to comprehend the vast amount of information he'd just received, Hiroaki made his way over to the door. "Think on it, Thomas. I would also suggest rather than taking this as truth from me that you write to your dear friend Louis and ask what you need to be satisfied. I have a hunch he will be truthful."

Thomas snorted. "Why would I involve him when he's probably in on this whole thing to begin with?"

"I can assure you he is not," Hiroaki responded curtly. "Because unlike the Madame, Louis loved your father immensely, probably more than I did. You as well. And no matter what anyone ever tells you, Thomas, he would never do anything to put Edward in danger."

Thomas was baffled. "How can you be so sure?"

Hiroaki didn't reply. He walked out of Thomas' study, as if he hadn't heard Thomas' last inquiry.

The brandy was gone when Thomas finished his letter, outlining everything he'd ascertained from Hiroaki and demanding any vindication Louis could offer. A knock came from the doorway and he glanced up to see Tony lingering, something noticeably upsetting him.

"Christ. Not you too, Tony."

"I'm sorry to disturb you, Sir, but this was marked urgent. It's... it's from the Madame, Sir. Would you like to read it or should I burn it like the others?"

Thomas' interest sparked. "How do you know it's urgent, Tony?"

The butler marched to him, his arm outstretched with the letter between his fingers. "It says must read on the envelope." He handed it over to Thomas, who examined it carefully. It was the Madame's handwriting, but it was sprawled, not penned out with it's usual precision.

"Sir, I know it's not my place, but perhaps you should—"

Releasing a heavy groan, Thomas had consumed just enough brandy to give into his interest. "All right, Tony. This day might just kill me."

Thomas,

I don't know if you've seen any of my prior letters, but if you have, you know how dire this situation is, though I am beginning to lose my hope that you are reading any of them.

Esther's sentencing hearing was this morning, and while we tried to prevent it, the police forced Celeste to testify against Esther. It wasn't pretty. The lawyers twisted her statement just enough to make it seem like Esther was the deranged one, not Timothy, and that she had been planning his murder for an extended period of time. Because Hope's body was not at the scene of the crime, any evidence regarding her rape and assault was thrown out...could have been anyone, they said.

It's fucking horrible.

Celeste cried and begged them to spare Esther as Timothy's wife and next of kin, but all to no avail. The record of Esther's police report against Timothy Adams from over the summer inexplicably happened to vanish as well.

Thomas…they sentenced her to death. She's going to hang.

I have been doing everything in my power to appeal her sentence, as has Samuel, but the judge is unyielding…a man in a position of power who looks as females as a lesser breed of animal. The lawyers the Adams family hired picked him purposefully to make an example of Esther. There's no hope for her. She has less than a month, and by the time this reaches you, half of that.

I don't know what to do, Thomas. Send her a letter. Anything to comfort her. She's losing her grip in that jail cell, with no hint of reprieve.

I am afraid I can't win this one.

M

This was too much to handle.

"No…" Thomas mumbled aloud. "No…I just…"

Tony stepped forward, his face full of concern. "What is it, Lord Turner? What's happened?"

Thomas drove himself up to his feet and made his way over to Tony, handing him the letter to read himself.

"The only good thing I had left…I should have listened…I should have fucking listened for once…"

When he'd read the contents through, Tony peered up from the paper at Thomas, his eyes horrified.

"But sir this says that Esther is…Esther is going to die. That she…she murdered Timothy Adams? How can this be possible?"

Thomas could only stare back at Tony, feeling as if the walls were closing in from every corner. Suddenly, the strength he had left to hold him upright abandoned him, and Thomas fell to the ground.

XXV.

A desperate knock on the door woke Celeste abruptly
from a dreamless sleep. The bedroom was dark, curtains drawn over
the windows in an attempt to block out the intense sunlight fighting
to stream in, and she buried her head in her pillow wishing for the
noise to stop. Her whole body ached, still in recovery from the damage of losing the baby, and the thump of her heartbeat pulsed hard
against her temples from a late night with far too much wine. The
only consolation Celeste received was in numbing out the pain of
all that surrounded her, though at the expense of feeling like Timothy had knocked her around again whenever she woke. What was
there really to live for? Her husband's family abandoned her, her best
friend's days were numbered as Esther awaited execution, her mother dead, her father in prison…soon enough, Celeste would have nowhere to go, no money for food, and no one left to turn to for help.

With a burdened heart, Celeste laboriously propped herself up
in her bed, rubbing her eyes as the knock came again, and she knew
she couldn't avoid it any longer.

"Ma'am? Ma'am are you all right?" Laura's voice was soothing
but worried. "The hotel manager is here to see you. I've just sat him
down for a cup of tea but…well…we both know why he's here."

"Shit," Celeste uttered to herself, pushing over to the side of the bed. "I'll be right out!" she called to Laura. "Tell him to give me just a few minutes to splash some water on my face."

The process was a slow one, as the bruising on her abdomen continued to pester her, but Celeste managed to amble out of bed toward the fresh bowl of water at her bedside. After a few refreshing soaks, she walked over to the windows and yanked the curtains apart, letting the light in at last and taking a deep breath, hoping to take in some of the power of the sunlight. When nothing else worked, a fresh burst from the sun brought her around again and, following another few breaths, Celeste could sense her energy returning. Circling around, she made her way to the wardrobe by her vanity – she didn't have enough time to fully dress and searched for her robe, which was hanging off the foot of the bed. Throwing it over her shoulders, Celeste fastened it tight around her waist, checking her vanity mirror and pinning her hair ever so slightly to avoid seeming as if she was only now just rising for the day.

With a quick pinch of her cheeks, she felt ready and made her way out of the bedroom and down the hall to the front sitting area of her hotel room. There, with a cup of tea in hand, sat the middle aged hotel manager, who must have once been a very handsome young man, though it was obvious the years in New York had done their work to wear him down. He smiled when he saw her and got to his feet, his eyes apologetic. Everyone at the hotel had been apologetic, along with every other acquaintance she had in that city. That horrible night was documented down to the last detail in almost every local paper and even some of the national ones as well, portraying her as the sick, feeble wife, unable to stop her insanely jealous and scorned friend from killing her doting husband right in front of her. The press had gone wild with it, especially when the details of her parents surfaced. No one cared about the facts…that Timothy had killed their child growing in her womb, that he raped and beat her on a regular basis, or that he'd also raped that jealous and scorned friend along with the poor girl who saved Celeste's life that night, and then tried to kill Celeste to cover it up.

No, none of that mattered to anyone, because to the lawyers, her testimony only consisted of one thing: she awoke just in time to see Esther shoot Timothy, and that was it. They didn't know she told Esther to do it, and they didn't care to acknowledge her former husband was a mass murderer from Virginia. There was no proof he had shoved her down the staircase earlier that evening, and the prosecution's lawyer tore her apart when she tried to explain the truth, pinning her as a hysterical and emotionally distraught female trying to save her dearest friend. It was that inescapable empathy that drove Celeste to isolation – she couldn't stand the stares or the gossip any longer.

"Mrs. Adams, I am so sorry to disturb you at this hour," the manager greeted her with a slight bow of his balding head. "I just had news to share with you and wanted to let you know as soon as possible to…to assess your options…"

"It is no problem at all!" she sang, taking a seat across from him as Laura poured her tea. "I was just taking a bit of time to relax and catch up on reading. These cold days have kept me indoors."

"Of course, of course. The weather is getting colder by the minute."

"Is this in regards to the funding for my room?" she asked, taking a small sip from her cup.

The manager clearly became uncomfortable. "Yes…I'm…I'm afraid your family…your mother-in-law, to be exact, will no longer be paying for your stay here at the end of the week. She was…adamant about canceling it."

Celeste nodded, attempting to not appear worried. "Understandably so. After what has happened, I daresay I am on my own. The funding will go until Friday, correct?"

"Actually Saturday…and…I will allow you to stay and pack up on Sunday, since you have been such a wonderful and hospitable guest. Do you…do you have other arrangements for housing?"

"I do," she replied lightheartedly. "And I will get you the address later this week for transportation's sake. I will be sorry to leave this beautiful hotel. It has been an absolute pleasure staying, but I guess it is time to move on."

The manager motioned for a refill of his tea, which Laura obliged. "I must say, Mrs. Adams, I am extremely relieved. There have been…there have been rumors your mother-in-law is leaving you without a dime or a place to go, and I…well I was concerned about what you might do next."

"Ah, now there is a bit of truth to that," she said, lowering her tone as if she wanted to prevent being overheard. "And please do take to calling me Miss Hiltmore, if you don't mind. I will no longer be associated with the Adams family…losing Timothy has caused a rift between us, but I am thankful I have many other great friends happy to take in a girl such as myself."

His brow furrowed knowingly. "I will do just that, Miss Hiltmore. And please, if there is anything I can do to help, all you need to do is ask."

Celeste smiled obligingly in return. "Thank you, for all the kindness you've shown me. It has not gone unnoticed."

The manager rose. "Well, thank you for the tea, Miss Hiltmore. It's always a pleasure. I'll send a bottle of Bordeaux up for you this evening, and perhaps I could convince you to have dinner in the dining room? It will be my treat."

She gasped excitedly. "That would be…lovely, just lovely. And you would be joining me?

"Of course. Let's say, seven o'clock?"

"I am very much looking forward to it, then."

The manager was delighted, gave his salutations one last time, and subsequently Laura showed him out. When she returned to the sitting room, Celeste dropped the act, more exhausted than when she'd risen from her bed.

"Christ, I don't know how I can keep doing this," she told Laura, sinking back into the couch. "Only a few more days and I'll be out on the streets."

"You even had me convinced everything was working out just fine," Laura responded, grabbing her own cup of tea. "Are you all right?"

"Yes," she stated automatically, then shook her head. "No, not particularly. I'm running out of options, Laura."

"Please, come back to Virginia with me. My family would adore you and you would be most welcome there."

Celeste had a drink of her tea. "I'm not going anywhere near the Adamses. My pride and my abhorrence will always win that battle." She got to her feet. "Help me dress and then take the day for yourself. I know you have arrangements to make before your travels. I think a bit of time alone to contemplate is what I need."

Once Laura had gone out, Celeste opened a bottle of wine and found herself back in the sitting room, mulling over the letter she received from her mother-in-law just a few days prior. They were, more or less, disowning her…Celeste's family and friends had brought the Adamses nothing but tragedy, and they wanted nothing to do with her. No money would be provided, no housing would be given…as far as they were concerned, she never existed. Celeste couldn't say she was surprised. In reality, she had been expecting something of the sort considering not one of them had any idea Timothy was truly a monster. Her former mother-in-law was infuriated Celeste accused him of such lewd behavior in a public trial, and took the prosecution's spin on her story word for word: that Celeste was trying to save Esther, and making up stories about her husband to justify the motive for his murder. Many different associates and acquaintances were called as character witnesses, every one denying they knew anything about Celeste's accusations of domestic violence. Despite the ensuing drama, Celeste didn't regret for a second what she'd said.

There would be a way out of this. She just had to think.

She went to her desk and flipped through her correspondence, wondering if there was anyone left to seek out. Amongst the letters Celeste kept close was one from her father she received months ago, begging to see her, though Timothy made her swear she would neither return his letter nor visit him under any condition. In fear, she obeyed Timothy's demands and never thought on the subject again. However, with the ground now shrinking beneath her feet, Celeste speculated if a visit to her father might help. Of course financially there was nothing left to the Hiltmore name, and her father would have no idea of what had happened in the outside world or the predicament she found herself in. But, Douglas was the smartest man Celeste had ever known, and guidance was something she urgently needed in this kind of a crisis. Time, in this regard, was not on her side.

The thought had crossed her mind a few times, predominantly after her mother killed herself. There was so much resentment in her heart for both of her parents, and for a time just the mention of them upset her. With such little remorse they lied to her, kept secrets of unspeakable things that went against every moral code of ethics they ever taught her, believing they would never be caught. Those atrocities alone should have made her despise them, but the one concept that haunted her most was that they let her marry Timothy, appreciating full and well what a bastard he was. It had been for the money…for the power, and Catherine and Douglas sent her off like a lamb to the slaughter, laughing as they did it.

She tried to think of anyone else to see, anyone else she could talk to, drinking one glass of wine and then another. Someone… anyone who didn't look at her as if she were a pitiful charity case and then go on to tell tell all of society she was nothing more than a homeless, spoiled brat who finally got a taste of what real life was like for everybody else. It was useless. Not a single name came to mind.

As she finished the bottle, Celeste made the choice to go to her father.

Minutes later, wrapped tightly beneath her fur coat, she was escorted out the front doors of the Grand Central Hotel to an unoccupied coach, ready to take her anywhere she desired. The driver leapt down and held the door for her, realizing who she was from the papers, removing the cap off of his head.

"Where would you like to go, Ma'am?" he asked benevolently, closing the door once she was settled.

Celeste slid over to the window and handed him a paper five out to him. "I need you to take me to the Tombs in lower Manhattan. And not tell a soul."

"The Tombs?" His eyes grew wide, dumbfounded for a few seconds. "Of course, right away Mrs. Adams." He gently took the money from her and resumed his post, and Celeste did her best to disappear inside, away from the crowded streets and anyone who could possibly recognize her.

As the carriage took off down the roadway, rocking back and forth, she was pleased she'd dressed warmer than necessary with the cool wind managing to blow through the carriage covers. It would be at least a twenty-minute ride, and Celeste struggled to put together any kind of plan as to what she would say to her father when they finally came face to face. At his trial, there was one distinct moment she remembered locking eyes with him while they dragged him off in shackles. It was one of the most haunting memories she had. Her father knew he'd let her down, and the look in his eyes wasn't pleading and showed no signs of fear: it was apologetic regret, understanding he'd handicapped her in a way she'd never recover from. During those few seconds Celeste could strangely read his mind: Douglas found no culpability in what he'd done to others or in the crimes he committed. It was only that Celeste was hurt in the process, and that notion made her ashamed, mainly because she couldn't decide if it made her love him or hate him more.

Her mother, on the other hand, she would never forgive. Celeste disliked Catherine's disposition, and as a child, loved her because she firmly believed their mirror-like appearances made them similar. Yet when she grew older and began to see the true side of the

729

woman who raised her, Celeste grew weary of her and discovered she greatly disliked her mother, though she never told a soul. Nothing was ever clandestine, and it took overhearing her mother mock her at a party over something Celeste confided in her to make her see the cruelness of Catherine's heart. Nothing was sacred to her, and in the duration of her ride to the Tombs, Celeste determined it must have been the poison of her mother that made her father do the things he'd done. And from that moment on, nothing would convince her otherwise.

Gradually, as the coach journeyed on, Celeste's thoughts ran to Esther, her throat tightening as she reminisced on the past. Esther was her consolation, her confidante, and Celeste lamented not telling her every day how important their friendship was to her. Without it, she wouldn't have survived Timothy…and would probably be dead. Heavy tears formed in Celeste's eyes. No, she couldn't think about Esther right now. She needed to prepare herself for what lay ahead.

The carriage came to a stop, and peeking out her window, Celeste saw they'd arrived. Out of respect to her wishes, the driver jogged over and opened the door, holding a hand out to her to help her down.

"The Tombs, Ma'am," he notified her quietly, keeping his head down. "Straight inside. The officer at the desk will help you. Do yourself a favor, Ma'am and don't stay too long."

Celeste stepped out of the passenger compartment and took another five out of her fur muff. "For your assistance."

He took the five, examined it closely, and then handed it back to her. "I won't accept this, Ma'am."

"Why not?"

"I ain't worthy of it. Five is more than I make in half a week, and all I done is bring you to the worst place in the city."

Stubbornly, Celeste stuffed it in the man's front jacket pocket. "Take it. Please. I'll feel insulted if you do not. Just do what I ask and please don't tell anyone you brought me here. I can't…I can't stand any more…" She could feel herself choking up. "You understand."

The driver bowed his head out of respect. "Yes, Mrs. Adams."

Her hand lingered, then drifted to his shoulder, which she gave a small squeeze. "Please call me Celeste."

There wasn't much to him – poxed with bad skin from working in the sooted streets, small and thin from years she could only assumed he starved, and only seven or eight teeth in the grin that formed on his face at her kind words. Her driver hinted to be near forty or fifty, though she contemplated if that was truly his age or the general wear and tear of life in this town. There were only a few hairs on his bare head when he took off his cap and politely gave her another slight bow before returning to his coach.

Celeste rotated around after watching him go, urging herself to step one foot in front of the other and up the stone steps toward the entrance of the Tombs. It was easy to make it this far in theory, but now that Celeste found herself just a few paces away, the trepidation of meeting her father in person following so much time apart was almost too much to handle. Overwhelmed yet resolute, she pushed onward, walking through the shadows of the pillars, people buzzing to and fro all around her. Every fiber of her being wanted to turn and head back to the hotel, and she had to remind herself there was nothing left for her uptown. Celeste steadied her breathing as she approached the front doors and yanked them open – this was her last and only option.

The main entryway was not nearly as crowded as the square. It was soundless save for the clacking of her shoes against the floor. With the exception of the wind, there was not much difference between the chill of the outside and the temperature indoors. The air was stale, the lighting dark, and the vast lobby stretched ahead pointing her exactly where she needed to go. Celeste didn't bother looking around, not wishing to bring any attention upon herself in case a familiar was nearby; instead, she went straight to the main

731

desk where an older officer stood, studying her closely from behind his spectacles. Whatever he was reading he immediately set down, all his concentration on her.

"Good day, Miss. How might I be of service?"

Celeste swallowed hard. "I'm here to see my father. Douglas Hiltmore."

His eyebrows rose, scanning her up and down. "Did you make an appointment? I can tell you right now it is not likely they'll let a pretty thing like you in to see him."

Without answering, Celeste sighed and reached into her purse, pulling out a solitaire diamond necklace of her mother's, one she was not very reluctant to part with. Prior to her departure from the hotel, Celeste wrapped it in a silk cloth, therefore making it a little less inconspicuous. It was the only bargaining tool in her grasp, as the money was running thin. She set it down in front of the policeman, motioning for him to open it.

When the officer saw what was inside, he was taken aback. "So you really are the girl from the papers, aren't you?"

"Yes, sir, I am."

He thought a moment, pocketed the necklace, and got to his feet. "Follow me," he instructed her. With a quick snap of his fingers, a guard standing by the doorway to Celeste's right assumed the newly abandoned desk. "Stay close to me," he ordered. "Don't' say a word to nobody. This ain't gonna be pretty, Miss."

Taking off to her left, Celeste did as she was told and made sure she was consistently no more than two paces behind him. He led her down a hallway, and a minute later they were passing a few rows of offices, loud voices ringing out in sharp contrast to where they'd just been. When they reached the end of it, he took another left and they came face to face with a guard holding the keys she could only assume would unlock the barred-up door opposite them.

"Stevens, this girl is here for visitation."

The man didn't budge. "Warden know about this, Robertson?"

"Nope. But I'll buy your first whiskey after work. Swear on my old lady."

Stevens hesitated, then flipped around, shuffling his keys. "First two whiskies, Robertson. You're lucky Warden is out today…otherwise this shit here wouldn't fly."

Officer Robertson turned to her. "This man here is gonna take you to see your dad. Remember what I said. Not a word to nobody."

Celeste nodded timidly and gave the man a slight curtsey. Rolling his eyes, Officer Stevens took her inside, and promptly Celeste identified that they had transferred from the working section of the prison to the housing portion. A smell filled her nose, more putrid than any she'd ever encountered, and it was so repulsive it made her eyes water. The air grew thick and hard to breathe, and muffled noises and shouts seemed to come from every direction. The walls, floor, and ceiling were stone and brick, the hall no wider than four feet across and the ceiling dripped with condensation. Celeste focused on her shoes and stayed closely behind Officer Stevens. They made a sharp right turn down a far smaller hallway, then descended a flight of stairs with steps so short Celeste nearly slipped a handful of times. When they were at the bottom, Officer Stevens stopped in his tracks and spun back around to her, his expression humorless. This was his final warning of what would lie ahead.

"We're going to pass eight cells before we get to your father's. He's fortunate, somehow pulled a few strings and has his own, so we don't have to worry about detaining any new friends he's made. Stay as close to this wall on your left as you can and don't you dare halt for any reason. I can't promise you won't hear things from these convicts, Ma'am, but you will be safe with me. Just try not to look at 'em."

The tone of his voice was unnerving, but Celeste pursed her lips and agreed, admittedly a little terrified. Officer Stevens strutted forward and she did the same, her palms gripped tight. The walk was no more than twenty yards; however, the things Celeste heard and saw in those few seconds would disturb her dreams for weeks afterward. Men barely alive in their cells, some cowering inside while others lurched at the bars. Each man was wearing clothes that hadn't been washed in God knows how long, covered she could only guess in a combination of dirt and their own feces. The smell was so pungent now that Celeste had to hold her breath to get by the last set of bars. The one common attribute that did not pass her observations was the men appeared as if they had been beaten badly, scabs and scars healing on their hands, arms, feet, and faces, some even still bleeding. Yet the worst were the voices…voices that sounded like the devil himself… "Rich cunt" … "Daddy's been waiting for ya, fuckin' ninny" … "Stupid bitch" … "Come closer" … "Let me out and I'll fuck ya right" … "Fuckin' whore."

It made her nights enduring Timothy seem tame.

Her last few steps, Celeste was recoiling inward in horror, not bothering to watch ahead, and ran into the back of Officer Stevens. Evidently he somewhat expected this, not appearing the least bit shocked and caught her just before she stumbled to the ground. Rather than comfort her, he gave her a moment to take a breath, and Celeste calmed down as the echoes of profanity faded away.

"When you're ready, I will let you in to talk with him. I'll be standing right outside. Just so you are aware, Ma'am, I will not be liable for you once you are in the cell alone. You get what I'm sayin'?"

Celeste peeked up, discreetly wiping away a few tears on her sleeve. "I'm ready, Officer."

Officer Stevens moved over toward the heavy steel door at the end of the hallway, with only a small barred window on the top. He took a key from his jacket pocket and unlocked it, holding it open for her to enter. No sound came from the room, no grasping clutches of dirty hands and broken fingernails; it stood open like an unknown abyss, and in spite of her fear, Celeste strode inside, holding her head high.

His prison was not what she envisaged. There were shelves to her left littered with books, sheets on the bed next to it, and curtains for the window at the far end. On a small side table in the far right corner was water and what she could only presume was wine, a half eaten apple, and her father's pocket watch, the one with the picture of her on the inside. And there, sitting at a desk right in front of her in the middle of the cell was her father, not dressed in fine clothes and yet clearly not the rags of the other inmates she'd witnessed on her scraping march alongside the hell this place was. His eyes stole up from the day's paper and were astonished at what he saw, as if she were a figment of his imagination. Slowly, Douglas lowered his reading material to his desk.

"Celeste?"

All she could do was stare. He was in grisly condition, with a scraggly beard covering half his face, a black eye, and nearly thirty pounds lighter since she'd seen her father last. On the other hand, he was in far better shape than she'd ever pictured in her mind. The accommodations did not make sense…nothing about the scene did…

Douglas leapt to his feet and slid his own chair outward, beckoning her to take it. "Please. I'll sit on my bed and we can…we can talk."

Pulling her wits together, Celeste took his offer and cautiously went to the chair to have a seat. She folded her hands and placed them into her lap as Douglas dropped down onto his straw mattress.

"I…I never heard from you," he started, an almost shy grin forming on his face. "I never thought you'd come to see me."

"I shouldn't have. We both know I shouldn't be here, father."

Douglas was mystified. "Then why are you here?"

Celeste cleared her throat, her eyes floating toward the paper. "I take it from seeing this, you know all about what's going on in the outside world. And I thought I had too much to share in one sitting."

He looked pained. "I tried not to believe any of it…you can't believe half of what these ass – pardon me, these people write. Did… did your mother really…?"

"Yes she did."

"And are you all right? Dealing with that alone?"

"I wasn't alone at the time," she remarked coldly. "I dealt with it. Mother was…mother. After she killed herself, I was very sad, but no part of me could ever forgive her for what she'd done."

Her father leaned forward. "What do you mean, Celeste? Forgive her for what?"

"You can't tell me she didn't know about Timothy. The question I have for you, father, is did you know? Before the marriage? That you were literally sending me into the hands of someone like that?"

Douglas' gaze did not waver. "I didn't know until your visit home, after the first time. I overheard your talk with your mother. When I confronted her about it, yes she did know. I was in the dark, Celeste. I had no idea she'd done that to you until it was too late."

"Don't lie to me. I want you to tell me the truth. Or I will leave you here and never come back."

"Why would I lie to you now?" he asked, slightly offended.

"Because I'm here and you don't want me to go," she suggested presumptively.

"Celeste, you have nowhere else to go, child. I don't see any point in not being sincere. We both have nothing but each other left, and the time for the truth has come."

Butterflies danced in her stomach as she prepared to question him about the things she needed answered, somehow managing to defeat the remainder of her cowardice.

"All right then. All of your convictions, all you've been accused of, those horrible things you did to those women and those people. Did you do them?"

"Oh, Celeste, please—"

"I want to hear you say it."

Douglas straightened up. "Yes, I did all of it. They were things I did to get ahead in the world and spoils I took along the way."

"Do you wish you could take it back?" she pressed. "Any of it?"

"Do you really want my honest answer, daughter?"

"I thought that's what we were doing. Being honest."

736

"You might not like it when you hear it." When Celeste didn't respond, Douglas went on. "I wouldn't have hurt the children, or the women for that matter. It was a barbaric thing I did as a young man, many times over and in the company of people who brought out the worst in me. That I would take back."

Mistakenly, she waited for more, and it didn't come. "There's nothing else? You have no other regrets?"

"This may come as a surprise to you, Celeste, but there is only one real regret I have in my life right now. And that is how my actions have affected you. If I had it my way, no, you never would have known about my past or any of my business operations and deals, and not only would I have found a way to get rid of your horrendous mother, I would have killed that bastard husband of yours with my own bare hands rather than make Esther shoot him dead in front of you. That is my regret in all of this."

Celeste was blown away, her expectation being that he would present excuses. This was a side of her father she had never seen before, one that alarmed her and left her in awe. Douglas was not lying, and yet she knew in her heart the better option...the more prudent decision was for her to stand up and leave, before he roped her in any tighter. Nevertheless, in her legs she found no strength, and in her heart there was no yearning to forsake this now, not when Celeste felt she finally saw whom her father really was. And not when a part of her still loved him for loving her so much.

Glimpsing around, she thought it best to change the topic, not knowing what else she had to say about it.

"How in the world did you get this, when men in the next cell over are rotting away and dying?"

"Actually, it's funny you should ask." There was a new lightness in her father's tone, indicating he appreciated the new topic of discussion. "My case is going through appeals," he clarified. "I would have been sent stateside already, but they kept me here and put me in the Mayor's quarters until the trial plays out. I am...I am very fortunate to have one friend remaining in this city. One that has seen to it that I don't…rot away, like you said."

Her heart raced. "Appeals? As in, going back to trial?"

Her father smiled again. "Back to trial in less than a month."

"On what premise?"

"Insufficient and falsified evidence."

"But…but the evidence they did have was…was real, right?"

Douglas looked toward the doorway, which was empty, then nodded, putting his finger to his lips. "You have to understand, Celeste. It's very easy for things to go missing in a place like this," he whispered. "Especially when you have the right friends."

"So what you're saying is you…you could be acquitted…and released…"

"I am hoping by the new year."

"That's…that's wonderful, father. I am happy for you."

His grin faded. "What is it? You don't want me to get out?"

"No, it's not that," she asserted. "It's just taking me a moment to soak this in. I mean, I don't know what I think about most of this new knowledge. I thought you were half dead, for God's sake! Not…not like this…"

"Then what is it?" he implored.

Celeste took a deep inhale – it was her time to tell the truth. "The Adams family has disowned me. My money runs out in two days, and I have nothing left. I could sell the little I still own off piece by piece and live on that while I can, or I can run off to Virginia with my maid who I can barely afford for the rest of today. I've…I've got nowhere to go, father. I don't know what to do. You were my last hope."

Douglas got up from the bed and moved toward her, squatting down and taking her folded hands in his. "Celeste, you should have told me right away so I could ease your worries. My friend, the one who set me up here that I spoke of, will take care of it. I promise you, you have no reason to suffer! I will make sure tomorrow morning you receive whatever it is you need."

She shook her head, tears forming in her eyes. "How can you do that? They...they took all the money, father. We have nothing left to give back!"

"If I am acquitted, Celeste, we will be refunded every dime. I have debts to pay, but you have no cause for apprehension. There is plenty sitting and waiting for us, and until then, I will take a loan from my friend, as that is what friendship is for. Now, are you down at the Grand Central?"

"Yes," she replied softly.

"Expect a visitor tomorrow morning, does that sound sufficient? Probably around eleven. Is that acceptable?"

"Of course it is!" she cried hastily, hating to admit how relieved she felt, "I don't...I don't know what to say...I thought coming here was a mistake..."

Douglas squeezed her hands. "Listen to me. I will not lie to you from this day forward. I am not a great man, Celeste, I never have been. I am greedy, selfish, and bitter about so much, but you are the one thing I put above all else, and you know that. Have faith in me again. You may not like the person I have been, and because of that I will try to be better. For you."

Celeste sniffed back tears. "Okay," she mumbled.

A loud clanging came to the door. "Time to go," Officer Steven's voice came from outside.

Douglas got up and reached into his pocket, pulling out a five-dollar bill and handing it to Celeste, chuckling at the expression on her face.

"It's fine. Tell Officer Stevens to take you to see Esther. If he argues, you say your father will compensate him double. Understood?"

"Esther?" Celeste had been so wrapped up in her own salvation and in seeing her father, she'd completely forgotten her best friend was in the women's wing of the Tombs, and most likely in far worse condition than Douglas.

The door swung open and Officer Stevens stood there, impatiently. "Let's go, Ma'am. It's getting late."

Douglas glimpsed at her, smiling one last time. "I'm so glad you came to see me, Celeste. It'll be all right. Remember what I told you. We'll get through this together."

Celeste couldn't suppress her happiness. It was wrong, and her conscience silently reprimanded her for it, while somehow, Celeste recognized she no longer cared about what was right and wrong. She'd gone into the prison empty-handed and was leaving with a future. Following the rules got her nowhere in life: married to a monster, losing most of her family and friends, and broke without a dollar to speak of. For another chance, Celeste would bend any rule – particularly if it meant she could keep her pride intact.

As Officer Stevens locked her father's cell door, Celeste held up the five dollars, a smirk on her face.

"Take me to the girl."

"What girl?" he posed, though she knew Officer Stevens knew exactly who she meant.

"Don't play dumb with me. If you want the money, and another five after from my father, take me to her this instant."

"Hah! So you're givin' the orders, then?"

"Yes."

"Well…shit," he chortled, amused by her confidence. "It's goin' to be a nasty trip, Ma'am. Hope you're ready for it."

Ten minutes later, they reached Esther's cell, and Celeste was sickened to discover that in this case, her presumptions had been right. In the back corner nearly hidden in the darkness was a skinny, crumpled girl, a flicker of the Esther she knew, huddling herself for warmth. Her clothing was ripped and tattered, her leather boots boasted a few holes, and the prickly, wool blanket she wrapped tightly around her shoulders looked as if it might do more damage to her skin than good. Esther's back was to them, away from the light and anyone who might pass by. For a moment, Celeste was incapacitated by the scene. Her best friend…her sister…she'd let her down. For nothing other than trying to save Celeste, here Esther was, huddled up on the freezing-cold stone floor suffering, and Celeste was mortified in guilt as she'd made no efforts to be there for her after the conclusion of the trial. In a rush, all the sobs she'd buried for Esther's fate emerged, and she ran in the second the barred door was open wide enough, falling to the floor and wrapping her arms around Esther.

Celeste cried hard as she pulled her friend in close, and Esther, once she realized who it was, hugged her back and began to cry too, and they stayed like that for a few minutes until Celeste released her. Pushing the hair out of Esther's eyes, Celeste studied her face and dried the tears from her friend's cheeks with the hem of her own dress. Esther's skin was dirtied and her lips were dry and cracked, the bottom one split and swollen from what had to have been a strike. Celeste kissed her forehead and then grabbed for Esther's hands, which were at least in slightly better condition than the male prisoner's she'd seen earlier.

"What are you doing here, Celeste?" Esther entreated her, baffled by her appearance. "You shouldn't be here. It's not safe."

"No…" Celeste wept. "I should have been here forever ago. I should have come sooner. I am a horrible, horrible friend. I just didn't know…I didn't know what to say, Es. I didn't know how to make it better or what to do about any of it. I'm sorry…I'm so… so sorry, Es…"

Esther shook her head. "You can't make it better. There's nothing you could have done. You know that."

Celeste tried to stop but the tears kept flowing. "I just don't understand. You saved me…you did it just to save us. And now you… you have to die. Why? Why is this happening?"

741

"I knew what I was doing," Esther disclosed. "I knew the risk. I didn't care. I wanted to kill him, Celeste. For both our sakes."

Esther shuffled slightly and bowed her head to the side, obviously trying to hide something on her neck with her hair.

"Wait," Celeste demanded, sobering from her distress. "Stop. Es, what is this?" She brushed the chunk of hair aside to reveal a giant bandage, from the edge of her collarbone at her shoulder to her jaw line. "Jesus Christ, Esther. What is this?"

Esther stifled a small grin. "Timothy's revenge, I'm afraid. You can look if you want. Should be almost done healing. They're just trying to prevent an infection so I don't die before I'm supposed to."

Carefully, Celeste lifted the bandage and uncovered a deep gash that must have taken dozens of stitches to patch up. The doctor hadn't done Esther any justice, and Celeste cringed to think of the scar it would leave behind on her friend's beautiful skin…and then she remembered it would not matter. Esther's skin would never heal fully because in three weeks' time she would be on the end of a rope in front of the mob of the city. Little by little, Celeste covered the wound back up, hating herself with such intensity she wanted to rip her own hair out. Her time fretting over the trivialities of her own life should have been spent with her friend, who had sacrificed everything for Celeste to live freely and was preparing herself to die for that cause.

"God dammit," she exclaimed, getting to her feet. "I have been wasting the precious time I have with you scrambling to come to grips with my own…my own bullshit. What is wrong with me, Es? What…what…have I become?"

"Hey, don't do that," Esther ordered, sitting up. "You have been through just as much as I have, and I know you have been fighting to secure your own livelihood. Louis has been telling me everything that's gone on. Celeste, there is no shame in that, and if you don't fix this, you'll be on the streets. That's not what I would have wanted. That's not why I did this."

742

"I should be in this cell with you," she muttered. "You shouldn't be dying because of me."

"You didn't pull the trigger, Celeste. I did. And I'm not dying for you, I'm dying for me and for what I've done."

Celeste couldn't accept that answer. "I'll come by every day and bring you bread…maybe some wine if I can get it inside. Apparently all you have to do is pay people around here to get what you want."

Esther paused. "What do you mean?"

"That's the only way I got in here. I had to pay. It was my mother's necklace, the solitaire…" her voice trailed off. Esther's eyes widened with anxiety.

"Which one brought you in here?"

"The one at the front desk brought me to him…Stevens is his name…"

The agitation evaporated. "Stevens is one of the only good coppers in this place. The rest…they're all foul bastards…and they take more than they should from a lot of the women in here."

Celeste was sickened in hearing her friend's words. "Es, has… has one of these guards touched you?!"

"Shhh, no," she hushed her, glancing toward the door. "Louis has taken care of that. Without him, though, let's just say what happened with Timothy would have been a cakewalk in comparison. I…I hear it at night, sometimes. It's fucking awful, Celeste. This place is worse than the Points or the 4th Ward."

Celeste sank back to the floor and hugged her again. "Listen, I will be back tomorrow. And every day until…"

She could feel Esther's warm tears on her dress. "Okay," she mumbled, then added. "I'm really scared, Celeste."

Celeste didn't know what to say. All she could do was pull her in tighter, letting Esther shed a few more tears before Officer Stevens put his hand on her back gently and told her they had to leave.

"Celeste?"

She stopped at the door. "What is it, Es? What can I bring you?"

743

"Just…on the steps…find Louis. He'll be there. He will want to talk with you."

"What do you mean?" Celeste entreated, now from the other side of the bars.

"Just do it for me," Esther told her. "Tomorrow?"

"Tomorrow. I promise."

"Thank you."

"I love you, Es."

"I love you too, Celeste."

Esther went back to her corner, and Celeste left her there, unable to stop herself from weeping the entire journey back to the outside world.

"You're a brave girl wandering into one of the worst prisons in the country alone," Louis quipped as they sauntered around the block. "How was she?"

Celeste had only just dried her eyes. "She's…she's not good, Louis. Scared. A little in denial, I think. I can't stand seeing this. It's too much."

"She needs you, Celeste," Louis pleaded to her. "Esther is on the verge of losing her mind. That place…the things that go on in there…if it weren't for my pull on things, she probably would already be…lost to us."

An idea occurred to her. "Louis, is there anything you could do to get her case appealed? Anything at all?"

Louis shook his head sadly. "This isn't a case like your father's. There was no room for error in judgment or evidence. It's completely out of our hands. Someone is going to have to hang for it, and it's going…it's going to be Esther." Celeste could have sworn Louis became choked up, but he rapidly recovered. "Be there for her as much as you can. Please. It'll make this easier for her and for us.

I'll see to it that you have access to her every afternoon without any problems, and if need be, I will escort you personally inside and out."

They didn't speak for a moment. "How do you know about my father, Louis?"

"It's my job to know these things."

They marched on wordlessly for another minute. "Louis, would you mind if I asked you to be here with me? I know you have other...other things to...to take care of...I would just feel better if...well...it were you with me, not another officer."

He almost laughed aloud. "You should know this takes precedent over anything else I have to 'take care of.' I would also feel more comfortable taking you myself. What time would you like to meet tomorrow? I'll find you right here."

"Two?"

"That works fine. Plans in the morning?"

"I...yes..." she acknowledged, remembering her father's appointment. "Sort of. It's a private matter."

Louis did not push her further. "I understand. Well then, Miss Hiltmore, I will see you at two. Don't be late."

"I won't be," she promised. "And...Louis?"

"Yes?"

"Thank you for...well for using that name."

He smiled at her. "I don't have the stomach to even think of calling you by the other. Nor would I want to offend you by doing so."

"Do you mind if I ask you one last thing?"

"Not at all."

It was hard to get the words out, still finding herself angry about it. "Why didn't you or the Madame testify? I was crucified on that stand and Esther is being put to death. Is that not enough to warrant an effort from either of you?"

Louis didn't show any hint of recoil. "I understand your resentment, Celeste. Nothing either of us said would have changed this, and we would have only been jailed as conspirators. The Madame

745

and I both know the system quite well, and the judge made up his mind before the trial even began. I think that was evident to everyone who sat through it."

Celeste refused to bite her tongue. "So you're going to let her die and do nothing? I know who you and the Madame are, and I'm not going to pretend I don't know what you're capable of. I at least tried. You two could have been character witnesses…anything other than just sit by and watch her be sentenced to death!"

"You can be mad at us all you like, Celeste, but our primary concern has always been Esther, and if you continue to doubt me, then frankly you can forget our arrangement. I've been here every day talking with her and keeping her in one piece. Where the hell have you been other than holed up in your hotel room feeling sorry for yourself?"

Louis' voice carried and a few pedestrians walking by gave them startled looks.

She persisted. "And what about the Madame? Does that mean she's actually been here?"

Louis glared at her and sat down on the steps, and Celeste did the same, not leaving until she had a response from him. Celeste was mortified and blameworthy for not coming sooner, but she'd be damned if she'd let Louis scold her like a small child after what she'd been through. Rather than respond, however, Louis drew two cigarettes out of his jacket pocket and handed one to her.

"I don't smoke," she lied, handing it back.

Louis didn't seem to care, and lit a match for her. "Sure you don't."

"Louis, answer me."

"I will if you have a smoke with me. There are a few things I think I need to educate you on, and better me than the Madame herself."

She allowed him to light the end of her tobacco and Celeste took one drag, then another, and another, the tension in her muscles subsiding. Then Louis spoke.

"I want you to listen to me, because I am only going to have this conversation with you one time. The Madame and I have loved Esther for most of her life. She has been in our care and protection despite being under your roof, and while you think this is devastating to you, I am telling you that you have no idea what devastation is. The Madame and I are the only two truly carrying that weight with the wolves biting at our ankles. We failed her, and we know that. From the moment your bastard husband laid a hand on her she was beyond saving, and I honestly don't know why she waited so long to pull that trigger. I wouldn't have.

"But to continue on in regards to your question, here is what you need to consider. Without the Madame, my dear Celeste, you would have been dead. She sent the one person in the world that knew how to save your life when you miscarried and endured Timothy's beating, rather than sending you to a hospital where there wouldn't have been a fucking chance. She kept an eye on your parent's enemies while you slept easy at night to make sure no harm came to you, and there are quite a few of them still lingering in the shadows whether you want to hear that or not. And while you were off gallivanting in your perfect uptown life, she spent every day encouraging your best friend that you were worth the trials she endured, including being raped by your husband. Oh, and to top that, your father's hearing stayed private because she paid off the papers with her own cash, all to ease your pain. The reason he's in the Mayor's quarters in the first place is because of her contacts and her generosity. So before you go insulting a woman who has gone to great lengths for you, for reasons I wish I could comprehend, you ought to get your story straight. Enjoy the cigarette. I'll bring more tomorrow."

Louis hopped to his feet and left her, not caring if she had anything to say in return.

She didn't.

"Good evening, Douglas," the Madame greeted, the steel door shutting behind her. "How are we today?"

"Would you like to take a seat?" he offered his chair.

"I'll stand, thank you. I heard you had a special visitor today, which I can only imagine has greatly improved your mood."

"It's true. Celeste came to see me," he announced, beaming as he told her. "And it's as you suspected. They've written her out of everything and she's on her last days of money."

The Madame leisurely skimmed his bookshelf with her fingertips, listening. "So our deal is settled then?"

"Yes." Douglas slid a piece of paper across his desk, which she instantly spun around and snatched up.

"This is it?"

"That's it," he replied. "This is the bank and the lock box where the hidden money is. I expect you to follow what has been pre-arranged."

"Lovely," she cooed, seeing the account and box number. "And as agreed, half for me, half for her?"

"And another bonus for you once I am acquitted."

She smirked. "Which will be soon, I am happy to report. Just think, Douglas, if we had worked together in the beginning, we could have avoided…well…perhaps we shouldn't think about that."

His cheeks flushed, though out of embarrassment rather than antagonism. "I can't argue with you there," he agreed. "I blame my wife, that stupid bitch. But it's getting fixed now. For the better."

"I concur! Well then, I will take care of Celeste, your trial will be at the end of this month, and when you are released from this disgusting place we will discuss our…understanding further."

Douglas shook his head. "I was sorry to hear about Esther. Really I was. She was a lovely girl and I always liked her."

The Madame left the books, turning her attention to him. "Correction. Esther is a lovely girl," she rectified. "And are you really sorry for her, Douglas, or sorry you couldn't kill Timothy first? From what I remember you wanted her dead."

"It was Catherine that despised her, not I. And what is this talk… is a lovely girl? Are you actually thinking she has a chance at escaping the end of the noose? I've seen the evidence, Madame…there is no hope for her."

"It's doubtful," she remarked casually. "Yet I am never one to try and make these kinds of predictions with so much in the balance. I can't say I'm not a little surprised to hear you have any sentimentality toward her."

"What mattered to me was her relationship with my daughter, which has proven to be more significant than I saw at the time."

"She saved Celeste's life," the Madame remarked. "A father can never repay that type of kindness."

"It's a disgrace I won't have the chance to amend for."

The Madame detected a note of remorse in his voice. "I am a little puzzled by your sympathy, Douglas. If you knew how much she meant to your daughter, why would you allow the hit to be ordered on her by Catherine? Or allow her police report to be covered up as if it never happened?"

"I think we both know the answer to that."

She took a rigid stance. "Enlighten me."

"You really did not figure this out?"

"Figure what out, Douglas?"

Douglas tilted his head, as if he were reflecting while he spoke. "When I found out the truth about Timothy…about the real person he was and Virginia…oh yes, Madame, I know about Virginia, he and his father threatened to kill Celeste and my wife, then expose me the same way you did. Within a week, Esther's report surfaced, and I had no choice but to pick my daughter over Esther and wait, hoping you would see it coming and stop it in time. The same move any father would make in such circumstances. It doesn't mean I was compliant. I was muscled."

"Does your precious Celeste know about this sacrifice?" she posed.

"If she asks me, I will tell her."

The Madame scoffed. "We'll see about that. Goodnight, Douglas." She turned to go, knocking on the door to be let out.

"She doesn't know it's you, Madame."

The guard appeared with the keys, and the Madame paused. "What do you mean she doesn't know it's me?"

"I mean Celeste. She doesn't know you are the only thing keeping us alive right now. And I'm not exactly sure how she'll take it."

For the first time in weeks, a sincerely entertained smile crossed her lips. "Don't worry yourself, Douglas. I am quite sure Louis let her know the truth this afternoon."

Douglas sighed. "Please be delicate with her tomorrow morning, if you can. She's not like us."

"Not yet," she declared. "But I'll do my best to break her in at a leisurely pace. Goodnight, Douglas." The Madame walked out of the cell, laughing under her breath at the irony in the reversal of circumstances. Perhaps in the end, Celeste would manage to fulfill the role the Madame envisioned for her long ago.

Only time would tell.

XXVI.

Louis couldn't decide who, in general, was doing worse: Danny or Esther. He and Danny took the afternoon to spend some time with Esther with barely a week until her execution, and as Danny sat on the cold stone floor holding Esther in her arms, for a moment he couldn't tell them apart. Their faces were gaunt and pale from lack of sleep and no desire to eat, causing the girls to easily drop two dress sizes since the night of tragedy. In addition to that, their dark manes were untamed and wild, falling long past their shoulders and no regard for what was considered appropriate. It was plain to see that Esther was on a plunging downward spiral with her days limited, though rather than losing her grip on reality as Louis predicted, she seemed to accept her fate and was already withering away with death on the horizon. Esther would not live to see the blooming flowers of spring, and at this rate, Louis wasn't sure if Danny would either.

Since Hope had been killed, Danny's quick wit and loud mouth vanished, and getting her to utter anything except a one-word answer was almost unattainable. Every night she drowned herself in wine, locked away in her room, though everyone at The Palace could hear her sobbing late into the night, cursing anyone who disturbed her. Where most might grieve and then progressively improve, Danny's condition continued to deteriorate. She would do whatever the Madame asked of her, which was not much in the aftermath of the night they chose never to speak of. The girls were informed of what happened, and they all cared deeply for Danny, but the show had to go on, with or without her participation. The Madame's weariness was starting to outweigh her compassion, and Louis saw it become a daily battle within herself of whether or not she could keep Danny on the premises to successfully run The Palace. The Madame had planned to 'retired' Danny, most likely to Esther's old apartments; however, Louis and the Madame also discussed the fear of what Danny would do without The Palace. They knew the answer already – she would have no reason to go on, not with Hope already in the afterlife, and they would most likely find her hanging from the rafters.

Esther closed her eyes, drifting off into a sound sleep. With a great sense of alleviation in observing her so peaceful, Louis lit a cigarette and rested against the cold stone wall. It was torture having to watch her rot away…there was no light at the end of the tunnel and nothing he could do to change it. On the outside, Louis was doing everything in his power to seem diligent and strong, yet on the inside he, too, was falling apart. They both thought with Ellis on their side and Timothy's record, a self-defense plea would be an easy verdict for any judge and jury. Instead, the prosecution turned out to be backed by a personal friend of Timothy's from his youth, and they had to sit back and watch Esther be decimated by the legal system. The evidence the Pinkertons offered was ruled out as coincidental, highlighting the point that their financial backers were 'emotionally compromised' by the loss of their family members and that the Pinkertons were an operation that technically no longer held any legal jurisdiction. Celeste's words were twisted and shoved into the template they wanted to create to portray Esther as the murderer and Timothy the victim, and not a single testimony swayed it her way.

The day they announced the verdict, Louis swore he'd never

seen the Madame more shattered in all the years he'd known her, and she didn't leave her office for nearly two days following the outcome.

What bothered Louis the most was neither him nor the Madame could testify, a point brought about by Celeste Hiltmore that pained Louis deeply. It was not because they didn't want to, but because if they did, they would only be thrown in with her as corroborators, not to mention the state would find all sorts of reasons to lock them up – it was no secret as to who they were and what business they were in. From the start, the judge and the prosecution wanted Esther to hang, and hang she would. Helplessly sitting in the back of the courtroom Louis watched it unfold, a fire building in his heart. Weeks had trickled by, and Louis scrambled to formulate a plan or method to save her, but it was entirely in vain. Nothing he could piece together would work, and unless it was impeccably thought through, Croker would never go for it. Louis had never felt like a bigger failure to anyone.

He took in a deep drag, leaning against the wall of Esther's cell, and finished his cigarette.

"Louis?"

Danny's voice snapped Louis out of his daze. "Yes Danny?" She glanced up while gently rocking Esther back and forth, who thankfully remained asleep. "You love her, don't you?"

His eyes began to water, and he nodded, dragging his cigarette across the wall to cease the burn.

"I have an idea."

"An idea?"

An air of revelation came to her cheeks, and it was the happiest he'd seen her in months. "Let me take her place."

The cigarette fell out of his hand and to the ground. "W-What? What do you mean?"

Danny's eyes went down to Esther, and she shook her head. "I don't want to live any more. She does. There's no reason for us both to die. And right now, unless you were really looking, there is no way to tell us apart."

"Danny, you have so much ahead of you…how can you–"

"No," she interrupted him harshly, "No, I don't. I can't live without Hope. I don't want to live without her, Louis."

"Yes, you can," he promised her. "You just need to let it go."

A single tear fell down her cheek. "I can't let it go. Don't you see? I've tried and tried, but I can't. This is what I want. This is what you want. It's the only way you could get Croker to back you, and you know it."

He was adamantly against it. "I won't let you," Louis contended. "You'll get better. You just need more time."

"You can't save me, Louis. Only Hope could. You can save Esther and you keep her safe, you understand me? I don't care what it takes, you tell that son of a bitch from Tammany this is how it'll go, all right?"

"Danny–"

"Just do it!" she insisted, angry tears forming in her eyes. "You've been trying to get her out of this, and that's the only reason you went to work for the Hall in the first place. This is what needs to happen, or your effort will have been for nothing."

Louis considered it for a minute or so, his morality battling back and forth; the one thing Louis knew far too well was that when Danny made up her mind, it was set and there was no changing it. Not him, not the Madame, not even Hope could talk Danny out of her own stubbornness. In reality, she'd already done the hard part for him.

"You're sure this is what you want?"

"Yes," she declared, caressing Esther's hair. "More than anything in all my life."

"Ok, Danny," he said. "I'll talk to Croker."

"I do have one condition that I think you of all people will get," she went on, glimpsing up into his eyes.

"What is it?" he pressed.

"We can't tell the Madame."

Louis was confused. "Danny, we have to tell her."

"That is my condition," Danny maintained. "The Madame can't know."

"But…but why?"

"Because it'll be good for her to realize she's lost everything she ever held close, all in her own doing." There was resentment in her words, a certain degree of spite Danny held on to after the Madame swore to her no harm would find Hope.

Louis got out another cigarette. "You don't mean that," he retorted. "She saved you and Hope. She took you in when you had nowhere else to go, and when most would have thrown you back out she let you stay to help her run The Palace. Have you forgotten all that?"

"The Madame also took away the only thing in my life that mattered."

"Danny, Timothy killed her, not the Madame—"

"It might as well have been her!" Danny snapped, causing Esther to stir and then, after a moment of stillness, fall into sleep again. "Louis, please. Just…just take her and get her out of this God damned place. That's the only condition I have. It has nothing to do with the Madame, and if I can save her, I want Esther to be free of this. Esther deserves that from us."

He could see the fury…the hatred fuming in her stare. The Madame never believed Danny blamed her for the incident, and on the contrary, Louis realized Danny blamed her for all of it. While his conscience told him to refuse this request and force Danny to come to grips with her own demons, it would do her no good. Apart from the Madame, she was the most tenacious and determined woman Louis had ever encountered. She wanted to die, and she wanted to save Esther in the process. No piece of him could deny her proposition was, in truth, quite brilliant. Anyone from more than five feet away would never know the difference between Danny and Esther. He had even made the observation himself not ten minutes ago. There was only one obstacle left to have the plan set in stone, and he would need Will's help to convince Croker it was the right move for everybody to move forward.

"I'll bring it to Croker tonight. And I won't tell the Madame. But Danny, if you agree to this, there is no backing out and no second chances. You are signing your own death sentence."

"It'll save me the trouble of doing it myself," she said nonchalantly.

Louis walked over and squatted down, studying Esther closely and putting his hand to her cheek. "She's not going to like this," he whispered to Danny. "When she finds out, she'll be furious."

"By the time she'll know, it'll be too late," Danny assured him. "We can't tell her until the switch. If she knows, she'll give herself away. It's too big a risk."

"I agree." He checked his pocket watch. "Time to go, Danny."

Danny nodded and squeezed Esther lightly, giving her forehead a kiss. "Es, it's time for me to go. Louis needs to get Celeste."

Esther woke easily. "Shit. I'm sorry. I drifted off again didn't I?"

"It's okay," Louis conveyed. "We're both glad you slept."

Esther sat up and hugged Danny close. "Will you…can you please come see me one more time?"

Danny grabbed her hand and kissed it. "Of course I will."

They all got to their feet and said their respective goodbyes, Louis pledging to return with Celeste sometime in the next hour. When Louis and Danny reached the outside, he spotted Celeste already waiting for him near the steps, trying to appear casual despite how uneasy the prison made her. He hadn't expected Celeste to live up to her word of seeing Esther every day, and to his amazement she actually had, spending hours with her friend and bringing her bread and wine hidden beneath her coat. In that short time, Celeste and Louis made a habit of having a cigarette prior to venturing into the Tombs, and it helped her to relax during her visits, which were not always the most pleasant considering the company surrounding Esther's cell. Seeing their approach, Celeste made her way toward Danny and Louis, though he perceived a flash of panic hit her face when she recognized who Danny was. Celeste hadn't seen her since the night of Hope's death, and he hoped their upcoming conversation wouldn't end up being awkward, or possibly hostile.

"Good afternoon, Miss Hiltmore," Louis greeted. "We were just wrapping up…Esther is excited to see you. You remember Danny?"

Celeste brought out her best charming smile. "Yes I do. Hi, Danny. It's nice to see you again."

Danny frowned at her for a few seconds. "Pardon me, Miss Hiltmore, but I must be going. Thank you for today, Louis. I'll see you tonight."

Celeste stayed silent as Danny left, though the second Danny was out of earshot, Louis felt the inquisition coming.

"What did I do, Louis? Does she think it's my fault?"

"No, she doesn't. That responsibility she places on someone else," he affirmed, grabbing their tobacco. "She just can't stand the sight of you, Celeste."

Celeste was visibly hurt by his comment. "Christ…why?"

"It's complicated."

"Is it because of what happened?"

Louis handed her cigarette over. "Not exactly. It's…well…you have to understand, you look just like Hope did, Celeste. Blonde hair, blue eyes, fair skin…I think it is just hard for her to stomach after that night." Celeste didn't respond, only gazed after Danny, her eyes full of pity.

When they'd each had a few drags, Louis ushered her inside. "Come along, before someone sees us. It's too damn cold to be standing out here for long."

He arrived first, followed closely by Will, and ultimately, Croker. Snow started to fall lightly in the cloudy night, almost warming the cold air biting at Louis' nose and throat in the late hour. Their meeting place was always the same, at the corner of 14th and 3rd between the streetlights, and they made a point to not be standing there together for more than a few minutes to thus avoid attracting any notice. Here, Croker would shell out the orders of what he needed done, and Louis and Will would comply. So far, Croker was extremely pleased the work they'd done together, proving to be more valuable than he originally thought. Tonight would be a muscle move, as Will had already forewarned Louis, which meant nothing particularly gruesome other than scaring someone into following Croker's orders. This one was concerning a small Irish neighborhood outside Hell's Kitchen where a health inspector condemned nearly six buildings Tammany had been housing immigrants in whilst they tried to find them steady work. Croker was livid, hating to be snubbed by someone he considered 'chump change,' and therefore Will and Louis would be sent to have a small discussion with the health inspector to convince him to retract his reports before being reviewed by City Hall.

All three men saluted one another as Croker drew near, peeking over their shoulders to be certain no one was watching or would overhear them. Louis and Will hadn't spoken a word to one another, only smoked and chewed their choice of tobacco and stood patiently. There would be plenty of time to talk later, and the last thing either of them wanted was to have Croker know more about what was going on between them than he should. Since the night in the park after Esther's arrest, neither Louis nor Will had mentioned what happened between them despite carrying out numerous other tasks for the Hall together. Louis couldn't stand it anymore. Once they'd finished their assignment, he was going to confront Will and put things back the way they were. Primarily, however, he needed this job to go smoothly – if they got through the night unscathed, Croker would be more apt to hear out Danny's proposition, and that currently mattered to Louis far above Will's feelings about him or some piece of shit health inspector.

"He'll be leaving City Hall in forty minutes, so you two had better walk fast," Croker told them. "Follow him, punish him, then tell him he will be rewarded for his…change of heart. You both know the drill by now."

"Do we have any side leverage?" Louis asked. "Anything we could use?"

Croker smirked. "He's a former morphine addict, subduing that with extensive cocaine use. Threaten to cut him off, and we'll see how terrified he really is."

Will spat onto the ground. "And will he go into withdrawal if we cut the son of a bitch off? I need to know how bad it'll be for him. Makes it easier to scare when ya've got a picture to paint."

"The withdrawal would be worse than morphine," Croker elucidated. "He would be bed-bound, unable to function with the fucking doses he takes." Croker's carriage rolled up behind them, and he tipped his hat. "I'll be in my office. See me when it's done."

When he'd gone, Louis and Will set off toward the front of City Hall, and the cumbersome silence making Louis more and more self-conscious.

"Will, we need to talk about it."

Will didn't lose pace. "What is there to talk about?"

"The park. We need to put this behind us." The snow started to fall harder, dusting the shoulders of Louis' coat and the top of his bowler hat, and he shook off the flakes every few steps as they strode on.

After a block or so without response, Will halted and turned to face him. "Ain't nothin' to talk about, brother. You'd had yourself a rough night is all, and I understand you had a lot of emotions runnin' thick in your blood. This ain't what it was twenty years ago. You've got nothin' ya need to say about it you ain't already said."

His face was stern, but Louis knew him better than that. "Will, this doesn't have to do with how I…how I look at you. This is to keep us…safe. From Croker and that Walsh bastard who's lurking around every corner."

"You're afraid they'll use us and try to put us against each oth-

759

er, eh? Don' think I hadn' already thought of that."

Louis took Will by the arm and kept walking, releasing it after a few paces. "They would put us against each other," he muttered. "We can't afford to…" Louis caught himself, resolving for once be candid with someone who meant so much to him. "I can't afford to lose another friend I trust. Or care about for that matter."

"I ain't goin' nowhere, brother. You know that. It'll take a lot more than that Irish mick to take us down. We ain't young like we once was, but we're sure as shit a lot smarter."

"You know it's not Croker I worry about."

"Walsh," Will huffed under his breath. "We gotta keep an eye on that son of a bitch. That night…with the Whyos…I still can't forget the way he…he owned them, brother. Plain and simple. And that ain't fuckin' good for nobody."

"The Madame thinks there's something bigger going on," Louis confided to him. "And I agree with her, but we'll get to that later." The snow and the cold were taking a toll on them physically. "Let's get this thing with the health inspector done fast. There's something else I need to run by you before we go back to see Croker."

"And just what might that be?"

"An idea. One I think Croker might go for."

This sparked Will's interest. "This 'bout our girl?"

"Yes. It has to do with saving Esther from hanging. And you know I can't do that without his say so."

"You really think he'll follow through on the promise he made you, brother? He told you…unless it's flawless…"

Louis smiled. "I think it's as close as we could possibly get to flawless."

Soon, they approached the front steps of City Hall, scouting the area quickly and then assuming a relatively hidden position to wait for the health inspector. Thankfully the snow let up, making it easier to observe the entrance from a somewhat precautious distance. For their spot, Will chose a tiny alley across the street and three buildings down, where they were shrouded in darkness and would go overlooked by anyone more than an arm's length from them. What the inspector was doing at City Hall so late, Louis couldn't say, yet it made their work much easier as most of the surrounding roads would be completely deserted that time of night.

"He's average height, portly, glasses, and extremely…clean," Will described, tacking off the list of attributes Croker provided them with. "Beard and moustache trimmed damn near perfect each mornin', and not a speck of dirt on his three times a day shined shoes. Not exactly the type of bastard to be pickin' livable conditions, in my opinion. Boy can barely stand a speck o' dirt on anythin'!"

Louis stifled a chuckle. "Should we just throw him in a fucking manure shack? That might be a better tactic than brute force."

"Nah. But we can threaten him with that for next time. That'll make his sorry ass piss his britches after we break a few of his fingers."

"Right or left?"

"Right hand. He's a lefty, and we still need him to be able to use a pen. Otherwise he won' be able to fix nothin'."

"Understood."

Through the clouds of steam from their breath, they spotted him a few minutes later, and Will's depiction couldn't have been spot on for the health inspector. He had to be the cleanest and most put together man Louis ever seen on the streets of New York, and he wondered how much extra time and sweat the man must spend each day on his appearance alone. If he ever managed to venture to the Points, the man would surely die of a heart attack from all the filth, and shockingly, Louis found he might actually enjoy this errand for Croker. A man who couldn't deal with a little dirt under his fingernails didn't know what it meant to live in poverty and spring from the ashes, like almost every immigrant in that city was forced to do. He could see why Croker disliked him, and an uptowner should by no means be the person choosing whether living conditions were good or bad for anyone, especially the lower classes.

761

Louis and Will glimpsed at one another and pursued from a few paces back, the idea being that they would get him just before he reached the carriage car as he headed north. As they were in pursuit, the inspector turned the corner of the next road and they did the same. Will then disappeared to Louis' left down a narrow lane, which connected at the end of the block to the intersecting street. Getting closer, Louis picked up his tempo, wanting to be only a few feet behind the health inspector when Will grabbed him. The snow made the streets slick, and despite his experience Louis slid a little as he kept up, the end of the road only a few feet away. The health inspector made a left and Louis whipped around the bend just in time to see their target get noiselessly yanked off the road by Will.

Within seconds Louis reached them: Will had the inspector pinned up against the wall, a knife at his throat and his other hand over the man's mouth. Louis stepped around Will and took the inspector's right hand in his, twisting his arm to make sure the pain from this encounter was excruciating.

"Hello, Inspector," Louis took the lead. "I want you to listen to me very carefully. First, I want you to nod to tell me you can hear every word I'm saying and that you are listening."

Louis tilted his head, scowling at him like he was nothing but an insect to be squashed. The inspector's eyes were bulging with fear, and the he nodded frantically, looking from Louis to Will, then back to Louis, desperately seeking some kind of mercy he wouldn't find.

"You're going to forgo condemning the Irish aid apartment buildings in Hell's Kitchen. I don't care how you do it, but you will make it happen, or the next time you see us, we will be the last things you see on this earth." Louis broke his pinky finger, and the man squealed from behind Will's grip, trying hard to pull away.

"Those buildings are property of Tammany Hall," he continued. "And if you cripple us, we cripple you." He broke the next finger, causing a loud moan and tears to fall from the inspector's eyes, "If you don't drop it first thing tomorrow, you will find no man in this city who will sell you your drug of choice at any price, and your body will begin to deteriorate from the inside out. You'll be bedridden, unable to do your job, and unable to stop us from killing you. Or throwing you into a manure pile and holding you there just to watch you fucking squirm."

For the final one, Louis mangled it enough to make it unfixable, wanting to leave a permanent mark of forewarning. A loud snap, and the inspector's muted cry of agony let him know he'd been successful. The point had been made.

"Don't make us come back again," he whispered into the man's ear. "Or I can promise you, it'll be the biggest mistake of your life."

Louis released his hand, and Will tossed him to the ground in a heap of misery. Without a moment to spare, they took off the way they'd come, tracing their steps back the direction of the Hall in case somehow they might have been heard, though from the emptiness of the streets as they ran it was evident they were in the clear. When they'd gone three blocks, Will and Louis slowed to a march, and suddenly Will started to laugh aloud. For no reason at all, Louis laughed too, putting his arm around Will's shoulder like two teenage boys who'd just barely escaped trouble. It had been easy for them since day one, and even with two decades apart, they both found themselves astonished at how well they worked together. The pair went on like that for another block, chuckling most of the way, until people ahead came into view and Louis let his arm fall back to his side with a quick clear of his throat.

"Well, that went well," he offered, not sure what else to say.

Will grinned at him. "Easy as pie, brother. Like all the others."

As soon as the other pedestrians were passed, Louis laughed again. "God dammit, Will. Why is it so much better when we're together?"

"'Cause that's how we learned from the get go," he answered bluntly. "More efficient with two, faster with two, more fun with two."

"And it has nothing to do with the fact that we…well…"

"Have feelin's for each other?" Will remarked sarcastically. "Nah, couldn' be that."

Those words coming from Will took Louis off guard, though Will knew him well enough to recognize the impact his quip made, and abruptly changed their banter to business once again.

"So, brother, what exactly is this plan you wanna run by Croker?"

The fire was burning hot in Croker's office, and he anticipated their return with a plethora of whiskey and his finest cigars at hand. With open arms he welcomed them back, handing them each a full glass with a flashy, politician smile from ear to ear, beckoning them to sit down and warm up. Louis was happy just to take note of Walsh's absence. Walsh typically accompanied Croker for their post-errand revelry, though never for long, and keeping in mind the night by the Bowery, Louis queried whether or not Walsh was there to try and intimidate him and Will...or Croker.

"Everything went according to plan, yes?" Croker entreated the two, sliding down into his armchair behind his desk – internally, Louis perceived Croker's behavior closely resembled that of the Madame, and tried to hide a smirk at her copycat. "He's such a fucking pussy, that one. I have a feeling he won't be out of bed for days. When I found out he was the problem, I knew we could get it fixed."

"If it goes to committee tomorrow, that poor bastard will pay for it," Louis responded, taking a sip of whiskey. "And by pay for it, I mean Will and I will throw him in the filthiest place we can find and make him wish he was dead."

"That's what I like to hear! Will, you need matches for that cigar?"

"Got 'em, thanks Boss."

Louis took a cigarette out of his pocket and received an almost offended look from Croker.

"It's nothing personal," he declared. "I just honestly don't enjoy cigars the way I enjoy these. The best tobacco you can buy in the city, and I roll them myself. It's a hard practice to break."

"Been doin' that since I knew him," Will chimed in. "But he'll drink ya clean of whiskey, that one."

The stiffness in Croker's countenance immediately eased. "Whiskey is the key to a man's heart. Wonderful work tonight, gentlemen. I've got your money on my desk. Louis, anything new springing up from The Palace? I'm thinking I might need her for another…night of entertainment with a few colleagues sometime next month. She's the best in her business…one of a kind…I don't know how she does it, but some of the tips she passed me have proven to be…well, game changing for us, I'd say. I'm beginning to wonder how the fuck we didn't partner sooner and spent so many years at odds."

Louis had more than a few answers to that, but he managed to keep them to himself regardless of the irrepressible urge to break Croker's skull.

"Actually, sir, there is something I wanted to discuss with you," Louis spoke up. "Separate from anything with the Madame."

"Anything, Louis. We are a family here. What is it?"

Louis peered at Will, who nodded encouragingly. "I want to propose a plan that would…well…save Esther from execution."

Croker reclined back in his chair. "I know she means a lot to you. Like a daughter, am I correct, or is there something else I'm missing?"

"No, sir, I just care a lot for her. Like a daughter, as you said."

"You know my hands are tied in this regard, and Will has been pressuring me when you are not around to try and dissuade the judge who decided to make her a fucking personal statement. It won't matter what I hit this asshole with, Louis, he's out for blood. This women's liberation front is making all these chauvinist bastards cringe, and they want to maintain their power with these incessant protests and incidents to prevent its rise. Esther killing that ingrate was a blessing to this city, but it doesn't make a God damned difference. Even the prosecution sees this as a threat. They don't want women

thinking they can take up arms as men do and get away with it…
they're swatting them all down. Even the Madame ought to watch
herself closely."

"That night, when we met, you promised me if I could find a
solution on my own that was flawless you would back me."

"Yes, I did."

"Well, Mr. Croker, I have a flawless solution."

Croker's attentiveness peaked. "Oh? What's that? The catch,
Louis, is that there's no way around the death sentence. Someone has
got to hang, so unless Esther has a twin sister hiding somewhere—"

"That's just it," Louis interrupted. "The…the prostitute Timothy Adams murdered that night…the one that died in the hospital? Her, well her…partner…might as well be Esther's double. Their
features match exactly, and after Hope's death, this girl came to me
wanting to take Esther's place and save her. She's…well, sir, she is
more than happy to take the fall."

Will choked on his whiskey. "Are you fuckin' kiddin' me?!"

Croker's eyebrows rose, his eyes wide. "You're not serious,
are you?"

"Yes, sir. I am perfectly serious about this. It'd be a clean swap.
No one would ever know."

"And what does the Madame think of this? One of her best going to the hangman's noose on her own fucking accord? Sounds a
little too good to be true."

"The Madame doesn't know about this," Louis clarified. "And
I've made a promise she will never know, either. This girl doesn't
want to live anymore, and wants to get Esther out of New York."

"Why is that?"

"I'm not sure. But if that's the way we are doing this, it would
be easier without the Madame's involvement."

Croker rubbed his chin, deep in deliberation. "Will, what do
you think? Put it openly, like you would if the Frog wasn't here."

"I think it'll work, Boss. There's gotta be conditions though, like she can't start waltzin' around Fifth Avenue again like nothin' happened—"

Croker stroked his beard, considering it. "Before we get to that, there is a bigger question at hand. Her mental state." He locked eyes with Louis. "How bad is it?"

"Well, she thinks she's going to die in a week. How would you be, sir?"

"So she's a disaster, that is what you're telling me?"

"Yes," Will responded for him, sensing Louis' sensitivity to Esther's condition.

"Christ," Croker thought aloud. "Give me a day, all right Louis? Just let me mull this whole thing over for a fucking day. There's a lot of ground to cover, and the three of us can't make a mistake here. Or we're all in deep shit."

Louis nodded. "I understand. I can get her out of New York, sir. Far away. No one will ever know she—"

"That's not the issue. This goes above you, you understand? It is my call, and if I can see a way to do this I will. I'm not trying to fuck you over, Louis, I'm trying to do this…vigilantly. I know she means a lot to you. And I want to keep you on board with me and the Hall."

Louis knew he wouldn't gain any more ground. "Thank you, sir. Saving her is the only thing that matters to me right now. I apologize if I was too forthright."

Croker stood up from his desk and grabbed Louis' envelope of money, tossing it in his lap. "Go home and sleep this off. Come by in the morning and I'll give you my answer. Until then, you're dismissed."

Will wouldn't give up. "Boss, it sounds like it'll work—"

"No, not tonight," Croker reiterated, holding up a hand to stop him. "I'm not the type of man to make a rash decision. Take the money and go. Goodnight, Louis. Will, you stay. We have other matters to discuss."

There was no other way around it. Louis got to his feet, finished his whiskey, and left Croker's office with the money in hand. One of

767

the things he hated most about Croker was the way he manipulated each one of his "employees" to try and make them feel more important than the other. It was a management tactic that, after many years with the Madame, he could see through, and hoped Will did too. His quick dismissal of Louis until the next morning and order Will to stay behind was meant to show him he had room to climb the ranks, yet Louis couldn't give a damn. At the end of the day, Croker needed him and Will working together to get things done, and Will would never hide anything from him. As Louis descended down the main hall stair and out the front doors of Tammany Hall, he found himself sneering: Croker thought Louis was in his pocket, that he was disgruntled in his employment with the Madame and was spying for him. That on it's own was enough to keep Louis' temper at bay, and even make his time with the bastard all the more entertaining.

The Madame would be looking forward to his return, wanting to hear how the day progressed in the hopes that their plan was moving forward. No specifics prior to that afternoon had been given to Louis in regards to Danny's offer for Esther's life, but the Madame had mentioned to him something might present itself, and he should be prepared to handle it. At first he really didn't believe her, almost to the degree of supposing the Madame was losing her grip on reality. Now he could see it all from her perspective: she'd set it up on her own, probably placing the idea in Danny's head without the poor girl even realizing it, setting into motion events that would drastically change their fates. The Madame more than likely predicted from the moment she'd found Hope about to die on the floor Danny's heart would go with her, and while she cared deeply for Danny, they'd all watched her mentally and physically regress over the last few months with no prospect of improvement.

Together, they would turn something tragic into a miracle. Together, they would save Esther, and take the upper hand against Croker.

She sat behind her desk, half the bottle of Casper's already consumed, observing him as he entered her office.

"Did it work?" she asked, pulling off her spectacles.

Louis collapsed into the chair. "How'd you get her to come up with that? How could you not tell me?"

"I didn't come up with it. Danny did that all by herself. I only… by mistake of course…called her Esther when she came in to see me yesterday. Things took off from there."

Louis sighed. "Do you have any clue as to why she doesn't want you in on the trade, Madame?"

The fire in the corner crackled loudly to fill the gap of discussion. "So she blames me for the whole fucking catastrophe, does she?"

The Madame slid an empty glass and the bottle over to Louis from across her desk, and he leaned forward to pour himself a share.

"I don't know, Madame. Wouldn't you, if you saw it from her end?" He thought she might grow angry, but instead she was steadfast. "I guess I might. But I've never been attached to another being in that way, so I can't say I understand her reasoning."

"I can't either," he granted, taking a sip. "Night went well. Pitched it to Croker, and he took the bait."

"Perfect."

"Madame, there's no way in hell he's going to let her stay in New York."

"Ah," she retorted playfully. "And what makes you think that?"

"Esther is supposed to be dead," he stressed. "If anyone who knows her catches her out and about, it'll be catastrophic."

"What makes you think Croker will be so apt to let Esther off the fucking hook without making her pay her dues?" the Madame posed. "When has he ever, in all the time we've known of him, given anyone around him anything without the expectation of something in return?"

Louis deliberated on it. "What are you saying, that he will want to use her? What could he possibly use her for? It's not as if Esther can return to Fifth Avenue and spy for him the way she did for us."

"That's what disturbs me, and why no matter what happens you don't let that bastard hold the control over this. I'm afraid…" her voice trailed off, like she didn't want to admit what was plaguing her.

"What is it?"

"I'm afraid he's going to take advantage of what we haven't…and send her to all the places she…she can go…without being recognized."

Louis was thrown. "No. There's no way. How could he ever manage that? How could she? She's not trained to survive in that type of environment. It would take someone with a heightened familiarity…someone who'd lived there for decades and knew every nook and cranny…"

"Or two men with extensive experience of running the Points and the Bowery when they were young?"

It was not what Louis wanted to hear. "You…you think he would have me and Will…what…train her?"

"I'm not sure, Louis. I am only speculating. But if I was him… that is precisely what I would do. You are two of the best hits I've ever come into contact with, and I'm fucking lucky to have you at my side. Croker wants young blood to build an empire, and he's going to need his old guard dogs to find new ones and get them in line, particularly since Walsh doesn't play well with others." She motioned for him to pass over his glass and she refilled it. "When is he giving you his final say?"

"Tomorrow morning. I'm going by before I take Celeste to see Esther."

She nodded, her eyes moving outside her windows. "Have you mentioned the Captain to her yet?"

"What about him?"

His too quick answer gave him away, and she turned on him fiercely. "I know he's not Thomas, Louis. I wish he was, but he isn't. You can't keep preventing him from visiting her. The man is going to lose his fucking mind."

"I really couldn't give a damn, Madame," he barked. "That's the last thing she needs right now."

"How do you know what the fuck she needs right now? This isn't about you, or me, it's about her!"

"This has never been about her!" Louis shot back angrily. "Your version of this being about Esther has been anything that suits her and, in turn, keeps in line with your own agenda! Out of all the people pulling on her puppet strings, I am the only one who gives a shit about her, and the only other person on this earth who does is across a fucking ocean, with no hopes of making it in time! For all we know, Thomas doesn't have a clue about anything that's gone on here in the past month, because if he did, you know he would have already come home!"

The Madame uncharacteristically remained unruffled. "And like Danny, you blame me for all of this?"

Louis let out a defeated breath. "No. No, I don't." He took of his hat and ran his hands over his shaved head. "Thomas' absence is Esther's own doing, I realize that. But Madame, if this does work, all her attachments, all the things she enjoyed in her life, they won't exist for her anymore."

"And when was the last time you remember Esther ever happy before Thomas? Hmm? The only thing I seem to remember is a girl stuck between two worlds, wanting nothing more than an out and asking us to fucking help her. Fifth Avenue...the Hiltmores... the parties...that was never her place, Louis. Her place is with us, and it always will be. If that means she spends a few hard years in the Points paying off her debt to Croker then so be it."

Louis was fuming again. "So it doesn't matter at all what she wants, then? We are just making the decisions for her?" His hand was squeezing so tightly around his glass, it was a marvel it didn't break in his hand.

The Madame stood and made her way around to Louis, sitting in the open chair beside his. She was appealing, not attacking.

771

"Esther lost that privilege when she was arrested. We are doing anything we can to save her from death, Louis. Death. She is very fortunate to have someone like you to be there for her, especially if Croker does decide to make his own God damned use of her. But for every one our sakes, you need to stop making her a fucking martyr. She is far from innocent." It was then Louis noticed the Madame had something in her hand, and she placed an unopened letter in Louis' lap. "I could have read it, and I chose not to. With the histories and the information I have trusted you with, I will have faith in you to tell him what you think is best."

The seal on the envelope was one Louis immediately recognized: a bold T for Turner.

"This came today?" he asked.

She nodded. "I don't know what the letter says. I don't need to know either. I am almost positive Thomas has burned every fucking letter I've sent him without bothering to open one, and fuck him for that." The Madame rose, visibly dismayed, back to her desk where she was strongest. "I've fucking ruined my family, Louis, and for what? It's you and me versus an entire city of Irish thugs working for Croker. I frankly don't fucking know that anything we do will be able to bring down the king and his court. And Mary must be cursing me to hell right now."

"She is not. She can see you're doing your best."

The Madame smiled at him sadly and motioned toward the letter. "Go on, before we both go crazy wanting to read it."

Hurriedly, Louis tore open the envelope, and what he read came as quite a shock. In his absence, Thomas had somehow uncovered many of the unspoken truths from his father's past, and Louis had a feeling it wouldn't fare them well.

He got up and handed it to her. "I think you should see this."

The Madame took it instantly and skimmed the lines, and Louis watched as the comprehension of what was in her hands settled. Thomas discovered his father's death was no longer an accident, and he somehow also found out his mother had been alive at the time of Edward's death, though there was no theory or name attached to the little knowledge he'd obtained. And he wanted the rest of it.

"Edward must have told Hiroaki everything he knew before he died," Louis concluded as the Madame gave Louis back the letter.

"Tell me about the chink. In layman's terms."

"In layman's terms, he basically taught Edward how to be both a monk and an assassin."

The Madame laughed sarcastically. "An assassin?"

"Have you ever heard of a Japanese band of warriors called the Samurai?"

"Can't say I have, Louis. I've never met a chink that spoke English."

"They are the highest class of people in that country. Not soldiers...warriors that live a life of duty and honor. And Hiroaki was one of them."

The Madame picked up her glass and took a drink. "Edward was skilled, this I knew, but I had no idea it was...well...that..."

Louis enlightened her: "At the start, Edward took to the practice because it helped ease the pain. I think Edward's actual talent for killing others slept deep down within him unless absolutely necessary, though I do know when he and Thomas went to Rome a few years back, it was the first time Edward killed anyone in over a decade, and he killed about a dozen men—"

"A fucking dozen?!"

"Yes," Louis elucidated, trying not to grin, a little pride blossoming in his chest for his lost friend. "There have been a few other occasions, but from what he told me, being a Samurai for him was about the meditation to try and find a path in the darkness of his life, not about taking lives."

"That was why he wanted to help Esther," she deliberated. "He really did know what he was doing."

"In Edward's prime, he was, in all probability, better than Will or I ever were on our best day."

The Madame went over to the fire and crossed her arms, her back now to Louis. "So what do we do now?"

"With Thomas?"

"Yes. He wants to know the truth, right?"

"That's what he says, Madame."

She peeked over her shoulder to Louis. "Do you think he can fucking handle it?"

Louis was astonished. "Are you saying you want to tell Thomas? Now? With all this shit going on?"

The Madame shrugged. "What is the worst that could happen, Louis? Think about this from my standpoint, for one fucking second. We are bound to the one person we've sworn to destroy. What's going to happen when that friendship with Tammany and Croker inevitably sizzles down the road? We have got to be ready to strike those bastards first, or we're gone."

"We're going to need more than just us," he read her mind. "We've been scouting to build the army."

"We wanted this," she pronounced, "We wanted this from the beginning. It's time to think offensively, not defensively."

Louis got up and paced over to her. "Tell me what's going on in there," he said, pointing to her forehead.

"I want you to tell Thomas everything. All of it from start to finish."

"Why?"

"You told me once you could turn Will, if the time came. We have nothing but time to make those moves slowly…gradually if we need to. If we can save Esther…if Thomas finally appreciates that there has been one fucking man behind both his parent's murders, the same man who has brought us nothing but shit and misery…do you really think he's going to stay in England and pretend the first twenty-seven years of his life never fucking happened?"

"Madame, it took years for Hiroaki to train Edward…"

"Well, my darling Louis, you'd better not waste any time in writing him."

His gaze drew to the fire. "What about Esther? What do I tell him about her?"

"You tell him she's to die as scheduled, to protect everyone involved in her escape. And you tell him it was Croker's call."

"And what if Esther's death puts out that fire of revenge?"

The Madame snorted and spun around, heading to her desk. "I think you and I both know Thomas better than that. Write the letter and send it tonight. And Louis?"

"Yes, Madame?"

"Take Bernhardt to see Esther."

"When?"

"The last day, just before the switch."

He threw back the last of his drink and set the empty glass on the mantle. "Then you'll do me one favor."

"I'm listening," she called, putting her spectacles back on.

Louis looked her dead in the eyes. "You get the Hiltmores in on this."

At once, the spectacles came back off. "And why in the hell would I want to do that?"

"You'll do it, or I won't write Thomas. Esther is strong, but she won't have you anymore when she's working for Croker. She needs someone other than me and Will to trust, and Celeste is the only one."

"How in the hell do you expect me to pull that one off?" she retorted, the frustration leaking out in her tone.

"Think of something and make it happen," he insisted, moving toward the doors. "Just don't fuck him and ruin what we have with Ellis."

Louis shut the doors as he left, astounded yet humored at the shouts of profanity chasing him out of the Madame's office.

For the second time that night, the point had been made.

"If you're lying to me, Will, I can promise you the consequences will be pretty fucking bad."

Will laughed off Croker. It had taken him almost two hours after Louis' departure to convince him to save the poor girl in the Tombs, but luckily his slow progressing southern charm set in, and at last he'd secured Louis request.

Louis was Will's entire world. Their past, as far as he was concerned, was in the past, and he'd been granted a second chance to do things right this time – a chance most men like him don't ever get. He would do anything in his power for Louis, including putting his own ass on the line with the one man in New York City he shouldn't be double-crossing. In his years on the run, Will had made a lot of mistakes...too many mistakes. With Louis, those mistakes faded to black, and as if no time had passed they had begun again down their same treacherous path, each day growing closer to death but doing it together, and that was all he cared about. The one promise Will made to himself when he took the job with Croker was that he would find Louis and make amends. He'd had no idea that would lead to a total reconciliation in doing what they did best, and as that moment came and went, a new vow formed and branded to his soul. Wherever Louis went, Will would follow him, even if that meant to his rancorous end.

"I can promise ya, sir, this girl is like a daughter to him," Will went on. "Man helped raise her, for God's sake, keepin' her safe from them assholes on Fifth and from the Madame. I've known Louis most of my life and I ain' never seen him as fucked up as when the girl got locked up. You save her, and he will be yours until his judgment day. No question 'bout it."

Croker's eyes narrowed. "I'll do the swap. There's going to be certain...parameters for her to follow."

"Parameters, sir?" Will didn't know why, but he had an inclination as to where Croker was going with it.

"You, Louis, and Walsh are the best I have," Croker confessed to him. "Walsh is…his own animal, to say the very fucking least. Not one of you is getting any younger. I need new people, young people, better than what we have now. It's the only way we're going to survive politically. I need muscle, in every sense, and I need someone that can get me what I need or do what I need done without making a fuss or bringing any attention to…herself."

"Herself, eh?"

"Yes. Esther could be that missing piece for me and for the Hall."

"Right. So from what I can gather, you are wantin' me and Louis to teach the girl, then, that's what your sayin'?"

Croker held up his glass to cheers Will's. "That's why I need the best."

Will smirked. "From what Louis has been tellin' me, the girl is already a natural. Hell, she lost both of us that night, and neither Louis nor myself have ever lost a target we couldn' recover. Not once, Boss. Not to mention…a female…no one would ever suspect her… tiny and fast…it's ideal. Pretty damn brilliant."

"Exactly," Croker concurred. "Walsh is too busy with the Whyos downtown anyhow, and they're hard enough to keep a fucking eye on. I need you two to make her better than you are yourselves. I don't care what it takes."

"Well, sir, you can count me on board. The bigger issue is, what's gonna happen if the girl says no?"

"She won't."

"Really?"

Croker's countenance was no longer lighthearted. "There is no option for her, Will. This is it. She does this and lives, or I will let her hang and kill the other girl in front of her first. So sure, she can say no, and then suffer the repercussions of declining another chance at life. There is no third path. It's one way to live or they die, and that's the only fucking way you win. You've got to scare people, because without fear, there will never be respect. And without respect, no rule."

"Couldn' agree with you more, Richie," Will added, trying to appear relaxed. It was easy to see the reasoning behind Louis' fear of Croker finding out about their relationship – the man was all about the angles, and how to use everyone to his advantage.

"Best of all," Croker carried. "Is that this one…this one will be mine. The Madame will be out, and at long last, I will have the upper hand on her." A grin came to his face, and his eyes drifted off in the distance. "At last I'll really own her."

Will filled their glasses with another round, Croker's final statement burning a hole in his mind as he changed the subject to tomorrow's tasks.

Louis' calculations had been spot on.

Eventually, a line would be drawn between these power houses, and apart from her resources and unique collaboration of skill sets, there was no doubt in Will's mind the Madame's side was the losing side. Nonetheless, Will already made up his mind, and if Louis was standing beside the Madame, that's where he'd be. Unless she found a way to obtain more muscle…more people with more power…there was no way they could take down Tammany Hall. The only thing Will could hope for was that somehow in a last act of righteousness, the sins of the infinite dishonorable things he'd done in his life might be forgiven. Or that maybe then, with all his heart, Louis would forgive Will for the wrongs he'd never made right.

Then Will would be ready to die.

XXVII.

Curled up in the corner of her cell, Esther dozed in and out of dream-like hallucinations, fooling her into imagining she could hear the guards' footsteps coming to take her to her death. Her mind had been playing tricks on her all night in the darkness, perhaps it was because it was her last night alive on earth, and with no religion plaguing her heart, there was nothing she could do but wait for the end to come. When dawn broke, the tortures of her mind would become a reality, and it would be time to take her upstairs to the courtyard for the execution. She'd spent weeks attempting to mentally prepare herself for that moment, to be strong in her acceptance of her fate; yet as it drew closer, Esther realized that acknowledgement was a total misconception. She was terrified, shaking like a small child and crying in fits, holding herself tight and finding no comfort other than the fact that she'd saved her only friend. Nothing could have ever prepared her to die, no matter how justified she originally believed her cause might have been.

Somehow, Jonathan figured out a way to visit her earlier in the evening, and all it had done was electrify her nerves to such a despairing degree, Esther thought as she watched him leave she would certainly go mad. When he first arrived at her cell, Captain Bern-

779

hardt could only stand there and stare at her, unable to trust what his eyes were seeing. Esther appreciated how horrible she must look after a month in that cell and only twice to bathe, her body swimming in her dress and hair knotted up into a poorly woven braid. After a few minutes, the Captain broke down entirely, and spent the remainder of his visit incapable of letting her go, telling her how much he loved her and vowing he would love her until the day he died. He kissed her lips, her forehead, her hands, swearing to God he would never forgive Him for it, and it made Esther cry even harder and kiss him back. She didn't know if it was that she truly loved Jonathan, or the thought that tomorrow it wouldn't matter anyway, but for the duration of his brief visit, it was the most peace Esther experienced since the day she'd been tossed into that cell.

In spite of Jonathan's visit, and as much as she tried to ignore the sting, a small piece of her wished the one to come and say goodbye to her in such a way had been Thomas. Once she was alone again, Esther sobbed uncontrollably, hating herself with a fury for not understanding her own heart, and that maybe it was a blessing she wouldn't be around to ruin anyone else's happiness. Maybe her death would make her friend's lives a little easier...maybe things would really be better this way...

She felt a chill rush over her shoulders and Ester shivered from her neck to her toes, sniffing back what she hoped were the last of her tears. Her arms gripped her knees tighter, and she closed her eyes to say a prayer to no one in particular, wondering if there was anyone to hear it.

Suddenly, out of the night, she heard the strike of a match against the stone wall, and saw a glint of light from outside the bars. Esther rotated around and saw, to her bewilderment, the Madame sitting on the ground outside her cell, her legs outstretched parallel to the cage and leaning back against the stone frame. She didn't bother to glance Esther's direction, and instead took a long drag from the cigar in her hand and exhaled a large cloud of smoke.

"Hello, darling."

Esther began to second-guess herself, surmising as to whether or not this was another dream. Her eyes searched for any sign of Louis or George, and when neither came into view, Esther was even more convinced the Madame's presence was a fantasy of her own making.

"How are you here?" she asked, "You haven't…this is the first I've…" She frantically crawled over to her, grabbing the bars and gaping at the Madame, "Are we alone?"

"Louis doesn't even know I'm here," she conceded quietly, "Come closer. I'd rather not be shouting to the whole fucking wing of inmates."

Esther inched a little further so they were sitting side by side, only the wall of bars between them. "You…you haven't been to see me. Not once, Madame." She could feel hot tears on her face, hurt at being abandoned when Esther needed her most. "Why haven't you come?"

Between the bars, the Madame held a small cup, which she then filled with whiskey from a flask in her jacket. "Drink."

Esther grabbed up the cup and complied, and then immediately was handed a cigarette along with a box of matches.

"I didn't come because I fucking failed you," the Madame admitted, refusing to meet Esther's gaze. "I thought…well, I thought wrong. And because of that, I got you locked up in this God damned place, and I couldn't fix it. Nothing I would have said would have been a fucking consolation. It only would have made it a hell of a lot worse."

"I didn't need consolation," Esther replied. "I needed you. I needed someone to tell me it wasn't all for nothing."

"It wasn't all for nothing, darling. You've done nothing wrong."

Esther lit her cigarette, her hands shaking as she did it. "Then tell me…why do I have to die?"

The Madame was quiet and took a sip of her own drink. Then to Esther's surprise, the Madame let out a small chuckle and shook her head.

"You're not going to fucking die, Esther."

Esther glared at her. "You think playing these games with me now is a good idea? My execution is in a few hours—"

"Do I look like I'm kidding?"

Esther's whole body went cold. "What are you talking about? What in the hell is going on?"

"Shhh! For Christ's sake, keep your damn voice down!" the Madame reproached her. "I mean that you are not going to hang. We've…we've found a way. But darling it's…it's not going to be an easy road. For any of us, and especially not for you."

Her heart pulsed rapidly. "I'm…I'm not going to…not going to hang?" Struggling to comprehend it, Esther could feel herself hyperventilating, and the Madame subdued her by putting her hand through the bars and onto Esther's wrist.

"There are going to be costs, Esther. Costs you will have to pay on your own for this."

"But I thought…they said there was no way I'd be exonerated. They said someone was going to have to die for this…"

The Madame released her wrist, visibly exasperated. "Someone is going to die for you, Esther. In your place. Someone who has volunteered because she herself no longer wants to live."

"Someone is going to die…in my place? Who would…" Esther put the puzzle together and was horrorstruck. "No…no please…"

"The deal has already been made, darling."

"I don't want her to die for me…I don't want her to die at all!"

"Do you want to live?"

Esther's breathing became erratic again. "I…well yes, I…I want to live, but I don't want Danny to die!"

"Danny is going to die one way or another," the Madame stated harshly. "She's been on the brink of killing herself and I've been waiting to find her dead in her rooms every God damned morning. She wanted to fucking do this…even presented the plan on her own without anyone's suggestion, and if you want to live, you will go along with it, or both of you will end up six feet under, and that's nothing more than a shitty waste."

"Madame…I…I can't…"

She extended the flask through the cage again and poured more whiskey into Esther's cup. "This is the way it is. And it's not even remotely the worst of it, darling."

Esther couldn't form a full sentence. "…worst…worst of it?"

The Madame let out a big cloud of smoke. "Esther, I am going to tell you a story. A horrible fucking story you will not like in the slightest, but I am doing it because…well because I love you, and because when all of this is fucking over, I want you to be alive. Do you need a moment or can I go on?"

Esther squeaked out something incomprehensible, suspecting the Madame would go on without her permission anyway. She was so overcome with emotion she could barely keep from screaming out with confusion, overrun with hate, pain, sadness, and regardless of her shame, elation.

"In a few hours' time, you will be visited by Louis, a man named Will Sweeney, Danny, and a politician…Richard Croker. Now, first and foremost, you are under no fucking circumstances to ever trust him…he is a bastard, and will do anything to gain more power even if it means killing you off. Second…for the time being, you are never permitted to tell anyone but Louis that I know you are alive."

The Madame took another drag, and Esther cut in. "I don't understand what it is you're telling me…"

She had a sip of whiskey from the flask. "The deal made for your life is thus: you will do whatever Croker tells you for the time being, as in theory, you will owe your hide to him. He is under the impression I have no idea what will go on, and I will be straightforward with you, darling, I don't know what he has planned for you, but I have a feeling it will run along the same lines with what you did for me and for The Palace, yet in a much more…aggressive manner. What I want you to know is that this man…this man has been the cause of every fucking terrible thing that has happened to us, in one way or another, and you're going to have to pretend for all our sakes, he is your entire world."

Any reprieve Esther felt during the few minutes of hearing her death was postponed vanished. Her stomach twisted into knots, aggravated at being informed she was lucky enough to live and then only to be told her existence would be at the mercy of a man she should hate.

Esther swallowed back the forming tears. "What has he done to us?" she mumbled as she dumped whiskey down her throat.

"Excuse me, darling?"

"You say I should hate him. What has he done to us?"

She expected the Madame to tell her off for her manners, but for once, the reprimand didn't come. The Madame looked at her, her face without a touch of make up and imploring in a way that made Esther's antagonism fade.

"He is the man behind killing both of Thomas' parents for wanting to expose the truth behind his organization. He's the one who has ordered a few of my own girls killed to keep me in line and threatened me with destruction. He is the man who has slowly taken over this city through lying, extortion, murder, and stealing from anyone he can take from, all under the name Tammany, which is nothing more than a fucking disguise for criminality. He is the one who knew not only about Timothy Adams and continued to treat him as a colleague, but also the man who made sure to bury your police report. He has made my life hell on earth, and I expect he will do the fucking same to you, and there is not much we can do about it darling. At this moment, we are both working for him, and we are both at his clemency."

Esther was speechless, gawking at the Madame as the alcohol hit her stomach, the burning of it easing her overrun psyche.

"Darling, we don't have much time, all right? I need you to listen to me. Look at me, Esther." The Madame grasped her hand through the bars, locking eyes with her. "The reason I am telling you this is

784

now is because I want you to know you're not alone. We all have to fight to survive right now. It's the only fucking way. But there will come a time…a few months maybe, most likely in a few years, when we will finally be able to strike back. I need you to remember who you are… and not to ever forget it. He will try to win you over, darling, and he might for a while. But that anger that's sitting in your chest, that anger is reserved for him and him alone, do you understand me? The time will come, and when it does, we will put a fucking end to this."

"Does Thomas know?"

The Madame nodded. "He will. Within days."

Another epiphany struck, one that was hard for Esther to bear. "Madame…I'm going to have to kill people…aren't I?"

"In all likelihood, yes."

"And what if I choose to die instead?"

"I had a feeling you might say that." The Madame let her go and filled her whiskey cup one last time, rising to her feet. "I wouldn't blame you, darling. The choice is yours. You can die at dawn, or you can begin the life I think you were really meant for."

Esther was overcome with anger. "Murdering and spying on innocent people?! That's what I was meant for? Being another hit like Louis? For some politician who has…has fucking ruined the lives of everyone I love, including me?!"

"Innocent isn't exactly a word I would use to describe Croker's associates, darling. You can either die, or join the war. You decide. But your real family needs you."

"The only family I've ever had is across a fucking ocean," she spat. "And he won't have me. What reason do I have to live?"

Though she could barely make her out in the dark, Esther swore she saw the Madame smile. "And what makes you think I wasn't referring to Thomas, too, darling? You think once he realizes there is one man behind this he will sit it out?"

A sudden rustle of movement down the hallway startled them both, and the Madame clearly didn't care to stay and see who it was.

"They'll be here within the hour. Think about all I've said, and that I would prefer it if you didn't fucking die. I need you, darling. We all need you now more than ever."

Esther spent the next hour and a half lost in a fit of desolation, unable to wrap her head around the Madame's visit...if it happened to even be real in the first place...and whether or not she wanted to live or die. For years Esther had worked for the Madame, infiltrating the lives of the wealthy and contributing to the Madame's Vault, though her work was only through whispers, gossip, and listening in on conversations through the thin doors of the maid's passage. The plan all along had been for her to move up the ranks and be more involved within The Palace's enterprise until Esther's engagement to Thomas halted that progression, and with its disintegration there were no questions as to what she would do next. Without Thomas, Esther only had the Madame, Louis, and Celeste – her loyalties were to them and them alone.

Then she shot Timothy, and changed her future in a matter of seconds.

According to the Madame's story, Croker had his hand in just about every misfortune surrounding Esther in the previous year, a man she didn't know and who didn't know her either. Whether or not she believed it, she couldn't be sure, and as the shadows moved across the floor and the cell around her began to lighten, the moment was closing in where Esther had to make a decision. Death meant an escape from this hell once and for all, a way to leave it all behind her and not have to undergo the burden she would suffer for years to come. Life meant a debt, living each day to pursue the will of another with the false hope that someday he might release her. A man who, unlike her, had no loyalties, and would break down any walls in his way to get what he wanted...he killed the people she loved and buried her secrets…was the Madame right in that this man was the only one to blame? As she reflected on it, the Madame's testimony was clearer and clearer: this is the man who killed Mary… who took Thomas from her in the beginning. This is the man who tossed out a police statement to keep Timothy Adams' reputation in tact…and because of that Celeste lost the only light she had in this world. This is the man who murdered Edward and once again took Thomas from her. This was the man that caused her to shoot Timothy Adams and hang for it…who put her in that cell…who destroyed her life, one shred of it at a time…

From nowhere, Esther felt the misplaced rage in her chest the Madame spoke of…the hatred…the ferocity…and the fear, compiling just as it did the night she put the bullets in Timothy's chest. There was no way she would choose to die. She was the chameleon, the hidden weapon, and she would blend in and hide until the time came to strike back. Years had already passed where she'd done the same, hiding in the shadows, waiting. She would join the war, and hope that maybe someday, Thomas would too.

For Esther, that alone was worth living for.

She heard them coming. Not one of them spoke, yet after spending weeks in the pit of blackness, Esther could recognize the sound and tremor of the distant footsteps from those who came to see her. It was Louis and Danny, accompanied by two others, two she had never heard before and assumed that like the Madame predicted, one set belonged to Croker, and the other to the infamous Cat she'd only heard tall tales about.

There was less than a minute for Esther to fall back into character…a character she would have to pretend to be for quite some time. She couldn't let on she was remotely aware of what was about to occur, and that as dawn came she would be executed at the end of the rope. Scrambling, Esther retreated to her corner and wrapped her legs into her chest again, forcing tears to fall from her eyes and mumbling softly to herself a Hail Mary she learned as a child. This

was it. This was the beginning. She would have to be Croker's pet…
she would have to win him over, to make herself irreplaceable…and
as the Madame instructed, she would have to pretend he was the
only thing in the world that mattered to her.

They paused outside her cell and looked in, though Esther refused to budge, wanting to appear reluctant to see her execution-
ers. Hushed voices, and a few harsh whispers sent three sets of footsteps away from her cell, while a fourth jingled keys and unlocked
the door before heading straight to her.

Croker crouched down and put his hand on her wrist, rotating
Esther to look him in the eyes. It was then Esther recognized she'd
met this man before, outside the Hiltmores' mansion the night of
their final party, and had yet to make the connection that this man
who kindly asked her for a light was the same as the one who had
been wreaking havoc on those she cared about. They stared at each
other for what felt like hours, as if he were scrutinizing her down
to her soul, and with his own clean hands, Croker wiped the tears
from her damp cheeks.

"You have quite a few people wanting to save your life, my dear,"
he informed her, his tone warm and friendly.

Her bottom lip trembled. "S-S-Save me? What do you mean?"

"Save you from the noose, of course, and if I am being honest, I will say that I'm actually beginning to believe your value to us
could outweigh the damage you've done to society."

"I don't…I don't understand…"

He smirked. "Do you remember me? When we met months ago?"

Esther sniffed and nodded. "Yes sir. At the Hiltmores'."

"That's correct," he acquiesced. "Louis is here. Danny is here.
And another…friend of mine as well. But before we start, I wanted to have a little chat to explain the gravity of what is currently
about to happen. To you, and those of us involved in this little…
rescue mission."

"Rescue mission?" she choked. "But sir, I'm going to hang at dawn." Esther endeavored not to come across too despairing, but from Croker's expression it was just enough.

"No, you're not. Danny will take your place."

"D-D-Danny?"

"Yes, you know her quite well, I'm told."

"I can't…no…why…why would she…?"

Unlike the Madame's attempt to console her, Croker made it clear did not want to waste time. Firmly, he took Esther's chin in his grip and held her head steady, as if to snap her out of a fit.

"No blubbering. This is the way it is. She will take your place, and you will live on the condition that you will now work for me and the Hall, under the supervision of Louis and my other associate. Everyone excluding the four people leaving this cell will believe you to be dead, and any effort to see that otherwise will end with you at the bottom of the Hudson River. Any attempt to breach our contract, run away from your obligations and leave New York will also not only end in your death but also the death of everyone here you love. Louis, the Madame, Celeste…even Captain Jonathan Bernhardt. Do you understand what I'm saying?"

"But—"

His hand tightened. "But nothing. You are not to ever be seen in the uptown Fifth Avenue district or amongst high society ever again. You will not exist in their world, you will only exist amongst us, and it will stay that way. When Tammany is in total control, and when you have proven your worth and effectively helped me take over the city, you're to be gone from New York and never come back. You will be compensated…beyond your wildest dreams…and what you do after your service to me is entirely up to you. I look at this as a simple business transaction, Esther. I save your life, you pay me what is owed, and we call it even. Do you accept my terms?"

Esther did her best to scatter her breath and appear completely shocked. "I…I…"

"Yes or no. Right now. But do understand if you say no and

choose to die, I'll simply kill Danny and leave her body in your cell to rot with you until you hang. I have no qualms if you would rather die. This deal will not make or break me, but it will make or break you. Louis wants you alive, and he has become an invaluable asset to my organization, so I will do what I can to see it through. So, Esther, what will it be? Yes or no?"

She paused one moment longer – it was the only way to make it more real for him.

"Oh!" he exclaimed suddenly, "I almost forgot the most important part. Perhaps this will be the one thing to convince you to join us." As he let go of her chin, Croker stood up and reached into his jacket pocket, pulling out a letter. "Ah, to be young and in love. I do wonder what Lord Turner might think about your bubbling relationship with the handsome Captain…"

Esther's heart stopped. "What are you talking about?" she retorted defensively, all feigned sadness evaporating from her face.

Her manner caused Croker to grin viciously. "I was wondering when the real side of you would come out…the one Louis told me was sitting in there dormant, buried underneath the years of 'proper' upbringing. You know Thomas sent multiple wires almost every day since I assume he found out about your sentence. After awhile, the justice department had to send him a formal warning that his requests would not be heeded and to…well for lack of a better word… to fuck off. This came yesterday, I think he was hoping to reach you before it was too late."

Esther used the wall to prop herself up and stand. "Give it to me," she commanded, her hand reaching out.

Croker advanced right into her face holding the telegram in the air, making Esther withdraw. "So…this changes the tide, doesn't it? You were perfectly ready to let the others suffer on in misery, and one measly letter turns you from a sick cub to a hungry lioness." He straightened up again and exaggeratingly cleared his throat, reading from the paper:

"'Es…I wrote to you the moment I found out about what happened. I promise I will do anything I can to delay your execution and have your case sent to appeals. I don't know if I can reach you in time, and in case the worst happens, I want you to know I love you and this is all my fault.'" Croker peeked at her from over the top of the page, amused. "How touching…he goes on: 'I never should have left you there or let things get so out of hand. I hope you can find it in your heart to forgive me and know if I could do it again, I would have never let you doubt how much I loved you and wanted to spend my life with you.'" Esther clutched at her chest as she listened, her whole body aching. "No one…no one told me he'd sent wires…"

Croker tucked the letter away. "If you come work for me, you just may be able to see him again. If you love him, is that not incentive enough?"

Esther wanted more than anything to claw Croker's eyes out, fighting to keep her cool. The Madame said a time would come… but what if it didn't? What if she was the only hope they had to be rid of this bastard? What if…she could be the one to save them?

"I want to know that when I'm done I'm free. And not just me. All of us."

Croker was mystified. "All of you?"

"The Madame, Louis, and me. And I want to be guaranteed that once Tammany runs the city, I go my own way. No bullshit, infinite contract."

"Smart girl. You want a timeline."

"I want a number."

Croker crossed his arms, clearly enjoying their bartering. "You're afraid I'll bully you into staying."

Esther's vision spotted and she put a hand against the wall again – she hadn't stood for this long in weeks. "I know what you've done to the Madame. Unlike her, I like having an end in sight."

After a few seconds of silence, Croker unexpectedly let out a slight chortle. "God I like you already. You're nineteen, is that right?"

"Yes."

"Twenty-seven. Eight years of your life is what I want. Is that acceptable to you?"

Esther spit into her hand and held it out to shake. Croker did the same, however he stopped when their palms were only inches apart.

"Do not forget what I told you. No one but the four of us will know you're alive. That includes Thomas, Celeste, the Madame… you have eight years before you can see any of them. And your re-union will not be happening in my city."

She lurched her hand forward to grasp his. "I heard you the first time, Mr. Croker."

Firmly, they shook on it and let go. He was still grinning: "This is in your blood, you know. Swinging the votes."

"In my blood?"

"Yes. In your blood." His hands went into his pockets, and he rested against the wall beside her. "You see, Esther, we are connect-ed to a degree that is…somewhat startling, in ways that make me look forward to the work we can do together. We will make an im-peccable team, you and I. Me being the leader of the Hall at its strongest standpoint ever, and you being the bastard daughter of it's true founder. It's like…like a song, really. Somehow in the end everything ties together! But let's not do this now, we've got to get you out of here first."

Croker paced over to the cell door and whistled for the others. Louis, Will, and Danny came forward, and Will ushered Danny in-side, where she went straight to Esther and hugged her close.

"This is the way," she whispered into Esther's ear. "I know it's confusing. But I love you, Es. Let me do this and feel like I've done one good thing with my life."

Esther was very aware that their moment was being observed, but she didn't care. "Danny…Danny I'm so sorry…Hope should still be here…"

Danny let her go and kissed her forehead. "I will see her soon,

and we'll watch over you. When you feel alone, we will be right here."
She tapped on Esther's chest, pointing at her heart. "I swear to you."

"Time for the swap," Croker ordered. "Clothes for clothes. Danny, we've been over the details of your role in this. You know what needs to be done to conceal any suspicions."

She nodded as the men turned around and she stripped down, Esther following suit, feeling more and more like she was in some sort of crazy nightmare. In those last few minutes, Esther couldn't help but soak in Danny, each movement she made, the lines of her face, the contented expression she wore…Danny was far more at peace with her choice than Esther could have expected. In the years to come, the only solace Esther would find from that recollection was in Danny's confidence, with Danny knowing full and well what she was doing with every fiber of her being and wanting to do it. They handed garments back and forth until their exchange was complete, and Esther looked into Danny's eyes one last time. This was not just a goodbye to her friend, it was goodbye to everything she'd ever known.

Louis came over and embraced Danny, saying something to her no one else could hear. At the cell door, Croker and Will loitered, giving Louis his time. When it was done, Louis spun toward Esther and gestured toward the others, where she joined the three men who would own her for the next eight years of her life.

No more words were spoken. With one last glimpse at Danny in her old cage, Esther walked on, believing if she stayed much longer she would change her mind. Croker locked Danny inside and they each exchanged a respective nod before he led Esther, Louis, and Will out of the Tombs, dropping the keys onto an unconscious guard when they reached the staircase. Minutes later, Esther stepped out into the chilled morning air, the sun beginning to peek over the skyline.

It was the first time she'd been outside since the trial began, and as Esther breathed in the space around her, no longer bound by those three horrible stone walls and iron bars, she felt more liberated than any other time she could remember. The muscles in her legs moved freely into the great expanse ahead of her, the warmth of the sunshine tickling her skin. Esther was overcome with the thrill of freedom. To her, anything at this point was infinitely better than the confines of the Tombs, albeit if it meant giving eight of the best years of her life to Tammany Hall.

Croker led them two blocks away where a carriage sat, the driver obviously expecting the four of them. After tipping his hat to the driver, Croker climbed inside first, second was Louis, followed by her and then Will, who closed all the flaps of the car to give them absolute privacy. The spark of a match lit the dark confines of the seats as Louis lit a cigarette and handed it to Esther, then lit one for himself.

"Well isn't that touching," Croker remarked, taking the helm of their discussion. "All right, so it's finished. Our deal now stands firm. You two will start training Esther tomorrow at first light. You know what is to be done." He proceeded to reach into his jacket again and handed Esther Thomas' letter, followed by a flask of whiskey. "Have a drink. What you just did was by no means easy, and demonstrates courage far beyond your years."

Esther snatched the letter and tucked it into her vest. When it was safely put away, she removed the cap from the flask and took a long drink, happy to feel the burn of the whiskey hitting her stomach for the second time that day. She could use as much liquor as possible to help her relax and try to stay calm.

"I'll take her to the execution," Louis notified the party. "Will can meet us after it's done and we will get her set up in an apartment near Germantown. No one would recognize her there."

"No one will recognize her period after today. One reason being that the public never learned about that giant scar on her neck."

Esther was puzzled, taking another drag of her cigarette and sip from the flask. "And what is the other reason?"

Will and Louis exchanged glances. "Darlin', we're gonna have to cut all your hair off," Will informed her. "It's…well, it's better for fightin', and it'll make you look more like a young boy than a cute little girl lost in a bad neighborhood. Ya know what I'm sayin'?"

It was as if someone hit her hard across her face. "My…my hair?" Esther's hand holding her cigarette trembled, and Louis averted his eyes.

"I'm sorry, Esther," he pronounced. "It's…not negotiable."

"This is how it's done," Croker declared. "Now, I have business to attend to, and you have work to get done. I'll see you at lunchtime tomorrow." With a hard push from Croker, the carriage door flew open, signifying their meeting was at an end, and the moment the three of them were out, Croker's driver left them in the dust. Will took off his coat and wrapped it around Esther, and they trudged unhurriedly in the direction of the Tombs.

"Ya want a little somethin' to eat?" he beseeched her, clearly bothered by her thin frame.

She shook her head. "Not until…not until after, Mr. Sweeney. I don't want anything on my stomach. I'm afraid it won't stay."

"Will. Call me Will."

Strolling on for a time wordlessly, Esther could feel the nervousness between them, not one sure of what to say to make the situation any better and staying quiet in an effort to not make it worse. Outside the jail, a crowd was already drawing in, one much larger than Esther thought would come to see her die. People filtered in from every direction, heading toward the courtyard to observe the hanging, which was now considered to be more entertainment than a scare tactic.

"Louis, you make sure y'all stay in the back," Will reminded him. "Keep Esther hidden the best ya can. If it gets…nasty…just make a run for it and I'll come and find ya. I sure hope it ain't too bad."

"It won't be." Louis gaze flickered to Esther then back to the crowd.

Will nodded. "I'll meet ya at the spot after. And I'll get us somethin' to eat. Barbershop run by that ol' jew bastard, right?"

"Yeah apartment above it," Louis confirmed, speaking as if Esther weren't right beside him. "It'll be good for her to feel like she's... well...at home again."

Esther no longer was paying attention to him or to Will – she cringed as she took in the scene in front of her, shivering from cold and the onset of grief for Danny. There was no reversing it now. Another few seconds passed before Will departed, and she watched him go, her eyes then going to Louis. These two men would be her family...her mentors...her everything...for the next eight years of her life...them and no one else. She had so many questions to ask Louis, wanting to know more about her role, about what the Madame needed her to do, and the most important, if Will was on their side. For the rest of the morning, however, Esther remained in mourning for Danny and for the loss of the others she would leave behind. In a strange way, this too was her end.

The Madame was right...she always was.

She promised Esther they would take Croker down, and while the want of vengeance gripped hard on Esther's heart, the second she was outside the walls of the Tombs, she felt that desire was secondary to another more intrinsic intuition. She truly did want to stay alive. Not only for herself...but more than anything else, to see Thomas again. If the Madame held true to her word and Thomas did discover the facts behind Richard Croker and his parent's deaths, there was no speculation in her mind he would return and join them. Yet if they failed...if they failed, Esther swore she would serve her eight years and find Thomas, regardless of where he might be.

And maybe, just maybe, she'd be lucky enough to slit Richard Croker's throat before she left New York for the injustices he'd permitted, though she had a feeling the Madame would find a way to beat her to it.

"Es, we don't have to see this," Louis said, breaking her thought process. "It might be better to just move on. I really only mentioned the execution for Croker...I wanted him to see how tough you are."

They stood across the street, gazing at the great stone pillars and the staircase that lead to the courtyard. The mob funneling inside was abnormally hushed for a hanging with this much publicity, giving it a much more eerie sensation than normal.

"I need to see it, Louis. I want to be there for her."

Exhaling a cloud of steam reluctantly, Louis took out a scarf and handed it to Esther. "Wrap it around your head. In case someone might recognize you."

Esther did as she was instructed. "Louis…I'm…I'm…"

"I know, Esther. Have faith in me. I'll keep you safe."

She took his hand. "I'm ready."

They strode across the street together, Louis putting his arm across her shoulders, and the pair oddly blended into the crowd despite Louis' size. The stage was directly in the center, the audience circling around, and Louis led Esther to the far right where they could see well enough without being too close.

"It'll be a long drop," he enlightened her, pointing at the long wooden beams. "Should be quick. Painless. Over in half a second."

Esther didn't respond as her eyes absorbed it. Instantly she was nauseated from the whiskey, the heartache of losing her friend, and claustrophobia of the immense crowd, her body both cold and sweating at the same time. There must have been three hundred people present, no one speaking to one another above a soft tone – everyone waited tolerantly, as if they, too, were averse to being there. Esther took deep breaths, her anxiety consuming her like poison flowing through her veins. If not for Louis holding her tight, she would have sunk to the ground, finding it hard to keep herself standing. A few minutes passed and a hushed whisper spread through the crowd: a man was seen ascending the staircase, clad head to toe in black and accompanied by a man of the court. They stopped at the top of the platform, and the courtyard went silent, wanting to hear whatever was to be said next.

"Ladies and gentlemen!" the executioner shouted. "It is with great sorrow we are here today to witness the rightful and just execution of a young woman, accused of murder in the first degree, whose heinous and brutal crime was both premeditated and in cold blood. Judge and jury have ruled her guilty of these crimes with the overwhelming amount of evidence for conviction, and we pray to God that he might have mercy on her soul!"

Esther's eyes fluttered closed, pausing to hear the typical jeers and catcalls of the audience, and was surprised when nothing came. Another rush of whispers, and Esther opened her eyelids, searching to see what was causing the crowd's reaction. Two guards lead Danny toward the stage, her head downcast, and in her wake trudged the priest reading her final rights. Across the blurred masses, Esther spotted Celeste on the opposite side, sobbing uncontrollably and being held at bay by Jonathan, who was by no means in any better condition, and it made her throat choke as she tried to gulp down her own tears. Near the stage stood Croker with a few of his constituents, a few of which seemed familiar to her, and not ten people to his right was the Madame, looking far more solemn than Esther had ever seen her. Though she didn't spot them, Esther knew the Adamses were present, and she pondered if they had any idea of the monsters Timothy and his father had been – if they had, she hoped they burned in hell along with them.

Nothing could have prepared her for seeing Danny marching toward the noose…for feeling as if it should have been her. Esther fought with Louis' grip, trying to break free in sudden panic, wanting to save her.

Louis' arm around her shoulder was like steel. "No, Esther. You can't," he articulated softly. "It's too late."

"Louis…it shouldn't be her…I did this to her…I can't…I won't…"

"Shhh," he muttered. "She wanted this. She chose this. Even if you decided to go through with it, you would both would be dead." Esther persisted to try and fight it until abruptly Louis held her at arms length by her shoulders, intently gazing into her eyes. "Nothing can be done. You have to endure like the rest of us. I cannot lose you now...we need each other...and I...I need you."

Esther huffed in air, finding it hard to contain her sobs and Louis pulled her in yet again, this time his embrace for reassurance rather than restraint. Together, they watched Danny climb the stairs, and still the swarm did not react, the whole endeavor feeling almost like a funeral. There was a sense of sadness rather than nameless hatred, and it assisted in placating Esther's dread of having to witness Danny dying like a common criminal. Over the quiet, Celeste's pleading cries for mercy cut through the stale silence, so loud and heartrending it caused the women all around Esther to weep into their handkerchiefs. At last breaking down, Esther grabbed onto Louis and buried her face in his coat, feeling powerless and overwhelmingly guilty.

"Are there any last words from the accused?" the executioner called out, continuing to put on his spectacle despite the crowd's lack of enthusiasm for a bloodbath. Danny's hair was in her face, smartly done to make her appearance indistinguishable to Esther's, and her hands were shackled behind her back. Something inaudible came from her lips and the man moved closer to hear her.

"What'd she say?!" an onlooker yelled from the back.

"Yeah! What'd she say?" came another.

"She says..." the executioner stopped, his head falling forward as he bit his lip. "She says to tell Celeste she loves her!"

Celeste wailed and collapsed onto the ground, and Jonathan attempted to comfort her.

The next seconds passed quicker than Esther predicted. A dark sack was placed over Danny's head, followed by the noose, as the priest behind her said a prayer in Latin which Esther did not recognize. When the prayer concluded, the hangman stepped forward and tightened the rope with one tug then moved backwards, his hand resting on the lever. With an approving nod from the man of the court, he pushed the lever downward and the floor beneath Danny's feet gave way.

The snap of Danny's neck echoed through the courtyard as the rope jerked straight. And in an instant, it was over.

Danny was dead.

Running hard despite the weight in his arms, Hiroaki shepherded Thomas briskly through the side streets of the city, wanting to make it back to the docks before he could no longer sway Thomas' original opinion of leaving New York almost as quickly as they'd arrived. The shipping vessel would be gone within the hour, and he could easily read from Thomas' current disposition that his young counterpart wanted nothing more than to stay, but they both knew that was not a viable option. Thomas chose his path, and to unconditionally pursue that path, dawdling in a city where he was considered a political threat would only hinder their goal. Especially on this day. The man they knew as Richard Croker would anticipate some kind of retaliation from Thomas, particularly after their insistent efforts to halt the legal processes of the state.

It was Esther's execution day.

Regardless of the challenges, Hiroaki and Thomas managed to smuggle their way onto one of Turner S & D's own ships and into New York City, though their journey was by no means relaxing or pleasant during those days on the ocean. They'd made it just in time, cloaking themselves in disguise to not seem suspicious and taking off their separate ways, each with a task to accomplish in a very limited amount of time. Thomas had run the direction of downtown Manhattan, hoping to make it to Esther and see her one last time, not wanting her to feel as if he'd forsaken her and did not love her. Hiroaki, on the other hand, had prepared himself for something he had not done in many years…something he never thought he would have to do again after he saved Akemi.

He went to Blackwell, where he found and rescued Mary.

Now, with Mary unconsciously bobbling in his arms underneath his long coat and Thomas not two paces ahead of him, they raced toward the docks, trying to remain out of sight, the cold, clear winter day biting at their lungs as their chests heaved. Neither of them dared to speak, only threw one foot in front of the other, as the time to share their excursions would come later. For the time being, the only thing that mattered was getting out. And getting out unseen.

The harbor entrance came into view and their tempo increased when Connor's figure came into their line of sight. Waving vigorously, he flagged them down and took off toward the boat, his head whipping from side to side making sure they weren't being followed or no onlookers spotted them. Hiroaki was not thrilled at Thomas' suggestion of Connor's help in their trip over the Atlantic, yet the man had proven his devotion to Edward and gone above and beyond for Thomas, guarding him ardently. Without him, the trip would have been a failure, and Mary would be lost.

"What the hell took ya so long?!" Connor bellowed as they caught up to him, and his eyes grew wide the moment they set on Mary. "Holy Christ Almighty. She's actually alive!"

"Not now, Connor," Thomas interrupted him. "We need to be securely on the boat before we start this up."

"Just this way, Lord Turner. Two more vessels down. I've made sure the boys are at the pub and won't be back for at least another quarter of an hour."

"Thank you, Connor."

Hiroaki, Mary, Thomas, and Connor reached the boat and boarded, the only man in sight being a longtime employee and friend of Connor's, who kept an eye out in their absence.

"No one's been in or out!" he notified them. "Second deck is all yours. Got water waiting and everything the ch-...I mean, everything the Japper asked for." He looked at Mary, startled. "She gonna be all right?"

They pushed by him. "She's gonna be fine, boyo," Connor took over, letting the other two urgently scamper to the second deck. Hiroaki had the man find him an assortment of herbs, roots, and spices to blend one of Akemi's masterful teas in the hopes it would revive Mary, or at least make her withdrawal symptoms less immense and painful, though there certainly were no guarantees. Upon getting to her, she was heavily medicated, and he slipped her an extra something to put her into a deep sleep to make her extraction far easier on him. The responsibility cutting at him for snapping six of the guards' necks and taking down a few others vanished as he dashed through the hallways of Blackwell Asylum, the horrors of it surpassing any prison Hiroaki had ever been inside, even in Asia. The patients were filthy, crazed, starved, and drugged. When he found her, Mary was chained up in some sort of prison-like cell, her arm lacking any definitive blood flow as it hung above her head shackled against the wall. There were two others in there with her – one was already dead, the other not far from it, the three of them having sustained heavy trauma. It was a miracle he'd found her alive…another few hours, and she might not have been. Hiroaki had the atrocious notion that someone wanted Mary and her fellow prisoners to die undetected – they hadn't been tended to for days, as was apparent by their gaunt frames and the evidence and stench of human filth that resided both around them and on their clothes.

Hiroaki laid Mary down on the mattress put down for her, ordering Thomas to boil water, and then set to work arranging the concoction per Akemi's instructions.

"Hiro…what did they do to her?" Thomas entreated him, dabbing his mother's forehead with a wet cloth. "She's so…so small… her face is so pale…"

"They've been dosing her hard with opium and something else…I can't be quite sure." The brew sizzled as Hiroaki stirred it slowly. "She's not going to do well on the trip. Withdrawal will come. I will do my best to keep her as comfortable as I can."

Thomas perused the steaming cauldron. "How much longer until she wakes?"

"It could be hours, could be days…since we don't know how much they were giving her, we can't make a distinction before she drinks a bit of this. Then I'll be able to tell you more."

"All right."

Hiroaki studied him. "I expected to find you more…upset, Thomas, having just seen the woman you love suffer in such a way."

Thomas slid his hand into his mothers. "Esther didn't die, Hiro."

"So they called off the execution?"

"Not exactly."

His hand stopped stirring, shocked. "Explain it to me."

Thomas sat back against the wall of the boat, his legs stretching out beside his mother. "I went to The Tombs…got to the courtyard…stayed right in the back like you told me. No one had any clue it was me. I knew the moment I saw the girl come out of there it wasn't Esther…she was trying to hide her face, trying hard not to have anyone recognize it wasn't Esther. And then…"

"Then what, Thomas?"

A smirk came to Thomas' lips. "It's hard to miss Louis once you know him. When I saw where he was, I found her with him. She was safe, Hiro, and that's all that matters for now." He breathed out, relieved. "There was a catch."

"What was the catch?"

"I saw the Madame, and she saw me."

Another startling revelation. "What was her reaction?"

"She smiled, as if she known all along she'd see me there. God, how the fuck does she do this?"

"The same way you can. The same way you already do and have a knack for." Hiroaki pulled the spoon from the tea. "Grab me a cup, Thomas, her remedy is ready."

Thomas complied and brought the cup over for Hiroaki to fill, which he did cautiously. Bringing it to Mary, Hiroaki lowered to his knees as Thomas propped her upright, and cautiously he poured a little into her mouth. She swallowed it down, her eyes still closed despite being half awake and her head rested back.

Frustrated, Thomas ran his fingers through his hair. "She was sitting next to him, Hiro. Not directly, but close enough."

"To Richard Croker?" Hiroaki asked.

"Yes. It was until I saw him I remembered meeting him years ago. He was the fucking Fire Commissioner…and I can't help thinking…"

"Thinking what?"

"The Madame must be working with him. And if she is, Louis too. I just can't figure out how Esther fits into this!" In a pang of fury, Thomas slammed his fist onto the ground, causing Mary to stir, though thankfully not fully wake.

Hiro checked her breathing, which was miraculously steady, and then resumed their talk. "I believe Louis and the Madame will do what's necessary to stay alive, and I also wonder if the reason Esther was not executed might be in part to their teaming with Richard Croker. With their lives at stake, people will do anything to survive and save those they love, even if that means partnering with an enemy."

"Even though they know he killed my father…and did this to my mother…"

"Amongst so many other atrocities, I am sure."

Thomas shook his head. "Why would Esther ever agree to let someone else die for her? The Esther I know wouldn't dream of it."

Hiroaki could see where the exchange was going, along with the anger rising in Thomas' words.

"Because like them, she probably wasn't given a choice."

His jaw clenched. "Fuck him…fuck that son of a bitch…"

"Thomas, we should wait until England to discuss this when you have a more level head."

"I've already made my decision," Thomas spat, jumping to his feet. "If they're going to play along with this bastard…if they're going to be his puppets, then there is only one thing left for me to do."

"You are certain this is what you want?" Hiroaki pressed. "After all that has happened today? After what we've done to get your mother out of New York?"

"Yes." Thomas glimpsed down at Mary, his eyes pained. "I am going to destroy that bastard. I don't care what it takes. He did this to her…he murdered my father…it's obvious I am the only one that can and will stand up to him, and if I am the only one who will fight, I'm going to tear Richard Croker apart piece by piece." He looked directly into Hiroaki's eyes. "We start training the day after we return."

Hiroaki had one query left for Thomas to answer: "What is going to happen if the day comes, Thomas, and the Madame and Louis are on the other side? What will you do then?"

"It doesn't matter who it is anymore," Thomas retorted. "Anyone who stands between me and Richard Croker is going to die. And that's the way it's going to fucking be."

The Madame jolted awake to the sound of someone banging more than a little aggressively on her bedroom door. It was the night…or was it the morning…after Esther's, or rather Danny's execution, and the Madame had made sure to celebrate by drowning her sorrows in a few bottles of wine. Apparently, somehow she'd managed to drag herself all the way to her bedroom, passing out still fully clothed. Blinking her heavy eyes a few times, she sat up, rolling her shoulders back and taking a deep breath. If she didn't have a whiskey fast, along with some coffee, any hope of keeping her awake would not last long. Standing up, she wavered a moment in her spotty vision, then stumbled over to open her curtains, which was a giant mistake considering the sunny morning that greeted her.

"Madame! For God's sake!" Louis voice came through the door, "You need to open up right this second!"

"Fuck you I am going as fast as I can!" she shouted, her pounding head sending sharp pains down her neck, "Fucking bastards… can't leave me alone for one God damned night…"

Barely standing, the Madame went over to unlock her bedroom door and opened it, planning a verbal lashing for Louis in the meantime. However, when she saw what was waiting on the other side, the Madame had a hard dose of reality. It was not just Louis at her door: behind him stood the Cat, Richard Croker, and…lurking back in the shadows…that son of a bitch Walsh.

"What in God's name took you so long?" Croker barked at her, cigar hanging out of his mouth.

The Madame attempted to stay composed. "Louis…?"

Readily, Louis handed her a cup of coffee laced heavily with whiskey, and she gulped it down as fast as she could.

"Well now. Does someone want to tell me what the fuck is going on and why I am being woken up?"

"How can you account for being in such a state?" Croker went on. "It's nearly ten thirty!"

"Well, unlike you, Mr. Croker, yesterday I saw someone very dear to me get hung. So please excuse me for being a little upset about it. Not all of us are as iced over as you are."

He threw her a glaring look, but Will interjected. "Madame, you were here all last night, that correct?"

"I've been here since I arrived home from the execution, and from there I proceeded to close down operations and drink myself nearly to death. Anyone here can vouch for me. Why the fuck does that matter?"

Louis and Will exchanged uncertain glances. "Let's go to the office, Madame," Louis suggested. "I'll get you another coffee."

Croker let out a loud sigh. "Get me one of those too, for God's sake. I'm going to need it."

Louis led them down the hallway and yelled down to Marcy for an entire round of the Sunday Coffee. The Madame entered her office first, followed by the others, trying to seem as if Walsh's presence wasn't making her increasingly pissed off. With the men filing in, she took to her desk, and the others scattered across the room in her various armchairs and loveseats, though Croker went straight to the drink cart for a whiskey.

"Is someone going to tell me what the fuck is going on?" she asked, feeling the burn of alcohol on her stomach and the caffeine in her veins. "Or are we all just here waking me from my God damned beauty sleep for a little social outing we could have done at a later date?"

When the others didn't budge, she turned to Croker, who had put down an entire glass of whiskey and was refilling for another.

"Something happened last night. I thought it was you. But... God dammit...from seeing you in this state and understanding how you operate, I was definitively...wrong."

"So that's why this bastard is here?" The Madame peered over at Walsh, who sneered at her. "To fucking intimidate me? We had a fucking understanding, you prick, and you're on very dangerous ground."

Croker's head fell. "I was overzealous. Walsh? Out."

"You bring him back here again, our deal is off the table. Permanently," she snarled. "If you can't uphold your promises I'm not obligated to uphold any to you."

"And what's so wrong with me?" Walsh crooned. "We've had some lovely nights here, you and I, Madame. I won't ever forget them."

Louis leapt to his feet, his eyes furious, but the Madame didn't falter. "You're a sick bastard who is lucky to have someone like Mr. Croker employ you. But just because he does, doesn't mean I have to put up with your fucking games. You're a piece of shit, and in spite of the fact that you're his employee, I see no reason to put up with you. So back the fuck off or I'll have Louis make sure you don't smile again. And I'm sure Will would be happy to assist him."

Just as she anticipated, Will took a cue and rose, striding to Louis' side, the two men standing together a dangerous and menacing sight. Croker's jaw dropped and he didn't move, only stood paralyzed at the drink cart without any clue as to what to say or do. Then, as if planned, Marcy knocked and entered with a tray of drinks for the Madame's guests. The Madame motioned for her to set them down, which Marcy did speedily upon seeing the Madame's expression, and exited.

Walsh let out a raw and bitter snort when she'd gone, shaking his head. "Relax, please. I am not trying to step on toes. With respect, Madame, I will leave your establishment, only to return if Mr. Croker asks. You are right. You do not have to put up with me, but we are on the same side. All of us." His eyes flashed to Croker's, and a haunting grin came to his face. "Have a wonderful day, won't you?"

Spinning around, Walsh skipped out and left the Madame's office, the door loudly thudding closed in his wake.

"So, like I was getting to before," the Madame carried on as if nothing odd had happened. "Does someone want to tell me what the fuck is going on?"

Croker finished his second glass and placed it on the drink cart. "Mary's gone."

The Madame, who was greedily taking a sip of her Sunday Morning, choked on it and coughed violently. "Excuse me?" she sputtered, gasping for air.

"Gone," Will repeated. "Someone broke into that God damn asylum yesterday and broke her out. Whoever it was, son of a bitch killed nine people and badly injured seven more. All the witnesses say the same shit. Man moved faster than they've ever seen, and he wasn't from around here, if ya know what I'm sayin'."

"Not quite," the Madame replied, her heart beating faster. "Could you clarify that?"

"It was a Celestial, Madame," Louis revealed to her, and she knew instantaneously what this meant.

The Madame couldn't stop herself. She began to laugh, harder than she'd laughed in years. All three of the men stared at her astounded, wondering what the hell could be so funny.

"Oh my God. You don't see it, do you?" she huffed, her stomach hurting from the contractions. "This was better than anything I could have ever fucking put together. Ever!"

Croker drew closer, his finger outstretched at her. "You tell me everything you know this instant, or—"

"Or what?!" she bellowed. "She's gone, far out of your jurisdiction, Croker. I can't believe I didn't see it coming."

Louis didn't bother to try and fill the other two in. "Do you think he was here too? How could this happen?"

"Of course he was, Louis. He wanted to see her one last time. And save his mother. Who Mr. Croker lied about and told us she was dead…" Her gaze fixated on Croker. "I ought to fucking cut your throat for that, you son of a bitch. What the fuck else have you been lying to me about?"

Croker didn't hear her, his eyes seeming to bulge out of his head. "His…you said…his mother…"

It wasn't even a query – Croker instantly comprehended whom they were referring to, and didn't like it.

"He saw Esther's death, he sent his father's old master to save his mother, what's next?" the Madame bantered, the amusement and pride in Thomas trouncing Croker's deception, "Oh, Thomas, the surprises are endless."

Croker twisted around to Louis and Will. "Check the records at the harbor. See if any Turner S & D ships were docked that day, or if any left. I want to know as soon as you do."

The Madame finished her coffee and grabbed for another sitting idle on the tray. "And what would that do, Richard? Hm? Are you going to go to England yourself and take her back?"

"Well…no…but I could put together a team and embargo Turner S & D products in the city, and—"

"Hah! You're going to ban trade on the only supplier of packaged cigarettes from the south? You do realize this will literally cause fucking rioting in the streets, don't you?"

"How so?" Will asked, looking from the Madame to Croker.

"Because they are currently the one distributor in the world for it," Louis replied, walking over and picking up his own Sunday Morning from the tray.

The Madame stared at Croker. "You know as well as I do, Croker, that people don't start to give a shit about politics until it affects their fucking addictions, and that's when it becomes all out rioting."

Croker's face went white. "He…he must know, then…Jesus. That's the only reason he would…"

The Madame's head tilted curiously. "Must know what, Richard?"

He was about to say something when Will took over. "That Croker's the one who had Eddie murdered."

The words cut through the room like a knife, and the Madame saw Will chose them for a reason: he wanted Croker to know that no matter what deals they'd made, he wasn't and never would be approving of what happened to Edward Turner. And it gave her the smallest flicker of hope.

"Richard, listen to me," she went on, trying to salvage the situation. "Thomas is across the Atlantic Ocean. The Turners have sold their properties in New York. There is no plan of return, and I doubt there ever will be. Let him have Mary, for God's sake, and we can just fucking move on with our lives."

He filled up yet another glass of whiskey. "What happens if he does come back, then? What do you think he'd plan to do?"

"He won't."

"I'm not asking your opinion," he demanded, his vexation increasing. "I'm asking what will happen if he fucking does!"

Louis strode over and took the whiskey from Croker's hand, pouring every last drop down his own throat. Insolently, he handed the glass back to him, an incongruous, almost gratified expression on his face.

"Well, Mr. Croker, if he really is his father's son, I'd say you are utterly fucked."

XXVIII.

It was April before the darkness and gloom of winter started to finally to melt away, both around the iced up city of New York and in what was left of Celeste's broken heart. Months passed so sluggishly they felt like years while Celeste hid away in isolation, spending most days rising late and sitting by the fire with wine in the vague attempt of coping with a severe wretchedness she just couldn't exorcise. Initially she'd gone to Esther's execution with the notion that being present would help to alleviate some of Esther's fear. But while she tried to prepare herself to see her best friend go to meet God at the end of a noose, those efforts had been in vain. From the moment Celeste arrived at the courtyard of the Tombs, an ungodly force took hold of her, and every shred of her agony and misery could no longer be kept bottled away inside. Captain Bernhardt held her while she screamed and cried, cursing the people who put Esther on that stage in front of the massive crowd to die, and she did so without any care for preserving her dignity. Those final words she spoke kept Celeste awake until the early hours of the morning, replaying the image over and over until she was certain she was going insane. If not for her father and for Jonathan, she was certain she would have.

Through the New Year, Celeste was taken in by the last person in the world she ever imagined would be a friend. She was so inconsolable leaving the Tombs, Jonathan had taken her to his home where he stayed with his parents in the city, only to receive a rather unexpected visitor that evening. The Madame came to her bedside, declining the constant propositions to leave her, and then proceeded to move Celeste to The Palace, though not without incessant protest. The thought of staying in a whorehouse, no matter how upscale it might be, was absolutely degrading to Celeste; on the contrary, the level of impropriety for staying at a man's home on her own, especially a man that she was neither engaged nor married to, would only bury her reputation further. It was the Madame's, or back to her hotel alone, and bearing in mind what the Madame had done for her and her father, Celeste did not want to cause any unprovoked problems. Since her adolescence, Celeste had greatly disliked the Madame, and yet the more time she spent with her, the more she realized how much the woman really did mean to Esther. That alone began to soften her hardened attitude toward the Madame which had formed over the years, not to mention that without her, Celeste's father would never have seen the light of day again. Celeste learned her bias was merely the result of her late mother's prejudice against the Madame's profession, nothing more, and discovered herself giving the Madame another chance.

The Madame kept Celeste occupied during her stay – she was completely isolated from the "operations" of The Palace, and when Celeste couldn't find the strength to get out of bed, she was brought some of the best food she'd ever tasted, along with a few bottles of wine. Her hostess came and went at odd hours, sometimes only to make sure she was still breathing, others to tell her a story about Esther or reassure her of her father's upcoming release. Most of Celeste's time was spent in her room by the fire, not caring to venture outside and deal with reality. Jonathan ventured to The Palace and endeavored to call on her frequently, but it was no use: Celeste didn't want to see or speak to anyone, as she could barely stand the sight of her own reflection.

Eventually the day came when Celeste woke to find Louis knocking on her door, informing her that her father was going to be let out that afternoon and would be arriving at The Palace soon thereafter. She had wanted to rejoice, to fall into her father's arms and they might both start fresh. Conversely, in the days to follow, Celeste saw it was nothing more than a silly little girl's dream. Once she was honest with herself, any prospect of normalcy seemed far out of reach, and though she hated to admit it, normalcy was something she could never return to. So much had changed in just under a year. Celeste had transformed into an entirely altered person. Normal was a foreign concept to anyone who'd experienced what she had in such a short time, and she'd have to find a way to get passed it.

The charges against Douglas Hiltmore were officially dropped by the federal prosecution on the eighth day of January, 1884, due to some portion of the evidence against him more or less vanishing into thin air, and thus leaving the rest of it to be circumstantial at best. Somehow, the documentation that proved the illegality of his operations, which was the focal point of the entire case, had gone missing with no indication as to how or why. Because of this, the judge had no option other than to rule for Douglas to be exonerated and restored his original estate seized by the federal government. With one swing of the gavel, Celeste and her father were reunited with everything they once believed was lost for good.

It was an emotional reconciliation for them in the private dining room of The Palace, and after giving them a few minutes, the Madame explained she had scouted a few vacant residences on Fifth Avenue, as well as near East Midtown where the Hiltmores lived prior to the governmental seizure of their assets. Celeste observed her father scrupulously, and in his eyes, she saw the same hesitancy she also felt at the thought of immersing themselves back in the societal bubble of the uptown lifestyle. Just as she was preparing to politely remonstrate the Madame's suggestion, Douglas did so for her, and brought to light the silver lining she had been unaware of regarding his deal to get out of jail.

"Madame," Douglas started. "I cannot thank you enough for all that you've done for me…for us…but considering the circumstances of our arrangement, I think Celeste and I might do better to live somewhere with a new certain…zest. An alternative to what we're accustomed."

She smiled knowingly. "I thought this might be the case. What if I told you I had a friend in Greenwich Village, one opening one of the more colorful hotels in the area that would be suitable for anyone of the upper middle class?"

"Another hotel?" Celeste blurted out, and then withdrew. "I apologize. It was just the first thought that came to my mind."

"A hotel would be preferable, darling, because then if something were to go array, you can pick up and leave whenever you like."

"What's the name?" Douglas went on.

"It's The Hotel St. Stephan. Off of 11ᵗʰ Street."

Douglas turned to Celeste. "For now, would this be suitable for you, Celeste? Just until we get our bearings?"

"Of course, Father. Whatever you think is best."

"Perfect!" the Madame cried jovially, clapping her hands together. "I will let the Ryder family know this evening, and you both can be moved in tomorrow."

To Celeste's amazement, the Ryder family was more enthusiastic than the Madame let on in welcoming their new guests, and insisted that the Hiltmores would easily be moved in that night as well as cooked a feast to celebrate their arrival. The arrangements were made in the blink of an eye, and there was little opportunity to second-guess their decision: Celeste and her father were taken into the Hotel St. Stephan with open arms, a roast chicken to share, and the best bottle of wine she'd tasted in as long as she could remember. Greenwich was an up and coming neighborhood,

mainly filled with new money, artists, writers, and anyone wishing
to be caught up in the cultural center of New York City. She was
pleased to note the Hotel St. Stephan was beautifully renovated,
and though it was no Grand Central, the Hiltmores were given the
largest adjoining suites the Ryder's had available which were, by
any standard, extremely luxurious. Celeste's rooms were already
furnished, with two on hand maids at her service, a cellar of wine
at her disposal, and an extra wardrobe offered if for any reason she
might need more room for her gowns. There was plenty of space
to fill: a large bedroom with windows facing out to the street, a sitting room centered around a giant fireplace with brand new hand
carved furniture, a small study with a tiny collection of books and
desk to match, and last the joined dining room she shared with her
father, equipped with a table to seat sixteen and china that looked
to be as expensive as what was used at her and Timothy's wedding.
Any reluctance Celeste felt in moving into the unknown converted
into overwhelming excitement, and for the first few days of being
in their new home, she truly thought she and her father would be
able to have a new life. Unfortunately, she came to understand this
could not be further from the truth.

Douglas commenced work again, lobbying for himself down at
City Hall in the Financial District, and with the help of a few old
friends, he'd been able to make some progress and regain positions
on a few of the committees he used to run. Word spread like wildfire
around New York, and with the perception not only that Douglas
Hiltmore was released to society completely absolved of his charges
but also with his previous bank account, any timidity to keep him
excluded would be nothing short of futile stupidity for progress. He
had done the unfeasible: made his fortune, had it all taken away by
the government, and marvelously reclaimed it, ready to advise and
put his newfound knowledge of the system to work for the right price.
While some of his former constituents were still debating whether
his involvement would be beneficial or only harm their company's

name, all it took was a bit of cash as well as some benefiting whispers, and Douglas was cast back into the game.

January and February came and went while Celeste battled to recover from the blow of losing Esther, staying involved with her father but continuing to segregate herself from most of society. The initial happiness of their move and having her father out of jail faded, leaving her to deal with a spell of misery that paralleled the dark and dreary winter outside. As the end of February drew to a close, Celeste sensed her father was growing more and more concerned for her wellbeing. Every night they ate dinner together to discuss their days, which was Douglas' idea of keeping their relationship as open and direct as possible so he might prove he'd turned a new leaf. His progress was substantial, every day coming home with more good news of his ascension back up the ladder, and she couldn't miss the disappointment in his eyes as she described yet another day by the fire, reading, sleeping, and drinking too much wine, grappling with memories she feared would continue haunting her without fail.

Then one day, Douglas decided to take action devoid of consulting her, probably under the assumption she would refuse. After her father left for the morning, Celeste was surprised by a caller for tea. It was Jonathan, who had come on account of being written by Douglas to see if his company might help ease Celeste's depressive state. She was furious with her father at first for intruding on a subject he knew nothing about, though as time went on, having the Captain around lessened the sting of missing Esther considerably, and she started to really enjoy his company. They talked about everything, from the horror of witnessing someone they both loved die that day to the abusive marriage she tolerated with Timothy, not even realizing until she spoke the words aloud how great it felt to let it be in the open. For so long she she'd lived trying to suppress the objections in her heart for the sake of being respectable, and having Jonathan there to listen to her and work through those elements step by step made the weight slowly lighten. In mid March, Celeste was saddened to learn Jonathan was being sent to the frontier to deal with the drawn-out Indian Wars for an undisclosed amount of time. He, too, was visibly upset by this, though he promised to write from the territory he was stationed at, and it wasn't until he departed that Celeste realized he'd become one of her greatest friends. She'd made drastic improvements during the weeks of his visits, and was pleased to nearly feel like her old self again.

March passed rapidly, and while she dressed for the day on the fourth of April after sending her father off to work, another visitor dropped by, one she hadn't seen since she and her father were at The Palace. It was Louis, who was in the neighborhood and wanted to stop in to check on her with the winter now almost through.

They sat together by the fire, and before Louis could ask if she wanted a smoke, Celeste had already grabbed two from the small, silver container in her dress pocket, causing Louis to laugh.

"My tobacco?" he asked grinning. Louis may not have shown his face at her new home, but he had sent a few encouraging letters to Celeste, and his words helped her on the darker days when nothing else would. He'd also arranged a weekly shipment of his favorite tobacco to her, which was delivered by George on Mondays. Just as Louis foretold, she took quite a liking to the sensation of it, and now nothing else could even come close.

Celeste beamed at him. "What else?" She handed matches to Louis as her maid brought out coffee and biscuits. "I must admit I thought you'd visit sooner. It's been three months!"

"My, how time flies. I hadn't even realized. Accept my apology, and also understand I did not want to impose. People are often… thrown together under circumstances and become friends for a time, only to have that friendship fade away when the struggle has passed."

"That is not the case at all!" Celeste retorted. "I…well, I have not been well for the majority of the winter. The after effects of… of seeing Esther go that way…well I never should have gone. It was harder than I could have anticipated, and it took an overwhelming toll on my person."

"I can understand. And I am sorry for that."

"I too am sorry. You and the Madame have shown my father and I nothing but kindness, and I spent so many years misjudging you. All the poisoning of my mother, I think, in seeing the Madame as a threat."

Louis had a drink of coffee. "You are doing better? You look lovely."

"I think the sunshine has helped to cure my ills. I was also lucky to befriend Captain Bernhardt, and we have been able to work through much of this together."

"And he is now off fighting the natives, correct?"

"Yes," she said, letting out smoke. "He is hoping to return before the next winter, but they gave no set timeline for his stay. I am also glad to report my old maid, Laura, who I'm sure you remember, has moved up to New York with her fiancé. His family just struck gold west of here, and their fortune has grown tenfold. He is moving here to push the sale of their gold mine, and as of just last week, I've been gifted another close friend in my midst."

"That's happy news."

"Indeed," she chimed in. "If you don't mind my asking, how is Danny doing? She looked so ill in December, I can only hope things have gotten better for her."

Louis gaze dropped to his coffee cup. "I'm sorry to say, I can't tell you, Miss Hiltmore. She left us not long after Esther's execution, with no hint of her whereabouts."

Celeste was flummoxed. "Well…that was not exactly what I expected. Let us pray she finds peace, wherever she might be."

Their conversation grew quiet for a moment as they sipped their coffee. Then, Louis broke the silence.

"Can I offer you a suggestion, Miss Hiltmore?"

"Please…Celeste. We're far beyond formalities, Louis."

He smiled again. "Celeste…it might do you good to get back into your social circles. Have you considered that?"

"You're as bad as my father," she replied, setting her coffee aside. "Honestly, Louis, I don't see what good it would do. The pointless trivialities, the superficiality that used to consume my life and does for most of my old friends…well…that no longer interests me. That part of me died with Timothy, thank the Lord for that, and after Esther…I have no hopes of ever returning to society pretending it never happened and trying to relive my old routine."

"So it's something more you seek? Something with a more definitive purpose?"

"I guess you could say that. I am not ashamed to admit I have spent a lot of time thinking, what would Esther do if she were me in this moment? What would she make of this? If I'm not going to fall back into line with the others, what else can I do? My spirit is back, along with my energy, so yes, I guess you could say I'm searching for some sort of purpose."

Louis leaned back in his chair, eyeing her closely. "What about getting involved in the women's liberation movement? Or just more actively involved in the city? That's what most women do if all else fails – find a cause and stand behind it."

"If I had a cause, Louis, it would be to tear apart the prison that I was kept in for the sake of propriety. But if we're being fair, the times we are in would never allow it, and there is not a thing on this planet I could do to change that. I don't think I could stand putting out a worthless effort in a cause I actually believe in."

Louis was silent again for a few seconds, yet Celeste could sense he was considering her words more carefully than she said them.

"Would you permit me a visit tomorrow evening?"

"You are welcome any time!" she assured him. "Is this where you leave me?"

He put out the last of his cigarette and rose. "For now. You've given me a bit of inspiration, Celeste, and I thank you."

"Louis? Can I ask you one more thing?"

"Certainly."

She also put out her cigarette and stood up, walking nearer to him. "You seem like you're doing all right. Losing Esther, and all. I know it was extremely difficult…she loved you so much."

Louis nodded. "Difficult does not even begin to describe it. But I've found peace in my work. She's with me every day."

"I know she is. Sometimes I feel like I can hear her right next to me, making some sort of brassy remark…"

Louis snorted. "You have no idea, Celeste." He took a slight bow dismissively. "Good day to you. Expect me tomorrow and have some wine ready. We might need it."

"Why do you say that?"

"Oh, I have a long two days of…physical challenges ahead of me, that is all," Louis went to the door and opened it. "Enjoy the beautiful day, Celeste."

"Have wine ready?" Laura teased, as she and Celeste strolled through Central Park later that day. "What is he aiming at with all this? Letters first, then stopping by once Jonathan leaves? Are you sure he's not in pursuit of you?"

Celeste waved her off. "Hardly. I think I remember Esther telling me he had no interest in women whatsoever."

Laura hooted. "And yet he's coming over tomorrow night to see you, and wants wine ready? Please."

They took a left turn after reaching the end of a bridge, Celeste hoping to find a little more sunlight and a lot less shade.

Laura wouldn't let the subject go. "How old is he anyhow?"

"Too old for me," Celeste remarked passively. "I would say he is in his late forties. And it's not…well…it's not as if he has a reputable profession, Laura. He works for the Madame at The Palace, for Christ's sake. And I'm sure with that line of work he's hurt quite a few people in his time."

"You still haven't said you don't like him."

"I don't like him."

Both girls paused briefly, then burst into giggles. "Ah, well, it was worth a shot I suppose," Laura went on. "But speaking of prospects, have you talked to Captain Bernhardt?"

"Just through letters. He sends me about one a week."

"Are you still living in a state of denial about him?"

"The Captain? No!" Celeste contended, though she knew she was lying. "He's only a dear friend. He loves Esther, Laura."

Laura halted Celeste mid stride, rotating to face her friend. "Celeste, Esther is gone. She's been taken from us. It's been nearly four months, and you've got to move on with your life. Sure, Captain Bernhardt loved her, but you did too, and you deserve happiness. He likes you, or he wouldn't write to you or have taken so much time to see you almost every day for those weeks! Don't be silly. If you have feelings for him, let them out! There's no reason to ignore them."

"I don't know. It's just that I feel like if I did, I'd be betraying her," Celeste confessed. "I don't want that, Laura."

They proceeded strolling on their pathway once again. "Esther didn't love Jonathan, Celeste, we both know that. I think she really wanted to. In her heart, though, there was only Thomas."

Celeste felt a shred of resentment pang at the sound of his name. "Yes, and he didn't even bother to see her before it happened."

"Not once?!"

"Not once," Celeste repeated. "Cold to the very core. I think his British roots ran deeper than we could have assumed."

Laura scoffed, and their talking fell off for a moment when they finally found a bench sitting directly beneath the sun's beaming rays. The ladies eagerly raced to it laughing gaily and sat down, taking off their hats and not caring if the sun would darken their skin. All they wanted was to feel the heat of spring on their faces and enjoy the blissful sensation.

A few minutes later, Laura spoke again. "Do you ever think about it?"

"Think about what?"

"That night. When it all happened."

Celeste sighed. "I try not to, Laura. It hurts too much."

Another few seconds passed, and Laura straightened up and put her hat back on. "I've been afraid to discuss it. With you, or with anyone. Even Ralph, and we promised to tell each other everything."

Celeste followed her friend's lead, tying her hat firmly under her chin. "What do you mean?"

"I have nightmares, Celeste. Not every night, but every once in awhile, and they're so real, I wake up sweating and crying for no reason."

Celeste's worry grew. "Nightmares?"

"About that night mostly. About Timothy."

"What!" she cried, taking Laura's hands in hers. "Why have you never told me this before? All you ever said was he…he hit you and it all went dark."

She could see tears welling in Laura's eyes. "At first, yes, that was all I could remember. And then I started having dreams, reliving it, over and over again. It's horrifying Celeste, and it scares me so much."

"What do you see?" she pressed receptively.

"It's the same dream every time. I hear a commotion upstairs and am fearful you've gotten out of bed or something has happened. I run up and turn into your bedroom and…I walk into the room and see him…brutalizing that poor woman. I rush over and hit him, trying to knock him off, and he throws me off into the wall. The first few breaths I can't get any air, and then he drags me from the room…drags me by my hair, and just when we reach the staircase I know he's going to throw me…"

Laura began to cry softly and Celeste pulled her into a hug. "It's going to be all right, Laura."

"I know. I just wish I didn't remember any of it."

"Does he throw you?"

Trying to pull herself together, Laura sniffed and pulled her handkerchief out. "No. He just stares into my eyes, and there's so much hatred in them. Then it goes black and I wake up."

Celeste squeezed Laura. "Do you think it's what really happened, or it's just your mind playing a trick on you?"

"I can't really be sure. And I'm not sure I want to find out. I just don't want Ralph to know…he's such a good man! I don't want him to think badly of me."

"Laura, he will never think badly of you. He loves you!"

"Yes, but we've only just arrived and I don't want him to think I can't be in New York. I wanted to be here."

"I know," Celeste acknowledged, doing her best to be soothing, "Then I think we should make a promise to each other."

Laura nodded. "I'd do anything for you. You know that."

Celeste grinned. "From now on, whenever you have one of your dreams, you come and see me, and we can work through it. I don't care if it's every day. We can do this together. Does that sound all right to you?"

"Yes. Thank you, Celeste," she dabbed her eyes with her sleeve, "Jesus, I owe you so much."

"You owe me nothing. You have stuck by me through the best and worst of days."

"And I hope you know Ralph and I both plan on repaying you with the love and courtesy you showed me when I was nothing more than a measly maid."

"You mean six months ago?" Celeste joked, causing Laura to blush. "Oh for heaven's sake, I'm only teasing. I am so excited for you and your family. You fell in love and then two days after you're engaged you discover he's worth almost as much as my parents were in their prime. It doesn't get much better."

"No...no it doesn't," Sarah smiled. "Which is why I want to ask a favor."

"And that would be?"

Laura appeared to grow nervous. "Would you come to the Admiral's Ball? You and your father, with us? Please, Celeste, it would be absolutely spectacular. I know your father has already received his invitation which includes you of course, but we can go together...the four of us! And I thought..." Laura searched Celeste's face for any signs of agreement, "...I thought it would be good for you to...you know...get out into the world once more and be social."

Laura's sharp transition from total devastation to pleading with Celeste to attend a ball made her speculate whether or not her loyalty and faithfulness was real.

"I'm not sure, Laura. I really have no interest in balls or parties. Particularly one of that caliber."

"Please, I'm begging you," she pleaded. "I don't want to go alone, and you always were such a natural! You know if I'm with you then I won't have to deal with being publicly rejected the entire evening."

"Yes, and that's because I'll be the subject of every snide remark and interrogation of the evening," Celeste snapped, growing irritated.

Laura was stupefied for a few seconds by her harshness. "I'm sorry...I just thought it would be nice. Fun, even. I didn't think about what I was asking of you. Really...how stupid of me..."

Celeste tried to contain her annoyance, identifying that Laura had not been thinking at all. She hadn't considered how a public appearance would play out for Celeste: a mother who committed suicide, a father thrown in jail, a husband murdered by her best friend, and then having to suffer through a trial filled with lies by many of those who would be in attendance, every one of them vouching for Timothy without even once bearing in mind their lies would not only impact the finality of the trial, but also the death of Esther. No, Laura hadn't thought of that, or the backlash following her father's rise after being released along with the rumors Celeste had gone completely mad, locking herself away in Hotel St. Stephan. She didn't want to see those people, be near those people, or even hear them breathe. Yet she remembered her good conduct and realized she must self-correct, or face losing what felt like the only female friend she had left.

"I'm sorry, Laura," she apologized. "I overreacted. Will you give me a few days to think it over? You're right, a night out might be a great idea, and I've got a great dress that has yet to be worn. Let's get together for lunch on Saturday and discuss it then?"

Slamming the door shut behind her, Celeste let out a sigh of relief to escape Laura. At first when she received word Laura and her fiancé were moving to New York, Celeste was ecstatic to have her old companion to talk to and share her intimate feelings with once again; however, after this particular outing, a rush of melancholy hit Celeste, one that was quickly followed by shame. She realized what she'd wanted was another Esther, another friend who was more devoted than any blood she had, who she could confess her secrets to without judgment, and who, despite being younger, seemed to understand the world around them better than Celeste did. A lump grew in her throat, and Celeste leaned back against the front door, taking a few deep breaths to remind herself she'd cried enough tears. The hard truth was that Esther was gone, and she would never have another friend like her. Not for many lifetimes.

A sudden clinking of glasses and laughter caught Celeste's attention, and her head whipped to her left toward the dining hall she and her father shared. The door to the inside was closed, but a flickering light shone from underneath, and she stood motionless for a couple of seconds, wondering why her father wouldn't have told her they were expecting company at this hour. She thought back, trying to remember if she might have forgotten, and resolved that whoever her father was entertaining must have been unexpected, like many of their frequent guests.

"Good evening, Miss Celeste" one of the maids greeted, approaching from Celeste's sitting room. "How was your ride home from Central Park? Smooth I hope?"

"Too cold, I'm afraid," Celeste declared, removing her hat and handing it over. "Who is my father with?"

"I am not quite sure, I did not see them upon arrival," the maid told her. "But your father asked me to prepare one of your gowns to put on when you arrived home."

Celeste smirked. "He is always thinking ahead, isn't he? I wonder whom it could be...no matter. Will you help me dress?"

Minutes later, Celeste keenly made her way to the dining room, pulling her shoulders back and readying herself to play hostess for her father's friends. Douglas had picked out a beautiful, pastel purple gown with white silk trim he'd only just bought her, with gloves and a hairpiece to match. The coloring made her fair skin glow, and as she checked her appearance one last time in the mirror on the wall, Celeste swore she hadn't looked better. Cheerfully she pushed the door open, and was welcomed by a sight she didn't quite expect: her father had only one guest, the Madame of The Palace, and when they looked to see who disturbed their dialogue, their somewhat serious expressions became instantly jovial and lighthearted.

"Celeste!" her father beckoned, rising and motioning to the empty seat on his right. "Please, join us. Frank is fixing a feast for us, though I couldn't resist a little wine before dinner with our guest!"

A little anxious, Celeste threw on her best smile, and waltzed toward her father. "Thank you. Wine sounds lovely after being out in the cold."

The Madame nodded politely as Celeste took her seat, and she felt the Madame's eyes stay on her, making Celeste flush. There was no real reason for it – since they'd moved to Hotel St. Stephan, Celeste found she grew anxious whenever the Madame was mentioned, only because of the indignity she felt for being so cruel to a person who had taken her in without a second thought. Celeste had never found the opportunity to apologize or to thank her for her generosity, and as her father poured Celeste a glass of wine, she contemplated whether tonight might be the perfect occasion.

"We were just discussing how brutal the winter has been," her father alluded. "Did you have a nice time with Laura?"

"Well enough," she answered, taking a sip of her wine. "Madame, I had no idea you were coming to see us, or I would have returned sooner."

The Madame smiled. She was absolutely stunning, as she was every time Celeste saw her. The gown she wore was a contrasting dark, floral purple to Celeste's lighter pastel, and her hair was curled perfectly and pinned just right on her head. If not for the plunging neckline or the makeup on her face, the Madame would easily pass for a woman from uptown, yet Celeste knew that was the last thing on earth she sought out to do, and it made her like the Madame all the more.

"It's quite all right, darling. We knew you'd be home sooner or later, and while your father likes to…ease into certain subjects, I am one for blunt and upfront candor, as you have learned by now."

Douglas let out a defeated exhale, sinking back into his chair. "Madame, couldn't we wait until after dinner?"

"No, Douglas, we can't," she pronounced. "We need our night to discuss this, not avoid it."

"I don't understand," Celeste remarked, confused as she looked to her father for some sort of explanation.

The Madame got to her feet, picked up the bottle of wine between them, and filled Celeste's glass even more. "Do yourself a favor and take a large gulp or two," she instructed her, then resumed her seat. "It will help with…well…all of it."

"All of what?" Celeste did as she was told and downed part of her glass.

The Madame glanced from her to Douglas. "You first."

For a moment, Celeste's father didn't move; then, without warning, he got to his feet and started striding back and forth at the head of the table, making it palpable that whatever he had to say was somewhat of a challenge.

"Celeste," he initiated. "You and I made a deal when you came to see me at the Tombs. I promised you absolute honesty, no matter what the truth was. And you agreed to that, am I right?"

"Of course I did," she agreed with him. "That was the only way we could rebuild our relationship, father."

"And rebuild we have. In these last few months, I've regained much of the footing I lost in the Financial District, not to mention we were granted every penny we lost when I was arrested to begin with."

"Douglas," the Madame interrupted, "you're doing it again."

"For Christ's sake, let me talk!" he thundered at her, and the Madame unflinchingly rescinded. "Celeste, you are aware that the Madame is the reason we have survived. She is the reason we are both alive, we are both well, and we both have our financial livelihood back in our midst. This is not news to you."

"Yes, and we are undeniably grateful for that," she added respectfully, nodding at the Madame in acknowledgement.

Douglas stopped moving and rested his arms on the back of his chair. "There is some unfinished business she needs our help with, Celeste. Things only you and I have the ability to do because of... well...who we are. And we owe that to her tenfold."

At once, Celeste saw through his pandering. "You're telling me we are...obliged to assist her."

"In a matter of speaking, yes."

Celeste was irresolute in what to say next, and the Madame assumed her cue. "What your father is trying to tell you, Celeste, is

830

that since that I have helped you, I need your help with something I cannot do on my own."

"And what is that?" Celeste cried, exasperated. "I thought you saved us out of the dignity of your own heart! You saved us because we were a tool for you to utilize, and nothing more!"

"Celeste, you watch your tone!" her father reproached, but the Madame held up her hand to silence him, not breaking their eye contact.

"I saved your father because I needed him, though he needed me quite a bit more. I saved you for one reason alone: because Esther loved you, and it's what she would have wanted. I didn't need you at all, darling. It wasn't until I'd already saved you I saw your potential, and no one will force you. Douglas has…persuaded me to leave that decision up to you. You will be compensated, and the pay is more than fair, but you are under no bind with me. Only your father is."

Her bottom lip trembled. "Father…?"

Douglas shook his head. "I will never ask you to do anything you don't want to. I never lied after that day in prison, Celeste. I don't pretend to be a good man; however I will do everything in my power to be a good father. If you leave this dining room now, you are free of any of my owed debt to the Madame for good. If you stay, you stay on your terms, and we do this as a family."

Celeste felt completely trapped, not wanting to abandon her father. "I don't…I don't even know what I could do to help you, Madame…I have no…no…skill set…with men…in that way…"

The Madame let out a guffaw at her words. "Oh darling don't be ridiculous. That's not what I'm asking for," she said plainly. "What I am asking for, is for you to pick up where Esther left off."

This confused Celeste. "Pardon me, where Esther what?"

The Madame finished the wine in her glass. "Esther came to me one day, many years ago, facing a similar predicament that you face now. She was tired of the charade. Her life had no purpose, no fulfillment, and she was surrounded by people who didn't give

831

a damn about her other than yourself. Rather than allowing her to leave, I presented her with an alternative, one that facilitated many great conquests for The Palace and the balance we try to uphold."

"She was a spy, Celeste," her father stated. "Not one of us had any idea. Our family was never a target, but being our ward and your best friend, she had access to places the Madame and her constituents did not. It was a perfect set up."

"She was a spy?!" Celeste nearly shouted. "To what end?!"

"The Palace runs a business that stretches far beyond whoring," the Madame clarified. "Esther brought me any information she could find on the people I requested, all of which she obtained through social engagement she attended with you. This included eavesdropping, hiding in passageways, interjecting into conversation, even flirting her way into the confidence of others. And she was pretty damn good at it."

Celeste couldn't believe what she was hearing. "But Esther... she never told me...she would have told me!"

"Why would she? What she was doing had nothing to do with you, or your friendship, darling. It was her own way of fighting against never being accepted in society for who she was."

With her head spinning, Douglas and the Madame waited on Celeste to react. Her thoughts were scattered, reflecting on all the times they'd gone to balls, parties, or events, and when they had separated, sometimes only for a few minutes and others for nearly an hour. Celeste kicked herself for not spotting it sooner: Esther was not fond of most of her friends, chiefly those who often freely made snide remarks to remind Esther she was not one of them. It hadn't been an easy position for Celeste, either – Esther would be hurt and offended, and Celeste's social circle would constantly press her as to why Esther was there to begin with. The recollections made Celeste sick to her stomach. It was no mystery why Esther despised high society and sought a way to strike back, and Celeste had done absolutely nothing to stand up for her. For most of her life she'd been weak…going along with what others had told her was fitting and proper, not once taking a stand for what she believed in. Esther had, for herself and for Celeste, and as a consequence she was dead, taken from her. Ironically, for the first time in their friendship, Celeste felt she understood Esther entirely.

Douglas marched over to where Celeste sat, and gently put his hand to her cheek. "This is not a menial task, Celeste. It requires excessive amounts of courage, cunning, and deception, not to mention being constantly on your guard. Esther grew into it over time. You would be taking a big risk."

"Esther did this for you because it gave her purpose," Celeste reiterated, ignoring her father's embrace and facing the Madame.

"Yes."

"Was our friendship real, then? Or was it only to keep up the façade?"

"Celeste, please," her father entreated her. "That insinuation is ludicrous!"

Conversely, the Madame smirked again, only this time there was no kindness in it.

"Do you know how many times near the end I told her to leave you behind?" Her voice was as cold as ice. "So many I can count on my fingers and toes thrice over. You were a leech on her, doing nothing but making her worse and causing her to doubt herself when she was five times the woman you'll ever be. You didn't fully understand the unrelentingly loyal friend you had until your own life was in total uproar and she stood by you through the storm. You didn't deserve her. As far as I'm concerned, you still don't. So, to answer your immature and idiotic query, Celeste, your friendship was real to her, though I still do suspect it wasn't quite that way for you."

The complete alteration of the way the Madame addressed her was so unforeseen and painfully striking, Celeste found herself openly weeping in front of the Madame and her father. It was true, every bit of it: Celeste had been the incredibly selfish and spoiled friend, and took Esther's constancy for granted. She felt like a complete monster.

As Douglas took a few retreating steps and sank down into his chair, the Madame took this indication to abscond.

"I can see you could use a night to think it over," the Madame asserted. "Louis will take your answer tomorrow when he stops by and deliver it to me." The Madame got up effortlessly, her face devoid of all emotion. "You're a good girl, Celeste. Maybe now you'll appreciate the friend you had, and do her the justice of continuing on to finish what she started."

Celeste let out a small, angry snort as she pulled out a handkerchief. "What good could I possibly do tattling on the gossip of others?"

"It's not about gossip. It's finding the dirty laundry and the dark secrets so people don't wind up getting hurt. Like the case of your late husband, for example, and what could have been prevented had we been able to expose him sooner. Does that ring any bells, darling?" Celeste couldn't find the words to react, and the Madame went for the door. "Douglas, always a pleasure."

With that, the Madame swept out of the room, and Celeste felt the last of her vigor collapse and break down. Her father came to her side, trying to calm her, yet she thought nothing of it. Celeste jumped to her feet and rapidly exited the dining room, dashing away to be alone. When she reached her bedroom, Celeste slammed and locked the door, a fit of agony coming on fiercer than any she'd had in weeks. She tore off her dress, ripping it in multiple places as she fought to get the corset untied, not caring if it was ruined beyond repair. As the dress lay in shreds on the floor, Celeste ran to her side table and splashed water on her face over and over again, hoping to wash away the night like it had never happened. Glancing up to her mirror, Celeste hated what she saw: she was a self-centered princess, one who had been a terrible friend to the one person who loved her above any other. She stared at the reflection, wanting to break away but finding herself unable to pull back, tears streaming down her cheeks because of the detestation she felt at herself. Nothing could undo it. Nothing could ever undo what had happened.

The clock in the hallway struck nine, and at last Celeste broke her trance. She moved over and collapsed onto her bed, falling into another outburst of grief as she hit her mattress with her fist repeatedly in anger. Nothing could heal the hurt. Nothing could turn back time and bring Esther back. Nothing could undo the atrocities or what she hadn't done when she should have acted. Celeste cried for hours on her bed until she cried herself to sleep, tortured by the remembrance of her mistakes and the things she wished she could have done differently.

The morning came, and Celeste woke to the sound of birds singing outside her open bedroom window, an abnormally warm breeze blowing through. She stirred a moment, recalling the hell of her night before, then pushed herself upright and wiped her eyes. It was another beautiful spring day, without a cloud in the gorgeous blue sky, and the temperature felt more like early summer than that of the fading winter. Stretching her arms overhead, Celeste yawned deeply, trying to shake off the last bits of sleep and scooted to the left side of her bed. Her eyes traced the floor and noticed the destroyed dress on her rug, and she chided herself for being so careless in a fit of rage. The first thing she would do was go to her father and make it right, and together they would find a solution.

The warm breeze blew against her face again, and suddenly, it dawned on Celeste that she locked herself in her room the previous evening to avoid confrontation with her father. No windows in her room had been open when she went to sleep, and if they had, she would have noticed with the nights being so cold. Hoisting herself up to her feet, Celeste went to the window and shut it, the sensation of fear creeping up her spine. Hesitantly, she turned around to examine the rest of the room, her body tensing with apprehension…

And then, she saw it.

There, on a large canvas by her wardrobe, was a painting, one that definitely had not been present the night before and from its general appearance, was still drying. Celeste marched closer, mesmerized. It was one of the most beautiful paintings she'd ever seen, and the detail was extraordinary. Blossoming in a garden, the picture focused on a radiant white rose, not fully in bloom but getting close amongst the surrounding red roses already in their best form. The colors were exotic…vibrant…and intoxicating, making Celeste almost feel hypnotized by the incredible artistry. How it had gotten here, she couldn't be sure, but something about the style felt all too familiar…

Esther's passion was painting. She confided in Celeste on several occasions it was her only escape from the buzz around her…a moment of peace and quiet she never felt any place else. The colors she used were always bright and engrossing, like they wanted to give the onlooker a respite from the monotonous darkness of the world, and when she finished, Esther signed every one the same way. Unlike other painters, she never put her full name on them; instead, it was simply three horizontal lines, like an E, in the very corner of the painting, so fine that almost no one could notice.

As Celeste gaped unwaveringly at Esther's signature at the corner of the painting in front of her, a signature no one other than Celeste knew existed, she began to laugh, soft at first and then uncontrollably. Harder and harder the laughter came until there was no way to catch her breath as happy tears poured out of her eyes. She huffed for air and dropped to the ground, not sure if it was a dream or if, as she hoped, it was a message just for her to see. Relief rushed through her, and the last few months fell away with her heartache. Somehow, Esther was alive, and wanted to give Celeste a sign not to despair. It was for her, and her alone, a way of saying that somewhere out in the maddening crowd, Esther was there, guarding Celeste and watching out for her, the way she always had.

"I won't tell a soul," Celeste promised aloud. "I swear on my life I won't." She sniffed back her sobs and wiped her eyes. Her mind was made up: she would take the Madame's offer without compunction. She would do this for Esther, and she would push herself to do it better than her friend before her. Celeste had admitted it to Louis not a day prior – she wanted purpose, and in that purpose she wanted to cause a rift in the system. There was no task better suited for her than to assume her best friend's former charge.

Celeste spent the rest of the morning in her room admiring Esther's painting as it dried until a knock came to her door. Getting up, she went to the door to open it and found her father, whose concern became bewilderment at the sight of Celeste's current temperament.

"Celeste, is everything all right?" he asked, taking her hands. "I have to say you look far better than I thought you would this morning."

She smiled. "I've made my decision, father."

"Already? Are you sure you don't need more time?"

"I am sure," she replied, "I am going to take the Madame's offer. There is nothing that would please me more than to work with her."

Douglas stared at her. "What brought on this drastic change of heart?"

"I just needed a touch of inspiration. I want to make Esther proud, and considering her devout fondness for the Madame, I ought to give her the second chance I vowed I would."

Taking a step forward, Douglas hugged her. "Just promise me you won't get too involved."

"No, of course not," she pronounced, her head resting on his chest. "This will be good for me, father. And have faith. I highly doubt the time I spend with the Madame will significantly impact my character. Nobody on this earth is that cunning."

XXIX.

"It will take years, Lord Turner," Hiroaki tried to elucidate not two days after they returned from New York. "Years of hard labor and dedication. And we must discuss to what end you are seeking this."

They were walking leisurely through the stables, both bundled up from the freezing winter sleet that had finally ceased, icing over everything it touched.

Thomas looked at him. "To what end?"

"Yes, an end. You need a purpose...a goal. This rage you feel is what is currently driving you, and that grief and anger have the potential to distort what is most important. You need your logic... your concentration and focus, and you cannot have that clouded when you find yourself in a perilous state."

"Killing Richard Croker is what is most important. And all the bastards that work for him who did this to my family."

Hiroaki sighed in frustration. "You are making my argument for me, Thomas."

"Well what did you expect me to say, Hiro?" Thomas entreated him. "I thought that was the point. To take out the king and all of his court."

"You want your revenge, and you will have that I promise you.

But if your driving force is purely revenge, then those selfish motives will in turn destroy you. We must take into account the broader spectrum."

Thomas could feel his nails digging into his palms. The previous few weeks Thomas had been submersed in a rage that made his temper and his patience hard to regulate despite his best efforts to remain composed.

Hiroaki halted, feeling Thomas' exasperation, and rotated toward him. "Take a deep breath. In slowly, out slowly," Hiroaki regimented. Nodding, Thomas complied, counting to five as he inhaled and five again as he exhaled. Hiroaki was the only one who could keep Thomas from boiling over, and he wanted to refrain from having another episode like he had after finding Captain Bernhardt's ring in Esther's possession. Everything had gone red, and Thomas still could not account for demolishing his old room at William and Lucy's in New York. And he never wished for that to happen again.

A small fragment of self-control returned. "Better," Thomas conceded. "Thank you, Hiro."

His friend put a hand on his shoulder. "Thomas, you cannot lose your compassion. If you lose that, you lose what separates good from evil. With your anger you can channel it and use it to your advantage, and it will give you the power to do either great or horrible things. Many of us make poor decisions out of our own desperation, myself included. We must take these years not just to train you physically, but mentally, so that you will forgo any chance of making that kind of a mistake."

"Basically you want to get a lid on my anger so I don't lose it completely, is what you're telling me."

Though he tried to hide it, Thomas saw a slight smirk twitch onto Hiroaki's face. "In a matter of speaking, yes. I also want you to begin to realize what we have previously discussed. The breadth of people Richard Croker has cowering in fear is vast, and it's what aids him in sustaining his power. The Madame and Louis are included in this, because there is no possible way out for them other than death." He resumed their stroll, and Thomas followed. "The argument I am trying to make is that this cause, this goal, this purpose and end point I keep emphasizing must be for a greater good. For balance and honor. You want your vengeance, but I also want you to be driven to give vengeance to others, even if it is only the Madame, Louis, and…Esther."

The sound of her name made Thomas' heart beat a little bit harder. "Es," he involuntarily said aloud under his breath, and then straightened up.

"You saw it with your own eyes, Thomas. She's alive. They got her out, and Louis will see to it she's taken care of, I have no doubt of that."

"Yes but they don't know that I know she is alive."

"The Madame might. Why else would she have smiled at you when she spotted you?"

"With her, there could be thousands of reasons," Thomas responded, their walk now stretching out of the stables and to the frozen grounds of Amberleigh. "I don't have a fucking idea what exactly happened, but I do think you're correct in assuming the Madame and Louis made a bargain for her. I know how much the Madame cared for her."

Hiroaki agreed. "And Louis' letter brought the clarity you were seeking in regards to their involvement?"

"I suppose. I just wish…God dammit, I just wish I had known sooner." A letter was waiting for Thomas from Louis when they'd arrived home, wherein he confirmed Thomas' and Hiroaki's suspicions. It was, in fact, Richard Croker who had kidnapped and imprisoned his mother when she tried to turn his organization over to the Pinkertons. It was Richard Croker who ordered for Edward to be murdered after discovering Mary was being held at Blackwell. And it wasn't just Thomas' life he'd devastated. Thomas learned, to his horror, that Richard Croker helped to cover up for Timothy Adams following Esther's police report, and he'd even killed some of the Madame's girls and threatened Thomas and the Turners' lives on multiple occasions to make the Madame cooperate. The worst of Louis' report was what came last: Richard Croker was the head of Tammany Hall, and not only controlled the police force and numerous high-ranking politicians, but also the gangs in the Bowery, and bit by bit he was growing in power uptown where it really mattered. There was no way Louis or the Madame could touch him, and instead, they were being forced to work alongside him.

"I could have you ready in four years," Hiroaki broke their silence. "But we would have to work hard every day, harder than you've ever worked in your life."

"I am willing to do anything you want. I just want you to teach me and make me faster, smarter, and deadlier than anyone I could face."

"I can promise you will be," he affirmed. "I'll teach you how to be invisible and how to use the fear of your enemies against them. However, there will be a few small differences. In my past, there was no artillery."

"Guns, you mean?"

"Yes. We had our swords, and our swords were our sole defense. You will be dealing with weapons that have the potential to be more lethal."

"So your recommendation would be for me to carry a gun."

Hiroaki paused, thinking. "Your father hated the idea of guns, but in your case, I think it will be absolutely necessary."

Thomas reached underneath his jacket to the holster in the back of his pants, pulling out the Griswold he'd stolen from the Madame nearly nine years ago.

"Guess it was a good thing I ran off with this then." Hiroaki took it from him, examining it closely. "You want to implement this in the place of a sword?"

"Is that going to be a problem?"

"It's...a start," he replied. "Thomas, they make far better guns than these. The Confederacy made these things cheaply: they misfire, jam, and are extremely unreliable. I can talk with Tony and we can find something better."

"It's going to be this, Hiro. It has to be. I'll just have to be prepared for any…issues that might arise."

A grin came to Hiroaki's lips. "This is so she will know it is you."

"It's so there won't be a suspicion in her mind."

He handed the Griswold back to Thomas. "The first step to becoming one with your weapon is having a direct attachment to it. You already have established yours. Now you must master your expertise. Tony will begin making you shoot targets with your Griswold every afternoon out in the back hunting fields."

"Hiro, I have a clean shot with targets," Thomas griped, putting the gun back in its holster.

"Yes, you may have a clean standing shot. Not while you're running, moving side to side, or trying to defend yourself," Hiroaki told him frankly. "I highly doubt there will ever be a time in the future where you have a direct shot at anyone while you are standing still."

"Right. Practice with Tony. Got it," Thomas granted reluctantly. He shuddered, the bitter day taking its toll. "What about my training with you? When do we start?"

"The beginning of summer."

Thomas' jaw dropped. "The…the beginning of summer?! You cannot be serious! That's months away!"

"Yes, and until then, we need to condition you. Your muscles and your heart could not handle what we are about to embark upon in their current status. You will train…run every day, work with me in the stables, build your force and your might from the ground up."

Flustered, Thomas ran his hands through his hair. "And when I'm conditioned?"

"I will know when you are ready. Like I have verbalized repeatedly, this is going to take patience, time, and mental strength for you to persevere. Nothing will happen overnight. Four years, Thomas. Four years."

The pair drew near the trail back up to the house, and they stopped before parting ways. "So for now I just…run?"

"Run the property line on the outskirts. Start for about an hour per day. No less than an hour, and we will increase as you improve. I would recommend in the mornings before your day gets too busy with the company. It's going to hurt, and it will hurt badly, but push through, and don't start too fast. Pace yourself."

Thomas bowed to Hiroaki and turned, heading back up to the house. "Pace myself…" he mumbled, slightly amused. "Never been one of my strong suits…"

The first few days were horrendously painful, so much so that Thomas could barely stand on his own two feet in the aftermath. His feet and toes blistered, the muscles in his legs and his abdomen screamed, even his back started to dread the pounding up and down the hillside, fully sweating through his shirt and trousers. By the end of the first week, he had destroyed his most comfortable pair of hand-made leather boots. To his surprise, however, Hiroaki came forward the following morning Thomas planned to sleep in and brought him a new pair he'd created solely for his running, and they felt more like a second pair of skin than a pair of shoes. At the end of the third week, the soreness resided, and by the fourth his stride was becoming stronger. The March cold came and went in a flash, and with the warming breeze of April, Thomas was running ten miles per day and doing the majority of muscle work on the estate, leaner and tougher than he'd been since he could remember. As the days stretched longer, Thomas felt he was indestructible, and he would get through his runs without really breaking a sweat.

On one of the earliest days of summer, Hiroaki was waiting for Thomas on the last leg of his morning run, still a half-mile out from the house. Thomas immediately recognized that this was the beginning, and from here on out, they would spend hours of every day training to prepare him for the task ahead. Hiroaki placed himself in the middle of Thomas' path, in a tunic that looked almost like a costume, entirely black and cinched around the waist as if he were wearing a dress. The long hair he usually hid tucked away in a bun was now beautifully braided down his back, reaching all the way to his waist, and on his belt was a sheathed sword. The way Hiroaki stood was accepting, submissive even, though Thomas could sense this was a front to lure him in. His hands were in a prayer position at his chest, and his eyes stayed closed at his fingertips rather than open and on the advancing Thomas, who broke to a walk as he drew closer.

"So," he panted, catching his breath. "Is this it?"

"Is this what?" Hiroaki asked, not breaking his stance.

"Is this where we start?"

Hiroaki let his hands fall to his sides. "We begin our tactical methods today. But as we start this, there is one thing you need to consider."

"And that is?"

"Most Samurai have two methods of defense. The first is always the sword – it is the method by which we have mystified and conquered our enemies for centuries. Your sword will be your Griswold, which Tony has informed me you are increasingly more skilled with. However, there is always a second, always another unique skill a Samurai has in case there is no sword, and that is different for each of us. You will need to meditate on this and consider it."

Thomas was puzzled. "It can't be hand to hand combat?"

An amused look flickered across Hiroaki's face, then passed. "No. Hand to hand combat, in the way that we teach it, is intrinsic. It is like breathing air. You need a secondary very few could ever be as capable with as yourself."

"What about a—"

"No, I do not recommend a dagger, Thomas. There will be

too many of those in New York as it is, and lots of men skilled with them. Now, come forward and stand in front of me."

Thomas inched nearer to his teacher warily, his final few steps timid as he premeditated some sort of verbal insight or direction. Instead, the second Thomas was within an arm's reach of Hiroaki, Hiroaki struck him so suddenly and sharply across his cheekbone, Thomas practically fell to the ground.

"Jesus Christ!" he shouted, stumbling backward. "What was that for?!"

"Teaching you to know your enemy and predict the line of attack." Without warning, Hiroaki was upon him, and another blow came to Thomas, this time directly to his diaphragm so hard he keeled over, unable to breathe. "That's two hits and you're on your knees. Are you not going to even try to defend yourself?"

In a competitive fury, Thomas lunged at him, and Hiroaki lazily batted him aside, causing Thomas to trip and fall again. Scrambling, he leapt up with his fists clenched, unsure of what to do next.

"Well? Hit me, for God's sake!" Hiroaki baited him, not the slightest bit ruffled. Bearing in mind his limited options, Thomas came Hiroaki's way slowly, his fists tightening with each footstep. Instinctively, his final few strides picked up the pace, hoping to put momentum behind his aim at Hiroaki's nose. This round, however, Hiroaki deflected the attempt and then seized his fist in midair. He whipped Thomas' arm around his back, forcing him against a nearby tree and holding him there incapacitated.

"Shall we persist?" he harassed, thrusting Thomas' face harder into the trunk. "Or do you see my point?"

"What point?!" Thomas yelled. "I don't even have a chance!"

Hiroaki let go of his arm and retreated away from the tree, taking a long bow while Thomas twisted to face his attacker.

"Tomorrow, I want you to try and use your brain. Anticipate the attack, try to see what may come next."

Thomas tried to breathe. "You want me to...to what?"

"Anticipation is one of the greatest skills you can acquire. In time you will learn to use it."

"You mean you'll attack me the same way? And I'll learn from it?"

Hiroaki gave him a look of incredulity. "Of course I won't attack you the same way. But now you at least know I will be attacking you. When you can defend yourself well enough, I'll begin to teach you a more tactful approach, however until then, you need to learn to be…adaptive."

"That's it?" Thomas ranted. "That's my first day? How am I ever supposed to learn if this is all I get?"

"Today was to demonstrate how far we must go together. By the end of our four years, I will make sure you are better than I ever was, but you see now why we must take so long in your instruction. This will not happen overnight – I was taught since I was a child, and not considered a full Samurai until after puberty."

"I can take more. We can go another round."

"That's your pride talking now," Hiroaki took on a friendlier demeanor. "If I strike you hard again in your chest, I will do permanent damage, and we cannot have that. You may use that for the next few days, knowing it will be the one place I do not aim for."

Thomas was ultimately able to catch his breath and, leaning back against the tree, slid down to the ground. "We're starting this just before the heat of summer. What are we to do?"

"We continue. The weather should not matter. I will make sure you are sufficiently dressed to make it through heat, cold, rain, or snow. You think a man out to kill you would care if it was scorching hot?"

"No, I suppose not."

"Come," Hiroaki commanded, stretching out a hand to help Thomas to his feet. "Let us walk back to the house. I have a few thoughts you should consider."

Thomas took a hold and hopped to his feet. "These thoughts are?" he pressed as they meandered the trail home.

"I can recognize the many ways you have the advantage in your enterprise. Not just in your practice with me, but because of who you are and how you can use it. It is not something we have discussed yet, and it is extremely important."

Thomas scratched his head. "In English, please, not in Hiroaki."

Hiroaki scoffed and let out a small chuckle "Consider who you are fighting, Thomas. A man who seeks power above wealth, wanting to feel as if he rules the city without any objections…he has many connections, particularly within his organization, but he does not have the one thing that you do."

"And what might that be?"

"You have an inherent power, inherent nobility that no matter where you go in all the world, it deserves respect. The one goal you must have these next years is to take your father's company and make it even greater. Do you follow what I am saying?"

Thomas did. "You're saying that I need to expand my station as much as I can so that when I do arrive home, I'll be welcomed with open arms and have an immediate set of wealthy and influential friends."

"Exactly my point. You need to be New York's crown jewel, a man born from nothing who lived on to become one of the most successful people in that city. You must have success to be respected and awed by the upper class, and in doing that, you will make some very prominent colleagues. It will give you leeway so that no man could afford not to be your friend, and it will build your shield against the corrupt politics surrounding you. Publicly, then, Richard Croker could never touch you if he were to ever find out it was you behind his destruction."

"So I'll have to lead two separate lives. A public one where I make myself spectacle, and a private one to chase Croker down."

"No one can ever know your pursuit of Croker and his people. That is the only way to do this and win."

Thomas and Hiroaki stopped, staring down at the Turner estate, gleaming in the sunlight. "The hole is gone," Thomas uttered quietly.

"The hole you felt last fall?"

He nodded. "It's so strange, Hiro. I keep thinking on my life, where I've come from, where I am now, and I just can't help but feel…"

"Feel what, Thomas?"

"Like I was born to do this. I grew up on the hard side of life and under the influence of someone whose business tactics I observed, studied, and unknowingly adapted to my own personality, tactics that by no means are always honest."

"The Madame certainly passed off a few of her skills to you," Hiroaki permitted. "Skills that have made you an incredible businessman yourself."

"And then there was my time with Edward, all of this…and now you, here…my training…" He shook his head. "I used to brush off our talks regarding destiny and our future paths, believing it was a bunch of ritualistic bullshit. I was wrong. I've found my path. This is my destiny."

Hiroaki eyed him closely. "I believe you are right, Thomas. With all my soul."

Thomas and Hiroaki stood side by side for a moment, student and master, inwardly acknowledging that there was no turning back. In Thomas' mind, he unreservedly trusted that there never had been another option. The hole was gone. In those last few months, with newfound purpose, he was no longer lost. This was what was meant to be, and he embraced that concept wholeheartedly.

"So we start in the Points with the petty thieves and murderers for hire?" Thomas asked, his eyes wandering back to his friend.

"We start at the bottom, yes, and you and Tony will have to do your own hunting to find them."

Thomas smirked. "That shouldn't be a problem."

Hiroaki lead the way down toward the house. "Have faith in Tony, Thomas. He will serve you well, as he did your father. As you've learned, I trained him myself to protect William and Lucy in Edward's absence, and he's done a fine job of shielding the Turner family from harm in America."

"And you think he will be able to establish contact with his brother in New York? I thought they hadn't spoken in years."

"His brother was very well connected with the underbelly of New York's gangs. I have a feeling, if he is still alive when you return, Tony's brother could be a major asset to you. Tony has also confirmed that the last time the Turner family was in the city, he received word his brother was alive, and even had a brief visit with him over one of your extended stays in Virginia."

Thomas was astounded. "Tony never mentioned any of this to me."

"And why would he? During that time, he was only the friendly butler in your eyes."

Something in Hiroaki's tone gave Thomas suspicions. "I feel like you're hiding something from me, Hiro."

Before he could respond, Robert abruptly came into view on the path ahead of them, jogging their direction. "Lord Turner! Lord Turner! I have news, sir, it requires your attention at once!"

"What is it, Robert?" he called out.

His page held a piece of paper high above his head, waving it. "It's an embargo, sir! From New York City! A boycott of Turner S & D! It's pending federal investigation!"

Thomas left Hiroaki and shot ahead, trotting to Robert hurriedly. "What in God's name are you talking about, Robert?"

When they reached each other, Robert handed over the telegram. "No clue, sir," he panted. "But apparently they're launching an investigation and an audit to make sure everything is legal, and until then, Turner S & D will not be allowed to distribute or trade in the city limits of New York City."

Thomas' eyes scanned the page, the contents corroborating Robert's report. At the bottom was a list of the committee members performing the investigation, and one name stood out amongst the rest.

"That fucking son of a bitch…" Thomas murmured.

It was nearing mid June before Mary really started healing, parts of her old self returning little by little. Thomas spent the lengthy winter and spring months when not training or dealing with business ventures nursing her back to health. Her haggardly and starved physical appearance faded, though mentally, Thomas could see the fallout of nearly a decade in a tortuous prison, and it was not pretty. The first few weeks she would wake up terrified in the middle of the night, sometimes needing restraint, thinking Amberleigh was a hallucination or some sort of vindictive trick. Certain days she would walk around the house not speaking to anyone, sometimes talking to herself nonsensically, a perpetual state of denial encompassing her. Any kind of loud or sudden noises would cause Mary to jump or flinch, and as a result, put her on edge for hours. She was quiet, rarely saying more than a few words at a time, her eyes continuously tracing and examining every inch of whatever room she occupied like someone was coming to harm her. It took two months until she was finally able to keep much food down after a meal. For Thomas, as her main caretaker and her son, it was excruciatingly painful to behold, and for a time he was unconvinced recovery would come and relieve her. The woman Thomas adored who raised him as a boy was buried down beneath years of fear, malnourishment, and cruelty, and though he hated himself for even thinking it, Thomas did often wonder if death would have been a kinder punishment.

The spring rains let up early, and when the weather permitted, Thomas took Mary on walks through the gardens a few times per week, the fresh air doing wonders for her complexion. They wouldn't speak much, yet she would take his arm and hold it tight, as if she trusted him and him alone. Flowers blossomed from every angle in the warm sunshine, and Mary's favorite path to amble down was through the rose garden, where every color of rose imaginable bloomed around a gorgeous, white marbled fountain of a naked Aphrodite standing on a shell. Mary would stop and stare at her, sometimes for nearly a half hour, as if Aphrodite were alive amongst the dancing water beneath her. Thomas would sit back on a bench, allowing her to have the peaceful moment to herself. These were his favorite days – he would forget about New York City, about Croker and the others. The hate would give way to the love and benevolence he felt for his mother, and at having her home at Amberleigh where she belonged.

Somewhere, Edward was smiling.

On one of the first blistering hot days of July, she came to him as he worked in his study, running through business numbers to prove Croker's Federal investigation was nothing other than a witch hunt. Her steps were so gentle the only indication of her approach was the slight creak of the floor beneath her. Mary took a seat in one of his chairs in the sitting area, and motioned for him to join her, and he did, taking his glass of whiskey with him. Mary stared at him for a few seconds, then her eyes wandered to the ground.

"Your father would be so proud of you," she professed. "I've waited all my life to come to this place. And now I'm here, with you, and I have had a hard time accepting that it's real."

Thomas took a sip of his whiskey – this conversation had been a long time coming.

"Edward's one wish was to have you here with him."

Mary's hands folded into her lap. "How did you find him?"

"Well, I found him when I was trying to find you," Thomas described. "The Madame knew he was alive. She'd been hiding his letters for most of my life."

Mary's head fell, and Thomas could see tears glittering on her cheeks. "She hid them in that safe, didn't she?"

"Yes she did. How did you guess?"

"Christ," Mary breathed. "I always knew it. Something told me that whatever was in there was about me…about us…" Her voice trailed off. "I loved her…I believed so blindly that she wasn't capable of doing something that…that…"

"Insane?" Thomas offered.

"Hurtful," Mary added. "I swear to God, if I ever see her again, I don't know if I'll hug her or attack her."

Thomas grinned. "I think she would expect both."

"I suppose you're right."

"Mother, do you mind sharing with me how if it began?" Thomas asked. "I've never known the story."

"With the Madame?"

"Yes. Father told me a few…details…but I think I would understand your relationship with her a little better, and her relation to me, if you could just…"

Mary took Thomas' free hand in hers. "I understand. I'll just… start from the beginning." Mary straightened herself up. "For as long as I can remember the Madame took care of me. She was so young, I haven't the slightest idea how she managed. The Madame always claimed she found me in the street on her way home from work and just…kept me. Apparently the first few months I stayed with her until she found another family, who I lived with for many years. She came to see me three or four days a week, paid the family whatever she could to keep me under their roof, and would bring me sweets. They were very kind to me, treated me as their own. My first real memory of her was when I was six, and I was learning to read in school. I taught her as I learned, sitting in the living room of that family's house amongst their own children. The Madame could have been one of them – she was seventeen, only eleven years older than I was, and no education to speak of. First were books, then arithmetic, then languages…she loved it, and we formed what I thought was an unbreakable bond…a sister's bond…something special. It wasn't until I was nine I learned what she did for a living and…" Mary stopped and pointed towards Thomas' nearly empty cup. "Thomas…can I ask you for one of those?"

853

His eyes widened. "A whiskey?"

"Yes. I know…an offhand request. It's been years…but I think the time has come to resume…normality."

"I won't argue with that." He got up and grabbed the decanter from the drink cart, along with a spare glass. "So, I'll move onto the more…awkward part of this talk," he carried on. "How did you end up working for her at The Palace?"

"I glamorized her life, as young girls often do," Mary clarified, observing him as he poured her drink. "She was young, extremely beautiful, and had men fawning over her, always wearing the latest fashions and bringing me little gifts. When her original employer was run out of his business, she took it over single-handedly. She'd saved half of what she'd earned her whole life, and from the start that place was exceptional. A woman's touch makes a world of difference." Mary took a sip of the whiskey and began to cough violently, attempting to clear her throat. "Holy shit," she croaked, laughing a little. "I'd forgotten what that's like!"

Thomas chuckled. "Water?"

"No…no I think I'll try again in a few minutes…if I can swallow ever again…now where were we?"

"What did the family you lived with say when you ran off to be with the Madame?"

Mary's countenance grew downtrodden. "Actually, they were moving out of the city…the gangs, the rioting, the impending war, anyone with an extra ounce of money wanted out. They wanted me to go with them but I couldn't leave her. You have to understand, I loved her…adored her…and she offered me a chance at my own sort of freedom. So at fifteen, I took it."

"But…then it was three years, before you met Edward. I was under the impression you'd only just been employed there when he came along." Thomas thought he might be embarrassed discussing this with her, but Mary's ease helped his anxiousness.

"Well, it wasn't three years," Mary confessed. "I am not proud of it, but I lied to Edward about my age. I was fifteen when we met, not eighteen. And yes, I had just started working at The Palace, though it wasn't the one she's in now, I can tell you that much."

Thomas almost dropped his whiskey. "You were only fifteen?!"

"He was barely twenty-one, and a young one at that." Thomas didn't know how to respond and took a second, more lucrative drink of whiskey than the first. "It all happened so fast. Edward and I were so in love, and I easily passed for a girl a few years older. I didn't bother to tell him otherwise…it was dishonest but…."

"Astuteness and wile certainly seem to be something we both acquired from the Madame," Thomas reflected. "What about Louis? Where does he fit in all this?"

"Louis showed up at The Palace about a month after I met Edward. He was a mess when he first starting working for the Madame, nothing but brute strength and just…sheer fury. I never really knew why, and it took years before it passed. He was extremely protective of me, particularly after your father left and I discovered I was pregnant. They had an odd sort of friendship, those two."

"Yeah, I saw that firsthand," Thomas remarked. "And he was the only witness at your wedding." He paused, waiting to see her reaction.

"Thomas…how on earth did you know about that?"

"The Madame sent it to the House of Lords so that I would be… eligible as Edward's heir. At least it's good to know it wasn't a fake."

She grew quiet again, and Thomas sat patiently, not wanting to push her any further than she was willing to go.

"How did he die, Thomas? I've asked Lucy, and she told me I needed to hear it from you."

A pang of guilt hit Thomas' stomach, worried that this news would be a huge blow to Mary's psyche.

"Mother, I don't know how to tell you this because I'm still trying to piece it all together. Lucy and William don't really know the details, so what I tell you stays between us. Is that understood?"

Mary took in a shaky breath. "It was him, wasn't it?"

"From the letter Edward penned to Hiroaki just before he died, and from what Louis has more recently enlightened me with, I can only guess that Edward found you and was killed because he planned to get you out."

Her eyes teared up again, reaching for the whiskey decanter to refill her cup. "That fucking bastard…"

"If this is too much, we can carry on tomorrow or some other time," he tried to console her.

"I'm all right. Really. What I wonder is, what do you think happened when Croker realized I was taken?" Mary posed. "He's going to think the Madame did it somehow…"

"I doubt that," he retorted. "From what I can tell, he's watching them too closely – if they were to go behind his back, he would find out. Croker knew it was me. It's part of the reason I'm dealing with this embargo."

"He can't get us here," she asserted, as if convincing herself. "We're out of his reach. Safe."

Thomas scooted to the end of his chair, wanting to be a little nearer to her. "I need you to tell me why he put you in there. And I need you to tell me all of it. I know the basics, but I want to understand what it is that was so threatening to him."

"What does that matter? It's not as if it will change anything… we're here, together, and we don't have to go back."

"I need to know."

Mary's gaze intensified. "Thomas, what are you on about? You're not thinking of going back there. He'll kill you!"

"I have to face facts, mother. Bernard is there running our leg of the business, but a time will come when either William or I needs to go back, and I sure as hell am not sending William with that impending risk."

"But that's not all of it, is it?"

"All of what?"

"Your reasoning," she insisted. "You want to go back for Esther, don't you?"

Thomas shrugged her off. "Even if I wanted to go back for Esther, we both know she's long gone. Everyone in New York thinks she's dead. It's not like she can just pop up and pretend it never happened. She's gone, another city, another life I would expect, and I hope she is happy there."

"Then what is it? If I am sharing all my secrets, you owe it to me to share yours."

"Mother, I saved you. I've done my good deed and fulfilled everything Edward wanted. But this is my life and my livelihood. I'm not going to hide from Richard Croker and give him that kind of power over me."

She stared at him hard for a moment, and digressed. "I got offered the job by Billy O'Neill. I was...I am very good with numbers, organization, reading, and writing. I signed on, knowing that whatever I was getting involved in wasn't legal, but I didn't care. It was over three times what I was making, and I thought if I could get through a year or so, we would take that money and go west."

"Our original plan," Thomas said.

"Right. A few months went by, and I kept moving up, which granted me more and more responsibility. With that, I discovered all sorts of...numerical atrocities, and also that I was unofficially one of Tammany Hall's bookkeepers. Or fixers, I should say. I was given the job of hiding missing money that Tammany was using to bribe some of the gangs, police officers, brothel owners...even politicians, and how to distribute money they were pulling in through criminal ventures. At the end of every week, Seamus Murphy would give me a sealed envelope with all my work, and I went to an office at the Hall to put the envelope in a safe. And it wasn't always just the corrected numbers I had concocted either. Sometimes it was a list of who was supporting Tammany and who wasn't, or even reports on any investor's illicit activities."

"He was covering all of his bases," Thomas stated. "And you said he gave you the combination?"

Mary finished her whiskey. "Never Croker himself. It was passed along to me. The first time I met Richard Croker was just after Seamus picked me up, about to raid Croker's safe and give everything I could find to the Pinkertons."

"Fucking hell, mother. How did you find Pinkertons?!"

"Harry," she told him sadly. "Harry wanted to help. You remember Sally, who owned the bar beneath the jewelry store? She had two Pinkertons working there, more or less hiding out and looking for work. When they found out about me, they swore they could build a case to take down Tammany Hall permanently."

This was the part Thomas had been diligently waiting for. "Mother, was one of the men who helped you named John Erving?"

Mary's eyes went wider. "How in God's name do you know about John?"

"It wasn't me. It was Edward. He found John when he was looking for you years ago, and they had a short correspondence, though they both firmly believed you were dead."

"You're telling me John survived?!" she exclaimed. "How?!"

"I have no idea, and I've reached out to Sally, but she said he's been gone for over a year with no hint of his whereabouts. She thought he might have gone back to working for the Pinkertons in Virginia."

Again, Mary was quiet, and Thomas didn't press her. It was nearing ten minutes when she spoke: "But…but I just don't understand. How was Edward able to find out about John?"

Thomas smiled, pouring them each another round. "There are some things I think I need to tell you about Edward."

It was the nearing winter when he found her.

Thomas was out for his usual run, sporting a nasty swollen eye from his lesson with Hiroaki the morning prior and a few bruised ribs to match. Months passed rapidly, and Thomas was shocked at how fast he was learning and improving. While he was nowhere near the level of his master, he was growing more and more self-assured with his movements, his concentration, and his agility. Hiroaki had been hard on him, pushing Thomas to greater lengths than he'd ever been pushed in his life, making his body hurt in ways he never imagined it would. Akemi would always provide a tea when they came in from training, one that would ease the pain and relax his sore muscles, but it was becoming harder and harder to avoid questions from William, Lucy, and Mary, who openly speculated just what it was he and the Samurai were off doing in the woods.

He hadn't told them, of course, sensing if any of them found out his true plans they would do all they could to talk him out of it, particularly his mother. There would come a day when William would have to be up to date, yet that time was not anytime soon, and would not be for a long while. For now, it was only Thomas, Tony, and Hiroaki.

The embargo Croker raised earlier in the year was quickly thrown out in the early fall, and proliferated as more of an insult to Thomas. To Thomas' relief, it hadn't affected business. Stocks were selling at a huge rate, packs of cigarettes were in high demand and blowing up the marketplace, and not only did England and the rest of Europe want machine-rolled tobacco to save on labor costs, they also desired the technology behind the invention, which Turner S & D would soon provide. The investors were ecstatic, and the Turner's were, if possible, wealthier than ever.

Just as the sun drew over the hills, Thomas was sucking wind, pushing his legs as his muscles burned in protestation. It was the coldest morning he could remember running that season, and suddenly as he reached the far corner of the property, he heard a shriek so earsplitting it halted him in his tracks. It was sheer panic, fear even, and Thomas had never heard anything like that sound before. Then came another scream, and another, until he couldn't stand it. Using his senses the way Hiroaki taught him, Thomas closed his eyes, focusing solely on the sound of the cry. He guessed he was maybe a hundred yards from wherever the creature might be, and took off in the route he assumed was accurate. The shrieks grew louder and louder as he ran, and Thomas could feel the apprehension that he might not make it in time to save whatever this beast might be. It was definitely not human.

He came to a slight clearing in the trees and instantly found the source: pinned against a rotting log was a peregrine falcon, not more than a year old, one of her wings dragging at her side, broken and bleeding. Another stirring caught his attention, and Thomas soon saw the reason behind her cries. Her predator, an enormous golden eagle, was on the ground no more than a few feet away, trying to make her his breakfast. The bird was six, maybe seven times her size, and she screamed on, her wings fluttering and spreading despite her injury, doing whatever was necessary to stand her own ground as the eagle made snatches at her with his gigantic, sharp talons.

A twig under Thomas' foot snapped, and both birds turned, their eyes focused right on him. The eagle let out its own screech, deeper than the falcon and far more intimidating, as if he were telling Thomas to back off of his prey. However, when Thomas' eyes met the peregrine's, the reaction was something much different. They were filled with longing, pleading even – she couldn't get away from the eagle, and Thomas was the only chance she had at survival. He didn't know why he did it…it was almost as if some sort of spirit grabbed him and took hold of his wits. The Griswold was on his belt, and he grabbed for it, pointed it directly in the air, and fired.

The eagle took off in a blaze, and within a handful of seconds was completely out of sight. The falcon remained on the ground and rested her wings, her broken one tremoring slightly. She wasn't afraid of him, and her eyes did not leave him as he marched to her steadily, her gaze piercing him, penetrating through his body as if reading his thoughts. When he made it to her, Thomas slowly took off his coat and wrapped it around the small bird, who bizarrely did not fight or resist. With his coat around her, Thomas lightly tucked her under his arm and took off toward the manor, feeling somehow this falcon was not ordinary. It was as if she knew him the moment she saw him, like she'd been waiting there for him to come and save her.

In just under a quarter of an hour, Thomas was banging on the door of Hiroaki and Akemi's cottage, and Akemi flung the door open after a few minutes. Her expression was extremely annoyed at first, though it dissolved when she saw who her guest was. She motioned to what it was he was carrying, and he opened his jacket slightly so that Akemi caught sight of the bird. Without a word, Akemi gestured for Thomas to follow her inside, and Thomas obeyed. She shut the door behind him, and he gently placed the injured bird on her kitchen table.

"I think her wing is broken, Akemi," Thomas explained. "I found her just as a giant eagle was about to make her his meal."

Akemi was searching the shelves, her back to him. "Tommy, please tell me you did not kill the eagle?"

"No, of course not!" Thomas assured her. "Scared him off, is all. I wanted to save the falcon. She…Christ, she looks at me like she knows me."

Akemi moved over to the table with a few supplies. "She did not…erm…oppose you taking her?"

"Oppose…? Oh! No, she didn't. Not even a flutter. I picked her up and ran here without an ounce of defiance."

Akemi halted, her eyes flashing to the falcon, then toward to Thomas. "Not one cry of opposition?"

Thomas was confused. "No. Why? Is that not normal?"

She grinned. "This one is special. Go wake Hiro. I will get the rest set up and show you how to repair wing."

Hiroaki was snoring loudly when Thomas reached his and Akemi's room, and to Thomas' disgust, Hiroaki was wearing no clothing whatsoever.

"Hiro," he whispered, shaking his shoulders. "Hiro, wake up. I need you."

His master's eyes fluttered opened, and the naked Hiroaki was not pleased. "How did you get in here?" he yelled, pulling the sheet around him and causing Thomas to laugh.

"Akemi," he said, "we need you in the kitchen. And can you put some damn clothes on?"

"This is my house. If I choose to be—"

"Yeah, all right, Hiro. Just put trousers on for me. Please?"

A few minutes passed, and Hiroaki joined Akemi and Thomas in the kitchen, his eyes lighting up when he saw the bird.

"A peregrine?" He addressed Thomas and streamed to the falcon, observing the bird closely.

"Yes, badly wounded by an eagle. I found her and saved her on my run."

Akemi cleared her throat. "Hiro?"

"Mmm?" he mumbled, not bothering to glance up.

"Hiro, the bird went willingly."

He, like Akemi, stopped and gaped at Thomas. "No resistance?"

Thomas still didn't understand. "Would it matter?"

"Yes, yes it would!" Hiroaki insisted. "It means she chose you! This is very rare, and very extraordinary for you, Thomas. Stroke her head."

"Are you crazy?" Thomas exclaimed. "I want to keep my fingers intact, thank you very much."

Akemi didn't hesitate. She grasped Thomas hand without his permission and tenderly brushed it against the falcon's head, which remained tranquil and motionless. After a few strokes, the bird was pressing into his touch. It was odd – Thomas had never handled a raptor before. The feel of the falcon, in comparison to the warm-blooded creatures he was used to, was other-worldly to him.

Hiroaki was delighted. "We must heal her as quickly as we can, Akemi. Thomas, we have found your second weapon."

Thomas had taken to caressing the bird on his own, though not without caution. "Second weapon? How can a bird be a second weapon?"

"Birds are fickle beasts," Hiroaki dictated, as Akemi assembled a needle and string to repair the wing. "They are cold, reptilian, an ancient animal that existed long before man. Typically, these falcons are used for hunting, but with the right influence they can be persuaded to perform other undertakings. They will be submissive to humans if trained from infancy. In…extraordinary circumstances, birds will come to us. We do not know why, but in these cases, they become more than just another pet. They are like one with us. They can see what we see, read our thoughts…they want to be with us, and they unify with you. This is a gift, and we can train her to be your ally."

Thomas considered it. "We could teach her to be at my side, even somewhere with as many distractions as New York?"

"Yes we could."

"Could we get her to disarm a man with a gun?"

Hiroaki smirked. "We could teach her to gouge his eyes out if you wanted."

Thomas contemplated the idea of having a falcon, and in turn, she observed Thomas, feeling the connection building between them. "She's already a fighter. I saw that with my own eyes." He turned to Akemi. "Can you show me how I fix her wing?"

Akemi stepped to his side. "We will have to set the bone first, then we sew her wound closed, and put this remedy on the stitches to prevent infection. Put your hands on my hands…watch closely…"

When the task was finished and the wing was repaired, Thomas sat with the bird on his shoulder by the kitchen fire, admiring her with a cup of Akemi's tea.

"She's going to be a beauty," Akemi revered, cleaning up the table.

"Yes," Hiroaki agreed, "and she will have to go everywhere with you these first few months. To solidify the bond."

Thomas smiled broadly. "I have no problem with that," he retorted. "When can she fly again?"

"The break was very fine," Akemi described. "It should only take a few weeks or so I would expect. She will tell us when the time is right."

"You'll tell me when the time comes, yes?" Thomas uttered, as he began to stroke her head once again. "A fighter…and a warrior…"

"You must name her too," Hiroaki recommended, "Something suitable…an aggressor that is both vicious and beautiful."

Thomas thought on it. "How about Athena as your name then?"

The bird's eyes flashed, and Thomas took that as a yes.

"The female god of war," Hiroaki remarked, leaning back into his chair. "Quite fitting."

Thomas nodded, his attentions focused solely on his new companion. "It's settled then. You're my Athena, my goddess of war," he cooed. "And together, we are going to be invincible."

EPILOGUE
AMBERLEIGH, FEBRUARY 1885

"Excuse me, Lady Turner, may I enter?"

Mary straightened up. She had been reading down in Edward's den by the fireplace, deeply engrossed in one of his mission logs when she heard the familiar knock of the butler.

"Of course, Tony," she replied, setting the well-worn journal aside and reaching for her glass of wine. "What is it?"

Tony came into the den and bowed. "A Captain Connor O'Brian sent word ahead he will be arriving a few days earlier than expected for his visit. Since Thomas is away on business another day and William and Lucy are vacationing in Bath, I wanted to inquire whether or not you find this suitable."

"Yes, tell Connor I would greatly appreciate the company," Mary declared warmly. "Anything else?"

"A letter has come for you from New York," he informed her, marching toward Mary with a hint of reluctance. "And I am sorry to say that I know the address."

He held the letter out, and Mary politely took it from his hands. A smirk came to her face when she saw it was from The Palace – she'd been wondering if the Madame would ever return her letters, and at long last came an answer.

"Can I get anything else for you?" Tony solicited, lingering by her side.

"Actually, Tony, there is something I have been meaning to ask you. If you don't mind staying a moment."

"Whatever you need, Lady Turner."

Mary looked at him. "Please, do be seated."

Tony stared at her, confused. "I'm sorry?"

She set the letter on the side table. "Do me the courtesy of sitting. Then we can begin our conversation."

"As you wish, Lady Turner." Tony moved over and rested down opposite her in one of the large brown leather armchairs.

"There are rumors circulating this household," she started, taking a sip of her drink. "About what you, Hiroaki, and Thomas are doing out of doors in the dead of winter every day, and not just amongst the staff. William and Lucy have been speculating as well."

"Recreation," Tony responded, unwavering.

Mary's eyes narrowed. "Tony, please."

Tony's expression did not change. "You claim everyone else is requesting an explanation, but not you?" he asked her. "You have obviously found one of Edward's written accounts of his former exploits," he remarked, pointing to Edward's journal. "From what I remember, he hid those away years ago in the hopes they might not be found, though somehow you managed to uncover his secret. Therefore, I can only guess you have made an assumption as to what Thomas is doing with Hiroaki and myself, and only call on me for confirmation of your assumptions."

"That is correct."

"Well, why don't you share your hypothesis with me, then?"

Mary's head tilted to the side, studying him as her left eyebrow rose. "Hiroaki is training Thomas in the same ways Edward was trained, and you are assisting. I can hear the gunshots throughout the day. There is no possible way Thomas is 'improving his hunting skills,' or whatever sort of bullshit he feeds us every night. He's preparing for something."

Tony smiled at her. "Thomas has advised me that if this day should come, I am not to lie to you. The question I have in return for you Mary, is do you really want to know?"

"I am his mother. I absolutely want to know."

He crossed his arms over his chest, now in turn scrutinizing her. "It's because you are his mother, Mary, I am reluctant to share. Nothing you say or do will change his mind, and you might not like what I tell you."

Mary had another gulp of wine. "You aren't leaving that sofa until you talk."

Tony sighed, slumping back into his chair. "Thomas is indeed training in the same ways his father did with Hiroaki many years ago, but unlike Edward, Thomas has an exceptionally different aim for his new skills."

"And just what aim might that be?"

For a few seconds, Tony closed his eyes, as if regretting what he was about to disclose. "He's going back to New York with the sole purpose of destroying Richard Croker."

Mary nearly dropped her wine glass. "And he's…he's training with guns…Edward never used guns…it…it wasn't…"

"A part of his code?" Tony finished for her. "No, it wasn't. Thomas acquired a Griswold from the Madame a number of years ago, and plans on that revolver being his weapon of choice."

"Is he learning how to use other weapons?" Mary pressed.

"In a matter of speaking."

Her patience was growing thin. "Tony…"

"Athena," he told her curtly, "is his secondary."

"Jesus fucking Christ," she whispered under her breath. "I always speculated…I just never imagined he would really…God damn him. How does he think he can win this? It's…it's impossible! Croker is too powerful."

"Your son is also extremely powerful," Tony added. "And I do believe he will use that against Croker. In this case, Thomas' wealth and status can be used to his advantage. You must see that."

"Oh bullshit. One man cannot take on Croker with all of his resources. The odds are not in Thomas' favor."

"I am not certain he cares what the odds are, Mary," Tony admitted with a small shrug. "And to be fair, Thomas is already twice the fighter his father was. He has a drive, a sense of purpose that is intrinsic, and his skill level is…impeccable. He's a dead shot even on the move, and his progress is chilling. The determination Thomas has to see that man burn is…absurd."

Mary shook her head, her throat choking. "I want revenge too. But…"

"But what?"

"I don't want my only son to die."

"We all die," Tony said candidly. "Thomas would rather die for a cause…for revenge against a man who took away the things he loved most. And between us, I think if Thomas keeps progressing, he could potentially pull it off."

This last bit of information startled Mary. For years, she was locked away on Blackwell's Island in a mental institution by Richard Croker for trying to expose the corrupted Tammany Hall. She never dreamed she would get out of there alive, and as she sat across from Tony a year after being rescued from her prison, her own feebleness ashamed her. If anyone ought to want to kill Richard Croker and eliminate everything he'd built, she should; yet instead, she was more worried about keeping her son alive and hiding away at Amberleigh? She glimpsed internally at who she had become in that asylum in comparison to the woman she'd been upon her incarceration: what happened to the woman working for the Pinkertons who would stop at nothing to bring Croker down? The woman who, to that very day, had information that could assist in bringing about his downfall? She ought to be helping her son, and doing everything she could to divulge the knowledge she acquired working for his operation. With or without her permission, Thomas was going back to New York – the best thing she could do for him was put aside her apprehension and aid him in his preparations.

Mary didn't know what exactly was frightening her, but she chose to ignore that fear. Thomas didn't need her guilt, her anxiety, or her dread: he needed her to be Mary again, and she'd be God damned if he did this without her.

"I know the combination," Mary suddenly blurted out. "It took me some time but…only a few weeks ago it came screaming back to me in a dream."

Tony's eyes grew wide. "You know the combination…to what?"

"Croker's safe in his office at Tammany Hall. I know the combination. And that's only the beginning."

He gaped at her for a few seconds. "You remember these things?"

"Only just recently…once I was able to…control my nightmares of the asylum."

"Hiroaki wasn't sure you'd be able to recall anything before Blackwell," Tony replied. "You barely survived your withdrawal recovery. It should have killed you, and we presumed your recollections would be patchy at best."

Mary shook her head. "If I focus, it's clear as day. I want to help. Please let me help."

Tony was utterly baffled, his thoughts adrift somewhere else. "Yes…whatever you can give us…" After a moment, he was on his feet, taking a bow once again. "Mary, my deepest apologies, but you have to excuse me. I have to go find Hiroaki," he asserted, marching the way of the door that lead out of the den. "You will be a huge asset to us."

"Wait!" Mary shouted, and Tony paused by the door. "I want you to tell Thomas he has my full support on this. I want that bastard dead as much as he does."

Tony nodded. "Whatever you wish, Lady Turner. Thomas will be thrilled to hear of your encouragement."

In an instant, Tony was gone, and Mary was left to contemplate over the discussion they'd just had. She'd noticed during her recovery an abundance of nervousness and unease in her person, two qualities she rarely experienced prior to her time on Blackwell. The institution changed her, and Mary found she was desperately fighting to regain her old self little by little each day. The nightmares were becoming few and far between, though what haunted her most were the flashes of memories after Grace sent Nurse Montell to her death. When Croker discovered his sister-in-law had died in a tragic accident just hours after nearly beating Mary to death, the mercy previously shown to her disappeared. Croker isolated Mary, tortured her mentally with excessive bouts of the potion, physical beatings, and starvation until finally she couldn't stop herself from confessing what Grace told her that day in the hospital. Without hesitation, Mary, Bethany, and Grace were rounded up and locked in the dungeon, where they were drugged and given one meal of gruel a day. Nothing was provided during those early winter months to keep them warm, and Mary watched in horror as Bethany died in front of her of sickness and fever. She and Grace battled to stay alive, and on a bitterly cold morning Mary swore was her last, Hiroaki appeared in the cell door and took her away. In spite of his assurances that nothing could be done, Mary found it hard to forgive Hiroaki for leaving Grace behind, never knowing what happened to the best friend she'd ever had. Grace was, in all probability, long dead, and Mary placed the blame entirely on herself.

"It's all in God's way," she reminded herself, suppressing tears as she had some more wine, attempting to calm her nerves. It was then she remembered the Madame's letter. Clearing her throat and wiping her damp cheek dry, she reached over to grab it from the side table and tore it open. In the envelope she found a letter and something she had forgotten about in her time at Blackwell: the locket the Madame had given her when Thomas was born. A raw emotion came over her as she observed the necklace, still in perfect condition, and with shaking hands she put it around her neck, fastening it. The Madame must have cleaned the silver consistently throughout the years, and it made Mary miss her immensely. Taking the letter from the envelope, she opened the paper carefully.

Hi, darling.

It has taken me some time to write for many reasons, the first of which being an innate fear that our relationship might be irreparable. After receiving your letters, I came to understand that wasn't the case, and instead a different worry took over: what if I cannot provide you peace?

I want you to find peace in England — you are under no circumstance to come back to this place, and I believe that Thomas will agree with me on that. There is nothing for you here but tragedy. Admitting this is difficult for me because it brings about a truth I have a hard time accepting.

You and I will not ever meet again.

I held onto your necklace and locked it away in the hopes I might be able to give it to you personally, but instead I think this way is best.

I wish I could have been the one to free you from Croker, and I would have if I could. Your son is in very good hands with the chink, and I swear to you when Thomas does return to us, I will guard him like I always have and not let anything happen to him.

Over the years I've kept many things from you to protect you, and also to protect Thomas. This is no surprise to you: it's the way I do things to keep those I love safe. However, there is one secret I never should have kept from you, and it's one I want to disclose to you privately. I ask that you tell no one, not even Thomas, because it will cloud the responsibility he has taken on.

Yes, I do know of Thomas' plans, though I cannot tell you how.

The story I fabricated of how I found you on the streets when I was young was, in fact, a lie. The truth is much harder to admit — when I was nearing ten years old, I was orphaned and I had no money, so I began to sell myself on the street. And shortly thereafter, I became pregnant. With you.

I will spare you the details of what happened in the aftermath, but I kept you because a part of me couldn't find the strength to give you away, as I had given myself away so many other times. So I did the best I could, and chose to keep it a secret for most of my life.

You are my daughter, and I love you more than any other, but I never want to see you in New York again. I hope you will respect this last request I have of you, and also take into consideration my secondary request to withhold from Thomas that he, too, is my flesh and blood.

For both of our safety, this will be the one and only letter I write until the storm has passed. When you do see Thomas, please tell him I am greatly anticipating his return

Yours & etc,

M

Mary's hand reached up for the locket and gripped it tightly in her palm. For a moment, she could only sit in silence, the Madame's letter such a shock she couldn't think straight. Then, without warning, Mary fell into a happy sort of sob. How had she not seen this before? They were so similar...so strikingly similar! The Madame's hair, though darker than hers, was littered with the same red hue as Mary's. In addition, they both sported the same grey tone in their eyes, and the eyebrow...it was an expression she thought she'd acquired from being around the Madame, yet instead it turned out to be hereditary. Their overall temperaments were indistinguishable, and at times when Thomas was young, it was what frustrated him about the Madame and Mary teaming up on him. And now... Thomas had grown so much like the Madame in his adulthood, she wondered how she couldn't recognize it – the three of them were one in the same. They really were family.

Slowly, Mary realized that somewhere deep down she had known this truth all along. She wasn't sure what she would do next, however she respected the Madame enough to understand she was right: Mary would never go home to New York City, and the Madame